To Rocio,

be brave, Visualize,

I 3 I believe.

Mystic Dawn

SAM BANFIELD

BALBOA.
PRESS

A DIVISION OF HAY HOUSE

Balboa Press books may be ordered through booksellers or by contacting:

Balboa Press
A Division of Hay House
1663 Liberty Drive
Bloomington, IN 47403
www.balboapress.com
1 (877) 407-4847

Because of the dynamic nature of the Internet, any web addresses or links contained in this book may have changed since publication and may no longer be valid. The views expressed in this work are solely those of the author and do not necessarily reflect the views of the publisher, and the publisher hereby disclaims any responsibility for them.

The author of this book does not dispense medical advice or prescribe the use of any technique as a form of treatment for physical, emotional, or medical problems without the advice of a physician, either directly or indirectly. The intent of the author is only to offer information of a general nature to help you in your quest for emotional and spiritual well-being. In the event you use any of the information in this book for yourself, which is your constitutional right, the author and the publisher assume no responsibility for your actions.

Any people depicted in stock imagery provided by Thinkstock are models, and such images are being used for illustrative purposes only.
Certain stock imagery © Thinkstock.

Print information available on the last page.

ISBN: 978-1-5043-4158-5 (sc)
ISBN: 978-1-5043-4159-2 (e)

Balboa Press rev. date: 10/05/2015

Prologue

Sunlight cuts through the sheer bliss of a forest. Its lush leaves and branches sway lightly in the breeze. The green grass is soft, simple here. The sun is warm, passing between the blades of grass and touching the roots.

A farmer removes his straw hat to wipe his brow. He grazes his palms across a meadow. His hard rough hands pass between the tall of the grasses, for he knows what's coming.

A lady with a broom can smell the fresh scent of dandelions blowing between the breezes. Her blouse is moving in the direction of the wind. The wind makes her smile. It makes her feel safe. The brilliance that surrounds her moves with softness.

A robed man in black reaches for reins. Before he mounts his black nord (a black horse but with long floppy ears), he peers from under his hood and looks back at his men. His eyes are yellow as the sun, but with opposite intentions. They have the same slick of a snake. They have a daring look; it's almost as if they could slither towards the rising sun beyond.

The lady begins to sweep leaves from her property onto a nearby rocky road. The sky above is a much different story today then yesterday's gloomy. Her brassy eyes peer at the sun's magnificent rays, its very essence reflects upon her surroundings for it's almost deceiving, like the sky may turn cloudy at any moment. But the warmth lasts, for now.

A broken-heart approaches on the rocky road, a mother mounted by nord.

The brassy eyes couldn't share the fierce dread that this other is portraying, riding her way. She couldn't comprehend the pain and sorrow that lies within this rider's heart.

The rider wears a green cloak, with her hood up. It covers features that resemble her enemy; but this in no way imparts their means. She rides an unknown path, and she can sense a lady's innocence not too far off.

The lady's blouse moves in the winds. She continues to sweep just beyond the green-cloak-rider.

The rider is a mother, and her hands tighten on the reins. The site of the lady in the blouse offers a thought of innocence to the mother. It's overwhelming, a similar appearance that reminds the rider of her husband.

The brassy eyes look up from her broom, squinting with the sun in them; it's odd to see anyone, because there is only desertion beyond, only forest and more of it. So where is the rider planning to go?

The lady steps off the path to move out of the way, and quickly the rider passes by. It didn't seem the rider dared to stop, nor think of this pedestrian; but what cautions the lady in the blouse most – a sudden cry of a baby was overheard. It disappears, fading into the distance.

The rider does her best to hide behind her cloak, now entering the forest and attempting to stay away from the sunlight, as if the sun is trying to catch any sign of emotion. The rider felt this would make her feel defenceless at a time like this. She tightens the shroud around her face. Her throat feels tight when she swallows.

The hooded-one in black becomes more anxious as he nears his destination. His grip is tight around the rein. He rides and makes his way into a deeper forest path with his men enclosing behind.

With each step from the nord carrying the green-cloak-rider and the baby, the sky shuts out from behind them. Mother embraces the memory of her family one last time.

The farmer man positions his reaper to support his stance. His hat shades his features from the sun. There is a look in his eye, as if he is waiting for someone, and as he looks towards the distance where a forest surrounds him on all sides, his reaper begins to slip. Fighting his emotions back, it feels pitiful to him. The thoughts of his family are rushing him — he knows he must be strong. From underneath the sun, his grip tightens once more. His dark hair and deep blue eyes peer with freedom. But the sweat of his brow continues to weep.

The sunlight fights to reach the thick stumps and rugged branches. It is here the green-cloak-rider loses her warmth as she drifts farther and farther from her husband. The trunks begin to thin out, offering a lighter forest path for her to ride through. She dreads what looks like rising smoke ahead. The smell of burning firewood engulfs her senses. She slows down and is guided towards a thin pathway. A dim light flickers on the other end of this trail.

'Smoke at this time of day.' She asks herself. 'I didn't know anyone was out here.'

Ash lingers in the skies and is smothering a creek. It fills the air around her like flies turning everything black. The river seems to slither instead of glide. She wipes the tears from her baby's face, covering her face with a red scarf from flames around. Nearing the smothering smoke, the mother's hands tremble -- She looks back. There is a look of abandonment -- too far from him, too far to dread the thought of his dawning screams any longer.

The rider in black left the forest to approach a farm in the middle of its harbour. The rider signals his men to search through a field-house.

A few cloaks dismount.

The dark rider waits while his regime move to a barn next, but no one is found in either or.

The whole time a man had been waiting in the open farm. He stood, shading his features behind a straw hat with a reaper in hand. He never once looked up from behind his shading face, away from the approaching regime on foot and nord.

Finally, the leader who is still amount came forward; he brushed his soft hands across the wheat. His eyes have the look of the slither as he approaches the man in the cropping field.

The man's head is evermore hung toward the ground, his features invisible by his straw hat. He knew better, these were no *men*. Then, he drops his reaper helplessly when approached by the Errifics; the regime uncovers their hoods to get a better look at the man who still hides his features.

The leader dismounts and took one step closer, and then spoke for his clan, still staring at this helpless man.

'This means they got away. They still have *it*.'

The man never looks up to meet eyes with their leader, because the man knows they are slit, that they always slither, in pretence.

The leader took another step forward and spoke with further sentiment; 'why am I not surprised?'

She pulls her baby closer to her chest. No one to be seen, there's no sight of blood, but this camp engulfed in ash. The river curling over the rocky sands is all that speaks for the forgotten. She doesn't know what happened here, but marks of war are noticed. But if she were to guess, those who've come for her husband have come for her, perhaps. But if this were true, then where are the bodies? But most importantly, how could the Errifics know where she'd be?

A thought bares her mind.

I just passed into the Lady of the Forest. This is her dwelling and her doing. I must tread carefully. Her Dark Ones must have killed them and dragged the bodies away, for they're always watching... they're always doing her bidding...

The mother is careful as she treads her nord. She knows this forest and the dark stories that belong to it.

In the crop field, the air has a faint move to it. The man's sea blue eyes flash back and forth between the Errific's slit ones. The man slowly removes his straw hat, and rests it gently on the ground.

Four birds land on a barn in the distance, prancing along the edges of a rooftop.

The baby finally lays silent in her mother's arm. A cool breeze chills from within, like a warning for those who dare to dwell deeper within. Her mother swallows and makes her way inwards. This forest is untouched, beautiful as it is ancient. Birds and life cry all along. With a grunt she reaches in her saddle pouch and pulls out a small book.

'Ashnivarna...' her mother whispers. She holds her baby close again.

A blue light crashes from the book; like a blooming flower, light bristles. The light attracts the baby girl's attention. With wide eyes the baby watches. She isn't the only one watching, something other is and it's in the deep. This thing isn't human. It waits for a signal to strike.

The eyes of Mom's baby, a sea blue matches the crashing lights beauty. A book expands becoming heavier in Mother's grasp. And as the baby girl watches, silently the light flickers and dies away. Here, Mom stares back at it; its power rests in her palm. Mom is to protect her baby but what Mother may soon discover; a pair of careful eyes is protecting something of its own; this old forestry moves in a light breeze. Mom is in its territory... and beyond the forest's withering; Mother and her child have awakened an old legend, and one day its fight will have to be faced. Timidly, the Dark One will have to wait for the signal, until then; it carefully disappears back into forestry waiting for its master's command.

The leader's soft hands relax releasing his tight-fist. He speaks melodramatically.

'We're going to find it and when we do, there is no telling when it'll all begin.'

He then snaps his finger to one of the cloaks nearest. This cloak mounts and leaves in order to search the house again.

One of the birds from atop the roof flies west, separating from its family of four.

The man is quiet, when the leader is about to speak the man decided to interrupt. 'You won't find *it*, because they'll hide *it* from likes of *you*.'

'So there is another...' The leader says in his arbitrary ways and rubs his thumb toward his index.

His rider dismounts and hands him a small blanket.

The man's face drops, and then stares back into the face of fear.

'A child perhaps?' the leader asks, turning back to the man. A wide smile creases from the lips of many who fear, but the man is not afraid of this arbitrator's way. The leader removes his hood to reveal his features; his slit irises are yellow as the sun. He has sharp tipped ears that point skyward.

The man is about to speak, but before the leader let him, the leader shot a burning light from his open palm, smashing into the man and throwing him backwards. It instantly kills him.

A beast jumps out from behind a bush.

Mom halts her steed and the baby cries from the sudden stop. But the beast waits instead of attacks, blocking the way on.

'A Dark One...' Mother says under her hood, ready for it with her palm on the book, which is sitting in the saddle pouch.

But its eyes move towards something behind the rider and before Mother could turn to see, a swooping hand reached her baby and a flash from the other takes the life of Mom. Mom's shoulders droop and she slides off the nord crashing to the earth with a thump.

'You did well.' A soft voice says with the baby under the arm. The being moves to the beast and pats it. The being is suddenly reminded. 'Ah!' And moves towards the saddled nord and lifts the strap. 'Right were you should be. My dear Alas you are good,' and pulls out a massive book. The woman looks towards the beast. 'Tell me friend, what is the spell to relock the Book of Knowledge?'

The beast stares. It blinks once.

'Ah hah, thank you my dear.' She says in robes of white.

The baby begins to cry.

The Guardian gets down low in position to pounce.

With a snap of the lady's finger the beast drops its striking pose and its eyes droop. It gives a tedious exhalation at the white robe and then walks away.

The Lady of the Forest returns to the baby, 'just as Alas predicted.'

She looks down at the dead rider and places the baby on the earth. She removes the hood of the mother and finds the look of the enemy underneath. This is a surprise to her. 'I can always fix this.' She finally says and moves to the mother to pluck a hair, finding another step over the body and picking up the baby in arm again. The Lady of the Forest gave a short frown to the one in arm. 'You and I will get right along, you'll see.'

She places the baby into one of the saddle pouches, and then retrieved a serum from under her robe and places the plucked hair into mouth. 'For Alas,' she says tilting the vial back and swallows the hair and liquid. As she did this, she visualized the mother without the harsh features of the enemy. In adjustment, she pictured round ears and round irises.

A flash of green with a bluish tint came over the Lady of the Forest's body. A small glitter around her mirrors the appearance of the one on ground, alongside alterations. The bright glow around the Lady of the Forest dies.

She eyes the baby and smiles deeply. The lady noticed a look of unjust but it was enough to convince the little mystic eyes, and that's all the Lady of the Forest could ask for.

'Now I have your mother's eyes.' She said as a figure of speech and lifts the baby up and out of pouch.

Only two birds from the four remain and so they cross overhead passing the lady and baby below, into dawn.

- Chapter 1 -

Mystic Dawn

Sleeping under covers, safe and sound, a girl turns.

Just outside the wind blows. Cold and withered there is a forest that withers through the willow. The moonlight strikes across the skyline.

Evelyn wakes with a start and squints through her bedside window.

The beautiful night is silent just like it should.

She lays her head back down. Suddenly, she feels a rush, for today is Saturday. She sits up and rushes out of bed. Her hair is a thick-black and hangs over her shoulders. A love for it since it rarely can get out of place, even in the harshest of conditions. When it gets greasy from a few days without wash, it has a beautiful shine, which reflects nicely.

The air can be smelt of roasted oats. Evelyn puts on socks and jumps into overall's, which fits loosely, much like her coloured shirts. Her nose carries her downstairs to a table, where a hot bowl of porridge lay.

'Thanks Mom.' She says in recollection.

Mother will make Evelyn breakfast on most weekends, since weekdays are too busy most times.

The kitchen window is left wide open. Evelyn rubs her eyes to the cool room. She doesn't get much sleep whenever the weekends come along. And she stayed up especially late last night hanging out with her two best friends, Jason and Jonah.

Evelyn's mother is always trying to get her daughter to bed on time so Evelyn can arrive on time for school. "An accurate sleeping schedule" is how Mother put it. But Evelyn doesn't lead a very accurate lifestyle.

Katherine; otherwise known as Mom, knows what it means for her daughter to get older. It is like a shadow reminding Mom to let go, so Evelyn can learn to grow her own wings, and leave this town to make a life beyond its shrinking lifestyle. It may sound easy, but for most mothers letting go isn't.

Katherine's love only grows fonder for her child, naturally. Mom knows the other side of this fence, loved to be let go; a circular dilemma. Mom tries to keep her mind off what this town worries about on a daily basis. The question is, should they stay or should they go?

Evelyn watches out the window as she eats, thinking about this very thing also. What will time bring? What will she do? And what will become of her outside the only place she knows? It reaches at her deepest fear. She would like to stay here in Maesemer, a town she adores. Its history is fascinating, yet all to be forgotten if she moves to the city to the far east. A place outside the realm of farmers and any real history, a place of work, work, work and no real play, but most importantly, a place Evelyn believes one goes to sell their soul for a "Career".

Evelyn puts a spoon to mouth and her teeth clank it. She remembers what her teachers preach for a better life.

"Remember to arrive on time and get good grades, so you can further your career. Maesemer is thinning, and we only get so many chances."

And yet, Maesemer is the only place she wants to be. This could explain why she hates school so much. Actually, it's not that she hates it, but despises the thought of being told to be someone or something else. Beyond this, it's a piece of land that had been hoarded by the country's major educational district. There came a time when it was Maesemer property, when the town's teachers spoke of its town's history with a pride. But if the town wants to keep its train station open to receive supplies for hospitals and whatnot, then Maesemer has to abide by the capital's laws, even if they're deep to the east.

'Put back into its rightful place.' Evelyn rolls her eyes to the thought, one to do with history class two days ago, on the subject of magic. She continues to recollect, 'whose rightful place? Brunon's soulless self that is.'

Perhaps being told "You need to learn to be a lady so you can leave and go to Brunon to marry that gentleman" would make anyone go mad.

'Brunon,' she says and shudders at the capital city of Egerd, Egerd being the country of the beautiful Maesemer and the soulless east. What makes it worse; Brunon uses coin as exchange system. No trade or bargain. So her thought on the matter is:

What kind of fun is that going to be?

With very little room for country land, it's a place set in bars inside this girl's imagination.

She knows the stories of its concrete jungle and its way of life; an Industrial Revolution, and all she ever hears about is the factory workers putting in extra hours, whether man or woman, it's the city's way of life.

Evelyn shakes her head and moves toward fresh berries on the counter in a ceramic bowl, dropping them in her cereal. Placing her bowl down, a pair of leather boots usually for farming is put on. She places her pant legs over and with a quick swoop to her bowl, she leaves the house. Haulberries, Tayberries and even Coneberries jiggle in her bowl. And she comes down the front porch steps to the backyard.

'Hey Mom,' Evelyn says. 'I just came out to see what you were doing. I know today's going to be busy, so I'll get right to work.'

The sky is dark blue. A faint outline of the moon is seen.

In the family of Maelkyn; Mother is always up especially early to feed their chickens and livestock. Packing and storing crops, she'll jot her records down with pencil. One positive notion that came out of Brunon was the invention of the pencil, especially in Evelyn's opinion. She couldn't imagine using ink and quill, at least not in today's day and age.

Let's get some perspective here, adhere with time and era. Egerd is only six-hundred years old, being three-hundred for the Old Capital, which is now abandoned, and the remaining for those thereafter; to the far east. I'd recon; Egerd is somewhere Earth's time-line in the 1850s. How do I figure? Granted, time is primitive... but hear me out. On Earth the first pencil was invented sometime prior to about 1560.

I promise not to give a lecture on history. Hang on. Maybe I will.

Since before the goods and passenger steam railway began forty years from the Upheaval to begin building to the far east -- Asnin being the Old Capital, and the Upheaval being the time of its change. After the Upheaval commenced the birth of Brunon, Brunon no longer wielded ink and quill, lucky for Evelyn; and thus the concordance of two primitives.

Today, Evelyn has grown up in a time that has fully bloomed into an Industrial Revolution. Brunon is using heavy machinery -- Great right? Well, the machinery is transcendent to Earth's second Industrial Revolution, which begun on Earth in the 1850s, and ends in the early 1900s. Let's do the math; keeping in mind this is justifiable. We subtract 1560; the date of the first pencil, from the second Industrial Revolution. And what do we get? Three-hundred and ten Earth-years. Again, the premise is similar time ranges. In this perspective, you'd think Egerd's society would be coincided. But oddly enough, Egerd's dialect is Earth's "First World" Twenty-First Century, and its fashion is 1990s. So Brunon is ahead. I suppose Egerd's absence of mass destruction and only having a short civil war (a light way of putting it) was good for business.

Yikes, right? I mean, we're the ones with the true World war... It is hard to believe I live on the very planet (Earth... obviously) that faced such brutality... That stuff doesn't come cheap, and it certainly doesn't just fall out of ones imagination. I don't think I want to imagine any of it, anyways... Well, at least we know *someone* got it right. "Cough", Egerd. *Anyways*; it really makes me thankful to be living in one of the most amazing countries, Canada. Gloating is not cool... I know right? Tie me up and bind my hands. That's the amazing thing about time; you can't! I'm in the Twenty First Century – And yes, lucky us. This story, which you're in a ride for, would get me hung like many had during The Salem Witch Trials in 1692. Now that's food for thought. Still, I better be careful what I say...

With all of thee above, Brunon is sure coming up with new and aspiring ways to delight its time. No one in Egerd (that's the last time I'll be this literal) can forget the newest invention, electricity in the form of solar and wind turbine. In Maesemer, only the main streets receive this luxury.

Evelyn continues to watch the sky; she rubs her eyes again, tiredly. Today's the weekend and that means the market is expecting the Maelkyn's to deliver their vegetables and fruits that are usually ready for picking. The Maelkyn's own the second largest fruit and vegetable farm.

There's something unique about the morning in Maesemer, before the break of dusk. Crisp, the air has a fresh nip. If one is to ever go out before the sun touches the horizon, they'll notice the change around. The quietness surrounds.

Evelyn lights a match made of Oatiswax; Oatis insects gather this nectar from specimens and create a hive. It is done exactly how a bee worker passes their nectar to their species tongues, where the nectar evaporates and turns into sugars, and then the Oatis convert the sugars in their glands. This last step is created into "Honey", a term not comprehended by the people of this planet. A Planet called Thaera. The Maelkyn's and their society have their own tern for Honey. It's called "Nuetpate".

Evelyn takes the flaming match and opens a small hatch door of a lantern; she puts the flame to wick, igniting it. She closes the hatch door and ventures to Mother. There is a light mist, hovering above the ground. Evelyn's boots can barely be seen as she walks along its misty path, and she comes to the long rows of berry bush. Blue, red, purple and even orange berries are witnessed. Evelyn grabs a berry from a short branch and bites into it; it's cold on her lips, fresh like morning.

There to her left, leaning against the Maelkyn's backyard shed, a damaged shovel is. Evelyn passes it and ventures inside the shed to come to a low wrack. She grabs a pair of gloves, tossing them inside a steel bucket and leaves the many other tools and gardening equipment behind.

Outside the moon is hidden behind some cloud. Evelyn puts on her pair of gloves and retrieves her lantern, shining light along the dark path. She finds a simple bush to set up near, and begins picking from the short brush along her path.

Evelyn is a fit girl. She's a survivor, and she does what she can to get by with her mother. As a farmer, she must not only feed herself, but supply part of Maesemer. And with a town of farmers and tradesmen holding this place, these craftsmen and farmers are its only hope. And since coins don't meet much demand, this makes the way of life separate to Brunon, generating little to no economical growth.

'Mom, when are we going to get those new shovels? It's been on my mind lately.' Evelyn hunches below the bush. A few paces from Mom.

Her mother is overheard. 'The crops are almost grown, you know this, when the main harvest is ready for picking.'

Evelyn comes up from the brush. A large forest in the distance blocks all of Evelyn's view westward. Distant mountains of great lengths fight to be seen, cropped by the forest's high branches.

'Hey Mom, I was thinking about the forest. I know it's forbidden and all, but you can't help but be curious of what goes on at night.' Mom looks busy watering the fields, but Evelyn continues anyways. 'How can a few witches and their stirring pots bring so much fear into us?'

Her mother finally comes to a stare, but all she can see it the top of Evelyn's head since her daughter went back for more berry picking.

'Miss Madalyn might be cooped up on a lonely hill and speak of ghoulish stories, which is one thing, but her story on the witches could hold up, and that's why many of us still fear the forest and dislike Miss Mad for reminding us. You promise me, Evelyn, you promise me you won't cross over that forest. Not for your friends and not for me.'

But something in Mother's stare made Evelyn interested. Her daughter has a knack for looking for trouble. Like a cat, curious and clever.

'Witches are very powerful.' Her mother looks around, 'even if they're the last ones. Beyond myth, the reality of them could still remain. And besides all of this, you are not going in there to pick anymore of those darn Rooberries. I forbid it Evelyn... you know this.'

'Well, I was never going over there just to look for trouble. I came back out alive, didn't I?'

'Evelyn, you know it's not safe. You don't know what lurks in there. You were lucky, and you leave the hunters to picking those Rooberries. It's just not worth it.'

'I know.' Evelyn laughs off her mother's worries. 'But you have to admit, those berries came in good use.'

'I understand that. But it's not worth your life, now is it?'

Evelyn nods sheepishly, knowing there's no win to this argument.

'And I told you, I do believe the witches remain.' Katherine lightens up. 'I don't blame them for hiding, who wouldn't want to be the furthest from Brunon?'

'Interesting,' Evelyn responds. 'Maybe they'll come out of hiding once everyone empties out of Maesemer?'

Mother groans. 'I think that's the whole point, honey. Honestly, the capital wouldn't be too happy if their myth was found in reality,' and she goes back to watering.

The mist probes from the forest, moving more heavily between Evelyn and her mother's feet. The vegetables and fruits have a fresher appearance, dripping from condensation.

Evelyn punctures her finger on a prickly bush. 'Ouch,' yet retries for a juicy Haulberry.

'Did you hear that?' Mother calls.

Evelyn looks to where Mom had directed her focus, towards the forest; curiosity strikes. 'I don't see anything.' Evelyn said next with annoyingly, alongside her pain. She bends back down to continue picking more carefully.

A light grows across the expanse, deep beyond Evelyn's sea blue eyes. The forest's edges are now shining gold; she turns around to see the sun is up. 'It's beautiful.' Evelyn says, holding her hand to shield the light.

'Its morning,' her mother says and looks away from the forest to grab a barrel.

Evelyn rolls her eyes with a few Haulberries in mouth, 'which can only mean one thing.'

A rickety wheel squeaks and bumps. A small cart is pulled by the Maelkyn's family. Inside the cart are barrels filled with today's fresh picked berries.

A nord should be the one pulling, but they're too expensive to buy nowadays, and to take care of.

Evelyn holds one bar to the cart, and her mother the other, pulling with their back and chest muscles on the way to town.

The sky is bleak blue, and the nip is usual at this early-blue.

They continue to pull up hills and move nearer town, wearing their usual farmer clothes and heavy boots.

Maesemer bows to a castle in the southwest. In the shadow of early morning and in the black of night, the castle and its surrounding area is most quiet, and doesn't receive many visitors. But this place is no longer home to Maesemer or the far east. The castle remains a reminder of the dawning fate Maesemer could one day face; desertion. You see, Evelyn and her mother don't live in a time of medieval, those days were numbered. It's kind of ironic, since Maesemer is born from the ashes of Asnin's true found glory. Now that was a time of medieval.

Asnin was once proud by many, until the Upheaval left witchery for merely echoes. A civil war had gone on for many years, till finally, the witches were cast out into the forest. From then on, Asnin was liberated, and in not long, Brunon would take its place. But ever since the refugees of witches and what have you; those who ventured deep into the forest, disappeared… and forever, mind you. The people of Egerd knew the forest was no longer a safe place. History is what makes the Forbidden Forest… well, forbidden. When the revolution moved and built Brunon, come ash and memories, the remaining people, farmers and their land tied in their families names stayed behind and built a town out of rubble. You said it, Maesemer.

In time, some thievery from the Old Capital laid paranormal experiences to those who brought items back to the ashen-town. And from then on, the forest would become second to their worries. Maesemer swore never to set foot near the damned towers again. Of course, that never stopped the new generation born into this world. If anything, it only excites them further.

Those from the east call it an eager-to-hear "Wives tales" – Truly, the stories from the ashen-ones travel. But the town folk's with first eye of the Forbidden Forest know better. They've said it once before and they'll say it again, "The fall of Maesemer will be from the fool-hearted today".

Still accused as fool or not, Evelyn likes Maesemer. She likes the history and what it once represented before its civil war. It was said to be a place of freedom and rejoicing people, and this sparks her interest.

Yes, Asnin is a castle proud by few in numbers, and those mainly from town. Evelyn can't help but feel surrounded by the Old Capital's self. A history set farther back than the oldest of town folks residing. There's something about it that makes her question her own beliefs. In a time of spiritualism and inner-being, to her, it is a place reckoning with myth and power. For most, it's just stories to pass around dinner or an intriguing night time story.

Sure, nobody would miss its living standards. But the rule of thumb is simple; no more practice in magic, and this means there is something definitely going to go bump-in-the-night in that nearby forest. We both knew that was coming, didn't we?

'Mom,' Evelyn asks, seeing the town up ahead. 'I don't want to leave Maesemer.'

'Then don't,' her mother looks tired, having heard this a hundred times. 'I wouldn't judge you for it.'

'I just don't know what to do. What's it going to be like to have a career?'

Mother relaxes her speed to adjust to Evelyn's slower movement.

'Well, I'd assume it'd be a lot like farming, but you're doing a lot less work and way more studying.'

'Hmm. Don't like the sound of that,' and finds a frown. 'That sounds like work.'

'My goodness dear, do you really want to remain here as a farmer your whole life?'

'Why not, you're doing it.'

Mom is silent, but Evelyn can see a sad look on her face.

Hmm, no harm done... right?

'I know. I know. Life here is only temporary.' Evelyn says to her silence, figuring Mom sought through.

Mom spoke up. 'That is why we are trading for your books, so you can get into a good school, remember?'

Evelyn has a gaze someplace far off. Her lips move but her eyes stay glued forward. 'If I choose to leave, then I'm going to do something with money, perhaps an accountant. I heard it's the best career out there right now.'

Mom makes a face. 'Yuck.'

Evelyn never thought of how Mom would actually take it if she does decide to skip town. Could Katherine handle herself? Sure, it's going to be a lot more work on the farm being on her own, but Evelyn isn't worried about that part. Mom is built and can outwork any woman her age. But can she cope with the simplest fact and one being her weakest suit; her emotion? The distance could cause trouble for her... Who will she turn to if she gets sick, or just someone to talk to? Evelyn and Mom don't exactly have heartfelt chats. Still... doesn't a presence make the difference? One would think. Evelyn can't help but worry.

'Good.' Mom's voice picks up again, 'maybe you can teach me a thing or two about money. Either way, you're buying me somethin'. How about a nord so we can stop hauling this piece of junk?'

'Mom,' Evelyn's about to ask something more, but decided best to change tone. 'What will you ever do without me?'

'Well, the sooner you decide the sooner I'll have enough to trade our stuff for one of those nord's. You cost a lot to keep around, Missy.'

Evelyn nods her head.

That's just like her, always calculating what's best for her interests

'You think you'll manage?' Mom goes on to ask.

Evelyn's thoughts run.

Me? You're gonna ask me this?

'Yep,' Evelyn says and ponders afterwards. She picks up speech thereafter. 'I was only worried about making friends, is all.'

'Oh you'll be fine at that; I'd be more worried about their laws.'

Evelyn laughs. 'Well thanks for the vote of confidence.'

'Well, you're always up to something. Just make sure if you break anything, you can run faster than the person you're making trouble with.'

'Well, who's to say I'll be with someone?'

'Oh you're naughtier than I thought.'

Evelyn laughs. 'Oh, so you're giving me a lecture now? Because you're always the one up to something, yes, don't give me that look, disappearing and never telling me where you speed off to. You do remember when you said you were working on our neighbour's farm? I found that you weren't there. Where do you go to half the time? You know, something tells me you're up to no-good most of the time, also.'

'I had to go out shopping, silly.' Mom says playfully nudging her, 'and my dear *you're* your mother's daughter. *Alright,* I guess I really don't have to worry.'

Evelyn rolls her eyes. 'But do you ever take anything I have to say seriously? You never do keep to your promises.'

'Oh honey. I was only joking when I teased you. Seriously though, be smart and keep good grades and all will be fine,' she winks at her daughter. 'You'll see.'

'It's not the grades Mom; it's the whole new life-changing thing.'

'That's the best part. Trust me, moving out will be the best thing you ever did. I'm just hoping I'll get to see you again, once everything rolls over.'

Evelyn's brows lift. 'You really think I'll be that great?'

'Oh I do. I really do.'

The Maelkyn's pass the town houses on the outskirts to town central. The streets are lit with old lanterns, black from smoke and oil stains from Asnin's time. The pathway made from stone, the houses are made of this very same material, sedimentary rock.

A large tree comes into view. The Maelkyn's boots crunch under the dry weeds.

The moon can hardly be seen, still a celestial in the sky, where the sun is not too far off, shinning between the trees spanned arms.

The Maelkyn's trade their berries for greater needs at the market, mostly for eggs, bread and cheese. Very little folk showed up. Even the regulars were in low quantity, so meeting other demands fell short.

It made the Maelkyn's a little sad, but one thing was evident, Evelyn wasn't getting those new shovels she had hoped for. Even a rare commodity like berries can run for plenty, in a town as slow as this, eating is all anyone does, and berries are a great way to make a morning, evening or night, special.

Evelyn scratches her head and Katherine followed.

Mom says. 'I suppose no one will be having berry pie over dessert today...' -- Berry pies are another great delicacy.

'We can always try Mr Barkley's.' Evelyn tries to cheer things up.

Mom nods and the two pack their things to leave. They enter a shop on their way out of town central, where a sign sways. It reads, "Barkley's Inventions".

Inside is rather dark.

Every day the Maelkyn's stop by and find most of the items have already been discovered. In their encouragement to Mr Barkley, it helps him to create newer items, and much more will be on the shelves in no time.

The owner of the shop has "Grown" successful with his inventions, and to sell his uniqueness without lifting a finger on a farm. Brunon's rules restrict any conduct of invention. Not unless they approve can one have creativity on the streets, or commercial sale. That is why this man comes from the land of the many to sell his inventory.

Before Arnold Barkley was a well-known man in Maesemer, he felt he had to be an already success to grab everyone's attention in order to set up shop, which he arrived as an electrician who graduated from Brunon's top school, O.H. Occupational Hazard.

I'm joking. The school is a well known institution. Do you think you can guess its name? It's Brunon Institution of technology. Could have guessed it, right?

Evelyn taps on a metal and glass object situated on a shelf. Some items are for lower trade, all for the kids and adults in the slow move of things. It helps to spice up their lives, while the more important items are traded for berries and whatever Mr Barkley desires. It pays, or I should say "Trades" to get on his good side and know what his wants and needs are.

The store is dusty and hot; it reminds Evelyn of the dry summer days she spent here, with the cool breeze blowing in from the wide open door. To her, the shop is a perfect collection to town; allowing for the fast paces to settle down. There is dust accumulated between the floorboards from all the summer hazes, since.

'Ah ha...' Evelyn says. 'The solar light bulb – what else is new?'

Katherine gave Evelyn a frumpy look and turned to find the man at the back-store counter. 'Hey Arnold, do you have any new toys for me today?'

'Maybe, it depends on the gift you've brought me.' He says loosely with hunched shoulders, much like the fit of his clothes, reflecting that of the town's plainness.

'Sweet berries, of course.' Mom replies.

'Oh, very good ma'am,' he says with a swivel and disappears around back to return with something small and metal. He places it in her hands and says. 'This should be useful.'

'What is it?' Mom giggles back.

He exaggerates the moment. 'I call it… the "Quick Lantern".'

'A Quick-what?' She has a bored look. 'Mr Barkley, you promised me something grand.'

He reaches over and clicks a button on it. 'Indeed, I did.' He says and a light turns on, beaming wherever it goes in the palm of her hand.

'Oh my, this is interesting.' Mom says. She flashes herself once in the eye and then in Mr Barkley's, and then moves it around the room. There Mom points the light, to find Evelyn looking taken back by the new toy.

Evelyn puts her hands up and found Mom examining the thing. Evelyn decided it would be best to turn from site. Her daughter finds an item on shelf. 'Hey… is this new?' Evelyn asks figuratively, and then flicks a button on the side and got a little shock. 'Owe,' and places it right back down. 'Guess so… no wonder why it's at the back of the store and all…'

Still, to her, it is nice to see electricity work in such a little thing.

Evelyn turns to ask Mr Barkley now. 'Is this a compass that lights up, also? Is this the new invention you've been promising us for weeks now?'

'No.' He responds. 'I came up with that prototype just last night. I figured I could start incorporating light into all my littler gadgets after I came up with the Quick Lantern.' He scratching the back of his bushy head, 'and the item I promised is finished, yes.' He approaches Evelyn, who is still caught up in rubbing her thumb where it was buzzed. 'Sorry about that one,' he points. 'Some of these little buggers can be a bit wonkier. Best take that one away from yea'. Don't want anyone gettin' hurt, now do we?'

Evelyn gave him a short face. 'You probably should check all these others before putting them on isle.'

'Ah. But no need when I got you, ah?'

'You bugger.' She replies and finds another compass.

'You mean zapper?' He asks smartly.

Evelyn scoffs to his use of humour and flicks the light on. She mocks. 'But not clearly as bright as the Quick Lantern I see...'

'Still a neat device, no?'

'Rightly so,' she perks, forgetting about her last words, and moves toward more items.

He finds Katherine taping the lantern for more power, for the light is dimming.

'It is solar power.' The man says. 'Only in the sun can these miscellaneous conduct and extract light.'

'It's good...' Mom's eyes swivel, 'but you promised me something extraordinary.' Her eyes twinkle at a glass container, not far from where a cord is set up to a power box outside. She looks back at the torch in hand. 'What am I going to do with this when the sun goes down?'

'Mom, I'm sure it stores power.' Evelyn says, grabbing it.

Mother smirks.

'No doubt,' the man responds to Evelyn's statement, but Mom is silent, so Mr Barkley amends. 'Alright, fine.' He spoke in more of a rush. 'I was going to wait, more of an announcement, but since I had promised.'

He leaves again only to return with something small.

Evelyn grimaces.

Oh, another zapper?

He places the new device in Mom's hands. 'I have made a few. It works. It predicts the weather.'

Mom is silent, both Evelyn and the man aren't sure what she's thinking.

'W-What is it?' Mom finally asks. A look of hunger is in her stare. 'How does it work?'

He rubs the front of his forehead with his finger. 'Well, those are the temperatures, and the dial moves up and down, hotter, colder. Look, its one Cantatude right now.'

Cantatude is basically Celsius... it's... their way of defining things.

'The weather you say? Well *that's just* brilliant.' Mom hits Evelyn, making her jump.

'Well I know.' He smiles and finds Evelyn rubbing her arm a bit. 'Very good, will it be --'

Katherine is quick to speak. 'It's this,' closing her palm over the item. She leaves him with a goodbye, 'my lips are sealed!'

On Evelyn's way out, she stops at the usual toasters, bug zappers and a miniature greenhouse. She touches the greenhouse glass case, feeling the heat on her palm. A buzzing sound comes from a bright light bulb inside – to her glory; tomatoes are a bit plumper since yesterday, growing on a vine.

When he promised something extraordinary, Mom had hoped this was his new invention. She is ever curious if he could maximize its size. Evelyn feels much the same; still, the Maelkyn's remain happy, since the barometer is a gift of early brilliance.

Evelyn is quick to remember Mother and is fast to come outside. She finds Mom with an egger site.

Her daughter whispers. 'Can it really predict the weather, Mom?'

She jumps with glee. 'It can, it's a gift of gifts.'

'Well, since you're in such a cheerful mood --'

'Cheerful?' Mom eyes brighten, 'this is brilliance; he is a brilliant man that Mr Barkley.'

'Rightly so,' Evelyn says and then hesitates a little. 'Would it be fine if I worked tonight, with my friends and all? They found a great digging job for an old folk. I only wanted to do this because of the season. You said yourself I should start working, now that spring is among us.'

'Let me guess...' Mom eyes drop not having to look at her daughter. 'It's near the forest.'

Evelyn signs. She was sure Mom was fascinated *enough* by the gift. Evelyn would simply agree that Mom is still plainly aware, and will always and forever be... stubborn.

'Oh come on, Mom! It's for Rooberries, cheese and bread. Mr Barkley always said if we could make him a Rooberry pie, we could get something else. I think he's getting tired of our berries... and besides, we need some new shovels. And I can kill two birds with 'em Rooberries.'

Mom looks at her daughter. 'Rooberries...' Mom says and then nods in self acknowledgement, *'oh alright.'*

A look all too easy for her daughter and this makes Evelyn's eyes squint. 'So... what's the catch?'

'Oh nothing, only that you're home at the earliest, and if I find that you're out picking near that damn forest, then you're in big trouble.'

Evelyn's sapphires are bright.

This is not like Mom

15

'Well… alright then.' Evelyn says. 'I'm glad to hear you're trusting.'
'Oh… and one more thing.'
Evelyn has a careful look.
Here we go…
Mom has a smile.
'Oh mother… let me guess?'
'*Oh indeed.* If you want to go, then you guessed it right.'

It didn't take long for Evelyn to wait for the day to turn to darkness, even if she had to do homework from math class for taking her leave tonight. Don't get me wrong, working on the farm is hard work, but it's fun. But studying… however, you may as well guess it.

But what's ever more thorough, Evelyn's in for a treat as a new burden stirs, when a mystical fog lingers.

On the corner of Malvin Drive, there is one of the biggest lots found. Evelyn stops at its rocky trail leading past an open gate, which is never closed. Weeds pass her as she arrives at the front door steps. It's quiet around this part of town.

She comes up solid granite steps to use a silver door knocker, banging it loudly on one of the two large oak doors.

This house is very old, and it has always scared most kids around town. It's known for being haunted, yet those who live here never once said they've walked into a ghost, figuratively speaking. But Evelyn's found the parents have always been way too analytical without much care for sharing personal agendas, either. And the daughter that lives here would never spill the beans, not if it meant going against their word; which is just as much standing out in that case. That would mean a loss in the finer things in town… specialties, like Mr Barkley inventions, of course. I mean, what else is there to buy here?

Which reminds Evelyn, '*walked into…* no one has ever worded if they've *seen* or *heard one* have they?' She shakes her head. 'Cheeky --'

'Is that Evelyn?' A man's voice is overheard behind the door. The door opens. 'Evelyn!' He says. He's a tall guy who fits nicely in regular clothes, only because of his large frame. 'Don't look so stranded. Come on in.'

'Thanks Jason.' She replies, hugging him. She almost disappears into his arms. She's a thin girl from such a small bone size, and had always been thinner than most girls because of this.

It's warm. It's dark. A furnace can be heard. Evelyn steps inside and takes off her dirty work boots.

'Hey.' A brunette girl greets her.

Evelyn rubs herself. 'It's been a while,' and hugs Jonah to get one back.

Jonah went a little further to give her a warm rub on the back.

The three move into the living room. Lit candles are their source of light, flickering madly.

'It's chilly out there, huh?' Jonah asks her.

'Very.' She smiles, noticing they already have a drink in hand.

'Let's get you a drink. There in the kitchen.' Jason says.

'Besides, it's warmer.' Jonah agrees. 'And for crying out loud, you're only wearing a shirt under a jacket.'

'That's a start, a clean pair of genes for once.' Jason adds, noticing her outfit also.

'I know. It's just the rest was *all* way to dirty to wear. I figure it's a great way to ruin the last pair I have. Or should I say had?' She rolls her eyes. 'Oh well.'

Jonah scratches her head.

'That a girl.' Jason says, admiring the risk.

'It doesn't matter. You always looked g-great in whatever you wear.' Jonah says.

Evelyn raises her brows and spoke teasingly. 'Were you going to say something else?'

Jonah laughs it off. 'Yes,' and clears her throat. 'I was thinking grand, but decided great sounded better.'

Jason watches the two staring at each other. 'Is it me or is it getting romantic in here?'

'What?' Evelyn asks, knowing he'll do just about anything to change an awkward moment, awkward for him maybe. But when it comes to 'em girls, as the slang around town goes, it ain't.

Jonah hits him. 'I know right? This one has a lot of work to do. Hey mister, you're with me, remember?'

Evelyn smiles weakly. She finds herself at a frown as well. 'What is up with *these* candles tonight? It's new,' taking off her jacket. Sweat marks are noticeable on her armpits; she usually gets scared of what others will think of her body weight, and this paranoid feeling is the reasoning behind her profuse sweating.

The two notice her insecurity, but don't care. It's not the first time.

The kitchen isn't any brighter, where a few more candles are lit and spread out. But what is neat, are the solar powered light fixtures Mr Barkley installed. Evelyn had been looking up at it and came back to frowning at the two. Jonah is middle of the kitchen, leaning against the sink and Jason furthest, where the drinks are.

'It's,' Jonah starts laughing because she found it too humorous, 'Mr. Barkley's fault. He will be coming by tomorrow to fix them. For now, it's back to normal.'

'What went wrong?' Evelyn asks, admiring Jonah's soft sense of humour.

Jason found a frown and says. 'He might be wrong, but it's a brilliant thing we have him. God knows we'd be no different than those witches if it wasn't for him.'

Jonah answers Evelyn's earlier question.

'I don't know. It's his newest invention, but something went short in the wiring and now we don't have any lights.'

Jason sighs. 'That's because I told you, you shouldn't have trusted his newest ones. Anyways,' Jason turns to Evelyn next. 'Want a drink?'

Evelyn nods eagerly, 'Kaluberry?' She can feel her pits sticking to her sides. It's a yucky feeling. She tries to wear dark shirts so it is not noticeable, but sometimes, it hardly matters.

'Yeah, you're favourite right?' And he pours her a glass of the berry juice. He hands Jonah it, but teases her, pulling it back a couple of times. He spills a bit on himself, and Jonah laughs.

Evelyn just puts her hand to her face. 'You're both so adorable.'

'Really, you think so?' Jason asks.

'You don't even know when your best friend is being sarcastic, do you?' Jonah says and reaches in and grabs it, finally passing it to Evelyn. Jonah points at Evelyn's drink, finding it hard to hold when a finger is poking at her sides. 'We just picked some up this morning.' And turns back to slap his bugging hand, but missed. 'Ugh,' she sighs and makes sure to reach in and hit him.

'You picked it up just for me?' Evelyn asks, and the two nodded back.

Ugh, just focus on them and ignore the feeling. It always goes away afterwards. It happens; I'm just going to have to sweat and deal with it

'Okay, we should bounce.' Jason says.

Jonah gave him a stare.

'We were kind of having a moment -- Me and Evelyn.'

'We were?' Evelyn asks. She notices the moment and rolls with Jonah's humour. Evelyn smiles to Jason now. 'Yeah we kind of were.'

'Fine, when you two chickens are done flapping around this cage, I will be outside to see the two of you in one.' He says it with his single index raised and leaves.

Jonah just shakes her head. 'He's a weirdo. But that's why I love him.'

Evelyn frowns on a different subject. 'I'm surprised you didn't see us at the market today.'

'Who?'

'Me and my mother.'

'Oh... I was thinking the same. We must have just missed you guys. How are you and your mother doing, anyhow?'

'You know... she doesn't tell me much, mostly the same old same old.'

Jonah grimaces. 'I'm surprised she let you come.'

Jason voice picks-up from outside. 'Are you two *coming?*' He lingers the word.

'It's fine.' Evelyn says to Jonah, being interrupted and all. But Evelyn wasn't fine. It's been weeks since she brought up the subject or anything sentimentally close.

Jonah shakes her head after his interruption. 'We should burry him.'

'It would take the two of us, wouldn't it?'

'We do have shovels. And not a person would miss him, would they?'

Evelyn continues with their humour, 'were forgetting about his grandparents.'

'They never were serious when they said they wanted to take him in anyways. They wouldn't miss his messy self.'

Evelyn nods. 'Well, what are we waiting for?'

Evelyn ends up changing her pants into a pair Jonah gave her; they're roughly the same size. Jonah simply felt bad for the girl, not wanting her to ruin her favourite jean. That's why she gave her a different pair of pant.

Everyone knows Jonah's a rich girl of the town, because her father owns a distillery that exports to Brunon and sells locally. But nobody understands why they'd choose to live in Maesemer. Surely they could move house and still keep the business running? But Evelyn knows better, and that's why she likes Jonah, she's different -- a girl who likes the boonies over the cityscape. Someone who's not in it for the money, that's why she stayed behind; it's a figure of speech. She's in it for the free life this town can offer.

Jonah taps on the washroom door. 'Would you hurry up in there,' coming to a lean against it, only to find herself explaining the light fixtures as a subject matter. 'You know... It was my dad's idea. He always wants the newest thing when it comes out. I shouldn't have encouraged his rich taste for things.'

Evelyn opens the door. 'I wonder where you got *that* from.'

'Hey.' Jonah hits her playfully. 'I love my mom, Meanie.'

The two exchange glances. It's funny, because Jonah admires Evelyn's figure, but Evelyn adores the relationship she and Jason shares. It also makes Jonah more attractive, in Evelyn's opinion.

Evelyn swallows a little and Jonah passes her, smiling. They both knew, they felt it... but neither would tell one another of their little secret.

Jonah closes the door afterwards, speaking behind it. 'I didn't know he was moving so quickly on his part, Mr Barkley I mean.'

Evelyn leans now. 'I was just thinking that. I was there with my mother. She was really excited about --' she stops when she hears someone else talking.

'What, what is it?' Jonah asks worriedly.

Evelyn returns to her lean. '-- It's nothing, probably just Jason talking to himself.'

'Yeah, I thought I heard another voice...'

They both laugh.

'Anyways, it's his newest inventions. They're getting better.'

'Any news on that grand greenhouse of his?'

'Nothing yet, but my mother was happier today. She got a new toy of his. A "Quick Lantern", so he says.'

'Really, did she manage to smile?'

'Yeah,' Evelyn laughs.

'Well,' Jonah scoffs. 'That's a relief.'

Evelyn found a smirk in the silence. She turned her head away from the closed door to find a famous Mr Barkley invention on the counter. She's surprised she hadn't seen it sooner.

Oh sweet... one of his earlier inventions

She picks up a heavy toy car made of steel; a replica from Brunon's auto industry. Evelyn flips a button and its headlights turn on. She can overhear the voice again. She decides to check on it and moves back into the kitchen. The flash from the toy car finds Jason on the porch step. The man's talking to himself.

'Well...' She says; short minded, 'could be worse.'

Evelyn finds her place at the door again. Just then, the door opens and Evelyn almost fell. She stands right back up to find Jonah with her hand on her hip, who says. 'A Quick Lantern you say?'

Evelyn nods quickly, 'you bet.'

The girls come outside and he looked up with a grin.

The moon is above their heads. There is an early patch of clouds moving just beneath it, allowing for a silvery glow.

'Finally,' Jason says and Jonah leans in and kisses him.

'That'll shut him up, hopefully.' She says eyeing those mystic irises.

It caught Evelyn off guard. Does Jonah know about her little secret? Or perhaps Jonah shares the same one...

Jason and Jonah made their way down the front porch steps, but Evelyn waits. She frowns, and looks about. There's a smell of fire. But that's not why she hesitated, since fireplaces are common out here. Evelyn has got this feeling staring out from the porch. It starts from the bottom of her spine... something she couldn't explain – something she's never experienced before. And a slight shiver moves all the way up to her neck. She watches the two walk across the hill, together.

The moon watches them, and as Evelyn catches her breath after the chill, she moves down the steps and calls out.

'I'm coming you two, hold on up.' Now arriving at their sides, 'frankly, this whole place is beginning to give me the creeps,' hiding her hands beneath her sleeves.

'Finally,' Jason says who peers at her. He turns back to ask Jonah. 'It's been... what?'

'Too long,' she replies, and turns to Evelyn now. 'I've been trying to tell you this place is scary. I'm glad you've joined *our* senses.'

Evelyn scratches the back of her head. 'You guys didn't get a feeling just now, did you?'

'Now you're trying to scare us?' Jason asks.

'Sorry.' Evelyn looks away.

'That's not very convincing... Evelyn. But I don't want to know.' Jonah says and Jason agrees.

Evelyn ponders around and finally spoke up. 'It was just a feeling I got. Do you think this thing tonight will take longer than we've thought?'

'I don't know, but I hope you've ate something, it could be a *wild* night.' He jokes.

The three approach the neck of the woods.

'Where are we going exactly?' Evelyn asks them.

Jonah gave Jason an eerie look and the silence drew. Evelyn isn't sure what it means; perhaps it's the forest that scares her? Evelyn looks at Jason to find light, who gave Evelyn the exact look Jonah had. That said; he's definitely not afraid of the woods, so something else dark is at work.

'Are you serious?' Evelyn's voice drops when she figures it out. She turns to Jonah, 'we're going to Miss Madalyn's!?'

'Why are you barking at me?' She replies and then spoke with mockery. 'I also hear ghostly tales about that woman and her house.'

'Jonah, stop. Don't listen to her. It can't be any worse than Jonah's house.' He says, trying to reassure Evelyn.

'Oh Mom's going to kill me. You know I hate going this far out, least of all...' Evelyn stops when she crosses eyes with Jason. 'Sorry, but from what I've heard... she'll give me the creeps.'

'You have no idea.' He says, signifying his travesty of Miss Mad -- his aunt.

Jonah stops. 'Guys,' she points towards the woods, but the site is clear. 'I...' She stops and took one step back. 'I... I want to go home.'

'Yeah… Jonah… we clearly got the point.' He complains.

Jonah swallows. 'Jason, I was not kidding around! Take me home.'

He finds his frown, 'how come?'

'I saw a bear, or something like it.'

Evelyn looks between the two and took a step back, unsure.

'Jason, I want to go home. Now,' Jonah barks. 'Evelyn's right. I don't like the outside of town anymore then that damn castle.'

'You're just saying that because Evelyn said it.' He whines. 'Come on, let's keep moving already.'

Jason took a few steps till he sees the two still in their place.

Evelyn comes closer to Jonah and asks. 'Wait, you're being serious?'

Jonah nods her head, lost in a sort daze. A fear plain-to-see, 'I am.'

'I told you.' Evelyn says and turns to Jason now. 'It's in the air.' She whispers. 'I felt it.'

'Fine,' he exhales. 'We will take the long way around, instead of following the forest's edge.'

He waits, having little voice on this matter. Still, the girls have decided it's best to go with him instead of going home without the man.

The hills climb before them, where the moon fights to reach them again and again. Deer can be heard passing across the meadows. Slowly, they move closer and closer to the forest's edge, for the pathway must come to a close, which means they're close to the towers in black.

They can hear the slithers of a nearby river. It reminds them of this line of scrimmage. There, to the three's left, the land of the "Wives tales" remains tall. So many fears its darkness, hardly anyone enters. If Evelyn could cast a light on her face now, it would scream "Hurry".

Jason is in the lead. He points. 'We're almost there; it's just a little ways up this pathway.'

Evelyn looks away from Asnin in the distance. The towers are seen, peaked and pointy.

Jonah had been looking toward the forest on the right the whole time, being someway from them and off to their left. This confirmed the last of Evelyn and Jason's suspicions they may have had.

He leads them up this slope and they arrive to the boarders, on the outskirts if you will. The large castle can be seen more clearly, which overlooks them and a sneaking look towards the town at bay.

They've all heard the stories of Asnin's front gates being reopened, for they're no longer sealed like before, due to a prank by youngsters to enter its mysterious palace. Luckily, no one has been reported missing or hurt. With hundreds of acres of land to farm on, anyone is free to relish here at their own risk.

Weeds are overgrown and a few old buildings are noticeable, this far out.

They walk a little segregated town on the outskirts of ruin. It's a town remaining to those who feel for Asnin's heritage, but don't practice in it. Or at least, they're not supposed to.

Here, on this little rocky pathway, a large house stood out from the rest. Hidden from Maesemer, behind the tree line of the Forbidden Forest, and easily witnessed by the once and proud and mighty. The town folks don't participate in any chatter about the "Outsiders" of Maesemer. People who live on this outskirts, for they're always left alone, being the last "True" remnants to the shadow of the past.

'Is this it?' Evelyn asks the two.

'This is it.' He responds, dragging a foot to a stop.

Jonah stops behind them, breathing heavily. 'Well, it's... uh, a little happier than I pictured it.'

'Yeah but, who would ever want to live this far out?' Evelyn asks.

'Come on.' Jason says.

Small glowing rocks appear all around the house; Evelyn reaches out a hand to grab one. Its brilliance shines blue. She looks around and then stares up at the moon in curiosity, perhaps thinking the moon is the sake for this rock-light.

Jonah comes to a knee beside her.

Evelyn held the rock lazily. 'Odd, isn't it?'

'Frankly,' she replies, 'this whole place is way out of my comfort zone.'

Evelyn scoffs. 'Imagine that, now you know how I feel. But what do you reckon these are for?'

Jason takes a knee also. 'Well... I think it's safe to say it's not from around here.' He reaches down to touch one.

The girls grimace at him.

'We know that.' Jonah says to him. She looks away to stare at the forest again. 'Maybe it was just a wolf.' She finally took a deep breath in, letting it out slowly. It was utterly the first release of tension tonight.

'Oh come on.' He says, trying to cheer things up. 'It's been a weird night, sure, but let's not get ourselves twisted in all sorts of knots. We didn't come all the way out here to turn around now, have we?'

Jonah gave Evelyn a stare and Evelyn looks away. Evelyn saw the look in her eyes; something wasn't right about any of it.

He glances to the towers in thought, till he spoke them. 'Miss Mad has always been a little strange when it comes to her belief about Asnin and how it's a safer place then we all give it credit for.' He finds another rock to study. 'But this… this is something else. It must mean she's gotten them across the Forbidden Forest.'

'And that's why your aunt asked for us... I'd bet she knew we'd never tell anyone.' Evelyn responds and tosses her rock distastefully.

The three lingered there for a few moments before Jason stood up and walked towards the front door. The girls trail behind. Plants of all sorts are on the steps up, with more on the porch. Evelyn lingers here, finding more glowing rocks situated in flowerpots.

This must be the job, to plant them around house

Jason and Jonah stop at the front door that is in white, wondering if it'd be better to knock or just walk in. Before he turns the handle, Evelyn stops them.

'Wait, what was that?'

'Really,' Jonah cries. 'Can't you see I'm already on edge?'

'Shh,' she answers back. 'It sounded like a howl from the forest, not too far from here. Did you guys hear that?'

Jason finally stopped to listen. But it's Jonah who pushes through. 'Enough of this,' and enters slowly.

Jason gives the area a frown and then disappears after Jonah.

Evelyn follows in. It's dark, and it has a musty smell. She can see picture frames near Jonah, dusty like the walls. It's hard to make out the faces in photos. The floor creaks as Evelyn steps, and she turns around to find her friends staring in the wrong direction.

'Hey guys, I think we passed the staircase.' She whispers and squeezes past them. 'Okay, frankly, this whole place is terrifying.'

Jonah is furthest. 'Well, wait for me!' She says, grabbing onto Jason's arm.

He gives her a look. 'One moment you're all tough, and the next moment you're all scared. Make up your mind, woman.'

Evelyn comes up the steps to stop in front of another white door. She slowly turns the handle and enters a room.

An old lady looks up to meet eyes with her. The lady reaches out an arm and speaks. 'Are you the ones that have come to help me?' She fights to sit up, trying hard to look at the strangers that gather at the bed's end.

'Yes we are. These are my friends.' Evelyn replies, feeling insecure.

'You sure this is the right house?' Jonah whispers into Jason's ear.

Jason steps past ignoring his girlfriend. 'Oh hey Miss, it's Jason.'

'Oh Jason,' she looks like she could have had a heart attack. *'Well why didn't you say something sooner?'*

'Sorry, I thought you'd be expecting me... and my friends.' He says sheepishly.

'Yes, well... very well, you know where the shovels are. You may carry on.'

The curtains are open, with the windows shut tight. The room is dusted, being a relatively clean space.

Suddenly, the old lady asks Evelyn before her leave. 'Who are you? You have interesting eyes.'

Evelyn looks back at her friends, unsure. Her friends have wide eyes and they wait patiently for their leave. It felt odd, like somehow Evelyn's knew this old lady. She's only ever overheard the crazy stories this woman is rumoured for.

'Miss.' Jason asks. 'Are you alright? We aren't going to be doing this again, are we?'

She releases her stare. A gloomy look forms. 'No, no. You're right Jason. I doubt I'd find anything interesting anyhow.'

'Sorry?' Evelyn reacts.

Jason steps forward. 'This is Evelyn, a friend of mine, so be nice. You know... the one I said I would bring with me, for help. Remember?'

'Yes. Yes.' The lady gave them all a wave with her hand. 'You may go.'

'Sorry.' Jason whispers to Evelyn.

'It's fine.' Evelyn says a little coldly. 'But I'm curious Miss, where in the world did you just so happen to find those stones. The blue ones I'm talking about, just outside your house.'

A dark cloud moves over the lady, like Evelyn just crossed the line of scrimmage. 'Well, across the *falls,* of course.'

'S-So you ventured there alone you mean, and all by *yourself*?' Evelyn asks.

Her friends stared at Evelyn as if she was growing hair on her back.

'No, actually, I never would go that far into the forest. One of the hunters came and brought them to me. I paid him with Rooberries. I found a special spot that I know of, where many do not. I've gathered them and now I have plenty to grow in my garden. This is how I'm paying you all tonight. No risk. No reward. Am I right?'

'Come on. Let's just go.' Jason whispers in her ear again.

Evelyn moves away from him, because the lady's next words sunk deep.

'Ask me why I got the stones, because that's the question you seek. Isn't it my dear?'

Evelyn looks back at her friends again, before turning to the lady again. They have the same look as before.

Fine, if they won't ask, then I will

'Why did you get them, then?'

The old lady smiles, like she caught something in her web. 'To scare away what lurks in the forest, of course. That's the only way I could go picking that day. I brought them with me. It has to do with territory. The Dark Ones don't like the blue light, you see. It marks a different territory.'

Jason starts now. 'What did you say?' And steps forward to grab Evelyn's arm, but she tugs away.

Surprisingly, it is Jonah next, who steps forward and says. 'I think I saw what you're talking about. Are they like a bear, only... darker?' She turns to her friends' right after. 'Like a wolf, I'd say.'

'I'm afraid so dear. This means you're in a lot more trouble then worth mentioning, assuming it's crossed paths with you. Then you're all alone, I'm afraid. I'm sorry.'

The three faces fall.

Jason leans nearer Jonah and whispers. 'She's insane.'

Jonah nods, hopefully.

'Uh huh...' Evelyn responds. Not sure what to think.

'Naturally,' Miss says in a condescending manner. 'Since you're in trouble girl, it will be coming for you.'

Jason steps forwards again. 'I've never heard of this story before, and we all know you have many, but thank you Miss, *for that*. We'll be going now.'

'Careful Jason, watch where you're treading. I've told you countless times, one of these days you better watch your back. I have told you to be wary of the forest, but you still enter without a phase.'

'Jason.' Evelyn says. 'I think you're right. We should go.'

Jason shakes his head at the lady, not paying attention to Evelyn because of his anger. 'I know we've never seen eye to eye, but now's not the time for another one of your cruel stories. I mean, *really*? You want to do this now, in front of all my friends? And here I was just trying to do you a favour.' He turns to Evelyn next. 'Where is she?'

'In the washroom, crying.'

He turns a look at his aunt again, nodding his head a few times in contemplation. Evelyn was sure he would yell or something... maybe even curse, but he let this one go. *'Nice,'* is all he musters and he runs out the room.

'Don't let him fool you. You know better don't you?' Miss asks.

'I don't know.' She shakes her head with uncertainty. 'I'm out of here.'

'Don't go. Wait.' Miss calls and lifts her head for her to come a little closer.

Evelyn frowns, taking a few steps back inside the room. A question swirls her mind, so it was natural it would come up. 'What did you mean... by the *Dark Ones?*'

The lady sits up in her bed and dares for her to come a little closer.

Evelyn took a single step forward and swallows.

'They're hard to be seen. It hunts those who cross its path. So, once it chooses, then there's no going back. Best be lucky, Missy. I heard you've entered that forest as well. Let's hope it wasn't beyond their line of scrimmage.'

'Echoes Waterfall, you mean?' Evelyn asks. 'How do you know they can't be seen? What makes you so sure of any of this?'

'Ah, now you're asking the *right* questions. You're not like them, I see that.' She said with a head tilt, signifying the town folk. 'But you see... you and the rest of this town have it all backwards. The things that go-bump-in-the-night aren't all witches...' She leans forward. 'Oh no, but you've heard the stories, of everyone who've crossed the fall's and disappeared.

28

Oh yes. That's right. But I think the real question is who is really behind all of *this?*'

Suddenly, the downstairs front door slams shut.

Evelyn's head spins to its direction. 'What was that?' She asks, not caring for an answer back.

'Do be careful!' are the last words overheard before Evelyn skipped downstairs, racing down the front porch steps and out into the open.

'Jonah?' she yells out. 'Jason!?' doing a twirl, finding the night stars are brighter than ever with the moon in full bloom. She looks around some more, nothing. She moves closer into the clear. She sees something at the forest's edge. A lady holding a lantern, or it could have been something else… like she was holding that torch from Mr Barkley's shop.

Evelyn moves back, trying to compose herself. A soft fog lingers beneath the lady's self, covered in black. It appeared she's robed, but it's so hard to tell… Suddenly, the light fades and the lady goes back into the deep.

In the corner of Evelyn's eye, she can see a body moving downhill. It's Jason. Evelyn follows after him. Her heart beats faster and her quickness makes for a loss of footing, coming to a fall. She tumbles and rolls till she catches herself on the green. Her back slides and her jeans stained by the skid on bank. Half way on the hill, she can see Jonah too, running.

Evelyn gets herself up from grass to her feet, and watches something else move out of the forest just then. It's dark and hairy, like a bear but more sleek and long. It took Jonah, dragging her behind. And like that, she's gone. No screams were heard. No yells or a yelp for that matter. Only now does Jason; a man who is standing still, undoubtedly from shock. Yet from time, he'll soon have to face the next few days in tears, thereafter, his trying years alone.

Evelyn remains still. She is watching Jason from her spot. What she'll come to realize rather quickly is this; Jonah missing won't be the emotional battle for her. It'll be a constant reminder of what lurks beyond boarders…

And then they both hear it -- with Evelyn on her knees and Jason still tall -- a long drawn out howl.

It's a night Evelyn can never forget and a night so unbearable it was hard to manage the fear.

The stars were so far out; she remembers that they've never been more spread apart. A search party is accumulated over the days and the final result is of no body found. No tracks of any animal or any sign of an attacker. Evelyn and Jason go on trial for the murder of Jonah.

The town doesn't appeal, nor does Jonah's family. With no outstanding evidence against Evelyn and Jason, the two are not wrongly convicted and thus far, they're found not guilty in a court in Brunon. Case is closed.

A memorial service is set in place and Evelyn and Jason get back to say a few words. The mystery of the two are put into question, and their lives pick up where they last left off.

First Evelyn must face the night. The nightmares, which would awake her in a stir, it's always the same too -- her back is sweaty and her hands feel tingly and cold. She would awake with panic, and fear of going back to that dreadful place in her dream, where the dark one drags her away from her house and pulls her into the forest. Or like last night's dream, when she was sitting on the porch and heard something underneath it. And when she went to look, the Dark One is found huddled in the pitch black, all furry and dark, and rustled in leafs... Waiting...

The daylight hours should be safest. Bah... and when she has to go to school, here her story should be heard as well, right? Oh, it is. It's just once the story is passed around enough, it completely changes. Now this is where it gets interesting...

'Hey Madison,' Evelyn says.

Madison is a girl in all the same classes as Evelyn, and for the first time she ignores Evelyn and kept on walking. It's odd, because the first week of school was "We're so sorry" and "It must be so hard" from everyone she knows. And it's quick to see they've only said it to get by.

Soon, trouble-makers found a way of twisting things, about Evelyn's and Jason's story and it all blew out of proportion from there. Its Miss Mad's referred "Dark One" that got the students howling whenever Jason and Evelyn walk the halls. All of Evelyn's friends turn a head, and no longer walk with her. They fear she may have taken Jonah's life, or if she's just really "Cursed" like everyone's saying. What's worse is Miss Mad's stories have put Evelyn and Jason in jeopardy. To believe in the estranged couple's story would mean Miss Mad could be right about all her other stories, and nobody wants that.

If Evelyn thought the hallways were tough, the classroom and their bicker only got worse. If she knew what she knows now, she never would have tried so hard to hold onto Madison and her friends, for they joined in this bicker, also.

When Evelyn and Jason thought things would get better, the two will soon be degraded by not only students, but by teachers. And that's pun intended.

There was a time when Evelyn was invisible, until all eyes shifted to her because the more the story spread, the more the whispers gather whether it's in the school hallways or in the middle of town, it hardly matters. Evelyn and Jason would now be the talk of the town.

It's near the end of the semester. The two walk beside each other down the school hallway. 'It's as if *we're* the Dark Ones now.' Evelyn says to Jason. 'If not, then they're treating us forbiddingly, like we're the damn forest. People should be focused elsewhere and hunting the real threat out there.'

He says nothing. He just keeps his focus about him so that he'll get to class without making a mess of things. If anything, Jason's temper should be the biggest threat right about now. He got into a little scruff a few weeks back with a few taunting students.

You know those really good-looking hung up on themselves students? Yeah, you do. One of them looked at Evelyn just now, with an impression. It wasn't very obvious, but Evelyn's on edge and that was enough to set her off.

'Evelyn,' Jason says and reaches to grasp her, but she pulled away. He already knows what's about to happen for she just stopped in front of the group.

'Perfect.' Jason says, standing lonesome.

'You know what,' Evelyn says to a group made up of three guys and two girls. 'You guys think you're so god damn perfect, yet that's what so god damn hilarious. We all freaking hate you, so it's really just you and your perfect five friends. So who are the real losers now? And it's funny, because people like you need each other to give one another compliments on how good you look. Because if you didn't have him,' she points to one of the guys, 'beside you to let you know, you'd have no way of knowing and you couldn't live with yourselves. People like us. Ugly freaks, we don't need friends like that. We love ourselves. So the next time you care to look at me like I'm something unworthy in your eyes, remember that.'

'Wait what? You're not even bad-looking.' The dude she pointed at says.

'Yeah, you're... actually really damn pretty.' The girl that Evelyn nearly spat at says.

'...I am?' Evelyn asks.

'Yeah,' the same guy from before says and the rest of the group nods with.

Evelyn beams. *So this is what it feels like.*

'Yeah,' another one from group says.

'Great, isn't it?' The same girl asks her.

Evelyn no. Don't turn to the dark side!

'Yeah, actually,' she replies and scratches her head. 'You know... about what I said.' She does a bit of a twirl and scrunches her face. 'It sort of just *came* out quickly.' She expresses with her hands, 'sort of like blugh.'

They all step back and give her that face again. They all walk off. Well, except one -- That guy.

'Hey, wait.' Evelyn says and whines. 'You guys.'

'Just a tip, the next time you come up with some speech, you best bring some more people. After all, there are five of us and there's only one of you.' He winks.

'Yeah... look again.' She says and winks back.

He only smiles. And she returns the favour. It was actually a good moment. *Maybe it really was all in her head.*

'Wow,' Jason says when he catches up with her, and goes on to ask. 'So, what happened?'

She makes a sheepish face.

Aside from the town's disbelief of the "Dark Wolf" which was clearly stated by Evelyn over and over again that it's the "Dark One". The two set up plan to search for the body during Summer Break. Their plan goes ahead and they round up as many able bodies who have stuck with them through thick and thin. But Evelyn and Jason won't stop there, they can't. Evelyn wants to find the body as bad as Jason, for Jonah's family and to clear everybody's conscience. They confront the local sheriff for additional helping hands.

'I'm sorry, but the case is closed. We are to leave it alone. Let's not put the family through anymore pain then they've been through.' The sheriff remarks to Evelyn anxious request.

Evelyn saw the misery in her own reflection that day, but what hurt the most were the lost in Jason's eyes. He knows no one trusts them.

It is difficult to believe that the town's people don't see that these two are dying, metaphorically. Sure the two have thought of giving up, and taking their own lives. But it became clear, if they gave up, than it isn't just their lives that are spent. No… they cannot rest when the dark dwells so close to the reach, and so near to home. With that in mind, more lives would fall to the Dark One. With the unquestionable threat at bay, the two won't rest till they shine a light on what should not be forgotten.

Now at the age of twenty, being two years later, Evelyn still cannot convince the town of the reality of the *Dark One*. Jason has basically given up hope on his story, and tells the askers he doesn't know what he saw, for the sake of the town's denial, seeing that they've deemed the forest as simply "Cursed". Much fear Brunon will have the numbers to close down the town. For many years Maesemer and Brunon have been in opposition. But Evelyn knows better, with more disappearances happening and nothing to go in hand, it only goes to show Brunon has walked away, a long… long… time ago. It's clear to all, there's no intention of the east stepping foot on wicked lands.

Instead, this gives Jason the brilliant idea to start over in Brunon. By this time, it marks the end of school. She got the news of Jason taking his leave to Brunon from her one and only other friend, Corry. *But she damn as well made sure to surprise Jason* the moment she got out when the bell rang.

'How can you leave me to this place?' She calls half torn, storming and ready to cry.

'You don't know what it's been like?' He asks melodramatically. 'Do you not see the way they look at me?' Her look said enough. 'I can't stand another day here.' He says, looking around him.

She nods at him. There is a shiver, the one she felt years ago -- at a climb up her spine. A gust of wind blows, and she knew this fight wouldn't last any longer. There is no more energy in his eyes. She's seen that look before. She looks away, with the wind blowing in her face, and stares out towards the abyss of dust and dirt this town is built on. Their silence drew and this was it. Their fork in the road began.

Jason and Evelyn graduate, and he already has plans for his decent in a little under four weeks. With the dry season of fall at an end, her nightmares are nearly over, and one could say the stars have come back into focus.

She not only faced the people's questions, but survived their talk on a daily basis, birthing a new strength in her. She saw her mother grow braver, and Jason take up more challenges than to simply stay put. He started *another* town search before he departs. He managed it, and it went on during day, until it turned dark, and the search would have to be called off for fear of the shadow.

'Sorry Jason.' One of the town's people says to him, patting him on the back.

It's dark out, and Jason looks back at the forest, knowing it'll be his last search. Something dies down then and he slowly nodded a reply. He joins the rest of his friends and town folk the way home.

That is when the parents of Jonah have also decided to move on and go east. They leave for a personal coach and no longer reside on Malvin Drive.

Lately, with the final days with Jason, Evelyn will walk by Jonah's house with her in memory, just so they can remember the times the three once shared. Every time they do, a magical feeling crawl's over her shoulder's lifting her spirit. It tells her not to fear the shadow. It makes her want to run towards the forest and face whatever shows up. But she looks away, and the two walk the other way home. She looks back one more time, and Jason saw a new burning desire in her eyes. It told him she's not ready to leave Maesemer, that she's ready to face the darkness and confront that *thing*. If it shakes her to her knees, because of fear, then she'll not resist the challenge. After all, it's been like that for years now, and if anyone knows this feeling better, it's these two. So why doesn't she face it and get it over with? It's all about timing. For now the fire in her soul dims.

The girl comes back to the day around them.

He finds his tire, knowing it won't be long till he leaves. 'We'll have plenty of time to see each other before the weeks give up. Better yet, aren't you and your best friend meeting up tomorrow?'

She nods. 'We are.'

Evelyn's accomplished much, and has gone through more then she has expected, and on a particular rainy day, sitting across from her one and only other bestie -- one she made in her final school year – they talk of what's to come now that they're graduates.

'They say the beast hunts for the kill and then disappears without a trace. That's the basic story.' Corry says. He's a skinny boy with short brown hair.

Most around town give him credit for staying on the farm after an attack, with many more that have come to farm folk near the forest, within the last two years. He's been given more grace then Evelyn, and the town is starting to believe in the story Evelyn and Jason once told. She could roll her eyes.

Go figure.

Corry lost his nord to the forest when he and his friend went hunting for game. They left the nord behind, after tying him to a tree. The boys ventured out, and heard cries from Corry's steed. As soon as they returned fearing the worst had come, they found only this and much blood.

'Sometimes, I'll go searching for his remains...' He says, shaking his head. 'I cannot imagine what you two have gone through, especially with Jason.' He nods to his own premise. 'Anyways, I always bring my rifle in case the beast is ever to return.'

Can you guess where his friends are now? No, they're not eaten. They will be moving out of town. It seems all are finally getting the hint. The haunting of that day has always stayed with Corry, so naturally he can see Evelyn's readiness to want to stare fear in the eye. Even though she is angry with this town, she knows they're only scared, and have always been since high school. But now that school is over, she can finally take matters into her own hands.

And redeem what is ours – She might have thought.

Evelyn goes on to share her story in depth.

'I swore from that night on that I would never go near that damn forest again, but that time is over. It has been four years after that thing took the life of my best friend. I always thought Jason would be lost without her. Once I saw the look in his eyes then; I knew I was right. That night he sunk, he trembled, stumbling to his footing till he fell-a-foot. I was too far to catch him because that was supposed to be her job. It took him a surprisingly shorter time to get over it then I had... So I thought. He looked like he was getting better. Till his announcement to *you* --'

'To be fair,' Corry interrupts. 'He was going to tell you.'

She smiles and continues. 'I realize that. But it doesn't matter. That was his way of telling me he's had enough. Anyways, it never went away... and lately, I think it's only gotten worse. Still, one thing is for certain, the fear will keep coming back for the both of us. That's why I have to do this.'

Corry nods understandably and says. 'For me, my dreams were taunted with the image of the Dark One. Mostly being chased by its massive blackness, or at least, that how it keeps coming up as.'

'I know what you mean. It's the same thing, over and over again. It's long and thick, black like the night. Going back to my story, everyone including my mother saw my broken life for the first time. School life as I thought would be over. I thought... I thought I never would have cope with their lashing words, but I managed. The lady, Jason's aunt, she was approached again by the sheriff, and she still sticks by her story to this day... Well it's harsh... but she's right about one thing, which is that forest should not be meddled with.'

'But then, so aren't we.' He says with more focus about him. This is something she admires about Corry, his boldness along with his determination to find the Dark One. 'But tell me, why isn't Jason interested in finding it?'

'Oh I'll tell you why.' She raises a brow. 'It was late spring night, just two weeks ago. The memories came back to us. We tried to face the fear. There was a go-away party for graduation. Yes, I can't believe I graduated either.' She rolls her eyes. 'But I felt I had too. School surprisingly kept me focused, or at least... the homework did.'

He laughs with her.

Her eyes squint and she returns to her story. 'Unfortunately, at the party, it wasn't too far from the forest.'

Corry raises his brows, 'oh no.'

'Right? And I sat across from him at the fire, around a small group of us, pouring down our hearts. We overheard a howl just in the distance. We just got over the fact that it still exists, just for one night, that's all we asked for. All we wanted was to enjoy our graduation and forget about the terrible thing that stirs the forest. I looked up at him right afterwards and he stared right back. He raised his cup to me, and I knew then... he's really going to leave me to this town. The thought of the Dark One has been running through my mind ever since... Of course a few men made laughs, howling back, "Ouuuuuh" they chanted. But we knew better... it must have known we were here. It haunts us to this day. I think it's clear to say that that thing isn't going anywhere. Aside from that, this town has reminded us how much we've lost on a daily basis. But for me, and I can only speak for myself, it goes to show how much I need to fight in order to get back what is rightfully mine.'

'Like a little peace of mind?'

'Exactly,' she banters. 'It's clear to me; the Dark One isn't going *anywhere*. We thought maybe it's possible, maybe it would just back off and we could stay.' She shakes her head. 'But there's something else to this story you should know. This time I won't run, this time I will get my answers. Even if Jason is to leave because of the howl, after all these years of finding the strength to get over it and then *that* happens... I-I can't blame him.' She swallows. It's something far reaching in her stare that makes her change gears. 'Anyways, you know most of it already. It's not Jason's game anymore. It's mine. We humans have been underestimated by the Dark One for far too long, and I'm coming for that thing... because it's like you... stubborn.'

'*We*, you mean.'

'Yes.' She scratches under an eye. 'I also saw a witch that night. At least, that's the only thing I think it could've been. A lady and her forest is what I keep telling myself. I need to know who she is.'

'That's the secret you've been keeping from me all this time?'

She rubs her eye again. 'It's not exactly something I'd say I'm proud of. I don't --'

'I'm sorry.' He concludes. 'I might have over stepped when I said that. What I meant to say was I can't believe a witch could be behind all of this.'

'We don't know if she is, but we do know of one who will. I've wanted to go back; I just couldn't pull myself to do it…'

He asks with a raise of his brows, 'who?'

She waits, knowing he'll figure it out, and he does.

'No…' His voice drops. *'Evelyn, you can't.'*

'Oh… I will.' She leans forward. 'And you Mr are coming with me.'

He laughs. 'What?'

'Just bring your rifle; it wouldn't come out of its forest in the middle of daylight. Unless it's more stubborn then we thought.' She thought about it some more, stirring a frown. 'Best bring some extra bullets.'

The next day, on the beginning of summer, two graduates and one sick of being frightened pulls the image of Jonah's attacker from her head. She avoids the memory of that night.

'I've been waiting my whole life… so here we go again the place where it all began.' She says, knowing it sounds a little scrupulous.

He looks toward the forest and she follows his site.

He looks away. 'Come on.' He says and rubs her on the shoulder.

They move up the hill together and he unstraps his gun.

'I remember this climb with Jason and her. It's very odd.' She hugs herself and moves to the top. Asnin can be seen in the backdrop.

The two look behind them, noticing everything from this high up. He finds her site has moved to the black towers.

'Is this where it all happened?' He asks her.

'No,' and she points to where it had, aiming somewhere below the hill. They stare out, squinting with the sun in their eyes. They stayed like this for a few moments. Until finally, she eyes him and he turns his look toward the only house nearby. The two make their way there.

'I remember these steps.' She says, bending down to pluck a barley stalk and then places it in the side of her mouth. 'Now we can go,' and moves up the steps to walk with him towards the door.

He narrows his site and asks her before she knocks. 'You sure this is such a good idea?'

She peers around; the haze of the day is warming up. The bugs zip and hover over wet grass and tall weeds. There was a faint rain last night and so the air has a faint smell to it. It smells kind of musty. She turns her look to find the same flower pots, and those pots filled with stones, never moved.

She never realized this place in daylight, it's actually more frightening. Anyways, she doesn't reply, instead she lifts a stone from pot and says. 'I remember these babies. We found these blue stones that were glowing. I remember she said she got them across the forest and that they kept the Dark One away, because it reminds it of a different territory.'

He has a look of fear, approaching the flower pot. He leans forward to see it as she says. Perhaps he remembers the tales of the curses that people have said to have laid rest here. He looks curious.

She walks past him to the white front door again. It's pealing from age. Her hand reaches it and it opens.

'I didn't know we were being expected.' He says.

'We're not. She never locks her door. I don't think anyone out here is going to steal anything, do you?'

'No,' the boy says with a scanty look around, 'maybe just your childhood memories.' Weeds pass through the porch that offer an eerie look, 'and your livelihood.'

Evelyn chuckles and enters. She stops him halfway up the steps and this caught him by surprise. She stares back at him, making him more nervous then he already is.

'What?' He asks with flickering eyes. He's two steps below her.

'This reminds me, Miss Mad told me she found the stones in the forest, which some hunter got for her.'

'So?'

'*So*, she's not telling the whole truth,' taking a step down and one closer.

His brows look heavy from the heat of the moment. 'You're saying she's protected by the witch of the forest, is that it?'

'Yes. How else could she have known of where to find them? How else did she know they'd keep the Dark One at bay? This also makes me wonder.' Evelyn puts a thinking hand to her mouth. 'Why else would anyone want to be this far out... unless,' her eyes turn in the direction of Misses bedroom.

He fills it in. 'Unless she knows where the witch is.'

'Yeah,' she says slowly.

'I don't know Evelyn… this seems a bit far off.'

'Just be careful.' She says with eyes fixated on where she intends to get her answer.

'Um…' his frown became a little softer. 'I'm not sure what to say to that, knowing that it's all a little far-fetched.'

The lady doesn't look like she's aged a day. Corry enters behind Evelyn, standing nearly the same height and spoke while Evelyn took her time.

'Hi, sorry… about --'

'I know why you're here.' The lady says, not looking at him. She's watching Evelyn move around. 'You look older. And I can never forget those eyes. But sometimes, things change. But can you see it? Your eye tells me a different story than the last time you where here.'

Evelyn turns a look. It didn't seem like she cared. 'Thanks. You're not looking so bad yourself, Miss.'

The boy watches the two, noticing a little tension.

The lady is clearly more sympathizing this time. She gets to the point of this evening. 'A hunter that goes by the name of Claud, son of Dale Ashback has seen its ways. He's seen them cover their own tracks.'

'Wait one sec.' Corry steps in, 'you said *them*?'

'There's more than one?'

'Yes.' Miss replies for them.

'Well, that would explain not finding its tracks.' Corry says.

'Yeah but… how did it take the body and cover its tracks?'

'Clever one,' Miss points at Evelyn. 'But the one that took Jonah was the leader and he doesn't make mistakes. These animals hunt on their own time, but on a rare case such as yours, the leader was crossed. Normally, one of the pack would choose a pray; game and sorts and then they'll hunt for the thrill, and naturally, the kill. She would have had more time. Also, the pack never leaves the forest. That's what makes me think it was the leader.'

Evelyn nods, understanding.

'It was a clean kill.' Evelyn says.

'It wasn't playing around.' Miss replies without a doubt. 'Claud was careful. He found a mistake they make in their cover-up. He is the only one who can track them but he still hasn't found their den yet. He's made sure to clear his own tracks. But we can't be too sure of this. This is why we must be extra careful when around Claud.'

'I've heard it two weeks ago. The same roar from that night.' Evelyn says, looking around dangerously and chewing softly on the barley. 'Fighting is back in business, I suppose.'

Miss swallows. Not because she's scared, but to clear her throat. 'It's not like that at all. Don't be foolish. It's not helping your game anymore then you wish.'

'Right,' Evelyn rolls her eyes, pacing again.

The lady can see the look in the girl's eye. It didn't take much to notice the "Bad kid" is there. Miss goes on to smile and peers out her bedside window; remembering her time of adolescence. She sits herself up like she had four years ago. 'Evelyn.' She says painfully. 'They're not to be meddled with. You walk like they will just go down with one shot. This is not the case.'

'Then what do you suppose I do?'

'Not these kind. You must keep your distance. They're not to be taken lightly. They're not some "Curse" like everyone --'

Evelyn ignores the reminder of death. 'And where is this hunter you keep speaking of?'

The woman nods, taking her time. She notices the boy has a gentle look about him but kept her words with Evelyn. 'Do you always remember what people tell you?'

Evelyn shot an emotional look.

The lady made a smack with her lips. 'The hunter you seek never crosses the falls. At Dale's farm you must seek the man who's gone above and beyond. He's not to be reckoned with. He's looking more like your future everyday and not to mention your friend here, also.'

'Corry,' he says, interestingly. He has an undetermined look, whether to shake the lady's hand or not.

Evelyn gave a sigh and found her place. But it was the lady who spoke again.

'Why did you bring him into this? He's just a boy.'

Evelyn speaks lightly. 'He's none of your concern.'

'How's your mother of all days, then?'

Corry knew that one would be felt.

Evelyn's eyes pinch. 'How dare --'

'Dare I?' She replies, laughing. 'I know she wouldn't approve of where you stand. She keeps you on a tight leash. Ha! I hear people talking. I hear what they're saying about you and me whenever I go... downtown, mind you is looking a little rusty... I don't know if you've been down there lately or not. But what you're doing – you're just asking for trouble. She's right to worry about you, you know. I would if I were her.'

'Well,' Evelyn laughs a little. 'Thank god you're not.'

The boy steps in... well... two steps forward. 'Hold on ladies, it's time to get answers. That's why we're here, remember? Save your energy, you both look like you could use it.' He glances at the old lady and one Evelyn's way. 'You should keep your wits about you, Evelyn, for the fight.'

Evelyn ignores the boy, turning back to her. 'I know why you -- why you hate me so damn much.'

'Why?' The lady asks.

'I bet you blame yourself. Because you see yourself in me and that *scares* you.'

'A little,' the woman agrees. 'But look at you, now you got this boy doing your dirty work? Look, I'm not interested in this little tirade you two got going on, but to me, you're the one who's looking a bit on edge, as you should be.'

'*Oh no*, you can't change the subject now that I've put you on a tight leash, Missy.'

'Missy, who're you calling Missy? I should have you know, it's not that I despise or... hate, Evelyn.' Miss is trying to sit up again. 'I can't help it when I see you going down a --'

'Save it.' She whines.

'No, I will not. I broke both my legs falling down one of the old hiking trails in that forest. I also saw a witch then. She helped me. She's not your enemy, Evelyn. Why... why the Dark One attacked your,' she hesitates and licks her lips as if they're salty. 'I don't know why it did it.'

Evelyn's face drops, 'witch? What witch?'

'Evelyn.' Miss hesitates. 'I can't say a word. She has me sworn to her word. She's only out there to protect the forest.'

Evelyn took one step back. 'I can't believe this. You're so working with her. *You're* against this town. You're against *us*.'

'You're over reacting.' Miss replies.

Evelyn turns to ask him instead. 'Am I?'

Corry has a few glances between them.

Miss puts a hand to her mouth before speaking. 'She doesn't want to harm anyone. She told me about the stones. She's trying to protect *us*.'

'Right, and what did *she* say? What?' Evelyn barks, spitting her barely from the side of the mouth.

'She's trying to convince their kind to stay back – a light way of putting it.' She shakes her head now. 'It all started when the last of them went bad. It's hard to explain.'

Evelyn looks like she was about to say something, but stopped when she looked pleased.

Went bad, pf, that's one way of putting it

'This mean's she's not sure what to believe.' Corry says in regards to Evelyn's silence.

Neither woman has anything to say. But Evelyn finally turned to Corry, she was about to say something but closed her mouth, yet again. Thoughts linger, about burning the whole forest down and being done with it. Yet she found the eyes of Miss again.

Evelyn asks. 'Just tell me what I need to do so I can go in peace.'

Corry cringes.

'Figuratively speaking,' Evelyn filled-in before Miss could say anything.

'Hey, you said it kiddo.' She replies, regardless. She held a sad look, feeling a little bad for how she dealt with Evelyn this evening. Miss scratches her head. 'I can tell you this. The next time she came to me was in my dream.'

'Really, you expect me to believe that?'

'Hey, believe in what you want kiddo. Just don't go chasing butterflies. Instead, let them come to you.'

Evelyn nods slowly. 'In my dreams, I can talk to her you're saying?'

'I'm sure she has already tried, but you weren't listening.'

Corry raised his brows, looking mystified. He looked like he wanted to tell Evelyn something, but is easily side swiped.

'And what about this Claud man, this hunter.' Evelyn asks with a rotating hand to hurry things up. 'This is what I came for.'

Miss gave Corry the look, the same one she gave Evelyn. Hoping he could convince the girl to let this one go. He says nothing. 'Claud say's these beasties move in the deep. You will find Claud at his farm, or you can try town central where he might work with his father, Dale, at the butchery. If you seek revenge, then believe in him. I've heard he's the man for this sort of thing. Remember, the Dark Ones come out at night, so no strolling during hours. They've been around here plenty, but it's as he said, they hide their tracks. I can't find one either, nasty buggers. I've never seen a Dark One... mind you, but lately I've been hearing them all the time now.'

'Lucky for you, you have a witch to protect you.'

Miss ignores the girl's tone, knowing she wouldn't say such things if she knew the half of it. 'The dark ones have this name for a reason, but they weren't all bad. There once stood a time of good and balance of the forest. The witch that helps me told me they were called the "Guardians". Apart of a team of different race-animals that work for her. The Lady of the Forest is what she calls herself. She can talk to them and work with nature. That is what the remaining Guardians call her and she calls them... so she says.'

Corry asks as if asking one's self. 'They talk to each other?'

Miss nods a reply. She explains further. 'The Dark Ones are your enemy, and they work with three bashful witches. Dolona the White, all evil and no light, its sort ironic her name, and then there is Candy; a name she's given herself after the fall of Asnin, in order to stay up with the "Times". And then there's the last but least, the leader, who calls herself *Moora*. "An evil bitch" I recall the Lady of the Forest whispering in my latest dream. She also told me you were coming. Anyways, the Dark Ones were once Guardian pups, a Shaywolf is what they're called by our ancient ancestors, long before Maesemer's time.'

'And you expect me to believe in all this crap?' Evelyn asks, torn by what she saw years ago in the shadow, so she reinstates. 'I mean... I'm just not so sure what to think.'

'It's up to you. But the story goes; once the Shaywolf leader was slain, the clan can be persuaded and that's why the witches took advantage. Altogether they took the pups and banished the remaining Shaywolfs, which are the most threatening of *the lady's* Guardians.' The two look at one another and Miss Mad concludes. 'The rest of your answers will lay with Claud. I think I've told you enough for one day, yes?'

Evelyn walks past Corry and leans closer to his ear before walking out. 'Having fun yet?'

'Yes actually. It's kinda getting exciting.' He replies. He gave Miss a slight nod, and he leaves too.

'Evelyn, revenge is never the right answer.' Miss says louder after the two are heard moving down the stairs.

'So then threatening the town is?' Evelyn turned the question on Corry. 'No, she couldn't be anymore wrong. I think it's time to face the ones that walk the deep.'

'Evelyn, maybe we shouldn't go chasing after something we can't handle.' But Evelyn was already gone, pushing past him and moving down the steps.

The lady spoke as if to the dim of the room. 'If only you knew she was trying to protect you...'

'So what do we do?' He asks her, moving outside.

'Seek out the man she spoke of. He's the one. He will lead us further to finding her body, if not... then the den.'

The boy shakes his head feeling unsure of the bashful. 'Well what about the witches? You heard her; we just can't go waltzing in there alone, what with... a silly rifle on our backs?'

'We cannot.' Evelyn agrees turning a look to the porch steps where he waits. 'But with *his* help we can.'

'And what if I tell your mother? I know she'd never approve of any of this.'

Evelyn smiles largely. 'You're wise. But we both know you wouldn't tell her, not when the Dark One has so easily walked over you. Remember, it knows you. You're under its watch... we all are. Something tells me the Lady of the Forest will be coming for us, also. When she comes to you in your dreams, tell her *I'll be coming for her.*'

'Evelyn.' He runs down to grab a hold of her. He finds an uneasy look back. He says. 'She's not our enemy. She is on our side, remember?'

'Then she'll have to prove this. Until then, they're all our enemies.'

He watches her reckless-self move down the hill without stopping to think of who has the gun in the first place. 'Ugh.' He whines. 'Alright, fine. I'm coming with you.'

They stare back at the butchery in the middle of town. The sign sways in a gust and he grabs her arm again. 'No, wait. Think about what you're doing.'

'Are you seriously going to back down?'

'Look at you. This isn't the Evelyn I know.'

She sighs.

He throws his hands up and walks off. 'Well you know what; I am walking away, so sue me,' turning around to back pedal. 'You need to wait for tomorrow.'

She looks back at the building, instead of him.

A few heads turn when he yells out again, 'tomorrow, Evelyn.'

She watches him move through the streets with a little pep to his step and he's gone.

'I can't hold back now. I'm so close.' She says and steps forward. A reminder, it moves up her spine, that same feeling that once ticked. It makes her stop and swallow. She takes a step back. 'Alright,' she closes her eyes. 'I'll wait till tomorrow.' And she steps off the way home.

The day is picking up and it's becoming a scorch. Evelyn finds her way up the steps to enter the house.

'Hey mom, I'm home.' Evelyn says to find no answer back. She moves to the stairwell and calls out again, there is nothing. 'Hmm, must be out.'

Evelyn opens the icebox to make lunch. It's always stocked. She grabs ground beef, an egg, and vegetables and begins cooking. Firstly, she sets up the pan over the gas burner and lights a match, igniting it. She pours oil into the pan and places it on the burner. She chops vegetables, and in no time made a patty with the egg, and then seasons the burger meat, placing it in the frying pan along with the vegetables. She plates mashed potatoes from yesterday's leftovers, found in the icebox and finishes her burger with a poached egg.

'I wonder where she'd be of all days.' Evelyn thinks out loud during lunch. 'I'm guessing Coraline's.'

Coraline is a lady, one who is close with Katherine. But one who constantly requires the help of ploughing and farming. The madam trades well of course, and Evelyn can't help but agree with Mother being a pick of the crop; a darn good farmer who is sure to be getting a lot of work done with summer time here.

Something is heard moving outside and Evelyn stood up, and everything in her being felt as if this something could jump.

'Hi.' Evelyn says with wide eyes.

Katherine enters and returns the favour. She looks around the room, noticing nothing out of the ordinary. 'You look like you just saw a ghost.'

'I know. It's nothing.'

Mother looks behind her and then she knew. 'Honey, are you okay?'

Evelyn gets annoyed when Mom does this. This act always makes her pull away… and they've never really been buddy-buddy to begin with, if you know what I mean.

'Yes. I'm fine.' Evelyn finally says.

'Alright…'

The only time they usually get to talk to one another is around supper, and Evelyn likes it this way. It is short and not much time for chat is met.

After Mother finishes with the garden and Evelyn with her chores around house, the two found one another sitting on the porch for a break. Neither said much. It all changed on that frightful night, four years ago. Now, Mother and Evelyn have never been further apart. With Mother's constant worry, and Evelyn's experiences, both have become different people. Evelyn can't handle soft people any longer. Besides this, she can't shake Mother's clingy attitude. It makes Evelyn want to stretch or even go for a run. Heck, let's just go with both.

The day is coming to a close, and a cool wind blows through the kitchen window. Evelyn and Katherine don't have any electricity, only candlelight. The room flickers and cast shadows around the room. Evelyn dries her hands and turns around in thought, coming to a sit with the food in front of her. She sat there, for how long? Awhile, thinking of the Dark One, and how cool life is now that she is free from school. The thoughts of the Dark One picked up during late dinner preparation and haven't settled since. All the emotions of this morning have started a simmer inside her, and now the pot stirs -- She remembers that night…

'Honey…' Mom scares her. It snaps Evelyn out of it. There Mother's look returns. 'You've been farther away more than normal.'

'Sorry, I lost in thought.'

It doesn't take long for Evelyn to want to get up and leave. Oddly, Mother suggests for company outside on the porch. The weather is particularly calm, feeling it'd be good to bond on a warm start into summer and have their dinner here. It wasn't such a bad idea, so Evelyn joins her mother to get some fresh air.

'Wow, the winds are so warm.'

'It's nice.' Mother says.

The neighbour's farm is not too far from here. It's a much smaller property with two boys and their father. The mother divorced their father and moved to the big city. This seems to be the sprawling of the ages.

Evelyn's cheek lifts in thought of what life could be like in the far east.

'What are you smiling about?' Mom asks her playfully.

'Brunon.'

'Ah yes.' Mom says, and her next words are loud from a train of thought. 'The big city, a city... with tall buildings and hefty crowds, everything's much louder with beeping horns too, with everything requiring money to be paid for. Oh, not a thing is cheap; nothing bargained or traded, either.'

Evelyn thinks she can see a faint outline of a star. She giggles. 'It's not like that Mother. I was just imagining my way.'

Mom scratches her ear. 'Oh...'

It's kind of scary... Okay fine, maybe it's not that terrible. Silly to think... I've never been there. So how could I know? Maybe that's the first thing I should be thinking about though, is heading out of this town

Evelyn looks around and found her smirk.

Who knows...but this place is my home. I can't go. I don't want to go... I'm too happy here

She smiles at the thought of Corry now.

He's a funny one. Maybe – You know what, he's right. I have all of this and I'm frowning? What's up with me lately... what happened to me?

'Corry... you were right...'

'Right?' Mother asks with food in her mouth, 'right about out what?'

Evelyn smiles to herself, feeling calm come over her. 'Ah it's nothing.'

Her mother surely notices how much her girl's changed throughout the years, showing her quirkiness to all, and never losing herself to those who deemed her cursed.

With the sun finishing its trail of the day, the glow crosses the mystic dusk while the two sat in its end, watching the final light fade. A good moment came over them. It birthed their talk, and they got comfortable with explaining their day to one other, except for Evelyn's morning details of course. It was a nice talk, and they haven't bonded like this in some time.

They wash up and get ready for bed.

Evelyn finds herself cooped up on her bedside, lying back with her head near the window, watching outside and thinking of random faces and places. Sometimes, she'll even picture a whole new life for herself, with new friends and all – Whatever's most exciting to her and for what feels right. She got so caught up in her fantasies for a better world, she snaps out of a sort bit trance. She'll do this imagining whenever she feels compelled too, or lost. In other words, she's done this many times before.

The moon stares through Evelyn's bedside window, as if it had been watching her the whole night long. She puts her day to rest, slipping on her favourite pyjamas and snuggles under covers.

The wind taps on her bedside window. Outside the darkness is shuddering. Pitch black.

'What did she want from me?' She asks herself, thinking of the lady in the shadow. She shook a head, and begins imagining the ceiling is a skyline of twisting galaxies. Another question came to mind. 'Who am I?' scratching her neck.

Evelyn... let it go

The stars twirl onwards into a bigger universe inside her imagination. Here the moon is missing, and the sun is shining someplace on the other side of the world. She turns on her side smiling to her awesome use of imagery.

- Chapter 2 -

The Butchery

She twists in her bed. Her dream is a vivid one:

Out in an open landscape, Evelyn can be found.

The boys across the Maelkyn farm are rolling down their nearby hill. Evelyn can't help but feel lonely. She calls out their names but they continue to play on.

'Evelyn.' Her name is called. It was Mother's voice from home. Mother never chooses to yell and this is what frightens Evelyn. Evelyn finds herself running to the house in worry. She arrives at the front porch steps, 'Mom?' But there is no answer. Evelyn goes around back. The wind is blowing, and there is a storm picking up in the distance, just above the forest. She stops to the site of the storm's black and purple haze. She turns her attention below it. A churn inside her is due to the dwell of the forest, killing her funny side altogether. Her mother is there, standing at the edge of the forest. Or at least, she thinks it could be her.

Evelyn moves across the grassy floor. She nears the forestry and before she could get a good glimpse of this being, the image turns its back. This made Evelyn come to a halt.

'Mother,' Evelyn frowns. 'Isn't it you?'

A loud crash of thunder makes them both look up. Clouds move overhead. All of a sudden Evelyn finds herself on all fours to another loud shake. Down here on lower ground it makes her feel safer. Her creeping self moves towards the woman. Evelyn can see the being has long hair, just like Mom's. So who else could it be, if not her?

It's getting dark out fast. The moon is showing, when a few seconds ago it was mid day.

From her animal position, the girl tries to get a better glimpse of the woman's face. That's when Evelyn knows, if she wants to be sure, she'll have to reach for her attention.

Something in the air thickens, making it hard for Evelyn to swallow the saliva down her throat. She can feel ice under her knees, nipping her palms where she goes. She reaches out and her entire body shivers to this fast changing environment.

Before reaching to turn the woman, Evelyn whispers. 'What do you want from me?'

The woman's breath can be seen, all the while, Evelyn turns the figure around to find no face; only dark space.

The blank space speaks. 'What do you want from me?'

Evelyn falls back. 'F-From you?' and then she realizes the lady holds a mushroom in one of her hands. Evelyn clears her throat to speak again. 'Well, I-I want to know the truth.'

The being holds out the mushroom, it's blue. Evelyn hesitates, and the black gave a head tilt, sympathizing. Evelyn slowly reaches for it. The shadow puts a hand to mouth, signifying Evelyn to eat it. Evelyn takes it and eats.

'*Now* you'll have your answers.' The being says.

Evelyn looks up to a loud thunderstorm, and would have sworn the shade gave a smile. Evelyn freezes to another sound not too far off. It sounded in the forest.

'Mother?' Evelyn whispers again and brushes past the ghost to arrive in front of a bush. This large shrub shakes on the boarder of the Forbidden Forest. Evelyn reaches a palm, for the sake it could be her. A wolf pokes its head out and her hand lands on it.

Evelyn blinks. She's awake, feeling too frozen from fear to move. She lay still, until finally coming to a sit up position. She swallows and stares out her bedside window. A gaze that should have lasted only a few moments, lingers.

'What the heck was that about?'

She exhales deeply, and repeats this exercise till she feels safer, for her palms are clammy and cold. But what is next, is somehow her reality has changed... She lies back on her bed and rests there for a few moments, staring at the ceiling. Then it hits her; there's something definitely different. She feels like she is still dreaming, even though reality is still upon her. This is an odd feeling, and all she knows is this must have something to do with the dream. She clasps her face over and over again, trying to wake herself up.

'This can't be real... How can life all of a sudden become quasi? It appears as a dream.'

She can feel the fear. Her tears rush down her face. She feels numb. Her body shakes to her crying. She swipes the tears and looks down at her palms. She can feel vibrations moving through her body, similar to when someone get hairs standing up from being too cold, or experiencing an intense moment. It's this, except warmer.

'What the heck is happening to me?'

There are little to no thoughts, with a focus for the moment. It is... tranquility.

'The Lady of the Forest... that's who was in the dream.' She squint her eyes from the daylight coming through her window. 'Is that why this is all happening to me? But how could a dream have such a large effect on me?'

Feeling the fear, Evelyn gets up and gets dressed into what she wore yesterday. She heads down the steps, with her heart beating fast. She is stern when life is loose. Her hands reach for her face again, feeling a bit paranoid with all of this. It's more than just spacey – she feels like she is watching a scene of a movie, being the observer, instead of the actual character. She feels out of body, but isn't. Time feels slower, but it's really not. Her focus is in one place. It is all in the moment, with a mind that is quieter than usual. Her life feels new. There is a flow of emotions too that are making her excited. The only way to explain this totality would be one's first (virgin) alcohol intoxication. Only, without the time lag and brain fart.

A flash of sunlight bears on her skin. She notices the warm kiss of the ray. Sound is more crystal clear, too.

Could this be a dream?

As she thought it, she knew deep down this was no dream. Somehow...
eating that mushroom has put her in a new state of being and thus, the
dream has interfered with reality. Some kind of spiritual transformation,
if that's what one should call it.

'Mom,' Evelyn calls out and moves outside. It's surreal. It's like she
just walked through a portal to a new universe and is somehow awakened
to a deeper part of self. Feelings are creating new sensations over her
body; emotions are in greater tune, so much so, she can feel a pulsating.
A vibratory state, like the blood rushing through her veins is tickling as
it moves.

The feel of morning is fresher; bewildering her all the more. Where
it was dark, now there is light. Where there was weakness, she found her
strength.

With the help of that one terrifying night; she could feel herself coming
into her own. Not just her body, because she's grown into that beautifully,
but also her mind and soul. But today's new finding is something else.
She just hopes she'll be able to adapt to it in time before anyone notices
the change.

She found Mother in the back. As Evelyn walks towards her, Evelyn
can feel herself drifting further from all she once understood and in this
bizarre complexity... heck, that's one way of playing with words. But truly,
Evelyn would call it "An everlasting chill-bone of now" – I just know it.

'What? What is it honey, are you alright?' Mom asks, arriving sooner
than Evelyn would have expected. Mom notices her daughter's wide eyes.

Okay, maybe life isn't moving as slow as Evelyn may have thought.
With her mind hushed and every other second anew, everything smiles in
the clear. Evelyn saw a different woman in Mother, and is sure she saw the
woman without a face in her dream, now.

'Yeah,' Evelyn nods very slowly, holding herself. It is odd seeing Mom
this way. Besides, her pupils are dilated in comprehension, and that just
makes it freakier.

'What's wrong honey, are you okay? You look like you're seeing stars.'

Evelyn smiles big and looks away.

It looks and feels that way

Evelyn's blinking a few in hopes it'll phase expression. She returns
to her calmer appearance – tries, I should say. 'I noticed there was no

porridge, and I just thought...' Even Evelyn should know better than to act like "Porridge" was the reasoning for her hesitations. She doesn't think Mom knows? Well she does, and it's clear on Mother's face, but she never mentions it.

'Just thought?' Mom replies and goes on to tap the barometer.

'Nothing... I just had a *weird* dream.'

'Evelyn.' Mom's head bobs up from what she's doing. 'Are you going to tell me what is buried in your grave, or you going to leave it ten feet under?'

Life doesn't feel as embarrassing, because it feels less real. Actually, it feels more real, it's just Evelyn is not so used to it. It is this constant warmth, like this blanket over her, being that of emotions that keep her feeling this way.

She can see Mom wasn't sure about much when it came to her; still, after all this time, all Evelyn wants to do is hug her. She didn't care about what would be awkward about it and what would happen next.

Evelyn reaches in and closes her eyes; holding tighter then she imagined.

'Okay, what's going on?' Mom asks in that tone. You know... the one the parents use when they know something's not right with their child. They usually can sniff out a shift in the ego. 'Talk to me.' Katherine whispers; and even this found its day.

'Sorry.' Evelyn comes to a sore laugh. A drowning... 'Jason's aunt had some crazy stories about...' Evelyn stops. She thought about how crazy everything now sounded the next day, especially out loud and in front of the one person who worries about things most. But there Mom waits, with a frown, listening intently. This is new because she didn't jump on Evelyn, or come to some conclusion about visiting so near to the forest; anything to find a reason for Evelyn's odd behavior.

Evelyn stares back at Mother and felt some more stillness come over. *Who am I?*

But what is odder, there is something unnatural about Katherine. It's this feeling and one that keeps prying -- as natural as an animal's instinct to be cautious of fire.

Evelyn does her best to change the subject, getting scared by it. She tires her best to explain to Katherine. 'Well... you know, in the dream is what I meant.'

Just then a knock at the front door turns their attention. Evelyn looks surprised, like the time she was zapped by Mr Barkley's glitch of an invention.

Oh no, morning... I forgot about that

Evelyn holds her hand to the sun, the warmth and brightness is beating down.

'Evelyn?' Corry calls out somewhere near the front of the house. He moves around back. He caught her in the distance staring at her hand as if marvelled by its simplicity.

Mother simply smiles – A look of figuring something out and turns to confront her daughter.

'And who is this?'

Evelyn turns to find Corry through her transforming reality and replies. 'You know Corry. I told you about him a few weeks back. He's the one you met after graduation ceremony.'

'Oh so that was *him*...' Mother replies. She turns to him now. 'Yes, I remember you now.'

Corry looks out of place with Mother's tone.

'Hey you,' Evelyn said to him. She found her words easily. 'I didn't know you'd be here so soon.'

Mother clears her throat. 'And I didn't know you were coming at all.'

'I can go...' He points behind him.

'No.' Evelyn says. It almost came out as a whine.

'Alright,' he says. 'I'll just be on the porch... then.'

'Oh, there is another... is there...' Mother says drearily, seeing a man move into site.

'Hi.' This other says and gave Evelyn an awkward smile.

'Oh boy,' Evelyn waves back and turns to her mother. 'Okay, I should have told you Jason and Corry were coming. But how could I? You're always out.'

Mother puts her hand up to the three. 'Alright,' Mom says. The three froze. I mean, they knew she didn't approve of much when it came to danger, *but my goodness*. Mom quickly changes gears seeing their worry. She smiles and says. 'Why don't the three of you freshen up,' and spoke in more of a hurry. 'Oh, and you two probably could do with some oatmeal and tea.'

Evelyn jumps agreeably, 'tea.'

The two boys look at one another.

'Wow.' Corry swallows once inside the house. 'That was...'

'Bizarre?' Evelyn asks.

Jason responds. 'You don't say?'

The two boys snicker.

'You're in a good mood, also.' Corry says to her. 'But does your mother *even know?'*

'No,' Evelyn replies, figuring it's about the Dark One. She comes to a sit at the table with her bowl. Her focus is enhanced. The colors are brighter; a berry is put to mouth and reveals its taste. She could dance to its rhythm; it tastes that miraculous.

What's happening to me? I... this is just amazing. I feel amazing!

They gave her a stare, waiting for their promised meal.

'I know.' She says relaxingly or seemingly I should say. 'It's kind of sad how she's irrelevant to anything in my life. But she's been really odd lately.' The two frown to this, noticing Evelyn lack of self awareness. 'Letting me do things she normally doesn't, like letting me go to town. So I'm enjoying the change.'

'Yeah that's nice and all, but are we going to eat or what?' Jason asks.

'You haven't changed, much.' Evelyn says and gets up to grab the boys' bowls, filling them with three big scoops of porridge, and dabs her fingers in two different jars, retrieving a pinch of salt and sugar, sprinkling over each. She wants to tell them, but doesn't feel she can since she doesn't even know what *this is*, this thing that is happening to her.

'Nuts.' Corry says to her.

'Me?' She replies back.

'That too,' he laughs and points to a bowl on the counter filled with dry nuts.

She smirks and sprinkles some nuts into their bowls.

'Can't forget the fruit,' Jason says and the other boy agrees.

'Anything else, kids?'

'No.' Jason says. 'But you could use with a little more sugar.'

'Ha!' She gets the metaphor. 'Funny, cuz' my life is sweet enough, thanks. You two are lucky I'm in an impressive mood, or else I'd be sitting down and you two would be feeding me by spoon.'

'We know, and this change is scaring us.' Corry says. 'We haven't seen you smile like this in a while.' Observing her new glee, figuring it has to do with Mother's change of heart or something.

She places the bowls with a drop in front of them, scaring them a little. 'Look.' She says, leaning in. 'You guys can't --'

Mom comes up the front porch steps and moves into the kitchen. She gave them a frown noticing their silence and walks right past to enter into the living room.

Evelyn's hand grips the side of the kitchen table to steady her from such high emotions.

Corry gave Jason a look and then spoke up once Katherine is out of the room.

'Look, you can't act like that and expect her to give you freedom.'

'What?' She asks, releasing her grip.

The two boys look at one another again, surprised she doesn't notice her strangeness. Jason made a face and eyes edgily around him.

She turns her sapphires on him. 'What, what is it?'

Corry spoke up, but it wasn't for Evelyn. 'She won't find out.'

'Good.' Jason adds.

Evelyn puts her hand to her face, figuring they wouldn't tell her even if she wanted. 'Fine, keep it to yourselves...' and plops herself into a seat. She remembers the last time she got them in all sorts of trouble, figuring it has something to do with this. She brushes her hands off as if to signify her distaste.

'What happened to the good ol' harsh and rough girl, huh?' Jason teases her.

Corry made an odd face and says. 'It's this new phase she's going through.'

She spoke at the side of her mouth. 'You don't even know. Besides, you should have seen the look on her face when Jason-boy moved to the yard... priceless.'

The guys laugh, seeing she remains ignorant.

'So how exactly are we going to do this?' Jason asks them.

She turns to Corry. 'I can't believe you told him. Is that what the moment you just shared was about? It is, isn't it?'

He rolls his eyes. 'Well yeah I told him. Only what he needed to know. That we're going into town and you're going looking for someone at the butchery. Besides, he needed to come. He's your best friend, remember? Or have you let that slide also? The way you've been acting, it's the least I should do. You *should* be thanking me.'

Jason crosses his arms, 'great, is someone going to tell me what the catch is?'

Just then Mom enters.

'Hi.' Evelyn says to her. Mom smiles and shuffles past to go outside again.

Evelyn leans her head in and returns the favour to Jason. 'It's nothing.'

He nods and leans back in his chair with the bowl of porridge. He rests a foot up on the table. 'Alright, so don't tell me. What do I care?'

'What do you reckon the witch is up to nowadays?' Corry asks in his randomness.

'Probably picking her nose, I don't know.' Evelyn replies, leaning back also and filling her mouth.

Jason sounds sore. 'I don't want to know.'

'She's probably out there saving the world and taking care of business.' Evelyn says, just realizing his foot is up and she pushes it off. '...Which reminds me, this is something we should be doing right about now, instead of sitting here and eating bowls of porridge when the world clearly needs our help.'

Corry teases, grabbing her bowl of porridge, *'right.'*

Jason laughs. 'Well, as long as I don't know the details there's no worry here.'

Corry reaches for Jason's bowl too, but hesitates when he got the eye from the man, so Corry swallows and looks away to find his bowl missing now.

'Hey, where's mine at?'

Evelyn has it in an extended reach.

Mother walks into the room with a basket full of clothes. 'Evelyn, give your brother his bowl back,' is all she says and passes them into the living room.

Evelyn went red. Jason couldn't help but laugh, leaning forward and almost spilling his.

Corry frowns. 'I get the fear. But come on, she's not a witch or something. Give it a break.'

'He doesn't get it back for that.' Evelyn says holding the bowl father out.

'What why?' Corry whines.

'Because,' Jason says and leaves it at that.

'Because…?' Corry lingers.

'Because… I don't know why, but I know I won't be sticking around long enough to.'

Katherine walks in and moves to the kitchen to fill the tea container with more hot water and places it on the stove. She lights a match and turns the gas burner on, igniting the element.

Corry spoke. '…And what a beautiful day it is indeed outside, today. No rain I bet. That's a good sign, right guys?'

Jason and Evelyn lean forwards.

The man spoke undertone. '…Why are you so awkward?'

'Evelyn.' Mother says. 'Why don't the three of you head out into town and get me those new shovels we've intended. You know… the dull ones,' and turns to face them.

Evelyn's face was as red as an apple; she apparently spilt some porridge on herself and the floor, with Corry still in his reach to grab it. Yet its Mother's eyes that are straight on Jason, since he's clearly the one looking more normal these days. Something about that is just not right, in her eyes. And well; let's just say he was trying really hard not to laugh.

'Okay.' Evelyn finally swallows to Mother's usual seriousness. The opportunity to leave became quick and the three got up to do so. When Mother left the room, the three look back at the house.

'Wow. She's really done a real number on two you, huh?' Corry asks and dodges a playful hit from the both of them. 'You guys are really messed up.' Corry finishes his would-be-sentence and rushes further out from them.

Evelyn laughs, 'oh *boys.*'

The town lies not too far in the south.

Evelyn pulls a cart full of fruits and vegetables by a long handle, letting the cart drag behind with some ease. The three had to go picking first before leaving, in order to trade for shovels they intend on bargaining for.

Closer in an old lady watches from her porch. Evelyn frowns at the odd reminder of this day, and looks back at her friends. They're looking at the lady's rooftop, which are full of holes with windows boarded up, and weeds grown through the walkway. Jason frowns. Finally, it wasn't just Evelyn and Corry who notice these things.

'They're always something nice to look at while walking to town.' Jason remarks and goes on to tease. 'You know, I'm really gonna miss this place.'

'Stay.' Evelyn shrugs.

'Nope,' he shakes his head and laughs, '*no way*. I leave for the train in eight days and I plan on leaving when it arrives from its cross-country journey. Otherwise, it's another month wait and I cannot do another day in this god forsaken town.'

She nods and Corry moves farther out.

Evelyn smiles to the day and turns her attention to Jason. 'That kid's something else.'

'You don't say. Did you know he likes me?'

She almost laughs. '*And* how do you know this?'

'Well he didn't tell me, but… I can see the looks he gives me, *and* you. He always has this watch in his eye. It was the same way Jonah used to look at me.'

She laughs and the boy found a look back, but that didn't stop her. She spoke quieter, though.

'He doesn't. And if he does, it's because of all of this.' She says with her hands to Jason, signifying his hulk body. 'He just needs a father figure and he doesn't have one. It just means he admires you. Believe me, it's nothing like you think, *at all*.'

'And how do you know?'

She swallows. 'Well because he told me his life story. And I know.' She scoffs. 'He was hit when he was younger. That's got to play part. And I know when I see heart, and this kid has one. Besides,' she gave Jason a nudge. 'He's pretty cute.'

He moves away from her.

'I'm kiddin'. Sure, I've seen him giving you and me looks. But it's not all that bad. I really don't care if he likes men, woman, or ladies for that matter. The stuff he had to put up with during school, people teasing him for being too skinny.' She shakes her head. 'We both know it's not about this.' She opens a palm to touch Jason's bulky arm. 'And I think we know it has a lot more to do with this.' She touches the man's heart. She can feel it beating hard under his chest.

He smiles, which is a surprise to her. 'You know, we both wouldn't be talking this way if we didn't lose Jonah.'

'Yeah I know.' She smiles next. 'A lot has changed since she left, hasn't it?'

He could finally see the change in Evelyn. It made him look softer. 'I'm happy for you. I really am. You're going to do alright, I just know it.'

She wanted to hug him. But knew her emotions were already getting the best of her, and wants to focus on what she came for. Her site turns a little darker. It didn't matter what she did, she still feels happy, whether she walks the dark or not, she felt no difference now. It all felt like one big adventure.

'Look at him.' She points with a lift of her chin. 'He's always chipper. If anything, we don't need to worry.' She winks at Jason. 'I'll make sure he's safe.'

The rest of the way to town is a small stretch; houses built more steadily and clean. The heart of Maesemer is made up of only four three-storey buildings. There is a market that runs dead centre which lines the streets and boards the walkways.

The streets can get sandy here, and that's with the pun intended. Items can get hefty too, though the trade is not the greatest worry, what is would be something the younglings are trading for. A small risk when one trades items from the outskirts. Its imperative one knows their neighbours because some items are stolen from the ghostly wreck of Asnin. Empty as it is now, a belief of phantoms harbour its materials.

Dust from over-crowding fills the air, giving the town a gritty look. The people move about with ease and patience.

A man lay against the outside wall, smoking a pipe. His expressions are sharp while his body lay limp. He is always quiet, but is well-known to be crude to those who approach him.

Corry gives him a cheeky brow, and the two beside him nod their respect to the smoking man. Inside, the movement and trading crowds make things louder. The younger age-groups always trade someplace furthest from central, nearest the back walls. It's more of a "Phantom market" -- So the town calls it.

The three paces with energetic movement, following Evelyn who is leading.

Corry bumps into a man.

'Selling sun dried tomatoes.' The seller offers. 'It'll make some of yea' go as round as plump. I'll trade some here for 'em O'Cous your friend's got there,' and motions a look at Evelyn.

O'Cous is slang for an early blooming squash.

He turns his attention to Evelyn who has a responsive look. He asks, '...or how 'bout one of 'em gifts from Mr Barkley's shop? Have ya got any of those sitting around, ah?' The seller smile shows little teeth, having eight in total, 'so how about 'em Hun?'

Evelyn scratches the back of her neck and decides otherwise. 'No I think I'm good.'

And before she could walk away he spoke again. 'Youngster's like you, with 'em vegetables.' He gave her a curious look over, 'who's to say where you got 'em, ah? But I'm willing to be nice and throw in some extra if ya want.' He motions her forward, but she doesn't move. So he leans in a little. 'It can be our 'lil secret.' He stood up straighter, 'so how 'bout it darling?'

'Sure.' She says, walking in arms reach. Her heart is beating fast.

Jason and Corry watch, unsure why she suddenly decided to agree.

With a hand dragging behind her, she reaches down with her only free palm and puts a Sun-dried to mouth, winking at him and walking off.

The selling man raised his eyes. 'Hey ya, you'll have to pay for that!'

Jason steps in front of the man. 'I don't think so, *buddy*,' and he reaches down grabbing one himself.

The seller stepped back but doesn't hold his tongue. 'We've taken enough from younglings who's dealin' dirty by us townsfolk. *Cursed you are.*'

Evelyn has a look of sass.

And it's Jason who looks around as if Maesemer is cursed. His eyes fall back to the stare that is reminding him once more why he chooses to leave this place. He spoke.

'It is not *I* who is cursed, but that forest and its wicked ways. Why our fight is not with you, sir, nor is yours with us.'

The seller gave a short grunt to Jason's words, turning to look for whoever would be willing to participate in defence.

Jason walks away, overhearing the man's voice pick up again, but Jason decided to continue on with his friends while the man's words went on;

'I know a dirty deal when --' suddenly turning to realize who he almost done business with. He watches the girl, and looks as if he could spit something sitting on the top of his tongue. 'Bad omens, I almost did dealing with *them two?*' He could barley watch. He would have given all his Sun Dried Tomatoes to never cross paths with those who've crossed the Dark One. 'Cursed, cursed *they're...* this town is turning to ash. All because of 'em youngling's starting things with that forest -- messin' about. Going pick'en near Asnin and taunting the witches of the forest. They brought 'em bad omens on all of us!'

Evelyn passes a child at the age of seven who pulls on her mother. 'Mommy, Mommy! I'm scared! Why is that man yelling so loudly?'

Evelyn back peddles and bends down closet to the child. 'Don't worry he's just having a hard day.' Evelyn looks up at the little girl's mother. 'He's just a little...' She signifies his craziness with her free hand.

The mother drops her mouth and takes her daughter away.

'...What, I was only being honest.' Evelyn says, and turns away. 'This town could do with more of it.'

A sign sways in front of them further from the man who yelled. It reads, "Talaries Farm Workshop".

Evelyn stops to look up at it, and turns back to her friends to say. 'Why don't the two of you go get your bargain on and I'll do some business on the mystery I came for.' She passes the cart handle to Corry and kept her eyes down when she passes Jason, for fear of his questioning. Instead, she squeezes through the crowed in a hurry to get by.

'You know,' Jason says and peers at Corry. 'She's more afraid then she lets on. Don't let that girl train your mind. She's all soft and squishy on the inside, more then you know.'

'Really,' Corry asks, not believing a thing he's just heard. 'She's probably the toughest chick in this town.'

'Yeah... well, that's what she wants you to believe. It doesn't help that she's well-known, mind you.'

'And stubborn,' Corry agrees looking in the big man's eyes.

'But that's not all. She's going over there to figure something --'

'About the wolf, yes,' Corry says looking about, having an expression of cool-headedness.

Jason shakes his head. 'I'm a tough lad, but even I know better. I have to go, because she can't seem to. Forget what I said. All we can do now is wish the best for her. Come on, let's go trade.'

Corry grabs his arm. 'You wouldn't allow this, would you? You know she's doing this for you, for Jonah. I was so wrong to allow this to go on for as long as it has.'

'You know buddy... you're kind of a good lad. But it's not up to you, now is it?' Jason says and goes on to smile his next piece. 'You kind of remind me when I was a little younger, myself.' He eyes over the boy's shoulder, the way Evelyn went. He leans in close to the boy's ear. Corry can feel his breath on his cheek. 'Don't worry; your secret is safe with me kid.'

The boy's face went red as a tomato; he almost wanted to kiss the man for the heavenly feel that's sent down his body.

'You know?' He frowns back with the sun in his eyes, hoping it was bright enough so the man couldn't tell.

'Oh, I know. You don't think I know what she's up to? What she's really doing and what this tough act is all about? I've heard enough about the man who hunts the forest. It's a small town. Who else could she turn to for *revenge?'*

'Oh...' Corry says raising his brows. 'I've been thinking about this...' More like thinking about the man in front of him and the image of his naked self. He scratches his bottom lip in humiliation and shakes his head to the imagery. '... And I must say I don't really approve of any of it.'

The man's voice cracks. 'Then tell her to back off. This is scaring me also.'

'What? Why can't you tell her? You're her closest friend.'

'I don't convince. I can't convince that *chick*, as you perfectly put it. She seems to like you, a lot. She said she'll watch your back even. But I doubt you'll have one after you two go strolling in the forest, help or no help, so you best undo this twisted fate she's got going on for you both.'

'You love her don't you?'

'How on Thaera --'

'I see the way you look at her.' Corry says with a laughing tone and finishes with a long nod of encouragement.

'Funny... because you are the only one I've noticed eyeing about. Why it's you who has kept tabs on me.'

Corry flushes. 'I... I'm not... *that* interested.'

'Right,' the man laughs. 'I don't believe you.' He goes on to explain something after realizing what shock he put under the kid. 'I've lost two girls in my life. I don't want to lose another.'

He ignores the mockery. *'You can't just leave her to this.'*

The man grudges before he lightens up. 'Then she gives me no choice.'

'What do you mean?'

'Slower than usual,' he mocks again.

There is only silence from Corry.

'You and Evelyn are more alike than I thought.' Jason says to the quiet.

It hit Corry hard. Perhaps it's because he likes the man, but what dug deepest was the man's lack of understanding, and the understanding is this.

'You don't get it, do you?'

Jason gives him an unreasonable look.

'How,' Corry hesitates. 'How amazing you look.'

'What are you talkin' about?'

Corry scoffs. He nods a few and then turns back. 'If this is the time than so be it. Jason, what you have is something I've always wanted my whole miserable life. You don't know...'

'Okay?'

'Listen. You don't know how hard it is.' Corry fights to speak his words. 'Being pushed around, and not loving myself. And you walk around in that.' He points at him, his masculinity. 'It's tough. This feeling, I wouldn't wish it on anyone, not even the most evil. I'll never have what you have... but you know what, that's *okay*. Sometimes, I look around and I see one of you, and I think in my head... is it real? And yet here you stand in front of me. I don't care if it sounds stupid. You don't know how difficult it's been for me. How could you? And then you walk into my reality. So you see -- you don't know what I would give. What I could do if I was you.' Now Corry is pushed to tears, 'no one's going to get this, and I don't give a damn. But you should know this; I wish I could be you.' He wipes his eyes and changes the subject. 'And also... you can't let her go on with this.' Corry swallows his emotions back and it becomes clear to Jason, that the kid had been serious about all of it.

'Than I'll have to resort to my last ditch effort,' he replies, ignoring the boy's scene.

This time it caught on, and Corry wipes an eye again. 'You can't,' and grabs hold of Jason's arm again. 'Evelyn will kill you if you tell *her*.'

Jason smiles, looking down at the kids grip. Corry lets go in realization. 'This part is about growing up, son.'

'Son? Growing up? Oh screw you dude.' Corry says and pushes past Jason.

He reaches out and grabs Corry's arm. 'Well hold on there, buddy.'

'And here I was taking a risk by letting you see who I really am. You don't know the first thing about growing up. The shit... ha! The shit I have to put up with. I see the way people look at me. Like I don't belong because I'm this.' He points to himself. 'Someone has to watch my back. I guess it's just going to be me.'

'I don't know what it is like, so stop putting your shit on me.' And for the first time, Jason saw the man Corry really is. He can see the flame that burns in his soul as it does in Evelyn's. Only Evelyn's fighting to ease a damned past and Corry's fighting to prove his worthiness. It's clear to see the skies above, Corry's reasoning is. And like that, the power of Corry's will-power shows. Jason can see with ripeness, that this boy would be willing to fight him right here and now, all to stand up for his right to belong.

Jason puts his hulk of a hand on the boy's boney shoulder. 'And like I was saying, just maybe, Corry, maybe Evelyn will forgive me for putting my better use of judgment ahead of me. That or... well... you know, it's for the better... And I wouldn't mind seeing her take a few beatings from Mommy.' The site of the kid is horrified. 'I'm kidding.' Jason says, pushing him. 'Lighten up, would you? You gotta take it easy bud; you and that girl are way too alike. It'll do you both some good, that I can be sure of. Once she forgives me.' He laughs to another one of the kid's expression, 'alright, *hopefully then*. Hopefully that girl will take my advice, should it pay off. Either way, she's getting grounded for the rest of her damn miserable life. I just want her out... and I don't mean this town, but this damn stage she's walking through.'

'...You and me both,' he replies.

Evelyn stops at the butchery. The sign reads, "Dale's Baron".

She swallows once. 'Alright, let's do this.'

Inside chimes dabble when she enters, hanging from the top door crotch. There is sand hitting the windows; it's the only thing that reminds her of home, of her bedroom window. The rest of the room is chilly from a ventilation system. If this doesn't give her anymore chills, the lights of electricity beating down white, will. They're solar power that is charged by a massive battery at the back of the building, with panels on the roof tops to absorb energy, and a backup generator with it all.

She shivers to the butcher desk and finds Dale behind a large glass counter, assuming it's the owner. There are meats labelled and wrapped in brown paper behind counter to keep fresh.

'Dale?' Evelyn asks moving closer to the glass.

'Yes?' The man replies.

'Are you the father of Claud?'

He has an auspicious tone. 'Yes, what can I do you for?'

Evelyn isn't sure what to say, does she tell him the truth? Or will this cause trouble?

'What can I offer you?' The man asks again, looking around at his produce, but he notices the girl is more focused on him then anything he has to sell. This establishment takes both trade and coin. Coin because it imports from Brunon, making it more expensive and more technical compared to other competitors in town.

'I am the daughter of Katherine, from the Maelkyn's farm.'

He is silent, but finally speaks his mind. 'Ah... Evelyn is it? Yes I know of you. Alright, what can I do you for?'

'You see... I was just wondering about your son, Claud. If I could have a word about something he saw in the Forbidden Forest, while he was on a deed for Miss Mad, I mean Madalyn. You know the one who lives on the hill?'

He leans on the counter some. 'Ah yes, Miss Madalyn... I've overheard stories, yes, I think everybody has. She's not one to cross; I hear she has some believing witches and wolves were the sorts to the trouble you've been through. I know Jason from his grandparents. I haven't talked to them or him since. I hear you're close to him and had been with Jonah.' He releases his lean to move on. 'I'm sorry for your loss.'

'Wait. Miss Madalyn spoke of your son's findings. Do you know of anything?'

When he spoke this time, it is very slowly. 'I've only heard my son gathered some sort of precious material for the lady. He said he'd tracked a "Beast" and recalls seeing it back track its steps. After all, the forest is not to be meddled with, so who knows if his eyes were cheated by some spell. I mean... such odd sightings have been documented before. But nothing --'

'Please.' Evelyn pushes. 'I am interested in the words of your son, the story Miss Madalyn had mentioned was most convincing.'

The man places a hand to his face. 'I see... Claud is butchering today, so you're in luck lady. He's rarely here. Normally the boy's out trapping around this time of day. I will notify him of your presence. Stay here.'

Evelyn nodded and the man left. She looks around, appearing cautious.

The man returns and finds the girl looking ever more solace, giving her and this store something in common. Dale tells her his son agreed and she is allowed to go around back. That's when Evelyn feels a slight nervousness in the pit of her stomach. She leaves Dale's sides after he opens the counter gate for access. He watched her all the way to the back of the store, and she takes a turn and disappears from site.

Evelyn looks back walking alongside a white painted wall. She passed through revolving doors and at the very back; a large handsome man is witnessed inside the building's loading dock. It's cold inside.

Claud wipes his hands on a cloth and washes his bloody hands in a sink. Carcasses are hung and being drained of their blood.

Evelyn does her best to look away, keeping eyes on him.

'You shouldn't have come.' Claud says.

'Excuse me?'

He doesn't reply.

'I'm Evelyn, I'm --'

'I know who you are; you're the famous, or infamous to some, daughter of Maelkyn. What do you want?'

His face is perfectly positioned; his nose is a perfect length. His expression compliments his features, alongside a thick jaw structure. He has a mighty arm, wearing a blood stained apron. Quiet the first impression. The sound of blood taps on the floors, draining into a drain, centre room. There are also vents, which are a bit noisy. Evelyn looks down at her feet and then lifts her chest to reply. 'I was wondering about --'

'Of course,' he says all knowingly, putting down the cloth and wiping his hands some more.

She waits in silence. He looks up at her.

'Am I allowed to speak?' She asks, hinting at his manner.

'Go on.' He says looking down to clean his equipment again, right next to a large range of stainless steel saws and a conveyer belt.

'Well,' Evelyn voice cracks a bit. The hung carcass on hooks kept her focus on him. 'Lately I have been thinking about the forest and I remember what Miss Madalyn, a lady I had just spoken with, just yesterday morning,' she clears her throat, 'mentioned your name and the forest. This is about what you saw there.'

'Ah.' He only says, not looking up.

'...And I know this all seems silly and we hardly know one another, but... I... couldn't help but be curious, about what she mentioned.'

He looks at her, still cleaning. 'Are you in any sort of trouble?'

'No, nothing like that,' she swallows and he didn't let her finish.

'So she spilled the beans.'

Evelyn nods her reply. He exhales, probably tired of explaining this story to someone like Evelyn before, a kid who comes with baring questions. But not every day does one come marching into the butchery where he works. The only reason he didn't shoo her away was the fact of her experience four years ago.

'I was hard at work; hunting.' He says, stopping what he's doing to toss the cloth into the sink. 'And then it crossed paths. It's large and black.' He comes to a sit on a stool near a workbench. 'It never saw me that day. What, seven hundred pounds I should think? Maybe more, oh, and it appears much like a bear, perhaps more wolf orientated. It was a surprise because

I've never seen such unique features. But you know as I do the fear it sheds. When I first saw it, it was a whole new level of fear.'

'It never really goes away.'

'Oh... I didn't have to guess that.'

'Good... many don't know that about me. Can you tell me about Miss Madalyn? She says you're hunting it.'

'I am. My buddies and I will be going in five days from now.'

'I want to go with you.'

'Whoa. Now, *now* Missy, let's not get rash.'

She gives him a look, like she's not some kid.

He asks. 'Do you even know how to use a rifle?' and raises a brow. 'Have you ever gone hunting before?'

'No... And yes.' She scratches the back of her neck. 'I have gone hunting once before. But how hard is it to use a rifle? Take a breath and then you shoot.'

'Ha-ha, that's perfect, a girl who doesn't even know how to shoot.' He nods his premise and asks a different question. This doesn't tell her much if he approved or not. 'What else did she tell you?'

Evelyn shrugs. 'Enough, enough for me to want to go and get back what's mine,' she says.

'Like your pride?'

'No, my sanity, you and I along with the rest of this town know we deserve better. No one wants to be tangled in its weave any longer.'

But the man knows the truth; he shoots her a look. 'Going in there with a hunch is the last thing you'd want on your hands. Take a good look around you, because it'll be your last. No, you won't come. You will be a good girl and go back home telling your mother you stopped by to look for dear meat for this upcoming Summers Feast. You'll tell her that.' He shoos her. 'That's all.'

Summers Feast is a celebration of the game that comes out around this time and so the first feast is laid down in thanks.

The man gets up to leave.

'Who did you lose to that forest?' Evelyn asks him. 'More than your pride, I'm sure of it. Anyone can see that. So why not let me come? After all, we've both been cut from the same cloth, have we not? Have I not seen enough to earn this right?'

Evelyn knows this has nothing to do with earning. And yet she persists, knowing the power of her portal life; the awakening. It's giving her strength; otherwise she'd be shaking and sweating profusely. Instead, she's focused and calm.

He scratches his nose with the back of his thumb nail. There is blood under it.

'When I was a young boy, I always loved helping my father on the ranch. We always had the sort of animals that were easiest to love. Dogs, pigs and nords, there was always fun to be had. But he always told me to be careful of the forest. I was curious, I just wanted to know, but I never did risk it. It was because he used to tell me stories, stories Miss Madalyn, a time in her childhood had shared with him when he was just a boy. He told me when they got their chance to stay up late; Miss Madalyn would share her stories -- whether she got them from her mother or what.

'I suppose my father was only passing the tales along, trying to keep his boyhood memories alive.' He scratches his scruff. 'They were frightening. He spoke about the Dark Ones. The very ones you've awoken us to.'

'Tried,' she reminds him.

He goes on. 'But I always thought it was just a real good story. You know, to scare us. It wasn't till my adulthood, when I saw the beast with my own eyes...' He shakes his head. 'I just don't want you witnessing the same thing that I had.'

She takes a deep breath and spoke afterwards. 'I won't. If you've known what I've gone through, you'd know I can handle just about... everything.'

He nods his approval and explains. 'When I saw her, the Lady of the Forest, she smiled to me and then she was gone. The same lady from the stories, I just couldn't believe my eyes. She's not the same anymore, of course. I know this because she never would have allowed the witches to take over her forest. But I'm sure she's older now, hiding out from the witches that escaped the fall of Asnin. I'm sure Miss Mad has told you all about them, right?'

Evelyn nods attentively.

He continues. 'Well, all the stories I've heard as a child turned out to be real...' He laughs. 'Go figure. A reality that sounds too good to be true, turns out to be my life.'

'I want to know more.'

He goes on to smile. 'You're just hungry for tales I think – didn't get enough attention from Mother when you were a child, huh?' Evelyn gave him a sore look and he laughs it off and says. 'Maybe we are cut from the same cloth, then. I'm sorry, I guess I shouldn't tease. Well, the witches raised the beasts like their own. Bred to hate -- The witches were so determined to hunt us, that their beloved history was their demeanour. The era when Asnin stood proud and mighty, as you well know it, has crumbled. It's nothing but a staple of their forgotten sin, now how's that for a slap in the face -- am I right? Where the people once rejoiced and the merry could spell "Witchcraft" without worry. Then it all changed and many are likely abused or jailed for it today.

'Of course, even as the Lady of the Forest hides, she's doing a damn good job of keeping those beasts and their pack astray. Otherwise, there wouldn't be much of us hanging around, I'd say. And that's why I have to stop those Dark Ones, to help the Lady of the Forest. And that's why the Dark Ones are moving into town. I think the witches see a trap. They're trying to get the Lady of the Forest sniffed out. The witches wouldn't dare risk leaving their forest. Not with the famous Brunon hunters.' He goes on to scoff. 'If Brunon gets but a mention of witchcraft in Maesemer, we'd have Witch Hunters arriving by the next dawn.' And his next words sunk deeper. 'So you bring yourself along, Missy. If you can convince your mother or whoever that you are going hunting for Summers Feast, then I hope to see you there. We will be at Asnin before the break of dawn. Listen for the cry of cocks and you'll see us.'

'So just listen to you and the men, you mean?'

He makes a small sound and rubs across the bottom of his lip, very slowly. 'You just bring your bold self and we'll see how talented you really are with a rifle. I don't do this regularly, so you best behave yourself.'

She has an impressive look on her face, and accepts his invitation.

The walk home had been a fast moving one. Evelyn could barely contain the information she just learned. She had big eyes, but she wasn't the only one that day who seemed eager for something more.

The guys explained to her how they did with their bargain and won a great deal for the O'Cous they traded for, in order to get the shovels. They got four neat shovels, thanks to Corry's great use of humour and Jason's talented persuasion.

Evelyn perks. 'See, I knew you boys could *handle* yourselves, ha! Get it?'

She got a sore look from them both and Jason walked away. Normally a smile would suffice, but this time it seems everyone is going through a rough patch.

'What? I gave you guys a compliment, it's not like I said you were incompetent. What I mean to say is that you did well. *So*, thank you.'

Corry managed a nod, and the boys kept to themselves on the walk home.

The three arrive to the house in much silence, but Evelyn didn't recognize it, marvelling in her new self.

The two boys place the shovels down against the porch side and make their way in. Evelyn took the shovels and went around back to place them into the shed. When she returned, she found Corry and Jason chatting at the kitchen table, and when she entered, they hush.

She sat down and Jason got up.

'I have to use the washroom.' He says and leaves into the living room where Mother is seen folding clothes.

'What did I do know? Does he not know where the washroom is?' She asks Corry, having a giggle about it.

'He's...' Corry never did finish his sentence, for he gave her a dab of his head in the direction of her mother.

She eyes from her spot to see Jason and her mother talking. When Evelyn came back to Corry, she saw him nodding. And that's when it all became apparent.

'Oh... *no*...'

Evelyn shifts in her seat to watch, and sees Mom anger.

'Just a few more days,' Evelyn reminds herself, getting clear signs of her mother's expressions. Evelyn didn't care if Corry had no idea what she meant by it, or if Mom could read her lips. But one thing was for sure, with those expressions on Katherine's face -- Everyone knows what's coming.

Evelyn got a lecture, and was grounded as expected. But Mom took it way *better* than anyone had hoped for.

Evelyn couldn't really blame Jason for trying to "Save" her, so he said. He looked a little worried too, and the girl really did take a beating from Mom's furious self; words of passion and a few shouts of course. Evelyn hung her head and took it in. Before Jason left, he places a hand on her shoulder and let it slip off as he and Corry walk themselves out.

Evelyn is plenty glad the engagement with the hunters remains secret, or else this really could have blown up in her face... if it hadn't already.

When the boys left, Evelyn felt the fear sink in. Now Evelyn's alone. She saw the worry of Mom's impatience. It means there will be another talk. Fearing Mother will do something rash, like take away all privileges or have her cooped up in her room all night long; Evelyn decides it'd be best to not say a word, if not move at all.

'Going after the Dark Wolf? Are you crazy? What were --' Mother halts speech and shakes a head. 'Go on upstairs.'

As fast as the girl can put on a T-shirt; she slips out the room, leaving no humiliation for the "Walk of shame". All she could think about was Claud and the date now.

'Dark hunters,' Evelyn grimaces once in her bedroom. 'That's what we should be called.' And finds humour at the expense. She can hear Mother moving up the steps and she enters Evelyn's room in seconds.

'What am I supposed to do with you?'

'Are they mad at me?' Evelyn asks looking out the window, seeing them heading home.

'*Them?* I'm *mad* at you.' Mother says, standing between the doorway, 'I can't make you do homework, now can I?'

Evelyn was about to speak when she's interrupted.

'That wasn't a question.' Mom knows school is over, it was just… a matter of speech. 'Look at this messy room. I want you to clean it up and meet me downstairs. I wanna have a little chat with you.'

Oh god...

'Okay.' Evelyn replies.

Katherine let go of her gaze and left the room thereafter.

Evelyn could feel the heat in her ears burning as she picks up her clothes and keeps her mind on the hunters' engagement. Her things are placed back where they should be. This whole thing in Evelyn's mind felt rather useful, giving her some distraction while she "Cleans up". She found her favourite pair of socks she lost and a doll she got when she was much younger.

'You and I go way back.' She beams at the toy. She plops it onto her bed and gets down low to check beneath the cot. 'Seems like enough space,' and throws the rest of her dirty clothes that lay around the room, underneath. She smacks her hands together and Mother's voice calls her name from downstairs.

'Here we go.' Evelyn says to herself.

Evelyn took her sweet time walking down the steps, and the last few felt like the longest ones of her life. She finds her mother sitting in the living room, on a small couch, far from the window but facing it.

There is an old mantle place with pictures of Mother holding her baby, that of a drawn picture. No picture of any man in any of their lives.

Evelyn scratches her head and leans against an old bookshelf just inside the room.

Mom pats the couch and motions Evelyn to come sit. Evelyn moves slowly but surely, and finds her seat beside her.

'So... are you going to tell me what's going on?'

'Nothing that's --'

'Please. Jason shares with me that you were going into the forest to hunt the *Dark One*. Is this true? Evelyn, look at me. Jason wouldn't say this if he wasn't worried about you. And frankly, I'm worried about you.'

'I know,' Evelyn says getting the point, like it had been Mother's fault. 'I'm figuring this out on my own.'

'You can betcha you are. You aren't stepping a foot out this door until this house is clean and I don't want to hear another thing about it.'

Evelyn made her swore face. Still, it seemed Mother is being *way too easy*.

'And... You are not stepping away this feast. You stay in. You are going to be mine. I will need your help making dinner this time, instead of your usual running off with friends.'

'Okay.' Evelyn says.

Figures...

'Don't you get it? If I ever lost you, what would I do without you?' She looks deep into Evelyn's sea blue eyes, and for the first time Evelyn saw her point of view. But who's living whose life? So who's being the selfish one? – Evelyn has thought.

'I know your father was taken by it also... I know...'

Evelyn was about to say "Do you?" but held her tongue. She swallows, as if words could be swallowed and glanced at the picture frame over the fireplace.

Katherine is wary. 'But you're coming with me to the market tomorrow. Tonight I have to head out again. You Missy are stuck to me until I can figure out what I should do with you. I thought it was clear when I said "No going into the forest" but now I can't trust you, can I?'

Evelyn saw the hurt in her eyes and it made her rethink about seeing the hunters. But she feels she *has to go see them*.

The next day Mother was a little more forgiving. They talked, until Mom left to go out to help the lady with more ploughing. When Mom returns in the afternoon, she notices how clean it is around house. No socks lying on the floor, no shirts left on the kitchen chairs, the floors swept and the dishes are all finished. It was like a frat boy's house before she left, and to return and find the floors shinier is amazing. She didn't think Evelyn knew where the mop was, heck, Katherine couldn't even find clothes swept in the usual places, like under the living room coffee table. Mom moves into the kitchen and finds the tea towels are neatly placed where they should.

'Maybe she is coming around after all.' Mom says and reaches for a cup to make tea.

Evelyn came downstairs after taking a shower and flashes her smile, passing Mom to put on boots and asks, 'ready to head out to get the deer meat?'

'Of course,' Mother says, surprised to see her daughter so quick and in a jittery mood.

'Okay, I've been thinking since I have all this extra time on my hands, can we at least have Jason and Corry over? After all, they do deserve a little treat for putting up with me, don't they?'

'We'll see.' Mother says, placing her cup down. 'And we will have to do more talking.'

Evelyn looks at her feet. 'It's not like we haven't bonded already.'

'It's not a joke, Evelyn.'

'I know...' Evelyn looks at her.

'Okay, fine. But I'll be asking them myself. I hope you're up to all of this cooking.'

'It'll be fun.' Evelyn reassures her. 'I'm planning on inviting the kids over, too. We're going to need their help. Remember last year's party? It was madness without the extra hands. And we *always* end up needing the extra. Don't we?'

'Okay.' And she walks out the door with her.

They filled the cart again with berries, O'Cous, and pumpkin squash.

'I'm excited you know, about dinner.' Evelyn says in a new upbeat manner, with one arm free to express while the other is clung to the cart. 'We really could do with the Sheppard's coming over sooner. Remember last time when they showed up late? We hardly had enough time to finish at all.'

Mother didn't say a word. It made Evelyn feel even further from her. The sun is brighter today, though. It's a warmer day then most and the sky is wide open. It made Evelyn shed a tear since it reminds her of fun times during the summer.

'I'm not happy about you.' Mother says.

More tears creep down her face and Mother doesn't notice.

'It's like you don't even care what I think, about anything I say.' She turns to see Evelyn and the tears rushing down her face. 'Oh Evelyn...'

Evelyn drops the cart and falls into her mother's arms.

'I could have lost you, you know that?' Mother says, kissing her daughter on the forehead.

'I know.' Evelyn cries.

Mother begins tearing up also.

It was the hardest thing to do in front of *her mother*, to admit her wrong. She rarely shares any emotion, but it felt so good to see Mother believing in it, at first.

Mother knew better. She sure would have liked to believe it. Finally, if Evelyn were to get off clean, she would have to believe in her own lie. So she releases more tears. She stood weakly in her mother's arms. But then... something changed. It slowly all became too much to handle and she fell from Mother's grasp. Katherine tries to hold her up. She hasn't seen her grieve so hard in her life. It's beginning to make Mother teary again.

Was this real?

Some words from Evelyn in that moment forth. 'I lost myself. But now I can let go. I want to go home, Mom.' She looks up with a dripping nose from Mom's hold, into her eyes.

If this is fake... then Evelyn's either psychotic or... just maybe... Mom's searching eyes saw Evelyn's actual self.

'You do know I was going to tell you that I think you're doing well with all of this change, over the past years. It's just, if you did go into the forest... I could never forgive myself.' Mom says and finds Evelyn's eyes. 'But it's up to you, Evelyn. I can't hold you back any longer. If you choose to walk this path, then I will not stop you any longer.' Mother held a stronger face, standing up.

This scares Evelyn and she sinks to the earth.

She's letting me loose?

Evelyn sat there, baffled by Mother's decision. Who's fooling who now? Only Evelyn started out as a lie and fell into grieving. A process she didn't even know was under all of this... pain. But Mother didn't need to read her mind. Whatever her daughter is thinking here and now, Mom knew those eyes were determining what's best in Evelyn's interest.

Mom reaches a hand down, and Evelyn reaches for it, helping her daughter to her feet. And before Mother spoke, Evelyn does. 'Let's go get ourselves a feast.' And smiles with the best intentions and felt the pain. Evelyn's heart is showing.

Along the walk, a few more tears tumble and her heart felt as warm as it could have ever. Freedom is apparent and something deeper inside, long tucked away had been fighting to reach the light of day. It was so overwhelming it didn't matter what Mother thought anymore – Evelyn just wants to get it over with -- the past.

The town didn't have the same gritty feeling. In fact, the blistering sun was a charge. It fuels her with the best of summer that is sure to come. As things are finally turning around, it's no bother on either's faces of what could.

The store is met and Evelyn pushes through, walking inside its typical chill. She finds Mother at her sides and Dale is surprised to see Evelyn today. The young girl had a shine the moment she walked through the door, and the store didn't recognize the brightness.

'Hi.' Evelyn says to him.

He smiles his greeting. A slight glance was made to her mother, and then he asked as if it was just any other day. 'How do you folks do?'

'Good.' Mom replies. 'We were interested in getting a quarter of deer for Summers Feast.'

'Of course,' the man replies, looking at Evelyn and bends down to reach for a binder. 'Here we go.' He says placing it on the counter. He flips the manual cover over and skims through pages with names and addresses.

'I was thinking...' Evelyn stammers. 'You know Jason, right?' He didn't say anything. Fearing the contemplation, Evelyn turns to Mother. 'It's been three years. It'll be a good change for him to see some relatives. If anyone knows him, it's me. Besides this, he's leaving town in a few days, and I... I just want to at least give him a goodbye from those who knew him -- don't you think?'

Instead, he looks right at Katherine to see her reaction.

Mom is unsure what to say.

'I just thought...' Evelyn says swapping looks between them. 'We could use some more people over. I-I can't help but feel he'd appreciate having some friends around this time.' Evelyn looks back at the man, ignoring both their apprehensive. 'Alright then,' Evelyn says, looking bolder. *'I'm* inviting you. Come along, unless you have plans...?'

'Well.' The man says and laughs a bit. 'Well, this is a little unorthodox.'

'Evelyn, I'm sure he has plans like we do.'

'Actually,' he says. 'They were cancelled due to a change. So we wouldn't be having any friends over like we usually do. I'm glad you ask. I'd love to bring Claud and myself... over.' Turning to Katherine, '... If that's okay with you, Miss?' There is silence from Mom who looks down at Evelyn in thought, and the man spoke again. 'It does get lonely around this time of season. You'd think not, but everyone's always out and about, and I'm usually the only one at home or manning the store, as you can see.'

Evelyn smiles big, 'Jason will love it. There! It's set.' She says a little spunky before either could clarify the moment.

'Alright, it's a go.' Mother says, lost without clarity.

Evelyn's admiring the risk of Mom's decision.

Mother shakes his hand, and he returns the favour.

'Dale, of course,' he rolls his eyes.

Evelyn found a large smile for them both.

Maybe there's something more to be made here... and I'm thinking outside friendship

Evelyn and Mother left on a good note, stepping outside.

Mother's amuses. 'Well aren't you full of surprises today.'

It had been awhile since Evelyn overheard Mother laugh so delightedly. Evelyn knew better then to let the moment slide, and so she reaches in and gave Mother another big hug. It sure felt good.

- CHAPTER 3 -

In the Deep

Evelyn awoke early with a jolt, sitting up in her bed. She could hardly sleep with Summers Feast today. It was always just Evelyn, Mother and the Sheppard boys. The Sheppard's always brought their usual berry-spiced apple pie over. Last year the Maelkyn scored two pies and Evelyn still wasn't allowing the Sheppard's to take any home with them because it was so good. But now the Sheppard's know better. They're baking four pies for this event, one for Evelyn and her mother and another two so they can hopefully have some left over.

The imagery in mind made her wide eye.

'We better get something on this hunt, the heck are we going to feed all these guys?' She thought out loud. 'Why I've been giving grief to Mother all this time is beyond me. I kinda hope… we can get the Dark One… Imagine that surprise as talk over dinner; "So who enjoyed dinner? Surprise, we only ate the Dark One" Okay… maybe not. That's a little gross, even for my tastes.' She smiles to her pun.

Her choice is clear. With the change of heart and Mother allowing her to do whatever she wants, life has surely opened up. Evelyn plans on walking the path beyond her. Why? Well, let's start off with an excitement to see Claud. Two, she let her anger for the Dark One finally go after her grieving. Besides, today she walks the shadow and is going to dominate it. Dominate it like everything else she has so far, which makes that three. How's that for a good start?

Evelyn yaws too big, for its too early for breakfast. She leans on the windowsill, sleepily. More eagerness rumbles in her belly that helped her to stay up. It had been mostly this way all last night. Well, it's still considered the same night.

She eats breakfast and heads out in her favourite jacket. She smiles to this blissful night before the break into morning, and makes way for town.

There the dark forest is in shadow, but it's not dark, just a place filled with fireflies and glowing mushrooms. A place that's ready to light up with majesty.

Evelyn laughs out loudly, remembering a dream she had before she awoken this night. In it, she walked a blissful and enchanted forest. There was a house in it, and a book. One Mother used to read to her when she was much younger. It's all good memories and a sign of great change. That's why she's so much happier, too.

Evelyn arrives to Malvin Drive. It stood abandoned and closed off. The gate is closed. But instead of moving around it and taking the path on the outside to get to the hill, she climbs the gate and jumps over, landing with a thump to the earth. She looks around and moves towards the house without any phase. In fact, she ran her hand across the side. She feels free and no longer threatened. If anything, pure joy in the moment to see what comes next. The fire in her soul is burning, and it's roaring aflame.

All the memories of laughter and play beckon to her. And she kissed the house in memory of Jonah and leaves the building behind.

The morning is starry. And in a few hours the sun will kite the sky, casting eve.

She climbs the hill to the top and see's the house of Miss Madalyn's and walks right on past. She ventures the streets, heading to the south towards the Old Capital.

She rubs her arms with her hands, walking the calm night. She looks up to see the moon just in the sky. It's a bright shine, but one that's ever watchful of her. Still, it seemed to smile, with a bright glimmering glow. Evelyn smiles back with a similar confidence. She knows she's got what it takes. Otherwise, she believes Claud never would have invited her when he did, leading this far out.

She lets her arms fall to her sides and takes a deep breather in, letting it out slowly. A path leads her out of the outsiders' town. The many houses fall behind and her steps pace toward the ancient castle.

The gates of Asnin are tall and peaked. Finally at the end of the roadway she stops at its gate.

'Well, I made it...' She says, feeling stronger now. 'I'm not afraid of what they'll think of me. I don't care anymore. I was wrong to think less of me all those years. Being too skinny, ha, I shouldn't be saying that anymore. Just that I am beautiful. From now on, I fight for this.' She looks up at that big scary tower. 'I was wrong... yup. I'm not scared anymore. I'd rather be scared and fight for me then to ever go back there, that feeling...' She smiles. 'So here goes.'

There is an abundance of carriages, where all are similar. Evelyn moves to the first. Inside, intriguing designs are met. She moves closer in to find old fashion cushioning. She comes back out, feeling silly for messin' about. She looks up at the castle. Asnin stands as brave in the night and as mighty as one should. When Evelyn looks away, the igniting mystery in her eyes are reborn.

The gate is arched, with white stone that's dirty from age. With two busted doors, where a small hole was made from someone a long time ago, granting passage.

Slowly, the girl took her time, passing a few steps in and her foot tapped cobblestone.

A crow lands above her and then lands a few steps before her. Evelyn stopped and watched it, and suddenly laughed out. The suddenness of her voice shocked the crow and it flew off. Evelyn smiled wittily to herself and followed the shine of the moon off the cobblestone, leading her inside.

A few jocks croak, huddled in town circle, laughing to a joke one had made.

'I guess I was right.' She grimaces to her mockery.

Old wells are passed. Grasses are up to the heavens. Weeds overgrown through the cobble, just like it was through Misses porch. But not nearly as bundled as the corn patches alongside the outside wall. Patches run to the backyard and around most neighbouring houses. What used to be simple corn now represents a tradition known as Fallhallow; a time in memory of the wicked that fell three hundred years ago, during the reign of the civil war. The fall that happened midsummer and kept on for four years after.

Today, Fallhallow represents the dead in memory for one special day and one scary night, only.

Sweet corn pie is served as a delicacy with candy corn. It is the perfect time to tell scary tales around the dinner table, mostly about a famous warlock, a war and witches. Some may be myth, but all are sure to scare children and give good fright.

A most famous story about Mada, an evil witch who works with her cult called her "Jeer" is told over families Fallhallow feast. The Jeer would try and steal a boy and girl – the hardest ingredient to come by from the grand capital of Asnin, a time during flourish -- to cook a many ingredients with the two in a stew for everlasting life. It only works on the full moon. One sip and this would give the witches their wish. But Mada forgot the most important ingredient on this very special night -- salt.

'Bah.' Mada whines and spat at the fire. She sent her Jeer out of the forest to fetch some in town, and surely enough, no one answered their door. Children and adults of homes knew better, so the towns' people ran to the house on the hill and knocked on Mr Adar's wicked door. A tall and purple robed man answered. The town's people told him he could finally have his wish of everlasting power, but he would have to swear to save the two children held in captivity by Mada and her Jeer.

He said nothing, so the town's folk went ahead and told him anyway about Mada and her difficult brew. That was when the people witnessed his first crooked smile, ever.

Fearing to return to Mada without her ingredient, the witches risk a knock on the wise and powerful Mr Adar's door. After all, *there only asking for seasoning, right?*

He answered. He was dressed in his usual warlock wear, but his hat sat a little to the left. It looked crooked. This was unusual, because this man was always neat. What's more, he seemed in a rush when he's always calm, cool and collected. Nonetheless, he gathered them salt, holding out a bucket full of it. It was so large and heavy that no witch could carry. They asked if he could carry it along. When her Jeer returned to Mada, they saw her face go whiter then the bucket full of salt.

On this terrifying and frightful night, two children locked in cages are about to witness a rather nasty battle between their soon-to-be hero and the leader of the witches.

'Mada,' Mr Adar said to her. 'Your Jeer has been so nice I just thought I'd bring you a token of my appreciation.' He tilts his head. 'Why, you look as if you've seen your ghost.' He says.

Mr Adar defeated the leader of the witch and set the remaining that was under her command, free. He cooked Mada in the already prepared stew, for *she* was his last ingredient and he would now have his wish. He took one sip and got his everlasting power and gladly kept to his promise, setting the children free.

Traditionally, many children dress up as their favourite hero or villain, witch or ghost. And parents may also, all to swap paranormal stories and tales with friends, family and colleagues.

Adar (built as a scarecrow) is the fictional character in robes and a wizard hat. He's known to fight off the "Evils of the night". The Mr Adar ordainment is stuffed with the leftovers of cornhusks, using pillow cases and whatnot, since so much corn is used during this date. It is also said that Mr Adar scares away any ghosts and ghouls that come out during midnight's past.

It is ironic because Fallhallow's is a day when witchcraft is embellished and a night where magic-tricks are allowed. Chicken stuffed cream corn is the usual meal of choice around the holiday, accompanied with a side of smashed gold rooloff; a giant yellow vegetable with a spiky husk, but inside is mealy and heavenly protein. When cooked, the only thing that compares to the smell here on planet earth; eggplant and bratwurst, and for dessert, hot and runny cream corn pudding.

The entrance shows a large opening, where a fountain's centre. It's not dried out, it's actually flowing.

It gave the place a bloom, giving the area life and energy.

The homes around here are different then the outsiders. Asnin homes are taller, and more bunched together, being tight fitted. Their roofs are sharper, and wrecked. All of the city's doors are left open. Like everyone left the place in one big hurry. Glass is everywhere and carriages broken down. They have their wheels stripped.

Evelyn didn't care to notice and saw the beings she came for. As she walks towards the group, she overhears them mouthing.

'This place could get used to. Somebody give me a bucket full of paint and I'd make this place look just like new.'

'This place gives me the creeps. You go ahead and stay if you want, but it runs of ghosts.'

Evelyn clears her throat. 'Ghosts are a friendlier bunch then you all give them credit for. You just have to hang around the right ones.'

They're all quiet until suddenly Claud blurs out laughing and the group follows.

Another man nods and spoke. 'The large keep remains in black. Its wicked rooftops and towers make it twisted and old. It's called the "Dark Rise" today. The hall withers and run with the lost souls of the civil war who still chill the fortress, with an inner sanctum that is widely known as the "Dark Blackened Halls". They say the sons of noble men and woman still eat and drink in wait for their parents to return from battle.'

Evelyn asks intriguingly, 'really?'

Another in the group spoke. 'Yes, his father is a historian and knows all the tales best.'

Claud spoke. 'It's funny you mention that, Dean. Have you heard of the Lady Who Stirs? She sits at the head of the table, in the Dark Blackened Halls. The fireplace lights up when she's there. She only appears to those who have no fear, this way she can speak to you and even tell you of her tales about the civil war.'

In a pen not too far, the hunters' nords seem restless, rattling their reins. Evelyn could feel the chills, and probably those nords could as well.

'The halls, now that's no joke.' The man who spoke secondly, replies. 'We all know their monuments and pictures line the walls. Their eyes ever-watching, I wouldn't be surprised if they could talk.'

The words of the hunter didn't bother the huntress. Instead, Evelyn could imagine these streets full of people dancing in the middle of night. Awakening to the morning's glory, and setting up for their daily renewals. Ringing out clothes and washing dishes after a breakfast of cheese, bread, salad mix, with ale and wine. We can't forget the abundance of fruit and vegetables and a delicious spiced sausage or ham to go along with it all. Of course, we can't forget 'em good ol' eggs, either.

They're old streetlights and banners that are still hung from a clock tower behind the fountain. It too runs. It seems there was a carnival and it never finished, for the area is partially decorated and chairs are all over the place. Or… it may have finished, and we're looking at its aftermath. Whatever happened here, I think it's easy to see something went terribly wrong, a long, long time ago.

She takes the open environment in and breathes heavily. 'It's massive.' Evelyn says to the hunters.

'This is Evelyn. Meet Jamie Cunning.' Claud says with an open hand to a bloke with black hair and blue eyes who had only been laughing with. He's roughly Evelyn's height. He's a lean lad, having fifty pounds on Evelyn. Oh, but her eyes are that whole different level when we are speaking in the language of compelling. He shakes her hand, taking notice. 'Hi.' He says interestingly.

'Hi.' She bent forward to reach in and return the favour.

A man who's taller than Claud, if that's possible, being three inches higher with white hair and blue eyes, stood out. He's albino. Something about this man made her smile, and before introduction was made, he leans in with a hand and one that completely covers hers. 'Andrew Nero.' It's a cold morning touch. What made him even larger was his stalk build… talk about three peas in a pod. Or was it always two?

She spoke with her usual sass. 'I thought this place could use with a little more brightening up.'

Andrew laughs. 'Yes… well, we can't all be *stars* now can we?'

The group laughs and she turns to the final one.

'Dean.' He said and shook her hand. He is thin, *sort* of like Corry, but taller. He has sharp features, oddly unlike his face line. Evelyn couldn't help but smile. She always liked a man who has dark and soft complexities. It's a mysterious thing, and so are his hazel brown eyes.

'And last but not least,' Claud says and smiles. 'Well, me.'

The group chuckles again.

'Hi.' She smiles biggest, feeling self-conscious around them. She hasn't sweated in some time, but now may as well be a reasonable time. Still, she didn't resist the temptation and made sure to give him a hand to shake.

Sure, it went a little silent between everyone, and maybe it was a little awkward, but let me tell you, Claud didn't mind her touch.

There's a whip in the wind and Evelyn turns around to see a massive flag of Asnin in white, or she thinks it's white, it looks grey from dirt. It could be sun faded blue for all she knows.

'Evelyn, are you okay?' Claud asks her.

'Yeah,' she turns back.

The group wastes no time and moves out. They all come to the pen. Evelyn and Claud approach lastly. He opens the gate to the nord stall and helps her on his steed.

'Everyone is here to watch over you.' Claud reminds and mounts the front and takes rein.

'Yeah,' Dean says and mounts. He leans with one hand on his side; he overheard them in the pens to their right. 'Maybe we can get you back in time for this Summers Feast. That is if we aren't the flip side.'

She knows he's only teasing and turns to Claud to ask something, which comes out secretly. 'You're coming?'

'Yeah,' Andrew replies for him, on their left hand side. 'He's been talking about it all day ever since he got the news from papa-boy.'

'Okay guys.' Claud says and chuckles a little, waving his hand to wave them off.

Jamie is quietest, looking ready to move on.

The two men smile to Claud's embarrassment and they ride off, taking a path they know through the city of Asnin to get to the forest. Jamie is next, moving into the street.

Claud bumps his stirrups and off they go. 'This will take us straight to the backyard of Asnin. There we will start our search. If we can't find the Dark One's den, then we are going to hunt a dear and have a feast to remember. What do you think about that?'

'Sounds good,' Evelyn replies. 'That should make up for our losses; if it is meant to be, then so be it.'

'We'll find it. After all, we have all day.'

'Mostly,' she agrees, flashing a half-wittingly smile. The hooves are loud hitting the road. 'We can't see.' She says in his ear. She has a firm grip on his ribcage, which feels beefy. It's a new touch, than anything boney.

'Don't worry I've been here before.'

Every now and then they'll move behind the tall of the citadel and go back into darkness. The maze of townhouses finally pitches them to a close. The others ahead came to a stop for a break. The group is found and is approached. Claud's nord breathes heavily out to the stop.

Evelyn shrugs off the chills of this morning and watches the area around them. The group heads out again, this time together and takes to the north, leading a tight pathway to get out of the city, which will end through a large hole in the outside wall.

'Hold on tight!' Dean yells up ahead, his voice echoing off the thin of the alley.

Claud could feel the tightness tug at his chest, both her arms are now wrapped around him. Her fingers press on his body. A soft land and Evelyn comes down with a bump. The impact causes an arm to fly from her grasp while her other remains to his body. Claud didn't have time to look back, and Evelyn adjusts her slanted self as a means to rebalancing.

The girl looks back. The night makes one lost in those streets. But now they're far from the citadel and its madness; with its rolling stairways and climbing steps, getting lost outside compares none to the maze within those towers and hallways.

The group dismount outside Asnin, halfway from its wall and the Forbidden Forest. The men tie their steeds to a few trees here. Everyone looks happier to be closer to nature again and outside ruin. But she found her wariness. She knows what stirs in the deep.

Evelyn waits while the others gather their things. Lanterns are lit and one is handed out to her, who waits for Claud still preparing his weapon. When finished, he slings it over his shoulder and approaches the thicket of the damned with her.

The foot before the thicket is rather dramatic, being grassy with very little bush before the stalk.

She steps in between the men, and has looks around at the bewildering shadow. Moving in, one can hear everything at this time of night. There are frogs croaking someplace distant.

She jumps back to a jumping frog and Claud finds his humour at a moment like this. There is no place like forbidden territory.

The speaking within the group is at a minimal, at first. Once the men got used to the area, they spoke up, lighting up their chatter. It was nice, giving the forest a lighter feel.

Everything seemed to move faster and Evelyn moved away from the middle and stayed closest to Claud, near the back. He never did say much, just a few words. Everyone has a look of marching because of the thick. He helps her when she has to climb over bigger things; fallen trees from years back, or last week's thunder stricken. Moss covers entire surfaces, even halfway up bark lines.

Mushrooms are the star of the forest floor, making it that much more enchanted. Andrew you've been replaced. At least you can still glow fluorescently.

'Imagine this... I'm walking the forest. Not in a million years did I think --' she almost fell when she said it, and Claud caught her with a hand under the elbow. In not long her foot slipped into a hole and he helped her out also, leaning down to pull her out. He comes back up. He saw something in her eyes, metaphorically. He looks away.

'Try and keep up.' He says.

She nods, feeling all kinds of emotions. The whole time walking beside him she can smell his jacket; leather. When he made looks around, she would want to stray away from his site, but they kept her coming back for more. Damn, what it means to be attracted, am I right? Straight like an arrow onto his. There is no deviation on his part, either. Which made it all that much compelling, and it can only mean one thing.

He would smile sometimes to her liking, and vice versa. I mean come on, it's clear to see, and even now, he'd slow down just so she could catch up.

Something in the distance, away from the group on their left was scared. It's a rabbit, yet its suddenness caught her off guard too, and she jumps to Claud, wrapping an arm around him. She smiles weakly back and releases her touch.

'Tell me more about you.' He asks, after some.

Her life just lit up.

'Me?' She couldn't help but find herself asking. No one has ever asked this before, at least no one she really liked. For such a simple question, it sure felt harder. She thought about where she should start, and the whole time, which felt like a good five minutes, but only lasted a few moments, brought her attention back to him.

'Wait a second; aren't you going to teach me how to use a rifle? I thought that was a part of the plan?'

He smiles. 'No way, you'll be observing today.' And then turns his attention to find her lingering eyes on the thicket. A change, as if she forgotten where she was.

'Hurry up.' A voice echoes from one of the men, up ahead. It sounded like Dean's. Or maybe it was Andrew's?

'Come on.' Claud nudges her. 'Let's catch up.'

A fog lingers and Evelyn was sure she caught something move in it. For a tail of movement is left of something passing. She catches her breath and scratches her head to something she thought of, but held her tongue.

'...You best be careful, a lot of rabbit holes and dens around this part of town.' Claud says noticing their efforts are working.

Evelyn has a wary site along her paces. She watches the forest more closely, something she feels Claud should be doing more of so she can keep up. She wants to have her head up and keep her wits about her. I think Claud got the hint, so he remained by her side, all the while making sure they move more quickly over stumps and branches. After all, someone had to watch over her or else she'd fall into a pitfall for all he knew.

They regroup and they all take a breather. They found Evelyn had kept her eyes on the green fir most of the time, assuming it's her first time and all. Her eyes are usually widest with anticipation to see more of it – yet what Claud saw was only fear. He felt kinda bad for the girl; for he allowed her to come this far. Well, he had warned her and now it's time for her to walk the dark on her own. He can't hold her hand all day.

The group heads out and Claud moves someplace further ahead.

Her hand grips a tree, squishing in the wet to hold her climb over another broken down tree.

'What was that?' Evelyn asks, but no one seemed to notice. 'I saw something move in the fog.' She says and the group doesn't respond. Thankfully the fog is thinning and the call of wilderness is quieter, making all things heard. Lanterns dim and one of the men's voices calls. 'Shh,' she hears. Evelyn couldn't make out anybody's faces. They all had their backs slightly turned to her, being ahead. She's near the back of things again...

91

so that didn't help much. One turns around and it's Andrew, he is pointing his hand to signify something's up ahead. He unstraps his gear and moves to a small bank.

'It's a dear.' The men's voices chain to Evelyn who is with Jessie, Jessie because he was told to watch her, not because he's slow. So he kept to the far back.

Jessie moves past her. I suppose he had enough of it. She was going to reach out and say how much harder this is than it looks, but he moved quicker than she had.

Evelyn does her best to catch up, trying to move quicker. She kept getting hushes from them.

She comes to a soft frown next. All she could hear was the men's gear bouncing off their backs, if anything, *they were the loudest.*

'It's not like I do this everyday.' She says and sighs. 'Gosh, I'm here for the first time, what do they expect of me?'

She steps on a branch. Snap. She looks up and her face drops.

A dear in the clear is caught drinking in the Funicmorain River. It looks up from its drinking, but remained still. It's staring past the group, directly at her.

'Sorry.' She hisses in the faintest of voices, still watching the deer in the clear. Hands fly, telling her to get down. She lowers and waits. She scratches her head to a few glares she had gotten. The men peer back to find the deer drinking some more.

Claud is seen furthest out. So she crept on past the guys who had wide eyes, as if this could stonewall her. Do they not know who she is? She arrives to the sides of Claud and waits.

He moves his body to speak closer in her ear. 'Did you know if you follow the river you'll hit the waterfall, but we aren't going that way.'

She gave him a look; it was enough to tell him of her surprise.

'Yeah,' he responds to her expression. 'We're heading west, in the deep. That's where we will find *them* and not near the falls, you see.'

The men are heard moving behind her and she watches them lift their rifles, pointing them over her.

A bird lands on a branch, overlooking everyone.

Evelyn looks up, noticing that same crow from before. She finds the rifle again and goes ears down with both palms. A loud squawk from the crow makes them all jump, and one of the triggers is accidentally pulled. She let her hands fall to its dissipating rang; the sound of the gunshot echoes off the forest.

A sound of an animal making for its sprint was also heard. Evelyn looks up and the bird is gone. She turns around to the men's faces staring in the direction of the river. She peeks over the edge to find the Lady of the Forest on the other side of the bank.

The lady is dressed in all silvery and white robes alongside white hair. She smiles to them and returns almost as fast as she came to go back into the thicket.

'So...' Jessie who fired the gun said. He is unsure what to say next.

'I'm not so hungry anymore.' Claud says, standing up to see everyone.

The warning was clear from *her*. It didn't take them long to leave the forest and walk out the way they came.

Everyone has the same look from before, now stepping out into the clear. The sun is nearly up, giving the sky a blue tint. They don't have to use the lanterns any longer. The men blow out theirs, and Evelyn opens the cage and hunches down to do the same.

'I think you're going to have a few more hungry lads over tonight.' Claud says to Evelyn, nudging a look to his friends.

She looks over at them with easy eyes and turns back to him. She finds her fast beating heart again, and says. 'It's a plan then. I better head back before my Mother's up. Better yet, I should head out now so I can start on cooking after a good nap.' She goes on to smile. 'Don't you think?'

Claud smiles a response back. He asked if he could take her home and she nods her approval. They talked about the experience. Evelyn told him about the witch she saw during Jonah's attack. The one experience she never did mention to him.

'The same witch you're thinking of?' He asks her, already making their way into the streets of Maesemer.

'I'm guessing that.' She replies with a few bumps on the saddle. 'I'm really surprised she would have come so close this time.'

'Well, from my own experience, I'm not.'

'But did you know she'd show?'

'No, but I had a good feeling she'd show today.'

They sped out of town and around the market to make for her house.

'You know...' She says. 'I never did thank you for all of this.'

'Bah, there's no need. I had a feeling you wanted to go out there. I'm just glad we never did head out to the den. I think that's why she warned us. Otherwise it could have been deadly.'

'You and your feelings,' she teases.

'More than you know.'

'Like reading minds?'

He laughs, 'I wouldn't go that far. But maybe *she* can.'

Evelyn isn't sure what to say.

They arrive at the house and Evelyn dismounts.

'What time do you think?' He asks.

'Five o'clock.' And smiles generously, still, she felt emotional, like she could cry. She doesn't know why, it just... came over her. 'See you then.' She says moving to the first step. She smiles again and turns around; but he already speeds off.

She put her hands to her mouth, for heck Mother could have overheard. She moves into the house and tip toes up the stairs into her bedroom. Evelyn puts her hand to her head. 'What was I thinking...? I could have gotten hurt... This whole thing was a *bad* idea.' She stops and starts crying. She can feel the early morning taking its course and decides to close the door behind her.

She undresses and dresses into her pyjamas. She comes to a lay on her soft comfy bed. She is half torn from over-excitement and wanting more sleep. Her eyes scrunch and her mouth cringes to her silent weep, until her eyes close and she lays her head back down on her pillow. Oh the feeling. How great it feels to just nap. Such a simple thing, but so glorious -- In my opinion, and I'm sure in hers as well -- You can never get enough rest.

She did her best to shake the thoughts, the fears, and then slips her beautiful life asleep.

- CHAPTER 4 -

Summers Feast

When she awoke, saliva drools out the side of her mouth. It is cold and wet; she feels alive. She wipes it with the back of her sleeve and smells it. Yuck.

She rolls over her shoulder and sits up on the side of her bed and wipes her mouth again, being oblivious to the moment and what is required of her, which anytime now should make her jump up. She looks around easily, and then hears a chopping noise.

'Mom?' Evelyn asks and props herself up to peer outside her doorway. The sun is clearly up, shinning onto the floor before her from her bedroom window. She must have slept in, which means it's nearly afternoon.

It dawns on her, 'Summers Feast!'

Evelyn comes down the steps to the smell of spices. Mother is in the kitchen preparing up a storm, already having everything set up. For the stuffing, she has begun chopping ingredients on a board, placing individual mounts into a large ceramic bowl. And on the kitchen table, ingredients have already been laid out to make pie shells, but nothing started or measured yet. Still, it was a plus to have everything ready to get started on.

'Morning, you've slept in.' Mother says.

Evelyn jumps into the kitchen, hair untidy. 'You didn't wake me?'

'I came in, but I heard you snoring, so I guessed it was going to be another sleepy one.' Mom says, smiling and chopping up bread for the stuffing.

Evelyn smiles and moves toward the bowl, looking around eagerly. 'Where should I start?'

Mother ignores the question. 'What time did you get to bed? You only sleep in like that when you're up too late.'

'No, not always...'

'Alright, alright, help me with the pies.' Mother rolls her eyes, knowing there's no use in arguing with this one. 'I haven't started those yet.'

Evelyn moves to the sink and washes her hands; all to remember the guys and how many more they will need to feed tonight. 'I... I think we will be having a few more coming over,' and swallows, 'tonight.'

Mother scratches her face. 'Figures, then we should start making double everything.'

Evelyn looks surprised. 'I thought you were going to be mad.'

'W-Why would I be mad? You don't think I knew you were going to that damn hunting party?'

Evelyn swallows as a means of reply.

'Guess who told me your plans. It'll be the last person you'd expect, besides... I figured Dale might want to invite a few more people over. So, I thought I better double check seeing I should go into town to pick up some more butter anyways. I stopped by the butchery, and I found your friend Claud there. He was asking me to invite a few of his hunter buddies. So... naturally what was I going to say? No?' Mom shrugs. 'It was right in front of Dale. So I said alright.'

Evelyn was sure this wasn't real. Evelyn blinks from Mother's easy going manner and reacts quickly. 'Well lucky you did then.' Evelyn says scratching her neck. 'We have no time to lose.'

Mother nods very slowly... and goes back to using her hands to mesh the ingredients in bowl.

It took them nearly all evening to prepare a double of everything. They also plan to prepare and cook berry tarts, spiced squash, roast garlic vegetables and garlic toast, all to be made with butter. Mom has the stuffing down; made up of two loafs of bread, raisins, apples, spices and vegetables.

Mother starts stuffing the deer. While this is being done, Evelyn makes three different pies from scratch.

The deer is placed to cook in the oven, with the skin filled with stuffing, and… you said it, with butter. Basically, anywhere Mom could fit her magic ingredient. If there was another spot, she would have found it.

At the bottom of the oven, Evelyn's pies are placed on a lined rack to cook; one pear and apple, a pumpkin, and a strawberry-beet pie. Yum!

Evelyn wipes a brow. The day had already been warmer than usual. Evelyn looks towards the door with a dirty apron on – wiping herself off -- dust from flour falls onto the sunbeam floor. She finishes rolling the pie dough's for the berry tarts, firstly. She chilled them in the icebox so they were easier to roll out afterwards. Unlike handling her last three pie shells, which gives her this brilliant idea to begin with.

Jimmy enters.

'Hey Katherine, I didn't know what time to stop over. So I thought now would be okay?'

'Oh, don't worry Jim, we're just about done. I really do hope you're hungry.' She replies candidly. 'I know Evelyn is. She hadn't had anything since we started.' Mother turns to her daughter with a finger in mouth after tasting something delicious. 'Let's get the glasses out. That way we can start pouring drinks for the rest of the guests when they arrive.' She watches her daughter breathe the smells of cooking in that linger the room. Mom says. 'We'll be eating soon, so don't start now honey. Otherwise, you'll be full before anyone starts.'

Evelyn moves closer to the porcelain oven, breathing in again. It was as if the whiff of food that scents the air could be tasted. That's how much her stomach talks.

Jimmy made his way around easily, admiring the smells in the oven also. He heaves himself up on the kitchen counter beside Katherine who is doing a few dishes, and fills himself a glass of water by tap. He swigs a little and took another glass from the drying rack. He filled one for Evelyn and says. 'It'll help keep the appetite down,' handing it out for her.

'He's right you know.' Mother says, looking back at her, dusty and ingredient ridden.

'Alright,' Evelyn gets up from her crouched position in front of the stove to take the offering.

Thankfully, it won't be long till dinner. And Evelyn was right; they would have to hurry. Thirty minutes from Jimmy's arrival, his little brother; Sam, and his father; Percy, walked over with their usual delicious *raspberry-spiced apple pie*. Two pies held in Percy's hands, and the other two in Sam's. This means it won't be long till more guests arrive.

'Oh!' Evelyn greets the pies happily. Sam carefully hides the desserts behind his back and Evelyn looks evermore eager to see his. Finally, the young boy handed his over to her, and Percy gave his son a wink. Evelyn never stops to greet them, not with the warm deliciousness resting on both her upturn palms. She takes a big whiff in.

'Come on in.' Mother says whole heartedly, now hitting Evelyn attentively with an oven mitt.

'Oh *hi*,' Evelyn says getting the point and ducking the last one on the way to the kitchen. She carefully places them on the kitchen table, right beside her pumpkin pie, with the beet and apple still cooking.

The smells are wonderful, filling up the kitchen. Evelyn has a calm look, keeping her focus from the stirring hunger.

About another thirty minutes passes and Evelyn's remaining two pies are out of the oven and on the kitchen table. That's seven pies in total that line the table. She places her prepared berry pies in the oven now, and a whole O'Cous in its shell to roast. And Mother begins chopping vegetables for their last and final dish.

Sam watches Evelyn take the deer meat out of the oven. She lifts the lid and steam rushes out. She begins basting. Once Mom finishes chopping up vegetables for the final dish, she places them in a dish and adds her magic ingredient along with some simple seasonings. She places a lid overtop and puts the last dish of the night on the bottom rack to roast. Katherine was not about to stop now, now that they're nearly done. She starts on her heavenly gravy, right away, using the pan drippings. It took teamwork from the two. Evelyn would baste and then help by slowly dusting in flour for Mom, who stirs to thicken the gravy.

Evelyn would never attempt to do the gravy herself. What's a meal without gravy? Yeah, last time she had, she nearly ruined Summers Feast. Besides, Mom makes it best every time.

This whole time, Evelyn can't help but feel a little watched.

Sam's eyes are bright with anticipation. He always had a little bit of a crush on her, and everyone knows it. He always would stay around her, trying to do anything to see what she was doing, looking up at her while she least expects it.

She looks back at his big brown eyes. Even now he's doing it, standing next to her in the kitchen, watching her cut pieces of toast. Has time flown that fast? Evelyn hadn't noticed.

She spreads butter with garlic over it so that the hungry Sheppard's aren't the only ones going to be eating toast tonight. And no, she hadn't forgotten to put out the glasses on the dinning room table. She'd rather eat in her opinion, than drink anymore water.

On her move, she almost knocks the watchful boy over. In apology, she turns her attention back to the oven with oven mitts, gently taking out the tarts to put in the buttered garlic toast. The smell brought everyone, even Mom around.

Evelyn waits, counting the minutes, till she quickly spun and reopened the oven. Cooked toast fills their sensations. She places the toast on the stovetop with the little space that there is and puts her pies back in the oven.

She bobs back up. 'Dig in.' Evelyn says, passing a piece to Sam. The bread pieces are all taken. Licking fingers and blowing on riveted hot pieces -- everyone manages a large bite, only, Evelyn found herself putting it aside.

Guess who the culprit is.

'Dishes,' Mother spoke at the side of her mouth chewing on a piece of toast. Evelyn knew well what she meant; knowing Mother is still busy with the gravy. Mom hasn't gotten around to taking out the stuffing just yet and imagines she won't have enough time to.

'Okay.' Evelyn replies and turns to the watching one. She gave him a frown and bent down to pat his shaggy brown hair. 'Hey, are you up to drying my man?'

'I guess...' He says brushing his frazzled hair from his face.

She got Jimmy and Sam to work with her, and just when they finish and find some time to rest, Mother's restless voice picks up. 'We need to get more chairs for the dining room table.' Evelyn nods a sore look back and then Mother decides on something better. 'I don't think we will have enough room and chairs.' Mother wipes the top of her head with the back of her sleeve and goes on. 'Percy, do you think you could go grab a few of your chairs and bring them over? If we can squeeze everyone around the edges of the table, I think we'll be able to fit everybody in.'

'Of course,' he says and he left with Jimmy.

Evelyn could sing, finally a *break!* The cool air of outside blows in and it gives her another brilliant idea today to push it wide open to circulate some fresher air. She let a sigh of relief take over, and then Mother points her to fill the spot for the kid. Evelyn shoulders drop, and she droops herself over to the kitchen sink.

'Hey.' Evelyn says to Sam with no real intention, feeling Mother's redemption -- all because of the extra bodies coming over tonight – Evelyn's sure of it.

'Hey.' He said back with a little more energy.

Mother smiles big and goes back to business.

It was actually a good thing, the dishes. Evelyn could just stand and rest, circling a cloth in the mess until clean. She finishes the last few, moving from sink to look around the kitchen, finding Mom sitting at the dining room table.

'Easy-peasy,' Evelyn says, giving Sam a high five. They come to a sit next to Mom. Now the *glasses* and plates are to be set up, and in not long everyone who's coming over tonight will be touching elbow to elbow from lack of space. Evelyn looks over at Sam, raising her brows heavily. He's smiling back at her.

She asks. 'You want something to drink before we start to set up?'

He whines. 'Setting up...'

'Yes.' Katherine intervenes. 'And good team work you guys.' She gave them both high fives. It was a pleasant surprise, and it told Evelyn her secret punishment was over...

Percy came back with the chairs to find the table being unfolded by Evelyn. It's an average size table seating eight, when unfolded it seats two more.

'So dinner's going to be a little tight with twelve coming over...' Evelyn says eyeing those around.

It raised a good question, if they should take dinner outside just in case it gets too crowded. Yet it made everyone quiet. You see, the last time she mentioned it, it rained. They knew her question was about to come, so this time around everyone yelled an outstanding "No". I'd say with all that's happened in the past... say... couple of years, she had this one coming.

'Okay.' She says sounding a little standoffish.

Timmy gave a frown. 'Sam, did you even move from your spot?'

'Yeah,' he replies from his sitting spot, assorting smaller spoons from bigger ones that Evelyn got for him for the set up in the dinning room.

'Yeah,' Evelyn repeats in the boy's defence, only to disappear someplace in the kitchen to grab many stacked plates and places them down in the middle of the unfolded table.

Percy and Jimmy place the chairs around the table. Evelyn gave Sam a wink and did the final touch, candles and napkins. Mother is in the kitchen watching the cooking and digging out the stuffing into another deep dish.

'Evelyn, we will find a way.' Mother says arriving in the room and resting a hand on the back of a chair. She exhales gently to let loose. 'Now all we have to do is wait.'

Evelyn kept conversation up with Percy and his boys. She was always made centre of attention and probably would be for the rest of the night.

Mother takes out the last bit of cooking in the oven. The roast vegetables and squash are perfect, resting them, along with the berry tarts on the kitchen counter. She finds herself back at the dining room table and holds a glass of water, chugging it down, exhaling afterwards. She's happy everything's all ready and done with.

Jimmy jumps up and ran towards the door. 'It's Jason, and there's another.'

'Corry,' Evelyn says to everyone at the table.

Jason enters. 'Hey you guys.' Corry is behind him.

Everyone greets them. The two men come to find a hug from their favourite girl. She pours them water in their glasses from a jug on the table. The walk over would have been a hot one.

'Evelyn, this looks good.' Jason couldn't help but say, admiring the set up.

'Yeah, it's great.' Corry agrees.

She hands them their glass and they gladly accept the water.

'Who are these fellows?' Corry asks in order to shake one of the children's hands.

'I'm Sam,' the littler one follows-up.

Corry and Jason go on to introduce themselves to the Sheppard's and receive introduction back.

'Sorry, I suppose I should have introduced you all earlier.' Evelyn says watching Mother move into the room with a large deer meat, no longer stuffed; *who would have thought*? It steams on a ceramic plate. Its smell is wondrous and its size is great, but the juices were just too much for Evelyn at the moment, teasing her with every drip drop.

'Wow.' They all beam.

Mother's voice squeaks a little. 'And since you're all accompanying us tonight --'

There's a sound of nords and Evelyn was the first to get up. 'That must be Claud and his friends.'

'Who?' Jason is the first to ask amongst friends.

'I'll need some help getting all the dishes onto the table.' Mom says in sort panic, and the room gets up to assist.

Outside, Evelyn moves to the porch. She comes down the front porch steps and stops. The carriage pulls up. Claud steps out with a clean shave, wearing boots, blue gene and a plain white T-shirt. There his friends are. Stepping out is Andrew, Jessie and Dean who are dressed similarly, only Dean wares a sleek coat of leather. Evelyn smiles big to all of them, and Dale comes down from the front stirrups to greet her back.

The men notice a storm forming over the forest, a few hours away. They all look away to follow their noses instead. Claud moves to her sides and whispers so nobody can hear.

'He doesn't know, so she won't have to.'

Evelyn was about to comment about Mother already knowing about the hunt, assuming this is what he meant. Instead, she smiles to him and says. 'It's no harm done,' and walks with him to the house.

Claud found his fancy in this.

Mother came outside and greets them, allowing the guys to enter the house. She kept an eye out for Claud at the back with her daughter, while she held the door open for the other boys. They thank her and she smiles at Dale as he passes inside. It was a little difficult to see Mother unsure about the hunter Claud. It's that evident. Finally, Evelyn and Claud enter and without word.

Inside, Corry is placing the final dish, finding a seat beside Jason. Stacy is at the far end. He sat next to Jimmy. Evelyn comes to a sit beside Sam who has larger eyes with everyone in the room. And, Katherine sits beside Sam, leaving enough room for the rest of the men. Claud sat at the end and Dale the other, where the last three hunters sat in the spaces they could find.

The room eventually had to open up and make space for them, separating Evelyn and Mother from one another. Dishes are moved every time someone bumps. Forks move and the knives clank, and like that – the room bursts into chat.

'Hi.' Claud is the first to greet Corry around room.

He greets back. But Evelyn and everyone else could see the embarrassment on Corry's face, being between both men. He's not near their height, nor size... of course, a hundred and twenty pounds and healthy, and nearly half their weight.

'Hi.' Jason reaches around Corry to shake Claud's hand. Now Jason's a big boy, but Claud has forty pounds on him, being the second largest man in the room... and who's first? Who else? Andrew. Andrew sat much like a stone giant, with his big blue eyes.

Claud had been beaming around the room where he eventually found a pair of similar blue ones... gosh, if he had words for how beautiful...

It wasn't just the hair... nor her smile, which was apart of the mix, it has *got* to be her soul that just amplifies this perfect adjustment of her in a teeming reality of his.

Evelyn smiles at him and found Jason's eyes staring. Jason could see the stranger and her have something else in common. Did it make him a little jealous? No, just timid, but then again he did decide to let her go... so what's the point?

Evelyn tries to stay calm. Oddly, she was more nervous with the hunters sitting next to her. And somehow, Sam figured out a way of keeping his spot adjacent to her; when the final change in room had been made.

She looks down at him and smiles to his smiley self. Still, even with Dean next to her, and Andrew next to mother; who looks a little nervous by him -- There they all sat, laughing and passing information to one another.

It's hard for Evelyn to conjure such a moment, passing looks to the boys beside, just to smile her "Hi" And ugh... that other guy over there, still passing her looks. She wanted to put her hands to her face in such humility. It's the warmth of the room that is making everything so much hotter too, and finally, everyone is sweating! Thank god and up above or whoever for this, for the huntress is sweating and even the hunters, also!

When Evelyn finally put her hands to her face to a joke that made her laugh so hard her body jiggles -- her cold sweaty palms relieve her face, feeling her fingers imprints left over for a few good moments.

Oh, but it appears Corry had the biggest blush of them all. He didn't say much, after all, he was more like a pole stuck between two beams. But Evelyn and Jason knew better for the reasoning. It had been Claud who had hardly noticed anything with his eyes stuck on one.

Me

Evelyn found it appealing.

So Corry is squished, no doubt, with these two guys – not allowing much room for anything. Evelyn could hardly see the boy acting himself, being the most anxious tonight -- But Evelyn didn't stop for a second to ask if he was alright, she knew he didn't mind being so close to the guys, *one* bit.

Evelyn laughs big at Corry trying to find a way of making him relax; instead it brought her silly side out.

Jokes around the room are making everyone laugh. The jokes came from every boy and girl. Even Sam had some things to say.

'You best take your time, big ones.' The men halt their reach in mid air in their attempt for more food and listen; at least three of them had done this. 'We don't want anyone exploding now do we? You'll end up looking like the strawberry beet pie we got back there.'

'Hey.' Evelyn says cheekily. 'I worked hard on that thing,' and goes back to scooping vegetables onto her plate. She waits for Mom's heavenly gravy to be passed around before she eats. Her stomach rumbles, and her mouth is watering. 'Screw it.' Evelyn says, passing the roast vegetables dish into the person lap on her right so she can dig in.

It had been silent while the forks hit the plates. A few moaning and a little loud chewing can be heard.

Evelyn couldn't conceal her words. 'It's so amazing. Thank you up and beyond for everyone who created this wonderful food to be put into my mouth.'

There was a few looks and then their eyes fell right back onto their plates, digging in for more. She looks up at their faces, smiling about. Oh she knew they had some words of their own, but they just didn't care to spill anything with the deliciousness running mouth.

There are drinks of beer and wine. But Evelyn never did touch her glass, nor did Jason or Katherine for that matter. Claud had a bit, but he looked like he could handle much more then he let on. In not long, he turned back to water, noticing Evelyn hadn't touched her choice of wine.

Everyone's eyes swish to Percy's and Jason's conversation, for they spoke least during feast.

'When are you leaving, Jason?'

'In a few days, I'll be taking only a few things with me.'

'Are you going to be taking the whole way to Brunon?'

'Yeah,' he responds. 'I'll be staying onboard for the week. My sister will be waiting for me when I get in.'

Mother's voice picks up. 'I forgot you had a sister, that's right, Danny, wasn't her name?'

'Yeah, she works near a school, at the local clinic. She owns with her boyfriend, but I'll be able to bunk in their spare room.'

'Oh, well, that's not so bad.' Percy replies.

Claud's friends seemed to be enjoying themselves, eating quietly. Their forks clank on plates. Every now they'd do something silly, like throw a piece of food or dab something wet in a friend's ear. But mostly, they're better behaved than anyone expected. So *everyone else* thought.

'Yeah,' Jason hesitates, and the room noticed as well -- Andrew flicking water at Jamie from his glass. Jason went back to explaining. 'It's really not all that bad. It might be a little lonely at first. But I think it'll be okay.' The room nods, eating as they listen; including the two who continued to act like dorks. They had gotten the eye from Dale and settled down.

'Are you going to be taking school?' Claud asks Jason, trying to make up for his friends behaviour.

'Probably – I've been thinking about it.' He replies.

And in not long, Evelyn hasn't realized how cute Jason looks. He'll do that to her when she least expects it. She gives him a subtle look as he finished his piece.

'I was thinking about being a teacher. Actually, I heard there is good benefits, so why not?'

Evelyn looks surprised by this, for this is news to her.

'I'm going to miss you.' Evelyn says and the round is quiet. 'There's going to be a lot of hotties wanting to be in your class. I'm sure of it.'

Percy covers Jimmy's ears and Jim laughs a little. 'Dad,' he whines.

The laughs went on and Corry seemed to be able to pick up the crumbs. He sat a little straighter and allowed himself to breathe. He eventually surprised the room, coming up with the most jokes and making everyone laugh more.

Mother got up and Evelyn helps her clear plates. Jason also joined the girls while the rest of the guys sat, chatting to make good company. It was a good thing too, the kitchen could only hold so many near the sinks, one for drying, washing and putting away. Otherwise, it'd be more trouble than the extra numbers were worth.

'Thanks for dinner that was awesome.' Jason says, drying the dishes. He looked like he wanted to ask if things were better between Evelyn and her.

'Absolutely,' Katherine replies, scrubbing.

They finish the dishes and the three set up plates in the dining room for another round.

'Who's ready for dessert?' Evelyn asks the chatty. They're hungry eyes from Claud and his gang, but Corry, and about everyone else looks stuffed.

Evelyn couldn't resist a slice of that apple pie. Finally serving herself after her guests tasted theirs.

The parties taken outside and the Sheppard's end up staying, normally they'd go home around this time. But Jimmy and Sam tugged on Percy's sleeve when the room decided to take the party outside to start a fire in the pit.

'Alright but only for a few more boys,' he says and they cheer back, running outside to find Evelyn. She needed their help and they re-enter the house to gather chairs to her request.

Percy joins the sitting around the pit with a drink in hand, looking full as ever. That last piece of dessert has gotten everyone looking more than thankful.

It was Claud's friends who started making the fire.

Next, Evelyn sat to Percy. The cool winds blowing on her neck never felt better, allowing everyone some space and clear mindedness. She sat back, watching everyone settle in their chairs.

Claud and his boys can't seem to start the fire -- there is a wind. Finally, Claud looks up. 'A pretty bad storm is rolling in,' and he comes to a sit across from Evelyn. She shrugs – to be rather cooped up with everyone or to be inside again and all alone? No brainer for this one.

He would still watch her, and found laughs when his friends keep up on trying for the tenth time, to light kindling wood.

'We need smaller chips, or even dry grass.' Jessie whines, hunched over the pit.

Claud looks over at his dad. Dale rolls his eyes and got the message. He got up to go look for some.

Everyone sat quietly, sipping their drink and the children; their water.

Sam is next to Jimmy, watching the men cursing at the cold wind coming from the storm's direction. Jimmy put his hands to his ears, and Sam is trying to pry his hands down.

'Now, now boys,' Percy says to his sons, rubbing his hands together to keep them warmer. 'Sam, just leave him be.'

Evelyn looks around and couldn't find Mother anywhere in view. Evelyn looks back to the hunters and found a sore laugh at the entertainment they kept on bringing.

'Oh you boys are so silly.' She says to them. At first, the hunters thought she was talking about the children who were acting up; who were play-fighting, but she got up and walked toward the men. Before she was about to give it a try, Andrew placed some brush and Dean scrapped the flint rock -- Boom! Fire oozes and the men fall backwards. Evelyn had never looked this surprised in some time.

Everyone laughed at once, patting their shirt from spilling a bit on themselves or the next person over. And then everyone quieted down to the roaring pit, a shock.

'Maybe it was the wind?' Mother says coming back outside with another drink in hand. She has the same wide eye.

'Goodness.' Dean laughs. 'Finally, we have fire!'

'Now we're a part of the Stone Age.' Evelyn mocks, resting her palms behind her again. May as well, she thought, wet from spilling her drink all over her.

'Hey, Missy,' Andrew says. 'That's Stone Age and one stone warmer.'

'Yeah, Stone Age and still kick'n around that is.' Jessie points out the obvious, and then the flint rock at her.

'Alright,' she laughs, 'alright, you win. Point that thing someplace else. That thing is dangerous.'

They nod back with firebug eyes.

'Oh great, now they'll want to blow everything up.' Dale says, tossing the brush into the fire. 'You're not helping any.' He says to her, brushing his hands off.

'Why?' She replies.

He winks.

She smiles, wiping a palm on her wet clothes to dry. She swigs what's left and forgot Claud was still here. She gave him a look across the fire. He looked straight away when Mother caught his eye.

'Alright boys,' Percy says. 'I think it's time to go. What do you think?' He asks his sons. Jimmy looks like he's trying to hold back a yawn because it's getting late. Percy caught Sam in the middle of one and Jimmy gave Sam a nudge. 'Nice.'

'Goodnight.' Percy says to everyone and everyone said it back.

'Thank you for having us over.' Jimmy says in his humble manner.

'Always a pleasure,' Katherine replies, liking Jimmy and his behaviour. Sam's too, now that she thought about it.

'I'll be heading back soon, too.' Jason says, taking the last swig of the night.

It was Claud's buddies who didn't get the hint, and Dale was the one who took charge to get things up and leaving. With a whip from the wind the fire blew out. 'There, look's to be a sign.' The father said.

'Goodnight.' Claud said to Katherine who has a smile on her face. She says her goodbye, and they thanked her for a great dinner. Jason and Corry shook the hunters' hands and walked with Katherine to the house.

Evelyn got up slowly, who had been chatting with Dean. But it was Claud who was the last one to enter the carriage. Dale is above and he gave her a look. Whatever it meant, it doesn't seem to get to her. And she says her goodbye to Claud with a hug. She likes Claud, but there was no way she could have kissed him without Mother's watchful eye from the kitchen window.

Evelyn comes to the porch step to stare out into the distance, watching the carriage leave. She's about to think a private thought, having to do with Dale's son, when a flicker in the corner of her eye halts the notion. She moves down to get a better view. Her eyes widen and she speaks louder.

'What in the world? That's some storm we got here. That won't be long...'

Jason moves outside. He felt the change in the wind also. He found her look toward the forest.

'You think it'll be bad?' He asks her moving down the steps.

The wind pushes them and leaves fly.

'Mom,' Evelyn yells out, ignoring Jason for the moment.

Mother comes down the steps and stops in the middle, hairs are brushing.

'Jason, you're staying over tonight.' Katherine says.

He nods.

No one saw this one coming. The clouds are black and bruised, and they've changed ever quickly. They flicker and a sundering is seen, with a fogy blanket running the sky, which means rain's falling.

There's a loud bang and the hairs stand up on everybody's body.

'Get inside.' Evelyn's mother says. Katherine's hair twirls behind her. She turns to them, who are still watching the dangerous storm.

'It looks... like a hurricane.' Evelyn says marvellously.

'Inside,' Mother says. They heard her worry. Evelyn looked at Jason and the two leave.

Katherine took another step forward toward the looming thunder.

'This means a change is coming.'

- CHAPTER 5 -

Magic-ficent

Evelyn sat and watched rain out her bedside window. It starts to hail. She lays her head back down on her pillow. There are thoughts of Claud and she shook a head to them.

'I'll never get to sleep with thoughts of him.' Her eyes close. More thoughts taunt, so she sits up and focuses on the hail tapping her window, anything to help heed a clearer mind. Her mind passes to another hunter, and she shakes it off. A thought of Jason lingers, who had gone home with Corry. At the time, the storm moved direction and only held faint winds and some rain. It hailed a little too, but nothing as threatening as anyone expected.

Slowly, she lies back down after ten minutes of refocusing on the rain, and her thoughts have finally melted away. Her eyes shut. Evelyn falls asleep. It's going to be one of those deep dreams again.

Clear skies are above. She looks up to see clouds forming a cluster around town. Mom was in the kitchen a few moments ago, making breakfast. It didn't bother Evelyn that she can see through the kitchen ceiling, but Mother's sudden disappearance had.

Evelyn gets up from the kitchen chair and finds a step on a branch, crackling under a foot; it hurts, so a rub makes it feel better.

The walls around are disappearing; and so the house and all its appliances does as well. The kitchen table is the last to evaporate, and in not long, the chair Evelyn stood up from, dissipates.

She looks back up and shades the light of morning sun with a hand. The sky shows of a large hole in concreting clouds. She looks back down to a tickle, the grass is growing taller. The earth begins to tremble and trees begin to grow, causing a wake. The trees stretch and leafs bloom. With a final shake; a forest surrounds. Moss and mushrooms are evident, and she realizes now she's in the Forbidden Forest.

She walks, and more spontaneous things happen. Blooming flowers and running rivers flow. Slowly, in the move of enchantment, she walks. There is an end to its reach and its fast approaching. She reaches the other side of the dark forest; a premonition to its end. A path leads away and out of the woods. She takes it. It is hard to believe she's already crossed over, skipping all the wonders and the fears bewildering. And that's what she likes most about it.

A glance back shows only calm in the withering. Instead, Evelyn regains focus and looks away. She continues her stride. It is a wide open space. It's a desert. There are marks, slithers in sand beds. It takes her to a base of a pyramid. She stops and looks up; it will be a rather long climb. She takes the only stairway up. She raises a foot, placing it on the cold sandstone. Another foot and she climbed the large steps carved from an ancient time.

She glances to the top. She doesn't know what's up there, only that a feeling keeps her moving forward. When she nears the peak, a familiar feeling pits in her stomach -- Mother, Maesemer, and all that she's ever come to love, feels as far as dusk now.

'Where am I?' she asks herself, feeling much from such heights. One can see the world with new horizons; the brightness is overwhelming.

She shades her eyes from the sun and peers toward the forest in hopes of seeing town, one more time. There is not a peep of Maesemer or a glimpse of home.

There's a change in the wind. Also, the sun is going down rather quickly, like there's some sort of rush for dusk. It seems everything is in the mood for suddenness.

She looks straight up when a cool raindrop is felt. Another dabs at her palm facing the heavens. She puts another foot forward; a flicker in the skies has the effect to halt.

'This can't be real, can it be?'

The scene is ever changing. The sun touches the horizon now completing dusk. She blinks and the sun went almost as fast as it came. In accordance, she finds a silvery moon behind a cloud, allowing for a misty glow.

She hurries the climb to the top of the pyramid. Up here, a large archway offers a passageway inwards. She doesn't take it yet.

'What is this place?' She asks herself. The rain trickles on her nose and taps on the sandstone. She moves toward the archway and takes steps that lead her within and down. Inside, it leads the way. She reaches bottom. Lights draw a way. A corridor has opened up to her. She takes it. Flickering torches guide her to a darker abyss.

She looks to the left and finds a painted lady pointing the way on. Naturally, Evelyn follows the musty way. It's a bit claustrophobic but Evelyn manages more steps as her comfort should catch on.

The floor is sandy. A humid breeze moves within.

The corridor already appears smaller; so naturally she stops to analyze; she moves her head the way she came.

'I can't be sure...' She gleams. 'Are the halls getting thinner or is it just me?'

Another torch is reached and the girl stops to catch breath. She feels the walls for some doorway out, there's nothing, and another glance around shows only one way on. The darkness calls.

The whole while, she would have sworn she heard a clanking noise someplace close, and then realizes another replica of the lady is on the wall. The lady has the same pointing pose as before.

This odd occurrence isn't what's bothering Evelyn, it's the torches spanned out further from the next, which means each light is going to be a longer destination to reach.

The feeling of containment continues to carry on, yet the feeling of calling persists and Evelyn leaves the light to go into darkness again to reach to the next. Sand brushes below her feet, caught by a smooth breeze along the thinning pathway.

A feeling in the black of someone follows. After some time, the light comes in approach and she moves around to listen to the same clanking noise. It does make her frown and seek. She touches the sandy walls in hopes of finding a means to its reason, only to find nothing.

With many hesitant looks, Evelyn decides to keep her site to the wall. She doesn't want to look towards the next discouraging point. They all seem so far, in fact, it looks as if the next will be impossible to reach. There, beside the torch, with that same pointing to the deep, the lady is.

'Hmm, I was sure you weren't there.' Evelyn says. She bits a lip and takes a few steps backward into shadow.

A voice whispers. 'Run.'

It catches Evelyn off guard. Her eyes dab at the wall and she back peddles till her return under the light. The lady on the wall is slowly approached.

'Hold on… are you following me?'

The lady nods, which comes as a great surprise to Evelyn.

'Can you help me?' She asks the lady.

The lady says nothing, but moves. The paint shifts and the lady dug for something in her pocket. Her star ridden robe shakes and a candle is retrieved. She whispers something unique, and like magic the tip ignites. The lady's expression grows wary.

'We must hurry.' The lady says.

'We must hurry?' Evelyn finds herself repeating. 'W-Why must we hurry?'

A howl is overheard.

'It's coming.' The lady on the wall whispers.

'What's --'

'The way is dark.' She says, holding the candle closer. 'But this will light our way.'

Evelyn leans in a little closer, her eyes reflecting off the candlelight.

'The Dark One is coming. You must go.'

Evelyn darts a look behind, nodding back to the lady. 'Okay you're right, it's time to go.'

The lady threw a hand around the wick so it won't blow out, and off they go. Evelyn can hear clanking of jewellery and vials from her. Finally, the two stop underneath the nearing torch and the lady spoke with tire. 'I cannot go beyond. Here is where you must jump.'

Evelyn reacts. 'What?!' peering onward, and the distance to the next torch is barely noticeable. 'Jump you want?! I'm not jumping.'

'You must hurry.' The lady says and she takes off the way they came. Her voice lingers. 'Remember; Ashnavarna!'

The sound of clanking fades.

Evelyn's eyes turn back. 'Ashnavarna...?' She follows instructions. She waits to hit the ground, but hit a ledge instead. If she hadn't jumped, it would have been a far way down. Her hands grip tightly on an edge, her fingers gripping and sand brushes, dusting below.

She pulls herself up. Someplace new adjusts. The girl can no longer see the torch like she had before. A new surrounding is witnessed; it's one kind of dramatic. Flowerbeds are noticeable, just like the mushrooms and fireflies that light the way, glowing blue.

She walks this fantasy. She looks back, staring at where she had jumped; it's like a portal. The world of ancient sand is now closing shut. She rubs her eyes and looks away with evermore eagerness to move on.

Trees crawl of little glowing blue beetles that help to light the way.

She moves quietly. A cabin in the middle of the gleaming woods is found and entered. It's small. A feeling she's been here before. Something shifts; the emotions running through her are the cause for more dramatic change.

The small cabin changes into the Maelkyn house and Evelyn's standing in her living room right next to the sofa. She's taken back by the shift in reality. In the corner, the bookshelf, and a glowing book wedged in the plain. 'Hold on.' She says arriving to it. 'This is the book Mother used to read to me when I was a lot younger.'

She opens the book cover, and oddly, and this is why; symbols fall out. A symbol she's never read before; an "A" with the letter "V" is overlapped.

She gathers one with her other hand. It vibrates in her hold. Evelyn slowly looks up and away to something entirely else, a tapping sound made by crawlers above. To Evelyn's surprise, beetles on the ceiling suddenly fall onto her.

She screams and drops the book to stomp on the many. She jumps to shake them off and smacks the rest. She shakes a look around; a want to scream again, but fights instead. The beetles are hunting, hiking up and over her, blinding her. They move into the room at an unstoppable rate. The window bursts open by additional advancement.

She holds her breath and with both hands she covers her eyes. Their prickly feet climb. Their heaviness buckles her knees. She falls, praying for one last breath, looking up with only a pair of eyes showing. Drowning in a sea of glittering blue, she wants to breathe. She wants to take one last breath but fears the little bodies may crawl down her throat. Her eyes twinge and her mouth opens wide. They start funnelling as she screams out, 'Ashnavarna!'

She awakes, taking deep breaths. The room is dark. She looks out her bedside window. The moon behind a bit of cloud is over the Forbidden Forest.

'Whoa,' in remembrance of the dream. She wipes a brow – relieved it's over. 'The book,' she says and moves out her bedroom to tip toe into the hall. A peer around takes her downstairs. She walks toward the bookshelf. 'I feel like I'm right back in the dream. It's just like it.'

Her lingering self settles in front of the bookcase. She searches. 'Found you.' And takes the small book out, the very one from the dream, without the magic of course. 'What were the words spoken by the witch on the wall, Ashen-varna?'

No

This gives her a look.

It wasn't...

Naturally, it brought her back to that dramatic place in her dream. She stares up at the ceiling, receiving a shiver. She laughs out loud and places a hand to mouth, feeling silly. 'I hope that didn't wake Mom.'

She turns the book over and reads, 'Tales of the Green Burrow.'

A kid's story of a seven and an eight year old that have crash landed their canoe on an island. The brothers go down a burrow that leads to a small town of fictional characters, which help the brothers build a raft and get off the island, so they can get back home in Brunon.

Evelyn scratches her face and decides to go outside. She sits on the porch. The stars are as beautiful as they come. She turns attention elsewhere and finds herself staring up to the clouds.

Could this book be something other than a simple story book? With the dream being so realistic, there must be some reasoning, right?

It was hard to think anymore at the moment. Her dream is still vivid in her mind and her mind is tiresome from early wake.

Two birds, a small and big one come from the west and land in a nearby tree, beside the house. They began to chirp as they perched themselves to a branch.

Evelyn continued thinking as she tried to remember what the lady in the dream said.

Ashvarna -- was it? No, Ashnivarn -- I think it was?

Then she remembers.

'Ashnivarna!' She says with confidence. The little book bursts to life. She drops the book and shook from fright.

Bright blue light shines. The light engulfed the little book, scaring the bigger bird. It flew towards the dark skies, abandoning the littler one who remains perched.

The light dies and a giant book tilts on the edge of the porch step. Looking down at the black and blue cover – a beautiful green diamond is centre. Evelyn reaches down and lifts the massive book. The weight is nearly ten pounds. She drops it into her lap and runs her finger around the gem. It has the "A" and "V" overlapped symbol engraved in its stone. It has a star-like appearance.

'Just like the dream-symbol!'

The large cover reads; Alasmieria. Slowly, she turns the large cover over to reveal the first page. She reads a small lettering in her mind.

Headmaster Alas. Council members; Maeled, Dawnce, Knewt, Vael, Vim, and Fooragh -- Covenant of Reobigheon; words from a council of seven

We dedicate Alasmieria's secrets to achieve balance from our era to yours

'All I want now is somebody to be here with me.' She says under breath, finding it all so hard to believe. Eyes stuck on page. She catches her breath turning the next. Two different languages are realized. The first reads, *Dsgess yxmwt ceoti, nehhesiiohh...* And the second reads, *O'Dsp'ge'en'ss y'yxo'mu'wr't h'ce'ea'or'tt'i, c'ne'el'hhe'es'st'ii'ia'ol'hh...* – whatever they mean.

An English version is below.

Her breath moved across the page with fascinated eyes. 'Open your heart, Celestial. A flow will come about your spirit. Let it come without hesitation. You are the body of its soul.'

In the middle of page, a lady pointing an arm skyward is found in ink, wearing a star dotted robe and a star symbol showing on the palm.

Evelyn looks up. 'That's the lady from the dream... it looks exactly like her, almost exactly like her...' her eyes dot around. 'Is this really happening to me?'

In an hour, the sun will wake. She rubs her eyes and comes back down to read more.

The little bird continues to stare with its little eager eyes.

Evelyn gets up and moves down the steps after finishing instructions. She has the book open-faced in a shaking hand, because of its heaviness. She rereads instructions.

Feel the forces fill, when you are ready --

She finds two paragraphs down instructing on how to perform the spell.

Read aloud, Restorate Apolatus. Awake the ceremony and watch as the skies brighten to let know our heritage continues hence forth

She smiles silly at the way she stands. She mirrors the lady's image in picture and shouts. 'Restorate Apolatus!' A warm sensation is felt in her raised forearm, tingling from an odd vibration. The book fell from Evelyn's shock. It came to a thump on the ground.

'Oh no.' She says from worry.

A bolt of light shot from her palm; the light twinkles over the skyline and a tremendous shake blisters a thousand little stars, outwardly.

Evelyn took a step backwards in awe. Bits of colour trickle, leaving a fountain of light. Slowly the shine and colour dies out, leaving the skies in smoke, just able to make out in the moonlight.

What comes next takes Evelyn's breath away. The book shakes on the ground. A beam of gold light shot up and out from its emerald stone.

She took one step back to the newer site set in wonder; a site of brilliance colours the sky. You see, the beam of light lights up the clouds of smoke, igniting a gold smoky haze.

Mom comes outside, looking around to the trickling of gold dust.

Evelyn heard the door slam but never cared to look, being locked up in the moment.

Mom is overheard. 'Oh my...' She blows a few bits around her and finally turns her attention to the source. There the book lay on the ground and the stream of light, shatters. It caught them both off guard. But Mom knew better, that this was no ordinary light. Only one force could have created it.

A bright spot glows in the darkness; it's the gem on the book's cover, hot from the use of power.

Evelyn takes a few steps back and surprisingly backs into Mother. Evelyn cries out as she looks towards her. 'I didn't know that would happen!'

Mom's gaze is quite often not as sympathizing, but this time in all sorts of emotion, she was. There is a look of horror also. She stumbles with Evelyn in her arms; she stares past her daughter towards the glowing dust around them.

'Mom, what's happened?!' Evelyn cries out for an answer, anything would suffice.

Katherine does not squeal, brushing past Evelyn to retrieve the book carefully, and then she takes her daughter back into the house and does not speak until the door is closed.

'What did you use?' Mom says, lost in her own trace of thought while Evelyn searches for her answer.

'A spell? I don't know… I was reading and then I said… these words.' Evelyn says with a hand to her forehead. A small glow had been evident. I mean sure, there was dust, but this was different. I mean to say, her palm itself is physically brightened. But seeing Evelyn and her clear shock, she didn't notice. Mother put her daughter's hand down at once and Katherine's voice becomes lower. There is a confusion settling in.

'This happened so fast.'

It was hard to see each other's face in the dim lit of the kitchen. If the drapes to the kitchen weren't pulled back allowing for some moonlight, it would have been damn near impossible.

'We can't stay here any longer. This is my fault.' Mother clarifies and grudges in self acknowledgement. 'Witches are very powerful, yes. My dear girl, you have my sympathy, and a clear gift of insight I see.'

'What are you talking about? You're freaking me out.'

'Listen.' She whispers.

Its Mom's fixated sight at the window that scares Evelyn. For a few moments Mother said nothing. What was she doing? Listening to the sounds outside? Evelyn was sure Mother meant to listen to something she had to say, but clearly Mom meant what she said.

'Do you hear that?'

'No,' her daughter answers. 'Do I hear what?'

'The wind,' she says.

'I do.' Evelyn responds ingeniously.

'There is a change coming. The winds are telling me this. I can hear it echoing. I've been seeing signs for days now.' Mom stops and then continues. 'Before I go on… before I explain what is out there, we must deal with the matters at hand.'

Signs she says? Evelyn knows this was not like her. Then again, the moment is bizarre. Perhaps Mom meant something metaphorical?

Evelyn frowns, 'for starters?'

'The book,' she says matter-of-factly. 'It must remain under your protection. It's been hidden in the family from… a dangerous environment and an unlikely foe.' She gave a look to Evelyn and when Mom left her sides to return with the book in hand, Evelyn reacts.

'No! Keep that away from me.'

Katherine pushes. 'You must take it.'

'No, I don't want that!'

'Evelyn you must take it. It's your responsibility now,' Mother does this with ease; carefully placing one of Evelyn's hands on the cover and then passes it over. 'You were meant for great things honey. You've always have been. This book will guide you, and no matter what happens… I will always be with you.'

Evelyn has a hard time finding the right words to say, '…and what of my friends?'

Mother looks nervously around, ignoring Evelyn's question and spoke accordingly.

'It's time you know the truth. This won't be easy. Once you know what's out there --'

'Why do you keep saying that? What do you mean by what's *out there*?!'

'I'm talking about what is out there!' Her mother snaps, scaring Evelyn. 'You must know something. It was I who saved you from deaths graze. You're not who you think you are. The roof of Maesemer no longer serves purpose, you are meant for bigger things.'

Evelyn looks like she wants to hide, because this doesn't sound *anything* like her.

'No…' Evelyn cries. The warming of tears makes Evelyn feel weaker.

Dust whirls around the window, breaking the silence between them.

'Honey,' she says, grabbing Evelyn's shoulders. 'The book is yours and yours alone. You know the spell to unlock it from its original version. Always keep it unlocked in dangerous places. Whenever you're around others of a bad situation, use it. It can be a burden at times, but it saves lives.'

Evelyn stands statue. She found words to speak, but she remained still. 'Tell me who I am. Tell me what this book is for.'

'I am… truly sorry. I never wanted things to happen this way.'

She then slowly grabs Evelyn's right hand and tells her to repeat after her, putting Evelyn's hand on the book's cover – Mother's hand shaking from the heaviness of the large book held close, with the gem facing up. Evelyn looks afraid of the book, like Mom's asking for more danger.

'Say the words,' Mom demands, feeling the resistance in her daughter.

'No.' Evelyn looks haywire. 'I will not.'

Mother places the book down on the table and says, 'Ashnivarna.' A crashing blue light scares Evelyn, and the book of Alasmieria disappears into the concealed book of burrows. Something Evelyn had been put to sleep with has now put fear into her eyes. Tears no longer rush down her face, and Katherine wipes what is left of them away with a sleeve.

'It's your time to shine honey. We're no longer safe here.'

Mom looks to the window one last time.

'Mom, you're scaring me.'

'Well you know what? I didn't plan on leaving so soon, but now you've given us no choice. But most importantly, just listen to whatever I have to say and don't be a hero anytime soon. I mean really… because I don't have the time to explain everything right now. And I know you have all sorts of *questions*.'

Evelyn resists another attempt of Mother's grasp and says. 'No, I don't want to go with you. You're acting nuts.'

'Yes. We have to go.' Instead, Katherine turns to grab as many things as she can from the kitchen pantry and storage. 'They'll be here by sundown.'

'Right… "They'll be here by sundown". That's great. So do you wanna tell me who *they* are? Why… how can you tell me these things and expect me to believe you?'

'I'm sorry. It might sound crazy, but it's no lie.' Mom laughs, but it didn't sound like she was sorry, because she found her words easily. 'I just didn't want you to see me… as I really am. But I can't stand another day living this lie.'

'Good.' Evelyn angers, not really sure what Mom meant by this. But it sure felt good to release the tension.

'Tell me that you're ready then.' Mother says, not really convinced. 'If someone tells you to do something, no matter what, and you've convinced yourself of their life's work, would you do it?'

'What?' Evelyn asks, finding her frown again.

'You would, wouldn't you?'

'What -- Do what?' Evelyn's frown grows. 'What are you trying to tell me?'

The lady looks down and mutters a few words. A light veil falls. Green and bluish flickering and then an old lady with long grey and whitish hair, stares back. Standing near the same height and weight as Katherine would – The lady's clothes sag some.

Evelyn puts her hands to her face. 'Oh… no… this is a trap.'

Mother – The lady of the Forest -- Whoever she is, had caught Evelyn by the arm and spoke daringly. 'I never knew when this would happen,' and shakes her head miserably. 'But that this day would come…'

'Who…' Evelyn stops in motion to find the right words. 'Where is she? What do you want from me?'

Evelyn's emotions are overbearing so she took a step back, but the lady's grip persists.

'No my dear, I was hidden behind a spell to cheat the eyes of all. A very evil one, but I am a witch who can do good things. Now --'

'Where is she? Where… W-Where is my Mother?!'

'I'm sorry.' She lets go of Evelyn. 'I know this is too much to handle. Your mother… she's been gone all along. She died trying to protect you. She was crossed by one of the Dark Ones long ago. To the same one that took Jonah's life. The Dark One was after you that night and mistakenly took Jonah. Going back, before this, it was I who saved you from the wretched beast during your mother's darkest hour. But I could only save one of you...' The witch looks up at her to see how she's taking this all in. 'And that book... a book known to many. My, it is a treasure to bestow all. I knew then who your mother was running from. For all who carry the Book of Knowledge use it for good or evil. That day I saw your mother fight for you and I knew then, just by how she handled herself that she was a good person -- a witch who only wanted to hide it from the enemy... a powerful one. I vowed to hide our identity, and keep your mother's secret treasure safe.'

'You saved me... from these... foes?'

'Errifics, we call them. Beings of immense power and control over the natural elements of the world, and luckily, like them, I and you are witches with the exact same...' She hesitates. Some words are better off un-noted, 'craft.'

'Sure...' Evelyn nods her head. 'So you call this good? You have taken the book for your own, but raised me for revenge?'

'No darling.' The lady sounds appalled. 'My dear, not revenge. I saved you because I believed you are the one who must *claim* this book. You can finish what legacy your mother carried out. It's up to you. This is your *truth*, and you may find answers to both your mother's and father's past. But you must come with me, and I will show you *who you really are.*'

'A legacy...' Evelyn responds, breathing in and letting it out slowly.

'Still having a hard time believing?'

'Tell me.' Evelyn's voice lingers. 'What about Brunon and this world we live in. What about that future?'

'But that's what's so ironic!' The lady jumps eagerly. 'The world we live in is in discernment. It's full of lies. There is a whole history to this world and a whole lot more where it came from. But now is not the time to exchange lessons on Egerd and the world across the forest that we call Alasmieria. We must build you up for your arrival.'

Evelyn blinks and then shakes her head. 'Um no... I can't do this.'

'You mean you won't do this.' She states.

'Well you see I feel like I'm dying.' She shakes her head. 'This cannot be happening...'

'But this is real!' The lady roars. The voice echoes past Evelyn, hoping to snap her out of it. The lady finds her softer tone. 'It will pass. But first you must walk the dark. And I will come with you.'

Evelyn falls into one of the kitchen chairs. 'I feel... too tired. And I feel... lied to. You were always up to something, never being fully honest when the opportunity arises.'

'Evelyn, I couldn't tell you... how could I? There will be more time to discuss this. For now, that time remains for later.'

Evelyn only shakes her head, and then found her voice. 'What did I tell you about Jason when I first met him?'

The lady nods. 'You told me you felt nervous around him. You said this exactly; "I hope he doesn't find out, or else I fear he'll run away".'

Only Mother would know this...

'You cheated me. I feel... gone.' Evelyn pauses to reword, 'dead.'

'Ah, but you already know this isn't true! Why you've shown me how strong you really are, with that Claud-man. That's how I know you're ready!'

'But you're the one who put me up to this.' Evelyn barks, finding the lady shake her head in disagreement. 'You've put me up to this... somehow; the wolves and... and this book. How can I trust you? I can't.'

'Evelyn.' The old lady says a few times to get her attention. 'I am the one who saved you, remember? If you are angry at anyone, be mad at the enemy. Why they're the ones who chased your mother into death's grasp. Be angry at all the things that lurk out there.' She points in the direction of the forest. But something told Evelyn she is hinting beyond; in Alasmieria. 'Trust me. I will teach you how to focus this energy into something promising. This is your destiny to redeem what is rightfully yours. To put *back* the balance that is needed so much in the world.' She spoke quieter now, so that Evelyn would listen intently. 'That beam of light set off a sort of signal. It was used a long time ago to awaken a ceremony and let know that the birth of knowledge is alive and well in the world... a knowledge that once stood for something in a land not far. You've awoken all to its origin, in this new trying era. That means those of Brunon will have noticed, and those in Alasmieria will have, too.'

'Whatever.' Evelyn sulks and then scoffs. 'Brunon folk, please -- what do they care?'

The woman beams. 'Don't let Brunon faze you. There are secrets hidden deep within its society. Let's just hope the Witch Hunters don't reach us before I can show you all the incredible things in this world.' This scared Evelyn. 'So my deer, you best pucker up, because you have both sides of the world coming this way. This is the true beginning of your story.'

Evelyn gets up from her chair and hugs her. The girl's knees feel like they should buckle from the pressuring words.

The lady pulls Evelyn up and speaks more assertively. 'Now your journey beings, and... I kind of know how it feels.' The lady's next piece sounded like one big play she'd show on stage. 'So let's grab food for our journey onward.'

'...What? We can't go. Not now.'

'Oh believe me, you don't want to be here when they come looking.'

Evelyn only swallows, not sure what to believe anymore.

'Oh, and how rude of me, I am Tetlas.' She says extending a reaching hand. Evelyn gives the lady a serious look, but the lady shakes off the awkwardness. Instead, she steps away and stretches her arms out widely. 'Oh how good it feels. If I truly had some wings I would have to flap them freely. I felt so squished for the longest time.'

She leaves Evelyn with this and goes upstairs. When she returns, she finds Evelyn standing in the same position. The book is still in the same spot on the table, too. Evelyn watches Tetlas take cups and utensils, folding them over clothes to place safely at the bottom of a school bag.

'Where are we going?' Evelyn waits for the lady's response.

Tetlas ignores her and leaves the room to go back upstairs.

Lost in all this change, Evelyn can overhear the grunts of the stranger frantically grabbing supplies. Evelyn moves up the stairwell, slowly, step by step she comes into the hallway and finds the lady in her bedroom.

The lady stops what she's doing, having her back to Evelyn and finally turns to find the girl watching from the doorway.

'Let us pretend and go back to way things were, for now, yes?' She asks Evelyn.

Evelyn's only hope dies down. Her eyes flicker as silence draws. She starts to feel invisible as she watches Tetlas fill school backpacks. There are many from the years, with as much clothes as possible.

'You like these right?' The stranger asks holding the girl's pants in one hand and a pair of underwear in the other. Evelyn felt it was well beyond inappropriate with Katherine to do such a thing, but with Tetlas... and her old-being ways, touching all her clothes. It made Evelyn feel naked.

Tetlas fills it anyway and passes the girl to go downstairs. Evelyn picks up the pace, following her into the kitchen. It's watching a stranger act the way they do in a house that is all your own – a feeling of touching your emotions.

'Take these two packs and fill it with food.' Katherine says... At least, Evelyn tried to picture what was left of Katherine, what with Tetlas's white hair and wrinkles.

... Is it me or is she blunter? Perhaps it's the change that makes everything else seem so much more off

Evelyn reacts to a look Tetlas gave her and Evelyn quickly fills the bag with food.

'Wait.' Evelyn says, and stops what she is doing. 'You may have saved me from the Dark One, but what about my father? You never mentioned anything about him.'

The lady spoke in a hurry, filling packs. 'That is an answer you must seek in the world beyond us.'

They hurry and before they finish filling the packs with anymore supplies, Tetlas pulls out the book and puts it into hers. She put a pack on the front of herself and then one on the back, already full to the brim.

It left Evelyn with the two original packs. One pack is full of food and cutlery. She lifts this pack and puts it on the front, like Tetlas had. The last is an old hiking pack; it's placed on the back; full of folded clothes and a small rolled blanket, seizing from the open top. She does her best to keep up and talk as Tetlas moves.

'You mean from the other side of the forest. This is where this other world is?'

Tetlas nodded, already taking a step out the front door. It kept Evelyn on her toes and not thinking about too much. Evelyn steps outside also. She just left her entire life behind and didn't know it. Now the night is all that stands between Evelyn and what's to come next.

Tetlas notices this flow of action and smiles. 'You see, the Dark Ones were once defenders of the forest, a time when they were called the "Guardians". We're the keepers of the forest, making sure no one turns back. That is what we do, for as long as we can.'

Evelyn suddenly stops in her tracks. Tetlas didn't have to turn around -- knowing what's coming -- but chose to anyways. The words fall from Evelyn's mouth.

'So you're the Lady of the Forest.'

'Yes. I am. I am the one who showed myself that night, that night during Jonah's attack.' Tetlas says and stops to look around her. It wasn't fear, just reminiscence. 'I was the one who continued to watch over you, and yes... I was the one who knew the hunters and their plan to go hunting in the dark forest. Still, I couldn't have let you go. So I scared you home.'

'What makes you think I'll go any further with you? Aren't you evil?'

'Hmm,' she thinks out loud. 'Well, you have two choices. You can walk the other way and I think we both know well enough where that'll lead you. A trip with Jason to Brunon, am I right? Or, your other choice is with me and you walk the path of who you really are, who you've always been asking for. Why do you think you keep on having dreams of the forest? It's calling you home.' She clears her throat, fearing she's said too much. 'And yes, this is all happening much faster than I would have liked, but that is why I prepared you. All those times I showed myself, it was so you could trust me. I was only there to warn you. I hoped this would prepare you, because we must not falter.'

Evelyn stared out in the direction of Brunon. She thought about an everlasting thought. One she had in the garden, and how beautiful of a day it was. The heat on her skin was raw, the smell of soil; fresh, and the damp earth was from an earlier rain which made it soft. Yet, a part of her is called toward Tetlas. It pulls Evelyn towards her nature. It tells her, Tetlas is right. That Evelyn cannot go back -- that the time is now -- a time of yearning for something more.

Tetlas watches her and found it to be soothing, so she decided to pick up things and change Evelyn's contemplating. 'And Alasmieria is a word you'll hear plenty of. That is the world where I am from.'

Evelyn moves into the darkness with Tetlas; a metaphor no doubt. Evelyn listens, feeling a story coming on.

'It was Asnin's fall due to the Dark Ones, for magic in the Old Capital would change and be thought of as cursed.' And spoke melodramatically. 'The Dark Ones appeared and *something* encouraged the Dark Ones from that point on. Soon the beasts came to the edges of the forest. You probably heard of them. It was those three damn witches. Here the Dark Ones harvested and haunted the people of Asnin. You see, the witches didn't have to fight Asnin. They couldn't if they tried. But they could turn its power against itself. This was the age when Asnin began to crumble. Magic resembled a way of life, until the Dark Ones were thought to be a bad omen from the overuse of it... So Asnin feared what had happened to the Guardians, would happen to them. Without the constant heed from Asnin's witches, I became weak. I was Asnin's protector, known as the Forest Keeper.' Tetlas goes on to scoff. 'The Forest Keeper... that was a long time ago... Anyways, as you'd expect, Asnin would have their upheaval. They fed their only protection to the wolves, and surely enough, the three witches would get what they wanted, thwarting me. The three witches envied me. Now they rule what we call the Dark Blackened Halls. They rest in the highest tower in the tallest peak. Even now, I continue to fight to hold balance, distinguishing their contrasting ways. The three enjoy chaos, but I am the light. If the Easterners collide with our ancient ways, more than an upheaval will be met. The fall of two worlds will be found. I cannot let this happen.'

It began to sink in. Evelyn shudders. They're heading in the forest's direction. Tetlas was smart about it, she didn't go straight to the backyard, but lingered her footing till she slowly turned in the direction of it.

Tetlas keeps the tales rolling. 'That's what makes the forest impossible to cross, unless you know the tricks of the trade, sort to speak.' She looks back, there Evelyn stood, not one step more.

'I believe you Mom.' It sounded odd, but it felt right. 'But I can't go on.'

Tetlas didn't realize the depth that's held in the girl's eyes, of how much Evelyn really needed Katherine right about now.

'Wait!' Evelyn shouts running towards Tetlas – Mother – Whoever she is, for the lady took out a vial from her pocket and Evelyn damn well knew what would happen next. 'I don't want you to go back. I can't.' Evelyn says with tears rolling. 'Please.' Evelyn pleads under the twilight.

Tetlas looks fierce, like she doesn't have the time to waste. 'I could do this forever. You just say it and I'll remain Katherine.'

'No.' Evelyn responds, placing her palm on the vial. It told Tetlas she was tired of all the lies, that this... at least *felt* right. 'Can I still call you Mom though?'

The atmosphere is surprisingly warm. Dust dangles lightly in the mists around them; it shinned in Evelyn's eyes. Tetlas knew they will never be the same old ones, and Evelyn waited for her response. Instead, the lady only put the vial in pocket.

'For safe keeping,' Tetlas responds to her pocket. A look too embarrassed to eye the girl, but does her best to find her "Daughter's" stare. It told Evelyn she would agree to whatever made her feel more at ease, but that it wouldn't last. 'Of course, of course,' Tetlas finally says, longing for their ease. And it worked, it suddenly made Evelyn smile.

'Mom…' Evelyn says a little hesitant. 'What's the date today?'

'It's…' Mother halts, thinking, 'Tuesday.'

'Well, that would mean we can still catch the train then. We could still go with Jason.'

Tetlas stops. She lets out a small laugh. The look doesn't heed Tetlas's eyes.

'Is this a test?' She asks, not sure what Evelyn's up to.

'No. It is me who feels tested.'

'Well, I never intended to go to Brunon. I have no clue what to expect beyond that train station.' The lady says and turns in contemplation. 'My heart and world lies beyond that forest. That is where we must go. That is where we will be the safest.' Evelyn says nothing; she only stared in the direction of the bushy madness. 'Of all places, we must return to your birthright. There we will find answers to your past; there we will begin your training. That is what we must do. You will be tested, but we will have rest first. There's a cabin in the woods. We will have all the food and supplies for our journey. Now is the time to go, *now* Evelyn.'

It sounds like words of magic… promising or are they lies?

The dream… The cabin… It's all adding up. Maybe I am a witch

Tetlas had already walked this path; she's seen the brethren beyond. But how could Evelyn? Even at the edge of the forest with Tetlas's hand stretched for her… it still wasn't enough.

'Evelyn, it is time.'

'No.' Evelyn shakes a head. 'Not yet.' She tears and took one last look behind. She looks towards the Sheppard's boy's house. Maybe she thought they could help? Then she looks south. Perhaps her friends would? Then she remembers Claud's face – it gives her strength. She held her head up high and walks towards Mother. 'I don't want to walk with you.'

Tetlas whispers a word and her hand lights up in the night – hoping it was enough to encourage Evelyn and remind her of a witch's power.

'What's the point?' Evelyn whispers now. 'It's all a lie anyways.'

'I understand… but I can't let you stay. If the Errifics don't catch you, then Brunon will jail you, or worse. Evelyn, reach out your hand. You must.'

Evelyn closes her eyes and steps toward till she felt the light on her face and then the warmth.

Tetlas spoke. 'Don't you worry child. I've done this before.' And the two disappear into the forest.

Evelyn's eyes open to a new world. There are chirps from birds not too far in. Evelyn looks up. Their eyes are wild.

Tetlas can feel the child's hesitation.

Evelyn bites her lip. The feel of emotion is crawling up on her.

The bleak morning seeps throughout the forest. It's cold, sending tingles down her neck. Still, her hand is warm with the heed of the witch's hold.

Mountains are in the distance appearing from the gaps in the treetops. To Evelyn it felt like it foreshadowed her journey. Surely it will be an uphill climb? She quickly looks around, already fearing the beasts of the forest. She pats the two backpacks in forgetfulness, but it was Tetlas who has the book in hers. This relieved Evelyn, so she trailed the hand of light, breathing in some scenery.

The two stay the course. They can see their surroundings more clearly with the rising sun behind them. Life is opening up. Wild boar, exotic birds and deer moved around them. Like a new beginning, Evelyn moves more freely, letting go of the grip.

The boar moves closer. Birds follow and rabbits come out to peek. The animals trail beside with the Lady of the Forest taking her every step.

The cry of birds began to sound more of a song.

Evelyn and the witch stop for a simple breather. Evelyn's emotions stir fast because she knows what is beyond; it's mostly what she's leaving behind.

With a supporting hand, Tetlas helps Evelyn up and got things moving towards the reminder of change. All Evelyn wants to do is cry, but the adrenaline rush keeps telling her to push forward.

Tetlas knew, at the bed of the river what else it might have brought up. Claud and all her friends, for beyond this point is a place Evelyn's never gone before. And the stories of all who have passed have not returned. Still, Tetlas said nothing. Instead, the woman reaches out her glow of a hand for Evelyn to reach.

Evelyn knew, this is the time and this meant there would be no going back. She reached and crossed the cold waters of the Funicmorain with Tetlas.

Their backpacks were surprisingly quiet making little to no sound, but the weight is something else, making Evelyn's stomach rumble with hunger.

The same old dirt would be cold. The fresh scent of leaves made Evelyn feel aware but no longer safe. A child deep within her cries out to be alive and to move deeper into the unknown, and Evelyn calms her mind and her heart so she can come back to the moment and be this giver.

A long path of water can be heard crushing over rocks. As they came up to it, the clear blue stream stretches in its slithery and a large waterfall walls twenty feet from behold.

Evelyn bent down, while eyeing her surrounding in case the wolves should show up. She examines the floor, and finds those blue stones all around her. This helps her to feel at ease. Soon, she unlatches her backpack, arriving with Tetlas to the banks of the falls to get some rest. This is as far as Evelyn would go. She won't remind herself of whom she was; now she must turn a gaze towards the many steps to unfold.

Tetlas is close by and is quick to thank her surroundings, knowing exactly where they are and where to go next.

'And they're your protectors?' Evelyn asks, pulling out some food to eat. A deer moves closer to peek at what she's got. Evelyn pulls away. The deer scares and moves someplace away. More animals attempt their approach.

'Go, shoo!' Evelyn waves her hand a few times over.

'Yes.' Tetlas replies to her earlier question. 'My Guardians are what I call them.'

Evelyn got up and approaches the waters, nodding -- clearly not caring. It was an act to get away from said beasties and the wet that mists around.

'They're not to harm you.' Tetlas says and talks amongst friends of the forest.

The girl's hand reaches in the water.

'Don't you drink that,' Tetlas says and pausing her conversation with her furry kind to move closer to her. 'It's best to drink rain water. That river water is plagued. It's full of parasites.'

A squirrel moves from their huddle and moves up to Evelyn and twitches its noise. Evelyn looked away in disgust to find Tetlas frowning back.

'I don't want anything to do with these creatures. Why don't you get that? If anything, they're cursed like you are.'

'Please.' Tetlas says annoyed. Evelyn saw it hurt Mother to hear this, but think of what she's going through, so Evelyn ignored the signs, seeing an all too familiar stare back. There the squirrel too had its hand's on its hips.

'Clever one, isn't he?'

'Yup,' Evelyn says bitterly, eyeing the animal's disapproval. She says to him. 'If you come any closer, I'm going to smack that ugly face.'

'It doesn't fear you. Not like you fear us.'

Evelyn scratches a nose. 'Don't you fear them?' She points a chin toward the southwest.

'What, the Dark Ones? Of course I do. But I try not to dwell on it. Besides, they only reside to the caverns in the deep. They'll never come out this far, not in broad daylight.' She goes on to scoff her next words, 'and certainly not when most of my animals are up. The Dark Ones may be predators of the night, but in the day, they don't stand a chance against an entire forest of the light.'

'You mean, you and your little squishy-squirrelly, and soft --'

'Enough.' Tetlas says. 'I have other waking Guardians of all shapes and sizes. These are the soft ones you speak of, no doubt. But they however know as I do that they have nothing to prove. The fiercer ones you're so obliged of are staying away because they don't want to scare you. So please, have some respect.'

'You walk with them and chat with them, do yea'?'

'I see you're angry. But what's the point, that's not going to get us anywhere. Now is it?'

Evelyn still held a bit of water in her palm reverting her wrist and watching the water pour out. Just-about how she felt when she found out her mother was someone else. The last drip falls and Tetlas got the impression.

'Ready to go?' Tetlas asks ignoring Evelyn's every last moment.

Evelyn stands up with food in the other and Tetlas watches her put the last of it and her words into her front bag, closing the lid.

The daylight shines behind that white hair. The day is rounding up the atmosphere, bringing life to everything.

Evelyn rolled her eyes to such a magical time; she never thought it would have reflected her reality. She thinks about going back. Every time she does this, a part of her is torn apart, and when she least expects, a hand by Tetlas is out once more to help her carry through.

Evelyn thought about her mother, like she has never really gone. Choosing to remember only the fun times, and doing her best to hold back harsh ones. She smiles to a memory, for all she misses now are the pies that brought them together and the spices that filled her mouth with each bite. And it was all just yesterday.

Funny, when we think we know what we have. But if it were really gone, would we? Sure it's still "Mother" but... it's not the same looking her in the eye.

Evelyn finds herself laughing. An invincible feeling creeps over her. She wants to drop her things and lay here until the sunset comes down and watch the sun hit the horizon. But something tells her it's against survival, so she must continue to follow the lady.

Evelyn gets up from another resting place, already finishing what Tetlas had packed for breakfast.

She's my only hope... I better take better care in noticing her; otherwise it could end up being just me and this forest

Something in the forest calls out. It was a cry of an animal and it's the first time Evelyn heard something distant... like... from another world.

This really brought Evelyn to her senses; you could say they walk side by side. The forestry starts to widen by Tetlas's approach. The trees branches spread and bend so room is made. Whether Tetlas doing or by the tree's themselves, Evelyn does not know. Evelyn only watches the sun this time around. It gave her strength to travel lonesome over large boulders and dawning hilltops, knowing this forest or the lady *of it* has the power to destroy or protect. Now, it's all one big adventure in Evelyn's opinion. So who cares? Considering everything in her world is at a tumble. At least, that's the attitude she's given off. After all, she's got a witch and her forest to watch her every move. It's Mom all over again, just shedding her true colours. Don't you think?

The mountains lay in a scatter across the horizon, and the clouds just brushing their white glacial tips.

'Have we come this far?' Evelyn asks Tetlas.

'Oh yes. You've been pushing this old lady for quite some time now.'

'I may as well have a bit of fun. It's not like my life matters now that it's basically over.'

Tetlas ignores her. She looks up at the canopy instead.

Evelyn's been hoping to see a house or some kind of person to talk to, but it's been four hours since she's come in any contact with the outside world. Except the animals that finally got the clue when Evelyn barked to them to go away -- someplace, heck anywhere would suffice.

'Will we make it before nightfall?' Evelyn asks.

'I'm afraid not.'

Tetlas fears the nightmares. The dark will be out. She can see it in Evelyn eyes now; they both share the similar notion of what's to come. Neither wants to be in this forest at night hours, and that's saying a lot for a lady and *her* forest. This doesn't make Evelyn feel any better.

Evelyn looks up and around, in one big twirling motion as they walk. It's a good sign of allowing some life in.

No fantasy land of spiky mountains made of candy corn or white diamonds... yet...

Tetlas gave them a break from the rugged bushes. It's beautiful. It appears peaceful. Someplace that Evelyn just wants to sit and rest, and it's so nice she could even fall asleep here. Her legs pain dreadfully from the endless walks. She draws to the middle of a field.

'Don't go too far, Evelyn.' Tetlas voice is overheard.

To Evelyn, out here, she feels safer in the wide open. No more wildernesses. Thank goodness. That way she can see what will be coming.

She finds a safer place to rest, out on a small grassy hill in the lush surroundings. Bushes surround her sides, blocking the site of those outside.

She slides her legs on the soft forest grass. The ache and pains pound at her feet and up her sore back. She begins to feel safe for once in this quiet and peaceful place. Her mind feels more at ease in this calm, relaxing space. Her drowsy eyelids twitch and feel heavy. Slowly she can feel them closing.

A quick flash of blue light quickens her mind. She gets up feeling uneasy. She finds Tetlas standing nearby with a pointing hand towards the skies. Evelyn watches and finds a small flicker following a trail in the bleak day that stirs up the clouds. Like a funnel, the clouds attract to its source, draining like water would down a bath hole.

'Wait, what… the…' Evelyn says raising a hand to shade her eyes from day, having a difficult time figuring out what she's actually witnessing. 'W-What are you doing?'

'Well, what's a witch worth if she can't have a bit of fun?'

The sunlight begins to show through the clear and Tetlas control fades, dropping the condensed matter into a funneling, hitting the ground with a running.

'Wow…' Evelyn eyes light up. 'How is that even possible?'

'It's a part of our gift.' Tetlas responds, and then offers a grimace. 'But not as easy as it looks.'

'Well I believe you, for once. I mean… you just pulled the freakin' clouds out of the sky…'

'Yeah,' Tetlas smiles, 'few of them.'

The air has become still. And the trek on is making Evelyn's legs heavier, if that's anymore possible.

The two stop at a ledge; it's beautiful and dreadful at the same time. Dreadful because Evelyn didn't want to know how much more she would have to take. Mountains, streams and little pathways flood this majestic area. Just below and out in the clear, a village can be seen. Yes, it was a sudden surprise. And no, Evelyn doesn't listen. She rushes downhill for it.

'Evelyn no, wait!'

A furry animal in the distance appears from behind a massive boulder.

Evelyn decides to slow her motion and slides a bit. She stops and the rocky path continues to tumble past. Remaining still, she can't help but think of her survival.

'Evelyn.' Tetlas says, but is cut off by a fierce roar from the animal. It has a catlike face, but it's nothing like the bobcats Evelyn's seen. Its claws swipe the floor. It hisses with whiskers, showing teeth. Its body is white without fur. The animal is scaly like the rocks, and surprisingly slim.

There is a "Zip" sound and then a flash of blue light. Evelyn glances up the path where Tetlas is seen with the book of Alasmieria in hands.

'Tetlas... tell it to back off already.' Evelyn says, taking another step back. The hilltops are steep, and her chances of outrunning the beast are rough.

A ball of flame crashes near the feet of the animal. But it only waters the seed of danger. The beast comes down the hill in order to get to them.

Evelyn runs and naturally, screaming from fright.

'Oh Alas, help me with this one.' Tetlas says melodramatically.

A flickering flash and the animal is crush, sideways.

Evelyn comes to a sliding stop to witness the roars from the beast that's rolling to a stop. It is a haunting site, yet incredible. The magic tangles and rips at the animal. It roars one last time, trying to claw away and then it finally draws its last breath.

Evelyn took a few steps up to find Tetlas haunted site.

'Wait.' Tetlas says with a sharp hand, and looks around one last time and then suddenly droops her shoulders. '*You* are a hazard.'

'I thought...' Evelyn says torn by what had happened and amazed by the scene of magic. 'Can't you talk to it?'

Tetlas moves downhill, asking sarcastically. 'Can't you talk to me?'

'Oh... I didn't know. I thought they all responded to the lady of their forest.'

'I share it for crying out loud. You almost took our lives!'

'Sorry...' Evelyn cringes. Fearing the woman's wrath, she looks down and away.

'*Please* -- I didn't just go through an entire phase of life to defeat the purpose.' Tetlas says, seeing Evelyn's fright of her. Tetlas moves along and blows a hair in front of her face. 'Come on let's get moving.'

Evelyn looks back where the animal was crushed. The beast is near invisible, for it was turned into a stone scrapple, mirroring its last position before death; crawling in a harsh position.

Evelyn catches up. '*What was that thing?*'

'A very dangerous animal that trails the rocky parts, and in this case, it was only defending her territory.'

'No. I meant that amazing *spell*.'

'Ugh, what is the matter with you?' Tetlas signs, knowing there is no phasing the girl's expression. 'Its advanced magic to say the least, and it was a lucky shot.' Tetlas says, hopefully cutting the thrill in Evelyn's sites and awakening the seriousness on the matter.

Just the thought of seeing another animal might bring the girl to her senses. But out here, nothing feels right and nothing makes sense anymore.

Tetlas makes her way through the rugged bushes, and Evelyn knows it's best to follow. As the trees begin to spread out, a small wooden village opens up to them from the pathway. All the while, Tetlas carefully eyes around, for she has to keep two watches now, on the girl and what will move after the looming night hours.

Evelyn is the last to enter the middle of town and approaches a small well. She was hoping for water, but it's dead. Not a shred of evidence or life in the area.

She breathes tiredly. 'All I want to do is rest.'

'We can't stay here.' Tetlas replies.

'I know that.' Evelyn bites. 'Can't stay anywhere, can we?'

'Guess what? You're right.' She says with a push of Evelyn's backpack; an order to get a move on. Together the two leave behind the abandoned town and start heading back into the green abyss. The straps to their backpacks are hurting their shoulders. It's been rubbing and paining for hours. And a decent meal would be almost as dreamy as a good night's rest.

The night turns into its creeping self. The sounds and the colours of the fire flies trickle. Evelyn looks to her left to the sound of a swamp and its crickets. Toads croak and bugs zip. The moon is a blistering bubble in the sky, colouring the surroundings in its round glow, with a smear of orange backdrop.

'Evelyn?' Tetlas calls, shinning her Aura in a round.

'Mother?' Evelyn's voice calls back. Evelyn thankfully catches up with her being a little ways out.

'I thought I lost you.' Mother says, turning her site away so they can continue on.

'You'd think with all this magic and power; you'd do something with the night, maybe some light?'

'We can't. We're too close to the edges of new territory. Out here we can't afford to be seen. It's too dangerous. Mostly for me for the animals don't hesitate for an old gal like me.'

'What?' Evelyn swallows, looking about. 'So you're saying we're outside your forest?'

'Oh yes,' Tetlas smiles. 'We've been for miles.'

Was she lying? Hmm, who knows? What do they say? Oh that's right -- no rest for the wicked.

The cries of the wild are haunting after that. The sound of the wind howls and in the distance, nothing but pitch black puts Evelyn on guard. She's already past exhaustion, for Tetlas swore to have arrival by sundown.

A bat flaps by, squeaking and it's gone.

Evelyn made a dreadful face. 'Looks like you,' feeling very annoyed with her.

'Let me show you something my dear.' The old woman says, finding the young girl trailing further and further behind. 'Please try to remember my daughter; you have magic that runs in those veins also. I need you to use a spell to guide your way. I almost lost you back there. It's the best way for me to keep track of you and of your surroundings. Call out Tastraity.'

Evelyn has a hard time standing, let alone performing tricks. So she leans beside the shaded forestry to find more balance.

'Tastraity!' Evelyn calls helplessly. A few birds fly out of the trees. Evelyn rolls her eyes, and waits for further instructions.

'Breathe in deep and let go of any stress. It works best this way.'

'I tried.' Evelyn could barely bark, which came out wimpy.

'I know.' Tetlas replies trying hard not to laugh. 'Just continue repeating Tastraity, fixating on a happy image. You should feel your hands becoming warm. When you feel that you are ready, and you will know when, you will receive this sudden urge to yell out "Tastraity". Do so and you shall achieve the white magic called Cloradis. It will form from your fingertips, like mine.'

Evelyn breathes in deep. 'Okay. Okay.'

Sure her state of mind is weak, and her physical ability needs rest, but if Tetlas recommends something, she listens now. She had saved her life five hours ago, or was it six? I've lost track.

Before Evelyn had called out, she looks around, hearing the noises, mostly of the typical crickets and bats. She slowly closes her deep blue eyes. They feel like they've closed tightly and they're sealed shut. She already feels more relaxed. She stumbles and Tetlas is there to help her lean against the tree.

Tetlas whispers in her ear. 'Think easily on a happy time in life.'

Evelyn wants to roll her eyes at that one, but let her mind wander aimlessly instead. She's having a hard enough time trying to keep her stance from drifting too far off and hopefully, not fall asleep. She pictures light, and this light alone. She drifts too far off. The sleepy feeling starts. There's a loss of balance from the heaviness and she grips tightly to hold herself up.

'I can't do this.' Evelyn feels weaker.

'Good.' Tetlas replies.

'No, I said I *can't* do this.' She enlightens her.

Tetlas teases. 'Oh, it must have been my old bat ears.'

The air is silent, she feels cool and Tetlas whispers. 'Maybe imagine food.'

Evelyn closes her eyes, and a warm steak sandwich flushes her imagery. She quickly wants to taste its delicious textures. But she obviously can't and this plainly frustrates. She wants to eat now, not imagine food. But the imagination is pulling her forward and she finds herself smiling to an everlasting bite of a warm beef sandwich, dripping with succulent juices.

Evelyn whispers, 'Tastraity.' The warm sandwich soaks her fingers, and the succulent juices move down her hand. She slowly opens her eyes. A faint glowing light takes to her fingers; she moves in wonder of its glow.

'This is incredible.' She laughs out loudly. Fascinated with herself, she lights the way. It is the first time she's wielded magic. *But* not used, of course. She walks, touching her fingers together, rubbing them to see how it works.

The forest seems to be thinning out, so Tetlas starts to pick up pace. They've eaten the last bit of food, and now is the right time for another, which is impossible. The missed meal is a hunger harsh on the stomach, and a small headache starts to build.

Evelyn stumbles.

'Hold on tight baby girl.' Tetlas says. 'We are almost home.'

A large open field came into view. Just as the two enter this grassy expanse, a head rush hits Evelyn again. She looks dizzily around. She tried to call out Tetlas's name, but she's already the walking dead.

Evelyn falls to her knees. Her fingertips start to feel cold, and her head begins to turn. She had to lean against a tree, clawing herself up. As the light fades from her fingertips, the moon and all surroundings fades from her site. She drops to the floor on all fours. Like a wild animal, stranded, it feels impossible that she allowed herself to go on this far.

'We just --' Tetlas is stumbled by the clear site all around her. She looks around and see's no girl. 'Oh not again,' Tetlas whines. 'Evelyn.' She yells. She waits. Sounds of frogs croak back.

Tetlas traces her steps into the field. She finds the girl lying there, tiredly Evelyn must have collapsed. She is approached and Tetlas find's the girl miraculously still conscious.

'Oh my... Dear girl, what am I to do with you?' Tetlas suddenly looks up to the sky, as if stars could read lips. 'I'm sorry.'

Evelyn moans and her lips found words. 'I've must have fallen.'

Tetlas gave the stars a head tilt and then realized it was Evelyn's voice. 'Guess what.' Tetlas prods her next, as if she didn't notice her tiredness. 'We are here.'

Together, Evelyn's leaves with an arm around Tetlas, the open grassy field is left and from then on, Tetlas promises to never let her fall again.

Tetlas wastes no time and rushes Evelyn deeper inside and into a bedroom.

Evelyn drops her packs and falls dustily and dirty on soft covers.

Tetlas leaves and comes back to wipe the girls face with a wet cloth. She finds Evelyn has already fallen asleep. 'Goodnight baby girl, we are set free.' Raising a brow, 'we have set you towards destiny.'

CHAPTER 6

The Laws Within

Evelyn opens her eyes. She lies in a soft comfy bed. The room is small and it smells of oak, cedar and fresh herbs. Evelyn quickly realizes that she's not at home anymore... she's in someone else's home... how freaky, how amazing.

Evelyn's conscious is high; all the while she mesmerizes what happened last night. Oh, and the taste of food in mouth. Ha, she wishes. She curls her toes, feeling their hot and sweaty selves from much travel. When she looks over to her left, off the side of her bed, a feeling dawns on her, that there is no turning back; it's all one big adventure now.

'That was all real?' She asks, sitting right back up in bed. She has an uneasy look around. This place is definitely not home. She got up and looked around for her things. Her backpacks found sitting on the ground.

Her blood rushes to her head. Her mind spins; she feels dizzy with hunger striking. She puts her hands to her stomach, feeling it gargle. Slowly, a peer around the room is made by her, and she tip toes, leaving the dark room.

A kitchen is witnessed. It's amazing how small this house really is. Even with the hunger, her spirits remain warm. She feels her face, half dazed from waking up.

To the right, an oval door is found. Slowly, with a turn of the knob she looks in. The site of fresh herbs and plants are set up, and small pockets of rice and odd shaped beans lay on the counter next to a bed; a quaint folded bed I should add.

'So this is the home of the faithful Lady of the Forest?' She asks herself in her awe and aspiring moments. 'Wow Mom, you've really outdone yourself, haven't you?'

A small kitchen is seen next. On a table, there is fully prepared food waiting to be eaten. Evelyn's eyes brighten up. 'Is this for me?' And does a body twirl. 'Well... who else right?'

The girl dives in for some soft slices of bread, cheese and beans.

'I'm surprised I'm not eating something magical and organic-like. Maybe I didn't get the memo, or maybe there really is no magical land... like I thought. Don't get me wrong, cheese and beans are great.' She lingers a site around. 'But how it looks to me, is she got this from town. I mean... canned beans... really? What's up with that? I've had this a hundred times and *I know* she didn't pack beans because we didn't have any... Is this some sort of trick, I wonder?'

She looks around the room as she eats. The room is much smaller then she imagined it to be, but it sure makes for a comfy space.

Well I should at least be thankful for the food. After all, she did save my life, more than I know. Thanks Lady of the Forest

A chopping noise is heard from outside. Evelyn moves to the kitchen window, outside an old lady is chopping large bundles of wood with an axe. Evelyn puts her hands to her mouth.

'Is that what she looks like?' pushing away from the window. She sinks to the kitchen floor against the lower cabinets. '...Sure looks different in daylight,' rubbing her face in contemplation, which is surprisingly cleaner then yesterdays.

The old lady enters the kitchen from a front door and notices the girl pressed up against the sink cabinets.

A curious fellow, which looks like that of a squirrel that's fat and white, zipped in the room. It has long floppy ears. Its long bushy tail whips the air and it sniffs the ground like a hound dog would. It doesn't stop for Evelyn; indeed, it went down the hall to sniff out the new comer's room.

Tetlas didn't bother with the rodent, and retrieves a wood mug and pours water from a wooden jug. The old lady wore a silk white robe that dragged to the floor, its edges all dusty and dirtily. A short necklace hung to a crisscross-metal base, wherein a small crystal rests. It's a beautiful stone. The lady passed Evelyn once more, ignoring the girl's worrisome manner and headed back outside.

That's when it hit Evelyn… 'No way… this isn't a cottage. This is a… tree-home.' She looks around in wonder, and got to her feet to touch the walls. She thought she noticed a difference about this place; it's too oval to be regular shape. It's been carved straight out. Meaning…

'I can't believe I'm inside a tree. I can't believe this is real!'

Evelyn leaves the tree-home to go outside.

The lady is in a crouching position, planting seeds in her garden with a brown pouch in her right hand. She dangles white seeds onto the warm soils where holes had been made for planting. As she turns around to see Evelyn, she wore a greeting smile. 'Oh, there you are my dear.' She said with a calm tone and points yonder. 'Could you pass me the watering-can over there, please?'

Evelyn hesitates, and then turns away to look up at the giant tree-home. Her mouth drops. And she turns straight back. 'Okay,' nodding her approval. She hands over the water-can positioned near a different garden, nearest to home.

A stairwell wraps up the tree-home to stop midway, where a balcony extends from the front of the home, outwardly, and has a sling bridge to connect a smaller tree-home.

Evelyn turns her attention to the water flowing from the nozzle, but the site is not for long. Evelyn's steps are already wondering off to the wide space. She notices everything, even the grass her is bizarre, being the color of purple. 'How is this…?' Evelyn points and bends down to touch the purple grass. It has a yellowy base that fades into the earth.

'Can you imagine a sea of purple in all its divinity would appear?'

'You mean?'

Tetlas nods. 'There are places in Alasmieria, yes. They're sacred spots.'

The area around the house runs of small globes glowing yellowy-gold, filled of water. Tetlas is sure to point them out. 'Northiz, they're bugs that harbour the soils, building dens underwater. Like ants build in the dry earth, only Northiz pollute the water and make it glow, brightly. There are many pools that glow in the night, and these globes are a way of attracting them for my personal use of light. They're many ways to gather light in

Alasmieria, and Northiz is but a few ways of doing so. At night, this whole place lights up with male's flying in from their long journey hunting. They respond to a queen who must survive underwater. Since the females are water walkers -- so they cannot fly. That's why the colonies are so unique and the Northiz males, especially. They would never be found in Egerd of course, since they follow Alasmieria's magnetic field, a sort of pole, if you will. You are really standing in another world, which goes for the whole of our hub.'

'Okay but purple grass!?'

Tetlas laughs. 'I know, I thought you'd like it. It's such a magnificent color.' She goes on to clear her throat. 'That's some night we had.'

Evelyn doesn't quite respond. She feels she can't. Her face makes some movements till she finds her voice.

'It's hard to believe that this is all real, Tetlas.'

'Ah, I see.' Figuring "Mother" would have never last the following morning. The truth of the matter, Evelyn is glad to be alive with food and water in her belly. But for now, she can't find common place between them.

Evelyn turns away to find an area to be sanctioned. They're small pillars in white, in the distance. It resembles a temple. The stone looks ancient and the mass of room surrounding is simple.

'Could you pass me that pouch? I forgot I placed them there. I was admiring the morning and must have forgotten about them.' Tetlas says pointing at a small pouch of seeds left on a picnic table, near the temple.

Evelyn stops cautiously. Another one of those small furry rodents, with their large ears wiggles its long bushy tail with curiousness.

'What is it?' Evelyn stammers.

'Oh, that's Iyem. He's a little timid, but he'll get use to.'

'Y-You call them by name?'

'Oh yes, they come around these parts quite often.'

Evelyn reaches a pat, fearing a bite. 'I thought your forest and your animal-friends were a ways back?'

'Oh they're, but that wouldn't stop me from loving them.' She turns to the whiskery fellow and spoke in a baby voice. 'Now would it Mr Iyem?'

Evelyn pats him cautiously. He backs up, slowly. Getting down low and speeds off.

'But why purple grass?' Evelyn asks, waving a hand through it.

'They say it was created by our creator Alas, who taught us our beliefs are the creating aspect to our realities. So he turned the grass and trees in certain areas in Alasmieria purple. He wanted to show the people that we could have our ideals.'

'Wow... I see. And he's the one --'

'Indeed.' Tetlas replies, giving a sharp look around in her terrifying manner.

'But the hunch is; I don't want to hear any stories about goblins right now, nor any tales about dragons. If you're going to tell me something, either lie to me or say something to make me feel better, because honestly, I don't think I have what it takes to hear anything outside myself. I'm sorry; it's just too much to handle right now.' Evelyn says, playing with her fingers. '...And honestly, you never do expect what you've come to love so dearly to turn out to be something... other than, which is why I am having a hard time trusting you.'

'Honesty and I like it.' She smiles with a raise of her brow. 'Well, if only we could have had chats more like this back home.'

'Yeah but home is gone.' Evelyn says annoyingly.

'Certainly, and we can't stop pretending that the hour is no longer upon us, because it's here. Moving forward, the land you speak of, or at least, some of the dangers that you mentioned do exist, just not the way you described them. Now, let us not pretend anymore that I am your Mother, but I will take care of you like I always have. We both know there is no more toasting to the vial.'

Evelyn has a great nod, 'agreed.'

'Well...' Tetlas says in a changing manner, as she usually does. Where do you think Evelyn gets it from? 'I always did like the farm. Mostly because it meant more to you then it did to me.' And goes on to smile, 'I'm glad we've come to this part in this chapter of life.'

'Yes... me too...' Evelyn is lost to the touch of grass again. 'It's even softer than ours.'

'Well that's because you've been taught that grass is green and tough. The world is governed by our beliefs. That is why it is the way it is. So *he* says.'

Sure, it sounded grave with her confidence lacking in the witch, but now a positive outcome is in hopes.

'But I don't know how this works, because I don't know what you want from me.'

The lady could only laugh to the sudden bluntness.

'Hold on now.' Evelyn says. 'Y-You don't know what I've been through. You don't get to laugh.'

The lady lifts her head. 'If you're heading towards danger, then I'd prospect death. I wouldn't see you getting another ten miles back there, before the worst should come your way. Now, I'm assuming you are planning on leaving to go back?'

It was odd, because for the longest time, the lady sounded prompt with intelligence. Yet Evelyn wasn't thinking anything on the lines of this. But now that she mentioned it, it was only time before it should cross paths.

The lady has a selfish way about her, that's what Evelyn feels. Perhaps it's providence. She just feels tough, like a circle of something greater roams around this old being and her way of life. And what's up with this house in the middle of nowhere?

'I don't know... what am I to you?' Evelyn asks, trying to get to the point of things.

'It may seem that way to you now, but *you're* welcomed.' Tetlas replies stepping forward, but finds herself at a pause. She looks towards Evelyn with a powerful look, which told her that this was no game they are playing here. Tetlas turns away, brightening the darkness in her face. 'Then again if you've had a teacher or someone close to you in order to protect you, then that would be a different. You see, travellers don't get real far in these lands. It's those Dark Ones that travel lonesome, or the packs of dangers that lurk outside this little place I call home.'

'Then that is what I should do, because I don't fear them. I've made it this far out.' Evelyn felt a premonition coming on. 'If there is a town, or something beyond these lands, maybe with a map and some directions, I could make it.'

'You mean to go beyond, and by yourself?'

Is it Evelyn or does it feel like she has to explain everything twice to this woman? Evelyn felt she would ask this, and it was clear to see the cackle that's going on inside Tetlas, hiding it behind a little smile. The lady pats down the earth. There are exchanging expressions, both Evelyn and Tetlas begin filling with unimpressionable faces.

This only frustrates Evelyn further. It made her feel younger then she already is; it made her feel foolish when all Tetlas did was stay to herself. Like secrets she's keeping, a woman who won't tell her things.

'Well, you're not ready.' Tetlas finally says, eyeing the girl. 'You're not ready to leave. Not just yet.'

'Well, how can I argue with that?' Evelyn asks, looking around impatiently.

Tetlas was about to respond but pauses yet again, she thought better of it.

Evelyn looks away; her gaze is farther out.

'You must be hungry, darling.' Tetlas asks, changing the subject. 'You must have only had a few mouthfuls before I came in, yes? How about we make something warm?'

'What do you have in mind?'

And before the old lady replies, she has a new impression. She left Evelyn to enter house and in her return, she held out the small book in burrows. 'Before we do, I have to give you this. It's your property, remember?'

Obviously I remember

Evelyn hates the thing; still, she lifts her cheeks and takes it. 'Thank you.'

Nobody said I'd have to use it

It was a trusting thing, something Tetlas knew would help turn over a new leaf. And it worked, for Evelyn had been wondering if she could trust her. Evelyn figures its best in her palms than in mysterious ones. Who else?

'I'm making a specialty chicken soup, with new flavours and good ol' roast potatoes and carrots. It'll make you feel as good as new.' As Tetlas said it, she has an open palm in the direction of a fire pit.

Evelyn couldn't help but contemplate how good it actually sounded, how good chicken soup and roast vegetables would taste after much time spent on an empty stomach. Katherine was always good at cooking, so I don't think the vial lifting would have anything to impend upon this. That's the last thing Evelyn wanted to think about and puts the book down in misery. She felt a rush of emotions flush over her.

'Can I help you?' Evelyn asks quickly, anything to change the reminder.

'Yes, how did you know? I was just going to ask you.'

Evelyn smiles a response.

Together they start the soup and Tetlas took care of the chicken, severing the head, and then plucking and all.

Nasty bitch

Evelyn simply watched, and then follows her additional command to retrieve a few herbs from the garden for the chicken. When Evelyn returns, she finds Tetlas placing the prepared whole chicken in a large pot of water that's over the fire. Evelyn gets on the chopping of potatoes and carrots, and soon to place them in the pan to cook.

Evelyn frowns in the sunlight flipping the vegetables in pan, watching Tetlas tasting the soup so she can track the flavour, and adding in additional herbs if need be. The herbs look like cilantro. Or maybe it was parsley? It's odd; when Evelyn first picked them she swore they smelled of oregano.

Evelyn leans forward to get a better look and Tetlas explains. 'It's Splinterleaf.'

'But where do you get all these other things? Like the chickens in the coop.'

'I have my ways, just like I got the rice and feed from Maesemer. But I don't think I'll be returning there anytime. Not even for the basics.' Tetlas's dark look is back. 'We'll have to make do with what we have.'

Evelyn nods, giving her a careful look. Evelyn can't be too sure what she's up to, or what she plans for the future. It's scary. What can Evelyn do? She can't exactly go beyond. And there's no way she could make it home on her own. She looks at the chickens in coop, having a resembling look.

Ah, but there is a good chance of rainfall and I'm not talking about the weather, but an emotional one, and that is clouding now. In not long Evelyn will be on her knees. The white witch is clever as she is bright, as pun intended. So she won't be expecting anything extraordinary from Evelyn, anytime soon.

Tetlas offers a sip of broth and Evelyn blows on the large spoon to cool it down. 'Well, I suppose if you'd do me, now would be that time.' Tetlas says nothing, looking rather bored of this talk. Evelyn shrugs easily. 'It tastes alright.'

The lady's lightens and thought; *finally, a compliment!*

Tetlas wanted to be positive for the girl after showing her true colors -- If only this was the right time. She thought Evelyn just needed a little push, and that somehow the book would be a first step to seal their bond. But since, Evelyn's been further. Sure, Tetlas places more emphasis on emends, but it rubs with uncertainty. What I'm *trying* to say is… Evelyn could really use a friend right about now.

There is something about cooking. Doesn't it always bring people closer together? It sure makes Tetlas ponder in thought.

Perhaps I should give her a little more space and time. I just can't help but feel this is the opportunity to see it through

The lady adds more water to the soup. The soup pot has impressive engravings on the side, some small stars and a few odd symbols. Evelyn removes her pan from the heat and goes inside the house to find a dish to place the food in. She returns with just this.

'I'll be right back honey.' Tetlas reassures her.

Evelyn doesn't answer; she can't, it only reminds her of the gap in time. It's like everything is at a standstill. So she comes to a sit on the table, watching the lady soon return to her cooking.

Evelyn looked drained and Tetlas didn't mind her watching. Tetlas knew it would be just the space Evelyn needed.

The sun is warm on Evelyn's skin. Time is no longer tied, slipping away. She sat listening to the new sound of the lady's knife cutting into lettuce and fruits for a salad that she spontaneously planned. It has the reminder of the simplest of times.

Evelyn's eyes close. This felt good – slowly letting her resistance die. She can picture all the good times Mother and she had. Then it hit her. Honestly, it felt good to be a part of this territory; sure it's not Maesemer but it's the freest place she's ever witnessed. If she ever wanted anything, and as off putting as it is, it's this.

Slowly, her eyes open to a new glow. Evelyn saw Mother. She saw the happiness. That Katherine was right in her element; no wonder why Mom was so miserable all those years. Now look at her, she can't help but smile. And damn, Evelyn can't help but take permission to do so.

The energy out here is high and beautiful. It is a sympathy that makes smiling as easy as the light that shines from the sun.

Still, Evelyn doesn't realize the pain and hurt in Tetlas's heart. It's a two sided coin, since her daughter no longer looks at her the same… Mom's love has always been there for her and it sickens Tetlas to the core how she is the ghost and how Evelyn's stares goes straight through.

Tetlas had poured Evelyn a glass of water and she didn't even notice her. When Evelyn looks down and sees it, Tetlas asks near the fire pit. 'Tired?'

Evelyn nods her response. She finally takes a sip. Warm on her lips, but honestly Evelyn's soul felt so much more torn now – part delirious, like looking through the glass to offer life's new perspective -- in one hand, she sees a world in freedom and in this other... well that's just it. It's the world.

The sky looks unique, with clouds stretching their white self across the openness. It makes Evelyn think; how far is she really from home? She doesn't know. It doesn't matter now. Perhaps, that's because she's already arrived. And for the first time, this could be the hardest thought of the day.

The lady passes Evelyn, noticing a new stare in her eye. A look that told Tetlas she's opening up, and taking the risk to enjoy life once more. The lady knows magic can't do this, only time. It won't be long; with much change must come from pain of letting the past go.

'Could you fetch me the Natanas from the garden, the blue and spiky ones? It would be a lot of help.' Tetlas asks.

Evelyn nods, not sure what a Natana is, but sure.

Evelyn heads to the front of the house. She looks around. There the garden is found where a few hedges of green bushy tops hide the vegetables underneath.

The earth sinks on her first step. Listening to the wilderness; she lets it all sink in; the sun, the wind, the site of mountains, and the movement of birds passing overhead. She falls to her knees, feeling the cool squishy earth. Her hands sink into the dirt, feeling the cold mass between her fingers. The flight for freedom kicks in, and yet she wants to hide behind fears. The sorrow reaches for her and the little water droplets seed the earth.

As she cries, stirring, she can't recognize a simple thing like vegetables for the first time in her life. Natana... this really is becoming a whole new beginning. But if she can't handle this, how can she ever handle that? You know what *that* is. Even the trees look somewhat different. This adds to the brush of reality, painting more confusion, in a picture that resembles insanity.

Evelyn laughs under hands to cloud her face, receiving a flash of happiness now, for this place is as beautiful as undiscovered. But her past tugs her back and forth, between a fear that keeps on creeping up and trying to tie her down, whilst a lust and freedom reaches for the sky. The goal was simple, and the vegetables are still two inches from grasping.

She wants to give up, with the sun warming her back, suddenly; a warm hand touches her back, and the sound of something being plucked from the garden sounds. That's all Evelyn wanted, hiding behind her palms. The lady's touch reminded her it was a safe place one more time.

Evelyn naturally lets loose and the tears fall all over the place. About the past and so much more, soon her fears begin bleeding away. She fights, and her fears creep back in, making her feel smaller. She came between lightening up a smile and crying some more. She feels excited for what is, and sad for what was.

She gets up slowly to brush herself off after a good while. Cold sensations move over her. The emotions flood her being. This tells her she isn't finished, returning to ground. It's quieter now, and it helps to release the tension in her heart. The beating of her soul, thump, and bump – it's all downhill from here.

What was lost was only a new growing. And when she stood up, for what felt like a long time – and it had been – a feeling of knots, and tied up old-roots clinging to the bottom of her feet are sprung loose. She steps, ripping free and stretches her branches.

Evelyn finds her place near the fire pit. The sun down has put the stars nearly out. What can be coming now?

The atmosphere is a flimsy breeze. She can share this commonplace in her heart. Evelyn rests herself on a large blanket that she grabbed from her bed.

Tetlas and Evelyn have dinner, chewing down a bean and vegetable soup, with potatoes. Evelyn was cooped up all day in her room before now, mostly napping after she ate their chicken and vegetable soup. They didn't talk that much after that evening, either...

Tetlas is glad to see the girl relaxing now; this tells her the hard part is done and nearly over with.

'It's nice.' Evelyn says with palms stretched out behind her.

'Yes.' Tetlas says with a lot more excitement, coming to a seat on the table bench, behind. 'This is nice.'

'So a whole new world... huh,' Evelyn spoke softly, peering out. There's a feeling the moon will miss her tonight, in the sense it won't make its site. She won't miss its gloom.

'Think of it this way. It's a new start.' Tetlas says.

Something calls in the wilderness, an unknown cry to Evelyn's knowledge. She looked at Tetlas, who had a lighter stare about it.

'The world and this book, I guess there really is no place like home.' Evelyn said.

Tetlas laughs. 'You said it kiddo. You always did make me smile. Evelyn, to be here is to never go back.'

'Then I must stay to find out the answers to my birth mother's past, my father's, and who I really am. And this book... I don't know why my mother had it or what it represents -- but you know what? You're right. This is my legacy now.'

'Yup, I'm glad you see it this way. I think you will find once you cross into the Boarder Lands you will seek something beyond the discovery of your families past, but answers to your own destiny. I think you will find more exploring and this should help your foundation. Your people are out there,' Tetlas points beyond those mountains, 'and not here, and surely not in Maesemer. That was a place for dismal.'

'My destiny you keep calling it, as if...'

Tetlas smiles to her words, and spoke more funnily. 'You just wait and see; once you're out there you'll be sure to forget this conversation and all areas around it.'

Evelyn's eyes jerk. 'Is it really all that great?'

'Oh, it will be. You'll see...' Tetlas has a spark, 'soon enough,' and sits back with completion.

'I just don't know what to do, I miss my mother.' Evelyn stirs in position.

'And here she rests.' Tetlas points to her own heart, signifying just that. 'But I can't go back to... that lie, I was. In your heart is where that image of her will remain.'

'Yeah... I guess it's not *so* bad.'

Evelyn's plagues a thought.

Pfff... Yeah right

'Use it as your biggest strength. It'll never let anything happen to you. No one can take it away from you, either. That's the strongest thing that will allow you to love and forgive others, so that you can move on from the past.'

'Right,' she says needless. 'It's the strangest thing. But I understand why you did it... it's so odd, this twisted fate is.'

The lady places her hand to heart again. 'That is the nicest thing you've ever said to me.'

Evelyn frowns, 'really?'

'No.'

Evelyn laughs silly with her.

'Now you've found yourself.' Tetlas teases and continues. 'It's so good to see you laughing again.'

'Yeah,' she found her smile.

'Come on.' Tetlas smiles with. 'Let's get some sleep tonight. We'll both be wanting it.'

The lady took care of everything. For the first time, Evelyn felt appreciation for what is. She really could have been dead, or found by someone dangerous. But this, this is as brilliant as the mysterious land across peaks.

Evelyn washes her mouth out with water and uses a small toothbrush in the bathroom cabinet.

'Tetlas, I'm going to use this odd toothbrush, okay?'

'Of course,' Tetlas replies someplace in the house, 'don't worry, I never ended up using it anyway. I made it myself. There is mint for when after you brush.'

Evelyn nods, releasing her frown from the plant in the washroom. She's even gladder that Tetlas has plumbing this far out... She finishes brushing and places a mint leaf in her mouth for freshness. She comes out and enters the small room set up by Tetlas.

'Goodnight.' Tetlas says at the doorway.

'Goodnight and thank you.' Evelyn says slipping into bed.

Tetlas closes the door behind her. The dark room is haunting in its own tender way. Evelyn tries not to think about the dangers of the woodlands outside this little space. Then she smiles, remembering that crazy lady.

No one messes with a witch, right?

Evelyn found much comfort in this, thinking of Tetlas. Soon, Evelyn falls asleep.

'You hungry honey?' Katherine calls out.

'Yeah,' Evelyn responds. The day is bright in the kitchen. She finds herself going outside instead of eating. Perhaps to work on the field in order to give Mother that extra leg up on the day. It's rather warm today and one would be safe to say only clear skies to expect.

She raises a brow at the forest; she's never too sure about its self, the stories, and the theories of witches. She rolls her eyes to this, and the image of the Dark One reminds her of a different path she walked. She shakes her head, hoping to shake the thought.

She looks back at this simple day. Mom is still there, so why worry about anything else happening?

Evelyn smiles to the thought of Claud. Oh that big strong man, what she'd love to do to him if she had more time on her hands. Hey, she got a brilliant idea, she intends on stopping by the butchery today, just in case he'll be in town.

Evelyn shifts in bed, with a sweaty back, her eyes open. Damn, I guess you should have taken up on that offer when you had the chance, Hun. No, you don't like that eh? Most people don't even know what they have till it's gone. Yeah, it's that same crappy story. Guess I'll keep my eyes peeled today.

She gasps for air in a panic after the wary dream. Her eyes twinkle in the small room. She sits up slowly. There is an overwhelming look on her face.

The dream reminds. All she wants is a hug from Katherine, to make her feel safe again. But that's impossible; this is impossible -- a feeling of suffocation. So Evelyn hugs herself instead. This works for a little bit.

She moves into the small hall to see its day out. She stretches her arms tiredly and looks for Tetlas. She stops at Tetlas's door and knocks firstly. The door opens to the touch.

'Oops.' Evelyn says, just in case she's in there.

Daylight shines onto an empty bed through the bedroom glass window. The glass is unpolished, thick and clumpy and in no means clear. This glass is not Maesemer likelihood.

Evelyn looks around the room and stretches her arms. 'I must have slept in…' and closes the door to find no food on the kitchen table. She makes a face and decides to leave the house.

It's silent outside. Not a whistle from the wind or a cry in the wild or a sound from the birds.

A figure ventures from the woodlands moving toward the house. Evelyn squints to find Tetlas, who is holding a small brown basket. Tetlas ducks from a low branch, overhead. The basket looks light in her hand.

Evelyn walks for a little in her pyjamas till they meet.

'What's that?' Evelyn gestures towards the basket.

'It contains all sorts of flowers and herbs. I'm just returning from picking. I'll have to get you to come sometime.' She says with that gentle smile. 'Have you eaten?' She asks with all sorts of excitement. Evelyn shakes her head no.

They arrive back to the house. She places the basket on the wooden table.

'There's bread and eggs in storage. You can take whatever you please from the garden of course. But don't be nervous, get creative.'

Together the two of them set up sticks and logs in the fire pit. In not long, the glorious day fills with the sounds of wildlife.

Evelyn can feel the thrill of today, with new insights born from the area around. This only adds to her womanhood.

She projects.

A witch…

Is it Tetlas who starts the fire? Why it is, with a flick of her wrist the wood ignites on all sides. The lady walks away from home.

'Won't we be eating?' Evelyn asks her.

She let out a small chuckle and replies. 'Oh, but I've already ate, Hun. I'll be up in the caves. Follow the blue path and meet me there when you're finished up.'

Evelyn wonders around while Tetlas disappears into the wilderness.

Makes me wonder about much, maybe a little video gaming, I'm talking the one and only. Where do you think I get all my ideas? Oh yeah, I guess I can't say the name of it for copyright reasoning's. Ugh.

Well I better hurry up and eat then – Well yeah, you should; this chick thinks way too much.

Firstly, she is to grab a wooden plate, and then she slaps a thick slice of bread onto it. With a spatula in one hand, she tilts oil into a pan with the other and places the pan over the fireplace. She heads back to the wooden table. The basket is quickly searched and she tests her tastes with all kinds of sweet and sour flavours. She licks her salty lips to the virgin flavours in mouth and plucks a few odder vegetables in the making.

With a cutting board and knife, she places the fruit, berries and vegetables on the picnic table and begins dicing. Once finished, she moves her way around, and finds herself at the back of the house where a few chickens flock in cage. She opens the little wooden door. There is hesitation from Evelyn, fearing the chickens in coop. She is quick to take one large egg from under a small round basket full of cushioning hay.

She passes the crackling fireplace that spits oil from the pan -- Evelyn jumps back. 'Whoa,' moving a few steps around and places the vegetables carefully into the sizzling pan's heat. The meal is cooked in very short time. She slips her meal onto a plate and returns to the picnic table where she butters some bread, taking a big bite into its soft slice.

'Ugh.' She hums. 'Delicious.'

Today's hot and stuffy, with the sunlight beating down on everything.

After a full belly, she wipes her mouth with her sleeve, making sure to get dressed into something more suitable before she takes off toward the forest. She quickly does this. She returns to take a majestic path of bluestones which leads the way to the foothills.

Her greasy lips taste of seed oil. She climbs the rocky path and finds an open crevice in the rock. A slit in-between the rocky wall is passed through. She follows the cut and makes her way from the bluestones, the same kind from Miss Madalyn's property. Off the path, a natural crevice is found in the wall.

She moves closer to the gap. She squints to see if Tetlas is inside. With the brightness outside, it makes for a pitch black site inwards. This entrance is small, offering little to no room to squeeze through. She tries anyways, using an arm and a shoulder to get by -- The girl huffs and puffs -- Halfway in, and in one more inch she won't have enough room to breathe. She wiggles herself out. She hugs herself, feeling chilly after the cold rock to skin.

'Wow. Unless you can shrink yourself, I don't think you're in there... -- Tetlas?' Evelyn voice echoes within. She wonders if this is the right place Tetlas mentioned. Having a bad feeling about this, she heads back up the rocky hills, following the blue stones again. She found the stones end at a larger cavern entrance; this one really echoes when she yells out. From within, a gap lights the way, so naturally the girl found herself moving inside. A path leads to a narrow passageway. It's cold and it's really dark. To the left lays darkness in the shape of a shroud. She fears this. Her fear began a hallucination of the Dark One; she can imagine it standing on its hind legs, like a bear would, showing its large round eyes through the thick.

Evelyn takes a few steps back until she hits another part of the wall. Something she didn't even know was there. With the cave being too dark to really see in, it makes Evelyn want to run out. Before she does, a light catches her eye to the right. It's a path and one Evelyn risks. It leads deeper in. She moves with some more courage and more physical light. Soon, she finds a woman at the bottom of a large opening, all within the cave. A stairway leads down. The woman is sitting under a large beam of daylight.

'Tetlas?' Evelyn calls out, and as she is moving down the stairwell, she's not sure whether to look at the woman or a large beam of daylight coming from an opening from its dome ceiling. Once the woman is nearer, and Evelyn in fact sees that it is Tetlas, the girl hesitates to Tetlas's silence. Near the bottom, Evelyn looks up and around, and is rather cold from a dread of this chilly bat cave.

Oh god, no more bats please

Evelyn clears her throat, moving down to the last step. Tetlas remains in her crossed leg position with eyes closed. Evelyn swallows and finally speaks. 'I'm rather surprised you didn't hear me calling.'

'Shhh, that's because I'm meditating.'

'Oh...'

Evelyn's heard of people performing meditation, overhearing it's a peaceful practice and all – *But... damn*, she thought. She's a real bitch. No, I don't think that's what she thought.

How can one find any relaxation here?

Entering the beam of light, Evelyn squints up. At least the beam is warm. It shines great from a short tunnel opening so that enough light can fall. It appears to be carved out by some sort of mechanical device. Clearly that can't be, not with the isolation thus far... *so*... by what then?

This is more. A small stream carries from the centre of the rocky floor and carries out in separate streams to guide to an outer rim. Evelyn does a double take; she thought she stepped into water earlier and shakes a foot regardless.

This is interesting

'Come here my dear.' Tetlas says opening her eyes. She got up from her sitting position, near the fountain.

As Evelyn enters further in, the fountain and its guided structure are better witnessed, draining around the circle of the cavern in a calming motion. Evelyn crosses her arms, not convinced of its glory. She takes another step over a vertical line, draining from the fountain. She waits for Tetlas, knowing there is something bound to come out of today. Still, she doesn't quite know who she is, but Evelyn's hoping to find out more about herself than anyone, and hopefully to do some training today.

Tetlas smiles to the area and spoke. 'For you know a whole new world's beyond you, and if you're going to venture there, you'll need to leave everything you once knew behind, *and become* who you really are.'

'I know...' Evelyn says, but her voice still sounds a bit chilly, which told Tetlas she's unsure of the sacred picture around.

Tetlas clarifies, looking around the ring. 'This is a training circle that helps you control your inner focus. It's a tri-force, which stabilizes your energy to keep you in better control. This place is very -- how should I put it? Unique -- as simply put.'

Evelyn frowns, 'is it for magic wielders? Are there Errifics -- those things you said that were coming back for us. Remember, back at the house? Are t-they some of the ones who use this?'

'Of course, it's for magic wielders. And the Errifics are masters at stabilizing, so yes. Training starts with the sake of the mind, body and soul.'

Evelyn appears as though she's wants to hold onto something, but holds her ground.

'Another sweet thing, darling,' Tetlas begins to move in the round, around the girl. 'You'll be learning of the right pronunciations for your passage. Your old wounds – sorry, I meant words -- what you now know is not the correct terms used in the land of Caealon. The Caealonians are the "Good guys" in Alasmieria. Your current terms will only act as a barrier, squandering you from them and their way of life. We cannot allow this to happen. You must blend in.'

'Got it,' her look is intent. She is quick to look around, fearing the dark outside the circle. Who's to say the dark one isn't circling the round right now?

'The term we use in Caealon is a Celestial, a wielder of the forces of nature. Remember, we don't use the term witch. Our enemy go by the term Errific; which is their way of identifying themselves, just like you will be describing yourself as the means, Celestial. And on another note, there are a rare few who wield a more unique type of "Magic", and in this case we call this magic Cloradis. I fall under this class known as a Clairic who specializes in this. The enemy's "Clairic" are called a Trinidade.'

Whew, that's deep.

'…You my dear are beautiful in every sense of the word. So you keep on holding tight and we will discover what lies in the deep of your courage, a courage that runs in your every veins, giving your Celestial brothers and sisters the same power to wield Aura.'

'Aura… is the word for magic, I'm assuming?' Evelyn asks and receives a nod back. Evelyn says next. 'I get the impression that Aura is dark magic and Cloradis is white?'

'Kind of,' she replies squeamishly. 'I'll touch base with Cloradis later. We don't want to fall off track. Not just yet.' She winks and continues. 'We use the term Aura and force, instead of magic. For instance, a Celestial is those who wield the forces of nature, or in other words, can guide elements by the Aura, which flows through you and connects with the elemental plane.

God can we get past this already?

'…It's everlasting. You'll find, once you become your own person, your own identity in Alasmieria will be key. It's everything. I'm referring to your religion, a way of politics and finding your emotional balance. To uphold your actions will notify those around you that you support your beliefs. That is a worthy trait.'

'That's a leader!' Evelyn points out.

'Exactly!' Tetlas replicas her attitude.

'I'm glad we are having this talk now. If you told me last night, it would have been damn well impossible for me to follow. I would have been too tired.'

Tetlas pauses for a few seconds, seeing Evelyn is in the right train of thought. Still, throwing too much at her wouldn't be a good thing, and Tetlas knows this. She continues more carefully.

'Evelyn, since you are a Celestial you will be trained for this, but I will only teach you a few basic spells. I know a few defensive spells also, so you're in luck. There are many different spells you can pick up from around those in Alasmieria. But the ones you'll practice most are the basic elements from your kind, the Celestials. The kind your mother learned. Once you've mastered these, you can join other practises.'

'It's strange.' Evelyn eyes squint. 'My new abilities are. This doesn't mean I'm going to ride a broom... Or does it?'

'For now,' Tetlas says with a distinctive eye.

'W-What... *you mean to say?*'

'I'm joking.' The woman cackles.

'Can anyone learn magic?' Evelyn exhales exuberantly. 'I mean Aura.'

'No Evelyn. Only those with the blood of an Errific, you're mother had it, so genetically you'll have it too. But that's not always the case. But I ain't getting into this right now, either.'

'Okay... maybe for later then. You kind of lost me with the blood of Errifics running through our veins.'

Tetlas looks ever eager, she continues. 'Come on,' pointing towards a thick boulder that sticks out from the side of the wall, 'you must come and sit down.'

'I don't even know what they look like, the enemy.' Evelyn recollects, feeling the warning in the sun, for her soul has fallen grace, and the warmth is an inkling of the distance that follows.

'Yes, I know.' Tetlas replies. 'But for now, slow down. Your emotions are up and down. Know Evelyn, you won't have to be like them, our enemy. You stand with your people.'

'I swear -- I want to kill every single one of those damn things.' Evelyn speaks louder. 'They took my father. I just know it. It's because of that damn book, isn't it?'

Tetlas gentle face brightens Evelyn's every being, even when Evelyn's at her upmost limitations.

This circle really does work. I'm just glad I walked into it today otherwise I'd be pissy

'All I feel is hate and anger towards them.' Evelyn says impatiently.

'Yes, anger. But hate is a strong one.' Tetlas says in a relinquishing tone. 'I will only teach you love.'

Evelyn lifts her head. Her lips cringe and she says. 'Losing my mother was a real strong one,' she can feel her anger beginning to build again. Her *real* mother is what she means by this, not Tetlas and Tetlas knew that.

The lady looks down. 'Evelyn, you must find it in your heart for I will only train you *how* to defend yourself. If I follow a path to hate, how am I any different from our enemy?'

Evelyn follows Tetlas look and gazes away.

Yeah... I guess she's right

All Mother has taught her, it seemed so long ago. She looks back up to see the old lady's strange face, but the stare of Mother remains. It surely found its sadness and came to a slow look to the floor.

'Alright,' Evelyn takes a deep breath in, letting go of the hate that clenches her heart. Anything to rid that look Mother always did hold. It told Evelyn that all those years spent together were real.

A long breath vibrates Evelyn's entire being and so she begins to feel ready for what's next.

Tetlas touches the girl's heart. 'Trust this.'

'What do you mean by that?'

'Listen now. There is something I've been waiting to tell you ever since I raised you up from the little girl all those many years ago.' More like the little hellish land. '...And look at you now. My you've grown into a beautiful woman.'

'Okay.' Evelyn says unsurely and listens.

'Reality works in a few different ways then we've all been lead to believe. You know the man Alas I spoke of earlier?'

'Yes.'

'Well,' Tetlas takes a deep breath in, allowing it to ease out slowly and follows up, 'here's what he's taught me. And to many, his practices are nearly faded. Listen now. Life is like a mirror; just like the one you stand in front of to do your hair. With all other beings on this planet, it is the same. No exceptions, gift or no gift. The mirror represents reality. The one standing in front of the mirror represents their choices, or in other words, the one who focuses and monitors their emotions. I'll put this plainly. If you feel good -- life will harbour this. The analogy is, if you smile at the mirror, reality will smile back. Do you understand?'

'I guess so.'

'It's strange, I know. Yet it's something very practical yet widely unpractised.' Tetlas says, rather annoyed by Evelyn's response. 'It's as simple as this, so lighten up. A strong vision of what you want is wanted, and believing you can achieve it, even though it is not here and now can still make you happy. What we want is to be happy, obviously. So there's more to this than just feeling. You see, your happiness depends on your journey and that's how you will attract what you want. Now, a belief has to be stronger than your doubts. Doubts are fine, but the belief should be strong enough to propel your passion,

What the hell is this lady talking about...?

'...which indicates you are moving towards whatever that vision is. In time, the vision will be manifested. Of course, you must take the desired steps to achieve your dream. Keep following your passion, which should be automatically generated by the vision. It works like that. It's all focus and believing in order for achieving your dream. I will teach you how to do these steps, so your journey towards what is wanted will be attracted. Sometimes not always easily, but the laws of the universe will make see that you get to your destination; that which you've envisioned. The mind works like this, you see.

'Your vision navigates you on your journey towards it becoming a reality. How you feel is your indicator of where you are in regards to your vision. Your emotions act like a compass. Also, you will find opportunities otherwise invisible to you if you do not practice your compass. That's why it is important to get in greater touch with your emotions. I can teach you this. Once you do know how, you can use this to attract positive ideals, too. If you find you are lost, all you have to do is look inside and ask yourself this one simple question. "Is this thing I believe in, my joy?" or in other words, "Do I trust myself to lead me to my vision?" The funny thing is, all this universe "Stuff" is you. You're the creator of your reality and your thoughts and emotions which is a belief, harbours your reality.

'We always believe in something. It is not the question if we believe -- we do. The question is, what is it that we place our beliefs in, and thus, putting ourselves in? It may be a negative or positive notion, and whichever side we focus on, is the path we lead ourselves. The positive path is once again your vision. You see, we don't predict the future, we create it. In other words, our mission is to come back to the now. That's because that's all we have, and by doing so, we realign our path by refocusing on our vision.

'Going further, with the now out of question; it is up to you to monitor your beliefs. This is the part where I'll break this down. A belief is dissected into two parts, by an emotion and a thought. Your thoughts create, and your emotions encompass. Together, they lead by example and undoubtedly in time, your vision. Be easy about your life, and remember, if you are unsure of how you feel, check in with your thoughts. What kind of expectations are you having? Are they positive notions of the future or negative? After all, this is all your doing.'

Wow, that was… "Takes deep breath"

'Can I really attract anything I want?' Evelyn asks.

'In time, it could take months to see the manifestation. It depends on your focus and allowing. And how do you know if you're on track?'

'If I'm having fun?'

Oh I thought she was asking me that, god I must be tired.

'Exactly!' Tetlas says.

'But what of my vision?'

'A vision should keep you creating and coming back for more, over and over again because you can't get enough of it… It is this incredible feeling. It should make you high, because you want it so badly. It should make you want to cry a little if you stray too far from it.

I cry a lot. What does that mean?

'…A feeling of being excited.

What about depression?

'…Of eager, you'll be ready to jump up and do something – you'll want to get moving – it should be that natural. It'll feel as if nothing can stop you, and nothing will. Not for the entire wild in all its glory could not hold you back from achieving your vision. And why do I say that?'

'It's because I'm sending out good vibes of achieving?'

'Good,' Tetlas says.

Okay I'll shut up. I won't say anything here.

'So in other words, you just stay happy?'

'So simple yet so hard for so many, all because they have expectations and beliefs that keep them in a circle – it won't be till you change your story, and follow a new vision, will life react differently.'

'So how do you stay happy in a reality that is difficult to be in?'

'That is why I must train you to harbour your emotions, regardless of what is happening around you. If you simply react to what is, than your emotions are subjected to this. And if reality is reliant on how you feel, than this reaction will keep on creating more – keeping you in its vortex. Or as you'd put it, an endless wreck.'

Evelyn blinks and says, 'that's big.'

Okay guys, I gotta take a break from editing. My eyes are killing me.

'That's the journey.'

'It is not your job to lift others up. If you're dependable, you're subject. You must lead by example, and that's how others can trust in themselves and know of their own true power in order to lift others. Now, going back to you -- drop what feels wrong and follow what feels right – that's the power of following your compass. With a little focus on the vision, it'll be as simple as creating your own reality.'

'It's like that is it?'

Tetlas laughs, and nods next and says. 'The more you practice this, the more you get in touch with this, the faster you will be able to fill and swell like a balloon. The higher the joy, the faster you can attract your ideals and attract an overall exciting experience. If you're negative, it works like this, just oppositely. Once ones emotions and thoughts are in alignment, amazing things can start to happen. This is when you begin to participate with the universe!

'Since emotions follow what you imagine, and where you imagine yourself is based on your vision, than staying focused is essential. It works like this. Thoughts are the blueprint, and emotions are the engine, but always, they work in unison to achieving your belief. To visualize is simple, or at least for some I should say. But to believe that you can achieve something outside your reality, this is the real ass kicker.'

'So it's my choice… to be in a vortex of things going wrong, by my thoughts leading every deed and by words. My compass too you say.'

'Yes. That's the way to create a vortex of fun.' The lady replies. 'I will teach you how to do this. We sit in our emotions. You will feel the vibrations move up your body. This signifies positive motion, while down is negative. The indication is a swell of emotion, and when in higher brackets of joy; it physically feels of hairs standing up and over your body.'

'So… joy.' Evelyn says amazingly. 'Who knew it could be so fun, yet so powerful!?'

'Yes, it is true. The compass will be this first step to your training.' The lady nods to her own premonition now, 'there is one more thing.' She moves in closer to Evelyn. 'This desire you feel has more to its meaning and its intentions. To walk your vision is to overt interruption. You will literally walk over and around interruption; trouble and oppression, because you are not vibrating this out. A simple change in focus will change your world, your life. This is the most powerful tool in the universe. But let's not forget, because you have a part of your real Mother that also connects you and this world together, and that part is in your veins… so dare to dream, dare to believe. You tell me, what are you waiting for?'

Evelyn nods nobly. 'And what about the gift..?'

'The gift serves its own purpose.' Tetlas replies and forwards, 'if practiced right, there would be a lot less negativity in your world. Anyways, nothing can be done to take the gift and your imagination away. Joy is always flowing. Stay focused on what you want and joy will continue to come. Now is the time to move forward, and if we are to train right, than this must be done. The cleansing of the soul and mind is what I refer to. This is crucial if you are to enhance your laws within and drive your soul.'

Well that shut me up.

CHAPTER 7

Tales

She left Evelyn alone to let her roll things over, so to speak. Finally, Evelyn calls out to her and a voice rings from the dark.

'Sit and close your eyes. I will help you get in touch with your heart. If that is what you desire?'

Evelyn nods first. And it's silence. 'Yes.' Evelyn finally says and Tetlas guides Evelyn to a meditative state, and it took some time. Evelyn focused in on the breath and the sounds of the water trickling. It all helps to release the stirred thoughts, helping to clear her mind and ultimately getting in touch with how she feels. She will move into a more vibratory state that naturally puts the body and mind at peace.

Evelyn gets up and can feel the energy flowing. She wants to dance and move around room, already forgetting about the darkness inside herself, and outside the tri-circle. Her heart is true and beating in beauty -- she feels the power of love.

'What a feeling!' Evelyn yells out and does a twirl like she's beneath one big shining star.

Tetlas returns in the tri-force. 'Now, shall we?' and holds out her hand for Evelyn to come in the centre. 'You say you want to become a Celestial like your mother?'

Evelyn nods her yes.

'Then there is lots you need to learn.'

Evelyn looks anxious. 'Show me.'

'Well, first you need to know the following things before we start. One, you always follow as I say; you never try and do something that is not regarded by me, for your own safety and my own. Nobody needs to be a hero, for things are about to get quick and bumpy.'

Evelyn nods in agreement. Tetlas can tell she is serious about this.

'Two, you never use Aura on Egerd soils. This means you cannot return home. And I think you know why. If you return, this only puts pressure on everyone you know. Now, most commoners of Alasmieria have little to no knowledge of Egerd, nor should they. It is Caealon that will serve and protect you now. Remember, this is another part to your journey and only you can count on you, when out there.'

'*Alone*,' Evelyn says in the faintest of voices. Hearing this word really sunk deep. Evelyn's going to have to leave behind *another soul*. But this time, she will be prepared to take the next step, *so she hopes*.

'I know you may want to return to your world, Evelyn.' Tetlas rather states. 'That's a place that no longer fits you, from here on out that is. So you have to promise me this... you will not return.'

'Okay,' Evelyn replies. 'But I'm scared.'

'Oh honey, you haven't seen anything yet.' She giggles at Evelyn. 'And three, Honey Bun, Aura is not a game. It's best for defensive matters – people get hurt otherwise. Now, to do with the book, this is not regarded by my teachings. You will have to learn that on your own. Not everyone in Alasmieria will be as disciplined as you are. Or will be... as I should say. This will be because of your knowledge of the laws within. Now, not everyone will be familiar to you... so you must be strong. Always refer back to your compass, speaking general thoughts to ease your soul, until you feel you are absolute with your vision.'

'Ok.' Evelyn's mind brightens again. But Tetlas doesn't continue. 'Is that all?'

At this moment a growling beast shakes Evelyn's world. The war cry sends shivers up her body.

Tetlas spoke in a low tone. 'Come, I want to show you something.'

Evelyn eyes her, not sure whether she can trust her at this moment. Tetlas disappears and Evelyn decides to chase after her. Inside the tunnel she catches up and the two take their exit.

The sunlight causes Evelyn to shield it with her palm. A giant beast comes into view and moves behind a tree in defence. Evelyn leans against the warm rocky dome in hers.

A body sits on two massive hind legs that support the avis's weight. The bird has thick fur and bluish white feathers that cover its body, except a smooth white underbelly. The wings are thickest at the base and thin out to hands, claws are visible. A unique avis which has an even odder appearance to describe; its long neck is thick like a tree's base yet it is agile. It is similar to an elephant's trunk. It has two giant horns that span backwards that are in twist of a snake's slither. Its face is pulled back and flat with a long protruding snout. Its face looks like no other and has blue eyes as bright as Evelyn's.

It's curious as well as cautious. It peers over to the girl who stands petrified. The avis moves away from the tree making the tree look more like a twig in comparison.

It's hard for Evelyn to trust such a massive beast. But if it wanted to snatch her with its large snout, she would have been bit by now.

Damn, I would have shitted my pants by now.

It breathes out heavily, blowing dust and pebbles beneath its giant smooth underbelly.

'What in the world...' Evelyn doesn't know what else she should say to finish her sentence.

'He's a beauty ain't he?' Tetlas says.

'I'm too young to die.'

'Nonsense girl, I was going to tell you about him. But he shows up out of the blue, literally.' Tetlas teases, but Evelyn can't find much humour in this. The beast stares around, but its head is still fixated upon Evelyn. It wiggles a long sleek tail and stretching a single wing, widely. It flaps its feathery span and returns it.

'Gosh.' Evelyn cries, moving a few steps back by the beast's simple movements.

'I call him Willow after my dead husband.' Tetlas says. 'I guess I never told you about him.'

'Who, Willow or your dead husband?'

The avis's giant wings stretch out again, flapping.

Tetlas points, 'this means he's ready to fly.'

'Oh great,' Evelyn's in panic.

They take a few steps away, and a few more from Tetlas. The girl squints nervously from the blowing dust, which forces them to shield their faces. The sun flickers with its movement and then the bird flew.

'Come.' Tetlas says, brushing her face from the birds last blast of dirt, and finds another swipe to the face with the back of a sleeve.

Evelyn follows Tetlas down the hill looking nervous.

'It's a Niveus Avis; it's a very special kind. It's also known as a Hsietne in the Esphisc language, which is the language of the Errifics. Errifics are from the northern landscape of Alasmieria. "Fierce" is what Hsietne corresponds to. Those to the north live in their region called Calliskue.'

'Call-a-what? You know the language of the enemy or what?' Evelyn had been watching the sky, until she catches Tetlas stop.

'Parts,' she replies. 'I only remember the words that have the most relevance to me. It's very similar to English, and it's not hard to speak. There is another language too, that combines both English and Esphisc. This language came long after the birth of Alasmieria.' Tetlas says and laughs a little. 'I'm sorry, is this all too much for you right now?'

Evelyn shrugs, 'nah.'

'Okay. A better word to describe the language would be Reobigheon, where the city of Reobigheon is centre of Alasmieria. The city once reigned and now bares ruin. Going back, Before B.A, which is the Birth of Alasmieria, long before the Reobighians of Alasmieria, the man named Alas and his wife Mieria had come from the region of Calliskue. Together, a treaty was formed with Caealon, who was only in their early stages of nation; of course Caealon had a different name back when -- but let's just stay to the basics.

'Eventually the regions of Alasmieria were condensed into one massive and powerful city; Reobigheon. A council of seven was formed there and Alas and Mieria were at the top, being the headmasters. Until a few centuries after B.A, it took but one night to break the amazing civilization down.'

'Well what happened?'

'That is for later. You will find many unusual things have happened after the fall of Reobigheon. Let me just start out by saying it split Reobigheon in two, separating the nation... Friendships fell and much was lost, and by all means the treasures that were meant to be kept safe… along with documentation and its people. In time, the chaos, heroes and legends were born. Mind you, the guardians of this world, those of us and the Niveus Avis, disappeared. The Niveus Avis is a wondrous thing and can only be depicted today. Willow is an interesting one who has mastered the art of survival. He won't land anywhere near the fractured "Spirits" of Alasmieria, who've lost most of their genuine self today. They'd only cage him for a sell.'

Evelyn looks up and around. Tetlas thought it was about the bird, but something else caught Evelyn and her senses; a flowery scent. 'Is this the place where you go out picking from time to time?'

'No, but it does flourish with many wild berries and flowers.'

Evelyn nods slowly. 'I have to ask then, do you think we will be getting back to the cavern for some Aura training?' Evelyn has that brilliant look in eye. In hopes, I should say. But you get it.

'Perhaps, but I believe we should reframe from training today.' She thought out loud. 'Yes,' and speaks more on time. 'We should continue our speech on the world beyond those peaks.'

Evelyn has an unjustified eye to where they had come -- just in case the Niveus Avis will return. She replies. 'Alright, I guess tomorrow will be do.' And before Evelyn let Tetlas speak, she says. 'So why does Caealon call our Willow a Niveus Avis?'

Their steps quicken down slope on the bluestone path.

Tetlas answers. 'You will find many terms in Caealon to be different to comprehend. Such words usually date back from Reobigheon; with Alasmieria having an upper leg on history. Egerd trails in comparison, so bare with the new pronunciations and their unique definitions. Such a word is Niveus. I'm glad you brought it up, it is a great example. The word means "Sky blue" for the bird's blue and whitish underbelly. In the Reobigheon language, they call them the Hsreespirit, which means "Freespirit". If you had paper I could write down the word and you'd find Hsree is in Esphisc, and the other half to be spirit; the representation of English. This was the language tongued by Reobighians when their numbers were astonishing. A language named after its massive self. It's written brilliantly, so both regions could do well in communicate. Even now, I find Reobigheon more interesting than speaking Esphisc. It takes a sure tongue and one heck of a mindset to speak this. What has me in wraps, being a little nosy and all is our mirrored language that you and I share now; English. I was surprised when I ventured into Egerd, prepared to find a foreign language... yet I found fundamental English. There are many mysteries on Thaera but this is by far a means to discover. For two realms to be separated it sure has a major link that combines Alasmieria and Egerd together.'

'You think Egerd could be descendants of Alasmieria? After all, Asnin was famous for its witches.'

'One can only speculate. But it doesn't take a genius to see the signs. Asnin was a relatively young capital -- Two hundred years old, I think. In creation, it begins at the end of Reobigheon. This tells me that our buddy'ol pals over at Brunon are imprisoning their own birthright. So what's the point? I'll tell you. At the collapse of Reobigheon, parts of its kin refugee to an empty landscape and formed Egerd. Of course, without any documentation this is *only* in theory.'

Evelyn smiles, 'well, it would sure help if you told me what exactly happened that night. Maybe we could both put this together.'

'I wish we could, but a couple gals like us ain't gonna do it in a couple of minutes. *It's the biggest mystery of our time.* But to keep it relatively short, those at Caealon are all afraid of identifying themselves as our enemy. It's simply not black and white anymore. With the little descendants left in Caealon having half and half traits, all are having issues with trust. It's this way because the descendants may be foe.'

Evelyn frowns. 'Scary.'

They've reached the house. Evelyn comes to a sit on the table; a little unsure of what to say from the bombardment of information given.

'Shall I continue?' Tetlas looks wary of the girl's expressions.

'Yeah,' she scratches her forehead. 'It's interesting, but sounds a little... fictitious.'

Tetlas rolls her eyes. 'Well of course it sounds fake.' She smiles and continues where she last left off. 'By now, most Caealonians reverse to English. I still use the council's language from time to time. It's just a bit of habit from my earlier days. I would use it all the time if I could, but I've forgotten a lot of the little words, and mostly use the main ones I remember. I'll have to show you the alphabet one time. That's the only way to explain such a language.' She came to a sit beside the girl. 'The switch in language has been like this ever since.'

'Hmm.' Evelyn thinks. 'So... how is it that I have the blood of an Errific?'

'Reobigheon was a time of love making; they're the ones who passed the genes through many generations.'

'Alright, I have a different question now and it's about the seven council members. I think I came across their names in the book.'

The lady's stare had been someplace far off when Evelyn mentioned it. Evelyn can tell the lady's thoughts run, perhaps about the past, maybe about the question. Evelyn called out Tetlas name and found a stare to be penetrating; it told Evelyn something very old and wise is happening behind her eyes.

'I know what you're thinking.' Tetlas says with a little twinkle in her eye. Evelyn follows the same look with surprise. The sun is shining on Tetlas's back. The woman goes on to say. 'And you're right. You hold this power in your hands. The book from Reobigheon, it being the most treasured feature of our time... So you're asking, why you?'

Evelyn drops her look and scratches the inside of an ear, finding a different look around. She comes back. 'I was going to ask on the lines of what it was for.'

'It's for very powerful Aura.'

'Oh you're so ridiculous.' Evelyn says and squints in the sunlight. 'I already know that.'

'Oh.'

'But now that you mention this... it makes me think about how fast this all happened. I mean you awaken me to this new part of Aura in my life, and now this life has shrewd all I thought possible and look forward to.'

'Well of course it feels that way; you're but two days into this. Now to answer your question, you mentioned seven council members who were listed?'

Evelyn smirks.

What a witch – oh no, she said it.

'It mentioned...' Evelyn went silent for a few moments... then it clicked. Her eyes spark and her voice cracks. 'That man! Alas, and I know he is the headmaster of the council… but Mieria, together they created this place called Alasmieria, didn't they?'

'Yes, the two are the reasoning.'

'And this book means what to them?'

'*This book* is what started Caealon and Calliskue forming into Reobigheon. A book so powerful, because it contains knowledge of the seven council members and by doing so, captivating secrets to their legendary minds and that was otherwise hidden from society.'

Evelyn rubs an eye. 'So… you're telling me… this book is over five hundred years old, and not just that, but the masters of the council from the most brilliant time?'

'Something like that.' She replies and shakes a finger. 'But I won't be the one to teach you of its ways. It's a beautiful craftsmanship and not mine to meddle with. You will have to trace it on your own dime.'

'You keep saying that, but why?'

'It's not my property, it is yours. Most of it is self explanatory. You see, the book does all the work for you.'

'Does all the work for me?'

'It isn't called "The book" for no reason. Ironically, the book is known for its power, yet it has a healing stone in its cover. This is odd, since such a stone falls under a Caloric's expertise and the book falls under a Celestial's power. This common Clairic practice uses a stone in order to heal a subject, yet there the stone rests in the book's cover. We call the stone a Temporal Stone. It is capable of storing plenty of energy, which is then transferable using a series of techniques to heal those with Cloradis, because direct relations from the vein would take too much energy affecting a Clairic. That would be counterproductive. Somehow the book is using this stone to instantly create elemental spells. That's what makes it so special.

'It's odd… but I think Mieria being as brilliant as she was, had to have opened a pathway that allows for energy to take from the environment, as to create elements and elementals. This tells me that the stone is not a source but a direct link to Thaera's energy.'

'Hmm. Does that mean the book could be connected to the natural order of things?'

Tetlas nods a couple before her answer. 'Yes.'

'The ultimate weapon,' Evelyn says with a nod of encouragement.

'The day you've dreamt of it, ten years to mix elements and create a spell, and in just one instant. That is why you must learn the patient way. Think about it, the world would sink into cataclysm, assuming the Book of Knowledge gets out of your hands and then you're left dumbfounded. What then? You're left without a clue on how to alchemy a spell... a defenceless Celestial is what that is.'

'I see...'

'But it was the most brilliant mind of all, Alas who took the last step to forging the power. I believe he inscribed spells to connect to Mieria's Thaerian link. This tapped science allows a word or phrase to activate any spell given in the book. Not to mention, in order to create a summoning it would take an entire ritual of Celestials. This book is other worldly.'

'Tell me about Reobigheon. I want to know more.'

'When the new era came, so did new labels and discrimination in all areas of Alasmieria. Of course after the Great War, the biggest injustice was funded by the Errifics. Calliskue disapproved of appearances symbolic to human traits, mixed with their own kind; a better definition is... as you probably guessed it; Reobigheon. It is the appearance of Reobighians that favour in either nation. In Caealon, every Reobighian wants to look human. And in Calliskue, they're no exceptions, its purebred or dead; long tipped ears, slit iris, tall, fast metabolism and a strong lifeline. Still, they're no exact ways to tell if one is Reobighian or Errific. I'd assume those who appear purebred, being actual Reobighian, have been lurking within those zones for some time now.'

'Huh... Interesting,' Evelyn says with a face.

Mhm...

'"Who inherits the blood inherits Thaera" is a very powerful statement. That's why the Errifics are so abundant with the Gift of Birthright -- it's just another word for pureblood. Their knowledge dates back further than anyone's, even Reobigheon's.'

'Wait...' Evelyn musters. 'My father, could he be one of the folk in Caealon without the gift?'

Tetlas stands. 'Highly likely, your mother was Celestial, but your father is unknown. It's not uncommon if he was. There's nothing wrong with this, in fact it is safer. To an Errific, there's nothing worse than a half breed. You're a sure sign of this, a human who can wield Aura. Yet you cannot live longer than one because you're not pure. Very few humans are gifted with Hsm'ssp Hs'efi'iyx.'

'Hsm'?'

Jesus. I'm not saying that.

'Long levity,' she responds.

'What was that…? Esphisc?'

Tetlas nods. 'To outlive the human condition -- perhaps three hundred to a thousand years old -- each Reobighian has a different life cycle and traits likened to them. You my dear are lucky; your appearance serves you in Caealon. In Caealon we call this Rs'mmface meaning two-face in Reobigheon, because you can play both sides, human or Celestial. Just make sure you don't go wondering outside boarders,' she winks.

Evelyn wipes her brow to signify she's in the clear, for the most part.

Tetlas manages a funny frown. Silence draws and Tetlas passes Evelyn to head behind the house. Probably to fetch a few eggs in coop. Evelyn sits in wonder, she blinks a few watching Tetlas pass back and forth, guessing she's setting up for lunch. Tetlas returns for the third time, with a pot of water and this concludes for Evelyn. The beautiful white robe swishes to stop when a question is directed at the wearer.

'Does this mean that there are going to be dragons and goblins out there?'

Well what are you thinking -- we going for a Mickey ride here? No goofy costumes and tall princess castles where we're going.

Tetlas suddenly laughs.

'Okay, I had to ask,' Evelyn laughs along, feeling silly.

Tetlas grows a wider smile, 'dragons? They're long gone. Their time is overdue. Now goblins, there sure are.'

Evelyn swallows. The look on her face fell faster then she knew it. And it could have been the look Tetlas makes holding that same old smile that made it all that much more viable.

Evelyn finds her frown now. 'Well, what happened to the dragons then?'

Tetlas fills the pot over the fire pit with water and then began explaining. 'The Crwyn, they've been long before Alasmieria's time. A famous scroll tells of our oldest story of The Sleepy Mountain and the Crwyn sleeping there. Before humans migrated to the land, there were four who lavished the land, a land that had no name. The Crwyn who slumbered deep within their mountain harvesting lava for warmth that kept the volcano from overflowing. The Niveus Avis who loved the sky so much they roamed as kings up and above. Below, the Errifics lived with their Aura flourishing their love affair with their forests. And the water goddesses and keepers of the coral floor who lived for beauty.'

'The Errifics,' Evelyn says scratching the back of her neck. 'I didn't know they were *that* existent.'

'Oh yes, they are living history.' Tetlas says with eyes wide. 'The world was shaken by a mysterious arrival of Mongers and Maldocs, known as the Shadow. The Shadow fought for space and in their failed attempts, the rulers of sky, land and ocean continued to push back, but there was still one place the Shadow could go looking. The Shadow slipped past the sleeping Crywn to crawl deeper within The Sleepy Mountain. The Shadow was loud and obnoxious; they banged and dug the caverns. When they awoke the Crywn, the Crywn whined and spat their fire. But the Shadow remained safe behind burrowed walls, digging deeper within the caverns.

'The Crywn couldn't sleep. They took to the skies for plead of help, but the Niveus Avis would have been dethroned by its own sky lord, a lord who'd rather have power then offer any heed. So the Crywn left the snobby king above to seek out those on ground, but the Crywn was being shooed away, again. To offer a helping hand would mean the Errifics power would wane being so far from home, and thus their forests would blemish. Finally, the Crywn approached the last of the world, finding a place on the sandy beaches to plead once more; but the Manaphee worried for their beauty, for they'd age faster if outside their safe haven of water. The Crywns knew without their attendance to the mountain, the lava of The Sleepy Mountain would overflow. But the rulers didn't listen to their plea. The Shadow sprung from the deep and spread across the world as the land surrounding the mountain burned, turning forest into fire. The sky clouded, twisting black from ash. The sea bubbled as molten spread, turning the beautiful coral black from the land's oozing cauldron -- The once lavishers of the land blamed the Crywn and in the wake of the mountain's destruction they fumed a war against them.'

'Sounds metaphorically close to the fall of Reobigheon, am I right?' Evelyn asks, feeling smart.

'Yes. It seems both shares a time of great battle. It's mostly legend being the land's beginning and all, but there is some truth to it, I'd think. Regardless, the next historical phase follows the Old Kingdom, when men and Errific fought on the broken land to vanquish the Crywn who wreck catastrophe. This is our tales of heroes and what have you, but the main story follows the success of war and bringing the Crywn to their knees. A celebration of human and Errific -- in this, brought about the Reobigheon phase.'

'Ah, so that's when Caealon and this Calliskue came together to form their new beloved city.'

'Indeed. One megacity,' Tetlas adds.

'Wonderful.' Evelyn says sarcastically. 'So peace for five hundred years in the magical city and then I'm born into this era of separation.'

Tetlas finds humour. Evelyn realizes now why she's so happy most of the time. It's her vibrational state. It's high, and high is bliss. Ever since meditation, Evelyn can feel the change too in her own heart. My, what a world Tetlas must be living, now that she's finally rid of Maesemer.

'It's never as good in the light unless you've walked the dark.' Tetlas says. 'Yes, it's a time filled with glory, but there are many gaps; if you go looking you may uncover some mysteries of our time, but you will undoubtedly taste the range of dangers along with it.' Tetlas goes on to giggle before she continues. 'You know... stories get around and honestly, as dramatic as it sounds and I'm sure the rulers were, we can't believe everything we hear.' She winks at Evelyn again. 'Regardless, it's not all that bad. I would have just put the Crywn to sleep.'

'How so?'

'With any troublesome foe, all it takes is a simple binding spell. Heswit Onquara. It only works with an agreement between two separate forces. Then, once agreement is made, the two forces of equal grace are placed under the balance of nature. And so they fall asleep until woken by a force of equal nature. The Crywn and Niveus Avis love to battle, which makes me think they're under the spell. Anyways, you will need your strength for tomorrow's training. Come; let's put our questions aside for now.'

Evelyn sits quietly, still thinking about all that had been said. 'Wait,' she cries out towards her, just before Tetlas enters the house. 'What about your dead husband? You mentioned him when the rare one took off. I want to know more about your life story.'

Tetlas expression fades. The colour in her cheeks dies out and now she looks simply towards the girl.

'He was a great man, truly amazing.' She hesitates in her explanation. 'I met him on the frontline during an expedition. Quite ironic to your own story and I'll explain why. I lost him to the Errific, but it was because of something he was hiding. Later on I found out it was because of one the Regalia he had found on his expedition in Reobigheon. He was to help save a Caealonian. I was... devastated.'

Evelyn points to the necklace that hung on her neck.

Tetlas nods and says. 'One of the missing treasures lost from the council of seven, known as the Crystal Heart.'

- CHAPTER 8 -

Training Day

Evelyn sits up in her bed covers after she awoke from a dream. She takes a deep breath out. Again and again, but images remain in mind, that of an Errific and Mother. Slowly, she leaves the room disturbed by this and takes the burrows book she slept with along with her. After yesterdays talk, Evelyn's finally accustomed to its touch, regarded by those good memories of the read that once occurred to her.

Outside is cold, but it's great to relieve the thoughts in mind. Her feet hit the cold rocks.

Over the nights that have come, the dream has made a bit of habit of her and making her wake on hour.

It starts with a walk in a forest in the end of fall. Leaves spin and twirl of bright and beautiful orange, red and gold, falling. The air is humid too and the colours are ripe and rich, allowing for an organic stench. A stench Evelyn rather enjoys. The sun is always warm and shining through the clear, sanctioning a stream of shimmering light. A warm sensation moves up her body. The dream takes a shift. She is standing in a street looking down a long suburban road. The neighbourhood looks unique, so she'd assume it's somewhere in Brunon.

She rubs her eyes. This is the fourth time this week. She makes her way in the night to the picnic table. Time feels slower. She feels she's got a handle on the dream now, now that it's fresh in her mind. She finds a spot atop the table. I should mention, as she recalls this reoccurring dream of hers, towards the end, she is an Errific; at least, she had the features of one. Her eyes are the upmost discomforting; the irises of the enemy are sharper than a knife. Her eyes catch a glimpse of Katherine who is in the clear waving her hand. It is a friendly wave and one that says goodbye. And for whatever reason, Evelyn looks directly at the viewer of the dream, which is she. That's when Evelyn awakes.

Evelyn presumes Mother is a representation of the death of the past. And the street represents... she thought about it -- her eyes squinting towards those hilly peaks.

'Fear,' she recollects. 'Fear of the past, and...' She thinks about it some more. 'Brunon always feels cold.'

Those slit eyes; she remembers their fitter build too, tall and slim like Tetlas described them. Back in the dream, the image of leaves falling reminds Evelyn of aging.

The girl shuts her eyes. Not because of this, but a hurt is felt remembering Mom's face... She shakes her head to such a twisted fate, yet it is her own. What a time to have believed in an image for so long and still have feelings for that which was only a mask. Can she blame herself? No. After all, Aura can be a grand deceiver.

She slowly takes a deep breath in. Speaking of Aura, tomorrow she begins training. It only took a week to prepare her... and now that it is here, she's not sure she's ready for its arrival. After this upcoming training day, she'll then have to survive the woodlands.

Can she really make it to Alasmieria, and all on her own? Was Tetlas wrong to assume so much so soon?

Evelyn exhales slowly. It's like she hasn't taken a real breath until now. She wants to let go... but the past doesn't seem to want to. What can Evelyn expect? These past few days haven't exactly been easy on her; she's growing spiritually, mentally and physically. She's a wreck. Can one really adapt to so much change? I think it's safe to say she's a recluse.

The trees sway in a calm breeze. There was a time when a story of magic and tale was plenty. She's not sure which story she likes more, the new world beyond her or what had once been read to her. It still makes her smile whenever she thinks about the boys who ventures down the green burrows. Yet because of this, many scary feelings start to crawl up her... I think it's starting to sink in.

Tetlas says this is a good thing, since she's becoming more aware of her compass. Anything emotion related these past few days has been a "Good thing" in Tetlas's opinion.

Evelyn completed all the necessary steps of mind, body and soul. But Evelyn's not so sure she's so ready. If life really does represent a mirror and how she feels effects it, than she sure feels the road to ruin.

Better get my emotions in check

She rolls her eyes still in the same position atop the table. 'If she's right about one thing, I hope it's about my greater wisdom kicking in. Perhaps all the more dangerous and fearful things will fall to the hand of the book. Gosh, I'm sounding more like her everyday.'

She stares out at the stars again, crossing a leg in. Her reminiscence gently finds its wane, and she pulls herself back to the present moment.

'The now,' she thinks out loud. 'If it's so powerful, why do I fear what will become of me? Why am I still afraid to see what lurks beyond those peaks...?' She has her stare to the moon. 'Ugh, a part of me just wants to get this training over with. I just want to be done. I can't stand waiting. I need to see this land. It's all comparative in theory. What if it's not like she says? What if it's all bullshit?'

With meditation becoming a ritual, she's more accustomed to the changes she's experiencing. And a lot more joy is found here. But I will not lie; tonight she's feeling the nerves. As she lies back on the hard of the table, its sturdiness is felt and she likes this.

She puts down her stirring mind and starts her vision. She imagines what she desires. She's creating her world; a vision to start emotional abundance – obviously right? Well, she's been quite afraid to take the first step. A dream to reality, or in technical terms, "The link to the evidence of the mind" is what Tetlas keeps telling her.

Evelyn told Tetlas about the dreams. Tetlas feels they're doing her a service by showing her what she misses. And by showing her some of her fears, so Evelyn can overcome them before her descent.

'I need not worry.' Evelyn says to the stars. 'Alrighty, I should focus.'

She buckles up and closes her eyes. A man with much money is pictured. He's to take her and guide her to her destination. She imagines the purple grass too to help her chain the link to Alasmieria... just in case. This need not be, since it is a universal law... *Anyways*, she sees him with much fear. Scratch that. She pictures him confident, more than she. Oh and with power! He is to lead her to finding answers to her family's unanswered past. The bottom line is this makes her happy. A thought comes to bare, but it is not hers. It's sort of... hers, but it felt unlike hers is what I mean.

In time you will find your way

Shivers roll up Evelyn's back. It makes her feel good. She hears something. She puts the book down.

The night sings of crickets. Wait -- a sniff lingers about – she's sure of this. Evelyn turns in its direction. Branches snap. She hugs herself closer from her sat position. She is unable to see past the tree line during night.

A man about six feet tall lingers in the shadow. He sniffs the air once then moves along with a hunch.

'Hello?' Evelyn asks nervously moving away and in the direction of home.

He growls at her and runs off in the direction he came.

Evelyn screams at the top of her lungs. 'Tetlas!' running back for her book as quickly as her heart takes her.

Tetlas comes outside. Her white night robe twists. 'Honey is everything ok?'

'I saw a... a...' Evelyn said, still pointing in the direction from whence it came. 'I think it was a man and I think he was naked.'

'A man?' Tetlas asks and she comes to her sides. 'How come he was naked?' asking lightly.

The same call from before but louder makes Tetlas pucker. Evelyn can't read her expressions with her back to her.

'This was no man.' Tetlas finally says.

Evelyn moves past her, nearest the door. 'I think I want to go inside now.'

Another cry but in much fierce shakes the forest, even the crickets silence.

'They should know better than to wake Willow.' Tetlas says and joins Evelyn inside the house. Tetlas lights a candle on the kitchen table with a snap of her finger.

More roars of bronze, alarm. Evelyn came to a sit at the table looking a little shaken. Tetlas puts some wood already supplied under cabinet into the oven and lights it. In not long a boiling cup of tea is made and Tetlas turns around with a cup in hand. 'Tea honey?' she asks nicely. Just when the girl is about to reach for the cup, a similar roar shakes the house.

Evelyn ducks down. Tetlas looks about seemingly calm. She sits across Evelyn, adjusting her seat where she is now.

'I never really did like the woods now that I think about it.' Tetlas says.

Evelyn leans closer. 'What?'

'Some nights, you can hardly get any sleep,' and takes a sip of her tea. 'Oh honey, I was only joking, you must know me by now. Come, drink your tea. We have a busy morning tomorrow.' She pushes the steaming tea cup she left near Evelyn who didn't realize she put it down in the first place. 'You'll sleep like a baby.' She says pointing to the cup.

It was hard to believe all Willow's screeching would end. Evelyn rubs her ear to the last of his roars and takes her final sip.

'What was it anyways?' Evelyn asks.

'A giant "Goblin",' she whispers.

'It looked a little more like a man to me.'

'A young Maldoc I'd recon. A full grown are much larger then you say.' Tetlas says and frowns to her own choice of words. 'They normally don't hunt this far out.'

'Were I came from, we call them trolls.' Knowing Katherine probably heard of the term once before.

'Well then Missy, the troll was up to no good. If you saw it up close, you'd know it was no man. You're lucky it was young, for adults can tower. Most are the size of a tree, while others can grow up to thirty feet tall.'

'Well that would explain its insecurity.' Evelyn whimpers through her look.

The Clairic in her prime sits tall. She chuckles, 'before all of this happened, I was dreaming of something simple and then I heard a scream in my dream and awoke -- Was that you?'

Evelyn makes a face. 'It sort of barked. Then I naturally ran, yelling for you.'

The Clairic is sheepish. 'Good -- Wise I should think. If that was a full grown, no telling what it could do.'

'Could you do something to stop it, one of the full grown?'

'Honey, I'm no fighter. I'm afraid I really don't stand a chance.'

'I don't think I can sleep after that.'

Tetlas gets to her feet and takes the little book tightly clenched in Evelyn's hand. Evelyn releases her hold to Tetlas soft approach. 'Let's put this away. What do you say?' And Tetlas leaves to place it on Evelyn's bedside. She returns with another candle and lights it from a blow off her fingertip. A small burst of flame blew and ignites the little wick. 'Don't you fret; I put in a little something that puts the night for an easy rest.'

'Tetlas,' Evelyn says. 'Can I ask, what is the reasoning behind this Regalia? You never did finish telling me.'

Silence draws. Tetlas looks down and fiddles with her necklace.

Evelyn leans forward gleaming at it.

'Ah,' Tetlas says easily. 'I figured you'd ask. An old gal like me needs this ol' rock,' and looks back up. The moonlight caught a glow in her eye. 'It controls aging. Being the Lady of the Forest and all, someone's got to strive to defend the place. Life's easier with more time on your hands.'

It took some time for Evelyn to ask this. 'But… how old are you?'

'Ha,' the lady answers. 'Old enough to know our enemies from our allies, and not all Errific are as bad as you may think. But that doesn't discount their manner, so don't go testing one. Take that with a grain of salt or don't. But one thing is for sure, those three witches are ripe with evil, Dolona and *Candy*.' She goes on to scoff her next one. 'W-What a bunch of --' she holds her tongue. 'Now Moora, ha, I wouldn't mind getting her in a little bit of trouble. Ah, that being said, revenge is a bittersweet thing.'

'Is that why you're training me, to help you with this?'

'No my dear… I thought this was clear. This is a fight all to my own. Bah, don't go troubling your mind with those beasties.'

Evelyn nods.

'I think I'll retire tonight. An old gal like me still needs her beauty sleep. Otherwise, I'll end up looking like 'em old wiccans.' She smiles, 'night.'

'Goodnight.' Evelyn says and Tetlas blows out one of the candles nearest. The girl's eyes darken from the last dim light. It flickers once and Tetlas disappears.

A moment of stillness, a sense of adulthood takes hold. The quiet is intimidating to Evelyn. Thoughts run wild to the new adjustment. Her mind focuses back on the last candlelight, and the smells from her teabag.

It scents the room with a new hunger. She hugs herself and listens for anything that could still linger outside. Then and only then will she go to bed. The wind taps on the windows and the candlelight blows out.

She smiles to herself. 'My, what a world I live in.'

'Brilliant, ain't it?' Tetlas asks from the dark, leaning from the hall.

'W-Was that you?' Evelyn stands up.

She chuckles. 'Just the candle part,' and held out a hand. 'Come. Let's get you to bed.'

It's hard, Evelyn's nervous to leave her spot. Her nerves and thoughts linger before she said it.

'I wish I didn't have to face the world tomorrow.' And breathes out heavily, taking a step away from her seating place. 'But I guess you're right…' sounding of petty.

'H-Hun, it's going to work out better then you can imagine.' Tetlas says, still reaching.

Tetlas's hand feels lighter in Evelyn's hold. Evelyn's mind is still. It's nice to finally let Tetlas and her world in, no matter the difference. The night holds this similar stillness. They pass Tetlas's room. The smells of herbs are strongest here. It reminds Evelyn she has a friend. The darkness makes everything impossible to see. She trusts Tetlas who takes her into the hall and finally her bedroom. And Tetlas gets the last word of the night in. 'Goodnight Sweetie.'

The next morning, Evelyn awakes to the same musty atmosphere. But this time her day feels different, warm and brighter.

There on the kitchen table a prepared omelette, beside is a warm steamy bowl of vegetable soup. She eats quickly and heads out to the caverns to meet up with Tetlas, figuring she'd be there for today's training. In the darkness of the tunnel the tri-force training ground awaits and so does Tetlas.

'How was breakfast?' She asks.

'Amazing,' Evelyn replies with a larger smile.

'Great. Come on in.'

A breeze brushes past them. It's rather cool inside, but it sure feels good with the warm sunlight.

It scared Evelyn; all last night she thought about this moment today. Yet here it is, and it feels better then she predicted. That's got to count for something, right?

Tetlas goes on by saying. 'In Alasmieria your talents won't be easy. Evelyn, there are many obstacles you will be facing along your path to Esmehdar. The capital and most important city of Caealon; it will be your safe haven. But first, let me explain a few aspects of our training that I will be going into. The four total elements in the arsenal of a Celestial are Lyric, Clayast, Leveate and Sophair. To wield any element will require a force to move, combine and create elements. Can you guess which one it is?'

'The element of air?'

'Good. Sophair is this element. The fundamental one, if you ever see it on a chart or scroll, you will see it is in the middle of a pendulum being the balance of all elements. Lyric is the fire element, all graceful and swift. Clayast is the element of water, ever flowing and easily moved. Leveate is lightning, quick and tough to control.'

'Lightning,' Evelyn could cheer, 'how awesome.'

Tetlas suddenly clasps her hands together and this gave Evelyn a jump. 'Are you ready to try and launch your first element?'

Evelyn eyes widen. Her hands are in fists, hanging by her sides. She nods with enthusiasm. This was a clear sign to begin.

Tetlas fixates towards the wall and she steps a foot onto the fountain, covering the stream. 'Remember, concentrate lightly and you will see your result more clearly. First to focus on a happy moment and you will feel the flow. We will be practicing Clayast. It's easiest to picture yourself scooping the water, like you would drink from a well. This is a great way of distinguishing what is felt. It is a way of measuring mass.' She releases her foot and the water shot up from pressure. Tetlas does it now, taking control of Clayast. A small amount hovers before them.

'How does it work, Aura?' Evelyn asks excitedly.

She gladly tells, dropping her focus and the water drops. 'It's the connection we have, combined with the power of imagination or a translation of thought and physical movement that makes the change happen.' She instructs further. 'Your hands are always a guide in the direction of the movement of elements.'

Evelyn keeps her eyes fixed on Tetlas's foot.

It's time. Evelyn smiles her readiness. Tetlas removes her foot, and the Clayast shoots up again. Evelyn's fingers tingle and light up. The small stream is focused upon. She made a movement with her hands, scooping the air.

'It feels heavy.' Evelyn says with palms scooped. Her action works to control a ball of water, or more like a giant raindrop floating above the fountain.

'Yes.' Tetlas responds on the other side of it. 'For now you will only be able to lift what you can with your physical capability. The connection of air is an extension of yourself, so you will feel the weight, but never temperatures and that sort of thing. First timers are tough. Your mind distinguishes by what is lifted, in other words it calculates by your physical ability.'

Evelyn loses focus and the water falls, crashing to the floor.

Tetlas continues. 'As you get skilled, you will overcome old patterns of thought and belief systems. But for now, this is new to the mind. So your gift fights to be seen.'

'That was amazing! But what do you mean by all that?' Evelyn drops her palms to her sides, and the light to her fingertips fades.

'It's really to do with solidifying your bond... It's the simple act of imagination and belief that has awoken the gift in you. Like when I walked you through Tastraity, that night.'

'Wait... I could do this my whole life?! And you didn't tell me!?'

Tetlas quickly scratches the side of her head. 'The moment you'd figured it out would be the day we'd all be doomed.'

Evelyn smiles at her. Now that sounded like Katherine. And Evelyn gets right back at focusing. She's more successful this time and pitches her arm as if to toss a ball, and the floating water ball smacks against the outside wall.

Evelyn's eyes light up. 'Water fight?'

Tetlas laughs. 'I see you're having fun so how about we turn up the heat?'

'Wait!' Evelyn shouts in eager. 'What if I didn't have this tri-circle?'

'It'll take more convincing then. It's a natural stimulation of the mind as to relax it and let you lift even heavier things, like rocks and boulders. Even then, such things are best left for the masters.'

'Powerful.' Evelyn agrees.

'Yes. But the most one can wrap their brain around is double their body weight. Some masters can even act with little movement, to none. But it's the alchemy of elements that takes the most focus. After you perfect the basics, then the fun begins. This is when the first part of making a spell comes into play. We call this "Spellbinding" or a "Memory charm". In my opinion it's best to journal the art. You sit down and Auritate; a form of meditation that syncs up your brain while you imagine the spell you perfected, and go over the steps in mind, all the while, using a word and one that scrolls off the tongue easily. This is Spellbinding. When saying the word, the spell activates all the necessary steps you took. Whatever element you've mixed, formed, shaped, sized and so on, will produce automatically. When the word is pronounced, the mind goes into trance till all steps to the memory charm are completed. It's a faster way of performing any level of difficulty in sequential manner.'

'That's deep.'

'Yes, and it feels incredible too. A beautiful vibration moves over the body and hushes the mind. It's the same feeling you get while you Auritate. The trance to the spell can only be stopped if you're interrupted. *It* can be dangerous. It is best to keep to quick spells and not to perform any fancy tricks in the making or anything like that. It's just another one of those grand aspects to a Celestial we have over our human friends. You will need to keep a basic spell book. It's a way of documenting your spell. Only those who created the spell can use it, obviously.'

'This is perfect.' Evelyn excites further. 'I won't have to hide the Book of Knowledge then. Instead, I'll pretend it's my spell book. How's that for starters?'

'No silly. No Celestial in Alasmieria has the power to wield such Aura. You will have to learn like everyone else. The practice of writing spells.'

'Hmm.' Evelyn thinks out loud and asks another one of her questions. 'What if I damage the Book of Knowledge?'

'It won't. The book is protected by an enchantment, so don't worry about anything like that. This is why I must train you to learn of a Celestial's origin. Very few artefacts have such an enchantment.'

'But Tetlas, what if someone discovers *the book*?'

'If it's found, hide the truth for your protection. Let lies flow until proven guilty. You must act out as if it were a second part to your heritage. Any spell of difficult are normally passed down through family generations. Once you find passage and safety in Caealon, you may find you are treated with less suspicion on your journey beyond the Boarder Land. Until then, what I've offered will have to do. You may even say you're carrying this book for someone who goes to the best school in Esmehdar, the school of Avail.'

'Ok.' Evelyn shrugs. 'So in other words just "Wing it"?'

'Exactly,' and gives her a wink. 'So, are you ready to practice some more Aura? How's a fireball sound to you?'

'Let's let it rip!'

Tetlas pulls her hands out more clearly from behind her robe, with the foot to the hem swiping floor. With a snap of her wrist forward a gust within the ring formulates. The Sophair begins to move in the round around them to Tetlas's swirling-hand gestures. The veins on her wrists are sticking out from blood stimulation.

'I'm not very strong with this type of force, but I've had some practice with this. So brace yourself.'

The air whirls faster and faster, whistling loudly off their ears.

Evelyn calls. 'Maybe it would have been easier to just light a fire from the house,' brushing the hairs from her face.

Tetlas remains fixated on her task and the girl remains ready. The air around is suddenly sucked into a smaller section within the ring, surpassing them and giving Evelyn a bit of a shock. The air is quilted, if you'd please and is ahead of Tetlas and Evelyn.

'It's a means of creating a more powerful force.' Tetlas says quickly.

The sound of whistling has faded and the hairs that were flying, fallen. The air is turned into this rapid, yet small spinning sphere of Sophair.

Evelyn watches with some distance; her face closing in from fascination.

'Are you alright with trying to control this?' Tetlas calls out, with but a hand out and in the direction of the ball. She's using her imagination now to keep it constantly moving. Only a master can do this, for it takes much focus.

Evelyn nods a ready reply. She takes control with her hands whilst imagines the ball spinning. The vibrations are felt when she does. 'This is dangerous,' Evelyn's hands and body continues to shake.

'Condense it one more time and it should ignite from superheating.'

Evelyn packs her hands together as if making a snowball and like Tetlas says, the air goes; it does ignite into such a powerful thing.

Evelyn reaches her other hand out as a means of protection, being a few feet from the heat. Her hands glow bright for her protection, also. She yells and fell backwards from worry, covering her entire face with both palms.

Tetlas had jumped forward and does her best to control the heat.

'It's too damn hot!' Evelyn cries in the echoing chasm.

The fountain sores up onto the ball by the master's hand. Instantly smoke explodes from exhaust. It flash freezes the once fireball into a scrapple of spiked ice. It fell to a shatter and glitters its mess across the floor.

Evelyn moves backwards on all fours from fright. The hot steam rushes the cave, swirling to the top. Tetlas quickly pulls Evelyn out of the steam into the dark cavern.

Evelyn coughs at her. 'What happened?'

Tetlas's eyes sparkle, if eyes could under such depths. 'See what happens when you play with fire?!'

Evelyn nods, unable to find the words to speak.

'So are you ready for round two?' Tetlas asks, hardly making out each other's faces.

Evelyn is finding this to be craziness, but decides to face it by starting with a breath in. 'I can do this.'

Tetlas pats the girl reassuringly.

On their way out of the darkness and back to the circle, their shoes crack over icy crystals. And before they regain their places in the ring, Tetlas blows the shard covered surface with a powerful whip of her wrist. Like Aura does best; the ice is gusted by Sophair to the outside of the tri-circle.

Now they're ready.

Tetlas creates another sphere of Sohpair and passes the hovering sphere.

Evelyn's hands are up, acting out as if she's taking it. It remains focused for now, whistling as it goes.

Tetlas gives the signal to go.

With fingers alit, Evelyn condenses it until it becomes superheated. The glow of her hands returns to the superheated heat. Her hand recoils and she slings the ball towards the wall. The fire explodes.

Tetlas quickly raises the fountain, shooting the aqua in a powerful beam consuming the flames that are outside ring. For something so little, it sure produced a lot more flame then Evelyn had expected.

The atmosphere cools down. Still, Evelyn's emotions are running high, a realization of the energy she can behold!

CHAPTER 9

When Destiny Calls

C old water from the ocean floor carries upward. It is moving towards the ocean top. Sun rays appear. This cold water turns warmer, heading towards the piercing light above us. Sun rays get brighter and the warming current is blinded by the ocean ceiling.

Sea creatures call out; their echoes are heard by former races, igniting the ocean of the deep in mastery. The sea creatures move along this current. The sea level thins out and so does the current. It leaves behind these sea mammals to remain course; tickling colourful coral wherever it reaches, until finally the current touches a beach and cools in the open.

The sun blisters on the hot white sandy beach, and the water evaporates to change the air into a cooler current. The air carries up to distant trees. Deep depths of dark forests are passed, until the current is a breeze, now following between pinewood and exotic vegetation, leaving behind all that was to the ocean who will continue to beckon on, long afterwards.

Above, a large dark cave is nearing, it looks threatening. Closing in, a large hillside is passed, which is covered in forest.

The current finds its way seeping into its cold misty self, and somehow the air becomes ever chilly when it passes a small creature feasting on its own kind. The thing drags the small wrinkle of a flesh body away from its clan. The one dragging lets out a wary cry to the following. The small hungry beasts move their bodies, no larger than a child's, towards the feasting one. The hoarder snarls back. The group moves closer in, nearing in on the shrieking one for he is keen in his unwillingness to share.

The current passes them and heads out of this old cavern and out into the freshening air. Exotic life chirps loudest in a forest of bright green vegetation.

The air is warm again, and it hovers over a stream, which curls down a large valley. It comes down to play with the splashes of this cosmic game we deem life. As the current follows and tips to another fall, it drops into the rocky mists below.

Down here a forest is thickest, deemed to be darkened and full of unique animals. The air moves towards two creatures, with tusks that point out sharply from their heads, with two long antlers that point skyward. The animals chase into the wild. The current follows behind them on their backs. They gallop loudly and fiercely through the darken forestry. Above, a light just barely seeps through the treetops.

The animals pass a large broken tree trunk; in a territory that no beast is welcome. The rainforest lights up from gaps in the canopy. With each step, the animals' hooves seep into the wet grounds. It's quiet, and is this way for a pretty good reason.

Suddenly there is a yelp from one of the tusk ones, and then a massive bolt kills the other. It lays dead, burnt and smoking in the brush. A crackling noise echoes past the remainder, signifying a warning to it if it comes any closer. The animal tries to escape but is caught by a pounding light, knocking it backwards, instantly killing it. It lay burnt in another bush.

The smell carries on past a tall and slim being. His historical features are as slick like his snake-like-eyes that look towards the animals that nearly made it past his defending position.

A large gate is behind the being. He stands in the backyard, where a path to a mystery behind these tall sandstone walls, awaits. His look of danger withers but his palms remain white from Aura. They refuse to settle. His heart beats and he looks one last time to make sure all is in the clear.

The small breeze passes him by, pushing towards the open pathway and out of the giant forest plains that hang from old, yet abundant trees. What now comes into view; Tiniss, which is a great city of Calliskue.

Tiniss resides furthest of the region, privileged from the protection of its grand capital. A capital that faces the ruins of Reobigheon and to the far east the proud nation of Caealon resides. The capital of the Errifics, a place very evil, very dark, yet it's always flowery and beams life when the capital is not. Evaloak is shrewd.

Wind passes through Tiniss's domain and enters through the backyard gate. The forest branches hang over high walls. The buildings are made with concrete blocks and fortifying steel bars. There are engravings just like on Tetlas' pot, but more historical ones that tell of a structure of power, and of a religion. A story runs of tales and the plague of the old times, of Reobigheon. This history is imbedded along the inner city walls.

The city's floors have a base, implanted with stone blocks, made from sand off the beaches. It's gold and bright covering the earthen floor. The buildings are made with sands also.

The sandstone wall runs miles in a giant circular radius that greets its front gate, a gate that's greater than the one in the far back of the city. The wall in general stretches as high as the buildings.

The city is built upwardly, made of mostly towers. There is a strong foundation to the city which is implanted with block, so the city won't sink into the earth from the towers weight.

This place smells of an earthen plague, they ring the reins of the Reobigheon, and fame of the Great War, but neither side really understands the depths of power that was laid down during those times. It's all myth and tale, as I said. But be mindful, if one here is to tell us a story, it's already aggressive.

The lower city atmosphere smells of fresh cooking and burning wood. Higher, a scent of fresh flowers, it moves with the airflow. It carries past tall buildings, over a giant dome where Calliskons manufacture all sorts of goods. They're Calliskue's best tailors, crafting beautiful robes and items. Civilian robes are in yellow and white. For their infantry, a golden leaf embedded on each chest of an Errific of Tiniss. This symbolizes the power of nature and the way of these true Aura masters.

A small white petal with blue veins falls from a flower. It dangles from a tower's open windowsill. It slowly drifts in the air, flowing over the lovely city below, touching another tower and landing on one of its many balconies.

An old alke; a woman who has pointy ears with slick green irises waves her goodbye to a young kalec at the lower city grounds, a kalec is a male. This kalec is on a large four legged beast, known as a laeq; a beast not so easily tamed. The kalec and beast have something in common, they're feisty, and the kalec won the game of dominance, taking the laeq as his frightening prize from the wilderness to grounds.

It had become clear to all what type of kalec this was, a leader.

All Errifics are toned due to a healthy metabolism. It was their build that gave the tell tale signs of a purebred when they banished anyone Reobighian. Few purebreds are truly bulky, and… that was one major sign that set them apart, aside from those with ears and eyes like mine and likely yours. Errifics are always fit and gorgeous, simply put, beautiful is a sign of danger to any outsiders.

The kalec waves back from his animal to the lady, his aunt. His face is sharp and his irises yellowy, with slight blonde hair and a hint of gold in them.

His aunt yells out to him in Esphisc. 'Goodbye Heike!'

He squints in the daylight. Blinded by the suns warmth but manages to wave his goodbyes. Due to popular belief, they're all wrapped up in stories. Brutality and common place are within their hearts, till the end. The king, only he can stand tall amongst the ranks. It's a privilege, no a right to serve him. That's what they forage. Evelyn, stay the hell away from this place.

The birds are heard chirping. Like on a crisp summer morning, they sing because they know what's coming -- a flight of erratic circumstances, and so the real in life is signed up for. They know they've got to move on to keep up with the changing winds. Their song is alive, making for some background music.

Heike looks away, a cold shiver flows his blood. His heart hurts. The site of leaving home just hurts. He knows the lands beyond these gates are different, but as commander of a small portion of the city's platoon, his training will be matched. From birth he was gifted with courage, and now this dusty duty of power. But once he's out there, there's nothing, yet he is certain of this. It's wrong how he's been treated. But I guess poor him, right? Out there it's unfair, the lands run wild, but he's sure it's not home. It's not safe, and that's why it's calling him forwards. That's the only reasoning behind his going, to match his excel of unknowing.

His aunt still watches him. Her eyes have that same fiery glow. It is not the sun this time; the sun is too bright for both anyways. To him, he only sees its bright flower. I'm joking. Its power and he lives for its heat.

Heike commands those in lower rank, most with one gold leaf whilst he has four. His men get back in line, marching away from their family and friends so they can follow orders.

Since Heike was born with the eyes of Tiniss, he had been in the eyes of many... and with it had come much expectation. Still, he's exceeded them all.

With a kick of his heel, the laeq dashes to Heike's command. The laeq wears lots of gear that bounces on the side of the beast, but the kalec remains in control. He comes to the main section in town, where a great way points to the front gate. Hundreds of lining up nords and their riders grow hungry to move on.

Heike pushes by excitedly, and attempts one last glimpse back to see of his aunt in the looming distance. He doesn't care for his follow friends. He's got one thing on his mind – you said it. That lust for power. He cannot see her, and the smothering sun is the reasoning. He knows he'll never see her again. His emotions are high.

The line begins to move out as to follow their leader. An Errific enticed in black, with a crown of pearls on head is a few feet before the infantry. He's cutting Heike off; this was an act of putting Heike in his rightful place in the order of things.

A little further, the General of the Army is enticed in black and yellow with a gold leafy crown. He also wears a cape in white.

As the entire infantry moves out, alkes and kalecs above throw flowers in honour of these brave ones. Peddles trickle in rosy pink and yellow, landing on the gold beneath their steeds.

At the front gate, Heike waits in rank. He is not too far in line from the general.

A slow and heavy earthen beat of a drum sounds and it continues on with the cranking of the large opening of the gate. The final crank turns. Heike's heart beats a roaring thunder. The great gate towers over him casting a shadow upon all thou who shall pass. The heavy beat stops. They move within. One can barely see with only a few torches lit and the shadow swallows them. Wooden hinges and a few symbols of the Great

War are witnessed on the inner markings of this tunnelling below the gate. Some are seeing this for the very first time. Only those with the standard title of Errific may come and go. And this does not imply an easy regards.

Guards clothed in robes of the city, stand on the high-rise of the gate and nod their respects to the brave ones enticed to leave the city limits to go beyond, and perhaps forever.

Five hundred year old abundant trees are within reach. They shade the riders under their wet and humid selves.

Heike leaves the gate of Tiniss behind and the quickening of his heart thunders. The movement of the leaders quicken. Twenty four years since Heike's training within those city walls, starting at the age of fourteen to receive high rank of commander, when finally he can now leave home. Whew, that's a lot of work. Only with this title will he truly be set free and to set foot with more esteem outside this realm they call the "Gold Ring". His battalion and the others are graduating and are as ever eager for their glorious stay in the capital. There it will form together. Heike will be finding himself saying Evaloak's famous quote, "A bud shall seed its kingdom's rose but in unity we shall flower. Welcome home, Evaloakens."

Riding heavenly now, Heike also can't wait to get there and there is another who resides someplace far from his world, far from the roaming plains. His elation fills him for the change. For the eye that bare see. The steeds begin to push and brush along this forest path. Ah, out here the air is different. It smells like freedom.

- Chapter 10 -

The Path Unfolding

There's only one thing to do now. Two weeks has passed since Evelyn's Aura training. She comes outside and moves towards Tetlas who stands petrified at the front trail, looking out towards the wilderness. There are calls, unknowing, sometimes even to her knowledge.

'Eh... it's been awhile,' she says to the unrecognized. She has a different look, turning a look home. 'Those pesky things must have eaten all my vegetables and fruits.' Tetlas says under her breath. She can be seen rubbing a finger in a hole within a tree, next. Evelyn comes past these trees with holes in them that appear like bite marks. She wears a white robe that is short at the hem so it won't snag for travel and a full backpack. She stops where Tetlas stands.

'What's this?' Evelyn says and touches the bite marks.

'You remember the little ones I referred to as Mongers?'

'Yeah, a while ago -- how couldn't I...'

'Well they've been paying us a visit. You best be careful, they're coming out of zone to find some food. They are hungry.'

'You don't think they will go that far?' Evelyn points her head in the direction, away from the mountains.

'Don't you fret; the Dark Ones are an infestation territory that way.' She has that dark mean look. 'And Mongers stay to the hills, they normally stay in dark places, they don't like to come out of hiding.' She touches the bite marks again, 'this changes everything.'

197

'Right,' Evelyn has the same wary look, but smiles.

Tetlas pats at Evelyn's white robe, an old one of Tetlas's, lightening up, 'fits nicely.'

'Yeah, I like it. I'm just worried about the colour.'

Tetlas looks faulty her way, 'most your age will still be choosing their class. You remember the protection spell you've learnt from Auritation?'

'I do.' Evelyn pats her pockets where Tetlas had given her an empty note book, which acts as a spell book. They created simple Spellbinds together in the days they had together.

Hestife is a projectile of rock. Clayastlia is a pressured shot from a waterbed. Lyratlia is a burst of fire, thrown, and Sopharian; a very compressed air quilt, which is held closest to the chest that explodes outwardly. And the Book of Knowledge lay in her backpack. Another large backpack lay next to Tetlas.

Evelyn goes on to remind, 'sub-Sopharian.'

The word "Sub" is always placed first in front of the word so the spell isn't activated.

'Good. Then that is a basic protection spell most Clairic's already know. Knowing that Spellbind is enough to call oneself a traveler's Clairic. Later on you can find a suitable tailor for your Celestial needs.'

'Thanks, and thanks for everything... I'll be safe.' She says reassuringly.

Tetlas nods slowly having a sad look. She goes on to retrieve the large pack on the earth and places it on Evelyn's front, strapping the harness around her. Evelyn waits for Tetlas to talk; Tetlas does while she yanks to tighten one of the straps.

'You must walk a trail to the Twin Peaks; it's a few miles outside of Caealon; so once your past... you may find you are best to never return. In Caealon you'll learn of the right paths.' Evelyn swaying as Tetlas tugs on the last strap. 'I believe they're outposts designed to guide your way to nearby towns all along the roads to Esmehdar. That's where dealers may sell nords and tailored clothes. There's everything else there, like inns and such.' Tetlas finishes and stands up straighter. 'It'll be a two days journey to the boarders of Caealon... Remember, you'll come past the Twin Peaks first. And remember; don't listen to any of the stories people will lead you to believe about me.'

'Mom,' Evelyn says, trying to get her attention. 'It's going to be alright. I'll make it.'

Mom just stares at her emotionally and then spoke from term. 'They're not all true. And, whatever they say... I will always love you.' Evelyn wasn't sure what Tetlas meant by this and got a little push as a hint to get going. Tetlas calls her back. 'Wait I almost forgot. I'll grab your other belongings from the house.'

'There's more?' Evelyn tries to collect herself and Tetlas returns with another bag.

'You're wraps in case you're hurt out there and herb treatments.' She says and speaks firmly. 'We can't forget a toothbrush, some paste and nail cutters.' Tetlas stops to notice, picking up one of Evelyn's hands. 'Look at these. They need a cut! Oh, and I also packed some toilet paper and other personal things for a growing woman.'

Mothers...

Tetlas wipes a tear from face. She fills the last of Evelyn's bags with these items. There are a few silent sniffles and then Tetlas goes on to say. 'You should make it to the scenery of the vale by nightfall. It comes before the twins. It's best to set up camp and get some rest. The next day you'll march your way towards the noticeable peaks. You won't miss them. You have enough money for a mount. Get one as soon as you can, it'll carry all of your supplies and quicken your travels.'

Thankfully Evelyn knows how to ride a nord, quiet well too. She's handled many in the times of helping with ploughing and other things.

Tetlas reminds. 'Esmehdar is the key for getting started; they supply you with all your other basic needs, like housing, food, and fresh water. They're hugely abundant, though they may ask that you work a few hours on farms, here and there, just to get a helping hand – its only right,' and scratches her face. 'It's been so long since I've been back. I'd have to say they still offer this luxury. Anyways, the outskirts of the city live by xzena; money as we know it.'

'Right, I'll keep the xzena close to me.'

In a gust of wind, the brushing of leaves gives the forest an appearance of waves. Evelyn's robe moves with it.

'It's time.' Evelyn says peering around in it, noticing the change. She comes back to the sound of Tetlas's voice.

'Ah… the winds of change are blowing.' Her lips pucker and she speaks less on point. 'You should see a great tower overlooking the flats. It's white and stony and its height can't be missed.'

'Mom, it's going to be alright,' Evelyn says emotionally now.

'Yes, I know. Okay, it is known as The Great Watch. It overlooks the enemies to the west, go northeast of it and an outpost granting access into Caealon should be met.'

Evelyn nods and squints with a picture in mind.

'You take care of yourself dear. Keep an eye out at all times. Remember what I told you?'

'Yes… don't crossover the vale, but to follow the trail towards the Twin Peaks, there I'll cross the hill into the Boarder Land. Once I see the tower I'll stay northeast where I'll enter Caealon, following the roads that lead to the great capital, Esmehdar.'

'Good,' Tetlas says. 'Come here and give me a big kiss, Honey.' Evelyn does this and Tetlas speaks thereafter. 'Not till you cross the tower are you in the Boarder Land. Evelyn, be wary, for the dangerousness of the outskirts is no boundary you should cross.'

'I won't crossover.'

'And don't you let anyone trick you into buying something with xzena. Also, you may come between those you may feel you can trust, but always make sure you choose wisely.'

'I will.'

Tetlas takes a deep inhalation, 'good luck Honey… this world is nothing you'll be reminded of.'

Evelyn's robe swishes as she struggles with the gear to hug Tetlas again, and so Tetlas makes sure to give her another really big squeeze. With a smile, Evelyn heads off into the bushy madness. Tetlas watches the girl slowly disappear.

'If it doesn't work out…' Tetlas says to the surrounding area, 'there is always another…'

Cold shivers come up Evelyn's body to the suddenness of her clearance.

When Tetlas spoke to Evelyn about the journey earlier this morning and the trail towards destiny, believe me, all it felt like was similar to a dream. Right now Evelyn feels focused. With the completion of losing

Tetlas… everything feels further from whom she thought she was and closer to whom she really is. My how she looks older.

Evelyn stops on a hill, overlooking the tree-home in the distance. She sees more on the rise. There she sees the fire pit lit. This tells her that Tetlas has already gotten back to her cooking. You see, Tetlas ended up using up all her time to go get the girl ready for this early morning and had fed Evelyn instead.

Evelyn remembers their talk last night, about what to expect on her journey.

"Head to the Caealon region, were you will find those that will accompany you. Don't be deceived to trust in only those who mark the same resemblance as you, not all Caealonians are good. They may be hiding more then you may want to know. Go to find what you can of your parents, only then will you be able to shed some light on the truth of your past. Evelyn, there will be times you may feel the need to come back, you mustn't, there's nothing more I can teach you, you've already done that yourself. If you're worried, just trust in your heart and follow it for all your answers."

A new path opens up to Evelyn. She leaves behind the safe haven of home. The rush of freedom hit her. So it begins. The road to the first vale is quite the pace — there is plenty of time to prepare mentally. The air is nippy, and Evelyn hates the cold -- If that's her worries then she's got some more coming, doesn't she? Bah, don't blame her, I hate the cold too.

The knowing of dusk is far, but so is the fast moving environment. It feels that way, I should say. With her grasp on her new life, she carries through the bushes without contemplation.

The forestry can be a dangerous place. Don't worry, she's got that message already beat into her head by Tetlas. Figures, right?

She departs through the green haze before her, not peering back. Not looking for the smoke, because in time, it'll be too far from her.

A dashing comes through an open path out of the great lush forestry into an open grassy expanse; Heike comes slowly up a large hill from below the Calliskon landscape. The openness is nice. Even for an Errific, it's nice to see grass no longer under treetops. It's also a break from the bellowing avis that were in trees. The smoothness of the land will be an easy ride under the bright and open skies.

The rest trample loudly out of the forest depth into the open around him. A rush of freedom comes about Heike's soul, like he could just open his arms and let them fly. So, when nobody seems to notice, he does this. He comes back, almost losing his balance and carries out with his arms on his reins again. There's a few looks from his platoon because of Heike's action, but mostly they keep them forward. Heike amuses. They'll be there by sundown, and then they'll be Evaloaken.

Evelyn carries through the rough bushes, looking up to the blinding sun in the middle of the sky.

She cuts through the thick bushes until she comes to stop at a small village just below her, Evelyn being atop on a rocky trail.

Far below, a small village stands out in a little open path. She makes her way down the stretch, taking her some time to arrive to the scene. The houses are old and raggedy, lifeless among the tall patches of grasses and weeds; this place sends chills up her spine. Leaving this area, the bushes are thick, brushing against her gear. The weight is bound to slow her pacing.

It had been tough taking off her gear and placing it back on when she finished from a rest. It's been a few hours since, and in many more she stops for one of her feasts she's prepared, marking the peal of the day. The sky bleeds an orange colour. But it isn't till a four hour trek thereafter that the valley of the vale is recognized with the twins in place, pointing due north.

She stretches her arms, 'finally.'

At a hilltop, overlooking the trees, Evelyn comes out with hand shading. The sun is setting in her eyes. The winds brush along the stride of expansion. The forest below her is at a slope. A wavy waterfall bristles in a breeze not too far either. It's a warm site with the sun sinking, and the site of it all crashes; a brilliant life indeed alongside a waterfall sparking in its simplicity.

'It's beautiful.' Evelyn catches herself saying.

The peaks are caught in the glow. Here, Evelyn stands up high near the mountain's side. She's in an area that's flat. This will be her resting grounds.

The winds are chilly. A foreshadowing fear; though life looks peaceful now, in not long the wilderness will shade and creatures will creep. But beyond an everlasting feeling of now, something that keeps getting better, the girl opens her arms and feels the chill run past her reach. She opens a stare to the wilderness. To her, it resembles an open area ready to be explored -- A haven of green as far as the eye can see, and already she feels reborn.

Tetlas voice rings her memory.

"The sun always rises in the east and sets in the west."

Evelyn looks around with the peaks in site. The journey tonight will be put to a rest. She unpacks. Tomorrow she'll pick things back up. As camp is in the works of being set up, she makes sure to start on the fire pit before the area crawls of creepers and what have should come out. Better now to get to know the area before sun down.

All around her life roars loudly. Bugs zip in her ears and butterflies sore. Birds pass quickly by, soon to be bats in the looming dark, where a cave is noticeable just outside her perimeter. She gathers some wood and sticks.

'I wonder if there is a spell for protection.'

She returns to camp with this in mind. It feels great dropping the wood down.

The book is retrieved from her bag; it's hidden in its mask. She speaks the words and the soul reveals its face, shining in the handsome. She feels protected by its touch for the first time.

She closes her eyes and remembers what careful words Tetlas has said to her. Thoughts run. Evelyn nods in the still. She slowly closes the cover and pushes the power away. With that change of mind she begins building her fire for tonight.

A heavy wind has already begun, and she needs the wood to block it out to start it. If that doesn't work, she'll have to use the book; it's just getting comfortable with its power. She wants to light a fire but fears, alongside her better use of judgement, that the book could turn this forest into ash.

'Risky business,' Evelyn says. She is quick to retrieve something old fashioned from her supply bag. She gets down low and gets close to her fortified wood, with dry brush in hand it's placed within the pyramid. With a flint rock in hand, she does her best to light a fire. She looked over at the book in hesitation, not just because of its power, but out of fear of what the power might also attract this looming nightfall. Tetlas told her more than once to take it slow with the book, knowing Evelyn has a tendency to want to rush things.

'But there is no one around... So why not?' Evelyn spoke as if Tetlas was right here. 'Perhaps I should listen. It is safer.'

She looks at the book in the simplest of ways. Its craved gem on the front makes for a more appealing.

Evelyn sits up and wipes her brow. She takes a deep breath out and listens around; it's quiet. She tries another time using the flint rock, but the winds are making it improbable to light. She decides to look through her things for something more useful and comes across a small brown pouch, remembering again what Tetlas has said.

"The filaments and stigma are grounded and mixed. It's a simple technique, but requires a rare flower. It has a special name; it's known as a Burley. I go picking for them. There is an abundance of them in the wild life."

She hands the bag in Evelyn's hands, watching her expressions. Evelyn asks her, "what does it do?"

'It creates Lyric. When I go out to pick, the whole flower head is taken. The chemical reaction works when it's dried in the sun. I then take the filaments and crush them. With this powder, it takes two final ingredients, those with the gift and their breath.'

'Breath?'

'Yes. It's a powerful combination. A flower of rare potential, you see. Though, it can also be a burden for those who don't study it.' Tetlas says and goes on to laugh. 'I've had my share of problems with the Burley. As you can imagine, causing fires unintentionally. It is a mean craft to handle.'

Evelyn frowns. 'So it won't ignite if the flower is alive?'

'This is what makes it extra dangerous; it does, even when alive. The dry ones catch fire easiest; you must pick in lively months. The summer season is safest. Even then, holding your breath is most essential when getting close up...'

'I'm curious,' Evelyn asks. 'Why am I called a Celestial?'

'The definition of Celestial is when the sun and moon are noticeable in the sky. Caealon needed a new name after the Great War ended, to replace the term "Reobighian", which died long ago. So, Celestial was crowned. The sun represents Calliskue and the moon is for Caealon, thus a blood of two opposites.'

Evelyn reaches into the Burley sac, and pulls out a simple amount. She opens her palms and the wind moves the dry dust around. She carefully crouches and places a hand nearest the fort. She exhales. The flame gives more wit than expected. A burst of fire from her palm ignites the brush, inside.

She jumps back excitedly, clapping her hands in joy and the fireplace snaps at her. She ties the Burley powder shut placing it back in her pack. She notices her palm glowing white. She touches it frantically, watching the glow fade. Her memory moves over her again as she stares into the flame.

"What do the flowers look like?"

"What, the Burley? They're tiny. Red peddles the size of a fingernail. Yet they carry very fine filaments that look like white hairs."

Evelyn looks understanding. 'Are there more of these type of plants out there?'

'There are, but I'm afraid I'm not as fond of the others traits. Simply, the many of Burleys are the rarest and finest trade in Caealon.'

Evelyn eyes reflect the flames of fire. She pulls out two thin rolls of cloth from her pack. They will act as a lower layer for her bed tonight, also a heavy wool blanket and a small cloth for a pillow is taken. She allows herself to rest her back on the softness and then she stares up at the stars. She's already thinking about what there will be to expect. All the while, she imagines the places, all the races, their faces – she wonders how she'll cope. She decides to eat a meal, knowing it'll be a few before bedtime.

A small wooden crate separates food from the rest of her belongings. If she uses it right, it will last for the final trek to the Great Watch. Yikes. Let's hope man.

This is a scary time and in the midst of it, all she has is a little bag of Burley and a genius spell book to get her by. Man, that's rough. She rolls her eyes to the taunting thoughts. 'Nothing's going to hike up these hills and attack me this far up.'

There is a call, and one that causes fear. 'You know what!' Evelyn shouts. 'I'm not going to be scared anymore,' and gets up walking towards the edge of the cliff. 'I have the Book of Alasmieria baby! Don't even dare try to bring your scary bears – so there!'

Her voice echoes off the bushy madness. It's silent. She returns to her spot and eats happily. 'Better.'

And she returns to reminiscence.

"...But if you seek further information, you have to venture to the edifice of the Royal Bibliotheca to find your answers. It's in Esmehdar city."

"A library?"

'Not just any library, the bibliotheca has the most information from our times. There you will want to search for any missing clues to the whereabouts of your family. They may just have what you are looking for. Just be careful of those who may think suspicious of you; the information could be hard to come by, or restricted for that matter. Assuming your mother was famous for her finding of the Book of Knowledge, in which the Queen may want to keep this information hidden. Be cautious, Evelyn, that's all I'm saying.'

'I understand. I will lay low. I will find my answers, one way or another, with or without the universe's help.'

She snuggles up to the covers, sitting up and feeling satisfied with a full stomach. The Book of Knowledge sits heavily in her lap. There are more calls in the wild, nothing recognized, though possibly something dangerous.

'I'll be okay.' She whispers to herself and turns on her side, pulling the blankets over her. She pulls the book ever closer and flips the heavy cover to reveal the first page, which flashes memories, but none are focused on for long.

'Let's see...' She says with stirring eyes. 'There must be a spell to protect me... Should be somewhere...'

Now going deeper, she stops a few pages in, next to a diagram showing symbols of the four elements that make up a Celestial's power, yet there is a fifth element and this one isn't Cloradis. This one houses all elements, they being within. 'How did I miss this?' She skims. '"A *Clist?*"' and reads about it. '"All elements combined are called a Clist element." How neat. Still, I don't see anything that resembles Cloradis. Oh, hold on now here it is. "Cloradis, named after the Fourth Chapel's priest who discovered it early Reobigheon era. This element is separate from the family tree of elements and is otherwise known as Cloradis."'

The symbol for Clist represents the first letter "A" on the Book of Alasmieria. She places a hand over mouth, 'interesting. Now I know.'

The more she reads and understands, the less threatening the book feels to her.

'I wonder,' she skims again. 'Perhaps the spell I am looking for is under this section under Cloradis. I'm thinking some sort of ring of protection around me.' Her finger falls on it as she reads it, 'sub-Roguevine -- to entangle and trap foes. Let it move around you so those battle it instead of you.'

She looks up from the page. She fears the shrewd wilderness. She leaves the book on the earth and comes to a stand. 'Very well, let's try a test.' Her hand rises to the north slopes, 'Roguevine!'

She looks at her hands, nothing happens.

'I guess Tetlas was right about the gift being the first connection to the book.' She picks up the book this time and repeats it, 'Roguevine.'

A crackling sound in the forest sounds -- first thought to be Aura and it turns out to be branches moving. She took a single step back, one closer to the fire. The heat is felt on her back -- her hand already pointing as a weapon in the direction of caution. 'Hello?' She says and peers. 'Show yourself.' Her lips ready for her Sophairian Spellbind if needed.

Something crackles again. It's that same noise. She creeps in the direction. The tension is slow moving.

A vine creeps up at her feet. It taps her boot and then decides to swirl back into the darkness.

Evelyn finds herself laughing in amazement placing her hands on her mouth again, knowing it isn't there to harm her otherwise it would have by now. She got the feeling when it tapped her boot it was only out to make a friendly gesture and say "Hello".

'I do know one thing's for sure; it has a personality whatever it is. The book is something *alright*.' She begins to have a staring contest with the dark, in hopes the vine will clear. Suddenly, more vines are heard moving like a pair of snakes in grass.

She shuts the book and pulls it closer to her chest. Her eyes gloss the area over. The fear of its whereabouts makes her swallow.

Slowly and tiredly, and after some time she finally lays herself to bed. Every time she would close her eyes, the doubt would settle in; fear plays tricks on her. She can't help but imagine the vine tugging her into the wilderness. A simple thing like an itch on the foot or a tingling on the body will make her jump.

The thoughts continue to play on, until finally she opens her eyes one last time to a noise she heard. She turns to the darkness as if it has feelings.

'If you are going to get me... Well?' she says, waiting. 'Now is that time.' Her eyes move around to the silence. Only the crickets sing. 'Good then,' she says and her voice cracks. 'I want you to keep it down.' She nods to the stillness and finishes by saying. 'I guess that is goodnight, then.' And slowly closes her eyes.

- CHAPTER 11 -

The Boarder Land

The morning strikes a deep blue and yellow. The sun just broke the horizon.

Evelyn sits up with her hair dangling behind her. She stood up to notice the beauty around her. She sees no vines moving and the book rest where it should have. She shrugs and figures the spell must have worn off.

She gets a bite to eat, hearing the singing jays, or whatever birds are out here. She stays warm in her traveler robe. She packs her things, getting ready to move on. There is a slight chill, and her breath is still noticed. The days when she awoke to the morning's mist, honing from the forbidden forest. Now, she stares out from the other side.

Still, it feels good to be awoken at this time, and it feels even greater for her biological clock still in works.

'Goodbye.' She says to the area, in case the vine should show up. She takes off with her belongings all neatly packed, wearing them like before.

She keeps her strength up by taking rests in between the trek into the thicket. Thankfully, Evelyn is still safe behind the Twin Peaks that are seen, where she stands atop a large boulder. The girl rests here for a little while, eating many of the same high fibre vegetables; that which looks like a plumb and is hard and tastes like an apple. Tetlas calls it a Reoue, a fruit-vegetable if you will. It grows in the land of Alasmieria.

Evelyn gets back onto track. The land is more grassy and rocky than ever before. She lets a hand fall from her strap, feeling the tall grasses brush on her open palm and she lets it graze between her fingers.

The Twin Peaks are near. The mountain's once parallel view is now faced head on. It's rather thin for a mountain and has a shorter peak then most around it. It looks like a little gate, which acts more like a door from this place to the "Realm" behind it. From her view at the end of the forestry there is an open expanse that reaches to the gate. She notices at the base of the mountain, there lay a small open crevice in the wall, acting as an entrance. It's not carved, but a slit large enough for two men to walk and enter.

She crosses the field with the book in burrows in her backpack. The book in this form is light for travel, but not defensive savvy. That's why she's equipped with Spellbind in mind, with her sac of Burley close by; it acts as a safer means of protection. Plus her Spellbind works well with Burley to perform the simple fireball. A young Celestial she may be, still, there is much that heeds from simplicity, isn't there?

Evelyn approaches the expanse and stops to notice the greater detail, the finer workings if you will. First, she looks up. She can barely make out the tops of the Twin Peaks. It appears as if a quake had slid two separate mounts together, creating this giant two headed peak. I say this because there is also a massive still-effect, a spiky shattering near the bottom closest to Evelyn.

She moves closer to the rocky wreck. A mass of rocky spikes point from the mountain, where massive gashes are near the base. As she nears, she treads between these spikes, which stick out from the ground. She stops at the base to peer around and then decides to move towards the gap. Inside, she is able to see about ten feet in. Being careful now, taking her time as she moves in the cold depths. She stops ten feet, just where the sun beam dies out from the outside. She looks back at the expanse and it looks very small from the gap. She feels very uneasy about all of this. She turns back to the darkness, knowing it's only one more step into black.

There is no going back

She remembers a conversation Tetlas and she had, about preparing for what should come and any dangers that may lurk on her path, that there's a crossroads and that it's fairly predictable. She remembers the last few words, easiest.

"Don't look back, don't you dare. It's a brand new life, don't you ever come back."

Evelyn nods to the memory. 'I have to go forward. It's time.' She places her left hand in her pocket, feeling the Burley sac. Her right hand falls into her other pocket, feeling the spell book and her burrows safe in her pack. She pulls her hands out and tightens her packs straps. Then calls out, 'Tastraity!' The sensations move to her hands and light seeps out of her fingertips. With one hand on the sac, and her right held up; it lights the darkness. 'This has to be it.' Her voice echoes in the chasms. She moves in the deep, unsure if this is the right entrance or not. All the while, Tastraity creates moving shadows, reaching up the surfaces.

The area is tightly fitted and smells badly. A trickling of water is heard in the distance. A few looks here and there to noises.

The air has a cooler breeze in. She follows the way on. Blistering and spiky rock is pointing all around, from the ground to the walls and higher above. She remembers that talk of danger. To stay amidst her compass at all costs. There's a path, and feels she's to climb away and around it. Here she finds herself leading deeper in. Wherever this path shall take her, it feels right.

She wants to hold her nose to that smell, but keeps her right hand up and her left on the squishy sac. She moves around a corner and hears a noise – a sniffing sound and a scratching up ahead.

Ten feet up, something is heard moving where a thin rickety bridge built from rope, is now swaying.

She frowns to this and then notices the smell of fire and cooking. She stops and takes another good look up, hearing eerie squeaking noises; it sounded to be some form of communication, for a whimpering is heard and another is repeating the same.

'It must be Mongers,' Evelyn says with heavy breaths. She climbs a large spike gashing out of the wall, like a tree stuck through a narrow hallway, she carries up and over it.

Something small lands before her and she shines light to see. A little being no larger than a child looks up to reveal its large black bubbling eyes. This thing looks older, and has boney everything. He speaks with a humbling tone.

'You want to pass? I believe a courtesy is in order – don't you, friends?'

Her eyes widen, hearing others crawling around. 'I don't want any trouble.' She says, keeping her focus on him.

'Oh, but we are the gatekeepers. Our lord wouldn't be too fond of us if we were to just let any outsider wonder right through, now would he?'

She frowns at the enclosing Mongers and asks. 'What do you want?' She wants to run is what she would rather be doing.

'How about something fresh?' another spoke from the wilderness, crawling on the side of the wall higher above. It's a female, showing large sharp teeth grinding for something protein.

Evelyn swallows and follows her better use of judgement. She knows better than to deal with such fowl creatures.

The first one and his dark eyes swish to Evelyn's movement. His voice squeaks instantly. Darkness falls as she shifts her hand of light for some dust. Pulling a small pile, she exhales on her open palm. Like a dragon disturbed from sleep, flames uproar. The ones above scatter and those ahead jump backwards.

Evelyn runs, getting near misses of fallen edges. The Mongers above are tossing weapons, ringing the halls of bouncing knives and heavier things, like swords.

'Sophairian!' she yells and the beasts scatter as fast as her words spread. Sophair is condensed into four seconds of a massive explosion of air and debris. It knocks back knives and dust, vibrating the entire tunnel.

In response, there are screams of anger.

There, not too far is an opening. The ring of her Aura still echoes, and she exhales on more Burley so that the little ones continue to move in desperation, allowing for more room to get to the opening. She passes bones, broken glass and even stumbles into puddles. A roar shakes the tunnel. Evelyn stops dead in her tracks, swallowing but twenty feet from exit.

The Mongers whisper words of death. Crawling up the walls and moving deep into crevices of the cavern. 'The lord is woken. Now you've done it.'

She looks up and about. Many more Mongers approach the rocky cliffs of the cavern and look down to see the commotion. They hold torches, lighting up their shadows on the walls and brightens the look in their eyes. The room starts chanting, tapping their feet. 'Chant, we chant. He will break you and he will eat you, till all your flesh is gone.'

A closer roar comes from someplace within, the same one as last. It must be enclosing on her.

Evelyn takes a few steps back and finds her way outside. It's an open field and it's a stretch. Evelyn holds her hand to the light. On all sides, high rock and little trees surround. A beating heart makes life a little brighter and awake. She moves through the field fleeting in the moment. The way is clear and the smell of grass fills her lungs. The warm day is already picking up. She decides in her glory to face the door of darkness, now getting a feeling that this lord may be trailing.

A call comes from within, enough to hear his voice.

'Break you!' he speaks. A massive fully grown Maldoc ducks its head to get outside and moves away from the entrance.

Evelyn stands but twenty yards on Alasmierian soil and this is what she already has to face, a fully grown mountain troll? Dead is a word she can hear chanting all around her, and she just may agree. The Mongers shout from the hills...

I'm thinking now's the best time to start running

Her feet pick up and her heart is felt beating a little faster. The pound of the lord is heard beating behind her. He holds a forty pound club, old and battered. Standing fifteen feet tall, the beast moves with a slight hunched back. He has a long face and small eyes. Almost like a dogs, but with less length.

Her mind twists.

I can't outrun that thing!

There is more movement from the hilly sides. More little bodies look out to spectator the two below.

With a half a sec of Burley in her hand, it surely won't be enough to stop him. She turns to face the catastrophe.

He is trampling heavily her way. It's a daring site.

She reaches into her sac; 'Lyratlia!' flame twirls around her with the use of her guiding hands.

Please don't slip and fall.

She condenses a small flame ball and brings it in close. The ball of flame is released shooting a cannonball. It misses, landing with a bang behind him.

She creates another, only this time she allows for it to float before her as a means of arsenal.

The beast is suddenly at attack by roots. It surprises the both of them, but the vines attempts have no real effect. The Maldoc rips through the green with ease, killing the last of yesterday's protection spell.

She springs back as if to throw a javelin and launches the flame ball. It pitches and lands whimsy from the distance in front of him.

He looks down at the smoke at his feet. 'Pity,' he says, waving a hand to brush the smoke in the air. He suddenly lets out a humongous laugh. She could feel the vibration jerk her body. He smiles with large teeth. 'You are going to be my meal now.'

'Sophairian!' she yells out in her last attempt. The air is formed and the giant steps back carefully. The final effect gave him a slight push. She takes a few steps back and blinks.

Let her die. Let her die. Let her die. I know you're thinkin' it.

The beast raises its club and a terrifying roar shakes the bored look of those watching from the hills.

The giant turns to look and finds a massive avis diving. The Maldoc cries with distress and runs towards Evelyn, who also runs. The lord swings at the bird and finds its club being knocked from his hand. The club bounces someplace near Evelyn. She got down low and glances back at the battle.

Willow, being actually bigger and with his full wing span is much heavier in weight. He knocks the giant flat on his belly. Willow doesn't dig his claws into the giant's back. Instead, he pounces and flies higher up.

The Maldoc gets up and starts dashing in the direction of the cave.

'Heck yeah!' Evelyn cheers. More cries cover the hills. Evelyn turns a look, and decides to get a move on with her escape. She's afraid Willow can't stop all the others, for hundreds of Mongers move down the hills in a stampede after her. Burley fire won't be enough. That's when it hits her, and as soon as she tightens up those boots and sticks out her chest, the thought of her next plan is thwarted. Another loud roar comes from

Willow that vibrates her entire being. He swoops above, warning the Mongers' to back off. Its massive wing span reaches over her, casting shade where he soars.

Willow passes the hills and scares more away, but hundreds more are pouring out from the entrance and over the hills. The avis lands in the middle, surrounded by the many.

Here on earth we have such beautiful things built from plaster, metal, wood and synthetic material to give historical creatures such as dinosaurs and large mammals a realistic appeal. It sure captivates viewers, even today. But the Niveus Avis are so much more, so much more fierce too, and in Evelyn's opinion, absolute wonder. Like a monument in a zoo, he would stand for something extraordinary.

She blinks to its movements, but what's more shocking are the Mongers already on the field. With what little time she has, she grasps for some more Burley and puts the pouch back into her pocket. 'Lyratlia!' she shouts again. Instantly the Memory Charm focuses her into action. After exhaling, the flames swirl into the ball. The heat is felt, hovering above her hand. She throws the small ball in desperation.

From the side, there is a lung. Evelyn yelps, landing on all four. She can see where her fire landed in the open field ahead. A Monger has landed on her back. She flips her weight so its little back cracks while its head is bashed against the earth. Its fight from underneath her is short lived after receiving her futile body slam.

To the right there is two more that jump towards her. As she just got to her feet the Mongers collide with her to knock her back down. They scratch at her front pack, tarring holes and digging out clothes. She rolls, feeling the little bodies being tumbled. One squeals to her weight and falls while the other's caught in her front pack. The torn pack is pulled off with it. Evelyn runs. More jump in the action, scavenging through her things for something edible.

Evelyn blows what's left of her Burley and scares a few wretched that were enclosing.

Willow's pass clears the way with his claws. He roars and blasts Mongers with his wings.

She makes way for a hill. Little feet are heard behind her. Hissing noises by them, closing in from all sides – Just as she expects from her guardian saviour, Willow soars loudly, scarring them off as well. She can feel herself separating farther from the little beasts. Their hisses are dying off, literally squeaking too. She has to find her balance while Willow continues to clear the way.

She passes him on her left and makes up the hill.

Like a cat against mouse, Willow chases after the few opposing with his large flapping wings.

Evelyn suddenly stops when she reaches the top, where a massive slope down leads into a flatter land. There like a mighty jewel in the desert, a fortress is seen far out. Only it's connected to a long running wall, the fort being centerpiece. The wall blocks off the grasslands of the west. Behind the wall, a forest that is adequate to the Forbidden Forest.

'That must be the wall protecting Caealon. This must be the Boarder Land!'

She shakes her eyes off the run of the wall and comes back to the might of the fort bearing tall towers. She would say this is as safe as it gets for all who have the privilege of passing gate, and an even safer assumption of it being the land into Caealon.

She puts her hands to her mouth in much relief.

The fortress is made of stone, while taller than the run which is only made of wood. The fort acts as an inward square, using the wall as its forward facing protection. In other words, the fort is an interior which extends behind the wall. It has four easily noticeable pointing towers; two are stationary and two to the far back, closest the forest.

Evelyn has never seen such might. It is no Asnin of course, and doesn't compare in height or any elegance for that matter. But, the staple of craftsmanship is one of pure defence. It makes her wonder what Asnin may have had to defend during its prime. Its days like this that sparks her imagination.

She looks around to see if it's safe as she moves downhill. And it is. The way to the open grassy land is as wide and clear as the skies above her. She puts her hands in her pocket to feel it empty – this means she lost her spell book.

She kneels to take her pack off. She reaches in to find the book of burrows at the bottom of her things, right where it should be. She retrieves it and closes her pack.

'Safer this way, since it is my only spell book now.' She says, placing the book in one of her empty pockets and turns Willow's way. 'I can't go back now.'

Willow's roars are received.

She doesn't waste anymore time. She moves down the rest of the slope. She walks for a good mile until she reaches the fort. She was sure someone would have rode out to meet her by now, but they stayed put and she continues to move closer. A mighty flag whips the air, in blue, white and purple. What she noticed was a Niveus Avis in blue, centre of a large shield which is half-white and the other half-purple.

She moves to the gate, which has to be at least thirty feet tall being five feet above the run. She can see men holding bows on the upper decks who notice her as well. She lifts her palm shielding the sun and a squint of her eyes to find they have nothing to say, nor do they move, nor cock a bow.

Well it's better than a threatened look...

They watch her with their relaxed intent. For here the towers have archery machinery positioned in an open face position, facing the enemy to the west. Red banners are hanging over the fort's towers, and wrapped around its upper posts deck.

That large flag she spotted walking towards the fort is now seen through a small hole in the fence. Without doubt, she's sure it's the flag of Caealon. She watches it dwindling in the breeze and every now and then she can hear it smacking the wind.

'Hello?' She asks after a short while. She even looked behind her to make sure that this was the right way, that perhaps she missed something along the way. Something, anything, a sign or a post signifying the Boarder Land... Could she be wrong? Is this place something entirely else?

'Well hello,' a man's voice is overheard. 'I was wondering when you would say something.'

Evelyn looks caught off by this. She wants to stare back up at the bowmen in case it came from one of them, but felt something entirely else. She frowns with the sun peering through holes in the wall and before she got her chance to speak, the voice of the man picks up, being louder. 'What do you seek, Clairic?'

She glances at her torn robes, she forgot about the colour. 'I --'

The man interrupts. 'These lands hold no place for a traveler.'

She overhears another voice. 'Get rid of her.'

She frowns at this and steps back. She looked up at the bowmen, but they no longer stared back. She relaxed, for this told her they have no intent of harm. The first voice sounds again. 'The enemy flood these lands. I cannot let you in.'

Evelyn breathes heavily. 'Oh I know, trust me, for I too had come from the southern hills. But please, you see I was chased by Mongers. They came without notice. Please, I require your aid; I am unfamiliar to these lands. I am an outsider, no doubt, but I am worthy, I am --'

The second man's voice cuts like a sword. 'An outsider you say?' only a shade of him is seen between the brackets.

Evelyn breathes in deeply. 'Yes, I dearly seek... shelter and food.'

'What's your name?' he asks.

She hesitates. 'It's Evelyn.'

The men fall silent, and then whispering is heard between them. It has something to do with her appearance.

The first man asks her. 'Do you carry a port with you?'

A... what...? Tetlas never said anything about that

'No.' Evelyn answers. 'I'm from a small house to the south. It's... it was just me and my mother. But I had to leave...' What else could she say? So she spoke more clearly, unsure of what they'll think now. '...So it's just me now.'

The two bicker and finally the first man responds. 'I'm sorry, but I've seen enough in my time from those of you. I've made up my mind. Evelyn, you must not cross into Caealon. Please head back to where you've come from. It is just too dangerous for us to risk an outsider.' -- It sounded like it wasn't his decision to begin with.

She blinks many times and before she turned around to walk away, her mind is busy with the reminder of her way back.

Tetlas did not warn me of this... She led me into a pack of Mongers... and what's best, this gate won't open

Evelyn clasps her hand to her face. 'Can it really be over?'

Did I do something wrong?

Evelyn turns around to the second voice. 'Lady, your time has come, get moving!'

She wants to throw something at the fence, she wants to drag this other out and yell at him.

Slowly a small trap door opens. A young man pokes his head out. 'Surely you won't go that way?' He asks pushing his greasy hair to reveal more of his face. His brows are deep and thick like his wears are. His long draping coat matches that long greasy mop covering most of his features.

She frowns. 'But you've just said --'

'No, that was Maraen. I am Cander. But are you tested? That's the way into Calliskue. Surely you have another way?' His suggestion is received in hesitation and this gives him the impression he's done something wrong. He looks over his shoulder to see if Maraen is there and then left her for a few more moments, closing the door behind him. He returns and with that same look, it quickly shifts, which told her he doesn't have much time.

Evelyn shrugs awkwardly and points. 'But that is where I am from, past those peaks.'

'Those peaks?' He didn't need to point. 'Surely you didn't just arrive from the Lady of the Forest?' and gives her an awful look, 'and all on your own? You poor thing --' the man is cut off by the other.

'Are you still bickering to that woman? You best close that gate or else I am coming out.'

'Good,' Evelyn says in courageousness. She wanted so badly to bite the end of her tongue but if she had, she fears the bite of returning home will be much worse.

'Please,' Cander says for her sake. 'He'll come out and we'll both have trouble on our hands.'

Cander is suddenly pushed aside from the trap door. There Maraen steps out to show himself. He's no larger than Cander, having short hair and a beard, but that in no way implies he's a little man. No, they're both tall and stalky men, riveting with strength. Their health is in prime and the eyes are bright... She could roll her eyes; she's had enough beasts for the day and irregular cleanliness.

Only Maraen arrives seeing blasphemy. His garments are simple and his boots surpass the foot of the pant. His shirt is woolly and brown, with a soft white shirt underneath. He has a little bit of a belly, but he's still cute, where a little bit of hair protrudes from underneath the neckline.

Evelyn took a step back from the fire that twists in Maraen's eye.

'Please,' Evelyn pleads. She can feel her wild side creeping up to grant her strength. She eyes the men. 'Who is this Lady of the Forest, anyway?' – Yeah she did.

'Oh dear… this is too much. This woman is of her forces. Don't you see that Cander?'

'What?' Evelyn says, pretending to be shocked by his words. 'Please, I don't even know who the Lady of the Forest --'

'Save it.' Maraen said and took a step forward, looking the way Evelyn came. 'She is a mean one, a Celestial of untamed power. They all think I'm crazy, but I know of you and your kind. Oh yes, the Lady of the Forest has got us all scurrying in our boots. I've seen the nightmares, over and over from the beasts that crawl from those peaks. So you see Clairic… I don't believe in this veil you have us perceiving. Those who enter don't return. So you must be an evil. How else could you explain your travels from there?' He takes another step closer so she wouldn't dare speak. 'Why do you think the enemy only crosses from the northwest? All leave the dark forest and 'em Dark Ones to *her*.'

They know about the Dark Ones…?

Evelyn speaks. 'All I know is… a lady helped me get across those peaks. I don't know who she really was. But she was not related to me in any way, nor had she once come across as foe.' – And that's it. She's got to stop lying. She dots her eyes between the two. In retrospect, it's true, in its bluntness.

Maraen points at Evelyn. 'She is not to be trusted!'

'Please, Maraen,' Cander says, placing a calming hand on his shoulder. 'Let her explain, don't you see, this is a miracle, not a bad thing… We should be sheltering this woman.'

'No,' Maraen says pitifully, stepping before Cander, an act of defence to separate Cander from her.

Evelyn frowns and stood her place, but three steps from Maraen. She asks. 'The Lady of the Forest, what did she ever do to you?'

'Me?' Maraen swallows. 'Oh, I've heard stories, enough to know.'

'I see.' Evelyn nods carefully. She looks at Cander, signifying Maraen's insanity.

Cander remains calm. 'What if we were wrong Maraen? Perhaps there are those who do well in her company.'

Maraen ignores him. 'Do you have a message for us,' his eyes are bewildering, '*from her?*'

She makes a face. 'What...?'

'What I think he means to say,' he says and turns to Maraen, '-- oh for peat sakes, she is not a servant of evil!'

'You watch your tongue boy.' Maraen threatens and looks at the bowmen. 'Shoot her. She is evil!'

Evelyn's eyes widen. She looks to the arrows cocking. 'This can't be happening,' Evelyn says, taking a step back.

Maraen taunts her. 'What did *she* tell you...?'

Before she answers an arrow lands near her feet – she falls backwards.

'Wait.' Cander yells, throwing a hand up for the archers to see. He approaches Evelyn carefully and leans down to whisper something beyond Maraen's hearing. 'I know you're not evil, but you have to prove this.'

'Careful now,' Maraen says with some more distance. 'She could be the very thing who took our brothers.'

There is a look in Evelyn's eyes, a fire fills her now and she gets up to approach Maraen.

'You can't come in.' He says lifting a palm, and before he could taunt, Evelyn's words cut him down.

'If you don't believe me... go look for yourself -- before the entrance to the twins. I dropped my spell book and used up the last of my Burley.' She looks up and steps back to speak to those who are pointing arrows. 'Now why would a serpent of this evil ever need such a thing as Burley when you suppose I have so much power? I only know four spells, and I've had it up to here with the judgement and lies! I'm really hungry and I'm freaking out -- I just want some rest. So please, if you don't believe me, then go look yourself.'

Maraen bites his lip in hesitations and then looks Evelyn over. He places a hand to his face in thought.

'I believe her.' Cander said and steps beside her.

Maraen roll his eyes. 'My friend,' Maraen approaches Cander and places a palm on his shoulder, '...and I thought you were one of us.'

'I am,' he says, taking the man's palm off his shoulder. 'I just don't fall under prejudice so quickly, like you.'

221

Maraen points at her. 'And how do you suppose we trust her? And know she isn't thy witted one, disguised in this... pretty eye... perfect form? That calls herself, *Evelyn*.'

'I am here to seek information from the Royal Bibliotheca in Esmehdar about my separated family. I am in search of answers, clues to finding them and to seek further training in the field of Cloradis.' –More lies, kind of. There are looks of discouragement from Maraen because of her expertise.

He mocks her, *'right.'*

'We leave this to the general. He will know what to do.' Cander says. Maraen stares deadly at him, and Cander speaks up. 'He will want to know either way, Maraen.'

His eyes narrow. 'Fine,' he leaves them through the trap door.

'Come,' the calm lad says. 'You'll need a temporary port to pass into Caealon. They may keep you until you get one, but it requires questioning first. I'm afraid you will have to answer to the general now. Let's hope he's in a better mood then he is.'

'Right,' she replies and goes on to thank him.

He stops to turn around before entering the trap door. The shade of the wall is over him. 'Don't thank me yet,' and enters. She follows suit. There are men who scurry around. Watching her like a pack of hounds. Their eyes resemble this. She watches back, and waits...

Maraen isn't in site and Cander leaves Evelyn to enter deeper within the fort. She takes another step forwards, but a man raises his arm up, motioning her to stop.

Ugh this is humiliating... what if they find out I'm no Clairic...?

A man in a fur coat with a red eye patch approaches. His foot lands in a puddle of thick bulging mud. It flattens with one step. Her eyes wrinkle to the squash sound and she looks back up to his direct words.

'What do you seek?'

She's never felt such anger, such fear. All eyes watching with hands clenching to their weapons.

Did Tetlas not prepare me for this? She warned me of troubling times, but not like this

'I'm Evelyn.'

She wants to walk over and shake his hand, but feels the nerve which keeps her put. 'I come from the hills. It's not too far from here. It's a two days walk from here.' She wants to give up her reason, who she is and who she knows. That this was all Tetlas's fault. But before the man in charge replies, she slips some more in. 'I mentioned to your men that I don't know about these lands --'

'Save it,' Maraen steps forth. The general raises a hand to him. Maraen halts.

'Evelyn.' The general says. 'You may take what you need, but I need you out by nightfall.'

'Please,' she pleads to the man with one eye. Many men approach with their hands on their sheathed swords. One guard in a black robe takes her hands and places them in his to take her a few steps away, still facing the crowd. Slowly he takes off his hood and places a hand on her shoulder.

She notices he has long pointy ears with slit green eyes, and black hair down to his shoulders. He is a shorter man then the rest. It was odd to see, so she takes one step back and his arm stretches. She finds herself coming back to her position when the guards move closer.

She wipes her eyes before saying. 'I can't go back. Please, I can't go back out there. Not to those things. They'll have me for supper!'

The one in cloak speaks. 'This one's tragic. Should another night's rest be accepted -- she would be grateful sire.'

'No!' Maraen steps in. 'She came from the twins. She is a threat to the Queen's lands. We cannot let this evil into our lands!'

There is stillness from everyone. No one is sure what to think.

'Hmm.' The man with the eye patch thinks out loud. His fur coat is white with black specs. 'You're right Maraen, if she is one of her minions then we would not be doing our duty to protect our lands and utterly, the Queen herself.'

Maraen turns to Evelyn and finds her gloomy stare back. Maraen seems to smile. He finds glory in seeing her squander. He walks ever closer to say. *'She is not to be trusted, along with all those who walk the enchanted forest.'* He taunts on. 'This is the Queen's orders. Have you all forgotten the hansom ransom placed on the Lady of the Forest's head?' He lifts his chin and finishes by saying, 'Evelyn cannot be trusted. She must not be. *She must not go beyond these walls.'*

The general speaks taking a few steps forward. 'I shall remind you Maraen the Queen has no authority in the army. That responsibility remains to me. Seeing that I am general of this forefront, I will not allow this woman to bare the outside world any longer.'

Maraen words are shaken, 'no, please, but sire.'

'Maraen I have told you countless times, an evil does not prowl in the daylight. It does however, cower in places you'd least expect it too,' giving Evelyn an eerie look. 'Regardless, the Lady of the Forest is known to dwell and does not go searching beyond her realm.' The general looks around him one last time and gives his final attention to the one in cloaking black, 'that being said, this woman will be your responsibility; from now on you will watch and take good care of her.'

The look was clear. 'Yes sire.' The cloak one replies. 'I must ask. Will she be reported for mischievousness on her records?'

'No,' he says blatantly. 'She will not be marked. I will write up her temporary port. She will not be given grief along the path into Caealon.' The general turns to smile at the girl and says. 'Forgive Maraen, his words are harsh and he's always in pursuit, but I assure you, I have seen his heart. The man only seeks truth in an already clouded world.'

'I understand.' She replies. 'And thank you.'

The general opens his arms wide, 'your welcome.' And with a swish, he leaves.

The black cloak turns to Evelyn, placing his hood back up and his ears poke through holes in his roof. 'Would you like to join me at a table? You must be famished.'

Men bicker around; there Cander stood silent but its Maraen who gave Evelyn an uncomfortable wink as she passes with the one in black. Maraen joins the others in their chirp.

She thanks Cander with reading lips as she turns back to her saviour and replies. 'That would be nice. I am hungry.'

The inner sanctum of the fort is rather inviting, and much larger than expected. Cabins are seen far off in the distance, which she assumes are their living standards. She turns her attention to an inn that they approach. Once inside, there are men all around chattering about and chewing down a feast. To the far back is a fireplace. There are many tables in the middle, not set. Each with four chairs, and at the very front, a bar runs situated. The cloak one finds a seat at one of the many chairs accompanying the bar. There are only two windows, fashioned oval in shape, one on either side of the room. It's rather dark from the lack of light.

Evelyn takes off her backpack, having a bit of struggle but manages to drop it quietly on the floor.

She sits down beside him and exhales slowly. The floors are dirty and dark, but the hearts of these men seem different, they're laughing with groups and having themselves a good time -- something twisted of a situation from the passing of gate.

Evelyn tries not to stare at her saviour's ears through his hood. But what she does notice is a red band located on his arm. She looks around to see all the others wearing them also. It seems the same colour that was hanging from the fort towers.

He can see her fear. He could practically smell it when she entered the fort.

'Don't be frightened.' He says.

She looks at him. He's a cleaner fellow than the very first man she had met. Now that she looks around, everyone else has a cleaner shave and face. Perhaps Cander's just having a rough day?

'I'm fine,' is her reply.

'That's one old robe you got there.' He says.

'How do you know?' She responds, looking away from his black attire to her white.

'The make-up, it's before the first treaty. I'm sure of it.'

'Ah,' she says, unsure of this treaty, figuring it must be from some time ago.

A man approaches with two wooden cups filled with liquid and places them in front of his guests. She stares into it as if examining it.

'Thank you... I think.' She says to the barman.

The barman nods. He wears brown overalls and he walked kind of heavy, like his boots were made of stone.

'She's not from around here.' The cloak one finally says to him.

'Then water will do.' He says, retrieving her cup and leaves.

'So what brings you here to these lands, this seems quite the travel from afar, am I right?'

'Yes. Although I search for knowledge of my family in Caealon, so that's why I'm headed there.'

225

'Hmm, you know, we're technically already inside its borders.'

'Right,' she smiles at the table.

The bartender places another cup in front of her. 'What will we be having on this fine evening chap and Miss?' He asks.

The cloak man puts his hands to his lips. 'Labbrus and greens will do.'

Labbrus sounds neat. I bet it's some tasty protein

'Same for me, please.' She says to the bartender and takes a swig of her water.

The bar man gave her a short look and found nothing but staring eyes from the both of them. He clears his throat. 'Alright, I'll see what I can do.'

Her saviour's eyes follow the same look of the girl's to a lantern on counter. 'Did you have a ride, before you were ambushed?'

He can see her stare is gloomy, as if she's in a far away land.

'A ride?' she looks back up.

There's a loud chopping noise from the back of the house. She takes her eyes to its direction.

He stares, 'a steed?'

'No. But I should get one.'

He scratches his face. 'How far is your home?'

'Two days. It's been one heck of a trek.'

'I see. Then I shall see to it that your quarters are set up.'

'Wait.' She touches his arm, 'right now?'

'It's no bother.' He laughs lightly. 'I won't be long.' He leaves.

Evelyn got this feeling run over her entire body. She does a bit of a shiver. A feeling that tells her she doesn't have to pretend any longer. Who cares any longer for worrying? It reminded her that she's at the very edge of discovery being at the arrival of the Boarder Land. For crying out loud, if anything she feels she's done it -- survived the most terrible thing this world could probably throw her way. Ever since meditation, Evelyn's entire confidence has been soaring, and it's growing. Right now, she feels the focus and the effects are paying off. The world feels much of nothing she knows of. Tetlas was right. Of course, this can change, depending on her thoughts – so Tetlas says. But does Evelyn really believe thoughts are creating her reality?

She thinks about it on a deeper level. If life really wanted to take her down today, it sure had its chance. That doesn't mean it couldn't have. She never imagined such things in her meditation, so why did the giant ogre show up today? These questions are under observation.

Tetlas told her she could follow her compass. Today her feelings told her she'd make it through the Twin Peaks, and she did, even when travesty struck. Certainly she wasn't focusing on her vision when she embarked. Perhaps the vision doesn't have to be held in account twenty-four seven. Thank god for that.

Evelyn has more thoughts on this.

Wait one second, Tetlas said the energy I put out is the energy I get back… the reason I attracted the giant was not only emotion but also the upsetting thoughts. I remember being worried, but that I'd make it through. In other words, I was not clear with my focus. I think I put too much emphasis on my compass. I could have gotten hurt. Did Tetlas say in reference to the mirror analogy, that emotions where the deciding factor? I believe she said thoughts were superior. No, it's not like that at all. It can't be. Wait, that's it then! It's finally making sense. This would mean… I need a better grip on my thoughts and emotions; because they're there to work in unison. That's the only way the vision will work. I must get back to my vision; otherwise my fate will attract more unwanted circumstance! That's it! I can do things the hard way or the easy way. I will take the time to meditate tonight. I must admit though, I feel the way I was going about this was way too hard. I think I should get better in tune with my compass first before jumping starting this process – I'm taking on way too much too soon I think, too. I must sooth this feeling of feeling anxious to get it done. I just feel like I can't afford to be wrong again. Then again, I can't be too hard on myself. It only took a mountain troll to help me to figure this one out…

With her thoughts running -- I'll step in and start out by saying something happened that night during meditation with Tetlas. That's right. But Evelyn didn't have the heart to tell her. She feared being like her. I'm talking about the vibration that momentum builds over time and the more Evelyn can realize it, the faster she can produce a better vision. Sometimes when she's riding high with emotion, it makes her hairs stand up all over her body -- just like it had a few moments ago – just like Tetlas informed would happen.

That night on the porch, before the attack on Jonah, Evelyn's always believed to have some sort of spiritual connection and that's why she goes along with this emotional "Compass" thing.

She's finally seeing the words into motion, that of Tetlas's. It really all began with the heart of her. It really is a journey to the soul. Not the journey of that which we see with the eyes, or that which she can taste and touch; I'll put it this way; it makes life so much more surreal. The emotions in her body jump and dance, a wanting to play with the rest of life around. It feels that way. And I would know.

A few weeks ago, Evelyn had finished meditation and opened up her eyes for the second run, she saw a slightly different world then, and is awakening to something entirely new, now.

She gazes around the bar, reflecting life back to her.

A book in the form of legendary sits in her backpack. And then there is the Lady of the Forest who has adopted her this whole time. To her, that spells A.W.E.S.O.M.E. It takes one to get to know one, doesn't it?

More vibration move up her body. A feeling that makes her feel like everything is going to be ok. It would sound crazy to explain this out loud to someone, but the feeling is one of enlightenment. It is an irresistible sensation that encourages her to smile in its brilliance, catching the eye of the bartender in the making. He can't help himself from smiling back. He goes around to the kitchen in order to check on cooking.

Slowly, she's coming back to the room. She smiles again and whispers to herself under her breath.

'I think I'm ready for another adventure. It might be scary, but it's gonna be okay.'

The bartender comes over with a plate of hot meat and vegetables. He places the two plates on the table and she thanks him.

The one in black returns and sits back in his seat.

'Perfect timing,' she says, and Evelyn and him eat. They finish and he helps her with her backpack, getting her behind straps and then offered to show Evelyn to her quarters. She nodded to him and shrugged off the thought of having to pay for the food. Not once did she see anyone drop a dime, so she assumes it must be free.

Outside is warm. The sky is already more bright. The clouds are moving slowly.

'Evelyn, shall we?' He asks. His cloak swishing as he stops. His face is more shaded, hidden from the sun. It makes his eyes glare. It's almost as surreal as the image she stares at in the far distance. She smiles and looks away from her original gaze. He followed her old one like an invisible string. The only thing in clear view is a big white tower, which stands tall amongst the mountain side.

'She's beautiful, isn't she?' he asks, in regards to the monumental structure.

She nods.

I really made it

It's funny how he refers to it as a "She". I suppose some things never change, no matter how far one travels.

She looks at him, his features under his hood, and his eyes of a slight emerald. It kept everything everlasting.

'May I ask you a question?' Evelyn tries to sound more ladylike. 'Why did you help me?'

'Why do you ask?' He gestures at the question. 'Why you don't look like a foe nor did I believe the words of Maraen. Once I heard his bickering I knew you were just a traveler. He's usually wrong about these sorts of things. Now this is a curious world, but in my own opinion, very few are really as bad as he says.'

'So you took a risk. I appreciate it.'

What she really wanted to do was thank him better by telling him how amazing of an opportunity it presents her. Not only, but he and Cander may have saved her life.

'Yes, we see this look in many travelers today, the fearful one. And I don't believe I introduced myself. I am Tilsan.'

Evelyn shakes his hand. 'Oh, I almost forgot to ask.' Her hand still gripping his, 'where is the nearest town, I'm heading for Esmehdar.'

His grip releases and he points the way east, to deeper Caealon. 'You will have to follow the outposts that run; it's a short ride to the nearest outpost and is one that belongs to the Rebuins. The next one that follows is Telador.'

'The Rebuins and then the next is Telador? I see.' She scratches the inside of an ear.

'Yes.' He scratches his head now, noticing her confusion. 'Caszuin is a boarder housing those of the Rebuin faction; those of mostly Celestial and Clairic folk. Each outpost is situated alongside a boarder to a given province. Those at Caszuin meet many Calon passing through their boarder, being so close to the Boarder Land.'

'And what faction do you fall under? Is it Rebuin, the one that I fall into?'

'Oddly enough, I am of the other faction, the Calon. I inherited subtle signs of the Rebuin, like my appearance, but not all.' He opens his palm to his height. 'The gift doesn't flow in my veins either. It's rare, but it can happen. I'm the only one in my family of Rebuins who must remain in the Calon faction because of this.'

'Oh... so those without the gift are Calon, how interesting.'

'Yes. You will stumble on more Calon than ever on this quest of yours, seeing that it's the majority faction of Caealon. Now, once you're at Caszuin, they will point you to the next boarder. I am sure of it.'

'But sir?' she grabs his arm and then lets go slowly.

'What is it?'

'That brown nord.' She points to a pen not too from the front gate; she noticed them while she arrived outside the pub. 'Are they for sale?'

His eyes are just, and then he speaks. 'They're not tamed yet, you see.' He opens a palm to their direction. Two brown nords look agitated; they huff and puff while a black one has a fiercer glare.

'Tilsan, I'll need one to get me where I need to go. I have --' she almost said it, 'xzena... to pay for one. I know how to ride one.' She returns her attention. 'How about that one,' she points over his shoulder. 'He looks suitable.'

Tilsan has the same gaze. 'That black one?'

He is cut off by a different voice that pokes past her. He stands ahead to see their attention. Tilsan comes to his, giving the general a nod. Evelyn is quick to follow.

The general spoke. 'If you can pay for him then he's yours for six-hundred zen, and that's a steal worth taking.' The general says. The general waits and Evelyn nods a few from thought with his single eye staring. She gets down to get her bulging backpack off and takes out the pouch of silver coins. She tosses it to him.

The general's eye swishes to the silvery in hand.

Tilsan spoke. 'But sire, he is not tamed, remember?'

'There will be time; he'll be tamed before she leaves. I will make sure of it, Tilsan.'

Tilsan nods in response.

The boss looks intrigued with his hand in the bag, a look that scares Evelyn all too easy.

Tetlas explained the way of profit before Evelyn's descent.

"The way xzena works is quite different really from Brunon's reality. It is made up of a puzzle; the finished puzzle doubles your xzena. We don't have "Pocket change", nickels or dimes like we know of in Egerd. In Caealon the poor strive off the copper ones, called xen. And silver are the highest brackets, in hundreds. We call these zen. Thankfully with Caealonians exchange system, opposed to Egerd's, only the words and sorting is different, numerically it is similar. Xen brackets are broken down like this; ten, thirty, sixty and ninety. That's it. Zen is the same, it is just with one more zero, being one-hundred, three-hundred, six-hundred and nine-hundred."

Tetlas points to a finished zen puzzle that lay on the picnic table. The pieces fit in a flat.

"I see they're thick." Evelyn says lifting the flat; it is of the silver kind. The complete puzzle sits nicely in her palm.

Tetlas continues. 'This is the basic goal to xzena; to form the jigsaw is to complete the pieces, doubling your efforts.'

'How intriguing.'

'Yes it is.'

Evelyn now runs her finger along markings found on the zen flat. 'Is this the flag of Caealon?'

'It is.' Tetlas nods.

It's hard for Evelyn to make out, but a faint formation is found. There is a Niveus Avis centred. A sword and shield can be seen in the outline behind the avis.

'It's quite something.' Evelyn says.

'So, let's get to the point of all of this. Now we know the basics of xen and zen. To break down xzena, an individual piece is classified as a fold. To resemble a fold, we place an x in front, or a z, being xfold and zfold; I think it's quite clear which corresponds to which. A complete puzzle is called a halo. Halo's double your xzena.'

231

'A halo, this is so neat. So this is what you meant by doubling up. So we have folds and halos in xzena, classified with an x or z to explain which type of fold it is, gotcha.'

'Yes, and It's about to get intriguing.' Tetlas says. 'So best pucker up. There are two ways to play the game with xzena. The market is made up of two distinctive ways, order or chaos. Order is simple; any price point that matches a fold's worth.'

'I understand order and its simplicity, go on.' Evelyn replies.

'The other is chaos. Let's say you go to the market and an item is priced at twenty xen, this is out of order. Again, items in order match the fold's worth. Anything outside of order is called chaos. So, all you need is a ten, that being to round up. The goal is to break from chaos to get to order again, but ten's are controlled and in high demand. In other words, just get used to playing chaos, since everyone does, except the few who are rich because they control the tens. That means they don't have to play tricky numbers. The rich remain in the market of order.

'So let me give you a better example of chaos. Since the price is at twenty, you'd never use a ten to pay for that, because you must also take into account, you're looking, always looking to double up. Tens are always the last piece to the puzzle piece in the xen bracket. And one-hundreds for the zen bracket. Back to xen and its chaos market; the basic idea is to save in a game that costs extra. And that's basically it.'

'But that makes thirty's the bare minimum to spend with.' Evelyn asks.

'Indeed.' Tetlas says. 'It all messes with currency and those in order can control the markets of chaos. With tens and one-hundreds being gold, it makes everything backwards. Even if you were to get your hands on a ten or a one-hundred, the things you'd have to give up for it would cost you almost as much as doubling up in that bracket... so those in chaos don't really make a fortune... It's a vicious circle for the majority of us. It was created after the Great Separation by the new era's heir.'

'I understand, but won't all the tens and hundreds go dry? If the rich continue to double up, the class in between will dry up also, and won't that make a massive gap between the rich and the poor immense?'

'Yes. A small portion has the big bucks. Again, it is a game of control and power, created by one of the last king's rule. The last time I heard, the Queen *today, being the second heir after the new era, has been trying to change this terrible system in chaos – excuse the pun.'*

Evelyn laughs. 'So what does this mean for the future of Caealon?'

'My guess is a civil war. The corruption will have to stop one day. But you should know of one thing, unless the system collapses on itself, the Queen as new rule with her heart already purer then halos can't do it all on her own.'

The general opens the pouch. He shakes it a little and then starts calculating. 'Let's makes this easy. Say four xhalo's?'

'Four?' Evelyn says with brows higher.

'A thousand four-hundred and fifty,' says the general. 'I can see you have plenty to play with here. Not that it's any of my business, but the zfolds you just passed is enough to set some for life.'

'It's a deal.' She replies.

He tosses her zfold sac back and she swaps her sacs in her backpack to toss him the xen one. She looks around her, noticing she's gotten a few looks by men.

'Don't mind them.' Tilsan says, noticing her alarm. 'The men are trustworthy.'

Evelyn nods.

The general takes a step forward. 'My men wouldn't steal from a traveler, not a lady and not when I'm in charge. You have an escort Tilsan, and one who is very savvy.'

It's hard for Evelyn to bargain, a general who has offered protection and necessities; it's already a great deal in her opinion.

The general finishes retrieving the xen. 'I'll also throw in a saddle and you can stock up before you leave, with another night preferably.' He tosses the sac when she sees.

Evelyn finds Tilsan frowning between the two and the two look at the cloak one, who says. 'If only I've had some time. I've only got two in the banks. Lucky you are.'

The general smirks at his comrade and comes back to Evelyn, who looks more delighted by the additional offer.

'Sounds good,' she says to the general.

'Good.' The general says placing his halos in pocket. 'Tilsan will escort you to your quarters now. If you want, the boys and I will be drinking at the bar tonight, you are most welcome to join us. And the nord is yours. You do know to take care of one, yes?'

'Of course,' Evelyn nods.

With a swish of the general's robe he disappears the other way.

Tilsan takes her to a many small cabins nearest the fort walls.

'Your quarter's ma'am,' he says, appearing wary of a fowl cry in the day. This makes Evelyn wonder herself if she is safe behind walls. She had looked around as well, then came back to face Tilsan.

It's quiet here in this part of town. Evelyn is intrigued by small town-houses nearest her quarter. They look warmer; it's the colour of the wood, a cedar, each with its own outhouse, a fireplace and a well nearest too. It sure spells "Cozy" and is for the higher brackets in the army, no doubt.

As they walk, she notices his face looks softer behind his hood and his complexities blemish.

'Tell me.' She says, 'how many does this fort hold?'

'It boarders the enemy to the west, it's a major gate of Caealon, the first forefront and historically the longest withstanding. Its walls reach thirty feet high in a square mile.'

'So this is the first forefront. But does it have a name?'

'The fort?' he asks and then nodded a yes to her question. He says, 'I can understand your interest. As many men find it an honour to serve the first front. Still, back home, it's known as the "Shield", meaning the shield of the Caealonian army.'

'I see.'

'Well.' He smiles kindly, 'you should get comfortable. I'll be just a holler as I should be getting back on watch.'

'My mother was wrong about this place. It's safer and more pleasant then she described it.' She says, looking about.

He watches her, unsure what to say.

'I'm also referring to where I'm sleeping... tonight.'

He scratches his ear under his hood. 'Surely you won't worry?' He clears his throat. 'The men sleep separate from a ladies house. This is one of the general's rules.' He looks happy to notify her. 'Your cabin has been empty for quite some time.'

'Oh, I'm not worried about the men... though I think I can relate to how many feel about the Army...' she eyes around, '...being away from home and all.'

'Yes.' He says. A hesitation, 'please excuse me, I should be going.'

She nods a couple wishing she could have asked where "Home" was. A feeling of loneliness approaches. Talking of home, maybe it wasn't such a good idea. She scratches at the thought, but for once, she doesn't feel like she's the only one with this emotion.

She comes into the cabin. It smells of wood. She looks around in the dark. 'No lanterns. Odd, how would anyone ever manage if it wasn't for Aura?' She calls out Tastraity and lights her way. 'Maybe they just expect me to know everything. I am a *Clairic* after all.' She grimaces in the dark.

It's the same set up upstairs as it is for down. She takes the one up, fearing if anything were to happen, she would hear footsteps first. She drops the pack, putting it down somewhere close. It feels great with it off.

A bed cot, Evelyn came to a sit on the soft bed. She lifts a heavy blanket to find a linen sheet. A mattress filled with wool and a blanket that felt of the same material. Underneath is a feather bed, with a bed warmer on the counter, next to it all. She lies on her bed. She knows it's going to be a sleepy one. She stares up seeing shades created from the source from palm. She looks over to her left, and to her surprise a blue line crawl's on the wall of small tiny bugs, much like ants move in a marching order.

'Hmm. Sort of reminds me a little of the dream I had, that night before I discovered the Book of Knowledge and its ceremonial awakening.'

Suddenly there's a howl in the distance.

She sits up quickly still staring at the same wall... waiting, listening for anymore calls. There are none. 'I'm getting this odd feeling...'

She crawls over her bed and grabs her backpack off the floor. She pulls out the book. 'What am I going to do with you?' and returns to the bed. 'Ashnivarna,' the light from the little cover grows and dies with a flicker. 'There must be a spell to make it lighter to handle. This thing must weight twenty pounds.' – Ten. I know she's dramatic.

She flips through pages. 'Here we go,' she points a finger to page. 'Hmm -- wall of ice -- defensive spell. Let's keep reading there has got to be something.'

Another loud roar from outside, but Evelyn doesn't make anything of it and so she continues on skimming. 'Doesn't seem like there's anything...'

A voice rings the fort, 'Maldoc!'

She looks up from reading. 'Are you kidding me...' she says with fright. The darkness seems to thicken. She listens for at least twelve seconds. There's movement downstairs and she calls out. 'Who's there?'

'It's me, Tilsan.'

She moves to the stairs and sees him just before the doorway carrying a lantern, blinding the darkness. She rushes back to her bedside. More roars are overheard. They sounded nearer, towards the walls.

Angst shines Tilsan voice on his way up. 'Be warned, there is struggle near the watch. Evelyn you must be on guard.' She can hear his footsteps but he stops, never arriving to the top. 'Evelyn is everything alright?' for he had noticed a sudden crash of blue light and climbs the final flight to receive a response.

She nods quicker than she's ever had and spoke much the same. 'They don't expect me to fight do they?'

'Perhaps,' he says looking around with his eyes; he peers back to her who is standing bedside with her hand on a little book. She's breathing heavily. He replies. 'We receive warning regularly, but there has been more lately, than usual.' He becomes loose. 'It's my obligation to keep you safe and let you know of them.'

'From Mongers, from mostly Mongers you mean?' She adds.

'It used to be this way, but the Maldocs have made more scenery now. They've been hoarding our poachers as food, making it harder for us to get something to eat.' He has a suspicious look. 'I'll be on watch if you need me, near the gate.'

'Don't you think their attempts will be futile?'

'I don't know,' and he turns to leave downstairs, and then hesitates and turns back. 'Oh, I almost forgot.' He pulls out a folded sheet of paper and holds it out for her approach. She retrieves it.

'Keep that,' he points at it. 'It is your temporary port. Also, there are showers around back... if you...' he's embarrassed, 'require refreshing then feel free.'

'Thank you.' She says, and he leaves her. She wedges the paper in the book of burrows and leaves the book in a nearby dresser. She moves downstairs after this. The cries in the distance are picking up and there are shouts from men all round the Shield. Here the sun is showing brightly. She creeps around the doorway to hear more men yelling.

'The Maldocs have broken watch. They've scattered over the Brook and are making way, all men to the wall!'

Her eyes widen. She watches all the men gather to defend the walls. 'That hadn't taken long.' Evelyn says in regards to the threat.

Most Calon carry a sword and shield. Archers pass those to get to the higher ground along the front upper walls.

The cries of Maldocs are already outside post. They growl and sneer when up close, trying to protect from arrows with a wood club and shield.

'Maldocs never come out this far!' One of the soldiers is overheard saying beside a mount of soldiers at gate. A bang rings the fort walls, and a club hits the top fence, attempting to swipe an archer.

She can't find Tilsan, looking around. Another crash at the fence makes her jump back. She looks to see an archer trying to fight off a Maldoc with only arrows. The archer ducks a grasp from the Maldoc's long reach and the man springs a bat to the hedge.

'Somebody help him!' Evelyn yells out, trying to get anyone's attention and yells again to those at the gate. They don't seem to notice, being too busy with Mongers crawling over a nearby wall. Some Mongers being tossed over by the Maldoc, too.

Another archer calls from above. 'Jump!' warning the archer who required heed. The two find themselves jumping off the side planks to land near Evelyn. It's a twenty-five feet drop and luckily they landed on a large bed of hay near the nord pens. They're not naturally set up for safe-falling, good aiming I should think. The two came to a rolling stop, covered in bits of sprigs twigging out from pockets and clothes.

A crushing blow had come again, smashing the hedge where the archers were. Bringing wood and debris back. Evelyn cowers, covering her face. The Maldoc notices the girl through the hole. It's a terrifying site.

'It's the same one from before,' she says baffling. The heeding archer pushed past Evelyn to get back to defending.

'Wait!' The first archer who required heed yells out to his buddy.

She watches the two take a few step back while at a stare to the large gaping hole.

She turns around to ask them. 'Where'd it go...?'

The two archers look at one another and pull out daggers from their boots. They look sure of what's to come. Suddenly Mongers start jumping through the hole, or rather, being tossed by foe.

The archers fight, stabbing and kicking around her. A whistle in the air passes overhead, passing through the hole and colliding with the Maldoc's attempting strike. The Maldoc fell without cry by javelin.

'Traveler!' a man yells, breathing heavily from his lunging weapon. 'This is no place for you; go back where it is safer.'

Evelyn nods and runs for her cabin. All the while, chills running up and down her spine. The cries are fading, and the men are cheering. She stops in a halting slide from realization. She breathes out. 'We're winning.' But there's something else, when she turns around to a hissing sound, four Mongers find her.

'Hestife!' she cries out. A trance of Sophair traces the ground, but no rocks are found. The Mongers move slowly towards her, rocking with dirt and wind.

A being in a black cloak drops down on a Monger, digging a fresh dagger into it. The wretched one lets out a cry and dies to the final twist of dagger. The cloak kicks the second towards a cabin and the third lunges from behind. The black ducks and the beast missed the jump, just as; the cloak throws a throwing knife giving the third his precision throw, instantly killing it. Tilsan stood up, revealing himself.

A knife from darkness passes Tilsan and takes the kicked one's life. Evelyn's not sure who's knife that was, and the mystery remains as Tilsan and Evelyn watch the fourth Monger escape.

'Don't worry about that one.' Tilsan says. 'He won't last --' a shriek sounds its death.

'Gotcha,' a man's voice is heard from someplace near.

'Right,' Evelyn exhales at Tilsan. 'Thank you.

A cloak appears from around a corner and more move in the clear. When they gather, they approach Tilsan.

'My lord,' a woman spoke firstly. 'That should be the last of them.'

'Good.' Tilsan replies. 'The rest of you take to the back. They attack because they're hungry. So make sure no more is lingering.'

She disappears with the others and Tilsan turns back to Evelyn to say. 'Now, get inside,' with a jerk of his head in the cabins direction and he disappears before she could slip another word.

Inside, Evelyn comes to her bed. Knowing if anything is to happen, she'll be ready. There the book of burrows lay where she last left it. She pulls it out from the dresser and stares at the power it beholds, as she watches it, a feeling stirs in her every being. She remembers that feeling. An image of gold trickling dust; it all reminds her of its power. What more could it produce? It scares her and to think.

No

She resists its touch turning a look away.

She vows not to let anyone use its grace, not unless for a positive reason. The power is a mystery far beyond what she may ever known – too dangerous for a negative reason to get its hands on, especially when her own curiosity strikes.

The shouts die out. In the silence the curiously is getting bigger. She wants to study the Book of Knowledge. She looks around in the quiet. This tells her the daily battle against the mountain trolls must be over.

The curiosity brings her attention back to the book. A temping finger moves to the cover. She presses down on it. Light moves from underneath her finger. Doing this repeatedly from fascination, until finally she says the words and watches light bloom. Her finger opens the cover. A feeling fills her; a little afraid. Heck a little scared at this moment to go outside, after what she's been through.

'Tilsan will end his check up by the end of the night, I'm sure of this. So if I want to practice the power then I must do it now.' She flips pages and then it hits her. 'Well… I can't do it here.'

She gets up with intentions to go outside and into the forest of Caealon. After all, it's behind the wall.

She moves through the fortress with the book in burrows, fitting nicely in her robe pocket. It takes her fifteen minutes to walk the long range of the Shield. She finds the back of the fort with its entrance and its two towers. At a smaller gate, there is much less protection and fewer guards here. She asked for permission and the gate guard asked where she intends to head.

'I want to go out picking...' She says and swallows, 'you know... for remedies.' She then retrieves the burrows and takes out the paper document where she last left it, handing it over.

The man eyes narrow at the page in hand. He folds it in half and then looks back up. 'Do you normally go out picking during these hours? I don't believe now is the greatest time to go... picking, traveler.'

'But, I heard we drove them off. So how many times do they return in a day, am I right?' She asks in all sorts of change.

The man is caught by her words; he grins lightly and then smiles a gritty look. 'Very interesting, they're right you know. You are a fierce one. But we both know it's not picking you're after but a little space, *am I right?*'

'You could say that.' She responds impatiently, hoping he'll have to hand it back.

'Well then.' He says mischievously and folds the document a second time, forming a square. 'Why didn't you just say so?' with a raise of his hand, a man and a woman above turn a crank to open one of the gate doors. The land isn't far now, just a reach into that forest. Of all the wonders and secrets kept -- her mind wonders of its inner works.

'Do I get to come back?'

'No.' He says plainly. His cheeks lift and he slowly holds out the paper. He pulls back, teasing her. 'Of course you can, but you best be careful you know, otherwise you won't be coming back.'

'Right,' is all she says, taking it. She puts it in her pocket now. She doesn't intend to get eaten, not this far out. Of the risk and mastery in hand, ha! She's not planning on doing anything disastrous either.

'...And don't bring anything back with you, otherwise I'm not letting you in.'

She smiles his way.

It's like he knows me – she thinks scornfully.

'Well then,' she says with no fear in her eye, leaning in. 'I understand.' – a metaphor for the world she's walked and signed up for. They don't know this woman. And sometimes I don't think I do either. This scares me. And it should them, and if you ever met a woman like this – run.

Outside is nice, and indeed, so is the peace. With tall grass brushing her calves, she takes a look back at the fort being some ways from it.

'Let's hope I know what I am doing.' She lights her way with Tastraity, moving within the forest of Caealon. 'A little extra light will never hurt. I'm looking for a spot away from site.'

She treads south, towards The Great Watch. The tower can easily be seen through the canopy above. She notices a blue glow. So she drops her spell to witness the forest bark covered of bugs. Those that crawled up her cabin are the same that light the forest under the shade. With flying bug twinkling not too far out, it's like a walk of time. She finds a nice open area to practice where the trees cover the tower's view. 'It'll be safe here,' she looks up between the canopies noticing sunlight in view. She finds a place on the floor. A noise of water is close by. 'That must be a river.'

She sat there for awhile, listening to the sounds all around her, the sounds of the wild and water turning over rock. She places the book on her lap; its little covers read back those words her mother once read before she began her bedtime story.

With no past, well... no real one I should say. It's hard to find who she is. So, who is she? I guess that's why we're both reading to find out.

The secret words are whispered, and the blue light seems fitting with the already dim atmosphere. A look around every now and again, fearing the things that move. She begins reading. With her finger trailing, she finds those different languages.

So where to begin?

She sits up against a tree and takes a deep breath out. 'Let's focus on what we came for... whatever that was,' and flips more pages. 'Hmm,' stopping on a picture, 'let's see -- a spell on raising the dead? That's interesting. But it never turns out how it reads now does it? And that gate guard would never allow me back in with such a walking mess. Wait a second. It says to repeat the word of the spell backwards is to diminish the spell.' This makes her wonder, so she flips on. 'Here's something interesting. A spell to summon a Thaeran Defender,' with hands off the page, being careful not to make contact while she says any spell. The book is placed on the floor and she repeats the words from the page, 'Asshethial,' and then backwards, 'Laih-ehssa.'

Preparing for the real thing, she gets on her knees and places a palm on the book. She says, 'Asshethial.'

Parts of the forest move contracting organics together to form a body. Water hovers over grass from distances and bounds with rock and stick. It's all pretty loud, but the ripping of bark is nothing to compare. It attracts more of the area to its source. Evelyn starts to move back, way back.

Bodily parts are forming of a replica of the human anatomy. Stick and rock form the skeleton, where a layer of grass and mud create the insides and then the skin.

'W-What are you?' Evelyn asked this organic structure. She can see he's male, because he's naked. Standing thirty feet, the height of the gate of the Shield, this male takes Evelyn's breath away -- even having to take a few steps back to get a full view of him. For his shape, he's thinner than the average male. Still, it's a healthy look, and one defined all the more.

He makes a move, bending down to come closer to the girl who can only manage to stare back. She can now see his eyes are slit, and his ears are pointy too -- perhaps more Errific orientated then man. She stares intrigued by his features. 'Wait.' She says carefully, putting her hands up slowly, 'can you speak?'

He looked around from his knelt position, being careful of his surroundings.

At first, she thought what any person would, he's respecting her as if she is his master, and maybe she is. But he appears to seem lost. His head tilts to one side, just like Evelyn would whenever unfamiliar things are to come across in the book.

'Are you my protector?' She asks him.

The creation doesn't acknowledge her. It seems more focused on what it is looking at -- her. He doesn't dare touch her and he comes to a stand. Not a pebble falls, towering this little being below him.

She moves far around him watching his odd mannerism. Her creation is fascinated with his own hands, his muscle tone – like it's not his to begin with.

She frowns a little. 'You're big. And kind of... naked... how... unexpected.' His silence gives her chills. 'Alright Mr, I think this was a very *bad* idea.'

He suddenly walks, having his head down so that it doesn't hit the canopy. He's moving in the direction of the tower, away from Evelyn. The movements are loud; the sounds he makes when he steps makes Evelyn want to put her hands to her face.

She moves, following. 'Ok. Take it easy now.' His steps soon cause her to run. 'Where are you going? Because look Mr Giant, you're going to get us both in trouble. So you best slow down.'

He stops and looks down at her from his foliage.

She gets this lonely feel about him. 'I...' She says and hesitates to his look. 'I think I never should have done this.' Before she calls out his name backwards to create defeat, the giant points eastward and then motions her to move closer.

She looks around before saying. 'I don't know if this is a good idea,' but follows him anyway. They step into a large open area. All around her pieces of white stone is witnessed. More of the great tower's site is thankfully blocked by the canopy above.

She frowns to a ruin around her. A strange reminder of pillars, like there once stood an old building, now withered and old without rooftop.

The giant lowers his body till he came to a sit on a large stone, a stone separate from the building. He rests his head on his upright arm, sitting next to what appears to be a broken down tower. Its base is large, and its wreck starts midway, having a great deal to do with a mess that created an open range further from them. This old tower must have fallen from age or war. Either way, the top half has rolled down slope and crushed most in its wake.

'I-I never seen a man naked before.' She swallows to his stillness. 'And so large,' her face is going red. He looks down between his legs and looks back up. She swallows her humility, 'I mean to say y-your body.'

He turns in his position to stare someplace else. There is a slight humour in his look.

She asks. 'Did something happen here?' He is motionless, looking statue. She eyes around and frowns at him. 'Don't you speak?' She makes a face and finds herself nodding to his quiet. If it wasn't for the makeup of earth, it would be impossible to talk to him. But the green and mud makes him look so much more alien, so it's less intimidating to see him naked. He catches her staring at his parts and he smiles largely, standing up to flex his bicep.

Her eyes widen from surprise. 'Oh, okay now. That's not what I intended.' She hesitates, only to stare at his gloating stance. 'Well... you're certainly prettier then expected. I imagined you'd be... clothed for some reason. Gosh, this was such a bad idea!' She looks away.

The being sits back down and gloats a little more, showing a side smile. If it wasn't for his organics, she would have sworn his teeth are sharp, like a Monger's.

'You're silly.' She says with the heavy book, finally resting it down. She flips the pages to the Thaeran Defender spell. 'I... really am sorry.' She says and puts her palm on the knowledge to whisper the name backwards. It took twice to pronounce it correctly and once she does, the form is suddenly sucked back from where it spawned, dissipating into parts and automatically manoeuvring to the places of derivation.

Evelyn's mystics are booming a moon. The final parts of the water crash into the wet river water making for a horribly loud splash.

'Well... I was never expecting that to happen.'

She knocks on the gates with a horrible look on her face and a bundle of randomly picked grasses and colourful weeds. The door soon cranks open. She moves in. Her robe twirls from a quick breeze.

'Well look whose back, and you brought something back with you. How nice...' The gatekeeper says. She hands the bundle abruptly to him and he laughs out loud, not sure what to do with them.

At her cabin, the book is placed in her backpack and she slid it under bed. Her heart beats fast. She looks at the bed as if it is tainted. All she does is shake her head and stare for a moment. Then she decides to take a nap. When she awoke to a frightful dream, she opens her eyes and it still paces her mind – all that has happened today. She lies back down and breathes out slowly. Her stomach rumbles, 'you know what, these things can bugger off. A girl's gotta eat.'

She meditates firstly out back in the warm day. The weather is similar to Maesemer's, it's a dry spell. When she finishes sitting in her emotions -- finding a calming rhythm in her soul now, she looks up with the sun sitting on the edges. In a few hours it'll be down.

It didn't take her long to enter the pub either, in her white robe again. She can see how they would only prefer two windows on each side. With them open now, one circulates air while the other releases the heat of the day.

Her hair's a little damp and she found a seat at the bar.

'Hi there, anything to drink?' the same bartender from earlier today, greets.

'Yes and honestly, any meal will do. I'm starving from my late nap.'

'Coming right up,' he says, knowing when to shut up.

There are large wooden barrels and boxes in stacks behind the counter. Men laugh and talk amongst each other. All around the room, they seem in hype.

'What's all the commotion about?' She asks the bartender.

'Life in the army, that's what.' He says and leaves her sides. She notices the drinks lined up across the bar, a drink that men simply walk up and grab. She points at them, asking a man sitting beside her. 'Are these all free?'

'Will it be drought or smoth?' He answers. His voice is rather soft and his face has a cleaner scruff, along with long straight black hair.

Evelyn looks at the drinks around her trying to judge the differences by the liquids colour. 'Surprise me?'

'Looks to be smoth then,' the stranger says and places a large wood mug before her. He watches her and she finally decides to take a sip.

He asks. 'Surprised?'

'Ugh very,' she coughs. She moves her eyes around the room nervously. A similar reminder of what it was like on her second day of school, when yesterday's adrenaline has worn off and now she's left with the clammy hands and a feeling that's ever self conscious.

The bartender behind back can be heard clanging to boxes with a steel barbell, lifting lids and pulling out proteins. He begins chopping and then places slabs of meat on a hot grill. When he returns she asks him. 'Would you happen to have any more of those greens? I have a burning stomach for them.'

'I'll have to go check around back.' He replies, before he does so, he reaches a shaking hand. 'Oh, and my name's Bald.'

She shakes it. 'Evelyn.' She says and nods to his respect. The man sitting beside her scratches his scruff, there's something on his mind, for he found her amusing for some reason.

Evelyn scratches the inside of her ear and turns away.

Bald comes back with a plate of chopped greens and diced vegetables. He places the plate of mix before her. Evelyn thinks she can make out bits of similar vegetables, but others are unknown.

Bald scoffs his words. 'I guess it's true what they say about ye Rebuins, heavy lovers for their greens, eh?'

She nods. 'Well of course we do, why don't you? I mean, you have a whole brilliant garden outside.'

Bald laughs. 'Ah yes, but only a Rebuin asks.'

She nods again, looking around the room carefully, and found Tilsan in the corner eating alone. His hood is down. She looks away.

'Ye Tilsan?' he points with his chin to the cloak one. 'Good man, isn't he?'

'*Yes,*' she says sharply.

He giggles. 'I've heard you think he's a Celestial?'

'Well, because,' she puts her hood up signifying this. 'You know...' she's careful with her choice of words, 'the hood and all.'

'Ah. Normally a Celestial is witnessed through qualification of rank, the symbol of a Celestial, like a Clairic has that.' He points to a single silver line on her robe that she never knew existed. 'You really aren't from around here, huh?'

'Nope,' she scratches the silver line and puts her hood back down.

Bald goes on. 'Just means traveler, or beginner, a rank one, of however many you go up to.' He looks deep into her eyes. 'Look Missy, you must be careful treading out there. If you see a cloak, don't be so quick to assume friendly. These boarders hoard many things, and not all are friendly.'

The man sitting beside had been listening in, because he scoffs his words. 'There not all as scary like he says.'

Bald remarks, 'ah, glad you could join us. When's the last time you got caught up with anything yourself, eh?'

Evelyn leans back, wanting to lean away, but found both to be terrifying. She senses some remorse in Bald's tone and before the man beside her answers; he leans in and offers a shaking hand to her. 'I'm Cloud.'

'Nice to meet you,' she smiles, shaking it. His nails are clean, not like everyone else's. Even she finds it hard to keep hers clean like she likes them to be, but this man manages. They're trimmed differently then hers also, cut right across instead of round.

He turns his attention to Bald instead. '…And the last time I scouted, it was I who tracked an Errific and led the riders to it.'

Bald revolts, 'that was a novice. The old are full of runaways.'

Evelyn's not so sure if Cloud and Bald are friends, or what. 'What's the old?' She asks them.

'The old passage,' Cloud says who seems taken back by her unknowingness. 'You mean you don't know of the old passage? Girl, I don't know where you came from but it can't be anywhere close to around here.'

'That's because she's not from around.' The bartender concludes.

'Then where did you come from?' Cloud asks her, mystified.

Evelyn is thoughtful and then chooses her words carefully. 'From afar, I used to live in a small town.'

'Ah, an outsider, well, I welcome you to the Shield.'

'She's already been welcomed.' Bald says, waving a drying cloth at him, as if to shoo away a fly. 'It's not like she's just arrived out of thin air and then *poof, she's here.*'

'Poof,' he replies unbendingly. 'Well, I've seen a few of those in my time, if you know what I mean.' He nudges Evelyn and laughs to his own joke. He found Evelyn looking confused and Bald unimpressed by his referral to an Errific's power. '*Or,*' Cloud goes on to conclude. 'It could have been nobody *just* told me.'

Bald spoke under breath, probably to do with no one ever telling Cloud things. Regardless, Bald clears his throat. 'You know, we were having a perfectly good conversation before you snuck on in.'

'Well that's my job, remember?' Cloud says and turns to Evelyn. 'That's my job -- what we scouts do. We sneak.'

Bald turns away to clean a mug and spoke as if to the remnants, 'and what do scouts do… exactly?' He turns to Evelyn before Cloud had his fighting chance, 'nothing.'

Cloud leans back, crossing his arms. 'Well they certainly don't just stand and clean like you do.'

Evelyn doesn't say anything, eyeing back and forth between the two. Cloud finally scratches his ear and leaves his attention to the one in white – well, dirty white. 'We scout, and all scouts know well the area and any hidden pathways.'

Bald puts down the cup. 'Oh for peat sakes, you lord the lands for any sign of danger, that's about it. It's not some save and rescue mission.'

Evelyn giggles.

'Well, that's brave of you, because we have riders.' He remarks with brilliance. He turns his attention to her again, 'ever heard the expression, "Don't kill the messenger?"'

'Oh here we go…' Bald says, knowing what's coming next.

Anyone else find Cloud attractive?

'I've heard of it, why?'

Bald cut in. 'Well in his case, they message and run.'

Cloud is least empathetic, 'excuse me? Please.' And turns to her next, 'what we do is warn the Shield with a team of scouts, by signal. We've been using brush, waving it and such. Last time we used fire…' He makes a face, 'caught too much attention.'

Evelyn matches his face and found a touchy subject. 'So… why do the two of you get along again?'

'We do.' Bald says, catching her sarcasm early on. He stares at Cloud a little. 'Only when we feel like it,' the expression in Bald's manner lightens up. 'Besides, Cloud and I've seen much --'

Cloud vents. 'Just don't let anything he says hasten your demise. Trust in your own instincts.'

For some reason Evelyn thought of Tetlas when he said this. It makes her come back to her compass. She rolls her eyes next.

I think for this one damn night… ugh, forget it. I'm tired – just for one day, leave me alone

She nods back agreeably to the man's words as she thought this.

Bald looks away to rub another mug, talking to the insides, 'yes, yes, I do have a bit of a mouth, but ye Tilsan,' he said to Evelyn. 'Now he's a fighter.'

Cloud couldn't help but agree. 'Yeah, but he's a trained rogue and if I too had his tools I could deal a blow or two, just saying.'

'Oh my deer boy,' Bald replies reluctantly all but to turn happily the girl's way. 'Quick blows, that's a rogue's true deal.' With his finger he moves it over his chest and then his neck, 'deadly dealing darlin', to the arteries you see. We all know damn right what he can do. But in the regiment, it's not all skill, it also takes heart. Otherwise, what are we fighting for?'

'*Right,*' Cloud replies. His next piece got Bald's attention. 'But then that makes me special too.' He gets a funny look from her also. 'What... just saying.'

'You see what I'm dealing with, do you?'

Evelyn laughs between them.

Bald's condescending, '...my grand mate you are so well and special that I hardly know what to do with you have of the time.'

'Thank you!' Cloud shouts out and then a howl afterwards, putting his cup down harshly. It made Evelyn turn in her seat to hear only the fire crackle, well, *you see*, the pub turned solely Cloud's way. There are many faces frowning and even one who rolls his eyes in the back of his head. Evelyn looks back to see Cloud a little sunken in his chair.

A loud crack on the grill broke the silence.

'Oh my smoth, hold on Mieria!' Bald cries and runs to the back in a jiffy. Well, he stomps is more like it. Smoke rises and a few swears in Reobigheon is heard. When finished, he returns.

'Eh, it's all good.' He says Irish-like, or pirate-like. I dunno, but it's funny to Evelyn. She looks down at her plate; the burnt smell still lingered over the pub, like a bat hovering in the skies. Do bats hover?

He points down at her plate. 'Kind of forgot about that.' He says. It was turned on the medium side as to hide the backside which is black, where a pointy herb rests on this better half. Bald assures with an open palm. '...It's still good.'

Cloud nears a whisper. 'I wouldn't trust it,' and gets a bat from Bald's drying cloth.

'Don't listen to him, even well in doubt, I can still salvage.' He says, crossing his fingers and waits.

Evelyn frowns childishly back and puts her knife and fork to it and it cut gently through until it hit the backside. The fork slips and squeals onto the plate. Cloud made a wincing noise and the whole pub looks her way. She forces a cut through and quickly puts a piece to mouth.

'It tastes... good.' She says at the side of her mouth. 'And kind of burnt --'

'What?' Bald concludes with a pinching eye.

Her eyes widen and she adjusts her neck from a head tilt. It came out sounding more like a question. 'It has a great crunchy texture.'

'Ah! There, you see! What did I tell you,' he says smacking his hand on the counter and making everyone jump. Bald is smiley to the pub and turns back to her similarly. 'It's fresh spilk and just caught yesterday. So of course it's fresh!' He slaps her on the back and she almost lost the piece in mouth.

'Spilk?' Oh, *she had to ask.*

Cloud sat a little straighter. 'You know…' He says with a quick head adjustment. 'You're the oddest gal I've ever met, and I've met quite a few people in my times.'

'Do what you're good at, spying.' Bald says to him.

Evelyn smirks at Cloud and spoke in a fair bit unpredictable. 'Oh,' and reaches a hand for him to shake. 'I never introduced myself, I'm Evelyn.'

Cloud stares at the girl, finding a piece of burnt meat stuck in between her smile. Instead, he has a disgusting look Bald's way. 'You see, I told you.'

Bald ignores his judgment of her. Pitiful thing, he could say, but didn't. Evelyn drops her approach and picks at it. Oh god, she's gonna sweat. Just then a group of soldiers around the room suddenly stood up to a man in silver armour.

"Eye roll"

The general of the Shield stood beside this clever appearance. Bald is quick to inform Evelyn to do the same, to stand.

'The general,' Cloud whispers to her, 'from the tower. Don't move and stay put.'

Evelyn frowns. *Like* obviously.

Bald points at her teeth. We know! Still, he dabs vigorously at his own. She gets the message… and massages it with her tongue.

'Please.' The general of the tower says to the men around the room… and notices. 'And lady… Please sit.'

She smiles.

Oh god, why did I smile?

The room sits as commanded.

The general of The Great Watch continues. 'I've been informed that there was an unusual disturbance late this evening, in the forest by one of our evening scouts. Noble Alssek was informed which means additional riders will be passing through tonight, because of the suspicious manner.'

Evelyn follows the looks given by the general in silver and that of the Shield's. They eye nobody in particular.

The general of the Shield spoke. 'Since Vosk was informed, he thought prompt to have us unified --that they may pay us a visit. Please be ready for questioning. No one is to leave tonight. That is all.' He never once turned to look at Evelyn with his one eye or near anyone directly, only quick glances. He disappears out the door with Vosk, who has a sword sheathed and a shield with a beautiful ink of the Caealon flag, visible.

She puts her cold hands between her legs. 'This means what now?' She asks the two. They're only stares received. Waiting for them to say anything, but they don't say a thing.

Bald squint's his eyes and looks around the group, 'Alssek, the highest rank in noble affairs. She's the best.'

'A noble --' Evelyn's cut off.

Cloud declares. 'It means the best is coming to visit us. She's only the top of her class, a Celestial who trances. Most can't keep up with her wits.'

Evelyn's the only suspicious thing in here. Sure, she knows it; she knows what she's done. But does everybody else?

'Boldly riders,' Bald states, 'nobles of her majesty the Queen, a noble can overt any rank and they're the highest paid.'

'Yeah,' Cloud adjusts in spot. 'Basically, all of the warriors who were the cream of the crop are riders. Only they stay this far out, never returning to the capital. They harbour where they go. Nobody knows where they stay; probably having multiple hideouts as a camp I'd recon.'

A man comes through the doors in a long draping overcoat and joins a seat next to Cloud and says. 'Rather quiet in here tonight,' dotting looks around and found Bald's eyes. 'Did I miss a fight?'

'No, but the news is riders shall pass tonight. And you're in luck; no one is to leave till they question us about a disturbance in the forest.' Bald replies to this new comer.

The new comer looks Evelyn's way. 'Riders tonight,' he asks and turns in his chair to witness the hush at bar.

'Yes.' Evelyn says to the looking man. His face is sharp and well defined behind a huskier frame. It looked like the one who threw the javelin, but she can't be sure. They all look so much the same.

The man scratches his nose. 'Do you think it's because of the Maldocs that came?'

Bald states rather low in tone. 'Could be,' and goes on to introduce himself by shaking the man's hand.

'Travin,' the man returns the favour.

'Travin, meet Evelyn.' Bald says with an open hand to the one in scrappy-white.

Travin reaches and greets her, then picks up his mug for what he came for, a drink.

'I don't have to ask do I? Didn't you just see the generals walk in?' Bald asks.

'Oh? Was that the sires?' Travin scratches his face. 'I thought I recognized them.' And he goes on to laugh. 'You see, I just arrived to the Shield from the tower -- took me a bloody hour to get here. You are getting more transfers from the tower tonight -- so that's what all the long faces were about.' He nods in self acknowledgement. The silence grows in the room. He puts down his drink after a large gulp and asks the round. 'Do we know what this disturbance was about?'

Evelyn is sinking in her seat now, noticing their faces staring. Could they know? The quiet and the stillness that seems to be deafening only beckons more looks. She looks away and finds those small windows to stare though. It's easier. The moon shines on distances, just enough to bear witness. She shakes her head and sits up straighter, she won't sink she won't cower.

Bald suddenly puts down a clean mug that offers her a scare. She swallows. The three watch Bald rinse a cup. Next, he rubs it with his drying cloth and said. 'The general didn't seem happy, not after all that has happened with the Shield today and now this? That's two birds with one stone.'

Evelyn finishes what's left in her cup and puts it down slowly. Bald retrieves it, giving her a look.

Travin spoke. 'Then I can't help but agree with the general's worries. I heard some strange things... today.'

Evelyn's about to stand, she isn't about to get picked off like a sheep in white clothing. Not today. Suddenly, a voice from behind made her knees buckle and she sat right back down.

'Going somewhere?' Tilsan asks.

'Nope,' she sways in her chair uneasily from the awkward moment. Now she can feel the nerves.

'Elaborate.' Tilsan asks Travin, reaching for a refill over Evelyn's shoulder and takes a sip. She can feel him staring down at her, or at least his presence feels confining.

Travin breathes out deeply. 'Well,' he rubs his lip. 'I saw a cloak…' He rubs across his lip again and Evelyn does an eye roll. He continues. 'Not too long from now.'

'What colour?' Cloud asks in a softer manner.

Travin was surprised to see the man speak, for he was silent for all this time – so he knows.

'White,' he replies.

'I see.' Tilsan says and turns to sit beside Evelyn, on her open right. So she turns to look at him. There's a gloomy stare from him.

'Where did you go? You disappeared some time ago.' Tilsan asks her, surprising everyone, but as she stared into his eyes, she knew, there was no fooling him or anyone else.

'I-I… might have used Aura?' She replies, looking cautious.

'Might have?' Travin spoke louder. Not having to look over Cloud's shoulder to see the girl's worrisome matter.

Cloud leans back scratching the back of his head. There's a funny look on his face. He asks. '…For what reason?'

Her face is flush red, 'to practice… it's in my blood, remember?'

'So that's what all the noise was about?' Cloud asks in a high pitch tone.

'Who said anything about noise?' Bald asks the bewildering one.

Cloud points a thumb over his shoulder. 'I just overheard the group behind us saying something about it.'

They all turn in the direction.

Tilsan turns back to her. 'So you thought of all nights, this would be best to do this?'

She shrugs very slowly.

'Besides this,' Travin says. 'What scared me at the time wasn't the noise; Cloradis doesn't make that kind of noise, now does it boys?'

The men are in agreement.

Evelyn puts her hands to her face in more humiliation. She spoke behind them. 'I might have lied when I said I was a Clairic.'

Tilsan speaks. 'It's my fault; I was supposed to be watching her.'

'What kind of Aura were you doing out there...?' Cloud asks but nobody seems to notice.

'Ok. I'll tell the general of this incident.' Travin is overheard.

'No.' Tilsan replies. 'He'll just put her into the dungeons. Besides, she's my responsibility now; do you really think she's capable of... of harm?'

They all look at her. She looks back at their faces and spoke. 'I might have accidentally summoned a giant.'

A-All of a sudden, the men start to blur out laughing. She made a few uncontrollable faces and found the whole bar also join in. She sinks in her chair and looks up at Bald, he has a loud laughter going on, trying hard to hold himself up with his hands against the counter. Cloud too squeals and it only made things worse. She sat up a little straighter and saw the bar wiping their eyes and cheering a few toasts to her, for the good laugh.

Cloud starts speaking through the humour. 'Do you remember that time --'

'How couldn't we?!' Bald taps his hand on the counter, still losing it.

Evelyn frowns and decides to participate with.

Bald goes on, barely able to hold himself. 'It took four Errifics to cast that giant and the three frontiers watched as the riders fought them off, one by one.'

'Okay, okay boys.' Travin starts out by saying. He leans in to whisper now that the whole bar is awakened. 'I was lucky; I think I was the only one that heard, because I am *that* scout general Vosk spoke of.'

The four of them fall into a deep hush, listening nervously for his next choice of words. Cloud even leaned away dangerously from the man.

Travin spoke in a happier manner. 'You all can make jokes on the matter.' He sits back in release. 'Now that I know it's nothing to worry about. I won't tell Vosk, either.' Evelyn felt a huge relief come over her. He continues. 'But, do you even know what they'd do to a liar, to me now for keeping it secret, if they knew about your carelessness?'

Bald leans in on her behalf and keeps to a lower tone. 'She's just a girl; she doesn't know the half of it, let alone what riders are about. To cast a giant,' he points at her funnily and decides to let his humour fall the moment Tilsan caught an eye. Bald spoke quieter and with both elbows on the surface. 'I don't believe she could cast one, and if she could,' he looks at her and back again, 'then she is one hell of a spy for whoever she works for. But come on, even if she could, than there'd be nothing we could do to stop her.'

Just then Cloud jumps in, 'with this in question, we must take a vote.'

The other men are careful of their words, for they are reminded of who she could be – a spy for the Lady of the Forest for all they've heard. With what's been said around fort. Still, Bald believes she's a healthier character. None with this evil agenda attached to her kinder intentions.

'I knew there was something about you Missy, all good though.' Cloud says, noticing no one cares again.

'What will the four of you decide?' Tilsan asks them, leaving Evelyn out of question.

'Well I just won't say anything.' Tilsan says.

Bald nods and Cloud spoke more calmly. Cloud finally got the group's attention.

'I would suggest moving her to a new location, quickly, perhaps the hospital beds. Just in case the riders steal her in the night. We don't know who else seen. Either way, it's a waste of the riders' time. We all know the riders won't forgive after being fooled.' He looks at her naively, 'we trust you Evelyn, but it's our heads on the line if word gets out, so let's hurry you to someplace quiet.'

'Finally it's something worth mentioning,' Bald remarks.

Tilsan's hand is placed on Travin's shoulder, 'what will it be lad?'

The group waits.

Travin eyes widen, the rest fill with empathy and he slumps in his chair, 'that's what happens when you guys get a new captain. We hear Orian is as solid as Vosk. I hear plenty has changed since Vandal's quart marshal. Still, I doubt not as strict.'

'So is that a yes?' Evelyn asks the round. She was about to ask about Vandal instead, but thought her first question better suites.

The group nods her question.

Bald speaks. 'Well then, tonight we better drink to this,' and winks Travin's way. 'I'm just glad you aren't all as tight fisted as everybody says.'

Travin replies with glee. 'Yes, I am not quite like the others so well portrayed by most; still, I do well noticed,' and he lifts a finger undoubtedly, 'and this situation is luckily one of them.'

Evelyn speaks to the table as if it has feelings. 'Thank you Travin, and I'm sorry and that goes for the lot of you. I didn't mean to bring any harm to you; I thought I could protect myself. That's all I was trying to do, what with the fear that had happened today.'

'We know.' Bald says with better intentions.

Evelyn looks back at Tilsan, and then the other men. But it's Travin who spoke. 'I think we should be safe. The transfers late this night kept most watch unnoticed. That's the only fear general Vosk had, of an enemy attack whilst the Shield was weakened by the Maldoc.'

The scout speaks for her. 'Well, I'm surprised the search was even called. Errifics don't normally walk around busting a 'bout, if I don't say so --'

Bald interrupts. 'Then keep it to --' and Cloud is as quick to intercept.

'They're usually the quietest bunch. They'd never walk the forests so naturally with the bowmen.'

Travin only nods to Cloud's choice of words.

'Why, what's with the bowmen?' She asks.

Tilsan explains. 'Errifics believe it or not have a difficult time deflecting arrows. Swords aren't exactly going to cut it, if you know what I mean.' He winks. 'The swords are usual for the big ones while cleavers are meant for the littler ones. So we mostly supply bowmen for the real enemy. Though, we've been given a bit of a run for our shortage. Haven't we lads?'

The men agree.

'I see.' She replies.

'Well in that case, another smoth for the house!' Bald suggests happily to the round. The entire restaurant cheers and Bald's face falls, never intending for the *whole* to hear. '...Whoops.'

Travin spoke in the loud haze with the many Calon beginning to line up. 'Well, I'd love to stay for the treat, but I'm heading off now. Nice meeting you all.' It was the first smile she got from the man. The others said goodnight and he left.

There Tilsan reaches for his drink and Bald gave her a wink as he did. The pub approached to grab theirs and Evelyn remains quiet. Cloud's voice became a little louder and so had the voices around. The line begins to break and hands overreach their shoulders.

Cloud raises a toast to them all. 'At this point, let's hope the Errific get side tracked with the beasts of the mountain, instead of us. The Maldocs approach is spreading to their land I hear.'

The pub cheers back. He got a few pats on the shoulder and he almost tips his drink.

Evelyn wonders if best to stay out of conversation, yet matches Cloud's pitch anyway. 'Hopefully they reach the heart of the west before they attack ours.'

Hands cheer reaching past hers. She turns in her seat with a wild smile. She helps pass the rest out to the remaining.

'That'd be fine by me.' Bald answers her and wiping a brow. Finally happy the serving frenzy is over.

But Tilsan doesn't seem impressed by this, shaking his head in disagreement. 'No, no. No one deserves this. Maldocs are not humane enough, not for my taste.'

Evelyn sat loosely. She felt the night begin to slip. She notices Tilsan seems more at ease also, finally arriving at his seat beside her. He has a simple gaze and a look all too easy. He barely had a sip to drink, is what I mean. It makes her wonder if he is pretending as to protect himself. No one can be too sure of themselves this far out in the Boarder Lands. She cannot be too careful herself.

His hood still hides his black hair, and shades his light emerald eyes. Evelyn's eyes fall to him.

Where are his weapons hiding? If he is a rogue, it must be somewhere convenient, near his belt... or tucked away... perhaps...

'I just wanted to thank you again, really. I appreciate all you've done.' She says to him.

He only nods.

'You're pretty quiet.'

'Yes.' He replies.

'You know,' she looks behind her and back again. 'You don't have to hide behind that thing all the time.'

'Excuse me?'

'I think --'

'I don't think you really know what you're talking about.'

'Funny,' she says with a little more spunk. 'When I was younger, I used to be teased for being too skinny. I never told anyone that one -- funny how that happens.' She has a way with her next words. 'How you least expect it to come out.'

'W-What did you say to me?' He asks, looking down at her cup.

'Relax.' She says.

'I'm serious,' he chuckles.

She's diggin' a grave with this one…

She says nothing, having a cool look about her – oh, she's scared.

'You know…' She says. 'I knew a kid back in the day that was also teased. I can't imagine what life would be like for him, but mine was always not being good enough. You see, being different was tough, because I lived in a farm town and I always was told I was too scrawny for life and that I should eat more. I would do everything to prove I was something else, but it didn't matter. In the end, it always came down to me and what I taught me.'

'Yeah, and what's that?'

She faces it and says it, 'to love myself.'

He remarks with only a face.

'You're wrong.' She says to it. 'To be me was to go out of everyone's way, but not anymore. But the hardest thing of all was learning to not give a shit what others thought about. I was able to move on and set myself free.'

'That's great.' He says and toasts her with his drink. No, he's being sarcastic. 'But with that being said, being teased is not what fears me.' He finds a laugh after this. 'It's more a feeling like I don't belong to something. It's because I'm something other than.'

'That's what my friend said. It's always the same thing, fitting in. But screw that. Who are we fighting for? Were not, were just hiding, and that's what you're doing. And you're just wrong. You've forgotten who you are, but I haven't. Not that makes me a better person; it just means I care to say something because I remember.' – I don't know if everything she just said made sense, but I appreciate her fighting for herself.

'Where are you from again?'

She shuts up.

'I realize you only have nothing to prove to them and only yourself.'

'Oh?' She says back. She rubs her face now. 'Think about it.'

'I don't have to. I lived my whole life chasing my enemies.'

'Well that's good. But why are you something other then? You said it yourself. Is it because you look like them?'

He says nothing, but she saw his edgy look.

'Sorry…' She swallows.

'It's fine.'

'…But I think you have beautiful eyes. And someone who thinks otherwise is not worth your time.'

He smiles big to the choice of words, probably from a little humility as well. 'Well, that's easy for you to say.' He says. 'How'd a pretty girl like you get all the way out here on your own anyways?'

She looks away from his words to where Bald slaps on a slab of fresh meat for a consumer. The meat sizzles. He lifts a crate for his further orders, retrieving bottles of wine. It's nice with the fireplace burning in the back. It makes Evelyn look and then turn back.

Tilsan asks. 'Is sweating another one of those things you've been having trouble with?'

'Ha!' And goes on to scoff her words, 'that's probably because I haven't had the time to clean. It's been a rough two days, if you wanted to know. And yes, I do sweat when I'm nervous, but that's only when I forgot to look inwards, and then let myself go again.'

He makes a gesture with his eyebrow, but leaves it at that. I dunno, what would you say to that? She's an irregular girl, isn't she? But, that's what makes me love her.

'People have different ways of coping.'

Bald breaks in. 'You know… you're pretty young to be travelling all the way on your own, now that I think about it.'

Evelyn is unaware what to say, she is more appalled Bald overheard their conversation, so she decides to go with what she knows best. 'Well, I'm heading to Esmehdar.'

'Ah.' Bald replies. 'The great city of Esmehdar, I'm guessing you'll be getting your port there? That's why you're travelling?'

'Well, that's a start. But honestly I'm not sure what I will do.' She felt her heart sink just now. 'I am just going to do what I can do to survive, really.'

Since Evelyn's always liked farms and the country land that comes with it, she'll have this in mind -- since she heard about Alasmieria, she has hopes for someplace similar. 'I'm just looking for a new life; let's just say I'm starting anew.' Evelyn found an empty spot where Cloud used to be.

The spot reminds Tilsan. 'We should go.' He says.

She nods.

Tilsan and Evelyn say their goodbye to Bald and take their leave. On the way out, their plans are set in motion. So they stop at the cabin to retrieve her things.

The air is fresh and the breeze is cool. The guards standing post can't help but notice them passing along, or maybe it's being the only lady, with the off chute of the rogue that gives them away.

'Have everything?' He has her looking a bit nervous.

'Yeah,' she responds.

What's going to happen to me?

He takes her through a large part of the Shield to get to the hospital. It's a contrasting site with him in black and her in white, all the more with his emerald look and her sea blue eyes.

She wants to tell him of the book, the thoughts in her mind, and with no real place to go – at this point; she feels it's best to be more open and honest. If only the words could come out. With little to no plan, what will time bring? There's a lot of fear right now.

There in the distance, the lit of the great tower's peak is in the backdrop. It makes her wonder of what this world really looks like, far beyond the horizon that lay see. She crosses her fingers and hopes for her farm life, because the past few nights are making her feel more of a wreck and it's making her miss home.

He leaves her at the doorstep to the largest building in the fort. It has a gothic appeal, with pointy tips along its roof. The building is made of stone and has little glass windows. Two wood doors mark the entrance.

Evelyn turns around once at the top. 'Thank you.' She says.

'You will be safer here. Don't hesitate to ask for help, and let others know where you're leaving. It's better this way.' He says and walks down the steps to stop halfway. 'Oh and by the way, if it's noisy in the night, it'll be the riders passing through.'

'Great,' she exhales and he smiles back.

They exchange looks and Evelyn watches him easily slip into the night.

The view of the fort from here shows the small cabins she was just at, and the inn, which is not too far from it.

The Shield walls block most of the view to the outside plane. The archer towers stand high near the gates, and the forest of Caealon is proud.

She finally enters the hospital passing behind large doors. Beds are noticed, which are against the walls, at least twenty of them. A small staircase climbs to the left where a flag of Caealon is hung centre room. There is an opening in the second floor, which acts as a balcony. She makes no hesitations and heads upstairs for more privacy.

'Can I help you?' An older man asks. He holds a candleholder wherein a candle's lit.

'Yes.' She says. She notices a double star; a star within a star marked middle of his white robe. 'I was sent here to stay the night,' and she points behind her about to announce the rogue who put her up to this.

The old chap holds his hand up. 'I understand, say no more. I was only wondering if you had a place to stay, and now that you do, please follow me as I will allow you to your sleeping quarters.'

Evelyn has only seen one other Clairic before, but this Clairic is dressed with the times. The Clairic man has three silver ranks.

They pass a large sword that lay on a nearby shelve. A man sleeps in a nearby cot. The Clairic takes her down the hall to the end. 'Here we are.' The Clairic says with an open palm.

Evelyn sets her bag down as suggested and thanks the silver in ranks.

'The drawer is filled with cloth and bandage, so you may wash up. So please make yourself comfortable, and don't hesitate to ask for further assistance. I sleep downstairs in my own quarters, behind doors.'

'Thank you.' She says. 'And I appreciate all of this hospitality,' arriving to her bed drawer. She goes on to open it to find as he says, cloths, bandages and even a night robe.

He places a hand near the candle to light up his face a little more before leaving. 'Yes, indeed. It's not all Cloradis when you can use dressings to get the job done, right?'

She looks down at her robe. 'Oh yeah… right. Of course.' When she made eye contact again, she didn't have the heart to tell him. She moves her pack close to her bed. She undresses into the sleeping robe. In the lower shelves there are towels and bed sheets.

She came to a sit on her cot and wonders of a shower, but can't seem to pull herself to it. She feels incredibly tired.

A man sits up on his bedside and stretches his arms. Evelyn only hears the sound of his breaths. 'Who's there?' She calls, but no one answers. She lights up the upper floor with Tastraity. There, closer then she had expected, a man in cot. He places a hand up to shade his face.

'Sorry.' She says. There was a bow and some arrow in a quiver on top of his dresser next to his bed.

'I didn't mean to scare.' He responds in the dim of light. 'Well in any case, I'd be betting you're only here for some rest, too.'

She can see bandages around his left shoulder. His thin body has a scratch on it, and she notices on his arm, a yellow arm band. 'I see you got yourself in some sort of scruff,' she points with her other hand, having her Tastraity under covers. 'But you're from the other watch, am I right?'

'A pretty bad scruff indeed,' he says touching his wraps. 'Yes. I'm from the northeast forefront.'

'Northeast, oh… I didn't know there was one. How many forefronts are there?'

He frowns, 'not from around here?'

'No.'

'The Great Watch is the mark of our brothers in white; its tower is hard to miss. It watches from the south-eastern front; it faces very little movement from the enemy, because of its strength; therefore it oversees those in red, the Shield. The Shield overlooks the east, of course. The Shield helps the northeast forefront known as the Brook. We wear the mark in yellow.' He points at his arm, 'the Skillet River runs eastward, behind the run of the wall. You'll see it if you've entered the brush of Caealon.'

Evelyn nods. 'I've heard of the river… at least I think so.'

'Well if you don't know already, this watch is known as the "Shield". I'm sure you've heard the term before, if not, I should let you know it's a major district and is always heavily guarded by the tower, so it always can use backup. It's the Brook that doesn't have the luxury of The Great Watch.

And so, the Brook usually gets the most hits. Besides this, the Brook has an advantage, since it rests beside the Aelon Mountains, so it only watches a small portion of the northeast wall, instead of being smack middle like this watch is, which requires heavier aid.'

'I see. What are the Aelon Mountains?'

'A row of mountains that narrows the gap to the northeast, but these aren't any mountains. It's a part of The Spine of Alasmieria, a spine broken up in three parts. The Aelon, which runs across Caealon to The Forlorn running along the back of the ancient city that once lived in majesty; the Reobighians. And last but least there's The Deadman's Locker, which goes deep into Calliskue territory and ends at their coastal line. The Spine so inspired, so much so it was the first influential break down of the map into bits, like a spine is. So, soon after another great idea was made. We call this one The Ladder.'

Evelyn looks dumb, 'The Ladder?'

The man smirks, 'ha.' Not sure how else to react to this. 'Have you heard of "The stairway to Athebasca"?'

'No,' looking quite frank. 'I'm not from around here, remember?'

'No huh?' he smiles again. 'Well, The Ladder's a pretty important piece for a traveler like you. It's a row of boarders that you'll need to cross in order to get to each province. Each comes with their own post that bares the name of that given province. The outposts are there to simply supply you with all your needs. The Ladder runs through six provinces out of eight; the most important one is Erahe. There you will find Caealon's largest city and its capital, Esmehdar. Esmehdar is literally a condensed palace with a population of over one million inhabitants, making Erahe a melting pot to be in.

'Now beyond The Ladder is the seventh province, known as the Marshlands. Don't worry; no one in their right mind ever goes there, so you won't have to learn of its correct name. Alright,' he smiles lightly. 'I'm willing to be nice and give it to you. It's Zucone. Most pass the Marshlands to get to the final province or crossover to get back to the rest of civilization. If you get over Zucone, you'll find yourself at the pretty coastal waters of Caealon. It's the last stop from the city in shipwreck; Yieryun. One giant city made of ships. The Ladder starts with the Shield, being the foot, so if you're heading Esmehdar's way, you're already on track.'

'Oh...' She says. She points to his scruff marks. 'So you never did tell me what happened to you.'

The man chuckles, 'well, I thought that was evident, what with all the talk of Maldocs today. It's been pretty much the news for the day.'

'I know.' She says slowly. 'I meant your story; how it happened. Surely it wasn't a Maldoc that did this otherwise you wouldn't have an arm, right?'

'Oh,' caught off by her bluntness. 'Well I was hunting with my platoon last night. We set out together, hunting the mountain at dusk for some blue-eyed-yellowtail. We were hoping for some arghun and spilk since they come out at that time, especially at this time of year to graze on fresh dayadun. A great location that we always hunt -- then the Maldocs came at a surprise. We got separated and forced downhill. I was pushed away from home and so I had to make way for the Shield. But there was no turning back. I could see the Brook was surely surrounded.'

'And what happened with your platoon?'

'Basically we feared for our lives, we scattered and ended up finding each other on lower ground near the forest. It was just outside the Brook. We got separated by fleeing Maldocs. It turned out my platoon were the ones who made it home safely. They were spotted by scouts and hid with them in a secret place. They waited for the riders who were luckily visiting The Great Watch, so they weren't far. They eventually arrived to take them home. Meanwhile, I was trekking the forest, all along, keeping a watch out near the wall,' he scratches the inside of an ear, 'in case riders were passing. I had to have missed the riders so I remained moving north. I saw the Shield after an hour. I moved out to the clear and came to a run. A Maldoc must have been looking for me or escaped from the forefront, either one. She came after me. I passed between a large enough gash in the wall; one I could barely squeeze through. She was really hungry, because she dug through the hole until she could get through. I ended up running outside, alongside the run, making way for the Shield. It was a rider who witnessed me. Thank goodness.'

'Who was the rider?'

'A giant man in gold armour, he looked to be about seven feet tall. He's the second rider I've seen now, and one who called himself Vaughn. As soon as he dismounted from a wouback, he sung a great sword and the

Maldoc basically ran away, fearing for its life. No one messes with a rider and the Maldoc know this.'

Boots are heard tapping and in short Travin is seen making his way across the hall towards them. He didn't seem to notice the man in bed when he stops a foot from Evelyn's end. Evelyn's palm from under blanket is placed overtop so that the light from her fingertips can breathe a little brighter.

'I know it's not the best place to sleep, I apologize.' Travin says, moving closer to her bedside.

'No, no, it's fine. If anything, it is me who should be apologizing.'

'I don't know if it will be safe here tonight, from them riders, Evelyn.' Travin says. His eyes are straight as an arrow. 'But I'm glad you're here then sleeping in the bushes or somewhere else. And for whatever reason a young girl is doing out here, is none of my concern. But it's my duty to protect my people and I consider you one of them. I'm leaving for the tower. I wish you the best of luck on your travels. As soon as I heard that you were here, I felt I should check up on you.' There's a straighter face, 'keep out of trouble.' And before he leaves, he turns around. 'Oh and I almost forgot to mention…' he goes on to tell her of The Ladder and how she can follow the paths to Esmehdar. It was said a little too fast, but the names and places he mentions had a brilliant ring to them. She thanks him and without word, Travin leaves in peace.

'Well, I'm off to sleep.' The Brook man says, not really at a care for what that was about. '…If you don't mind.'

'Oh… okay,' a little unfamiliar with the times. Her hand sinks under covers and imagines her hand dimming. There is a regain in darkness again.

She slowly gets comfortable enough to leave her bedside. She retrieves her toothbrush, paste, soap and nail cutters from bag. Beside her, a bathroom with a shower is visible in the moonlight. Eagerly, she grabs a towel from the drawer and enters with her stuff, closing the door gently behind her. 'What a day it's been. It feels like a lifetime.' She says, lighting up the room with Tastraity and then putting her things onto the sink counter.

She didn't realize how dirty her face was until she stepped in front of the mirror. Her fingers trace through a few cuts in her robe. 'Well that's not any good.' She says tiredly. She undresses and looks her body over for any scratches or bruises. There are a few spots on her ankles and arms.

After she cleans up her act, she pushes curtains back from a bathtub and enters reclosing it over. A shower head is noticed with a lever, so she turns the lever to find a chilly blast of water spurting back. She is quick to turn handle till she felt some heat. There, it begins to flow. 'Ahhhh,' she breathes heavily to the incredible warmth. Her shivers die down and her cool body warms under the shower head. It feels so damn good man with the warm water crashing off her face, tasting the crystal clear water in mouth. She gargles, tasting the freshness, later to find a drinking of its deliciousness.

The dirt in her snipped nails is cleaned out with the head to the nail cutter. After, she reaches around to grab the bar of soap where she had left it on the counter, cleaning the rest of her body with it. The bubbly essence is smooth over her skin, its oh-so-soft. She lifts her head back and uses her fingers to clean her hair, washing it down to the back of her neck.

It wasn't till after her shower can she really see the beauty. Her face was pretty dirty. The same smile flourishes and her deep blue eyes surpass her glory. She didn't even notice the scratches in the shower, oddly, they didn't seem to hurt. I suppose they weren't so deep.

A sound outside the hospital brings her back to focus. She looks out the washroom window. The window shutters from winds. She can hear men calling. 'Open the gates,' they say. 'The Riders are coming.'

She lets her light dim and a bit of a sigh release. Now brushing her hair with a comb she found behind the mirror, which opens to a hide-away shelve. She finishes and leaves the bathroom with her things. The floor creeks on her way to bed and she puts her things back. Now is the time to picture something beautiful, she feels.

Outside the window across her; the sky's a dark blue tonight. Cold, a hazy wind knocks again. She watches now, with her comfort remaining strong. It's a whole new world here; she can't help but feel secure because of it. She focuses on her emotions; they help to place her in a calmer state of being.

'Ah, this is nice. Maybe I just needed some space from all this lazy, crazy, hazy... hectic...ness.' She whispers to herself.

She climbs into bed and closes her mind and lets the night slip away -- Yeah, it feels that good. A little exhale and her eyelids shut.

The whispering winds call to her in her sleeping dream.

Evelyn slips out of her bed, still feeling warm. She moves down the hall, noticing all the beds are empty. Outside the hospital, a faint wind echoes. It's so peaceful tonight. There, the moon is lit in the backdrop. She carries down the steps. She moves in her white robes gliding behind her and arrives at the inn. Inside, it appears darker then she remembers.

Bald's voice is overheard. 'Evelyn? Well aren't I surprised to see you again?'

Her eyes swivel to Bald who stands behind bar.

'Are yea' hungry, is that why yer here?'

'Yes. Very much so,' she replies and finds a nearby seat at the bar. She couldn't help but feel silly for some reason. This new face she's just met and now feeling so much trust for him. He goes on to smile and she looks towards the flames in the fireplace. They twist and twirl over and over again. 'Do you always stay up this late?' She asks him.

'No not always. I just wanted to make sure to see you one last time before I said goodnight.' He says and leaves to head to the back of house.

'Goodnight?' She asks confusingly. He doesn't answer her. 'Bald?'

He suddenly appears at her sides. She jumps and his voice rings in her ears. 'Evelyn. You must leave tonight.'

Breathing a little heavily, she awakes. The winds are calm, and the room is cold. She sits up and waits for her eyes to adjust to the dark. For a moment, she felt like this was real. She touches her face. 'That's because this is real...' She breathes, 'how odd.'

A feeling, the same one in her dream reminds her of what she must do. She couldn't explain it if she had to, for the feeling is strong. She undresses to slip into her dirty white robe and gathers all her things, strapping on her backpack. She opens her dresser and takes the book out and places it in her pocket. There the paper is where she last left it.

She whispers under breath. 'Hopefully tonight's not as cold in the winds like before.'

The dark sky leads her through the night. She walks amongst the quiet of the fort. Not sure what to expect on her travels, nor what lies beyond. You know it'll fill her with fear every time she leaves. Even now it's chasing her through it all. It reminds her how much she's letting go; further from Tetlas and the men who have been kind enough to help her.

She keeps images of the library in mind, and all that it will bare for her. It keeps her focused on what's the task is at hand. Hopefully, this will get her through the night.

The Shield is quieter around this time. There's a bit of chatter around fort, but nothing like daybreak. Many lanterns are lit around camp, flickering to the calm. She plans on restocking food. It was part of the deal she was given. Inside the inn, an unlit fireplace leaves only darkness. She beckons Tastraity; lighting her way to the barrels and crates behind bar. There is no Bald. She looks away from where he usually would stand and lifts the crate with a steel crowbar she found next to it. She starts to fills her bag with two loafs of bread, odd shaped fruits and vegetables, and a smile to dried meat. She gets fully stocked.

Outside, a hesitant glare is given to a fiercer one; her nord appears at her approach.

'Oh, this is a bad idea.' Evelyn says with hands on her hips, how silly it feels. Though the gate to the pens is shut, the hinges don't appear barricaded and last she checked, it was locked. Evelyn wonders if someone had forgotten.

She enters the pen house but can't find the saddle near her steed's gate. Normally, it would have been hung outside the gate. A scurry through the barn -- even on the hay scatter ground and she still can't find it.

'*Oh*... how am I going to do this…?'

No sooner then, a voice beckons. 'Looking for this?'

Evelyn turns to see a familiar face holding what she needs. He speaks. 'I see you have stolen food… do you really need that much?' He can see the difference in size before she entered the inn and after, to a new size of bulge in pack. 'You have a knack for trouble, don't you?'

'It was part of your general's deal.' Evelyn says offensively, holding her hand out for the saddle. 'Please can you hand it over? I'm leaving tonight. I want to reach Esmehdar quicker. All my questions I need answered will be there. I need a place to get started and they offer all the essentials I was told.'

'Yes, you're right Missy. But why leave so soon? You should stay a little, you have friends. There's no use in rushing, it's takes a long time to get to the centre of the world.'

'No.' Evelyn is steely. 'I cannot stay. I must move, now. If I get comfortable now, there's no way I'll have the courage to go on. You don't know how hard it is to leave behind friends and loved ones.'

Cloud can't help but toy with her assertiveness. 'Alright Missy, so Bald told me you bought a nord. This one is it?' He points at the black one.

She swallows at his amusement. 'Yes, it is.' She holds out her hand again. 'I can handle it.'

He nods with patience. 'Very well then my young Celestial. If you really are leaving so soon make sure to take the forestry behind us, there will be a road leading deeper south. It'll take you over a hill and the rest will be clear from then on. Mind you, stay off the roads of the Rebuin, once you're past their boarder that is.' He leans forward. 'They can be a bit touchy concerning new stragglers and all.' In reference to her pack, 'you could feed an army with that thing.'

Evelyn sighs. 'Look Cloud, I must get moving.'

'I have the authority to let anyone outside tonight.'

She raises a brow. 'I thought you only stay to the outside world?'

'Please, not tonight, it's too darn dark. I only get out in the daylight.'

'How brave of you...'

He scoffs, enjoying the bite.

She doesn't want to ask, but regrets it anyways. 'So... will you allow me outside then?'

'Sure.' He says cheekily, 'why not.'

Evelyn hadn't remembered his full face; he always would look straight ahead. She was expecting that cloudy looking one, more than a mischievous. He seems so much more relaxed this time too.

'That's why the door is unhinged, right?' She points at the pens this time around, 'because it seems like you knew I was up to leaving, somehow.'

He winks again. 'My, clever you are. I figured you'd sneak away. After all, it's something we're both good at, no?'

'No.'

He puts his hand up. 'I've only met you once but I can read you like a house of cards.' He gloats, 'it's a gift. I bet Bald forgot to mention that.'

Evelyn says nothing and wastes no more time, entering the nord gate to get inside. The nord doesn't appear as insecure as before. Inside, she approaches from the front and gradually arrives to his sides. She gives him a firm stroke. Before she thinks of mounting, she turns back to the dawn. A bit of light can be seen above the wall. An early morning, but more light will be needed to navigate for later on. Meanwhile, Evelyn has another problem assuming Cloud's done and over with, with playing games -- Evelyn's has ridden a nord plenty of times, but it's not the question of if she can; it's more on the lines of trusting the steed.

Cloud waits at the side of the gate, knowing what should come of this.

Evelyn approaches. Cloud recoils the saddle in hand when she reaches. There is another reluctant eye from her as a warning to him. He only smiles. She gets closer to him so this Cloud can *really* hear her. 'Look, I don't have time for games.'

'Ladies first,' he says, opening a palm to the nord.

She shakes her head disappointingly and uses the side fence to climb on the nord's back, with a leap she reaches him. The nord is fair in his movements. Cloud watches as she almost loses balance, finally, he rushes over to her. His amusement still hasn't gotten the best of him.

'I had to see that happen -- I wasn't actually going to make you ride him without a saddle.' He says helping Evelyn from the nord back onto the fence.

'Thanks.' She replies weakly.

He grins at her sore sarcasm. 'Here miserable one, let me put it on for you.'

'He seems so much calmer since before yesterday.'

Cloud nods. 'The general took him for a ride. He broke him in.' He finishes and helps her onto the saddle. 'You have no idea, but out here trust is everything. That's brave of the nord to give in so quickly.'

Evelyn rubs her nose. 'What's the general, the nord whisperer or something?'

Cloud laughs. 'That's a good one. So what are you up to calling him?' with a raise of brow to her steed.

She sits up straighter. 'I'm not sure honestly. It'll come to me I'm sure.' She appears wary again. He knows it's not the naming part, but the riding. He got the reins ready and hands it to her palms.

'Thanks.' She says in the lowest of tones.

'You betcha, and stay out of trouble, ok?' He goes on to open the gate.

Evelyn can feel the nord want to spree for the open but she gave him a short tug and he remains put. 'Did Bald put you up to this?'

He looks amused to see her ask such a thing. 'He told me there was a good chance of you leaving tonight... And... you remind me of my old gal, she looks a lot like you. She doesn't have your eyes. I don't think anyone does for that matter, but she's still my girl.' He pulls something out of his pocket, a wrinkly drawing of a girl. He shows her. Evelyn has the same nose as she.

'She has that smell of the summer.'

'Did you draw this?'

'No.'

'...What's her name?'

'Katherine.'

She nods very slowly. 'I see.' It's hard to look after that.

'I'll be heading back on my shift.' He says and she hands it over, looking emotional. 'You know how to ride him?'

'Sure do.'

He playfully laughs, 'good.' And then taps the animal on the side and off they go. He watches her disappear, as she does best. One minute it's everything she wants and the next, it's gone. Something she didn't even know she had had been there. This time, she felt it. Otherwise a man would never give such grief if he hadn't already had feelings. She doesn't blame him, being so far from home. Being lonely like that can make a human do some really weird and crazy stuff. Besides... he's cute, and so she thanks him in her own tender way.

The moon blooms as it always does, shining in the dimly lit sky to guide her way. Soon, the sun will be up and a celestial will expose.

She struggles hard to stay on her nord and continues to move forward. A few pulls back and they slow to an arrival at the back gate. A new gatekeeper lets her through without word and wishes her the best on her travels.

Evelyn thanks him and the gates open to dawn.

Cloud is watching Evelyn from atop the wall, seeing her leave the fort. It doesn't take much for him to notice her troubling balancing, but all he can do is laugh – because out there, she's all on her own.

271

Evelyn knows this and she's not afraid anymore. She's got her compass and it's leading her right. A lean to the left with a snap and her steed moves as directed. She snaps the rope back, slowing him down. 'Whoa, whoa boy,' she can't help but laugh nervously. 'Oh we'll get along just fine you and me.' She pats him easily. 'Slow and steady now, slow and steady.'

- CHAPTER 12 -

Her Vision Comes to Life

The morning begins. It is young and wild; she looks for the trail that Cloud spoke of. She grips her steed tightly and pushes forward, deeper into this gothic blue shining forest, they ride. It is a realm like no any. The sound of grasshoppers, it runs wild around her, stringing emotions with the blue fantasy – those glowing bugs, and that vegetation – and memories of Mom in the fields. She wasn't sure what this had to do with Mother; surely it's the forests uniqueness that ignites this once exciting recollection.

'Gosh... this place is something else.'

Evelyn tries hard to press her emotions back. The image of Mom continues to fight. Evelyn breathes heavily, her eyes watery as it's been awhile since she's felt this, allowing it slowly in. She has to slow her steed. Evelyn's watery eyes make it difficult to see; it's always been Tetlas, still, the emotions tell her the time they spent were real.

She looks around. No dirt road of any kind. She's been riding in this direction for some time now; her steed gallops onwards. The song crickets sing enriches life. When Evelyn feels she's gone too far, a large blue light catches her eye. The light is nothing like the bugs that crawl. The light is disguised in a lingering fog.

An outpost?

The forest trunks still glittering with bugs and the blue fog shines ahead, yet the forest floor has no dirt road – doesn't sound like an outpost to me.

Could I have gone off track?

She leans forward; she first mistaken the light for more vegetation and bug behind the fog, till it becomes clear.

A shadowy figure behind a purple cloak appears ahead. He moves from the fog and comes to a stop in front of her, blocking her way on. His cat-like irises glisten. He can see she appears busy. She's looking at a massive tree house above.

'Whoa!' She yells, halting her steed. They stop three feet from the figure. He didn't move an inch. Easily she's surprised by this. She's not sure what to watch, him or the fog flowing beneath her. 'I was just heading to Caealon.' She says. He has pointy ears, and those eyes continue to glare. 'I came from the fortress, the Shield I mean, just a mile back.' Her nord breaths match her fearful ones. There is untrusting within; the feeling as if destiny is going to die tonight. She holds back any tears; if she's going to die, then it will come fast and swift. Before she could react, the figure spoke.

'What are you carrying?'

Evelyn speaks quickly, 'food and water.'

'Dismount, show me your belongings Clairic.'

'Ok… just take it easy now.' Evelyn says, slowly flopping off her steed to the earth. Uneasily, she does as she is told, holding back any emotions that stir in her midst. The fog passes her feet and she removes her backpack, taking out everything and placing belongings on the misty ground.

He gave her a shady look before he sifts through her things. The food she took from the inn, some clothes, and her bathroom stuff is sorted on the floor. The figure stands up and moves away lightly with better witness. He brushes his hand in the air and the fog moves away from them.

Evelyn notices his fingerprints are lit.

A Celestial perhaps?

He asks. 'What's in the saddle pouches?' His eyes can't be hidden. Still, darkness surrounds his face behind the shroud. His tall tip ears poke through the top. He is standing with his back to the blue shimmer, the site before she nearly ran into him.

'Nothing, it's empty,' showing him by padding the nord's sides. Her breaths are faster. 'Now look, I have papers to prove myself,' and found herself a light laugh in the making. 'And I am no threat.' She places a hand in her pocket to pull it out, but the figure raises his palm halting her action.

'No.' He says flatly. 'Empty your pockets, Clairic. I want them inside out.'

Evelyn gave him a look and then reaches in to do so. A book bounces on the earth.

'A book?' he points and he fixates. 'You should have told me you had this. And yet you say you only carry food and water for your journey?'

'I know! It's --'

'Don't dare lie to me Clairic,' he shouts. 'Fileet Vien!' his palm shot a seeking light; it crashes with a bright bang throwing the book towards her. She jumps forward and reaches the book as it becomes heavier in her hands. The masking spell is broken. Blue light flashes madly off her expanding grasp.

The figure walks a circle around her, moving closer till he's at reach.

She does everything in her power to shield it from his site. Her hands cover the Book of Alasmieria.

He takes another step forward and finds a bit of a flinching action.

'I am no fool, that's not Cloradis. Why are you trying to fool me, Celestial?'

'I... I had too. I'm just a traveler disguised from Errifics and intruders!' She slows her pace. 'It was just a disguise to keep me safer while I travel to Esmehdar city.'

He stands straighter. The girl doesn't dare stand up. He tries to get a peek at the book, noticing the large covers. He fears she may be more than just a Celestial in disguise.

'Well... I would like to see it. Hand it over.'

Her eyes glare. 'No. You can't just take it from me.'

His observation is blunt. 'You will do as I ask,' with a hand already in stretch. She slowly came to her feet from its weight and the book is handed over. His look is figurative, brushing a hand over the cover. He studies its weight and then opens the cover to witness the page of introduction. 'What is this?' He asks awkwardly. Thankfully, he doesn't come across the council and flips a few more pages to witness spells written.

'Please. It's my mothers.' She thinks about that one. 'Well, I mean to say. It was.' Her sea blue eyes are big with notion.

'A family heirloom,' he nods and held his other hand up like he had before. He then closes it and hands it back. 'Something as big as this would take a generation to fill -- you may place it back in its protection. It's your business, Celestial. It's smart to do so in these lands as you say. The Errific are trailing at night hours, keeping in protection is keen.' He then frowns. 'Though I would like to know where you've come from.'

'From outside the wall -- It was just a small house -- One not too far.'

His frown grows. 'Hand over your paper.' She finds it on the ground. It fell out of her pocket when she turned the pockets out. He takes it and reads it over. His eyes move back and forth. He looks back up and says. 'Very well, you may take your belongings. I can give you a more suitable robe so you won't fall upon this mess again. This is just the way it has to be... Oh, and welcome to Caealon. You've just entered the province of Caszuin. We are near its major city, being the second outpost to The Ladder.'

'Wait, so... Caszuin is the second outpost. But you say it's also the major city?'

'Caszuin runs few in numbers, so the outpost is its only city and also remains the only city in the province, which is the smallest of the eight provinces.'

'Yeah but, even smaller then the Marshlands?' she asks him smartly.

He finally caught on to her playfulness. 'Why it is.'

'Well I'm glad you told me.' Evelyn lightens up also. 'I thought I would have been lost. There was no sign. There was no telling, or any lights for that matter. I... I must have gotten lucky.'

He crosses his arms. 'That's because you had. This is the back entrance. Half a mile and you would have found the path to the visitor's entrance. Regardless, all should know their way when traveling in the Boarder Lands. Only the highest of rank should be out here.'

She nods to his fuss. She returns the book back in burrows. The kalec watches and then speaks, having a hand to shade the light as he steps between her things. 'You know it's illegal to have done what you have. You're lucky the Rebuin are more tolerable to these types of acts; it's only understandable for us. But not for the Calon.'

I guess a lot has changed since the days of Reobigheon's passing. Yet, he seems written with all kinds of battle scars. I can see it in his stare, with the eyes of the past. He is... mysterious, yet intimidating.

Evelyn knows he has great knowledge with the use of Aura – he certainly acts it. Thankfully, the Rebuin's heart is pure and in alliance with hers.

...It's an honour, but there is something else... about this, this being. He's passive and so beautiful. I wonder if all Rebuins walk with as much majesty as he. I remember the color of purple on that Caealon flag outside the Shield. Purple just like this Rebuin's robe -- That's it! The Rebuin, this is surely what the color resembles, next to blue which must be Calon

This makes her think of what Errifics are like. He's spot on in her imagination in comparison to the enemies once described complexities. It's as close as it gets, if not... exactly... comparable. The feeling of being next to him is fearful, for instance a snake and one that doesn't care and has patience... with an ability to talk.

Evelyn gives a survey of the area with her eyes.

The Rebuin flicks a wrist and the fog dissipates. He then grabs hold of the reins pulling her steed that looks wild again, as if the nord's taming had been shrugged off when he saw the slit irises.

Evelyn straps in her pack. She stands and comes to the kalec's side. Well I think it's safe to assume he's not a rogue, not when he's towering at six' two. No, this one is surely Celestial. She notices a symbol on his chest, a leaf in silver on his beautiful and sleek robe. In part, he reflects those of the Shield, proud... and strong and certainly walks his height. The rest is unknowing.

His hood blocks most features from her. When he observes her, it is all nearly revealing. His hair colour and facial structure is blanketed. But those eyes... yes, they cannot hide in the dark.

Her robe brushes his arm accidentally and his look finds her. She looks from perplexity. Blue lights shine above; it caught a lively attention. She wants to look away, hoping not to look too foreign to these new surroundings. It makes her look a bit stiff.

Higher above, interior homes carved from thick trees, where the littler ones have an exterior home, built by ply wood. The houses are separate form others, not joint. To her surprise, they're actually watch posts. Guards look out, with a bow in a hand. The bow-guards return inside. This must imply the bigger outpost is on the horizon. After all, Evelyn has already passed behind the wall of Caealon, allowing for a lower degree of conduct.

With lacing fingers the kalec reveals his face by pulling his hood back. Evelyn knows she can trust him. Still, there is an edgy feeling she cannot shake of an all too easy slither in her stomach.

His pointy ears are loose, pointing behind him. A unique face is revealed within the vicinity of blue. He has sharp cheek bones, but a soft round nose with a hair of gold and a mind inherently bright.

Consumed by it all, she hesitates, not sure what to think. His features perfectly smooth, great skin and those eyes... if it wasn't for those eyes, she would slip away into attraction. But they're always fiery. A stare she can't quite get a hold of. It makes her think twice about his beauty which is tangling with his haunting yellow eyes.

There is a fuel in her blood; she wants to know his thoughts on how he felt about her. Her robe brushes his and he felt ever closer... Perhaps they are in the same panel.

Shifting her attention, she focuses on these illuminated balls of blue that shine without fire. These spheres come into better view awarding a certain glow mounted atop a large pillar. The light has an underwater appeal. It's of sunrays. Evelyn catches a better glimpse. Closer, the air has a smell of fish. The top half is cropped, where leaves cover the surface. To add to its account, a sudden fish swishes inside the sphere. It pokes an emitting head out. The visibility makes it hard to bear and its tongue catches bugs that hover nearby.

What would you call this? How about a Star-frog? It surely looked it, and there's more than one shining inside the bowl.

Shining Fish-frog in a bowl...?

'Lighting the way, I see.' Evelyn says tapping the bowl. Her eyes reflect off the glass.

The escort and Evelyn pass the final watch together. The movement nearby is scarce. More pillars of Star-frog occupy a nearby stone wall. Odd engravings and a language are in its rock.

The language looks Reobighian

The Rebuin hands the nord to its owner. A word slips the escort's tongue in Reobighian.

Evelyn looks up to notice houses behind the wall but loses her concentration to a sound of a crank. A large part of the wall moves. Blended with deep engravings, a door appears like it never existed and it begins to creep open. Evelyn would have blended too, like one in the ranks if she hadn't acted so surprised.

The capital of Caszuin... The size of a small city shines brightly blue from Star-frog in all directions. The pillars are on pathways, leading into the city centre. This pathway leads straight into the wilderness of homes, homes that glitter from more Star-frog above and below. There are many stairs that mark an entrance, and a special kind in a swirl to the highest of levels.

Evelyn looks up to see balconies all connected by bridges with kalec and alke running, not walking across. They desire a site of this new comer.

Evelyn leans forward, with eyes wide open her mouth drops to something entirely else. Some of the houses, being nearest her are actually a part of a fort. But what takes her breath away is even mightier than this, trees so large mark the distance along a main stretch, much larger than those outside and ahead. Trees four times the size, such a thing must have been seeds from someplace other. And she thought those outside were great?

Evelyn steps in closer and the gate slowly closes. With only a few steps in, movement is at bay – the kalec and alke are here and there. Their eyes glare in the moonlight. The light is just cutting through a seep in the open canopy. But Evelyn's not looking at them anymore; she's shifted to a glare of their overall creations. This one big city made out of wood.

The escort takes the steed from Evelyn's weak grasp.

The Rebuins ears point up whenever an abnormal alert beckons in the deep, and so the fiery returns.

Guards stand at posts along the wall robed in purple, holding bows in purple design. They have the same encrusting as the escort, but with a bronze leaf.

The outer wall stretches in a large radius; like Tiniss does, though smaller. The trees within Caszuin reach high, stretching out their thickness. They block the sky from most light shining in. Even their trunks are Tetlas house-thick. The branches hardly move in the winds above. If the bark could talk; it would be a calming voice. Evelyn can only hope the overall Rebuin share a similar trait.

Doorways are at the base of tree bunks.

Evelyn watches the little turquoise faces; children crossing her path. The atmosphere covers all with a lukewarm tint. They laugh and giggle as they pass, it's contagious and Evelyn can't help but give one forward. The alkes of homes nod nobly to the new adjustment and carry back inside, but the little ones continue to watch, pointing at this outside-girl.

Evelyn's steed clumps on clay below which is an engraved stone. It reminds Evelyn of the symbols on Tetlas's fire pot.

The escort takes her steadily through the fort. The road is a curvy stretch, which evidently leads to more overwhelm. To the left, a pond is wide open, glowing with enchantment from swimming Star-fish. Small wooden canoes sit docked to the grassy banks. Everything is glistening off the atmosphere, yet never too much to ever make the eyes sore.

They continue to come to a turn along this pathway around large grassy banks, and leaving the way to the fort which would later lead to the home district. The escort leads her south of these mighty trees, leaving the enforcement area of the back gate.

His silence is like the moon and the stars above. His yellow irises are of knives to cut the desire, making her breath a little quicker. It is building. The more she looks at him the more he reminds of the enemy -- If only she could stop.

Where are you taking me?

A rather large tree-bunk is found. Two cloaked Rebuins guard a station. One is kalec and the other is alke. Evelyn nods slightly to the female. Although the alke pays no attention to her action, the male seems fitting, nodding to Evelyn's respects.

The escort ties Evelyn's steed to a nearby tree. 'Stay here.' He says and returns momentarily alongside a Rebuin high-ranking officer. A gold leaf is on her chest. She's a mid forties alke who holds in her right hand a blue robe and in the other a purple.

'Fitting,' Evelyn says to her.

She replies. 'We only have these kinds of robes. It was that of the Reobighians before the Great Separation. The robe is as you'd expect, very old, but still a better suit and will be approached as traditional.'

The escort spoke in Reobighian to his commanding officer. The alke nods, having long silvery white hair and steel-blue slits for irises. It's a wedding site. She turns back to Evelyn. 'But I must ask, are you sure you want to go down this path?'

'What do you mean?' She asks, looking between the two.

'You don't know?' Her escort asks carefully, mystified by this.

She shakes her head at him. In a moment of pause she looks towards the guards at the station.

The alke spoke to the silver-ranking one in tongue. He nods back afterwards and he leaves them. Evelyn looks back at the lady alke.

The alke spoke. 'It is an easier life to become a Calon. You have the appearance of one and could easily slip unnoticed. We can grant you temporary papers. This makes your travels easier to get a port for wherever you're going.'

Evelyn's not sure what to say. She is so fascinated with their eyes; it took her voice away.

'The Calon would be an easier life, Evelyn. And since you reside without a port, you are at this moment in life a free woman. You have the option of choosing a faction. And I promise, if you do so, they'd never know.'

Evelyn nods slowly. She is given time to think. Evelyn looks at her nord and then the guards again. The alke's voice brings her back. 'But if you choose Calon, I shall say, you can never use Aura in the face of anyone. Otherwise it's treason for lying.'

'But that's just... silly.'

'What is...?'

'I meant, who would ever run from who they are and to live a life in lie? I won't,' Evelyn shakes a head. 'I won't. There is no man, there is no woman, let me tell you, who will ever tell me what I am capable of. It's so silly. You may go ahead and mark me down as Rebuin because I see my heritage right here.'

The escort looks empathetic. 'Very well, I hope you know what you're in for. But I honour your courage, young one.'

Evelyn kept her head high. 'I think I'll manage,' thinking of the Book of Knowledge to give her strength and knowledge on her journey.

The alke lifts her head also, being a few feet taller than Evelyn. 'Since you are a traveler and you come without a seal, your current robe is unfit for your progression.' She notices the holes in Evelyn's outfit, even touching one before she went on. 'You must wear this,' and holds out a beautiful purple one. 'It is a standard robe that marks the symbol of the Rebuin. I will get you your new papers, and you can get dressed in one of the rooms stationed to your left.'

I didn't know Clairics require a seal... I guess Tetlas really meant what she said when she said she was away from Alasmieria for sometime...

'Ok.' She replies and gets dressed in this silky purple robe. It's loose at the hem and tighter at the chest and shoulders. She returns with her original robe over an arm.

No wonder they stand so straight... I can hardly breathe

Evelyn looks at the motionless faces of the two standing post, who rarely find interest.

'Do you like it?' The high commander asks with impression.

'Yes. It's quite...' she fiddles with the tight neckline to scratch under it, 'snug.'

The paper is handed over, having a signifying stamp and signature. The lady of wedding raises an eyebrow at the girl and simply walks away.

Evelyn found one of two side pockets to place it in. Her smiley self blooms. 'I think she likes me.' She says proudly, brushing her hands alongside her new fitting. A female guard has Evelyn looking over her shoulder.

'In today's age, how you've managed to pass through without a true identification is beyond me. The Shield is getting sloppy.' The alke guard took a single step forward and continues. 'Although you should know, your appearance blinds them, I would have not been so keen to allow you access.'

Slowly, Evelyn fully turns. 'Then why does the high ranking one help me?'

The alke turns her head in spontaneity. 'She is like them. The higher in rank; the more they're consumed in persuasion by those above us.'

'Those being the Calon?'

'Precisely,' she replies. 'And those who look like you.'

'But I am not them. As you can see, I've made my decision.'

The alke says something spiteful in Reobighian.

The kalec is alarmed by her use of tongue. 'Kalisia,' he bites.

Kalisia held her hand up to him and then turned back to the girl. 'We speak in truth. To me, you are not much different from *them*,' pointing west. 'You may say you remember who you are, but even I know better than to trust an outsider. Otherwise, you would speak in tongue. *So*, I beg to ask. What is your true nature?'

'I understand your anger,' Evelyn says. 'But I did not come here to persuade you. I don't care if you are disconnected from,' she looks for the right word to say, 'from this other faction. I know who I am, and I stand with your people.'

The alke guard shakes her head in disappointment.

The kalec raises a hand to the alke this time and spoke on the alke's behalf. 'Then you are a pure soul.'

Evelyn nods slowly.

His tone remains. 'We stand under the Branch of Life. That is the way of our people. I understand you see this world differently – even then, I can see it in your eyes – I commend you for your courage. Take it as a gift. Out there many things will show you, to teach you. I can see why the alke chose you,' in referral to the high ranking one. 'You have a pure heart and your choice represents this. Be brave, young soul. Never forget this.'

'Alke... you say?' Evelyn asks.

'Yes. It means woman.' He replies.

'I see.'

'Kytiun is correct.' The alke says with an open palm. 'I was wrong to judge you. You are a guest inside the walls of Caszuin. Though you are required to report to head officials in Esmehdar, there you will retrieve your port. There you'll truly become one of us.'

Evelyn nods to her change of heart. 'Thank you.'

The alke was impressed to see a kalec interrupt on Evelyn's part. It is a risk to stand up for an outsider, so it must mean he saw something grand. This kept Evelyn more open hearted too. She got a shiver and felt their conversation meant something more -- that a guard's candid is rare and doesn't happen on a regular biases.

Evelyn points to the Rebuin male. 'Kalec, you say?'

He nods to her question.

Evelyn repeats their words in fascination. Not soon after she came to a sit on a stump to rest the legs. She shivers in awe. Here the temples of grace surround her. To the shinning orbs of Rebuin hold, even the Rebuin attitude appears more graceful, matching their inner beauty.

It's much easier to feel in place then out, for it only took a few moments – a conversation to awaken Evelyn's emotional heart. It makes her wonder about herself. With a face of the east and the blood of the west, it remains unsure how many more likewise there'll be. One thing is for certain. If there were ever Rebuins in her high school days, they'd be the popular and beautiful looking ones.

Evelyn looks up, seeing the treetops moving in the west from a gust.

A kalec in an odd wardrobe moves around with little to no comfort for the area. He wears a white robe with a blue stripe on one shoulder and there's a purple on the other. A crest of Caealon on the left chest is visible. There are many gold and silver strips below the crest; it signifies to Evelyn some sort of master in command. Her eyes squint to his oddness, for his creations are misleading, and his wears... it only took a few thoughts and then it clicks.

Calon... or is he Rebuin? Or is he representing both factions?

If we were to play high school all over again, then he's the one who is most viable and is privileged in some way. But truly lost when it comes to admitting he needs help finding class on the first day of school. He's the one friend who will get everything... or... he already has it.

Evelyn gets a whiff of something that makes her plug her nose. It takes her attention away from the odd one and instantly to her steed. 'Ugh man...' She makes a sore face.

I forgot they do that... -- I really got to get you a name

Her memory finds the odd one again. With robes of white... and a symbol of a star she had not located till now which is centre chest. It can only mean one thing...

A Clairic!

This odd appears is summoning her, but she remains put. The Clairic disappears around corner and his voice is overheard. 'I can't find nordshoes. Would you happen to know where I can find them?'

A lady's response comes from out of the blue, which sounded of cynicism. 'Oh my, I'm so very sorry Clairic as I'm quite new to these surroundings, just try asking one of the guards. I'm sure they'd *love* to help one of her majesty's nobility.'

'I see.' He replies. 'Very well then if that's how it shall be.'

The Clairic moves in Evelyn's site, though again seemingly lost to find help. He's tall like the others, with yellow eyes and blond hair. He approaches the station. Evelyn found herself coming to a stand to make herself known... or maybe she thought to honour his rank? I tell you, I don't always know what this girl is thinking. Let it be known, she adjusts her white robe over the arm, probably having to do with being more ladylike or something.

'Ah guards.' The noble says, and then turns to Evelyn and smiles. 'Quite bold,' he ponders at her. 'I haven't seen a Clairic in these parts for quite some time.'

'She's no Clairic.' The alke interrupts, looking him down to up.

The Clairic frowns at Evelyn in correspondence to the alke's words and looks back at the guard. 'I see. Misinformed am I?'

Evelyn sits back down.

The noble couldn't help but ask to everyone's stillness. 'I haven't stumbled on an interrogation of some sort, have I?'

'No.' Evelyn says, not standing up this time. 'Just a mix up for the robe, on my travels I mean. It got me in a little bit of trouble.'

'Trouble?' The noble is quick to pronounce, making Evelyn seem uneasy. He then turns to ask the guards. 'Where is she headed, exactly?'

'Oh my,' the alke says with an odd exaggeration. 'Wouldn't you like to know? Oh my, I'm sorry, I've forgotten my place *your nobility the grand*.' -- And I thought Evelyn looked stiff?

I tell you, only the sound of crickets sing. For a moment Evelyn turns the eye where she swore she heard a croak of bullfrog.

The noble brushes his robe to speak humbly. 'What concerns me is why we have a young traveler out here. It's forbidden, and dangerous for her sake. It's written in class five that a rank two companion be with her at all times when on The Ladder.'

'Does it?' The alke asks, clearly not caring.

Kytiun held a hand up at Kalisia. He spoke to the Clairic. 'Perhaps you should hold your tongue. Reframing from your heritage and denying our respects is what's discouraging.'

Evelyn looks like she wants to hide; first about to say something but hesitates. She's faced the wrath and doesn't intend on it for seconds.

For some reason, as they argue over her, she feels evermore lost in this unknown universe. It's the way their ears flop as they use their arms in their usual manner. Right now a look back at her olden school days; it makes her feel at ease and it helps things feel, well a lot less real.

On a late school afternoon, her head is heavy and the air is stuffy. All the while, outside beams of light, but it's too bright to see the sky through such a small frame of the classroom window. A small room full of students; the stuffy and hazy ones look at the chalkboard. Only now does it remind Evelyn of the uneasy movements of the teacher's steps. Soon the school day will end with the same suffice as before, the stuffiness is drowning, it makes you want to roll over and die. The way home... *home*, Evelyn misses it -- The air, the sun, the simple walk back.

She awakes back. There they are, still bickering. Tall ears that are pointy, and my, they sure can argue over something irrelevant to her virgin-diplomatic ears. Evelyn looks away. A sun ray blooms through the canopy. It's a rather warm feeling that brings her back...

A young blond student keeps to herself. Whirling her pencil through her hair, to Evelyn it's like the whole world isn't on her shoulders.

Sometimes, Evelyn just wanted to be like that, to let go of the pressure of school life from back when. It would have been too easy if she only felt the same way as she does today.

She looks away from the ray of light, noticing the very clean robe of this noble one. His vials hanging from his belt, in them dried herbs and mushrooms.

'We'll it's nice to have met you too, brother.' The noble one replies sarcastically to his fellow kalec. Kytiun only ignores further. One could assume Kytiun has safely chosen to butt out. Ha, good for him. But it's the alke who continues to temper, having many more objections.

That's when it clicks. Evelyn would like to speak to the Clairic.

The noble bickers back to defend something on the lines of politics with a bewildered look. 'I doubt this veteran. I am only concerned that's all.'

The whole time Kytiun watches Evelyn; his eyes seemingly focus to hers now. Evelyn wasn't sure if he was looking at her, or straight through her. It appears she's not the only one drifting off into space from words of oppression. Finally, the kalec snaps out of his time-out and takes a step forward to end this old tirade of the Clairic's "Disloyalty" to his people. 'This is quite the concern Clairic of her majesty the finest. So please my noble, what would you have us do now?'

The Clairic looks surprised by the standoffish question; like it's some sort of trick. Maybe it was the tone used too… I don't know man.

'No please.' Evelyn butts in, a little unsure what the Clairic plans to do next. She gets all three's attention. 'You search for nordshoes… maybe I can help you find them, if I'm need be?'

'Nordshoes… How did you know? You sure this one isn't Clairic?' The noble asks them, and they frown to his misconception.

'He's a typical noble. Only they speak this highly of themselves.' The alke says with a roll of her eyes. Evelyn could actually look at her as relatively human. It seems the alke pulled an *Evelyn*, one might say.

Evelyn has a lighter tone to the master in command. 'Where will you be heading if you don't mind my asking?'

The tall Clairic twists to look down at her, where she remained a-sit and on the sideline of things. His robe looks shinier in the sunlight, 'Telahire on the way to Eslr, why?' There is a look in his eyes like something just escaped them. There is a sense of warning too. Evelyn doesn't care for it. If it is as he says it is, then she'll have to have his help and what better than the Queen's right hand?

'Clearly you're heading back to Esmehdar after?' A twinkle in her eye signs hopefully. This could also mean a guide to get her to the Royal Bibliotheca.

'Yes.' He replies.

'Will you be heading to Telador? One of the men from the Shield said it was on the way.'

He frowns, bringing his full attention to her. 'Well yes. I must in order to move through Tenor. That's the point of The Ladder.'

'Wait so… so is the next province over Telador? Or is it Tenor? I'm a little confused.' Evelyn asks, feeling a flush of nerves.

He finds her insecure, not having to glance her over. 'Telador is in Tenor. The great Tenor is next.' He turns to the guards with a little shock. The master has a simple look but one that told them they should be worried by her lack of knowledge. Of course they say nothing. He turned back to the girl. 'Well… along the way is as you've put it. It is where the great Celestials of Telador reside. Is this where you intend to go to further your training?'

'No…' She says a little boring. 'I honestly didn't even know where that was until you mentioned it.'

'Oh Alas, you are lost.' He says with a single twinkle in his eyes. 'Well… in any case the mighty Calons of Telahire is on the way to Eslr.'

She frowns likewise and her dwindling expression says it all.

He turns to the guards. 'She needs a map.'

They move from station to find one, when they do, they hand it over to him.

'You see traveler.' The noble says opening it – Evelyn gets up and helps him by taking hold of the other end. He retains speech. '…Firstly you have this, the wall of Caealon. And then you get Caszuin.' He points to a small dot on the map that said "Caszuin". But she is already consumed with all the other places. There are towns in the form of dots. And cities further out, having concept art for each one. She can see The Spine of Caealon and so much more. A large drawing of a ruin is centre of Alasmieria, but her focus is quickly redirected by the noble's coming voice. 'After Caszuin, then comes the woodland of Tenor. Tenor harbours two cities, Telador and Telahire. Beyond the woodlands is the third province wherein my destination resides. In this province of Eslr you will find the might of all Calon, where the mighty city of Rhion and all other Calon staples rest.' He says with pride, looking up at the Rebuin guards this time. The guards squint their eyes and he's quick to return his to the map. 'Beyond this province of Eslr lay the heart --'

'I know.' Evelyn interrupts. 'Of Caealon, the fourth province Erahe from which Caszuin and the fifth boarder from the Boarder Land lands,' her finger taps excitedly to the city on map. 'This is where the capital and major city resides, also known as the centre of the world by some.'

'*Oh*, and I missed an introduction?' He asks and playfully looks around to come back again. 'You did well.'

The alke voice is overheard. 'Centre of the world. I've never heard that one.'

Evelyn replies to her. 'I heard it at the Shield.'

'Ah,' she remarks, '*figures*.'

The noble closes the map and hands it over to Evelyn. She stuffs it inside her Clairic robe which is now under an arm.

The noble speaks to Evelyn. 'I'm here for medical supplies for a patient. I am in no rush like you. And for your information, it all appears small on map but takes a lot longer to travel then it looks. So take your time. Just know it's a month's journey to the centre of the world by nord.' He turns back to the guards and spoke in his dignified manner. 'I will trust she will receive a companion in Caszuin to guide her to her next destination.'

'Yes.' The alke says, even though her eyes are as slick as rock.

The Clairic nods. 'Very well then,' and he turns to leave.

'Wait!' Evelyn cries. 'If it's truly as you say, that I should have a companion... if it is all the same to you then why not you?'

The escort from before appears just then, noticing a noble when he sees one. He approaches and is now aware of Evelyn in her new fitting.

'Ah, you look great.' The escort says. 'It was once worn by all members of Reobigheon society.' Her cheeks lift. 'Now it's just a sign of novice.' They fall. He stood a little straighter and says. 'I'm glad all things are in order. Do be careful now on this journey of yours. Lady Aisa has you in good faith I hear.'

'She does?' She asks, she didn't realize what she had done and speaks up, 'yeah, she was very nice to me,' in assumption that lady Aisa refers to the gold ranking officer. 'And I will. Thank you.'

'You may buy what you need. You are very much welcomed in Caszuin. I hope you understand that.' Evelyn wanted to say "Cool" but um... she says "Thanks" instead. The escort takes her Clairic robe off her hands and she makes sure to retrieve her map and folds it again, slipping it in her only free pocket.

The escort finds the noble's attention and nods honourably. 'I do hope that our grandest is enjoying their stay?'

'He's a friend.' Evelyn says -- not sure if he will get along like the others did.

The two turn to look at her with much surprise and the escort spoke slowly. 'A... A friend of yours? Well then, I will leave you to your companionship.' He suddenly leaves as quickly as he came.

The Clairic frowns at her and he too departs without anymore notice.

'Wait,' she says but he kept on moving. She looks at the two remaining and they raise their brows at her. Evelyn reacts and quickly unties her steed; she couldn't help but ponder, peering back at the station.

I really am glad I've met them. This whole place is so much more then I imagined it to be. It's better

Evelyn catches up with her *companion* -- fingers crossed. She found the noble not too far out. Breathing heavily now, she comes to his sides with her reins in hand. Her steed is lagging behind.

'So, when do we plan on leaving?' She asks, adjusting her slanted pack for better.

He stops in his tracks, and the nord nearly bumps into the back of her.

'That's some petty pack you got there. I think you better buy some supplies before your travels, traveler.'

'Yes, good point…'

'Anyways,' he looks at her funnily. He peers at her fashion, which just comes off as old fashioned to him. 'I need some things for my steed and medical supply, as I was saying, for my patient.' He peers around, and Evelyn can't help but feel out of place again. 'I probably should have taken more time to be kinder instead of… well you know, you were there. They didn't like me very much, do they?'

'Very true,' Evelyn says with deep conviction.

He stops and frowns slow. It took some time, a little more. 'You really are one of them.'

She swallows.

Still, her innocence gave him a handle. He pulls out a few xfolds and places them in her hand. 'I need those nordshoes. Here, prove your innocence and talk to a different pair of Rebuin. After all, you're one of them now, right? I'll be in the main trade district to look for some myself, but I have a great feeling no one wants to deal with me. If you complete your task before I leave, then your allegiance is with me.'

She frowns.

'Oh for Alas sake, I will take you where you need to go.'

'Oh! Sweet.'

A wild frown crosses. 'Indeed… sweet.'

She remains a put with the xfolds in hand and peers around with bigger eyes.

'There's enough there, surely.' He says and readjusts. 'Oh, only come if successful. I have faith in you.' He relieves himself of the girl and her steed.

She looks around insecurely -- four thirty's in one hand and a leash in the other. Her quest is simple. The hard part was trying not to look up at all the pointy eared ones that move above on sling bridges; even on the balconies above her. It's her fascination.

She feels a rush of confidence in the idea of having to find the nordshoes. She's been pretty successful thus far on her journey; so what's a little more?

She finds wobbly ears near a station. Another similar looking pair of guards is approached. 'Oh, excuse me. Where could I buy nordshoes?' directing her question to the friendlier looking one. He looks down at her perfectly fine nordshoes on her steed.

It's the alke that surprises Evelyn. 'There are side shops just to your left, two blocks southwest where the pens lay,' she points to an open road ahead.

'Oh. Thank you.' Evelyn replies candidly. Finding her way to the road again, it takes her to a tree-bend. Like a crescent moon there is a little bit of a hidden area.

Two kalec's man the shop and she stops dead centre to peer for the item. Behind her, nords breathe heavily in a large pen. She turns to the sound of their feet flopping and decides to tie her steed to a nearby tree. She approaches the wooden moon more curiously.

'Do you guys have any nordshoes for sale?'

'Why we do.' One of the kalec cheerfully replies and his eyes are wide with anticipation. Evelyn smiles weakly, for this will have to take some time to get used to. The way they watch her, it looks.... unnatural. One of the kalec's moves down the row like a cat following, whilst the other clamps down at a wood box and asks, 'individual for twenty or a sixty for four, so how many Celestial?'

She takes her eyes off the follower. 'Oh. Four please.' She places two thirty folds on the counter and he counts.

He replies. 'Ah, you are a little short I'm afraid.'

'Oh… I am? you're right. Silly me, I thought you meant the amount of sixty for four, but you require a sixty fold for them… I must have missed that.'

'Right well, if this was the high society of order then you would've been correct; otherwise you're stealing from me. That would have been a crime. What game are you playing at?'

'Sorry,' she says slowly.

So four thirties for four, gotcha

She places four thirty's on the counter and waits for the kalec's response. The kalec smiles gladly. 'Perfect,' pulling the xfold into palm and passes her her token of success.

'Perfect. Thanks.' Evelyn says as her smiley self. 'Hey, do you know where the trade district is?'

He responds with as much cheer as possible. 'Why I do! It's dead centre, you can't miss it Celestial.' His pointy ears move again. It is an amusing site.

She and her nord move on with their proven innocence. She mounts leaving this place behind. She takes the pathway to the main strip. The road narrows and so does the street. The trees here are a little thicker and taller.

'This must be the home district.' Evelyn whispers to her steed.

It's still, and it's quiet. Soon the narrowing street comes to a sharp end that is connected by an archway leading into a new area. Blah, she enters. The same blue milky floors shine by those glowing globes atop pillars. Her eyes light up. '...And this must be the trade district.'

Chatter and quick movement is in the masses. She feels she must come to a stop for the magnificence of this district. It lies in a great circle -- A massive tree with its middle removed. The ground space occupies shops. The massive tree is actually an incredible two sided husk, in the form of two giant half-moon shapes. The hub has divots allowing for shops on its multi-levels. Sling bridges connect one side to another.

Evelyn waits at the northwest entrance in sort amazement. The frontier of space is nothing like before all this. Ah, now the claustrophobic feel is withered and gone.

Spheres glow from beneath the sling bridges, hung in baskets, creating the same unique ambience within this little world one could easily get caught up in calling home. Of all the scary things that go bump-in-the-night outside the safe haven of Caszuin, this district sure places a calm presence in anyone's heart. Robes and cloaks squeeze by with anxious faces, never wanting to exit, being a part of the great attraction.

A young pretty alke in a long purple and white dress grabs hold of Evelyn's leash.

It happens. The withering -- just when Evelyn thought it was over — all of whom Evelyn steps aside from. The perfectionist appears and "The woman she ought to be" is frozen in time. Observe away.

Normally, Evelyn would look away when she focuses on self lack. Blah, that's like saying there is magical kingdoms where money grows on trees, right? Yeah well, not always on target. The fact of the matter, she misses confidence. Staring back at a part she misses, her sapphires fade. The alke's beauty holds a power that has no reflection. And to Evelyn, were to step, where to go? Where in front of it aren't we? You know what I say, we're playing mirror, mirror, all over again…

The woman's weight and height only adds to her appeal. The alke fits her dress like the fairest.

Evelyn blinks, not sure why she romanticizes over an alke, and why at a time like this. Not knowing whether to apologize or thank the woman for taking her away from the crowd, Evelyn becomes stagnant. The alke ties Evelyn's leash to a given tree. Here, spotted nords are in lines. They're feeding on hay.

Gosh, how do we get so damn low? For looks… I wish I could say the same and not care like she, but I'm not. I'm just as terrible as she, and so damn weak. And sadly, I don't care if this book makes sense any more. I've lost myself in my own life, I'm alive but I'm alone. I wish I could go back to all the fun I had — even as I write this, the voices in my head tell me to stop, maybe that's just my editor inside trying to make everything fit and go smoothly. But life isn't that way. And I don't care.

Evelyn can't stop, and when her heart wants no more, the beating of her fantasies strike. It didn't help that the woman smelt wonderful either.

It took but a moment for Evelyn's withering to start, and the shock of its fast imbedding has already set her on a course for turmoil. No matter how hard Evelyn tries, how many times she has sobbed for her perfect image, the feeling won't change.

She looks down at her wrists, and this is what she sees – "Not good enough". She looks away from a shiver crawling down her spine, and guess who's packing their bags for a little time away? Her soul, and I'm positive it would say 'I'm out of here.' because it sees her forthcoming.

Evelyn sinks.

In fearing she's done something wrong, Evelyn apologizes to the lady. The woman's dark hair and light blue eyes have no delay of wonder, as if the world around her couldn't be any more blissful. Evelyn got the hint and rephrases. 'Thank you.'

The lady draws a smile.

Sure, Evelyn finds her beauty to be empowering, and those in Egerd may think otherwise, but this place holds no place for their loyalists.

Evelyn tries to tell her she has to use the bathroom.

The lady can't find the right words for the job, so she points to a door to a small hub in a nearby tree.

Evelyn opens the door and says. 'Oh, I see. Thank you.'

She nodded at Evelyn and disappears around the corner into the trade.

In this tree bunk only part of it is used for its size is enormous. It's dark with the smell of oak. It smells… of something else, but nothing unsettling. Evelyn closes the door behind her. The dark is lit up. This is no Aura. Better yet, little beetles crawl with a glow. Evelyn shakes her head in disbelief to the thousands upon the wood. They're smooth to the touch and never moving to it.

They inspire her to venture back out after her business is finished and she rejoins the trading crowd. With goods at her fingertips it makes her navigate here and there; she's already forgotten about her awaiting Clairic for the time being. Her eyes glisten off gems for sale. Stones of unique cuts sparkle with marvel.

'New prices for new Thundercott coats,' a kalec wearing purple at a coat station calls. He catches Evelyn's attention. She fights to cross a road to get a peek. Civilians call out to the kalec; it seems not only Evelyn had been attracted. The seller is showing off the same one for sale.

'How much?' the crowds ask.

Evelyn notices how much she really stands out, even in her robe. Their ears and eyes are just too much for her. It's alien. She takes a deep breath in. She's surrounded and bumped by the many. Her soft body twists gently. That's when she saw him on a balcony, a balcony sticking out of the grand scale of things.

A chill moves up her spine, to realize she's the only one around with circle pupils and short ears. It makes her inhale less. Time felt slow. All she can see is the oddness of their faces. Then it hit her.

Do they look at me the same way? Am I as alien to them?

She recognizes something similar just then staring up at the Clairic; watching him as she stood statue. There he remains, only...

He's sitting all alone and I don't seem to see anyone with him. Maybe I am needed more than I know?

Maybe, maybe more than you know. What? It's a worthy thought.

The shivers hit her again. Oh how good it feels to feel the rush of home again.

A ramp on one of the half-moon leads her to the upper levels. It has levels of its own and houses shops as a way of consumer convenience. On her way up, a special shop caught her attention. A sign reads; "Burley Bright".

Goods lay out on a counter. Some brown pouches have markings on them, playing as a label. One reads, "Burley frost".

Why am I so damn cynical? You know, I felt like killing myself today. Come on... I wouldn't actually do it. It's just that feeling, you know? Yeah, sad story, no wonder I write about someone one else's. But it's not like that. I'm not always this miserable; it's just the days I have to lose. Welcome to my therapy session. Ha... I shouldn't share this.

Evelyn's sea blue eyes twinkle back with modesty. 'What do these do?' She asks the alke at the counter, but the alke is too busy with other guests for her to get hold of. The shop produces a strong smell, from all the herbs lay out, caressing a majestic scent. Evelyn drops her pack from her shoulders to retrieve xzena, looking to make contact with the sellers' eyes. The alke finally smiles back.

Evelyn slides her fingers around something new with confidence. It's a pouch of Burley frost. The smell is unique, and its touch is cold. A small blue leaf is pinned to it. The pouch has a price point of ninety xen.

'Blueskirth huh?' she says noticing Evelyn's grasp, 'the rare one of its kind. What kind of lady would likely need this for? Beside your class, aren't you a little young?'

Evelyn responds. 'Well... yes, but what's it --'

'What's it for?' Her short and bold spiky-hair from a natural gel to keep it in place is extreme. Not to mention, it gives her an appearance of being stricken by thunder. And yet, she smells of... a cold winter. 'If you are asking what it does, then you need not need it.' The alke moves with a glide and disappears behind shop. She left Evelyn with nip of frost, no pun intended, but it's quickly shaken off once Evelyn places the pouch down.

The alke returns moments later, 'I've decided to be gentle, but I need to see your port.' She carries more supplies for the thinning products on the counter.

Evelyn's quickly spoken. 'I have papers.' She has it out for the alke. The woman puts her things down.

'I figured. But sorry young one, rules are rules. Official ports only.' She lifts a chin, 'you know this.'

Evelyn smirks... if only she knew how much she doesn't. And so it doesn't get across... bah, who cares. This surely finds Evelyn's focus to change. The change is a large balcony that sticks out from above.

'Alright,' Evelyn says staring up. 'At least a girl tried. Can't blame me for that, am I right?' And she leaves the alke who has a raising brow.

On her way up she finds more shops and stops at one that sells books.

Its funny how you meet people you never expect to, when you least expect to when they shine a light that they didn't even know that was there. She picks up a book to glance over. A being behind her accidentally bumps into her and she drops her book. She looks back sort of crudely at how off putting it was.

'This yours?' The man surprises her, picking it up.

She stares back for a moment, never responding.

'What, did I say something offensive?'

'No.' She giggles, 'sorry, I just... I'd never expected to see another human here.'

'Yeah,' he says with a light tone. He reaches down and picks it up. They exchange smiles and he hands her the book. His hands are dirty. At first it puts her off.

They talk; Evelyn had mostly been playing along, just agreeing to what she heard, for now. She did do her best to keep her eyes on his and off his dirty attire. Something sort of nice happens -- he happens to be dorky and makes her laugh. It's not short of confidence, or beautiful – Evelyn enjoys his simplicity. He's not trying to impress. A different bloke then those in Maesemer, he's… happier in his skin, to say the least.

She picks up another book and looks up to the balcony again.

'Expected somewhere?' He asks.

'Yeah, sort of.'

'Have you read that one?' He asks pointing at the book in her hand.

'No, what's it about?'

'Basically a fight club, one that fallows a man who lead a separate life which you find he's a family man by day and a fighter by night.'

'Oh… No,' she shakes her head simply, 'I wouldn't read this.'

'How come?'

'Because… it's gross… fighting, and all that blood,' she isn't shy of faces. He says nothing.

'I'm not a fighter, I'm a lover.' She says putting the book back. She gets closer to him, whose looking over more reads. It was just nice to be in his presence. She skims more books, in reality, just enjoying her mood. He reaches over her and grabs another book.

She asks, stepping back. 'What kind of books do you mostly read?'

'Oh, I enjoy Alf Addor's, his work is brilliant.'

'Oh…'

'Never heard of it?'

'Nope,' but what it does do is makes her wonder about this man on a whole different level. Where do these people sleep? Is he homeless? What is his life like? Do homeless people have families? If so, where are they? Does anybody have thoughts like she does? Do people ever wonder about these people? Or is everyone else just living on individual islands and not caring for passing ships? What most, is he reminds her a little like the man who has his smoking pipe, leaning on the outside town wall. Only better looking of course, and without the stark. Normally, even this slight adjustment would have put her off, but she decides to trust him, for his mannerism is soothing. That's a true mystery in her opinion, that's a person who she wants to be more like – persona. Someone that doesn't care about what they look like. It makes her wonder what his reality is really like. Is it a hard life? To her, it takes a pretty incredible man to stand on his own -- Ugh, she just wants to let go and ware pyjamas all day… that's the life.

In not long, he has to slip into daybreak.

Damn

Evelyn smiles to herself. He reminded her how beautiful she is, without having to be anything but herself.

She used to get caught up in the memories of what was wanted back at home on her bedside. Imagining all the things that could be, and still, the unexpected realities are so much better than anything that she can bring up in her mind. Beyond her fantasies, she'll crawl for another moment like this, especially for it's unorthodox. Now if she could just stop her sweating, then she thinks she'd be golden.

Evelyn follows into a small gateway of a large tree trunk that runs a spiral stairway to get to the higher levels, faster. Inside, the air smells of cedar and the area is lit by candles on holders sticking out from the wall. Evelyn follows the way up and ventures out. She quickly notices the height. It's a great space punctured in trunk. It has a long layer of wood to mass as the fourth floor, of how many more levels there are. It's more beautiful then she pictured it, and it gets even better with the balcony. She stops to look up and around, 'damn, that's one site to remember. Talk about wonder.' She hasn't been around that much in life, aside from her awakening, but this really can't be matched. Plenty of bridges connecting the two half-moons together are in better witness.

In clean white, the Clairic is easily noticeable. Evelyn approaches and the noble is quick to notice her also. He invites her to a seat at his table.

'Sorry.' He says. 'I forgot to mention I was hungry. I couldn't resist their toteai bean strought.'

She leans over to see olives, beans, unique vegetables with a mix of nuts and a smell of spices she's never smelt before, all in bowl.

'Ah… smells great.' She says, happily to notice a few ingredients still thrive in this part of the world. She grabs one of the wood stools, but it's heavy, so she rolls it, and then heaves it up. She takes a seat. 'It's a lot more peaceful up here and so much more quiet, too.'

The sound of birds can be heard chirping more clearly. The smell of cooking is rather fantastic as well.

'Your nordshoes?'

She teases, 'my nordshoes are on my nord, of course,' and tries to get comfortable in the chair's surface that belches inwards so one has greater support for their back.

'I mean to say, do you have *my* nordshoes?'

She didn't have to read his impressionable face. 'Yes. They're in my saddle pouch.'

He gives her another look.

'What? You'll just wait and trust me I suppose.'

He finally smiles back, catching her sense of humour. 'Hungry?' He suggests, pushing his bowl towards her.

'Um, do I get my own spoon?'

'I'm offering, and not unless you're buying your own meal... so no.'

Evelyn looks at him and then stares at the bowl. 'Ah, what the heck,' she grabs his spoon and gives it a try. He frowns at her expression when she bites into something blue on the outside but brown on the inside. Her face quenches on its bitter taste. 'Ugh! What is this?'

He laughs. 'I never said you would like it. You just don't know how to appreciate a good meal.' He pulls the bowl back.

'No,' she says taking it back. 'No it's fine.'

'Uh huh, that's what I thought.'

She nods, 'hey, this is actually pretty good once you get around those brown ones,' dabbing a few aside with her spoon.

He seems so interested in her. 'So, you're a Celestial?' He adds with a raise of his brow.

She looks around insecurely. 'Well, you know... a traveler.'

'That's how everyone starts. Will you be considering changing faction? I'm assuming you'll want to be Calon once you get out of this uncivilized territory.'

'What do you mean?'

He smiles. 'First of all, as Calon, you serve the grandest portion of this country and you get plenty of xzena for doing so.' Evelyn looks all around, noticing the stares from the Rebuin folk. The Clairic doesn't seem to focus on it and if he did, he probably wouldn't as long. 'If you serve the Calon they will treat you much better than the Rebuin do. That's why I joined.'

'But you're Rebuin by appearance. The only way I could go Calon is because I slip under their scope. So how did you join?'

The Clairic wipes his mouth and gives her a slight smirk. Could have laughed, but didn't. 'It doesn't matter what these foreigners say. Anyone can be a part of any faction. Very few know this. But if one would want to become important, and if their appearance separates them, than one would be better off proving their worthiness. I used Law of Wish to get me through this.' It's funny, well to me, since he said it with an unlawful look. 'It isn't so difficult like everyone has themselves believing.'

'Wait, Law of what?'

'Ok, it's a basic law discovered by Alas. He's the one who taught most it. It's a dying knowledge... many don't participate when it reminds them of back when.'

'But you do?' She asks with a squint of her eyes and pushes. 'What's it about?'

'Well its simple really... how do I put it? Alright I'll start with this. There's the law of gravity. It works like this, instead of things going up and back coming down, when you ask for what you want and you focus, it forms in your reality. But you have to believe in this firstly; otherwise you'll be getting what you're putting out. If you disbelieve than life will show you just this. In any case, Law of Wish is always working for us, whether we believe it or not. That's what's so ironic; we are always playing this game. Ever tried to convince someone otherwise when they're in opposition of your point of view? It's because we're always getting what we're thinking is our truth.'

'Yeah,' Evelyn laughs in agreement. 'Never works out.'

'Exactly, anyway, it's funny, because I never argue. Now going back to what I said earlier. I used this law to get me through training and exams. It's all you need to know, really.' She gives him a smirk and before she spoke, he says. 'It's about training your belief. You just have to focus on what you really want and know it'll come around once you've let it go. The first timers usually get themselves caught up in the timing. After a month or so then they should receive their wish, because that's how long it took them to actually believe and give in to the feeling. The feeling comes first.'

'Interesting,' she smiles. It's fascinating to meet another. But she doesn't intend to share her knowledge. Not just yet. She'd rather listen. After all, it's his reality and her choice now. So what difference does it make? To her none – she figures, like I that it's always about having fun. When we have the universe wrapped around our finger like we both do, sparks happen.

He laughs big. 'Yes, that is the only way to do this. In order to receive you must believe. Regardless, in my experience, the universe gives you the benefit of the doubt and always has your back.'

'Neat.'

'Yeah,' he heckles. 'You'll get the hang of it.'

'Well wait, I'm more interested about the factions,' Evelyn takes more bites of food and spoke more on his tone. 'It goes like this, you see, we are all the same. I don't count appearances. We all share the same gift; and I'm talking about love. What is the use of freedom if we cannot express ourselves?'

'I like that point of view. It's just the Calon don't like being reminded of their enemy. So I think you can guess what the Calon arguments with the Rebuin are, since they feel the Rebuin are in "Their" country. But most of the time, it's the usual racial slurs that are found to be most staggering.'

She frowns with the very image of Tilsan in mind. Maybe Tilsan was right... But Evelyn won't stop there; she'll have to know more about this, instead of judging a book by its cover.

'But how can one tell the difference?'

'From the enemy?' He asks and she nods her response. 'Well,' laughing a bit. 'There are ways, but in short, proof of passage. Relatives and families from Reobigheon could only pass. That's what makes my life so interesting and for those who look like me. We look like the enemy, but aren't. Ceaelon took a big risk allowing the last of the Reobighians in.' He shrugs next. 'But then there are those of you, the bridging ones. It's good to play on that strength, because you're the only link to rebuilding that trust between factions.'

'Strength... how is that strength if all I'm doing is... being something to relax others? No, you're wrong.'

A frown crosses, making her nervous. 'You should really consider finishing chewing before you speak.'

She doesn't know if he was kidding or being serious. She swallows the food she forgot was in her mouth and looks away, only to find his words again.

'Are you going to give me your name at least?'

'It's,' Evelyn hesitates to an off putting call in the wild, reminding her where she comes from and how far that is. 'It's Evelyn.'

'That took some time.'

'I was thinking...'

He raises that brow again and extends a reaching hand. 'Well, mine's Jale.'

'Interesting,' she says gladly shaking it. 'And here I was expecting something different,' and laughs nervously to his silence.

His ears wobble and those cat-like eyes become more fixated. 'That's because it's actually Jalelilian, but I don't take after it since it's my heritage name. I had to blend in and become more like... well, you. It came in handy when I was training with the Calon.'

'I figured.'

He finds her staring at everything and everyone. It's an insecure look. She wanted to remark on his mannerism. She finds this world completely different... it's literally impossible to cope with all the change. Sure, it's a lot better, but she can't help but feel restricted from her lack of experience in Alasmieria and her knowledge about... this other.

He asks her. 'So how about the new treaty, I think it was right, don't you?'

Evelyn looks like a deer caught in the headlights.

'You do know what I mean?' He asks her as if she's *supposed* to know this.

'No. What do you mean?' Trying to stay calm and not trying to drift away to the faces that stare. 'You don't care that they stare? Don't you find it annoying?'

He reflects. 'What do you mean?'

'The faces, they stare and watch every other second.'

'They tend to do that, the Rebuin folk. We are the new age folk, you being Rebuin who looks Calon and me, well, do I need to say anymore? You and I aren't exactly typical folk.'

She thought she had it all figured out, but she finds the more she speaks to him, the further everything is.

His voice makes her shake. 'You seem so much more confused. What was there not to understand? You'd have to be off the edge of the planet to not know of the treaty,' lifting his spoon and dips it into the bowl, taking the last bite. It came off spitefully sharp even though I don't think the kalec meant anything of it.

She watches him, not sure what to do about him.

'So?' He asks. 'Where have you been the last couple of years? I guess I never did ask you where you were from.'

'It's just too much. All of this.' She says, and he looks evermore confused. She notices his face; it's even harder when he's good-looking. She tries to keep it together. 'I'm just not sure, remind me is all.'

She can hear her words sound bothersome, but what's worse; is the world that swirls around her. She can see the eyes watching. She can feel her face flushing with heat. She swallows hard and there's a tension in her chest. It's this feeling of needing to catch a breath of fresh air -- but can't. It's like one of those damn dreams, and one she cannot escape -- It's not like she can all of a sudden wake up when she feels like it. This is reality were playing in here.

Where's mom? What happened? How did all of this change so god damn fast?

He sits back slowly, just watching her. 'I'm not sure what to say.'

His voice makes her head spin. It's not tension anymore but lightheadedness. When she wants to yell out he spoke.

'Who are you?'

'It's... too complicated,' when all she wants to do is cry now and maybe yell out loudly that she doesn't know.

She stops to look around some more. More faces pass her by, eyes slick, it makes her feel sick. Surrounded by a race that doesn't even understand what it means to be from a place called Maesemer. She can't help but feel out of place here. She feels herself slipping from realizing she's just *some other girl* with a robe on. She has to try so hard for them, for all of this, to fit in and be "Normal". It's just... unjust, and it feels like no one bothers to care.

Their eyes are catching the look in her eye. 'I can't do this,' she says and gets up and leaves.

He blinks twice, puzzled. Finally he gets up after her. 'Wait. What did I do?'

Evelyn pauses at another face; the cat-like eyes catch hold of her. A couple of moments ago it would have been tough, but now it's just dizzying. Their faces never smiling at Evelyn, these ones only stare. Evelyn rushes past the beings to get to the stairway down.

Jale following behind her, 'wait, Evelyn!' And he catches her arm.

'Let go of me!'

He can see her eyes are watery now. He makes sure he has a strong hold. 'Wait.'

'Let go of me!' She pleads, pushing him back against the wall; her world spinning with tears flooding her sight. All around her they watch, clogging the stairwell. Jale places a hand on her shoulder, watching her fall into a crouch against the wall. Every time she comes back up for air, their heads poke around to show their scary-looking eyes.

They took your father

'Go away...' She shivers; she gets up and pushes past the bottom crowd. The trade district is neat with more. She comes down the ramp into the open. Her thoughts twist and she yells. 'What do you want from me!?' Her movements are futile. 'I don't know what you want from me...' He reaches her. 'Go away!' She cries again. But his grip is strong enough to ignore her behaviour altogether.

'Evelyn.' He sighs.

She fights back and gets free. She bumps into a few pedestrian who didn't realize her in their midst. Other, naturally crowding around to see if this girl is alright, sort terrified themselves. They had a look, a similar one of *why*, why is she trying to escape a noble's grasp?

'Just leave me alone!' She pushes and falls in the middle of the trade district. He's right behind her and he wraps his arms around the girl who sinks in his arms. 'Just leave me alone...' She mopes.

'Just needs a little space.' Jale says to the crowd.

His hands feel warm around her and her mind feels more at ease as he places a hand on her forehead. 'Easy now,' his lips sound in her ear.

'No more...' She feels like her heart is burning hot; all she feels she can do is cry. 'All I want is...' The area is about to fade. 'My... m-m...' The light of day slowly dims and she faints by Jale's use of white-magic.

CHAPTER 13

Playing With Fire

Falling, her world comes to a slow landing; her boots touch Alasmierian soils. It's a chill here. Her breath can be seen.

A nord rides to her; it appears from a mysterious forest beyond. Evelyn feels wide awake with the night reflecting bright stars off her glassy eyes in reach of a look to the skies. She tightens her fists in the frosty night. She can easily see the stars up above. Looking away to the approaching nord now, there the friendly face comes, her steed. Evelyn lightly steps and finds herself mounting her steed; he takes her towards the forest. The movement reminds her of freedom because her body is off the ground. It feels good. The smell of pine is a gentle brush along the winds. They enter the forest.

A small village is seen within, with torches lit, it's a heavenly look. She smiles to a mysterious feeling that awakens her senses evermore.

She turns in her bed, twitching every now and then.

They stop at an edge of a pond just outside the sake of town for her steed wants a drink. She notices in reflection off the waterbed. It's beautiful. She is.

Ripples glide along the waterbed; her watch follows its wave and then it bumps into a paw on the other side. Her heart beats a little faster. She slowly looks up to see its onslaught face. A surprise no doubt.

She frowns at its deadly face, yet a great awakening is taking place in her soul – a willpower flows through her like no other. There where the town was and only now a valley is. This emotional change is changing her reality, it seems.

'Dark One…' She says. 'You are rather beautiful, yet if it wasn't for all that snarling maybe you could be loved.'

The beast is still.

Evelyn walks the outer rim of the pond, gently and slowly on the earth she moves towards the beast.

The Dark One places one paw after the other, getting low to her approach.

Evelyn looks down to find she isn't walking but gliding across the ground. She can hear the treads of her steed rushing in opposition from fear of the beast's enclosing, but her nord doesn't seem to travel, not going anywhere. The area is loud from its kicks, and he remains stuck there. Stubbornly, her steed rips up grass where it struggles. But Evelyn knows better. She looks back to see the beast further from them. The distance has suddenly grown between them.

Odd

So she frowns and stares into those large dark brown eyes. 'Oh I don't think so. Not today Mr.' She says and smoothly moves across the waterbed to regain approach.

The beast panics. Yes, it is time for it to run for it thought it could taunt, but it knows now it has no effect. There is no escape of loves gentle touch; the girl reaches a hand out to touch the animal. It lunges to bite and does all it can to resist her feel, to survive in shadow. A finger reaches its skin, brushing beneath the hairs on its back. It struggles and whines as if a knife has pierced skin; an emotional pain to say the least, for no skin is. The beast can feel a magical feeling from her touch, a powerful sensation, and one that continues to persist. The girl doesn't fear the bite that snaps back. The Dark One twists and turns as if something unnatural has overcome it and holds it down. Slowly, the beast begins to sink -- slipping from her grasp -- a drowning in the earth from struggle.

She too submerges like quicksand. 'Shhh,' she says to the furry one. And soon both release their resistance. The Dark One melts away. And too, the feeling of tickle consumes her.

Evelyn awakes.

The room is dark; she jolts up and is quick to remember Jalelilian's face. A window is seen and it is open. The air that blows through is warm. She pushes a blanket off her, seeing her robe is still on.

Searching, she finds her bag on the floor.

'Wow that was some awesome dream I had there... Hold on, where am I?' She almost jumped from her spot to find a bird staring from a railing outside the bedroom, on a balcony. It creates a unique call, similar to a loon's and it flies away. This is a bird she has never seen before.

She frowns at the suddenness. She is reminded by flooding images of importance. 'The book,' and finds it inside her bag. She recloses the lid. 'Thank Alas,' she says with some sassiness. She pats her pockets to find her map and paper as well.

Evelyn straps in her backpack and moves to the balcony, she takes her leave and is upon a unique scent -- one that smells sort of like lavender, but tangier. Her world is evermore dreamlike only because of the magic of this place – giving her a hard time from distinguishing reality from a deep sleep.

Flowers are clung to the outside tree-building; they're fully in bloom on vines. The vines wrap around steps leading to lower levels. The scent from these floral is deliciously overwhelming.

She scoffs.

What's a dream but life anyways?

Without any railings noticeable, the realization of height is a far ways down. Looking down, it's a good tree drop. Up here, it's a cozy spot, being just beneath the canopy.

Birds glide below, making their loon call. She remembers hearing this very sound when she was sitting across from the Clairic. She wondered what it looked like. It resembled a part of Alasmieria not yet discovered... Well now that it is, she feels upturn. Perhaps it is a sign?

With an open view of things, she can see many houses and their spiral stairways. No bridges are anywhere near. She does her best to stay closest to the wall, descending down the stairs.

In another clear, she gets a better view of the area, being midway on this giant tree house. For some reason she receives a glimpse of happiness and smiles. Down more steps to get to the bottom, she carries to a clerk at a front counter. His expression turns from patient to wide eye as Evelyn spoke early.

'How long ago did a man in white pass?'

'Oh, I'd have to say forty minutes ago.' He responds.

Evelyn pauses, not sure what to think. All of a sudden, her mind sparks.

'Miss, are you alright?'

Wait one second. I created this. All of this. I remember asking specifically for a man who is rich and powerful, who will lead me through the lands on this journey to the centre of the world. My focus is what creates my reality. Tetlas is right

She nods more enthusiastic now, feeling a little frumpy with her bag. She asks. 'Did he ever mention where he might be going?'

'No, he never mentioned anything,' he puts a thinking hand to his mouth. 'He ordered a room for you and then he took you upstairs. He returned ten minutes after. That's all I know.' His unique features matched the room's atmosphere, they're warm.

'Oh.' She says and leaves the counter with that in mind. She found a few more stairwells and finds her way to ground level. The area is unknown. Looking back now there is a hazy site at the sunlight where a giant structure wraps up a massive tree beside this bright spot.

'Well... I'm just glad I didn't get lost in there.' She goes on to wonder. 'I couldn't have slept for too long. Maybe I can still find him?' She glimpses around the premises. 'I must be in the heart of the living district.'

Her heart beats faster; and before she said it, she finds her nord in a small pen eating grass and hay.

Evelyn scratches her head. 'When was the last time I fed him?' She opens the pen gate for him. 'You'll have lots of time to eat later, *I promise.* I have tons of fruits and vegetables so that we can snack on for later.' She suddenly finds herself holding her nose. 'All you eat is grass and hay -- how can that smell so badly?'

The nord makes a musty look and shakes his head. His ears flop.

'Okay... that one was new.' Evelyn says.

She mounts him and rides in search for the gate. She came to a stop at a new place and finds herself trailing the wall to the front gate location. The gate has an archway, being the same material as the wall and has thick wooden doors beneath its tall. Evelyn halts her steed at the wood, handing her paper over to a gatekeeper. He gives her a look of respect.

Oh yeah... I am one of them now!

'Open the gateway,' the gatekeeper commands those above. 'Have a safe trip, Celestial.' The gatekeeper says, passing her paper back.

Evelyn puts it back. 'Hey, has a noble Clairic passed through these parts?'

'Yes.' The gatekeeper says and he is paused by another kalec manning the lever above.

'He passed, just a few minutes ago.'

The door opens to the wilderness.

'Which way did he go?' Evelyn asks the one on the tall.

'Down the narrow trail,' he points her way east of the road, the one Evelyn originally was supposed to be on, before her intervene. She thanks them and grabs tight of her leash. The trail is brighter; she knows she must ride quickly if she's ever to catch up. With a light bump of her heel, there's a swift start into the growing morning. She slides and bumps heavily. This scenic route takes her through the unexplored land.

A river is heard near the path, and the road forms to a bumpy hill. From higher -- the overlooking part of it all tells of a picture. A wonderful waterfall crashes down, from the river dancing into a vale. But the valley has no bridge in site to get to the other side.

'A vale,' Evelyn says. Her heart beats a little faster; she calls out Tastraity. She imaged Jale by her sides. This helps her to believe she'll catch up to him. After all, he is the one person that helped her, that finally saw her vulnerable. This is something she rarely shares and she wants to show more of. Her passion makes for a brighter effect. Brighten fingertips engulfs into something more, a brighten hand.

She rides, manoeuvring around the simplest objects that are on the rocky roadway. She doesn't want to face the world without him by her sides. He said he would help her on her journey. All she needs now is to get the gentlemen's attention so he will hopefully stop for her.

She slows her steed to a stop, pulling her pack around to find the book. She grasps it tightly in her hands while calling out the magic word, 'Ashnivarna!' The book unravels. It pushes her hands outwards as the book expands heavily. 'There's no turning back. I promise if I find him, I'll never complain again.'

Even the birds around her don't confess familiarity, of all the creatures of this world; she wishes to be by Jale's sides.

She flips through the pages and comes to a stop at Tastraity -- the spell – never aware that it was there to begin with. She flips past and goes on to skim over many more spells in search for one that can grant greater light. 'Come on there's got to be -- found it, sub-Forskies; a light for guidance in darkness. Ok, ok, just give me those damn instructions... Ok screw it, Forskies!'

Heat begins to seer up her arm to her fingertips. Her hand shakes. Images of Jale flips her mind and she gets the impression to stare up at the dimly lit sky. A bright shot of light bursts from her hand and it scares her. Her nord trembles.

'Whoa. Whoa!' Evelyn calls. The burst of white energy creates a bright spot. It rises; like a fizzing firecracker, it crosses the sky.

Her steed calms and the words are placed to shrink the book back. She places it in her robe's pocket, just in case she'll need to reach it again.

Boom -- the flicker explodes as if a star had been born -- a ripple of small sparks spread across, oozingm fume. They slowly sail till they stay put, leaving a trail of stardust in illumination.

Another nord cries, not too far from Evelyn.

'That's got to be him!' Evelyn shouts.

It's mysteriously wide open; from here she finds a path and follows it. With the light immense, the shade beneath the trees will now be lessened. For some time now, she rides to be out of the shadowy depths, covered beneath giant trees of this forest, she fights to be in polarity. Since the starlight is so bright, it tends to create greater contrast.

She hears hooves echoing off the pathway, not sure how far away they could be.

That must be him. It's gotta be!

Not too far ahead, a white cloak is seen climbing a hill, mounted on a white nord.

Evelyn continues down the narrow trail in conviction it's him. A quick swerve looks fatal and her traction rumbles. 'Whoa nordy!' she says near the ledge, never knowing it was there to begin with and the white cloak disappears. Evelyn gets back on track.

'I can't see a thing with these trees, if Jale is ahead or what.' The book shakes madly in her pocket. She holds on tighter to her steed, getting lower on him.

'The light…' She looks up to see it blocked by the canopy. Only now in the bleakness can she hear her steed breathing intensely. Evelyn comes out of the forest and the hill is climbed, 'Jale,' Evelyn yells out once she reaches the top. She can see he's not too far, and a curve is up ahead. If she goes off track she may be able to shortcut her way to him. Evelyn gets low and goes off road. The trees brush past her, the weeds beneath snap with much speed.

A quicker skitter of feet swerve behind her. The girl snaps a look back; there a fowl beast chases. Its teeth show wide.

'Oh no.' She finds herself in a sudden breath. The starlight lingers above. She looks forward then back again and the beast is gone. 'You've got to be kidding me.'

The Dark One who feeds her disbelief is someplace within the forest.

She grips tighter on the leash. She gets ever low, almost close enough to kiss the steed's neck. She breathes off his back, keeping her eyes forward, hearing the beast tumbling behind her again. There's no telling how close the Dark One is nor how far the white rider could be, and so the chills run. She dares not to look back. In not long, she looms toward the curve in road. There is a shout and it's not by her or the one trailing. It was a man's voice and he had stepped out of the bush and onto her path.

'Joulate!'

A jolt of light collides with Evelyn knocking her off nord. She comes down tumbling to the earth in utter shock. Her breathes are shaky. Her nord yelps, rising on its hind legs. Only to find something furry and black to frighten it further. Evelyn's steed dashes for safety. A fearful cry from it echoes off the valley walls.

Evelyn looks down, hanging from an edge of a cliff by her pack. She gasps, fearing the fall.

The figure in white rushes out from the bleakness to grip the girl.

'Evelyn!' Jale yells with a hand by the cloth of her robe. He suddenly looks up to a flicker from the starlight, which is falling very slowly. There's a cry from Jale's steed and Jale turns a look back and sees it. He loses grip of the girl.

Evelyn fell to a slide, rolling helplessly, much like a toboggan on a wintery trail. She misses a tree and tumbles to a roll onto the open valley below. Lying on her back, she can hear yelling and thumps from the cliff, but found she cannot turn to look.

The light from Forskies flickers a little, signifying its looming death. They're a few bangs from the cliff's edge, and no one's yelling this time around.

It's like a thunderstorm with the silent flickering of starlight.

She breathes heavily. The sounds of crickets sing in her ears. Lying still on a bed of tall grasses, she kicks her feet. Her fingers are numb as is most of her body. She kicks again, squinting back in the light. She wants to call out Jale's name, to see if he's ok, but it came out more of a hum. She wants to run to him, to hide, but the spell has taken control of her entire body. As she fights to move, slowly, feeling comes back to her feet. Her neck thrums and her palms tingle. She tilts a look at the cliff's edge.

Silence, there is stillness...

Her hands get feeling back. She fights with her mind, and manages to prop herself up on one side, with a looming look towards the drop. Her control of her body is slow in coming back. She manages to get up, limping from ache. Those once stiff legs and arms now pound painfully. She breathes frantically at the final life returning to her body.

Something tumbles from the hillside of the valley, cracking branches as it goes.

Her eyes widen, 'Jale?' She almost fell and returns to balance. She then finds the strength to yell. 'Jale, can you hear me?' A few warm tears skitter down her face. She knows what it could be...

A figure is seen at the edge of the cliff where she fell, looking tiresome and beat.

'Jale!?' Evelyn yells out again.

His voice echoes. 'Evelyn, you must go.' He looks weak. 'You must!'

She has a look to the moving bushes. Her eye is flushing with some dirt in it and her body twinges too.

No time to panic

The beast dashes for her. It's mouth showing wide.

Evelyn yells as fast as her arm flings towards it. Its body swishes at her as she gets the breath out, 'Hestife!' Rock and mud spurt from behind and manoeuvres around her to project debris forward. The beast is slowed and it jumps to get out of way. It turns to another cry from the Celestial. 'Clayastlia!'

A bolt of water is ejected from a nearby riverbed. The jet-shot misses her target, hitting ground with a smack.

Far and appearing unexpectedly, a pulse of Sophair hits between the two separating them and knocking Evelyn further back from such a powerful force. She rolls to her hands and flings her hair back. Her eyes glare, and so does *its*. She manages the heat in the sky, using Sophair to attract it to a spot ahead of her.

The Dark One is already up and in pounce.

Swoosh! A storm of light and fire crashes down. She runs, dodging the heat. Like missiles, the sky rains and sizzle's fire, shaking the both of them. The beast jumps back and watches as the girl escapes in opposition, moving in panic. The animal is rocked, retreating back by flame and bouncing spark. In a long drawn-out-way, its anger dissipates and the Dark One leaves.

The shattered star is a mess on the earth, spitting and kicking tantrums and then it dies out.

Evelyn lets her arms droop and knees touches to ground. The earth is wet, it's so cold. She listens for anymore movement. Tiredly, all she wants to do is close her eyelids.

Jale comes hurtling down now with both hands lit from casting his Sophair shot, crackling branches as he does, holding onto trees to support him from the steepness.

'Evelyn!' She over hears him and his steps slashing through muddy grounds. He arrives by her sides.

She moans at him. 'Surprise…' Her one eye twitches and the other is squinting and wet. He lets out a sigh of relief. He looks around and then bends over her to treat her wounds. She thought it would hurt, but it didn't. Instead, it feels warm and tingly. There was blood and he stops it from flowing, something she didn't realize he was doing in the heat of the moment.

'Argh, it hurts.' She says with agony.

Jale regains focus to the wound, for he'd taken his eyes off for a moment and thus the pain is felt. He tries to relax a little, knowing this may be some time.

Suddenly, she begins to moan, feeling more of the pain.

'My Alas, this is really annoying.' He makes a few glances around and comes back to the wound. He fears what lingers outside their boarders. 'I can heal it without it becoming a scar.'

It becomes apparent; another part on her arm is found torn open, probably on a sharp object. Her heart raises and another warm hand puts her at ease.

She spoke weakly. 'Am I... Am I --'

'No. You'll be alright.' He says. 'I'm just glad you didn't break anything. These wounds I can fix, but not bones. Something we Clairics can quicken the healing process only,' he hesitates. 'Please eat something from your bag.'

The mud succumbed bag is still on her back, it had taken most of the damage.

'I'm taking energy from you in order to heal you. So you need to consume energy from food in order to get me to do this.'

She nods and he helps her down to a sit in the cold mud, and slowly tries to relieve her of her pack. She whinces at the final attempt, finally, he gets it off. She grits her teeth from pain, 'all because you paralyzed me.'

'What! I thought you were an Errific for crying out loud!'

She finds her gingerly expression. And he lightens up a little. She hands out food with her good arm so he can eat.

Jale talks with food in his mouth while mending the gash. 'You know that's all anyone worries about around here?'

She scoffs. 'And yet I haven't seen one yet.'

He sat up from his crouching position over the arm. 'And you don't want to, ever.'

She feels the pain. 'I know... it was a joke...'

He looks around. The wilderness has a faint call, some birds, other animals and the crickets.

'Well it looks like you're stuck with me.' He says as he concentrates more Cloradis which comes off as light from his fingertips. He makes no physical touch; instead the light does the work. 'Well, at least I know you don't take no for an answer.' He looks back up at her when he said it.

'Ha... I didn't think you'd leave me,' taking a bite into some odd shape of a fruit.

'I didn't think you'd want to come, after that ordeal back when.' He looks at her boringly. Those eyes are big and wet. But something told her something deeper was behind them. Aside from his mannerism back at the food court – heck, she forgives him. I mean she can't be upset when he's just saved her life...

She looks around, fearing what could be still out there. He too had the same fear, but held a calmer presence.

'You know, I never got to name my nord.' She says.

'Well, you're in luck. Now you don't have to. And this situation defeats being chased by those *things*.'

She frowns helplessly, 'yeah. I guess...' She digs for more food and Jale sits up, longing for his concentration because of it. He waits, overhearing the same crickets instead. There is a tame smell in the wild.

He finds something in her pack too. 'Why was it after you? They never come out this far from the dark forest, especially at this time of day, regardless of all that, they'd never chase a steed.' He exhales in the bag. 'This one must have been needy.'

She pauses and exhales too. When he's done searching, she goes back to looking for something other than bread and fruit to eat. 'It was probably following me.'

'Why would it be following you?'

Evelyn is wary and sits back on the wet earth with a small vegetable in hand. 'I don't know... alright I do. But are you sure you want to know?'

'Yes.' He asks, going back to mending the wound.

'Well I guess now would be a good time as any... I swore to say nothing.' Her site is becoming dizzy, and her energy is lessening. 'Anyways... I never... originally... was born here, my whole life I mean -- I'm like you and the others, technically speaking.' She doesn't look at him, 'but...' now she does, 'I was raised in a place a lot different than Alasmieria, in a town called Maesemer.'

'What? And try not to move.' He says and puts his food back so he can concentrate again. 'I'm almost done cleaning this wound.'

She lets what she mentioned go for now. An awesome sensation moves over her arm. It puts her at ease. When he finishes his work, it feels like an invisible bandage had been glued to the spot, which completely has taken the pain, gone. The tingle is stronger when she moves her body.

'Okay, that just feels weird.'

'Better than no arm,' he remarks.

He got a look back from it.

'I'm joking.' He says. 'There, I'm done. You may move too, but the feeling takes a bit longer to get used to.'

'Thank you.' She says looking a little hazy. She can see the wound has ceased; the gash has pulled itself together and sealed by his magic touch. Yes, I said magic touch. There is only a stain of blood too wherein she would have bled to death if it was not for him.

"Smily face"

The blood must have been sucked back into her body as part of replenishment. Only a massive bruise remains. It is all purply, black and blue. Sort of like her robe, an appearance as if ink has rubbed off on her skin.

'And to think I just got this thing…' touching the cuts in her ruined robe.

He smirks. 'Ok and you were saying? Something about someplace outside of Alasmieria.'

Evelyn can feel the rush of hunger, and so she takes more bites of bread and then leans forward. '*And* you say?' not looking convinced she got the message across. 'Look. We are here,' she says this matter of factly as if he should know where "Here" is. 'And say this… here, this is Caealon.' She draws a map with her finger in the mud, feeling the tingles all over her body when she does. 'Ok, now, I was born here.' She points at a dot much farther from the rest.

He stares firstly, and then realizes, 'in the mountains?' but frowns afterwards. 'Uh, don't tell me you were raised by Houlladdians?'

'Oh my god, *what*? No,' she shakes her head. 'No,' and pausing.

I'm not sure if he was being funny, or?

She moves on as if he hasn't really paying any attention to her. 'This dot is placed outside of Alasmieria.'

'Right, we all call this the Outlands. That's to pass the Twin Peaks and walk the land of the lady and her forest.'

'Right, but... you don't really get it... at least I don't think you do,' and doesn't refuse to stop where she last left off. 'Well since I was raised in the town of Maesemer, I soon stumbled on something.' shaking her head to her own imagination. 'Wow, that's one way of putting it, but yeah.'

'Evelyn...'

She finds herself slipping in all sorts of knots. 'Wait, just let me explain. It's hard to explain.'

'Okay.' He says tiredly.

'Alright,' she says. 'I lost my mother to the same kind of beast that attacked today; I know this because it's been haunting us for some time now. Now, once I passed into Alasmieria... I... I didn't think it still knew I existed. But obviously,' she shrugs. 'It all started when I used Aura near the forest. I suppose the Dark Ones protect intruders from... well, you know -- this place.'

He rubs an eye. 'So you're saying there's a place outside the outskirts?'

'Exactly -- You'll either believe me or not.' She banters now, 'so you'll see there is a lot more than meets the eye. There's a whole new world beyond this realm you call *Alasmieria*. I mean, I've gone to school my whole life in Maesemer, and that's just for starters. Trust me, they don't teach anything Aura related either, especially not in Brunon -- which is five million people.'

'What?' He sounds annoyed by her. She looks taken back, *is* taken back.

How could he not care?

He sits back slowly. There is a look of concern about the number she just mentioned and the kalec finds some laughter. 'That's double the population of Alasmieria. Is that what you're telling me, that a world like this exists out there, similarly?'

She nods right back. 'The country where I came from is called Egerd. Their culture is almost irrelevant to yours. Out there, they have many different rights, and out there, of all the people, none are aware of Alasmieria. I wish I brought one of the inventions from Mr Barkley's shop as proof to show you. We were always told as young that witches were a means to trouble – I mean Celestials -- that's what we call them, witches. Back there, I mean.'

There's a worried look by her. And... he's not buying any of this.

'Look,' he says. 'I knew you were a little different, but...'

'I know.' She says. 'But just hear me out. I didn't really expect you to move so quickly. To be me was tough. But believe me,' she knew that one was counterintuitive. 'Look, I hope this will help you --'

'Wait.' He says, 'what about the Dark One? Is it still coming back for us?'

'No, not after that little ordeal, did you not see what I did back there?'

'Yeah, yeah I saw. I've never seen a Celestial perform such a show.' A little lost in memory.

'I didn't even know what I was doing to be honest.'

The two are silent, reflecting back on how lucky she was. Evelyn goes back to digging through her things. They go on to eat dried meat and whatever's left, leaving only uncooked beans in her bag – something Tetlas gave her. Evelyn picks it up and reflects in memory. It makes her smile, thinking of her. She puts it back slowly, forgetting that he has been watching.

He hands over the dried meat and finds something else at the bottom of her things. 'Oh good, you got a Toegar.' He finally says, holding up a fruit.

'Are they any good?'

He shrugs, pealing the ripe skin. He leans over and tells her to take a bite. A bite of everlasting, the taste is.

'Oh wow, it's rather creamy.' She replies, a taste of something tangier then mango. He takes a bite himself and then used his hands as an expression for her to get back to the story.

'Right,' she replies at the side of her mouth but he doesn't let her finish.

'Ok, I'll budge. The world you come form is rather odd... but I choose to believe you. Now you have me wondering, how can this place help Alasmieria?'

'Why the change of heart?'

'Because,' he says.

She raises her brows.

'Just cause,' he says and swallows what's left in his mouth. 'They're so many mysteries to this world, so why not one more?'

'I thought you'd say something like that,' and a quirky look forms. 'That's how I've been getting through all of this. Ok, before all this happened, you've got to take a good look at this; I have the kicker,' she searches her bag. 'It's sort of like proof, though I'm told it's from your lands.'

He watches her. She digs through her supplies, past the paper document, the map and the beans -- but there's no book. Her eyes squint, a little lost about this. 'Where the... where did I put you last?' Then she remembers and reaches in her pocket. 'Oh no...'

'Evelyn...' he says, the belief in her story dwindling.

She gets up and moves around. 'Hold on,' she says like those in Caszuin do, palm facing him.

'Where are you going?'

She continues to search, moving further from her spot, until she sees a bright glow in a puddle. She approaches and reaches down to its magical touch. He sees a small booklet in her palm. Then he sees a look of insanity in her eye.

Standing there with it, the words slip her mouth, 'Ashnivarna.' The book brews into something beautiful, until a large piece of history reveals and grows itself. There the sanity is reborn in her eyes. She returns to him and sits down in the mud, having the book in her lap. Well, it's hardly a book.

No words come from his lips. He places a hand out and she uses both hands to hand it into his single reaching. His other fingers trace its grace. And something serious -- aside from Evelyn's mysterious eyes, she's found something in his now.

'The Regalia,' he can hardly breathe out. And before anyone could say something else, he knew what it meant now, that look that stirred her eye. Still, and without her knowing, he doesn't appear fearsome of the book, nor worried, only expectant, like he's seen it before.

'My mom had it in her possessions.'

Then like a match to light him up, the kalec spoke. 'Do you even know what this is, what it means to have it?'

Her eyes are a reflection. 'So you know what it is?'

'I know of it.' He replies, 'this is dangerous.' He hands it back carefully. 'Too dangerous if it's really... the... one.'

'Good,' she drops it back in his lap, startling him. 'I was hoping you would know more about it, because I have no clue what it's for. I only know what it does.'

His eyes glare across the secret cover. He flips it open and moves his hands over the written words. 'There must be a thousand spells,' he says and presses on one. The protection spell glows where his pressure goes. 'I must say, at first I thought --'

'I was going crazy?'

'That, but I was going to be polite about it.' He says and she laughs about it. 'But where'd you get it again?'

'I told you. My mom had it, that's why I came all the way out here. I have questions I need answered. And I'm hoping you're the one who can help me find the clues to them.'

He gave her a look, a little shocked by everything that's been said and seen.

'You know this is one of our biggest mysteries in the world? And I'm holding it.' He says, looking like he could barely breathe.

Evelyn raises her brows.

He looks up at her. 'You don't even seem to care, Evelyn. Perhaps it's for a reason?'

She smiles playfully. 'What reason?'

'Why did it find you, why does it come up now after all these years? Is this why it's been lost, with you and this place beyond Alasmieria that you call home?'

'Once called home… but yeah,' she says and shrugs. 'All I know is I miss a lot more then what that thing has to offer.'

'For starters?'

'The town,' she replies. 'Where my mother… well, let's just say I lost her the moment I crossed into the forest.'

'I'm sorry.' He is quiet now, unsure of "The forest" and gives her a moment anyway. But she didn't seem like she needed it. 'I got the feeling something had been taken away from you. From the first moment I set eyes on you. I got this feeling before. You know… someone mentioned you, before I had met you. It was a guard who told me you passed through, probably just to let me know the news of the day… people tend to do this because of my title. So this isn't odd, but the feeling I got was. You, the…' He looks around but never finishes it.

She only nods knowing it's up to him to spill the beans.

The dark look is back. He finds the words, 'the lost soul.'

She looks away, not sure what to say. She could have been more upset, yet he's the one with that look. She could tell he wants to tell her something else, but couldn't.

'So, no going back I'm guessing?'

She shrugs at him, 'I guess.'

He puts his hands to his face. 'I-I knew something was different about you... but this? You're... how do I put this...' Evelyn doesn't seem in the mood, for anything that'll cause her emotions to show, they're already stirring by what he'd brought up. 'Unique beyond measure, you're as much as an importance as *this*.' He sits back with the book in hand and collects himself.

'I never thought I was going to make it.' She recalls in memory. She can't swallow. The emotions make her feel cold on the outside, but very warm on the inside. Excited to be alive, but not trusting when she has to take the next step forward. After all, this is what she wanted, daydreaming of another world on her bed, staring out her bedside window for hours at end, for days and the nights that passes and have gone...

She looks up at the stars now. They seem so far away now. The same way they showed up in her old reality. But so much changed then and so much is new now. So what happened? All those days of dreaming of a distance world, a world that made her feel safe, alive and free. Is she not here? Has she not arrived? So why be down now? So the question is simple. Does she see this?

She shakes her head. 'It's all too much. All of it, what does anyone expect of me? How could anything let this happen to me?'

He puts a hand to his mouth in wonder, in wonder because he's sympathizing. 'Tell me Evelyn. What are you going to do now?'

'I don't know -- what kind of stupid question is that?' She looks up to the skies. He rubs below his eye again. She can feel the tears roll down her face, stopping at her lips. 'I've felt like giving up. Believe me. But now that I have you, and this book -- just this now, someone to talk, it all helps. I think I just need rest, you know, to sleep in harmony for once?'

He couldn't help but laugh to her overwhelmed state of self. *He's been there*. 'Well, what it's like there?' He tries to take her away from her gaze. It scares him -- he doesn't know what she's thinking.

His words almost slipped her ears. 'It's actually a pretty neat place. It is, and it's quite nice. It seems more… calm.' And she spoke almost quieter then a whisper. 'I miss her.'

He stands up in the deep of emotion and spoke something irrelevant to her knowing. 'I miss him.'

They both stare up at the distance.

Evelyn frowns and watches his eyes prance through thought. She knows better than to ask who he spoke of, for he won't tell her. Surely this would be for another time, just like hers is a best kept secret to him, I'm sure. Both look at each other, knowing they're bearing one. Life… what can I say?

She asks around the moment. 'What are you thinking of?'

He can't help but smile, 'mostly about the book.'

'You know. Maybe… just maybe… this book could give us a little bit of a fresh start.'

CHAPTER 14

Places of Gold

He hands her the book and she places the book in masquerade.

Jale watches as the light tumbles and a small book rests in her hands. He frowns, not able to make out the title. He moves closer to get a better look and Evelyn hands him the book. He reads out loud, 'Tales of the Green Burrow?'

She nods at him. 'It's a very short story my mother used to read to me as a child.'

'I see.' He says and looks it over. It's unrecognizable. He opens the cover and flips to the first page.

She says. 'It's a picture book about a fictional character that goes on a quest to find his lost brother who escaped down a green burrows, which lead the two brothers to become closer in a world undisclosed. They have to fight to find their way back to Brunon.'

He nods slowly and notices the publisher and writer, neither does he recognize. He gives it back to her. 'That's enough proof.' He says playfully. 'Why didn't you just show me this?'

'I don't know.' She says with laughter, placing burrows back into her pocket.

He nods and looks around. 'Now, how do we intend on getting back up there?' motioning to the slopes.

Evelyn straps into her bag with ease, its light without food. She responds as she's doing this. 'There's got to be a path someplace? I don't know. This is your world remember?'

He smirks, and leads the way. They find a small pathway, using trees to help boost their weight as they climb on the muddy slopes. They make their way up to the top. Looking back now, Evelyn didn't realize how far it was, the whole time climbing, it was hard to believe she fell down such steep slopes and with only two gashes. She's lucky she didn't break her neck.

Together now, Jale and Evelyn come closer to his white steed. It is still tied to that tree. Evelyn might have thought it was attacked by the Dark One, because it's been so quiet. Luckily, Jale's steed is tied a few yards from trouble and this explains his safety; out of the way of things. Jale pats his white steed, and then mounts him afterwards. He speaks atop. 'I don't have a double saddle so it might get a little bumpy.'

It's bizarre. This moment, right here in time. If I could show it to you now, I would. It is a feeling of everything she's ever wanted. She's never had a companion before. I should say to her, "Let me remind you, silly girl, he's everything you've ever wanted".

'I understand.' Evelyn replies, leaning her weight on the nord with her arms and with a great hop she mounts the back.

'We have to go to Telahire. I have business there that needs finishing. But first we must cross the border into Tenor; there we will rest at the outpost. We can even skip Telador to get to Telahire quicker. I know of a shortcut.'

'I remember, for your patient you said. Let's go around Telador then, if it's safer.'

The steed's master nods, with a whistle from Jale, they take off. All the while, Evelyn thinks.

How could I have ever managed without him? I'm just happy I have Jale now

'He's beautiful.' Evelyn says and peers deeper within the forestry.

'Thank you.' He replies, patting his white nord.

The wind blows on their faces. It is cold but feels good, perhaps not as grand as the thoughts that swirl her mind.

Could it be out there, watching us?

Her thoughts linger... watching the wilderness. The valley is beautiful with the sunlight striking brightly; there is no need for another spell from the Regalia.

Her thoughts are a jumble, until stubbornly she decides to let go and just enjoy the surroundings, letting go never felt so nice.

'You smell good.' She says, with her head close to his back – his robe is wondrously soft.

'I smell good?'

She is quiet and he can tell she's thinking. Her voice is heard behind his ears. 'Like a flower.'

'You smell a little like soil.'

They laugh together. The wind isn't cold anymore, it's *nice*. The mud covered girl is rather comfortable with her change of mind. After all, it's not the first time she's been covered in mud for a farm girl.

He didn't look back to see her reaction. He couldn't, he's watching the roads. 'I sampled one. Not too soon after I saw the Aura light up the sky, just beyond the hill where I shackled you.'

'So that's what that was?' She asks funnily.

'Yeah and you're lucky I stopped for a flower. I'm lucky it caught my eye; otherwise, you never would have caught up. Was this Aura... from the Regalia? I've never seen such a thing, so I assumed Errific and waited for the Errific to come by. But clearly that wasn't the case.'

Evelyn laughed a little, 'yes it was from the "Regalia". I used it to get your attention.'

He smiles, figuring she couldn't have conjured the spell, 'there are spells for this, ones not as extreme. I will have to show you the ones I know once were near Tenor, within the Great Forest. Not much light get's through, in fact, its pitch dark during all hours.'

'Oh... sound's scary. But I'm curious, what's with the sampling of flowers for?'

'They're good medicine. I stock up for myself and give the rest to the academy in Esmehdar – it's a school thing.'

'Interesting, well, we train doctors in Egerd... and I think they use herbs for medicine too.'

'In Egerd?' he asks.

'Oh, right.' She says forgetting. 'It's the country from where I came from. You know, Maesemer and all that stuff.'

'Right and doctors you say? That's definitely a new name.'

'We also have universities. This is where Egerdians train for their degree; a symbol of recognition for completing their study for doctorate and what not. I find herbalists a neat thing too. But I don't think we have degrees for herbalists.'

He nods. 'A Practicist is a special flower, which we named our profession after. Unlike your herbalists, a Practicist requires training for a seal to be recognized. I have a friend who requires certain herbs for his medicine. He's a professional.'

'And this flower was one of them?'

'No, not by any means, it was a Zwauna, normally for treating headaches. I am no herbalist, but I know the basic flowers for minimal care.'

His body is warm on her hands held around his waist. 'I'm actually more curious about you.' She says.

He twists a little. 'I? Yes, I am interesting.' His smiles generously, 'what you've discovered from the Regalia is an interesting one as well.'

'Is this the word we use for the Book of Knowledge now?'

'It's the only word known for the ancient artefact. Is that its actual name, the "Book of Knowledge"?'

'Well, no. It's the book of Alasmieria. Inside I came across a list of names a while back. Seven council members; one was Mieria and Alas, coincidence that it pertains to the word of this realm?'

'No. It is as you put it, the man who created the Regalia was the headmaster of the council, a visionary and everyone knows this, but very few know of his wife --'

'Mieria.'

'Yes. Many know of her power. It was she who taught him the way of Aura. It was she who was the master and he the student, only she died early on during Reobigheon and Alas led the way with her knowledge and his vision.' His voice is louder now so Evelyn can hear it in a gust of wind. 'But it's not like this at all. Most have it backwards. Alas was no greater than any other student Mieria trained. This is why it has me believing that he was passed her power. She gave him her life-force, for lack of a better word, then and only then could he bare a great lifespan and the power to carry out his vision.'

'She could really do that?'

'Most definitely, she was unlike any other alke, Alas being kalec of course. How else does one explain his grand power after her passing? Well, either way, I find it blind to see that one is to believe Alas could conjure such power on his own. I don't know if you know, but if you carry between the two opposing regions, Caealon and Calliskue, therein lay the remains of the Great War.'

'I've heard. It's to do with the fall of Reobigheon. I want to know more.'

'Well, the landscape remains a great scar. The council of Reobigheon was held in the mighty Emgacia; a city within Reobigheon – it's like a city within a city. That's how large Reobigheon was. Emgacia was named the capital within its parts. In a citadel of Emgacia, many treaties were held, between the two regions that exist today. After Mieria's death, then came the formation of Alas's council members. It was in Emgecia that seven secrets were created by Alas for his council. The book is one of them. Alas always planned ahead. He created the council to fill the book with extraordinary spells from all corners of Alasmieria, which was the secret duty of the Regalia. Going further, each secret was created to suppress any who threatened the safe keeping of the Regalia. Or correctly termed the book of Alasmieria now,' he snickers. 'But that's not all. The real secret is; why create the book in the first place? Spells like this only do good in battle...'

'Weird... so you're saying he must have known the Great War was coming?'

'Rightfully so, today they say that whenever one prays, Alas answers. That is why many pray to him, in hopes his lingering spirit will grant wishes, since he's always been seen as a god. But I know better than to pray to a ghost who doesn't do such things. He was not our creator, oh no, he was a troubled man who was good at planning and hiding things.'

'What makes you think this?'

'Because he lied when he said his knowledge grew over the years, she only taught him to an extent, like I said. He lied when he said he created the council to create balance and a democracy. He was always up to something; why else would the council have turned on him?'

'They turned on him?' She sounds surprised.

'I've studied. Instead, others would rather be told a "Truth" that is no more than a grand fable – I found it all so... demeaning. But I continued to dig further. I know he did something to cause the Great Collapse, it was only time when the secrets became too much for him to handle.'

'You think he was hiding something?'

'Yeah I do.'

'So... whatever happened to the remaining six secrets then?' She knows of another -- the beauty and simplicity that is arond Tetlas's neck.

'By my research, they're objects held in pictures and paintings. I found all my scrolls on the council from families, *not* from the bibliotheca. I got them from real people; their ancestors that witnessed the true possessions. It's not proof, but it adds up when you ask the source; the people are the truth.'

'Of what sorts... of possessions?'

'Necklaces, gems, swords -- all kinds of possessions, for all we know, one could appear as a simple goblet of a thousand that was drank from in Emgecia. The speculation goes on. Witnessed by nobles who dwelled in the citadel, but not one artefact has been found since.'

'Until today,' Evelyn says with a large smile.

'Right,' watching a swerve in the road. He spoke when it was clear again. 'You see, the very first image of the Regalia is in a portrait with Alas holding it with both hands. This portrait is our oldest and can be found in the Octum Museum in Esmehdar. We know the first treaty of Alasmieria was signed in the Regalia. When I first saw the book tonight, I knew it was an exact match, but I can only tell if it really is the Regalia if the treaty is signed by Alas himself, and by former council members.'

'Yes, it is. I've seen it,' scratching the back of her head and gets a handful of dirt. She brushes it off and focuses on his next words.

'I see. Then the Regalia could be a major reason why the Great War manifested. We are best to keep it secret. Many presume Alas turned on his council for his mind was overcome by power. I could speculate on this matter, but the fundamentals are lost leaving me with no real bread crumbs to follow. It's a burial. And right now, this knowledge is about six feet under with the rest of those artefacts.'

'Then why not study it as soon as we can? We have to use it for good, whenever you don't know what to do with something, always good. We don't have to do side quests anymore.'

'You've made me a believer now. But I promised I would finish my quest for a good friend. It's on the way to Eslr. I'm held in good faith for it, Evelyn.'

She takes a deep breath in and lets it out slowly. 'Ok.'

Six and a half hours of riding, they come to a stop near a patch of trees. It's exciting to Evelyn, traveling deeper within this amazing land. This land is hilly, away from the thicket they've rode for the time being. Evelyn yawns tiredly and they intend to eat together for the second time. Hopefully with more ease this time and less worry. She stretches her arms out widely watching Jale tie the white nord to a nearby tree. They take food from his saddle pouch and come to a sit under a tree.

Evelyn gets comfortable on the grassy beds of Alasmieria and Jale passes out dry toasted tree nuts and bread, with cheese and fruit. With very little words swapped, they enjoy themselves. She smiles with a mouthful and he smiles back.

He tells her they'll need to get their strength up for the long ride into night. It's an eight hour trip to the next province.

The kalec watch is on the surroundings, and as he chews, Evelyn can't help but wonder what spell he will use once the moon is out. She reminds herself of the Great Forest where the moon's light cannot go. That'll be a first for her. Still, it's exciting and thrilling.

Jale stands, and leaves her sides to retrieve a crystal form his saddle pouch, he puts it in his pocket. Why a stone? She has no idea why. Closer than before, the white nord is eating grass. It made her think about her lost steed. 'I suppose he's better off now.' She says lightly, watching Jale take out a fruit and vegetable, feeding his nord.

He returns to Evelyn with the crystal in palm. She can see its clear white and it looks expensive. Much like his unique wears, with vials and a gold pocket watch, though he never uses time and nor does she. The only time she found it pliable was during school, otherwise, the farmland and most of Alasmieria appears much the same. What can I say? It's timeless on most parts of Thaera, except the one and only, Brunon.

329

Jale kneels beside her and places the stone between his palms and breathes on the crystal, like to warm up his hands in a cold winter night. A bright light ignites within his grasp. His eyes close now. The brightness begins to shine brighter. There he sat, with legs crossed and eyes closed praying to a god he called Suyphun, and waits to receive word back in his mind. To those in Brunon, this may be condemned, but Evelyn knows the truth to their fearfulness, it's not magic, it's Cloradis.

She waits, looking around this unique world. The smell in the air is flowery from plants nearby.

Jale opens his eyes. He moves his palm and the stone begins floating. He touches it and it dabbles in the air, finding its balance.

Evelyn leans and touches it also.

'How do you do it?' She asks him neatly, watching it gently come back to centring.

'I Spellbound Cloradis to the stone so I can easily repeat it, that way it makes a quick way to have light.' And he moves the stone higher above them with Sophair, shinning it brighter. 'It's a great spell. I figured this one out all on my own. Most are taught The Way of the Light nowadays, that's what it's called. I learn much on my own. It is great, isn't it?'

'Yes.' Evelyn laughs with astonishment. 'But why pray to a god?'

He nods to her inkling. 'If you don't know already, Cloradis is a new type of Aura. It was discovered late into Reobigheon. Neither Alas nor Mieria knew of its source, odd right?'

She nods.

He moves the stone over her head and down, just above the nose. She giggles. He explains his new piece. 'Sohlie was a famous alke and is a legend today. She found Cloradis when she practiced meditation. She was never interested in the way of the Celestial and actually began to encourage all Reobigheon and those with the gift to move away from Aura. She said Aura held a memory bank of the old, which had a connection to pre-war and control. It's rare to find an alke who doesn't practice their gift – well, back then this was. You see, Cloradis is different. Clists nowadays who're practicing advanced Aura is as rare as Sohlie herself.'

'Ah yes a Clist.'

'You've heard of the term used before?'

'I've come across it in the book.'

'I see.' And he continues his earlier speech. 'Even for me, Cloradis has a different feel then Aura. The only way to explain it is Cloradis has a faster vibration, making it feel lighter while Aura is always a slower vibration, making it feel heavier.' He smiles. 'Sohlie first practiced at the Temple of the Moon in Reobigheon, on the outskirts of Emgacia, a famous meditation spot. She got famous for her discovery of a god who came to her in her meditation and called himself Suyphun. She got all her knowledge from him, and learned of his teachings. She began preaching aura's predisposition to only a handful of close friends and teaching Cloradis instead.'

'Intense.'

'It's actually a glimmer of information. Scholars today study her ways and just found out there is a new being channelling this amazing god, Suyphun. I won't get too far into this, but what I will say is Suyphun is encouraging us that anyone can learn of its ways, not just those with the gift. I found out about the man; who is not well known, but is growing in recognition. He is Calon. I imagine a new world of Cloradis for all, all the time now. Can you imagine a world of peace, one greater then Reobigheon?'

She shrugs her word. 'Beautiful.'

'Well, I'll have to end this; after all it was a rough night for the both of us.'

'No way, are you kidding me? Go on.'

'Well then, what I will say is, Sohlie soon became the headmaster of the temple, removing the word "Moon" with "Suyphun". This is near the end of Reobigheon, when nearly all of Alasmieria was in Reobigheon. After the Great War, her ways shatters and her knowledge scatters. In a huge way, the Great War played a role in opening the doors to her knowledge. So that's why I pray to the source, in respect to Suyphun and his adept.'

Evelyn looks up at the stone. He had moved it someplace above them again.

He glances too. It hovers his playing with it, having it in a circle around them. 'I only use the basic elements of Sophair to control it. It's more convenient. All with the gift should know how to use Sophair; it's a basic tool I should think. There is a rhythm to Sophair too. Find it and that's when your balance becomes second nature.'

'Really?' She reaches out to try and touch its passing; she almost falls to her far extension. She scoffs to his playful ways. 'I guess you're right. But I'm still finding it hard, especially with the heavier things. I don't know how to lift and then launch items with very much speed.'

'Ah. I found my balance hard with heavier things also, but that just takes practice. In time, the balance will come and then the speed.'

Genuinely, she thanks him.

'Do you have a god?' with distinctive. 'Do your people pray to one?'

She looked away and found her way back to him, relaxed by the calls in the wild. 'Yeah, Egerdians believe in much the same as you and I, I'd say. They give thanks and enjoy the amazing gift of life.'

'Traditions seem linked. It's a universal thing I suppose. A lot like those of the Errific, believing in nurturing nature, but I don't know how many follow that nowadays.' He suddenly blurs out laughing.

'Oh boy, now I see why they aren't fond of us. Well, surely it can't be as bad as praying to Alas?'

He props himself up to stand, 'fair enough.'

'This makes me think. I wonder how Alas felt about the divine power of Cloradis. Did he ever mention this power in any scribes or whatever?'

Jale shakes his head. 'It was never around.'

'Really? Nothing?'

'It's possible. The only way to know for sure is if Cloradis is in the book of Alasmieria. We can't do it here. We will read it someplace safer, but not in the open.'

'Alright,' she stands and stretches. She'll keep the spoiler to herself. He'll have to keep the guessing for this one, because she isn't giving it up.

Jale mounts first, and then the girl and they leave this quiet place behind.

The whistling of winds come and go, the thicket moves closer to the edges of a dirt path. Five and a half hours into riding, they stop at the forest.

'Wow... it's *huge*.' She says.

'A blanket of three tiers, it's… pitch black in there.'

'Is it dangerous?'

'The most, it's not called the Great Forest for no reason honey. In retrospect, it's called the forest of Truke. It's actually warm in there, because of hot springs, heating up the dome. It's an incredible sanction.'

They enter. The Way of the Light lit up their path before them, being at a glide ahead of them. The light kept Evelyn's focus for the next twenty minutes, but another hour into riding, all she wants to do is get a warm meal. At this point, the bumping keeps her mind sleepy. If they were to stop to eat, she's not sure if she would want to. It's this darkness, for it reminds of those furry paws. It could be out there, still treading about.

Even the seemingly unreal things have their wear offs – Evelyn looks away from the light. She can see when Jale too drifts off from riding, either the source of light withers or it moves further from the path. It's a great tool for keeping them both focused and awake. She is quick to give him a nudge to get him to refocus again.

A call in the wild is offering. It sends chills across her body. It sounded like a whale's cry, but deeper. It's too scary to look to the left or right. A blanket that covers them in abyss, Evelyn and Jale are well submerged in the dark. Evelyn manages to turn and look behind. Not a flicker of light. 'Hello black,' she says and overhears Jale snicker.

It's a very neat forest, where parts light up, having colours of blue in some and others in red. On Evelyn and Jale's passing, many things are changing and happening. One thing that stood out more so was yellow glowing vegetation and the unique way the plant life presented itself.

'It's enchanting.' She whispers. She doesn't know where they are geographically, if they're up in the hills or if they're in the clear, if there are more paths to the left or right, or how close they are to a ledge. Now she knows why it's called the Great Forest, for a glimpse of glowing pools and glowing spotted salamanders-things show up. It is short lived, for nothing seems to last when the speed Jale is taking them through is fast. Sometimes, the birds are bright from reflective feathers. Other times, in the pitch dark, the top of the forest will twinkle like stars.

'Beautiful.' She says, hinting at the ceiling. It's the only thing for a mile.

'Butterflies are caught in its invisible web.'

'What do you mean, web?'

'Well, you see, those shiny dots are the insects for a mother's feast, Naralasa are a nasty thing.'

'T-Those are spiders?'

He's void of shaky. 'I don't know what world you come from, but we call them Naralasa here, and they pry on the weak.'

She has an eerie look up and she points ahead. 'Keep those sarcastic eyes on the road.' And he has a playful smile back. She has her eyes focused deadly on the rise for most of the time, and he kept his eyes ahead. He makes a pincer sound and reaching back to pinch at her.

She hits him. 'Stop it.'

He laughs. By this time they've spent a good two hours in the thick of things – a bright winged beetle zips past her, just missing. She turns to watch it jitter behind, dissipating into the pure unknown. There are many beautiful things in this forest, and that beetle is but one of them.

A many of Lyricicen, which is another type of butterfly, will spot its light similarly to a dragonfly's.

Evelyn and Jale come to a curve in the road. In not long, the scenery turns neon purple, covering the entire forest in its viny grove.

'It's so beautiful.' She beams.

'Yeah,' he scoffs. 'Right… you don't even know what you're talking about. You step off this path – you see that?' He points quickly.

'I do.' She says pretentiously.

'One touch and it's.' He uses a hand across his neck and made a splutter sound with his lips. God those hot lips – Can they have sex already?

She pats him thankfully and calms herself in her seat. Many more dangerous looking plants oozing with neon drooling poison is lookin' quite pretty. She's just glad she's with noble-buddy otherwise this would have been a quick read.

'How close are we?' Evelyn asks him finally. They are moving away from the neon into pitch again. The silence from Jale makes her slowly close her eyes. She opens every now and again, feeling a shock from tilting. She has no idea how much time has passed. Until finally she leans her head forward, tiredly, she leans on his back. It's moments like these she could use that gold pocket watch.

'This is not safe for us, Evelyn.'

She can hear his voice, but the tiredness just makes her want to stay there longer. 'Ok.' She rubs her eyes and moves her head up again. The forest floor is sparkling.

Something thin and tall moves not too far out, if it wasn't for the glow of things, she never would have seen it. It was camouflaged with much of the same light, so when it moved, she made out its body shape from its glow. It appeared tall and stalky. It was definitely not human or related in any manner. Any such bug that large should only make her awake.

'Freaky.' She says and finds a refreshing site in Jale's distance. There is a path of spruce trees and it is fast approaching. She's thinking she's hallucinating. 'Whew, I knew I must be tired, but man, that can't be real.'

'No... that's real.' Jale responds.

A cast of moonlight shows. Finally, at its peak, the outline is breathtaking. This means they're leaving the forest of Truke. The wilderness around is thinning. They enter the spruce forest.

An hour and a half after passing into this new area, something new is also upon them. They ride alongside a wall made of stone. It's a fair size. She looks away, feeling her sleepiness, that heavy feeling still in motion. Jale promised they'd be there long before now.

'Oh, just when I thought you were going to fall asleep.' Jale's voice sounds.

Evelyn isn't sure what he meant by this. She notices this wall still running, which tells her it's going to lead them to somewhere...

She can hear crackles of fire someplace close. It takes her eyes off the run of the wall to look around. It creates a warm sensation in her mind. The crackles come and go, echoing far off into this bushy abyss. Before she could ask where it's coming from, there above the run, small orange lights are witnessed.

Fireplaces!

The land is already at a shift and they slow their speed because they're nearing a gate that is at the base of a slope, which appears to be a hill.

'What is this place?' She asks.

'The way into Tenor,' he says finally.

She points to a shade of a structure that stands out behind the gate. She doesn't know how far it's behind walls. The night plays tricks on her eyes.

She points at it. 'What is that?' Her voice is louder than before.

'A pyramid and a piece of mastery that these people occupy.'

She wants to stretch her legs. Can you imagine if she hadn't of chosen to stretch nine and a half hours ago? She would have been regretting it now. I know it. She decides to sit up straighter, 'you mean... people live in that thing?'

'Oh yes.' He nods. The steed came to a trotting and then Jalelilian closes his eyes, repeating a word and the light around them dies. Darkness crawls on them. Jale retrieves his stone and places it back into his saddle pouch. Evelyn can feel their speed nearly stop. A light blooms in the distance and the open canopy allows more light from the moon to shine their way to the outpost's gate.

A man walks towards them with a hand on the butt of his sword and with the other holding a lantern, which is breathing light on them. 'Good evening chaps.' He says and then realizes Evelyn. 'Oh, I'm Miss, I must have missed yeah,' wearing a long brown overcoat.

Jale speaks. 'It's just the two of us.'

The man peers lightly at them and then waves another guard over. The guard comes and spoke for the man with the lantern. 'Good evening,' he said to the two and then tilted his head at Evelyn. 'Celestial, do you have a port?'

Evelyn cringes. 'I don't have one. But I do have a temporary paper.' Her voice rings in her ears. The stillness of the forest makes this so.

The guard that was just called over is an official boarder guard. His uniform gave this away. He smiles lightly at her youth. 'Very well, can I ask the two of you to dismount and step aside while we perform a search of your things?' It didn't sound like he's asking.

He's pretty. Evelyn finds him attractive.

'This search is protocol noble.' The border guard says to him, with the one with the lantern standing aside. The guards wear blue clothes, and the border guard has a symbol of a shield marking his jacket. After all, Calon dominate in numbers, and power, so basically they do all the running of things.

'Yes, as always.' Jale replies and dismounts, stepping aside. Evelyn follows and watches the first man with his hand still on his sheathe. Her eyes fall back to the good looking man and she retrieves her paper from her pocket and waits with it in hand. She has this look around though, of something's not right. She has to look to her left, away from the gate and wall. It's because she fears something is moving just beyond sites. She took one step closer to the noble.

The border guard notices this mud spat girl. It's all over her. Then he sees she's rather covered from head to toe. He leans a little closer to see her mud stricken hair, smudged and dry.

'Did we get into an accident?' He finally asks the two, not having to point out the messy girl.

She touches her face where spits of mud are dots all along her face. She forgot about this. The back of her head is reminded of its sand like texture, which also covers the backsides of her sleeves. Even Jale seems timid of her appearance. Yet it is his beautiful robe that's rather muddy at the hem and this is an unusual site to have a noble so dirty. The border guard saw him as the utmost unjust.

'Practicing Aura, you know how it can be.' Evelyn says, keeping a straight face.

The guard frowns and looks away from the girl suspiciously, glancing at the lantern man for his opinion.

Jale leans a little away from her, not sure why she said this. Still, Jale said nothing, which surprised the guards all the more.

'It's as if the likes of you got yourselves in a bit of a scruff.' The man with the lantern says.

Nobody answers and finally the border guard spoke. 'That's fine, out there is expected. To be honest, I really don't care.' He turns to point next. 'Behind those walls of the post, there will be none of that. Is that clear?' He asks the girl, not looking to the noble.

Jale gave him a look and the man forgot his place, clearing his throat. The guard drops the idea and asks to see her paper instead. She does so and he reads it over. His brows are deep, and his eyes are blue, like hers. Hers a reflection of being lost in time, but only now can he see there is a woman behind all this mud. If secrets could tell; the guard wouldn't have the air to speak of her heart wrenching beauty.

She looks up at him with her eyes. He slowly hands it back, having nothing further to comment on the matter. When she looks at Jale, his confidence told her to believe in him instead. She looks away, a power she fears. Jale smiles anyway. The smile he wore, how nice it was to see it on his face. But what did it mean to her? It could have been soothing, but the yellowy only haunts more.

'Very good, I hope you two are getting along and enjoying your journey?' The border guard asks.

'Yes, very much,' Evelyn says, scratching the back of her neck with a single finger.

Oh believe me, Jale can see her insecurity. He only raises an eyebrow to her and looks up to the next words directed at him.

'My dear noble, of her majesty the finest, may I?' The border guard asks next, holding out his palm for his paper.

'Why of course.' He responds, handing it over.

Evelyn should have known better then to look away from such perfect slit eyes, but she's still young, no?

The border guard smiles to Jale, noticing something similar he likes in him also. He hands it back without a word. The border guard clears his throat to whistle for a third guard to start the search.

Just outside the stone gate, Evelyn still fears – she looks around them while they wait. She could feel the abandonment. She couldn't have made it on her own and she knows it.

It is cold on the earth standing on the paved roadway. The movement of Evelyn's rocking feet is due to shivers. She can't help but feel the Dark One's eyes watching, imagining it someplace not too far from them. The bushes are too thick to see through; the dark makes it more impossible. A Dark One could literally be standing behind it and nobody would notice.

She moves again a little closer to Jale and the guard. Neither appears nervous in the dark. She literally wants to light up the skies with her Aura, or get Jale to use another one of his god-spoken-spells to light up the place. She manages to stay calm, swallowing ever now and then.

Jale looks at her. She looks up and away. She focuses on the large structure instead. It's dwarfing, nearly a black shadow in the moonlight. She crosses her fingers, hoping she'll cross boarders sometime soon. It doesn't help with the fresh scent of firewood and the sound of laughter in the distance.

They had to wait for the rightful guard to search them. The man with the lantern moves closer to shine more light on the scenery and the third guard approaches. The third is told to search the both of them. He moves closer in the light and stops when he got a better glimpse of her. She smirks weakly. He's a younger man then the two lads, and he moves slowly, almost carefully. She couldn't help but cringe when she notices him hesitate to touch her.

'Oh for Pete's sake boy, get in there and stop waiting for Alas,' the man with the lantern says.

She felt the dirt on her sides as he pats her down. She smirks to the crumbling and he pulls away quickly, he then asks her to remove her pack. She does so, and he searches the remnants. He finds some essentials, and… beans. He holds it out and found a frown, dropping the sac back.

Evelyn shrugs, looking at Jale and then back at the young man. 'I couldn't find a way to eat them.'

'Hmm.' The young man replies and hands her bag back. 'Hit a rough patch?'

'Something like that.' She replies.

He moves to the white cloak one. The young man looks scared. He pats him quickly and says. 'You're fine.'

The guards can relate and they let a hand signal fly for the gate to open.

Evelyn's smile couldn't light up any bigger than this. She wants to scream "Yes" to the gate guards and hug them for the sake of letting them in. Finally, a place to wash up and get a warm meal inside, with all night to rest! She wants to light a fire and start right away.

The darkness behind her stares again and she mounts after Jale. They carry past wood doors of the boarder, and up the hill they go. Another guard at a post greets them, midway. Jale pays him for a card numbered "601" on one side, and the other "Route 29" in return for their stay.

'You'll be staying for one night, sire.'

Jale thanks the man and they continue up the slope.

'What about the Dark One, shouldn't we mention that to him?' She asks Jale.

'Absolutely not, they're capable of protecting the province.'

Evelyn relaxes, dropping her hands to her sides. She looks up. 'It's huge. How many live here?' the world becoming brighter being out in the open. The populace climbs with them, only to witness more torches and tents on their way up, seeing them out in the open stretch. But what also catches her eye is the outpost at the top of the hill. They ride this easy path guided by torches on all sides of them.

This is a night to remember

'The pyramid can hold very little. It is mainly for historical purposes and sightseeing. Though the pyramids and temples is a way of life in Tenor, it's a fairground for tents all along the province. Convenience is a way of life in Tenor for it's the land of traveling.' He turns his attention elsewhere. 'It helps with beautiful things like the pyramid, don't you agree?'

Evelyn turns around to look out at the wilderness behind them. She can see the gate closing. She looks forward again exhaling her retention. The large pyramid is up ahead and behind the hill, on her right. It is partially blocked by the outpost in plain view. 'Yes, it sure is.'

At the very top of the trail, Evelyn waits outside the outpost and Jale enters through the portal gate. He must have told them to open the gate, because it did. Rebuins move quickly to take hold of the noble's white steed taking the reins and leading Evelyn inside where Jale resides.

She witnesses from the top of the hill the other side. All the tents scattered beyond the forestry below, lighting up like stars in the night sky. Someone must be playing music; the sound of drums creates an earthly feeling – even the area smells of sod and mud, or… that could just be her.

There the Pyramid is in full view. It is heaviest surrounded with tents, small and large tepees. A large monument of stairs allows anyone to the pyramid's top.

The Rebuin takes her to the pens and helped Evelyn dismount. Jale asks her to get their supplies for some night's rest. He hands her the card and points to a station with tents, it is next to the tents drop-off station.

As she walks slowly, wilderness of campfire lights are easily witnessed from the heights, bright and trickling away to the far open scenery into Tenor. There is a lot of movement near the top, even for a quiet night. It's nice to know there safe for once, everyone, not just Evelyn.

She comes to the station and hands over the card given, getting a large heavy rug and tent in return. Evelyn struggles to handle just the rug so the Rebuin at the station helps her out, carrying the tent to the pens where the white steed waits. Evelyn drags the rug. She got halfway and the Rebuin helped her with the rest of the way. She huffs and puffs, finally dropping it to the sod. 'Thank you.' She says to the Rebuin.

His irises are nearly two blades of grass, slashing in the moonlight. He has hair let loose, down to his shoulders; a light brown.

'Of course, Celestial,' He replies smiling generously.

Carriages are also parked near the pens. A fine white and silky blue dress of a lady, along with her daughter at the age of ten; they struggle to get a tent inside their carriage's side door, with blue drapes and lanterns flashing on the outside of a window on either side. The back of the carriage is wide open, where a boy at the age of twelve struggles to put the rug in.

Evelyn runs over and helps the boy out, getting a whiff of his cologne.

He knew she was offering a helping hand, greeting her first. 'Celan,' he says with his other hand and she shook it back and says.

'Evelyn.'

Who could easily overhear the boy's mother and the little girl finally give up, dropping the tent with a thump. The children's mother has disappeared someplace other, probably to get help by staff.

'Thank you.' The boy says getting ready to heave the tent on his side. 'Where are you from?' He asks Evelyn.

'Oh, I came from Caszuin. I only just arrived here.' She responds, grabbing an end. They breathe heavier with it in hand.

'Oh wow.' The boy says with much surprise. And the boy's end is placed on the carriage edge and then Evelyn pushed from her side to get it fully inside. It slides on the carriage floor and fits in place.

His little sister appears and spoke, smacking the dirt off her hands from her troubles. 'Yes, we wouldn't dare go near that place. This is far enough; Mother is already treacherous being this far out.'

'Oh, where did you come from?' Evelyn asks the girl in surprise by her suddenness.

'Me? I should be the one to ask you that question.'

'Oh.' The boy sighs. 'Don't mind her. I'm sure she was eavesdropping someplace in the ride.' He pulls Evelyn away from the girl who then sticks her tongue out at them. He takes Evelyn to the front door where the other tent remains. 'We came from Rhion. These lands are not for us city folk.'

'Rhion,' Evelyn nods casually. She wanted to ask where Rhion is but pointed at the tent and the boy nods back. The little girl watches the two struggling a little with this one. 'It's a lot heavier.' The boy says, and Evelyn can't help but laugh from its weight.

'Oh, let me help!' The girl whines, joining her brother's side.

'No Anasea, take from the middle.' She does, lifting from here and the three manage to get the tent inside.

'*So* you're from where?' The little girl asks Evelyn.

'Caszuin,' she replies easily.

'It's a scary place where you've came from.' The Mother says, arriving to the scene.

Evelyn turns on her heel to see their mother in her beautiful wears, wearing that long and sleek.

'I survived.' Evelyn says, feeling self conscious around her cleanliness.

The Mother doesn't care about Evelyn's dirt covered self, though she surely notices. 'Thank you for your help, I gave up and went looking for my husband, wherever he is...'

'You too...? I see.' Evelyn says, and hopefully by no means to imply she had a husband, but instead, referring to the lack of muscle around.

She gave Evelyn a smile. 'Two peas in a pod I see.' Evelyn shrugs greatly at her words and the lady laughs her next piece. 'What can I say,' looking around some more. 'Men.'

Evelyn turns slightly to see Jale arriving. 'Here comes the cavalry.'

'Well hello there.' He says to the children firstly before anyone could make introduction.

They smile back and Jale reaches a hand out to their mother. 'Jalelilian,' he introduces.

'Cara.' She shakes his hand. 'I haven't met a noble yet. So this is a first,' and laughs candidly.

'We are scarce with our time, but I am generous, so you're in luck.' He says cheekily.

'I haven't met a noble Clairic, but I've seen a noble Calon before. She was pretty nice.' Anasea says.

'Oh? I hope she was.' Jale responds.

'Yeah, the last noble I saw was a Celestial. He was like you.' The boy says pointing at Evelyn.

'Oh,' Evelyn responds with as much bluntness.

Their father moves around to find the group in a bunch.

'We thought we lost you.' The Mother says, and the husband looks a little stranded with the strangers around, until he notices the noble wares, and takes a step back before ever offering to shake a hand. 'Well hello there, it's my honour my noble Clairic.' The man says, a little nervous by him. He moves in and held out a quivering hand.

'Yes.' Jale replies, watching his manners.

'I hope we aren't in some sort of trouble?' The Father asks.

And before anyone could speak, the little girl eyes Evelyn. 'Why are you all muddy?'

'Ana.' The Mother says with embarrassment. 'I'm sorry... she's not short of shy I'm afraid. We've been so far from the city on a personal matter; where are your manners?' The Mother asks giving her daughter a look.

The husband rubs her wife's arm. It was clear to see that they lost someone dear and that's the reasoning for their travels.

Jale crouches and responds to her little one. 'Well, let's just say it's been a late night for the both of us.' He stands. 'We should get going, but I do hope your stay is enjoyable.'

The family thanks him graciously.

He laughs when out of the family's hearing range. 'We've got to get you to the showers.'

'I know.' She whispers. 'I was trying so hard not to laugh before their personal agenda.'

Evelyn and Jale mount to take a small trail down the slope that seemingly leads farther away from the rest of the sites. They breathe heavier with the bumps in the road. The sound of distant drums die behind them and the sound of birds pick up. Evelyn asks. 'Are they expecting us to trek to the mountains or something?'

The moon is higher in the sky, making its mark. It casts a glow all too familiar in a land not so much. It's a land and story untold to her soul. She's dying to see what's next. Oh no... this means nightfall is upon us. What does this mean? Where will it leads us? All questions that stir her mind, oh, but she doesn't get to know the future. Which is a question for you; would you rather live the moment or the far reaching semester of what could be? I'll tell you this now; I'll give you my luck.

Do you wish you could reach for the stars or the things not so far off in the distance? Let's face it; we all want something that is outside of ourselves right here and now. Whether it be a dream, or a reality we think we want and can face. Whether it is a better relationship or just getting your mother to bugger off your back about the silliest of things, either way, do you know what it takes to get there? – I don't know either, but I'm willing to find out. Its funny how we sit and read about others lives, but what if we found that out was being read? Maybe we'd be more cautious of those around us? No? Would we act differently? Would you? Would you open your eyes to the possibilities? I know I am. Let's keep reading and find out.

Small wood polls mark numbers on them in white.

'The kalec who gave me the tent said it was close. I'm surprised myself.' He says.

'You don't think it's really this far out, do you?'

'I doubt it.'

They stride past a pair of larger trees and bundles of wood can be seen. The distances from the rest of tents are becoming grave. Not far now, a river is seen off the flash of moonlight.

'Oh look, we're here.' He says.

Evelyn was about to say something when the weight of the canvas rolled into him. She laughs similarly.

Jale gets the idea and dismounts to tie his steed to the nearest tree. He retrieves the tent over his shoulder, next. Evelyn touches earth and helps Jale who looks like he was struggling. They drop it near a fire pit.

He wipes his brow. 'Let's say we start a fire first, I saw some wood earlier. Stay here, I'll be back.'

'Alright,' she responds, not really focusing on firewood right now. With trees blocking the moon, the camp site is plain chills to bring. She calls out to him. 'Remember, it's still out there.'

'We're safe, Evelyn.' And his treads stray further from site.

Evelyn wants to yell out to him again for him to hurry up. She comes to sit on the rug instead and lights the surrounding with Tastraity. 'I wonder why it followed me so far...' She says, lost in thought about the Dark One. Then she peers at the curling river. 'It's out there...'

The camp is made up of a fire pit and a surrounding open space. She looks around. Crackles of fires are heard in the distance, but nothing is seen. She hugs herself with the unlit hand. 'All I want is to be someplace closer to the hundreds of people camped out near each other. Someplace safer... is that so hard?' Jale steed breathes out heavily from tiredness. She looks his way shinning the light at him. 'Not just me, you too huh?' she suddenly jumps to the sound of movement. 'Who's there?'

He laughs lightly, 'just a beast to come and eat you.'

Her laugh builds, becoming louder than ever before. She calms herself down and he knows it's because she's tired. 'That was fast.' She finally replies.

'It was nearby,' and drops the wood close to the pit. 'Let's start the fire.'

'With Lyric?'

'We are not aloud.' And he smirks his words. 'You know Aura is considered a weapon in public spaces?' His face is blinded by her hand of light. 'And besides,' he bends over and places her hand to her side. 'It's safer this way, fire keeps animals at bay.'

Evelyn leans forward; the darkness is closer to their faces. She asks. 'We just passed through gates though,' and swallows, 'aren't we safer behind them like you said we'd be?'

His face is closer, she wonders if it's the dark. 'Evelyn. You can never be too safe.'

She smirks and lets the light fall. She moves her eyes around but cannot see his face, only the remaining light reflecting off the riverbed glimmers. 'Fine, have it your way.' She says and waits. In not long the two are standing still. He hears Evelyn trying really hard not to laugh right about now, for nothing could ever get done in this grim.

'Alright,' he whines. Their lights are back on – his hand brightens to a full palm, being advanced and the finger tips lit for her.

'It's only one night.' She says sorely, moving around and goes out of site. She steps over a few branches, little ones crunch under boot and picks up the biggest ones for the fire. She returns to site and puts them down.

He didn't mind. He could see her smile just as he imagined it – and he liked it that way.

'It's not like we are with the rest of them campers. We are out in the middle of nowhere. So I say... a little Aura would do me and you some good.'

He laughs lightly. 'They did pitch us farther from the rest. I wonder if they knew we'd use Aura. Nobody likes the sun up earlier then it should be.'

'Really? I really love the sun. If I had it my way, this whole place would be morning.'

He scoffs. 'Well, when you come from another part of the world, I can't help but agree with you.' He turns to her reluctantly, knowing there's a grin on her face somewhere. 'Look, I have no idea what time your sun is up. Now, let's get this rug a push and pitch this tent.'

Evelyn makes sure her smirk is seen; knowing he's being overdramatic about the time-differences and helps him anyway. They roll out the tent. A simple way made the tent pitch, which makes Evelyn feel so much more thankful for the moment, but not because of the tent, alright, in part, yes, but for all the really great things that are here in her life. Did you know it's the first tent she's seen in her life? She's only heard of those in Brunon who camp out, a famous site near a large lake on the outskirts of Brunon. And what better then to set up structure in another part of the world, and with another race? I mean, that's an adventure worth mentioning.

'Perfect,' Jale's voice sounds from around the tent. 'A simple tepee, this will do.'

Evelyn places her paper and the book of burrows in the tent. 'I'll start the fire.'

'Perfect. I hope nothing too crazy though. We were only given a few logs.'

Evelyn laughs, which comes out sounding silly. 'Oh my good lord, you worry so much, just relax.'

He gives her a look; it was enough to see in the dim of her light.

She scratches an ear. 'Just joking...?'

He chuckles. 'I think I will unload our things now, and then I'll grab us a meal for tonight. I know you're starving.'

'Okay.'

He returns holding blankets from his saddle supply and all his other sleeping supplies. 'I'll see if I can buy you some clothes too. You aren't sleeping in those I hope.' He says tossing everything inside.

She makes a face at her clothes, not feeling the same. 'I guess not. Thanks Jalelilian.' She sounds genuine.

'Of course,' he says and leaves her. He and his steed return to the trek in order to get to the outpost on top of the hill.

She listens for the sound of them wondering off, leaving the night and Evelyn together again. She thinks about it, the book of Alasmieria. Evelyn stops at the door of the tent then goes through. Inside is a large enough room for at least six people to sleep comfortably. Animal skins used for flooring with a simple but heavy task of polls and pegs supporting the structure. It amazes her how such simplicity makes a unique structure – If only she knew how difficult a process it takes to create these materials...

Evelyn moves around feeling safer, walking around her pack. She touches the book's cover, opening the book and being instantly reminded of memories. Her eyes move in hesitation. She shuts the book nervously. 'Ok, if I'm going to do this I better not get caught, and least of all... not from Jale.'

The words are spoken; the book lights a blue within the tent. She flips the pages in search for spells to light a fire. She stops at one. 'Perhaps Tetlas never knew the power it beholds. Then again, I could just as easily be wrong. This would be so much easier if I had some burley on me. I'm surly not ready to attempt the true craft of a Celestial's nature. It's too... unsafe.' She looks around and thought she heard a sound in the wild. It gave her shivers. 'Ok, I'm going to use the book.'

She leaves the safe place with the massive book in hands to return to the pits. A fort is slowly built with the bundles of wood. With her Aura lit, she reads the words with the book spread out on the ground. If she only had a caldron; it would be a witch and her ritual. She finds just the right spell and closes her eyes, repeating the word from the book of Alasmieria. Following instructions, she focuses on the wood in her mind. The wood ignites. She claps her hands with excitement and they ignite also.

'Naenulaen!' the spell is said backwards and both fires blow out. Her hands glow with protection. She rubs them. 'Oh thank Alas I'm okay. Okay, maybe I did something wrong – Tetlas was right, *this* is way too dangerous!' Her thoughts dreadfully think of everything she would ignite if she would have to use it again.

She keeps searching for something simpler, but it only gets more sophisticated. So she gets an idea to try it again, this time, instead of her hands, her hair ignites – blazing aflame. Evelyn wants to scream, but focuses and repeats the words. Flames of Lyric defuse, but oddly enough, the fireplace remains alit.

She pats her hair, feeling the same hair where it was. She licks her palms a few and pats it again, in case any burnt residue should show… there is none. But what does show is a small glow on her hair. Her eyes wide from last moment's adrenaline. 'Wicked,' she blinks. 'I guess my own Aura cannot hurt me.' She thought about that one again, getting images of training with Tetlas. 'Okay… maybe the book doesn't hurt me then, because I'm its wielder. Wow, if so, than that is really neat. But then, how could you ever stop someone with this thing?'

Jale returns to camp ten minutes later. He oversees a blazing fire in the pit. He dismounts and ties his steed. He comes into range with a sack over a shoulder and places it down near the tent. With plenty of wears neatly folded under his other arm, he places it in the tent near blanket beds. She must have made them while he was out, he thinks. There beside one of the bed the book in burrow beside her map and paper.

'I got just a few clothes for sleeping and for staying warm tonight.'

'Thank you.' She says near the pit, brushing her hands together to keep them warm.

'A toothbrush and paste in case it's needed.' He says holding it up for her to see and throws it on her bed.

She nods in acknowledgement, enjoying the warmth of the fire.

He leaves to return with a cutting board and knife from his supply. He makes his way to her.

'I see you have things in order.' He says looking around the wilderness. He places his things down nearest.

'Yeah, you could say that,' turning her attention to something else. 'I see you've brought dinner. What is it…?'

'You'll see.' He says. He then stops and leans in a little closer. 'Are you okay? You seem a little frazzled.'

She breathes in slowly and breathes out. 'Oh yeah, I'm alright.'

He nods and walks away, picking up the sac near the tent where he last left it, making his way towards the fire and comes to a sit on the grass. 'So, how did you start it?' pulling out a little brown sac from the inside of a pocket for her to see. 'I forgot to give you this.'

'Burley fire, you bought me this?'

'Yeah,' tossing it to her. 'I figured we'd need one.'

She catches. 'Thanks.'

'It's nothing; I could have bought you a hundred more.'

'You're rich?'

'Oh course, I'm a noble, remember?'

Her mouth drops. 'I… didn't know.' And she slowly places it inside her pocket. 'I started the fire the traditional way, of course.'

He smiles to himself. Evelyn could see he knew something but never cared to share it. He got up to set up station with a cutting board and knife with a few bowls and lidded pots.

'Do you want any help with anything?'

He shrugs, 'alright.'

He looks around one more time and pulls a slab of meet out and drops it on the board. 'This is Lunan.' He says.

'Lunan?' she asks right away.

'That's right. Its beef, it's going to be the best. A simple pot cook will do the trick. A Tenor favourite I should say. It comes with vegetables and fruit,' and doesn't hesitate to start preparing for dinner. 'There is a bag with tools and cutlery in the saddle pouch.'

Evelyn listens, going where he directs. Her voice picks up in the distance. 'Shouldn't we take off the saddle, giving him a break?'

'Oh right.' He says. He approaches and together they take it off his steed. 'You know, all the way out here… it's quite nice.'

'I was just going to say that.' She says, smiling at him.

'You can see great shooting stars like no other in Tenor. It's known for that.'

'I remember those long quiet days.' She says, picking up the cutlery and cutting board and moves towards the pit.

He smiles to himself again, happy she can take care of things. 'Must have been nice,' he says, coming to a sit at his location again.

She nods at him, both lost in their reminiscence.

'It's amazing how much we change in life, looking back its incredible what I've become.' He says and pokes the fire with a stick to get it to settle. His ears jiggle at the tip. The darkness portrays the best of one's features at night. But for Evelyn, it's more of a fixation of his eyes, because they're so different.

There's some difference about him also. He's quieter at times but always with a confidence, yet he can be out going -- unlike her, for her usual all over the place. Even now, there's something else again; like he wants to say something about his past, but won't share it.

'Well. I'm impressed by your mannerism.' She says kindly. 'How you're handling yourself. You're the kindest and most intelligent being I've met,' as it suddenly feels silly for saying it out loud, it felt good. It doesn't feel that way for long. It's those eyes that remind her it's all a real life fable and she likes it -- she can risk it all, she feels. After what she's been through, no words, no thoughts could draw her away from who she really is.

He nods. 'Yes,' and begins chopping the meat into strips, and then cubes. He could see she is opening up to his features, so he looks directly into her eyes. 'Even if you are from another place, it's no different. But that is what makes it all so worth it. That's how one finds oneself -- the more people you or I meet, the sooner we will know. Then, will our heart --'

'Find its way?' She asks and goes on to sit up a little, daring to not look into those eyes anymore.

'Precisely,' he says, cutting his look through her like a knife on bread.

She clears her throat, caught off by this.

He smirks to a thought he just had. 'I never would have agreed to this companionship unless I felt you could handle it. It's like I said, the moment I met you, I felt something was different.' He places the cubes into a bowl and put them aside to retrieve a pot. He gathers his board and knife along with it. He leaves Evelyn to go down to the river to wash off the blood stained board and knife. He fills the pot with river water. He returns finding Evelyn chopping vegetables into cubes like he had done with the meat.

He places the filled pot right into the fireplace, so it can boil. They finish chopping the rest of the vegetables together and after a good while the water boils. He left it to boil another ten minutes in order to rid of parasites. He first places a bag of grain in and then scrapes the cubes of vegetables into the boiling, and then dumps the cubes of meat in also. 'Thanks. Just toss yours in.'

She does so. 'I'm just glad I've changed. Now I'm attracting everything and everyone I want in order to get me where I want to go, you know?'

'I do.' He says simply, seasoning the brew. He leaves to find a cover for the pot. When he returns, he places it on top, slanted so the steam can rush out. He returns to his board, taking out fruit to chop up. 'I'm going to add the fruit in for later.'

It feels even better that she can share her opinions with another, and so openly. Besides this, the topic of choice is one of unorthodox, yet that's what's so beautiful about it.

Those eyes, they scare her but she risks another look. 'It looks like it will taste good. I don't think I've ever cooked vegetables and fruit together, though.'

'It's good.' He doesn't look up. He smiles, peeling a fruit with his knife in hand.

Evelyn leans back, the chills are coming back. It floats up her chest – the tingly sensation. He's a mystery to her, with her mind playing tricks on her; there is no telling what this night will bring to her.

I like him. He's more mysterious than ever before – She wonders if it's just the moonlight getting to her head.

He raises an eyebrow to the silence.

'Let me help you.' She asks him. She hopes he can't read her mind – I mean you never can be too safe. His words, not mine. She hangs in there, managing to peel a fresh fruit, and then dicing it, discarding the skin into the bush. She gets up and carefully takes off the lid with her sleeve. She brushes a Pio, a type of fruit that is both bitter and sweet into the pot, replacing the lid. She licks a finger and came back to a sit.

'I'm pretty tired. I'm feeling a little sleepy tonight.'

'Are you?' He asks, seeing a change. Watching her through the fire; the flames slither up and down, side to side.

I see it in his eye. He's a stranger, but I can't help but follow him; he's like Alasmieria soils in the flesh and bone, walking and breathing – *he knows this place better than anybody else, which is why I must continue with this friendship*

She nods back and says. 'I think I'm just going to go sit in the tent for a bit.'

The top pot shakes with bubbly fume; Jale slides it away from the flames with a sleeve, 'alright.'

Evelyn takes her boots off and walks across the cool grass. She enters through curtain doors and closes it behind her. The cold grass is off her feet; she closes her eyes and breathes out slowly -- a look to the fireplace. He's moving towards the tent.

'Evelyn?' His head pokes inside. 'Is everything alright?'

She just stares back. It felt long. 'No.' She replies, not wanting to lie but not wanting to tell him what's on her mind either. She feels like she's going to faint. Holding her breath in anxiety, finally she lets it go and tears begin to fall from her eyes.

He just watches. He didn't know what to do, but instead walks in and sits beside her. He doesn't know if he should hug her or... what, but reaches.

'I just miss her so much!' Evelyn says.

He pulls back.

She leans and grasps him, falling in his arms -- a safe place in this world, just like she remembered it. The same feeling when he grasped her in Caszuin. Her mind runs with thought.

He closes his eyes and remains patient knowing she'll come around anytime soon.

She stops after a few minutes of brooding and comes back up for air. She looks up into those eyes -- she moves back where she was sitting and stares at the ground, unsure what to do. 'I'm sorry.' She decides to say.

'No, I mean, it's a bit of a surprise but what you're going through is a lot of change.' His next voice is soft. 'Look at me.'

A faint look is mustered.

He giggles. 'I forgot what I was going to say.'

She finally giggles with him, lightening up her mood.

'I know what you're going through.'

'You do?' She asks with eyes staring up at him, a sea blue and those that he believes should never be stormy in the first place.

'Yes. Look...' He says and breathes out, but just can't find the right words to speak again.

Evelyn only nods, knowing this is hard for the both of them.

He raises an eyebrow. 'It wasn't till I gave up being something for others that I was then free.'

His words scare her a little. It's odd because it struck home. She tries not to stare at him. 'I know exactly what you mean.'

'I'm glad.' He says. 'I miss my parents too, you know. And whatever happened with you, and you don't have to tell me anything -- it's a grand thing, finding your way.'

She smiles back. It's quiet for a bit. The fire crackles in the distance. A warm hush hums over her being, like a blanket to sooth the mind. No need for Cloradis this time, but natural peace of mind.

'Man I'm hungry.' -- Jale sounding more like Evelyn already -- Must mean he *likes* her.

'You're right.' She laughs, 'me too.'

They serve themselves and eat on wood plates, with steal forks all provided by him, of course.

'Where are your parents?' Evelyn asks carefully.

'Well.' He laughs. 'It's perfectly normal to want to know my history. I just don't talk about my past anymore.'

He looks to the tent. And she is unsure what he is thinking. A look of caution in his eye, 'I know. This is something else. This land and I, but I can only offer who I am.'

She nods, understanding how he felt. 'It's like you said with Law of Wish – I'm only here because I want to be… right?' She stands up and yells out, 'thank you Law of Wish for this amazing life!'

'Ha-ha, well now you're catching on! Oh! We better freshen up if we are to have a clean sleep.'

Evelyn looks towards the river. 'You can't be serious?'

'Oh yes.'

They finish eating and place their dirty dishes into the river to clean up. The water is rather cool. But to dip entirely one's body during night hours is something entirely else. Jale is already undressing. This makes Evelyn nervous, so she takes the plates and places them on a rock bed next to them.

Jalelilian removes his socks, stripping down his robe to a pair of underpants.

This is a new site for her, but a good one altogether. He makes no mistakes showing the best parts of his lean body, intimidating all the same. She looks away, taking off her boots. She doesn't wear socks. She came to the shore first and tip toes into the water. Her robe touching at the seams, covered in sand.

He takes off his last piece of clothing and tumbles in behind her, slashing.

She tiptoes and stops at her calves. 'It's freezing!'

'No it's not. It's warm. See.' He twirls around.

She moves in deeper and he comes up to Evelyn, looking about.

'Don't you dare splash me,' she says. He looks up at her and laughs at her silly words. 'Jale, I'm serious.'

'Oh alright,' he grins. 'I'll take all mine off if you take all of yours off.'

She smiles at his pretty face. 'Silly, you can't fool me. I know you're naked. I saw you.'

He smiles at her body image. It's smooth, perfectly curved. She undresses from her robe, which took some time and shows more skin. Wearing underwear and having one hand across her bare chest, she tosses her robe at him teasingly.

'It's tempting?' He swims closer to her with the robe in hand.

'No Jale.' She says shaking her head at him, looking cautious.

'Oh alright,' he whines.

Evelyn knowing well enough he wanted to splash her, or pull her in.

The way her sharp hips show is a feminine stature anyone would risk for a peek.

'I'm not comfortable with any of this.' She says pointing at herself.

'Ok.' He swims away.

She let a faint sigh of worry out and screams as she enters the pool -- a strong few seconds later and the cool fades.

'See?'

'Better.' She finally says, spouting water at him. He dips under, disappearing for awhile. Evelyn looks around, not sure how far off he could go. It's quite shallow, so she moves in a little deeper, looking down. All there's is black.

He appears in front of her with his chest above the water. All she can do is make a face. He disappears the second time.

'Jale, we aren't playing any silly games here, who knows what lies under these depths?'

The current has a slight push.

'Over here.' She overhears him.

She squints. 'Where?' and comes to feel the bottom in a shallower area. She catches a glimpse of him and something moves over the water – she thought it was a fish. Rather, a ball of water tumbling over the surface to flow out and dissipate. She swims to him. More water rolls, tumbling off her. 'Clayast?' she touches them, melting off her open palm, others pushing her fingers with a stronger flow.

'A tricky one,' he says.

She smiles largely. 'It's beautiful.'

'I know right?'

But she wasn't looking at the rolling anymore. A perfect statue in the moonlight, every muscle dances with the movement of his thin arms, beautifully in shape. Standing six feet, she's never seen such a toned looking man in so much joy before.

His palms move, shifting from one angle to next. Clayast is moved, swirling and haunting to the skies. He brought it back down and a stream literally snakes around her, swivelling five eight. In fascination, Evelyn's eyes sparkle like the magnificence as if it were sapphires.

'You any good with Clayast?' he asks her and drops the swirl of water around her with one splash.

She laughs a little wiping her face. 'I've only tried it a few times. But this one's not too hard.' She does her best with Sophair; blowing a splash of water at him.

'Not bad.' Jale replies with a wipe to an eye. He goes on forming more shapes and sizes.

'I've created a fireball before by superheating Sophair. I have a few more tricks up my sleeve, but nothing more than the basics.'

'I see. That will have to change.'

'Jale,' she asks.

'Yeah?' he stops, dropping his Clayast.

'Tell me all the strangest things, so there are no more surprises.'

He smiles at her. 'Come, let us get some rest. Let's put the talk for tomorrow.' He can see worry on her face. The worry of the world, to wake up and face it all tomorrow is always the nerve wracking part.

They wash their clothes, with Tastraity relit. Evelyn can see the rocky bed below. A few fish will glide by when she's most still. She washes her hair, ridding of all the sandy bits, between her toes and on her body.

They dry off near the warm coals of the pit, hanging their wrung out clothes over branches. Evelyn disappears into the tent. She waits till his back is turned to her and she closes the tent with him still outside. 'Ashnivarna,' she whispers.

Jale notices a glow of blue; he turns towards the tent curiously. Now he finds her voice calling.

'Want to see something I can do that's pretty neat as well?'

Jale gave a cautious look.

'Nealunean,' he overhears. The coals blow out in one whip and darkness falls upon him.

'Evelyn.' Jale voice whispers. But then he thought about it, lightening up. 'I've never seen a spell make me feel so enticing before. My, the power of the council is mighty.' He approaches the tent and finds her with a wide smile.

'Now you've done it.' He says playfully and runs in after her.

She screams playfully back.

The following morning was much more magical, though she didn't expect for the kalec to be up so early. She yawns and stretches her body, pointing her fingers towards the wall. Her body is naked, underneath smooth covers. She looks around, wondering if they had done something last night she didn't remember.

'How did I get undressed?' She says under her breath. Worrying if there is some sort of spell to make her lose her memory, she's in the mood to make sure she gets her answers.

Jale enters through the drapes and walks around. He stops; his notice of her becomes apparent. There she peers at him. His long white robe with gold outlining brings Evelyn's memory back to the place where she roams once more.

He smiles.

'Hi.' She says. 'We didn't?'

'No,' shaking his head. 'We went to bed as soon as you blew out the fire.'

Evelyn is still, knowing quite well he didn't approve of that surprise. They go on to agree on using the book only when together and it clears the air between them.

He looks away and spoke. 'I made breakfast. I can't find... there it is.' He reaches over her. Blankets in a bundle, curled all over the place. 'Forgot my things,' he grabs a brown booklet and a pouch nearest her and heads back out.

Evelyn lays her head back and takes a deep breath out. 'Yikes, that was a lot to handle.' She gets up to find her clothes neatly folded in the corner of the tent. 'I definitely didn't do that.' This random kind of act from Jale made her smile.

She dresses into her sleeping clothes to go outside. Sunlight is blinding, shining right onto her face. And the air is warm. A chill runs up her spine though, prickling as it goes.

There Jale approaches with her Rebuin robe in hand, passing it over.

She awakens to her senses. The long travels of today are ahead of them, she must be prepared. She gets dressed leaving her sleeping clothes in the tent and joins him for breakfast. He carries his own cooking oil and so much more.

For breakfast, they have chopped Olums; which are potatoes, there is also vegetables tossed with salt, and protein from yesterday's buy, which was placed away in a canister to keep sanitary and locking its scent from animals. Evelyn leans over the pan smelling it all. They split breakfast in half and eat on the grass on this warm summer day. The bugs zip and the sun beats. The fire pit embers, crackling in the new dawn.

Evelyn wipes her mouth. 'We never did finish our last conversation about the book of Alasmieria, did we?'

'This is true.' He replies and scrapes the last of the potatoes from pot with a spoon to plate. 'You've been through a lot, no? With the incident back at Caszuin, and the dark one, you sure you're up to studying?'

'I am. We can't slow, I'm just too eager lately! Curiosity seems to be getting the best of me. And by the way, thanks for all of this, for everything.'

'You're welcome. Curiosity does that. Then first I must ask what do you know of Alasmieria's history?'

'Not a lot. Tell me more.'

'Of course,' he nods readily. 'The Reobigheon city; I believe we discussed the basic fact but never its origins?'

'Yeah, but more about the council and its treasuries, I believe.'

'Alright,' he explains. 'Reobigheon is a wasteland, separating the two regions to date. The great city Evaloak isn't too far to travel from there, which resides as the capital of Calliskue. A dangerous place, their home is no place to cross; anyone who enters will find a tough return.'

The feeling of frisky runs about her, 'tell me more about the history, after the Great Battle. What happened to all of the Reobighians?'

Perhaps it will lead to explaining his past in familiar parts

He explains as they eat. 'The Great Collapse, Separation, however you put it,' clanking fork to plate, 'for it has a different pronunciation to everyone. The day after the Great War, or Battle as you put it, put the people of Reobigheon in the most difficult situation.' He spoke at the side of his mouth as he chews. 'When they turned to Calliskue, they were pushed away. The Errifics returned to normality of their origin but their rules had changed. Calliskue didn't accept any mix bloods, just thy pure because they blamed everyone else for the Collapse.

'The Reobighians had one last choice, Caealon. It is difficult to tell the difference from Errifics and Reobighians, but there are tell tale signs, of course. The Caealon criteria were simple, no Errific allowed. Reobighians had to prove this in order to be allowed access. This era is known as The First Act.'

'What kinds of signs though -- like height?'

'Exactly, Caealon found it easy to allow access to Reobighians; the only problem during the Great War was losing paper and documentation.'

Makes me wonder about all the families misplaced and separated because of differences

'Alright Mr, so what happened next?' She asks.

'The Second Act and the riskiest of all; final outcasts of Alasmieria, those of purebred Errific were aloud passage into Caealon -- why? I'll tell you why. Calliskue closed its doors to all, including purebreds after Caealon's act hit Callikons rule. Thy king wasn't too happy about this.' He says with muse. 'Anyone who left Calliskue had to fend without citizenship. When Calliskue announced this, Ceaelon was shocked; we didn't have the heart to leave Errifics without a home – how could we? Heartless bastards -- this was not the world we would stand for, and that is how The Second Act was formed; being four years after the first.'

She thought about it, looking up at the clear skies. 'Caealon took a huge risk with this. I can see why Calon and Rebuin had to be formed today…'

'Yes. Anyone could flow in and out of the country for a certain timeframe. This would allow access to the run-away-Errifics who were meant to make it here safely. As soon as Calliskue's ruler found out -- he immediately interferes.'

'What happened next?'

'Think of it this way, just a Calliskon mentioning something against rule would put them up for treason, forget about planning as many as they could for an escape. When we saw them crossing between Reobigheon, I remembering thinking what our world has come to, watching them kill on the very plane that housed friendships -- our families, our brothers and sisters.' He stops and starts tearing up. 'It's so hard,' he can hardly speak, 'to watch that. I remember a man yelling out in the thousands of our county's line, waiting to help. He keeps yelling, 'Do something!' in the ranks, 'we have to do something!' over and over as we watched our families fall.' Jale weeps again and she holds him. He breathes in her arms and tries to collect himself. 'We watched them burn -- their screams in massive numbers, each one someone we came to reunite. We were supposed to be fighting for them. What would you do if that was your mother on the line?' He shakes his head. 'It was an ambush. We stood there and watched, for a good minute, watching their humanity fall apart, and the run-aways hold on for their lives. They would just have to pass the line of scrimmage between Reobigheon and our land before we could help. Otherwise our interference would be considered an "Act of war". I remember, the man continued to yell, 'Do something!' I remember he roared and all of a sudden...' He pauses, looking hazed until he found his words. 'We stepped in. I've never seen as many riders, and arrows fly in defence. We aren't a tyrant raid, but we fought for our loved ones that day and crushed everything in our wake without blinking. Somehow, we found a way. We knew it was impossible to stop Errifics apposing, but we did...'

Evelyn shakes a head. 'I can only imagine the run-aways difficult task of escaping the woods, and to go for miles?'

He nods. 'They were running low on food, and to cross the dangerous lands was enough.' He says spitefully. 'But their own to wipe them out?' he just shakes his head and then continues. 'After the battle took place, the stories from that day forward would never be forgotten. We knew then what our country would stand for, and peace would remain for as long as we could stand for.' He finds laughter in the moment. 'You couldn't imagine the runaways' euphoria. It all seems so simple, but to gather but a whisper of mentioning something against the throne would be treason in Calliskue, let alone planning thousands to make their great escape? Amazing, and I remember they smelled of pine and Dark Spice; something known as Krapilla -- harvested from the dark bark in the depths of Evaloak.

'After the battle on the field, we returned to the boarder of Caealon. And there they are, all huddled around. At first, the runaway eyes reflected all but an echo. But, when they saw their friends and family again, their hearts broke free and Caealon celebrated in reunion. This was what shocked the hearts of the nation, giving Caealon the acknowledgment of peace once more. Freedom was the answer and still remains for us.'

Evelyn sobs and after some moments she looks up at him. 'But… that leads me to you.'

'What about?'

'You look exactly like an Errific.'

'Yeah,' he says. 'I am misplaced in the eyes of our friends, but both my father and mother were born Reobighian. Their ports led me passage into Caealon. You yourself are a Rebuin for your blood is Reobigheon, yet the Aura of an Errific runs in you. But you appear Calon, despite your differences. It's the appearance that gets to everyone – not the blood. You will still be treated as one, Evelyn. As long as the Calon see them in you, you will be given grace.'

'Yeah I got that lesson early on at Caszuin… with those guards.' Her tone is serious now, 'how many had been saved in the Second Act?'

'Not much.' He shakes his head. 'I wish it was everyone. Our population is estimated a little over two point three million, which includes the few Reobighians who decided to stay, instead of perishing to some other land – that I believe. Calliskue is seventy five thousand, most purebred. Reobigheon was four million back when. No more than ten thousand died during the Great War. Still, that leaves one point six million deserters who never returned to a side.'

'…Wait, you say the Calliskue only have seventy five thousand? That's not very much.'

'Even though, they still outnumber us,' he says. 'Their infantry is twenty percent their nation. Ours is approximately ten, giving us two hundred and thirty thousand troops, if I'm not correct.'

Evelyn thinks out loud. 'Okay, but what's twenty percent of seventy five? About...'

'Fifteen thousand Errific,' he says with a smile. 'It's very low, I know. Here's the breakdown. For every one Errific, it's equal to ten royal troops.'

Evelyn is quick to frown. 'Still though, we would nearly double them, even if they're ten times our unit. Add a zero to fifteen thousand and that leaves one hundred and fifty thousand for them.'

He nods. 'But here comes the kicker, the Caealonian's army is broken down into half the Royal Guard and the Army of Caealon. The Army is nothing more than bow, sword and shield with little tactic. The Errific would light them up, much like a matchstick to a haystack, so... that leaves the Royal Guard left, who are our major protectors in Esmehdar. The Royal Guard are the ones that fought on the forefront for our families -- an army that's made up of supreme swordsmen, rogues, Celestials, Clairics and the best-known lot from all across Caealon. So in retrospect, we can only compare our Royal Guard, placing us at half our units. We're about fifteen thousand disadvantaged.'

'You don't think we could survive their wrath?'

He seems taken back. 'We are not a fighting nation. We are kind. We all know if Calliskue would start war, they could obliterate. Either way, it would come down to every able man and woman in Esmehdar, including the queen who rests in her chambers to fend off those beasts.'

'Hold on. She doesn't rest in Rhion; I would only expect that, no?'

'Understandable, but no -- the Calon are a people trying to get this pushed, and they're in numbers, but her majesty feels she must respect all people of the nation and not only a soul party; that of Rhion represents. Anyways,' he says. 'We have a long day ahead.' He gets up with his plate and takes Evelyn's. 'Let's take the tent down. The sooner we head out, the sooner we can get to Eslr, the sooner we can get the answers you seek in Esmehdar.'

More bugs zip and buzz in their ears. Evelyn can smell fire and she can also hear faintly, deep earthly drums.

'Is there more to this quest then you say, or simply to get a move on? You never did tell me what it *really* was for.'

Jale smiles, 'I know, but all we need to concern with is packing, the faster things go, the sooner things move around here. And plus, don't you want to read once we get there?'

Evelyn agrees, his words are attractive – he's only saved her life and helped her sleep under a roof or two. If anything, she believes now is as good a time as any to have more faith in the kalec; it's only because she's worries about his stupid quest.

They attend to the tent, and first clearing out the blankets and pillows, the exterior came next. For such a simple way of living, Evelyn feels she could do it regularly. It's comfortable. The sun beams down on their backs. Jale's face has changed yet again, something entirely noticeable in people. The appearance is still the same, but the way she feels about them changes course – she notices new features that she might have overlooked. The way his iris appears in the light, to the way he acts. To her, there's nothing better than watching a kalec do his line of work, throwing around large objects, even if she can't see what's moving around behind that robe of his.

'Well, to be honest, I didn't expect this camping thing to work out so well.' Evelyn says. Jale is quiet beside her. They pull off the skin drapes together. 'It's really comfortable, this sort of space of our own and all.'

'I'd think so.' He says and looks up to see a smile. 'The weather has picked up lately, summer is here.' He looks to the skies next. The sun is golden and blinding, like thunder, if thunder could remain constant.

When they look up, they can only feel the heat on their faces. Evelyn wipes her brow. Her bruise showing through the opening on the arm of her robe is noticeable.

They finish packing and ride with their supplies to the top of Tenor outpost. Evelyn can feel the book in burrows in her pocket. Her pack was filled with her new clothes and supplies that Jale picked up for her last night – what a sweetheart, right? Her paper document is safely packed in as well.

Together they dismount at the station, tying the nord to a nearby tree. The scenery is great in daylight. Nords are heard drinking in the pens behind them, where carriages are seen not too far, with people leaving and coming, some unpack for stay, others leave to go.

A woman approaches the station and struggles to lift her rug on the counter; Evelyn was about to help her but stops when Jale steps in to. He manages to get it up all on his own.

'My Alas,' the woman says. 'Aren't you two a cute couple?'

'Thanks.' Jale says in hesitation and turns back to the station when a kalec asked for his site card.

'Oh, we aren't together.' Evelyn says and squints at the woman because the sun's beating in her eyes.

'No?' The woman asks, nudging Evelyn and giving Jale a raise of her eyebrow or two. Evelyn did not like this; in fact she frowned and stepped away. Nobody touches her. Not unless she says it's ok to do so. The woman continues, getting the hint by her body motion. 'Where are you two heading, if you don't mind my asking?'

'We come from Caszuin.' Evelyn responds and swallows at the girl's pushiness. She's a middle age woman, a dirty blond. Evelyn caught a glimpse into Jale's eyes after, but looks away. It suddenly made her think of the woman's suggestions.

'Are you going deeper east?' The blond asks lightly, raising her hand to shed her face under the sun's heat.

'Yeah, we're heading to Esmehdar together.' She responds.

The woman leans in a little closer, and breathes in deeply. Was she smelling Evelyn or... just happy to see her? 'I'm betting you've been up close to The Spine then, seeing you're from the land ajar?'

'No. But I'm sure Jale here would be glad to tell you.' Evelyn replies and steps back again.

'Oh.' She says, giving him a look over again. Her eyes widen to his uniform.

Evelyn lightens up – It's a beautiful day, so why not? 'But what caught my eye most was the Great Watch.' Evelyn replies, and even manages a smile.

'Magnificent isn't he?' The blond asks her, a focus still remaining on Jale's body, a little lost in imagination I think... She turns back at Evelyn in her mysterious manner. 'Have you've ever heard of the stairway to heaven? I wouldn't mind taking you there.'

Evelyn blinks. The woman's words surely caught Jale's attention too. A man approached just then, leaning on the blonds' shoulder. 'Hi honey.'

He says, noticing the "Pair". He wears a country hat… if that's what one would call it. It's basically a cowboy hat. This signifies to Jale the far travels from Rhion, the capital of that. Evelyn's never seen such an odd looking hat. Evelyn only has seen a cap, which started in Egerd.

'This is him, my husband, John.'

The man smiles to her introduction. He has a scruffy face and nice eyes. He has a plaid shirt which smells of hay.

You never mentioned anything about him…

Jale raises his brows. The woman and man are staring at them like they're the last two sizzling pieces of steak on a burner. Before Jale could step in, Evelyn shakes the man's hand and Jale reaches in for his introduction next, only more slowly – hoping Evelyn will get his point.

'So where do you come from?' Evelyn asks, unsure of their conversation.

The blond responds. 'We moved from Rhion to the beautiful city of Esmehdar.'

'Oh, are you serious?' Evelyn asks.

The woman could see Evelyn's eyes glow, and the woman offers an imaginative expression. 'It's such a beautiful place. You can see the mountain tops where white peaks are.' Her flattery blooms, 'me and John here used to go traveling up in the hills by Rhion all the time, but those compare none to the beautiful mountains of Esmehdar, which are really, really…' The woman said it while looking into Jale's big slit eyes, 'really big.'

Evelyn clears her throat. 'Well, I'm glad we are heading that way. I'm really eager to get there, right Jale?'

He nods unintelligently. Evelyn frowns at it.

'So are we.' The woman replies. 'A city of dreams, I still get shivers when I arrive home.'

'Jale,' Evelyn says and turns to him with bigger eyes. 'You hear that?'

'Oh I sure did. It's a beautiful place, Evelyn.' A hilarious tone used – Evelyn frowns again, knowing it's not like him… to find it uncanny. There is an awkward moment and the woman compromises.

'Why don't the two of you stay for a while,' while reaching in to touch Evelyn's arm.

'Oh.' Evelyn moves back, not sure of that one.

Jale has a humorous look. 'Yeah, what do you think Evelyn?'

Evelyn gave him another look, and turns back. 'Well no, no we really *should* be going, we have places to be.' And lightly backhands him in the solar plexus when he's not looking. He let out a wheeze and Evelyn finds the man who has straight eyes on her.

Oh no...

She has a hard time looking away. Her site blooms.

Jale leans a tinge closer to Evelyn. 'You're blushing.'

'Shut up.' She whispers. He blocks another sneaking hit.

The country man smiles his words. 'We are heading down to the market. You two look like you could do with something more before you head out. What do you say you tag along? We could use some extra hands for breakfast.'

Evelyn glances at Jale's who has eyes wider, hoping she's finally getting the picture.

His wife adds. 'We plan on making our favourite, sloppy Joes.'

Evelyn looks confused, like she's trying to figure something out. 'Oh, you don't say? Sounds like fun...' looking for Jale's opinion.

The man leans in and hugs an arm around Jale. 'Well you smell pretty good. What do you think -- sloppy Johns?'

'Joes,' Evelyn snorts the reminder.

They all look stiff. It took but a moment for her to realize what had been happening.

Jale releases the man's arm on his shoulder and spoke more loosely. 'We've got a lot of work ahead us.'

'Oh we *know* you do.' He replies.

Evelyn gets a wink from the woman.

Evelyn's mouth drops. '...How about next time?' raising brows at Jale to get going. Evelyn and Jale run off.

He has to ask. 'Did you say maybe next time?'

'It's all I could think of,' in sort panic.

He finds his humour again. 'Aren't you glad you've met me?'

'Right,' she finds hers.

They arrive to Jale's steed. He spoke, looking far off. '...The last time I did it, it hurt. Chains, whips, you name it.'

'*Oh* you're *so* toying with me.'

'Ha-ha,' he backs off. 'Alright, but if I had to guess, they probably must have had a dozen toys. You ruined their --'

'You finish that and you're dead.' She teases.

'Right,' he laughs. 'Okay let's get out of here.'

'Why? They wouldn't --' she turns before she finishes to see their eyes glancing around, and finding their eyes on hers again. 'Okay, let's go.'

They restock on supplies and food before their leave. Jale unties the steed with the reins in hand and Evelyn follows behind; loving the site of the pyramid, one of a sandy texture. It glimmers gold, with heat waves moving along the diagonal structure.

They stop at a clean spring water pump, refilling water jugs that hang from the sides of the steed. The steed breathes heavily at him and Jale pats him softly. Soon after, they buy food and refill the saddle pockets with fruits and vegetables. Evelyn places loaf of rye bread and jars of seeds within the pouch, with a jar of honey and Coranut butter; in resemblance to peanut butter, only crushed. A shiver runs along her body and she stops to face the pyramid again. 'I remember that dream... with the pyramid. Huh... looks just like it.' She decides to let this one go.

Evelyn finishes and mounts. She can see only forestry tops ahead. Where she imagines farms and mills are occupying the remainder land outside of Tenor, in the realm of Eslr. Jale mounts afterward and takes them to an easier path down the slopes, a better way for carriages and nords that can't handle the steep slopes down. It's a curvy road. It comes to more bends, along unlit torches that mark the way.

Sunlight cuts through the Tenor tree lines, the same kind of bird that was heard in Caszuin calls. Evelyn can see it in the treetop. Tall and feathery, with blond colors; it sang as mysterious as the playpen she's going to enter now -- an unexplored land -- here we come.

The great pyramid is no longer in view. The caverns of the gold burrow deep into ground, for additional shelter, something she wishes she could have witnessed as a way of Tenor's living.

A man raises his arm. Other watchmen approach, halting Evelyn and Jale when they get closer to the gate, leading out of the post and towards the forest.

Jale answers a few questions and Evelyn relaxes as the man and kalec talk. She moves over so she can lift the saddle pouch lid and grab an exotic fruit. She looks down to see the guard boots are dusty, but their swords and shields are clean.

'A fine day, wouldn't you say, noble Clairic?' The man asks.

'Indeed. As fine as our stay.'

'Good, I'm glad you enjoyed it.'

The man in the coat looks at Evelyn chewing happily, she raises a fruit in hand to say hello. He nods at her and then at the noble gentlemen. 'Very good, you two have yourself a swell day.' He says, letting them through.

Evelyn opens the pouch lid and whistles, tossing the gate guard a fruit. 'Cheers.' He toasts her.

The gates are behind them. A carriage approaches. There is a canvas attached atop. On the sides, a flag flaps. A woman riding aboard nods Evelyn and Jale's way, wearing a simple green dress. Evelyn can see a younger man and an even younger boy, inside. The flag waves by and they leave a dusty trail behind.

'The flag of Caealon?' Evelyn asks Jale, watching the carriage enter post and the gates close behind them. She looks forward, a wilderness not of zanny... nothing compares to that Truke.

'Yes. They ride from Erahe, since they bare the flag of Esmehdar, with the four mighty towers in black. The nation's avis is dead centre. A rare bird known as the Niveus Avis, it is our symbol of freedom.'

Evelyn looks up and says. 'I've heard of them.'

Jale's head turns a look. 'I wouldn't keep those fingers crossed.' He says and turns back.

Evelyn keeps her focus to the skies. She can see a figure move; if she didn't have to squint she was sure she might have just seen Willow.

Oh I won't...

The winds are warm. The sunlight catches the best in all. The grass is lush, its heights nearer to a fence they ride alongside. The road ahead slips east and then breaks up, with another heading north. They come to the crossroads and Jale took the main road, leading east.

Evelyn is not sure how far Telahire is, but if she asks, it could be this that makes her fear the long dread of a journey. Its better off not knowing, she feels.

They stop here and there for breaks.

'Oh, this is so much better than the hours we spent on getting to that damn forest.' She kids.

A weapon for the spells was studied and they found them to be helpful as well as destructive. They performed in fields. They'll decide to do this during night hours, figuring it's *probably* best. Just like the Thaeran Defender she used but never told him about. Instead, many other spells are summoned. Jale believes in the power of *the book of Alas* – as they've decided to reference.

Seven days on and off the road, they pass Telador without visit. On the cusp of Tenor, Telahire will be the last stop for this province. Beyond this point is the land of farmers, where Jale intends to reach its provincial outpost, today. Benched on a cliff, Eslr outpost overlooks the main agricultural grounds for its kingdom core; Rhion, A place with different kinds of wheat, known for bread, beef and smoth. Rhion is a massive city made up of tall buildings that's similar to Asnin, only not as tall, with surrounding rich farmland. On the outside are ranches, and best of all… great looking men and women – but you didn't hear me say that.

They awake without eating, and Evelyn is promised their desirable destination won't be far. She rubs her eye to their two hour-after arrival.

'Telahire,' he says with a smile and she nods. They take rest here. It's a small city sanctioned in the middle of a forest. Townhouses are crowded in a tight radius. Very little green and grass is needed. It is a society unknown to the ways of the forest.

'A little bizarre how its location is in an ancient forest,' she says, clearly seeing how its walls ignore any Rebuin symbolism and culture. 'It's a bit of a slap in the face, considering Telador is but two hours away. It's like they don't want us to *like them*.'

'No, I think you have it the other way around.'

'Right,' she scoffs. 'Now I see Caszuins point of view.'

'Nah, they just found me too pretty.'

'Cocky, which is my point exactly,' she says.

'How can you take their side?'

'It's only right.'

He wipes his forehead. 'It's too hard to fight in this heat.'

'Well maybe if we had some trees, and they didn't break down our precious forests, we'd have some shade.'

'Look at you all "This is my world now" going all anti activist.'

'Look, all I'm saying is they could have at least allowed from some green. It has a perfect look to this place... which gives it a cold feeling.'

'Were do you think I get it from, babe?'

Her stomach growls at him. She doesn't have the patience, and hardly makes a face.

Evelyn and Jale pass through its living quarters, to find restaurants and carriages lined on the streets. Streetlights are from a different place, nothing she's ever seen yet. Her best guess, from Rhion or Esmehdar.

Telahire uses their limits right to the last square inch, making up with taller buildings, all fitting in a one square mile circumference. It's a Caszuin made of stone, metal and glass.

Mounted, they trot pass a bar, with large glass windows. Inside, tabards of Calon are worn amongst the friendly faces.

More stores are bunched up amongst each other. But as Jale led them further in, Evelyn got this feeling they're heading to the centre. And behold tall and white castles in white stone, middle.

'The royal quarters,' Jale says, not having to point them out. Now she rolls her eyes. They can hardly see with the blazing sun, reflecting off all the white. The weather is in its prime today, and she thought last week was hot? Ha.

A large statute of the Queen is island, situated in the middle of a road. Many carriages occupy this traffic zone. Evelyn looks up at the Queen's simple face. They pass along, leaving her to the busy mayhem.

The two arrive to the headquarters. They dismount and Evelyn is asked to wait outside with his steed, otherwise disclosed some time ago as "Bud".

She has the look and he knows he better hurry if he doesn't want Miss Grumpy.

'I'll be quick.' He says with his hands and climbs tall stone steps to enter through white doors. It's a place filled with high ranking Calon. All this clean cloth and proper makes her want to scream. They smile when she doesn't want to. She hasn't slept decently in two days and her hair is a mess from this morning's early spree. She takes one look down at her wrinkly clothes and rolls her eyes melodramatically. It's not just that, she hasn't gotten a decent meal in her stomach – Jale has been rushing her all yesterday so they can to get to this Telahire, quicker. They hit a storm two days ago and it held them back – the man's on a tight schedule, you could say.

'Ugh.' She says smelling under pit. 'I knew I should have showered last night, when I had my chance.' She didn't realize a guard had been watching. She looks away. She's tapping a hand to her thy. She smells something off. She takes a sniff in. 'Is that my breath?' She scrunches her lips. 'I hate bad breath. Jale... you're ridiculous. I'm never doing this again. As soon as I can, I'm jumping this train.' She slowly turns back and finds the guard's eyes. He winks.

'Flattered...' She shakes her head, and shakes it again. 'Boys...'

There is another place deeper that's cut off to commonplace. The royal palace, but Jale won't be going there anytime soon.

Many are found with shading hands over their eyes from the overuse of stone, reflecting off the sun. There is redder in the sky, allowing for a rosy pink on the palace.

As much as Evelyn disapproves of this town, it is an architectural marvel no Rebuin could resist. Something more, Calon nod a respect to Evelyn. It is a great surprise; in fact, it taught her something great – that not all Calon are crude. The Calon move in and out of this palace, wearing clean and tidy blue and white wears, some with silver and gold rankings, marked noticeably. She wants to take a peek beyond those pair of white doors. So she takes a step closer when one of the guards halts her, and she's stood from walking in. She took a step back and in perfect time too. Jalelilian returned through doors. He looked taller in his realm amongst his party. He's given a salute by the two men who halted her.

Jale's début with army officials reveal themselves. They pass Evelyn and Jale to go down the stairs, making those in public salute some more.

Jalelilian is quick to lead Evelyn away from the royal monastery and he promises her something better. 'Let's go get something to eat at a pub. It's not fancy. We'll freshen ourselves up after, I promise,' and their steed is taken away by a snap of his finger.

370

'Well that was quick.' She says, referring to his command. 'You already got me on a tight leash.' It didn't help much, not with her watching the novice take care of his steed, feeling similar to bud.

'Come.' Jale takes Evelyn's hand, knowing she must be as hungry as him and they enter a nearby restaurant. He's so tall, so handsome. How in the world did she end up with him? He makes everyone turn head, even the men. Oh what can I say, she's got her dream boy. Doesn't that just make her down attitude for looking grosser that much worse?

He's sure, that this is the reason for her attitude, and he's probably right. Inside, a royal rug and animal's fur is on the first floor. Antlers hung on the wall. Their host approaches and asks them to follow to their request. They're seated in a booth for privacy.

'Wow this is amazing.' She says with a raise of her brow. 'So what happened to "Not fancy"?'

He finds his smirk. 'No, no one's going to judge. And besides, we are outside of army jurisdiction. So can you relax? I just needed to know my updates.' She nods very slowly. He starts to get off topic. 'This is an old building to begin and oddly shaped too, nearly a spiralling structure. It's interesting, much like a piece of art. But I've always loved inside, since it's elegant instead of sophisticated.'

'Like outside?'

'Precisely, good eye,' he replies. 'Around these parts, we don't get too much of this. It's a site that actually gives the forestry a battle for creation. It's nothing like before, but evermore Telahire great.' He's using his technique to get her mind off her negativity, by distracting her thoughts and its working.

Evelyn smiles to his handsome and the Calon already inside are looking more curious.

It seems in Jale's life, there is no shortness of looks. Not in Caszuin and certainly not in Calon territory; and it's a beautiful thing. Evelyn is gorgeous too, so why doesn't she get looks? Of course she does! But um... you know -- Jale's simply more kickass at the moment. Man... he's got the look.

'These booths are cozy.' She says, finally relaxing. Flags of Caealon are hung from the beams of the ceilings. Finally, she found some bare wood.

371

A waitress with hair tied in a bun and neatly dressed in a black gown, approaches. She pulls a pencil out of her apron to ask for their drinks first. Jale orders their meals after and the waitress nods gladly to him and takes her leave.

'It's so nice we are finally here,' Evelyn finds herself saying.

'Indeed.' He says, brushing his hand through his hair. He finds her still looking bothered. 'It's fine Evelyn.' He says and then laughs a little and leans in a little closer. 'Nobody cares. This isn't like your world. We don't judge people on how we look. Anyway,' he says rather quickly. 'Eslr is our next destination. I can't say too much about my matters, tough, as it's --'

'Classified, I know. You don't have to tell me,' Evelyn says, giving him a soft look – knowing his last remark was only because he's trying to be nice. 'Just know you can trust me.' She says placing her hand on his.

He nods, 'yeah, I know. I'm just worried it'll be too much for you.'

The waitress places down drinks and gave Evelyn a look, then quickly turns and walks off when Jale notices.

Evelyn, let it go. After all, she's got Jale, so why care for some other? She's been to Caszuin, and survived their staring eyes... just barely, I should say. So her beautiful soul saw the waitress as a bark to what could have been a bite, if it wasn't for her past experiences.

'I have a better idea.' He says with a little more glee this time. 'How about we leave the diplomatic affairs and eat. I know you're hungry and want to just rest from all the travels. When we get there, I'll share it.'

'Okay, agreed.'

After a few, a burger and steel cut fries are served, with a glass of red merlot for Jale and a smoth for her.

'It's so good,' Evelyn says with a stuffed mouth, not an ounce of green on her plate.

'Welcome to the Calon,' smiling and digging into his own greasy delicious gourmet burger.

'This is a great change; it's exactly the food I'd expect from Calons. If I was to ever return here...' and clears her throat to the thought. 'It's from all the food we've been surviving on, living town by town – but a burger? Now this is exactly what I needed,' taking a bite of her hunger, and speaks at the side of her mouth. 'God I love this, my life's majesty.'

'That's good. I'm glad for you, so you should fall in love with your life.' He changes his tone. 'You remember how we spoke about the book and swearing not to tell anyone?'

She nods, dipping her potato fry into sauce. 'Go on.' She says happier, whirling it at him.

'You know I must say, you'd look great with a sword in your hand, swirling that fry at me and all. You sure you're not Calon? You got the looks babe.'

He's been calling her babe pretty lately too. It's not new.

She smirks. 'I'll think about it, *dude.*' This is a term he's still struggling with. When she first laughed at him calling her babe a few days ago, she had to call him dude; explaining its meaning. Meaning sleek, for the word cool didn't come across like she had hoped for; reminding him of something cold.

He continues on his first subject. 'Well, I know a friend near the cusp of Esmehdar who may know more on what we should do.'

'Alright, well that doesn't surprise me considering your position. And I overreacted earlier. I'm sorry,' taking a drink of smoth. She licks her salty lips, with cheese dripping from the sides of her burger, and maybe there is a little guilty pleasure too... Bacon does that.

He smiles at her apology. He finds the opportunity presenting itself. 'Happy moments?' he asks now.

Okay, over the past week they been asking one another random questions to get to know a little more of each other.

'Ha, that's an easy one, this food for sure.' She replies.

'Ha-ha, no doubt.'

She smiles back, she doesn't recognize him anymore. Like he's a whole new kalec, blooming since she's last remembered him at the post of Tenor. He's one dude that puts her mouth into her lap most of the time. The world she's seen, all because she surrendered herself to his luxurious life. All she can do is think about him. If she could get another pleasure, it would be him in her arm; though she'd have to get rid of that pride; the Rebuin are the best in her opinion.

Sometimes she'll give him a look, which always tells him "Just don't go away". Sometimes he gives them too. This may be a fantasy in a world all the more. The emotions she's endured and finally tamed on her accord makes her that much more awesome to him, and for her too for that matter. Rightly so, their perspectives have merged. Now they're both beginning to go crazy. They feel they can't survive without one another.

'Alright,' she says, swirling another fry. 'What's your best moment in life?'

'This one,' he tells.

'Awe, that's sweet. Alright, greatest learning experience?'

'Hmm, let me think about this one for a second.' And hesitates on something he was going to say, then changes his mind. 'No, I think the experience when I slept with a man during my time at the Avail School.'

Evelyn coughs. 'What... you slept with a man?'

He leans a little back. 'Of course,' there is hesitation. 'Oh...' his face drops to her bewilderment. 'Did I do something wrong?'

'No. I mean...' She laughs. 'It's just a little forbidden is all.'

'No.' He says. 'No it's not.'

'Well in Egerd,' she swallows. 'Is what I mean.'

'It's been a part of Alasmierian heritage forever.' He says letting go of his strong gaze.

'I see. So everyone can celebrate same-sex?'

'That's the basic theme, yes.' He replies and smirks at her worrisome matter.

'Is it... any fun?'

'Um...' He frowns. 'You're going to ask me if it's fun? I mean, you don't appear comfortable with this.'

'No, I'm okay with this.'

'Come on.' He says. 'Admit it, you're scared.'

'Bah.'

'Have you ever...?' He asks.

'Have I what?'

'Have you had sex?'

She makes another face, which obviously meant "No".

'Alright,' he says and gets up to walk across the restaurant to arrive at a small table.

'What the?' she says from his suddenness and gets up to join after him.

'Calm,' he says with his hands. 'I wasn't leaving you.'

'Chill, I think is what you meant.' She replies.

'Well, it sounded better when I said it.'

She scoffs with boredom and brushes past him. He goes on to explain the name of the game. 'It's a pocket game. You have to sink certain colors in a row, having to pocket all balls in identical color before I do.'

They relax playing this easy but fun game. A few good looks from Jale and a few more laughs went down as fast as their drinks in hand. Evelyn had to start sticking to water, she's starting to act a little frumpy, and Jale decided on water too. A few more cool breaths and they're out the doors both winners. They took an easier look around, enjoying the synergy between them.

She knew it wouldn't last for long. And she's right. They head back onto the open road, how couldn't they? It's just too much of a beautiful day to stay in for too long. They continue to take the road north. The path leads over a hilly road, furthest from forestry and finally out into the open grasslands.

'Say goodbye to Tenor.' He says.

Evelyn waves her hand in the wind, hoping to see some farms later on. They ride like this for two hours, with the sun high over the skyline. Evelyn barely noticed the time. It passed as fast as the day did. It may have had to do with tipping the glasses earlier on, if you get what I mean.

Jale takes them through a bumpy path, but to Evelyn, it's all the same, one big magical land. And everything is interesting. They had rested, having lunch under a Joshua tree, on a hilltop overlooking the landscape around them, only but a road to lead them on – how romantic, right?

It feels good to be at another resting spot with him. With the book in her lap once more. The sunlight gazes down on them and they gaze down at the book of Alas. As they flip through pages, all Jale wants to do is watch her. With nothing to lose, and everything to gain, it's not only mastery for her, but him too. Jale is at her sides, kneeling down. Noticing her hair flying in the winds, she looks up at the sun beyond them.

He leans and points a finger to page. 'The council members,' he says. 'The treaty, the signatures that created the council that brought both factions together, Caealon and Calliskue… this is amazing.'

'You smell good. How come I didn't notice that earlier?'

'Hey, what's this,' he asks around her statement.

'The names of the members,' Evelyn's finger goes down the page. 'How come I forgot to show you that?'

'I guess we've been too busy practicing Aura. We never did stop to look at the first couple of pages together.'

She smiles up at him from a crossed leg position. 'Did you know we all call Aura magic in Egerd?'

'Magic,' he repeats. 'No I didn't know that.'

Evelyn flips past the introduction to find something new herself. 'Oh, well then, this is neat, isn't it?' She says, reading on, 'Bridge of Shropestone? It says it began 10 B.A; Birth of Alasmieria and completed 50 B.A.'

He nods and explains. 'It's a bridge that connects The Spine to Reobigheon. The rock was used from The Spine. The mountains were called The Backbone, back when. The bridge was built for easier movement of materials to build Reobigheon. Later on had it found a grander purpose; Calliskue built an exact replica over their lands because the stone wouldn't disturb their nature below. It became the main trading road between nations.'

She flips the page. 'The Brook's Pass, it says it began 20 B.A. and finished 65 B.A. What's The Brook's Pass?'

'The Great Pass is what it's called today and it's heavily guarded by the Royal Guard, in case anyone tries to slip into Caealon unnoticed. Unlike the shropestone bridge that is not guarded at all. Walking towards Calliskue is really the last thing any Caealonian would want, so it doesn't need any defence. Anyways, if you don't know already, The Great Pass starts from Esmehdar, where the mountains with the white peaks are. It cuts right through The Spine, all the way to Reobigheon.'

'The Great Pass,' Evelyn points to the page. 'It says it was created ten years after the Bridge of Shropestone.' Her eyes mesmerize. 'Smart idea for Caealon to join efforts, in regards to the connection Calliskue built.'

'Yes, you're right.' He replies. 'Since it was a major feat for Caealon, through land, cutting down the trees and burrowing through rock and valley, The Great Pass became a symbol of Caealon's engineering. It took much time to build. I'd say by that time, Reobigheon became the centre of Alasmieria and the council formed not soon after. The story is grand, but to cut one short, to build Reobigheon would call for wood, but Calliskue wouldn't touch their forests. So Caealon stepped up and that's when The Great Pass came together.'

Evelyn raises her eyebrows. 'Can we go see it one day?'

'Yeah, sure,' -- That means no. And Evelyn can already tell of the sign – something dark returns to his stare. She can hardly get to talk to him when the book comes out, the only time he does this and starts getting sarcastic. It's always a few cool looks, and that's it. Ever since they've started summoning, Evelyn can't help but feel he changes. He gets miserable and condescending. Sometimes, she just wants to get off this trip, and go on her own. She never planned on finding him, and his messy mind, but she feels she really needs his help.

'So we dug through Alasmieria's forests? That should have been the first sign of trouble between Calliskue and Caealon.'

He laughs with some amusement. 'I suppose.'

Evelyn flips through some more pages and he interrupts with a finger to page when they came to the summoning section.

He spoke. 'Summoning is an interesting craft. But it appears all of Alas's spells in this section only deal with massive beings, nothing smaller then fifteen feet.' Jale has only seen a few in his lifetime, but none are as large as these beings. He stands up with his hands to his face, watching her study. 'What's that one? It looks dangerous.'

'Oh, this one?' she points back and laughs her next words. 'The first summoning spell I used when I was at Caealon boarders, the night I arrived to the Shield.'

'Really, is it another tall one like we've seen before?'

'Yes. It's a mystery those beings, don't you think?'

'Yes,' finding a frown now. 'I've heard of giants, but we are talking before the dragons. So it's not even worth mentioning.' His frown crunches, 'and what were you doing at the boarder casting such madness? That's a bit careless, no?'

'Jale, I'm a Celestial. You have to respect my ability to want to use Aura.'

'Magic, I thought that was the correct term we use now?'

'No,' she laughs sarcastically. 'I can't believe you are going to use that, what if someone hears?'

'Alright, I guess you're right.' And his dark look is back. His eyes get like daggers.

'It was you who said we need to lighten up, maybe you a little more.' She says, noticing it.

'Right, yet I'm not the one who's afraid half the time.'

'Me?' She looks taken back. 'Oh don't worry. I can handle what's coming.'

'Show me this spell of yours.'

'No way,' she replies. 'You remember the last time we summoned? You got silly and it got dangerous.'

'Show me, I want to see again. No one's around.'

'No,' she scoffs. 'What are you going to do?' She taunts. And before he can speak she doesn't let him. 'I thought we went over this, it's not safe out here in the open. What if someone sees? We decided against this. I'm not about to break that. Not for you.'

'What?'

'I've seen the way you look at this thing, and frankly, you scare me.' She says and gets up with it in hand. She knows the Thaeran Defender has a personality. She can't stand seeing them used for their attraction and services.

'How about we retry this? Let's start over.' He says.

'You're not sounding any different.' She says and suddenly shuts the book. 'Yeah right buddy.'

'Wait.' He says and bends over her, reopening it. His finger flips back to the Thaeran Defender spell. 'So you can say the riddle, and it appears as easy as all the others did?'

'Just like magic, isn't it?'

'Magic... indeed.' He replies. His eyes are distant, and Evelyn's graze is on his wondrous taunting eyes. His are on the all the words scattered across page. 'May I?' He asks.

'Will you take my advice?'

'No.'

'Ok.' She says and shuts the book. She moves away.

'Hey,' he says and reaches. 'You're not going anywhere.'

'Let go,' she twists and he reaches it. The book is pulled and she pushes him. The book slips and falls to a landing. He lunges for it and she jumps on his back, and they start rolling down the hill clung to each other. The book is tight in his grasp and she slaps him on the face. She gets off him and runs with the book towards the tree. He chases after her, easily catching up. She blasts him with a burst of Sophair. He resists, using his against hers. A tunnel swirls between the two and explodes after pressure, knocking them back. The book tumbles. She gets up, rushing for it and he reaches as she does. She stood up, and his hand is on it.

'Trust me, it works.' She says with a plain stare to see. 'It's a sad thing to see them arrive and then disposed of. I feel like I'm using them.'

Something dark vanished just then, 'right.' He breathes a little more. Both faces flushed. 'Of course, what was I thinking?' He releases his touch. She puts the spell it its place. The blue shines in the bright day.

'It's ok,' she says breathing heavily. 'But thank you for being the hero.'

He reaches again and steals the book.

'Jale!' she angers and chases after him. He's laughing but she's serious and throws her whole body onto him, tackling him to the ground. She pulls on the book till it's ripped out of his grip.

'Whoa... okay there.' He says with hands up, under her. 'Chill you.'

She wipes her hair back from her face. 'Never touch something of mine, especially when I said no.'

He kisses her and she leans back from surprise. He leans in again and she spreads his arms behind him. She gets down close to his lips, smiling.

The older one looks away. 'Are we done here? We should head back on the road, and we're not far either,' a gloomy appearance.

Evelyn agrees, still over him. He flips her now and he's the one on top. She laughs, 'excellent,' staring up at him. 'And I'm hoping before nightfall?'

He smiles back.

'So, are you going to get off of me?' She asks.

'Are you going to apologize for slapping me?'

She smiles weakly and nods her approval. 'Alright, I'm sorry. But we both know you couldn't take me, even if you tried.' And she pushes him off.

He scratches behind an ear.

She gets up to hold the book up high, and her arm shakes from its weight. 'Come and get it, pansy.'

He gets up, and she screams. She runs in the opposite direction.

He laughs. 'Where are you going to go?' He yells out. 'You can't get that far. Remember the wolves?' He stops to look around. there's nothing for a mile in that direction. 'Alright, let's play.' He says and manages to catch up with her. He tackles her and she falls now. They roll a little and he presses his lips to hers. They kiss and giggle some more until he lies on his back.

She follows, looking up at the sky. 'You've got some issues...' She breathes and he nods straight back.

'My goodness that was fun but rough,' sitting up. He watches her get up and walks in the other direction, still with the book in hand. 'Come on now, I was only joking.'

She raises her brows, 'we got places to be, remember?'

'Wait,' she overhears him shouting out. 'Wait on up.'

'You know what? I don't need you anymore.'

'Wait.' He says and reaches her arm. 'What?' He grabs her and twists her around.

She laughs. 'Gotcha,' and runs towards Bud.

'Alright,' he says squeamishly. 'I get it, you don't need anyone.'

Her laugh is heard, 'come on.' She says still running from him. 'Let's get going already.'

'You're nothing I thought you'd turn out to be.' He shouts and starts running.

'I know.'

'I can hardly bear you,' he replies from the distance.

'Good,' she yells back.

'Wait, I remember you saying something about you liking me -- whatever happened to that?'

'Oh shut up,' she laughs.

It's hard when she smells so damn good all the time. Even when she hasn't showered in two days, he's gotten to liking her smell, heck her smelly breath. The last time she showered, he offered for them to shower together. She said no. She screamed afterward when he dumped cold water over her, still under the showerhead. She made sure to hit him, really, really hard when she got out afterward. He won't be doing that anytime soon. And don't worry; she plans on getting him back.

They ride for Eslr.

She just gives him a look when he looks back to check on her.

The day felt different, calm and quiet. It's beautiful. An hour into riding, they stop at a small town on the way. They took some time away from each other. It was a peaceful thing for them. Evelyn hasn't been off his belt in a few days, and this was what they both needed. She found a place to sit and clear her mind with meditation, and Jale bought some food for the last hour into travel – he's always eating something when he can. When they both meet up after an hour of time apart, Evelyn shows up in different clothes; she bought some farmer clothes, only less baggy and raggy, and new and tight – gene shorts, a cotton shirt that brought out her eyes from its white, and new boots; cowboy boots that go up to the calves.

He only nods and says nothing. But we know what he thought then, don't we? *She looks good.*

'Oh, and I almost forgot, the seller said it's a country tradition,' she pulls something out from a bag and puts on one of those cowboy hats on her head. 'Now we can go.'

- CHAPTER 15 -

Prince and Princess

On the highest peak, a castle rests on a hillside. Evelyn can't see the land beyond its masses, but surely more land is reachable beyond a drop. Wind soars around the tall towers of this castle, which overlooks the valley below.

Lanterns are lit on a nearing bridge – a simple long and flat one made of white stone. Down below, a crevice moves with rapids. Evelyn can taste the earthiness in mouth, and the sound of a waterfall crashes closely.

'Oh my, we're here.' Evelyn breathes; he can tell she's excited about this one.

'Yes.' He says, 'its Caealon's finest outpost.'

Evelyn and Jale arrive to the boarder. The wondrous world is a scene. Travelers from all around are witnessed carrying caged birds and animals within carriage. Most people are of royal counterparts from all around Esmehdar and Rhion, who come to this crossroad in order to reach the other.

Evelyn wallows in the scenery and Jale parks them in a guarded steed lot, and together they dismount and walk towards the castle. Nerves seize and excitement soars in the air.

They made it by supper. Her cowboy look is unfit for those around in intricate wardrobe. Even the noble Jalelilian is given a match for his glorious title. And as the two walked towards the castle, she felt a confidence lift her up. She isn't going to focus on anybody else anymore. She's going to keep her nose right where it should be, out of everybody else's business and keep it right here; on hers. It gave Jalelilian and the rest a run for their xzena, sort to speak. It's quite the unique match these two, creating a great attraction; two outsiders who surely can shine. People turn head to get a look, which are making their way up the stone steps of Caealon's crossroad.

Evelyn looks up at balconies of Eslr before entering the castle. They're large and would be a grand experience to see the land from these heights. Inside warms her. Red carpets and animal fur -- a glorious Telahire no doubt... or is it the other way around?

A great hall is crossed, guided by large stone pillars that are ignited atop within a large silvery bowl, filled of oil for fuel. The heat is felt as Evelyn and Jale pass by. The two arrive in a little line to the concierge. Evelyn can smell cologne and perfume.

Held in cages, being atop luggage, minute birds squawk and move around.

A female squirrel-looking thing moves around the room, between the feet of others and getting a climb up on others luggage. The birds flap their wings in fear of the little rodent, flying around in angst. There are some who are calmer, nipping at their feet and feathery selves.

A larger cage is place down by someone ahead in line and Evelyn got a view of new species. They are bird-like and have a large frame and bright colors, with a large puffy face. Another furry face prances, to make that two in the cage, finding its place on a crossbar and remaining relatively still. It appears it got a glimpse of the rodent and wasn't sure. But its perched brother doesn't seem to bother.

The sound of the little birds continues to find their site of the feline rodent upsetting.

A lady nearly steps on her tail, and Evelyn saw, cringing.

'It's alright, this is normal.' Jale notifies Evelyn.

Evelyn frowns at him. 'This is not normal,' and turns back in fascination, watching it move around the feet of guests. They're relaxed, moving without notice. It's the children that can't get enough, trying to catch it even though they have their own little friends to attend to.

She passes Evelyn and gets down low, nearing the pitching squawks, now filling the hall. A sound of pecking bars and flapping wings are a cry of alarm with the little beast taunting. The squirrel-thingy stops, and watches intently.

'Gotcha,' a little boy manages to catch her, carrying his red face back to his family that make sure to place this squirmy girl in her cage.

An older woman ahead of Jale and Evelyn hold's a fury animal over her shoulder. The feline is similar to a cat, painting softly in the heat of today. She has longer ears that flop down like a nord does. It's white with a contrasting rose color; swirled from belly to back.

Evelyn asks if she could pat the animal and the woman thought nothing of it. Its plush fur sinks Evelyn's touch. A beautiful match to the lady's white hair and a white fur coat she wears.

The feline looks at Evelyn. Its black eyes resembles of a bigger thing back when. Does it ring any bells? She pats it edgily and thanks the woman.

Evelyn turns back to Jale. 'This is awesome,' she whispers. A small smile he gave. It's wondrous and alive with heartthrob.

The skin color of everyone is tinted from the sun, tanned all over, whilst others have a more natural dark skin, to African American in color. The dark skin ones wore thick and raw jewellery, having bold color.

There to Evelyn's left, in a line, a group of Rebuin stood out. They had a scent all to their own, a good one, and to the right, woman with hazel skin. Their eyes are like a Persian cats; bright, revealing intelligence beside sleek brown features -- stunning and ripe with draping blue gowns. Evelyn's never seen such skin color and pretty looking eyes. They wore brown hazel bracelets, to gold. Their features are soft, just like sands from faraway lands.

'Mommy look a noble and Celestial,' a little pulp redhead girl with freckles calls out in a left line. On both sides of Evelyn held commoners, lined specifically to get rooms on the lower floors because of lower prices. The people are also well taken care of by staff, mind you. There are no shortages of luggage handlers at this post. These lines are much larger; they have more children and fewer cages and wear simple garments that wait patiently in line like anybody else.

The lady ahead of Evelyn and Jale wore a black beaded necklace with a tiny white jewel, middle. It's quite daunting, and dazzling for such a little thing. Evelyn has to get a better look and got a whiff of the lady's perfume. It's a peachy smell that gave the woman a more adorable approach.

The lady orders herself a room and turns to smile peachy at Jalelilian, leaving the concierge with that.

Evelyn frowns for what she can't figure out, but Jale had been smiling the whole time he orders a grand room. Then it clicks for Evelyn.

'Was she hitting on you?'

A few heads turn her way. Jale swaps xzena from the concierge and receives a key in return. He hurries her from the crowd. They leave the hall to arrive to a carpet stairway, reaching as far as they can see.

He makes a face. 'I'm used to it...' and gave the stairway a similar look. 'And besides... this could take a while.'

'It's because you're cute.'

He lifts his eyebrows in response.

'Come on; let's do this.' She pushes forward. She is eager to see their room, even if it's a daunting path, and one that looks as if it could lead to the stars.

A proud man noticed Jale on his way down and gave him a short look, noticing his fine title but said nothing. He didn't have any animals, but had men to carry his luggage. Evelyn did notice a fine rock on his finger, surrounded by white gold. Evelyn's eyes widen to its approach and the man caught her glimpse. He spoke lightly.

'Oh honey *if only* you knew what it took to get it... I almost want to give it away...' He says melodramatically, and another man beside him hit him lightly, and the two walk the way down. Evelyn couldn't believe the words and Jale laughed when they were higher up.

'It's not all about xzena, trust me.' Jale says and got some whispers from the descending flamboyant ones.

'Good. I'm glad to hear it.' She laughs.

The area around is bright with large open windows. As they climb, hallways get smaller and doors further from the next. Evelyn could easily get lost in this maze of stairs. They rest near the tops and watch out a window. She's mesmerized by the scene. You'd think they'd had enough movement for a day -- but Evelyn hasn't, her heart has been skipping a beat ever since she met him, so it makes it all that much cheesier. Speaking of food, she's hungry for something more. I'm not saying anything else on this matter.

'We aren't far.' He says watching carriages below pull up near the castle grounds. The two continue on and move along floors that are made from the wood of Tenor. Many more windows are passed, showing the widespread of land. There is nothing like this floor, it is different because there are no doors around, still, plenty of space to look around. The area is covered with orange and red flowers in flower pots, it matches decor. The area smells very wonderful.

Jale turns to her. 'You think that's a new view? Wait until we get to our room.' And he opens a door not too far along. He was right. Evelyn steps inside to find a balcony at the end of their long room. This room takes up the entire top floor.

'W-Wow this is nice.' She says moving inside.

'It is. It's a plaza.'

She looks taken back by the site of the room, dropping her things in joy. All she wants to do is hug him and so she does, and then runs through a hall of rooms to finally jump on a bed; king-size. Fruit and baked goods were passed, so much so that she backpedals to find them lined on tables. 'Not only does the decor match, but the food compliment also!'

Jale leans against the inside door frame, watching her gaze away.

A wind blows warmly through white curtains. The sound of birds chirping in a tree on their courtyard is loud. This courtyard has many things, including gardens. She slowly turns a look and came to notice that this was no ordinary balcony. 'Oh… my --'

'Alas.' He finishes with sass, grabbing a pastry to bite into.

'It's humongous!'

'Yes!' He matches, going on to relax in a cozy chair like a prince.

Evelyn moves around the curtains. Being this high up, it's quite blissful for her. She's never been to a castle top. She moves through the gardens, past flowers, and all along beds of unique greens and even fruit trees. At a ledge, she's mesmerized by the site. It's pretty -- ha, that's one way of putting it -- where she can see similar gardens below on much smaller courtyards. A few towers are witnessed, tall and thick on the outer rim. They're huge enough for a comfortable stay for two at its peak.

'This is a fantasy.' She says breathtakingly.

'I know.' He surprises her. Ears tickled by a whisper. 'And to think... it's all to ourselves,' sending shivers up her spine. 'We should head out.' He says, still in her ear, tickling as he leaves.

From so high up, the final forest of Tenor before Eslr is seen over the tundra. It's but a dot in this open landscape. It's too far to get a good glimpse. She can't see southwest from here, she may have been able to witness thy mighty Rhion.

She looks back at Jale, with wide eye, and filled with glee. 'It's just... beautiful.' She says and moves over the ledge to get a better feel. He watches her climb, and then he slowly moves towards her again.

'It's nice,' she says looking far west again, and finding a look down. 'And I thought I would have gotten over all this...' Her legs wrap tightly around the railing. And she lifts her arms, like a bird ready to fly.

It sort reminds her of what Asnin would be like if they were somewhere near the top. But this castle is cleaner and not as old, so she feels. If anything, Eslr outpost is more elegant than not.

Eastward, the sun is blocked by towers of this castle's soaring height. A glow of orange is stretched outwardly, where a massive shade is created by the castle onto the grounds.

'Jale...' She says.

'I know.' He says and then goes on. 'But it's going to be dark out soon. When we come back later; the city is going to light up with candlelight. It's quite something.'

She looks back and nods, climbing down with the breeze on their faces. She takes a breath and looks back one last time. It's just been so long since she had time to rest. They're always on the move. Always things to do, so this was really damn nice, putting it lightly. Chirps in the wind call out to her again. Carriages far below can be heard moving.

There are caretakers attending the trees in the many courtyards. The castle has pathways too, almost like roads for its major size that can be taken to reach the next courtyard below that one.

I would seriously want to roar like a lion and be proud, letting all know who roams this tower. No? Alright... I'll do it with less dramatics then.

People are walking along the courts below and looking about. Evelyn waves her hands and they can see her, pointing back.

She laughs with astonishment and Jale smiles and gets her to come back into their room. A marble fireplace is passed. They leave it behind and find the table of treats once more. Not far from orange-red drapes that hang beside, more food on round tables; glorious fruits, cheeses, dried meats, other proteins and spiced breads lay. It fills the room of essence. They chew with plenty to enjoy, spreading a silvery butter knife over soft loafs of bread. There's aged cheeses and homemade jams too!

'Evelyn, you're drooling.' He says with a little more sass.

'Man, it's so good.' She can't help herself.

'It's all day fresh, made daily. From churned butter to loafs of bread. They have some of the best bakeries in town.'

She leans in for a kiss and he pulls away. She gave a look of surprise, and then he leans back in.

'Teaser,' she says and takes food and puts it to his mouth.

They took to the beds where they finish eating.

'Just one more,' she teases him with a chocolate covered strawberry close to his face.

'Yeah alright,' he says with stomachs already satisfied. In their lazy compromises, he opens his mouth and she watches his lips taste the sweet kiss of the strawberry.

He begins to unbutton his robe.

'What are you doing?' She asks him.

He swallows deeply and says nothing.

'So this how you'd do things, you bring me to this suite of yours to booze me up and then get your way with me?'

'Evelyn --'

Her laugh catches him off guard. 'Oh... you poor *sucker*.'

He completely looks shocked; it didn't take long to pull himself together, 'oh you naughty girl.'

She laughs and helps him take it off, all but underpants. She does her best to take off her shirt as fast as she could, and it gets caught halfway over her.

'The damn --'

There is a knock at the door and Evelyn screams a little. She laughs with him and he gets up to arrive to the door, hiding behind it.

'I see a… service man.' He says cheekily, peeking through a peephole. Evelyn is still, still with the shirt over her. She hears him open the door.

'Hello.' Jale says to the service man with some ridiculous charm. The service man nods his respects, getting the impression to stay away and hands him a bottle of wine.

'On the house,' the servicer says.

'Why thank you,' Jalelilian says and takes it. He almost forgot to tip the man, running back to his robe on the floor and finding xzena in his pocket. He returns again to hand a fair amount. He offers the man some of their treats too, knowing they have so many, but the service man knew better.

'No thank you.' He rejects politely.

Jale returns to his damsel in distress. When they finally get it off she looks back, red faced. He wasn't sure if it was the robe or her embarrassment. Well… either way, it made no difference, because they end up having dessert after all. Hint. Hint. Okay *that's* my last cheesy line. Wink.

'Right, I suppose we should head out then. We're having a ball tonight.' He says, buttoning up his robe.

'I know I'm having so much fun.'

'I mean, literally; a ball.'

'A ball?'

'You've never been?'

'No,' she giggles.

'You're going to have a blast; it's basically a party but with some elegance and dance. They're people I want you to meet, too.' He says, with a light flicker of his eyes.

There seems to be no shortage and that's how she would have it, the rich life. She takes a few treats and together they intend to take a stroll through the castle. He closes the doors behind him and locks it with their room key. In the hall, there are a few knocks on doors by gentlemen serving a hot meal on plate, carried by a silver tray.

A warm breeze moves through the open windows, a cast of sunlight on the upper floors, and the smell of food blows around. Feet tap here and there. But not all are wearing posh wear. Construction moves outside on the courtyards where others employees are caring for plants and gardens. Guests sit quietly with a paper in hand, reading about the times. Others are attending to their animals, patting them. Evelyn does double takes to the animals' uniqueness. Meanwhile, a pair of children with slit eyes and their little pointy ears is playing tag alongside Calon kids, soaking up the sun.

The two leave the stroll of the public courtyard to head back inside. A garden is met. One that is unique, it's indoor, where one must walk across stones to get across a pond.

Evelyn looks down to see colourful fish. Evelyn and Jale leave this place. They move down flights of stairs and pass the commons to once more arrive in the main hall.

Jale takes a moment to attend to his mail. Behind a counter, a large safe containing many boxes with a keyhole for each are seen. Jale spoke to a mailman behind counter and flashed his port. The man unlocks Jale's safe box with Jale's name and port number on it. Besides all this, Evelyn notices a large doorway hemmed in gold across the hall, with a giant gold door knocker. It's odd, because it's positioned so publicly.'

An alke knocks on the door, wearing a silver and diamond rim necklace. It is stiff in the middle and loosens for comfort at the neck. Evelyn steps forward from curiosity, still watching the scene.

The door opens and a guard on the other side answers, letting the lady in. She wore a crown and has irises of green. The gem reminded Evelyn of the Lady of the Forest who has a similar taste for richness.

The lady looks like she has power, but doesn't get a curtsy from the people inside. Instead, many appear to be busy studying, having their eyes glued to a page. Beside the Rebuin who now entered, a friend or perhaps husband had been holding a crystal bowl. It is full of water. He enters behind her. Evelyn hasn't been so interested like this before, it's the exotic looking alke and her riches. And the man with his… well, bowl.

There is another call from inside and the guard leaves the watch of the door to help another guest who request's immediate assistance.

A scent of flowers passes Evelyn nose and she looks around. She came back to the site inside the room. It's a large bright area lit by candlelight. Evelyn was sure it was for those of royalty, for the wood is a brassy-cedar color with an elegant finish.

Evelyn waits by Jale who is still busy reading his letters. As she watched the large room from afar, she sees the man place the bowl down and the alke thanks him, finding himself a seat adjacently. She looks up at Evelyn. I suppose she found something appealing in the girl, also. And then the alke tips a candle over the bowl, watching the wax fall to the bottom. It swirls all on its own and then became stiff, forming a shape. Like a new sort of magic, she takes out this wax piece and studies it beside the man.

'Are you okay?' Jale asks, making Evelyn jump.

What was she doing that for?

'Yeah…' she replies; clearly having something on her mind. Before she could ask, a man spoke.

'You know, it's not nice to stare.'

'What?' Evelyn turns to find… a Rebuin? I mean to say, he doesn't dress like one, or a Calon for that matter. It surprises her. There is a reason she feels this way. His slit irises are brown, but his ears are short like hers. A scar runs from his lip to his chin. His good looks are spiking hairs on her arms. The Rebuin finds a stare by her.

'Day,' Jale says shaking an old friends' hand. 'It's been awhile, hasn't it?'

'Yes, my noble. It has. On another quest I see.' He says, keeping an eye out.

'Always,' Jale replies.

'Aren't you going to introduce me to your --'

'Friend,' Jale is quick to say.

If Evelyn thought Jale was good looking, then this one has it also. He's as tall as Jale, but has a lot more muscle weight. He wears a jacket that is part leather and cotton. His collar is up and it flairs nicely around his light brown hair, pushed back. Because his weight is thick, it makes for a thick waist-line. He is unlike a gentlemen Evelyn would imagine in Brunon. Though there are similarities. For one, it's the combed hair, or maybe by the lick of the palm to keep it stuck back. It's just those eyes that don't fit the bill, and the overuse of muscle. If he really was spotted in Brunon, he probably would be feared. Either way, it's a whole new look and one she approves of.

His coat could blanket Evelyn's entire body. It covers to his calves. He's wearing intriguing boots in cedar-leather, with duel silver trinkets. They're of a face. It can hardly be recognize. Of a nord's perhaps, but looks kind of fox-like... so it's hard to make right.

'Evelyn.' Jale says with an open palm to Evelyn as a means of introduction for Day. She's unsure why Jale didn't mention their togetherness. She appears a little unsure now, reaching a hand out for the Rebuin to shake. Was Day someone she should be worried about?

'Mind if I do?' Day says, reaching in and kissing the back of her hand.

Yuck. That's too classy for me

She blinked at Jale right afterwards.

Jale finally got the hint and removes himself from his occupying letters, placing them down. 'Well my friend, will we be seeing you at the ball tonight?'

'Count me in, Jalelilian. Do excuse me, but I am already expectant someplace else.' He says, watching Jale's eye and then the two nods gently back and Day leaves the way out the castle. In her opinion, it was odd watching the men react the way they did. Like two snakes ready to attack if one were to cross the line.

'Who was that?' She asks Jale.

'A man of his crowd, he's helped me with a few errands. A great friend to say the least,' and surprisingly he winced. 'You can't let *anyone* hear me just say that, it'll put his life and my good faith in jeopardy -- secrecy from a vigilante.' He says, nudging her.

'Okay, maybe I just read that wrong? I thought you two were enemies, they way you dealt.'

'You're definitely wrong.' He replies. 'We're just this way.'

'So Day huh? Interesting...' Evelyn says, forgetting about her fuss.

'Indeed, and a damn good one,' looking evermore intelligent the way he came. Jale came back to find Evelyn looking still, watching the gold-hemmed door now. He points with a chin. 'I'm betting you want to know what's in that room.'

'No,' she says. 'I think I figured it out. *That's* the ballroom.'

'Indeed,' smiling at his gold pocket watch. 'Very well, I have to head off to do some business. I won't be long.'

'Oh.' She frowns to the surprise, 'alright.'

Ladies smile and gentlemen greet in the hall. Carriages are heard parking outside and families moving in and out of the quarter.

He looks back up from a bite of his nail. 'I-I won't be long.' She could tell something was on his mind, but decided to let him figure this one out on his own. He's a big boy. Besides, he didn't look like he has the time to explain. 'Meet me up at our room. I'll be waiting for you there.' And hands her plenty xzena.

'I'm going shopping now?'

'Yeah,' he says and thinks about this. 'Well, shopping for a new robe I suppose.' She forgot about her torn robe. 'And perhaps... something pretty for the ball tonight?'

'*Oh alright*,' she says cheekily back.

The mail he read is placed back inside a steel box and he kept one envelope, placing it inside one of his pockets. He hands the box over to the mailman.

Jale smiles back at her. 'Have some fun,' and turns to leave up the stairs.

'Well then...' She says to his suddenness, watching him leave. 'I'll just have to find something to buy then.'

Outside carriages pull up and Evelyn smiles wondrously back to those stepping out. The sun is caught in the imagination of what is already a beautiful day. Evelyn walks down the steps of the castle to enter town, finding many more looking joyfully around. A wonderful idea it was for her to be out and about, especially on a day like today.

The day is nicely lit by lantern. The air is still quite warm and the smell of fire is cooking somewhere. She takes to the shops. Inside, she finds similar trinkets Day wore. Other shops offer different goodies, but none had any burley shops. She'd love to spend time studying the many kinds, if only she had the time to do this back in Caszuin.

At the far back of the store, she finds something from a much earlier time. 'Ah, pitch forks.' Evelyn says. She stared back with a smile on her face and breathed in her glory.

The sun beats through a window. The air is clean, unlike the dusty dirty town central of Maesemer. Bah, she moves on and walks out the store, glad to rid of the full blooming memory of her past. After exploring most of the town's gift shops and clothing goods, she finds a few pieces that interest her. In realization; if she's ever to return home she's got to have proof. Wouldn't you?

She lingers around for a little till she finds herself near the backyard of the castle, near the bluff overlooking the below. The magnificent sunrays catch a look and she finds one similar, looking back. There the horizon is where it should be, a place among the rays, catching her nearsightedness. There are rays of orange, stricken on the stone thick railing. It's grey, whitish stone that acts as a gate before the fall.

'Where is he?' She wonders back at the horizon, thinking of Willow. It's quiet here. She climbs the railing and sits atop, looking down to see it's a forty five feet drop. 'Pretty high,' she says with nobody around. Birds in the sky cross over and carry off into the sunset. 'I want to see how far this journey can take me. And to think,' she laughs out loud. 'I'm sitting on the edge of the world, overlooking a landscape no one back home would ever believe. And yet, here we are.' She looks smiley. 'I can't really believe how much it all changed.' Her eyes squint. 'I was only having supper with Mother a month ago,' she blinks. 'Summers Feast. Can it really all be gone?' She looks to her left and then her right. A bearing feeling, 'it feels so long ago…'

The stars will be out soon and there's only one thing she misses. She looks up higher to find a balcony similar to Jale's suite. She's always imagined a place that would take her breath away… and this is it, how freaky. But the world is already taking a shift; it's all inner beauty she finds. The more she reminds herself of the Law of Wish the more she realises all that time pent up in her room imagining, which was what helped to create this reality. She held pretty high emotions, allowing for the energy to formulate into this.

This girl vortex's a soul she loves more and more, she's in love with being, with life and all other things, from the flowers to the feeling of being nourished.

'I'm craving my own life experience. I love it… well, you know what? This is already amazing. Right here and now… so I'm going to sit and indulge.' She looks to the skies. A few clouds harbour, moving like ducks docked on a lake during a gentle breeze. 'I bet he's not too far out, enjoying the view.' -- The thought of Willow passes and like ducks, they glide away. Her mind clicks and something else forms -- an inspiring toss up of emotions -- a momentum. It's funny how things can change in a moment's pause. She picks up a leaf that's beside her; it's full of life and richness.

Spinning it by the stem, and tosses it into the breeze. It goes free, along with all her cares and worries, carrying like the two birds before who're just a few dots in the still.

'Do be careful.' A man says and Evelyn turns around to see.

'What are you doing all alone on a day like this?' She asks him, feeling adventurous.

This is it. I'll imprint myself. Do you remember the times she had back when? It's all coming to a close. How will it end? Will she find the answers? She can feel it, the looming of what's next. Thinking about the good times won't stop what's to come. Nope. Now is the time to turn page and see, to discover. Ha, it's on and this one calls for a little more than a stir in the wind. Look to the moon and hear the shouts, because tonight it's all bad blood baby.

'I was just walking the castle, you?'

She nods. 'Yeah, pretty much the same.'

'It's beautiful, isn't it?' He points out.

She nods his point.

'You know...' She says mystified. 'It really is...' She got down and leans beside this stranger she's never seen before. And the comfort of the entire world hovers over her. 'I'm getting glued to it.' She laughs, sort embarrassed by how stuck in the now she is.

He finds his words. 'I feel the same way.'

'You remind me of someone... from a far away land I came from.'

'Oh? Would this place happen to be Esmehdar?'

'No, but that's where I am headed.'

He nods, and then spoke. 'And who's this one I remind you of?'

She feels silly for bringing it up, shaking off the whole concept.

He pries and she gives in.

'His name was Jason.'

'That's an unorthodox sort of name. I hope you don't mind my asking, but where do you come from?'

Evelyn doesn't answer just yet. She feels so much has changed. You ever notice when you do, all your old friends become boring? They do the same old thing and have that way too familiar thing going on... It's... tiring and unsettling. Evelyn's ready for something different.

'Far... Maybe too far to explain right now -- but what I will say is, all there really is, is right now.' He couldn't help but agree. She asks now, 'so how about you?'

He smiles and benches himself up on the ledge like she had before, and kept his site towards the open landscape.

'I come from Rhion. I'm here to meet my sister.'

'Is it far?'

He responds shockingly, 'you've never been?'

'No, can't say I have.'

'Well... where you're heading is a lot more fun. Mind you, you may find you'll miss the Baskaloes and Cowts.'

Evelyn isn't sure what to say from her lack of knowledge, so she romanticizes her thought, 'can't say I know of them.' She finds an easy look from him.

The humour caught them both. He got the message -- she's new to this part of the world.

'I hear Esmehdar is magnetic, I can't wait.' She says. 'I remember when I was a child, I would always dream of something like this place and just thought never possible... you know?'

'Sure, I have a few ones of my own.'

'Well this is sort of my wish, this castle and now.' She says.

'You know what? Now that I think about it, this spot is always a beautiful surprise, no matter how many times I arrive I always find myself at ease,' he goes on to add. 'I always find myself lost in the moment.'

Evelyn returns the favour, yet she just wants to tell him of her story, but knows she mustn't.

'Well, I better head off now.' He says.

She doesn't say anything. He turns back from his leave to catch the only thing in his moment, a glimpse of unique.

In some time, Evelyn and Jale meet up. He held out a surprise for her -- a new dress, white and gold, with a red lace hanging from the back. Thankfully, she *forgot* to get fitted like she was going too. Being lost in paradise does that to a person. Sometimes, she thinks the kalec can read her mind.

'Beautiful.' He says. She asks him how he knew and he replies. 'I honestly didn't. I saw a beautiful robe and thought how great it would look on you, and would let you decide if you wanted to wear it.' He admires her in her dress from his position in the open bedroom of their plaza.

'Yeah,' she says lazily while brushing her teeth. There is a hood to her dress, and a long intrigued design on the shoulder; it's woven in black.

He wore a black suit with one side clothed in drapes and the other in sleek purple. A white cloth underneath and a necklace of silvery white hung in the middle.

'Are you ready?' He asks after applying cologne.

She spits into the bathroom sink adjourn the bedroom and nods, washing her mouth out. She laughs a little, putting her toothbrush aside and takes his hand. They head out.

The rooms flood with dresses and gowns predestined for greatness, Evelyn feels; some are better then she would have designed. The woman and alke also wore flat bottom shoes, whilst men and the kalec wore something different in places that are made-up to enhance their appearance. Most of the males wears are unique. Jale's, who's is more simple and fancy, has a ring of raspberry stone in white gold, and another in a diamond blue with surrounding gold.

Downstairs, in the hall, a line for the ball is met and Evelyn and Jale pass under the gold-hemmed doorway. Inside, a line of guards are noticeable, standing watch.

Afterwards, the two find their seats and wait while the rest of the castle is sat. Half the town can be sited, having four floors to house everyone. There are steps layered with red carpet to connect every desirable tier.

The first thing that caught Evelyn's eye was the color of the room. Flowers of blue, red, yellow and orange brighten the ball, with candlelight in the backdrop, and rosy centre pieces on tables. Evelyn looks up at beautiful chandeliers; they have a twist to them.

Evelyn and Jale end up finding Day with his friends and join them at a table. Day wore a face mask, which fitted him perfectly with his already mysterious ways. He wore tight pants, which fits his perfectly formed ass. Secrecy of a vigilantly, ha, mixed with a little face-fetish is always fun. She could sit or stand, watching his behind all night long.

It's a gold wavy-mask that took away his appearances and offering nostalgic. A woman right next to him wore an all white, with dirty-white furred collar and cuff dress, a simple, but elegant fit.

'I just want to make a toast,' a kalec stood up in the corner of the room saying. 'For all the nights I can remember, tonight is one that will surely bring surprises and joy, and to the brothers and sisters from around, cheers!'

Evelyn and Jale find themselves clapping and looking around to toasts. Later, Evelyn and Jale end up moving out of their seats to get something to eat. They pass a large buffet of glorious foods with people waiting in lines to grab a bite to eat. The smell is rich as they pass to go outside, deciding to wait it out on a patio instead. They find this overlooks the way to Rhion.

'Wow... it's so quiet.' Jale says, leaning on the railing.

'It amazes me still,' she says, both lost in their moment. 'I can't help but keep wanting more,' turning around to face the way in. The crowds are many, and the house is full. There are three more balconies for those higher tiers, becoming smaller with each level. She turns to ask him. 'So this quest of yours, will we be doing it together?'

'Altogether,' Day says, arriving at Jale's side, furthest from her.

She's about to respond and Jale toss's her something small.

'Burley Frost?' She asks. 'I didn't know I needed one.'

'Oh you will.' Day responds, and pulls something out from his jacket pocket. He tosses her another three pouches that are cold to the touch. 'There's nothing more exciting then ice, am I right?' When he said it, it was directed towards Jale.

Jale looks amused and continued their chemistry. 'We leave tonight.'

'We're leaving tonight? To go --'

'On a quest,' Day sounds assuring.

'And that's what this is for.' She rather states, holding it up. 'Aren't these a little... expensive?'

Day laughs. And Jale responds. 'Oh... don't worry kid. It's a small price. You coming will be your way of paying me back.'

Evelyn leans.

Kid?

She's unsure now, offering looks between the two. The moon is behind them and a howl is overheard. The three turn head in the direction. Day gave her a slight look.

'You hear that?' Jale asks her.

'Yeah,' she replies.

'It's deceiving, its call... part man... part --'

'Don't worry kid.' Day interrupts him in turn to her. 'We've gone through this many times.'

'Is anyone going to tell me what's going on here?'

Evelyn's never seen this part of Jale. Heck, she didn't think he had it in him. It must be in the stars.

Jale keeps an eye out for his buddy-pal and walks towards the ball. 'How about we get something to eat, and get a little dance in before I tell?' and stops under the doorway when he finds Evelyn looking evermore lost. He swore he caught her look up to the sky, glancing things over. 'Come on,' he says catching her attention. 'You'll want to eat a meal before we go.'

She had still been holding her Blueskirth. Her palm is fire-red from the cold. She put them down.

Day points and says, 'I usually throw the cold ones straight into water. Burley Frost makes for a big bang.'

Evelyn's about to throw them off the balcony and Jale jumps, 'no, he meant for later on.'

'Anyways,' Day says, rather enjoying this. 'You two have some catching up, I can see this. I have something to do before I see you two there.' And he leaves.

She scoffs to her unknowing of "There" and decides to trust in Jale. 'Alright, I won't bite. Instead, let's have some fun, but I won't be holding these *all* night.'

He smiles and holds out a hand.

She walks up to him and places the Burley into it.

He smirks and puts them inside his pocket.

'Now,' she finds his palms and opens them to intertwine her fingers with his. 'We can dance.'

He was about to lead her into the ball.

'No,' she resists, 'right here.'

He raises his brows. Then nods and takes her hands. 'Follow my steps.'

'I know how to dance.'

They toe step under the stars. She looks up every now and then – and to think she used to lie in bed and imagine everything she wanted; staring up at her ceiling never got old, thinking of the exact same stars. She looks away to find his eyes. In the background, the music isn't electric, and it works, playing a symphony.

Yeah… this is so much better

She finally smiles and takes him aside… they share a kiss.

'You treat me too good.' He says.

'I'm only here for the fun too you know.'

He raises his cheek and they return to the room of crowds. Food is all around a large oak table. Carved symbols out of the legs, as thick as Evelyn. Torches flicker around room. The guards from before are no longer on watch.

The ballroom is getting busier, she feels like a princess in her castle. She eats all different kinds of pastries. She feels, as she may as well enjoy herself, before leaving on a mysterious quest.

Evelyn separates from Jale, both filling up their plates with more than they could probably finish. A funny thing happens when she opens up, she finds the guards grabbing a plate and decides to approach one. Feeling a bit naked, she asked to join them. At first, there had been a few awkward looks, until one of the guards thought nothing of her request and finally the rest shrugged their approval. The biggest shock came when they realized she is with a noble.

They shook their heads to the site and gladly shook his hand. She knew it'd make their day. She's never felt as confident as now.

'What an honour, I haven't met a noble in quite some time.' One says.

Another agrees, 'yes this is my first time.'

He thanks the lads and offers them to sit. Evelyn sits with them and starts with salad. She has loafs of bread, and some pork, where she hopes she'll have enough room for finishing with desert. The guards sat at the end of the table, looking hesitant with the food before them. Finally, they lighten up and decide to eat with the grand noble across them.

I would be nervous, wouldn't you? This doesn't happen regularly, and I don't think Evelyn realizes the fire she put under their arses. But we already know what she'd say, don't we? *'Let's have some fun.'*

'This is new for us.' One of the guards says tenderly. His helm is still on; he has the appearance of a clear stare. What he meant to say, was he's never sat and ate with a noble of her majesty the finest. Bah, what does he have to worry, he's a cute lad – I say relax.

Evelyn couldn't help but laugh to his serious manner. After all, everyone's surrounded by bumping and cheering crowds – now is the time to screw-up.

Evelyn had to ask. 'Are you going to try and eat through that thing?'

'No ma'am.' He chuckles and slowly takes off his helm. 'Are you going to try and escape while I feast on the many bellies of game?' He teases, having open arms to the table.

'No sire.' She giggles back to a shorthaired man, with blue eyes and a small bearded scruff. He rests his sword beside his helm on the floor and nodded his head nobly to Jale. The rest of the men watched.

'Well go on then, eat lads.' Jale says in his usual straightforwardness.

'It's really good.' She says in her usual glee.

The goblets they drink from are of silver and gold. Symbols and carvings are of the flag of Eslr, and other decorations which include a nord with a hill and castle, behind it.

There are little footsteps to be heard in the chattering room. The dancing is dying down and the atmosphere is getting intriguing. The candlelight flickers. The scenery is great; red drapes. The floor is that cherry dark. Rugs look of royalty and so do the massive decorations around, of statues of mighty Calon in armour.

'It's a really large place.' She says looking about.

Jale breaks his silence. 'It is, sort of creepy really. This castle is the second oldest in the nation.'

'Is it really?' A different guard asks him.

'It is.' Another guard of the bunch agrees with the noble. His voice picks up, turning his attention to the girl. 'Are you two visiting?'

'Yes.' She replies. 'We're on casual business.'

'Ah, very good,' the man replies, still a little shocked he's eating with the royal.

'Do you live here?' Evelyn asks him.

'This place? No Miss.'

'Oh I definitely can relate. Well in that case, I'm Evelyn.'

'I'm Joules.' He reaches in across from her to introduce himself.

On Joules side, a different bloke asks. 'I'm glad you have a bit of food in front of yeah. I know it's not always easy on the travels.'

'I hear you.' She replies. 'But I've been taken care of *pretty* well.' She says snazzy and the men chuckle. She turns back to Joules. 'What a good name. Are you from afar?'

The distance between them is short; still, they'd have to shout because the noise is picking up.

'Yes.' He laughs at her bluntness.

She nods to herself. 'How far, may I ask?'

'In the Outlands.'

'No me too! This is interesting, tell me more.'

He manages a smile, looking differently between her and Jale, making sure he wasn't over stepping. Jale didn't seem to mind, knowing Evelyn can clearly take care of herself.

'A small place called Caeslar.' Joules responds.

Evelyn looks at Jale unknowingly, hoping he could help her out. He says nothing.

'I'm not familiar with this place.' She finally replies.

'It's a smaller town in the mountains. The snow falls on winter covering all the trees. Sometimes it reaches up to our windows-high. It can be a burial.' He laughs some, 'but we are a proud people who love our way of life.'

'I see.' She places a silver spoon into cake, nearly stuffing down most of her food because she has been so hungry. The cake is an amount too much for any one person to finish. Out of the blue, Evelyn can overhear a clock ticking for midnight. She doesn't know how she couldn't, it was so loud. She turns in her seat to discover its beauty in the corner; brassy wood, old, ancient, yet completely a new site.

She spoke up. 'Do you wish you could go back, to all the things that life once offered? You know, to be free with the ones you truly love.' Her eyes squint with focus, 'that nothing else matters, not the pudding cake in front of you or the glass of wine, only to see your loved ones again. You know how much you would give, but it would be worth it, just even... for a moment.'

'Yes.' He agrees without a doubt, a little stumbled by her steepness. He looked around at the men and found casual looks back, even from Jalelilian.

The clock finishes. And suddenly a door opens widely, the leaves of outside brush into the ballroom. Jale nods at the guards and they all stood up. Jale signals them to sit, allowing them their feast and he makes his way to speak to an official approaching.

Evelyn couldn't help feel invisible with the guards' eyes on Jale. This is new for her. Jale moves out of site and she stood up.

Joules offers an open palm to her. 'Stay, you're amongst friends.'

'Can't,' she says with a little more energy. 'I'm on another one of my glorious quests,' shrugging with palms up. She disappears out the gold-rim door and heads into the hall in search for Jale.

The guards watch her leave. Joules turns back to the table, there are more treats then he could possibly fathom. He takes a glass of ice-water and pours it into his gold goblet and puts it to his lips. He looks around in memory, being reminded of his family. The moonlight flashes on his back; the leaves are still in the rustle of a breeze. He looks up one more time and looks down at the ice in his cup; it makes him think about home some more. He smiles to himself. He grabs his sword and stands up, placing it in his holster. 'Goodbye lads, I've got to go home.'

The men cheer to his surprise, happy to see one of their own finding their way. With that, he turns around and walks out the gold-hemmed way.

Evelyn catches up with Jale outside the castle, finding him on the steps down. 'Jale,' she calls.

'Evelyn? I thought I was going to meet you back inside. Well, either way, I got everything set up before I returned --'

'I know, but I couldn't wait.'

'Well in good timing then, the concierge packed our things. He was just telling me that our staff had finished for us.'

Evelyn nods, eyeing the area. She got one of those feelings run up her spine. The same one she got four years ago... The moon is striking on her face. But not this time, and this time she'll be ready for what's to come.

This is going to be one heck of a night... I can feel it

He puts his hood up and his dark face is back. His back is away from the sky's glow. 'Alright then, hop on.'

- CHAPTER 16 -

A Mystery to Remember

They checked out of Eslr castle still wearing their elegant wears. The night is an old and brittle one. This road takes them along a paved roadway with a history, broken, chipped, with a bent formation. A whip in the winds shows off a flag pole. The flag is ripped and the color of red catching in the breeze.

The two ride with all their supplies to a top of a hill, leaving Eslr miles behind. At the very top, they overlook a dead city.

'What is this place?' She asks with the book safely tucked away in her side pocket and her papers in the other.

'A place of broken nature,' he replies.

They ride down and come to its gates. Tower, the first thing seen in the distance, a singular black spiral behind a massive stone gate made of dark stone. The city wall is out of epoch, a design unlike anything else.

'Welcome to the Old Kingdom.' Jale says and dismounts. He takes the reins.

Evelyn jumps off Bud's back landing on a rocky trail, 'the Old Kingdom?'

'Yes.' Jale leads. 'A place separate from Eslr and Esmehdar. It was built between the hilltops, and a forward facing mountain. It was a mighty fortress that was distinguished by its motives, for mining, everything from crystal to ore.'

Evelyn looks taken back, she touches the gates. There are cracks and markings. It is one giant piece of history.

'A mining city,' she replies.

'Yes. What they found down there...' He turns away to look up the mountain. It is in view, of course being far behind the gates, '...was nothing short of ancient, I'm saying more than just rocks and stones.'

'Mining the Alps, they found Mongers, didn't they?' Evelyn asks with a tone of speech, since she's found they usually stay to the hills and caverns. She didn't have to look where he had. When they just arrived in, she saw this large facing mountain and the hills that surrounded the historical site.

'Well not quite...' Jale says. He takes them over a short bridge to get to the city. The three pass through a large hole in the city wall. They move around what looks like molten debris. Jale continues with his speech. 'That's close. But you see Evelyn, the Old Kingdom was formally known as Tother Bale.' He walks and she follows. 'King Raja of Bale was the first settler with his men from overseas. They arrived before the birth of Alasmieria, during a time when the land is unwritten. A place to freely roam until those of Calliskue were discovered and treaties between nations would later come into effect.'

Evelyn looks past him into the night of stone and debris. 'What kind of a treaty was made?'

'A simple one for a simpler time; the two nations first took time to discover each other's story. The story of Caealon's beginning starts with a shipwreck from sailors that came from the Lost Shores, dangerous islands just off our coast. The settlers rejoiced in their discovery of new land. The land unwritten, the settlers found it offered much more resources and peace for their kin. So word spread to their ruler Raja. He soon moved his nation to grow a bigger, safer and in turn, a happier empire. He would now marry. Later, the queen of his armies gave birth to two children.'

They move deeper in, passing over broken rock from a cause of a battle long ago. To their left in the brush, the crickets sing.

'The offspring decided to expand the territory with the approval of their parents. Prince Kaln, and their daughter Princess Mear, searched for new territory in the land, away from the hilly mountains and the dry-rugged terrain of Tother Bale. They found their promising territory, and formed a city on the cliffs, overlooking lush scenery below. The city is stapled as Apas, which rightfully took passage.'

'Sounds promising,' Evelyn agrees, imagining the vision he setup for her.

'The children gain rule after their parents passing. The sister becomes overseer of the new capital, and her brother as the ruler over Bale. Can you guess what Apas would later become?'

Could it be Esmehdar?

Then a different thought arises and it comes out loud, 'Caealon?'

He smiles, trying to give her the intent. 'The country was known as The Kingdom back when.'

'Oh, so it was Esmehdar.'

He nods to her conclusion. 'Now, going back to Kaln's rein; Tother Bale became a military fortress and the main mining establishment. Kaln digs further then his father had ever. This got Kaln in a little bit of trouble. That's when Kaln had discovered something else.'

'Wow, so this was how Bale was destroyed. But what was down there?' She asks, observing the wreckage.

Jale says no words but walks over crumbled rock. Evelyn carefully steps around too, as they pass under a large bridge together; it is dark and the rubble is much less evident. Their shoes crunch under its phantom experience. They exit and a new revealing exercise is on the other side.

Evelyn hesitates in her tracks, between the mess and the painted picture before them. 'Won't you tell me?' She asks.

'Of course, it only had me thinking. But to answer your question, it was Crywn down there.' He says. 'You see, Tother Bale was lost with Kaln, it mirrors the fall of Reobigheon overnight. Many assume Crywns destroyed Bale as fast as Reobigheon had abandoned. But if you look closely,' he says and bends down to touch a broken piece of bone. 'You will see signs of battle that entails Bale lasted throughout the many years to come.'

Evelyn takes a step back, and she sees it. They're standing in the remnants of a Crywn – they're that big. She nods before she spoke. 'Bale stood up a fight.' She can also see parts of the city molten to ruin and others are left standing. There are bones of men and Crywn all over the place, but what is most neat, is a Crywn skeleton lying over a broken tower not too far from here. It must have been shot down and crash landed there.

'Yes.' He replies. 'They did. Mear feared if Kaln were to dig any further, then the plot would thicken. Oh it surely it surely did. She was right to fear the nasty Shadow. But no one, not they, you or I could ever expect to see Crywn down there.'

'The Shadow...' She says and lingers before picking up pace again. 'Are we talking about the legends before time? The rulers I'm speaking of, of Alasmieria, the story that goes way back, about The Sleepy Mountain.'

Jale takes a deep breath in and lets it out slowly. 'This is indeed about The Sleepy Mountain.' He then points to the mountain and says. 'Kaln's greed was deep, and that's pun intended. He wanted to become rich in the mountain's vein; yet that would forever depend upon an entirely different treasure to defend the empire. I'm talking the one and only, the winged masters of sky who bear a heavy heart.'

'The Niveus Avis,' Evelyn eyes light up.

'Yes,' with a resembling tone. 'Now, the further Kaln had Bale dig the more Crywn crawled from those tunnels. Three, three things help bring the stronghold of Bale down to its knees. If it weren't for these three, Bale might have stood a chance against the foul Crywn. The three slogans today are "An old enemy", "The travellers curse" and "The mountains guardians".'

Evelyn's eyes are widening. Evelyn and Jale move deeper into the ruin of Tother Bale. Bud is at Jale's side with Jale at the leash.

He continues. 'Today, many things were expected when Caealon first discovered the ruin of Bale, but to find the reasons for almost all would take time. The most troubling in my findings, had to have been his greed. That what was so devastating to me.'

'So where did Calliskue come in during this age of the Crywn?'

'You're ahead of the game, but let us continue --'

'Wait, you said we'd be doing a side quest, so what are we doing down here?'

'We aren't far, that's why we can spare time.' He said rather ready, as if he could explain it in more detail. This told Evelyn without words that something else is on his mind, that he's about to get into something that'll unravel the mystery of him.

'Now going further, without documentation we can't be sure of anything. And, I'll get into the three slogans later on. Yet, what still doesn't quite fit right is this; if the Crywn did demolished Bale, what would stop them from causing cataclysm all over the world? A large gap in history has gone missing here, don't you think? This is a place in time when I can't help but find myself agreeing with the many. Well, we assume heroes were raised and had fallen in order to rid the fell. This is an era known as the Wrath of Ages.'

Evelyn scratches her face to all of this, then spoke. 'Well, what happened to Apas during this Wrath of Ages?'

'At the death of Bale alongside its Kaln, Mear arrives at the podium to defend the kingdom's core. There is a document that pertains of a man who took the reign during the Wrath of Ages; his name is Altus who thrones the line of Apas.'

'Her son?' She asks.

'Perhaps... We assume she brought up a son in the time of chaos, a time when Apas's land grew red from blood and the skies burgundy from ash and flame. The problem here is some don't believe he was of blood. Either way, he sought up efforts and took up reign during this time. But this is all speculation. Later on, on the last forefront of Apas, we do know Mear dies in battle fending off the malicious scaled ones. We found proof of her remains. With the line of royalty deceased, no one knows of the true heir, today.'

'Sounds to me Altus seeks out the opportunity to rule.'

'Either way,' Jale says happy to see her performing in all of this. 'Altus's record tells us that the next few reigns of royal ship would be horrific, and in a land of terror. In the Wrath of Ages it wouldn't be easy. This is why many missing heroes must have gone off record.'

'So what happens next?'

'All that we know of is... is of one more crowning. The gap between Altus and the last one before B.A. is large.'

'Wait, only one?' Placing a hand to her cheek and her thinking stirs a little before she spoke. 'Well that sums that up. Even if Altus was the wrongful heir, it doesn't matter now. This gap in history is the problem you're dealing with now.'

'That's right.'

He can see Evelyn nodding at his lecture, ready to ask the next question. 'Who was the last to reign on record?'

'I'll tell you, and it's our most heroic tale. Long after the phase of Altus's reign, he left a morbid country in the hands of a boy. The new limelight shined. The lord sought out a new calling, one of faith instead of bloodshed, which is funny since it creates the greatest battle of men against Crywn. At the time he believed in something *more* when all else failed. Maeled is his name, and he went on a search, which gave the people some hope. But he left the cold place of underground to enter the wake of ash and death to bring the Crywn down... that's all there is too it. He's known for taking them down. And this brings us to the first stages of Alasmieria.'

'That's all we know!?' Evelyn yells, laughing.

He has a presumptuous shrug.

'Hesquit Anquara?' Evelyn asks indifferent.

He stops. 'You know about... -- How do you know about that spell, the spell of slumber?'

'I-I've been told by a wise lady that a force of two equal powers can be put to rest with it.'

He laughs with quality. He has a brief look and one of figuring something out. He drops it entirely and returns to their conclusions. 'But the question is... how? How could a man without the blood of an Errific do such a thing?'

'Alas.'

'Right and my finger points to Alas and Mieria also, who *must* have been found on this faithful journey of his,' with a little speculation of his own, 'if so, then the first relationship of man and Errific happened at this time -- he found Alas. So, the council of three lead an army of Errific and men who took out the terror in sky. This is the coming of Alasmieria.'

Evelyn moves from her spot, finally, and looks up at the black tower that is a swirl to its pinnacle.

Jale found her eyes and she saw his dreary look.

He explains. 'These times are so thin in documentation, with only speculation it's more fictional then real, but the parts make up the masses.'

A horribly bad mass... in thought of the ruin around them, *And I thought Asnin was in pretty bad shape?* She snickers.

A look further from her symbolises something else was at bay for the death of Bale. It made her think of the three slogans not yet discussed. But then again, if they're only "Playing a small part" as Jale put it, she might just choose to believe in tale.

She asks now, climbing over some rock. 'And you got all this by speculation?'

'No.' Jale finds an easier path with Bud, around. 'I knew a trustworthy source that once lived to see these days.'

He finds her laughing in astonishment to say the least -- 'Oh really? You mind sharing this source, for they would have to be more than a hundred years --'

'At least,' he says, recalling. 'From the first settlers of Bale to the crowning of Maeled, was three hundred years that we know of. Now, as far as Caealon is convinced, our journey starts with Reobigheon, which lasted five hundred years. It's only been two hundred and sixteen years since Reobigheon. We lost the last bit of documentation of time in the vaults of Reobigheon. The Great War was the reckoning, making the day 716 today. We should be dated at 1016 – but we live in a broken history...'

He walks again, moving his steps over glass and stone.

Evelyn thought about Egerd's date. It is only six hundred years old; three hundred from the birth of Asnin, with another three by its revolution to the south.

They walk across a large bridge overlooking a river below. It's a slow lazy river. Jale clears his throat. 'My father must have seen an opportunity beyond the threats around Maeled; he must have seen something in Maeled that was worth helping the man on his quest to rid the fell. He was planning Reobigheon long before the first settlements arrived.' He says and continues slower. 'I'm still figuring things out after Alas's passing. I know it doesn't make sense now. Just think how I've felt after all these years.' He looks around and comes back to her again. 'My father told me only parts, but it's enough for me to start somewhere.'

Evelyn has flickering eyes. 'What are you trying to tell me? You can dress and hide your words, but this doesn't really sound like the Jale I know.'

He laughs a little. 'You miss the right question. It's what aren't I telling you. It's all a part of the bigger picture, can't you see that? I think it was an opportunity that presented itself, and that was Maeled. From then on we were all... Alas's pawns to be played.' He spoke with boredom but his eyes still have flair. 'Alas forged a necklace from Mieria, who gave her life to forge it and the birth of everlasting life, was born. It would give longer life to anyone who wore it. Alas handed it to Maeled. Maeled; king of Caealon in the coming of ages would oversee the heir of Caealon for hundreds of years to come, all under the rule of Alas, Maeled's closet companion. Maeled was one of the seven. Mieria was never a part of the seven.' He laughs with this, 'she died long before this. And not of old age like everyone has themselves believing. I bet she gave her life as soon as Alas's plans came into effect, all to create Reobigheon. The rest of the plan to overthrow the council would come afterwards. But why and why would Alas create a council to create their defeat?'

Evelyn frowns first. 'Interesting...' She says, watching him closer.

'It doesn't make sense right? Or does it? This is why my theory has me thinking Alas did something wrong, tampering with his power; he changed something,' and nods to his premise, 'he did something changing the course of the future. And then he saw it, long before its coming – a future that was meant to be perfected and last much longer then Reobigheon had, yet it would now crumble. I'm saying, Alas witnessed the death of Reobigheon, he saw it all through his foresight. And I think this is why on this journey of Reobigheon he forged the Regalias. He used the council – I don't know what for, and I don't know how, but that is why they were created. And from then on he was on this plan to change what he had done...' Evelyn is still as he continues. 'Do you really think that he *needed* them – I ask, for what? Close friends, advice?' He shakes his head. 'No. They were for so much more, more then partners... It's our job to piece it all together and walk this part to *reverse* a looming cataclysm and restore balance.'

She hesitates, 'we've talked about this already... but you're implying something more. What are we? Are you trying to tell me that we're to bring balance to the living... with this... book?'

'*Think bigger.* Beyond all this, Evelyn, two nations coming together to form Reobigheon was Alas's doing, but the reason was for something much more then freedom. Reobigheon stood for a hidden secret. When his city fell, so did the secret to something more.' He comes closer. 'I thought he was just doing this to restore Reobigheon, a valid reason, but no... he always told me Reobigheon was a key to a door. Now… this secret I am still looking for.' He watches her. Evelyn appears lost, like he's first witnessed her back at the Rebuin hold.

'You father… is…' She almost couldn't say it. 'Alas?'

'Was, and my mother was *her*,' Jale says with a raise of his eyebrow.

She now stands between a hole in the ground and a sword pieced in its shatter. A frown crosses her brow.

If Caealonians have no idea about how this place fell, and if what he says is true… then perhaps it's time to believe in miracles

Jale hesitates before he spoke. 'This was something I was hoping to tell you. Now, how the book got to you is just another part of the plan. It's his doing. He told me I would find a girl and that the book would be her destiny. Not mine. You are the last piece to the puzzle and I have to protect you.'

'Okay… yeah, I'm sorry…' She drops her hands. 'You know what… I've had enough of this. This is all I've wanted to do ever since I found it.' She takes the book out and throws it off the bridge.

Jale mouth drops. He suddenly starts laughing and finds his voice. 'This actually feels kind of great. You know… you got some bad blood in you,' he looks up to the stars next. 'I've been pretty angry with him too, ever since he left me with many unanswered questions. No disrespect dad, but that's how I've felt for the longest time.'

'Yeah… whatever…' She says unabiding, walking off into the distance.

'Wait.' He says, looking between the entire world he's ever known and the new one she walks. 'Oh screw this. I'm coming with you!'

She's surprised to hear him say this and he catches up with her, and the rubble of the world is leaving behind them. 'Can we still go to finish my quest at least?'

'Yeah,' she says and shrugs. 'Eh… why not… -- I bet your father didn't see that one coming.'

He laughs in a toasting manner. 'Well, here goes to the end of the world.'

'Well, I'm off to Esmehdar before it ends then.' She says in a chipper sarcastic way.

'Ha-ha I'm with you.'

She laughs with.

- CHAPTER 17 -

The Traveler's Curse

'So what now…' She asks him.

'Well now we go and finish the promise I made.'

Evelyn treks on and spoke. 'Something tells me you won't just give away the secrets you've uncovered.'

He moves with Bud beside the girl and Jale takes a deep breath in. They move deeper into the city. 'Ah yes, you refer to an old enemy, a travelers curse and the mountains guardians.'

'Was there a hint of sarcasm in your voice?' Evelyn asks the kalec, smiling.

'Yes, two hundred years of hunting for answers will do that I suppose.'

They pass a large pillar in the middle of the streets. There's a gothic look to it. A manor is empty. It's a large building faded and rubbed off by war and whatever else walked the planet centuries ago.

'Well guess what, it's a riddle you'll have to figure out on your own.' He says. 'I'm not giving it away this time.'

Evelyn perks. 'Care to explain more about the promise you've made then?'

'A lady is in need of help.' He looks up at the sky. Evelyn follows his site. The moon is the only thing that stands out.

'Is she close by?'

'Yes.' He says and moves forward. The three walk a long stretch into the middle of the city. The spiral tower is closer.

They enter a larger opening. The debris is great, surrounding the many structures. Some large human sculptures are carved from stone in the buildings walls, holding a carved shape of what looks to be a gem in hand, with the other palm pressed to the ceiling.

They enter through a blast hole and a few moments of darkness creeps over them.

Evelyn spoke once they leave the darkness and arrive on the other side of an opening. 'It's... very large.' She sworn her voice echoed and they begin to walk a tall grassy field.

'It's an arena. And that's the Mountain's Grace.' He says, pointing at the tower.

The grasses are up to their waists.

She points to the spiral tower too. 'That's what Tother Bale called it? Did Alas tell you all of this too?'

'Yes. He told me of their history. I've always been a keen questioner. I can remember one night we sat down together, I asked him about the Old Kingdom and that's how I learned of Raja and the others. He only told me the basics; the rest was filled in by my own theorizing.'

Evelyn nods. 'Yes, that was a ton of information for one night.' Stepping over an unsmooth surface, 'I'm sorry about the book... it just frustrated me to think someone had control over my destiny. Maybe it wasn't the best of my judgement, but what can you do, right?'

Evelyn feels it is the greatest seeing Jale in his line of work, and her leaning on every word to fit the slogan puzzle. She's getting a dark feeling he'll be the one she's going to be glued too, becoming best friends with. Of all people to bear with, she couldn't have picked a better friend in Alasmieria. The fact he's kalec, she finds this ever so brilliant. It makes all his words that much more interesting because of his uniqueness. It's not like she *really* needs him and all... a little sarcasm here.

It's the way he laughs, and it makes her want to lean in for a little kiss.

'Alright,' he sighs and then gave a little chuckle.

'Give in?' She asks, knowing he wants to give it over.

'Yes.' He laughs. 'Funny thing is... is the mountain guardians are a whole new race, one you're surely unaware of. The old enemy was not only Mongers but Maldocs also.'

'I knew it!' She shouts, jumping up from excitement. Her hands pass along the tall grasses. 'I figured they'd have a hand in Bale's ruin.'

'Yes, but not just on Bale, but the whole of Alasmieria. Drilling those holes not only brought the old enemy, but the last secret hidden within those rocks.'

'Now, I'd be safe to say this is the travelers curse?'

'Yes.'

They continue the long stretch out in the long grassy space. Evelyn moves in a new direction, getting a feel for the place. She arrives to the far side. She decides to go look around – sightseeing if you will, climbing stairs to the tower entrance, which is connected to this part of the stadium. 'Well this place sure dug up a lot more than they bargained for, that's for sure.'

He speaks, arriving at the bottom steps. He waits for her. 'Basically, they stirred up the entire whole.'

She returns in site. 'Is that a play on words?'

He smiles at her.

'You don't think I baffled your father after I threw his book into the river, do you? Assuming he's watching us.'

'I think water's the last thing on his mind.' And then laughs, 'assuming he's watching us.'

A rock falls in the quiet.

'That was a sign.' He says.

'A sign? What for?'

Jale takes the reins and moves on. Suddenly a howl in the distance is heard, clear as day, or in this case, the night.

'Jale, w-what are you talking about?'

'We should keep moving. Day is going to be there anytime soon.'

'You know how I never ask where we are going, or at least I try not to?'

'Ok?' He laughs a little. 'What's this about?'

'Well… now would be a *great* time.' She exhales her next words, jumbled by her movement. 'Could you tell me? I'm feeling this… bad feeling here.'

Jale stops. He looks around, looking for a way out of the stadium.

This only adds to her nerves. 'What's wrong, is it another one of those signs?'

'No, it's more like one of those bad feelings. Now how do we --'

'Over here.'

They come through a dark tunnel out of the stadium and find bushes on the other side. They pass into a courtyard. Evelyn steps slower, 'what is this place?'

'Keep moving.'

In a maze of brush, bushes are all around them. Ferns and fruit trees are passed and Bud wants to stop to get a bite to eat, but Jale pushes on.

Jale is seen out of the clear with the reins in hand. He moves quicker where he finds another bridge. It stood high, allowing for a great view of the city from its arching peak. It doesn't have railings and there is a flush of water beneath it. A rocky pathway leads to its end that'll take them up the mountain side and out of Tother.

Evelyn carefully peers over the bridge.

'Jump on.' He says, already mounted. 'That book's long gone. It's my father's plan, and if it truly does exist, however he does it, then it'll have to show up somehow, right?'

Evelyn looks carefully away from the river to give him the look, asking next. 'And if it doesn't?'

He is silent, and she knew she caught the yellow-eye-bushy-tail by its tongue. She's never really imagined what it looked like... till now, tilting her with it head in mind.

'Are you coming?' He asks finding his humour.

She nods and jumps on the back of Bud. She adjusts herself to get back into the feel of things for their journey onwards. They carry on up through the mountain and Evelyn looks taken back by the city. The view is great! It's the humility of travesty! The higher up, the fewer trees are.

Jale spoke eagerly. 'This is the pathway up and out, a shortcut leading to where we need to go.' They move into a clear rocky area. 'It will lead us back to the roads, on the way to Esmehdar.'

'Ok.' She replies.

'I think I said something about the traveler's curse?'

'No sire.' Evelyn says, not remembering anything he's mentioned on that part.

He shakes a finger. 'You don't ever have to call me that, ever.'

'I know I was just having a bit of fun with you.'

'Well, that's where we are heading now, the traveler's curse.'

Evelyn can feel her lips coming to a pinch. 'Should I be smiling or worried about that?'

'Stay close to me, at all times and all should be a knockout-swell. My quest is to help the sick woman, hopefully we aren't too late.'

'Jale, what does that even mean?'

'Don't worry about it.'

She looks up at the moon. Now she can feel the world and all of its bizarre complexities compelling her forward. But she can't figure out why she can't stop, to tell him it's all too much. The fear, the bizarre intricate, and for the love of *oh,* the world's consuming her in for just a little more. She swallows hard, and for once, she can depend upon one person who may just hold her fate in the rest of his daily adventurous hands.

Not everything in this night life remains brittle like before. Oh no, not compared to that old patch of a city. For a patch of fireflies near a river bed flicker instead, reflecting off Evelyn's deep blue eyes filled with that grand sympathy. It was something of beauty... only, when she passed it by; it felt as if she was leaving behind a part of her safety in these majestic plains. Even if they're in Caealon, it's a far ways from any means of a civilization from here on out.

'This is it.' He says dismounting.

'We're already here?'

'Yeah.'

Evelyn gets off very slowly, for this town is as abandoned as she imagined it. Jale slips off and begins to tie Bud away from the scene. Bud breathes out, and Jale got the hint. Jale opens the saddle pouch and pulls out a fruit. 'Here.' Jale says holding it out for him, and pats his buddy'o pal with his other hand. Bud takes the offering gladly and huffs, coming to a lay-down on the grass.

Evelyn's already on the move of things. She's walking the area, knowing Jale's not too far behind. 'Well this is just grand, it's nothing more then what we just saw.'

'Is that sarcasm I suspect from you?' He calls, still tying Bud to a given tree.

'I don't know, probably?'

He jogs to catch up.

'Oh no, Evelyn, I think you are taking after me now.'

417

'*Oh no,*' she teases back.

They make their way into the deserted town. The skies bluish, wherein the weeds growing form underneath the dry earth has found its way in nearly every grassy patch as it could have mustered; huddling its glory underneath a town's solace.

Evelyn stomps on a weed patch from under her boot. It reminded her of the dry spell in the drizzling sun, and as much as she loves the grand memory, she doesn't miss the weeds. She always had to dig them out from the garden soil before any planting could be done.

'Day should be here…' Jale states rather obligatory. They move around and don't find anyone. 'Day?' Jale shouts out.

'This place is damn eerie.' She says and gets a feeling rush over her, telling her it's going to be okay, whatever may come. 'Day,' Evelyn yells out now.

The two spread out to make more ground. After awhile, Evelyn and Jale arrive to place, centre town.

'I don't know.' Jale only says, knowing what she's thinking. He leads her to a small house. 'This is the house with the patient.'

The door has scratch marks all across it. On Jale's way up, the steps creek. He shivers and gave Evelyn a swivelling look.

She nods with agreement. 'Creepy.'

His knuckles pound on the front door, ignoring the whole silence scene. The door sways open from his touch. Still, he waits, but there is no answer. He suddenly warns Evelyn to stay back – raising his hand like those in Caszuin would.

Evelyn acknowledges him, looking afraid of the area around her.

He spoke. 'Miss, its Jalelilian. I had gotten a letter signifying your husband had gone missing. Miss Dolora, I am here to help you. I hear you are terribly sick. I am going to come inside now.'

He enters the dark home; with a hiss of his voice his hand brightens the room. The kalec moves slowly. His Tastraity shines to an old sofa that has tares in it. The walls are all ripped up, and the floors are madly scratched.

'Evelyn.' He whispers. 'Get in here.'

'Tastraity,' she whispers, and finds him with the raise of an eyebrow, signifying the mess. She takes a deep breath in and lets it out slowly, signifying her uncanny. He moves into the living room and she follows. Their guiding light is making him feel like a target.

He keeps his watch on the windows and started listening for any noise. But he hears nothing. Slowly, he moves into a new space, the kitchen. Boarded up windows are seen with a few ripped from their hinges. Just outside the wind blows and the branches sway in a light breeze.

He decides to move on, passing a door that's been ripped from hinge. He looks back, but can't find Evelyn. When he turns to look around, he notices a gateway that leads to a basement. That's when a horrible stench comes to his sense of smell. He jumps when he looks down to see the same beast that had attacked them at the cliff -- the Dark One. It lay silent, the body bloody... drenched and appearing lifeless.

Jale reappears from the dark, breathing hard. He finds Evelyn near the front house doorway, looking grimly.

'Sorry...' She tweaks, 'I got nervous.'

But he doesn't say a word, so he slides his finger up a scratched railing and looks back at her. She understood what that stare meant; so she took a step back with caution. Oddly, she gets this feeling of being watched by someone, or something.

The floorboard above them creeks and Evelyn looks up.

Jale continues to make his way to the second level. He slides his hand against the wall; his fingers catches hold, so he naturally stops.

'Jale, I don't like this anymore... lets go.' She says and he stops to pull something small from the wall, but Evelyn can't make out what it is. She can see him examining it. 'What is it?' She whispers. She becomes aware of the fury texture from where she stood. He says nothing, but instead dusts it off with a flick of his finger and the piece descends to the floor.

She remembers what Day at Eslr said about the deceiving ones.

His robe gets caught on the stairway. He leans down to detach it, as he does so he closes a look on Evelyn from the twist of his body. 'Something else has been down here and recently.'

'You think she'll be alright?'

He wasn't sure if she was being funny or serious. He comes back up with a twist. 'Miss Dolora?' He calls arriving to the top, looking over the railing. A heavy slide is heard, like a dog pulling its paws together.

Jale freezes.

A loud sniff comes from a crack above Evelyn, where the master bedroom is; a sound of an animal snorts back out.

'Umm yeah, it's time to go.' Evelyn says to the ceiling.

Jale moves down the stairwell until he leans near Evelyn, looking up; all to find an eyeball peering through a small hole in the floorboard above her, with eyes of black; pupils blended with a dark cornea. Jale begins to pull Evelyn away. The eye swishes a look towards him. The animal's breath becomes louder. Evelyn can feel Jale's other arm reaching carefully, and he pulls her away. They rush down the front porch steps and out into the open.

Evelyn stands close, almost back to back. 'If that's one of those things I heard howling tonight, then I don't think Miss Dolora is coming back anytime soon.'

Jale whispers. 'And I don't think your unwanted friend will be paying us a visit, anytime either.'

Evelyn eyes shift. 'You mean that thing killed the Dark One?'

'Yes,' and looking anxious to speak his next words. 'When I mentioned to treat; I meant the lady's curse. That's why they sent me, and not some defenceless Clairic. She must have gotten bitten by her husband, which is a foal; a different kind of beast then the Dark One. The Dark One must have looked for other sources of food when it didn't get us. It fought for its life here... This means Dolora changed before I could reach her. You know... this would have been a lot easier if she hadn't.'

'Wait. You mean... that's Dolora up there? And you plan on curing that thing? You cannot be serious Jale? That's mad!'

A man arrives and he's suddenly noticed.

'Day!' Evelyn shouts out.

'Hey guys.' Day says, wearing his long draping coat with a large travelers pack. It's deflated. He turns away from the girl to peek at Jale and says for him to hear. 'Is this one always this tragic?'

'Hey,' she frowns. 'I heard that. Hold on a second, how did you get here?'

'He's... what you'd call a Moen.'

'A what?' Evelyn asks them.

'Basically,' Day informs. 'I can transform into any animal.'

'Any *land* animal.' Jale adds.

'No one likes a give-away.' And he turns to her next. 'And I *know* what you're thinking, but it's the Aura that infuses me, granting me forms.'

Evelyn raises her brows, unsure what to say.

Jale leans an arm on his buddy's shoulder. 'This one comes from the Marshlands. Mean place. He's one of few who can do this.'

Evelyn nods, looking around. 'Remind me to never cross into those lands.'

'There you go.' Day nudges her. 'Now you look like you got some color into your face. Oh! I found this.' He pulls out the book of burrows. 'From the river crossing my way over here -- Cute little thing.'

'Evelyn.' Jale says boastingly.

'Well what's with the face?' Day asks him, and then he refers back to Evelyn. 'You okay darlin'?'

She's about to respond -- even Jale could barely speak before Day figured it out.

'Let me guess,' pointing her over. 'A worried expression – you get that a lot with Jale – a bit of pale...' He slowly turns to eye the house next. 'I'm guessing we have a little beastie in there?' And finds him a smile, 'no, that's not all of it, there's more...' He turns to Jale, adding one plus one. 'By the look you give, and with hers,' he holds the book up and she has a hesitant reach. 'You told her your long dreary papa story... didn't you? Damn boy, you're *just* lucky she didn't throw you into that river also.'

Evelyn can't help but laugh. 'How do you know all *this*?'

'How?' he asks and she nods. 'I'll tell you the first time he told me, I almost ran him off the road. That's how. Assuming you loved this little thing so much, you probably threw it at him, missing him and landing in the river behind him. Close?'

The two nod saying, 'something like that,' for the sake of saving time.

Day offers the little-read over to her.

Evelyn gladly takes it. 'Great.' And exhales with it in hand, 'so three heroes to try and save the world. Well, what are we waiting for?'

'I like this girl.' Day nudges Jale. Day removes his backpack and hands it to him who accepts it. 'Relax.' Day says to him and puts his large palm on her shoulder now. 'Trust me.' Day says to her and she gives him a brief look. They watch as the Rebuin remove his coat, which he places it over Jale's shoulder, as if he's a coat hanger. Jale gave a bored look back and let the big coat fall. Day smiles gingerly in a pair of briefs and removes his boots, showing a large tattoo of a sun and moon on either side of his large rib cage. Evelyn found it all… a bit amusing, Jale… not so much, until… there is a smell of sweat from Day. Before Evelyn could ask what was going on, Jale interrupts.

'Here.' He offers holding the bag open for her. She folds the coat and places it inside, having a bewildered look all over the place.

Day hands her the boots and she found a smelly-look back, and drops them in too.

'Anything else?' She asks, a little unsure if she should have. He removes his underwear and she looks away. She smiles, 'ha-ha, nope, that's your job.'

Jale loosens the straps around Day, eyeing around a little. Jale took a step back and the Rebuin smiles. 'This should go swell,' and suddenly he shape-shifts. White light consumes him, like Aura would of the finger and his body goes blinding white. His shape grows, moving away from light and into a wild animal, standing eight feet on his hind legs, fitting his straps perfectly.

'Cool right?' Jale asks Evelyn.

She sways and slides, fainting sideways.

Jale caught her in his grasp. 'Oh man, bad idea.' Jale says.

The wild-looking animal overreaches Jale by two feet, and being quadruple that of Jale's overall weight.

'She signed up for this… no?' Day asks, scratching his head. He reaches down and slaps the girl with a furry paw on the cheek. 'Wake up honey; we've gotta get you up for battle.'

She opens her eyes and looks dizzily around. 'I'm alright.' She wanted to laugh but caught another look of the lion-like animal. He's one without a mane; he also has long ears and a furry red face and back, where the sun and moon are stretch marks on his sides. Mostly, it's a pair of slit irises that are by far the meanest.

'Evelyn, just ignore his eyes, they freak me out also.'

'Oh…' She says and finds a noise not too far out, perching herself right up. 'Shouldn't you be right at home, though?'

'Hah.' Day barks on his behalf, and adds a remark directed to her. 'Hey, don't worry kid, the dead father thing, it'll pass.'

Evelyn shifts her attention to Jale after the reminder. 'How old are you?'

Before Jale could answer, a howl causes heartthrob in the three who now stand closer to one another. Day falls to his paws with a heavy thump, speaking lower in tone. 'Oh... there's so much more to this world then you or I, Evelyn.' With eyes wide, 'you can be sure of that.' And his back is turned away from his friends, so he's ready to face the dangers that lurk his statement.

'She's weak from the fight. That's why the house is torn apart.' Jale concludes.

'So that's the husband?' Evelyn asks in regards to the noise they heard.

More movement sounds from Dolora's home, and then a shake is heard from the upper floor and down the hallway steps. Suddenly, a loud thump came to the backyard.

'Okay, so now we got two of them. Do we leave?' Evelyn asks in a hoping manner. They shake their heads "No". She finds a different expression. She quickly suggests. 'Here, this is what I'll do,' she approaches Day. 'I mount him... and... Jale you run back for buddy'pal over there.'

Jale just gave her a look. 'Yeah *right,* look, all I need is a clear shot on her and she'll cure.'

'Yeah, we came here to finish this.' Day adds.

Evelyn looks impossibly the enemies' way. All that she knows is that those things are definitely not human, and the lady's original size has taken shape into something much bigger – whatever these foal things are. If Tetlas was right about one thing, it's tonight. Tetlas told her to be wary of those with dangerous lives. Ironic though, don't you think?

'There's a spell to lift such a curse?' She asks next.

Day answers. 'Well... it's not as simple as that.'

Evelyn slowly turns to him reluctantly. 'Try me.'

'We need to try and paralyze her, reversing the curse and turning her back into human transformation. The rest is the easy part, to combine Blubainic pressed against the chest. A spell, directed to the heart so it will reach the core. This will lift the curse while she's down. Only problem is, catching her before she does us. The foal move so quickly. They rather circle than rush, and they hide in the darkest --' Day halts his speech when movement is heard again.

'But they're easy to hit, right?' She asks, but doesn't get a response. 'Alright then,' she says shakily and slides the book out from her pocket. 'Just keep us protected.'

423

Jale looks around. 'You mean, just keep *you* protected right?'

'Same difference,' she responds.

They both gave her a look.

'I'm joking...' She replies.

Jale eyes forward. 'And what exactly are you planning?'

'Ashnivarna,' the seer of light brightens up the surrounding. 'My plan is to save us.'

Day watches the book in wonder. 'Well, surprise, surprises.' He finds himself saying. She finds him smirking – it's this site of a large kitty cat making a "Cool" face. 'It's nice to see I'm not the only one who has some tricks up my sleeve.'

Freakish

A foal comes into site and another behind a house. The suddenness interrupts Evelyn. Jale bumps her aside and steps forward. The night twinkles like stars; sparks fly from Jale's palm. 'Joulate!' he shouts.

To the sound of spells pound, Evelyn crouches with the book in hands. She can see furry paws circling, their steps aimless. Sometimes the foals move in a hop, dancing from near misses. They have thick black fur with white feet and a white underbelly. They pound their feet from hops, becoming harder to see, from a hazy dust cloud being created by their quickening movements. Their large with claws life size which are always scary and their snouts are wet from anticipation.

With the blast of spells, it makes the air dusty. It is difficult to see in.

Evelyn crawls closer to Jale. She opens the book and flips pages. 'Instant sorcery' to 'mastery of spells' came at her.

'Anything Evelyn!' Jale yells out when he got the chance. 'Use anything!'

His spells spin, twirl and upheavals the earth. It all makes a loud crashing noise. Anything to push those threats back.

Day swats his claw, thwarting the foal's further attempts. But it doesn't last. The enemy's heavy paws push closer, their snouts nearer. After a binding spell touches earth, by the use of the book, it came close to defeating the purpose -- knocking Evelyn and Jale to a stumble. That's how close the foal got.

'Sorry!' She yells. Soon, a different spell is activated. Her body begins to vibrate. Her world doubles from the shake and a large unforgettable face forces at her, reaching her dangling hood and pulling her with a yelp.

'Evelyn!' Jale yells.

She's tossed onto the earth, canceling her spell altogether and rolls outside Jale's protection. The beast comes her way. She can hear her name being called, and a flickering light lands with a flash, giving the foal a jolt of fear.

She gets to her feet with a grasp on the book, 'Zylamort!' She yells. A loud thundering crash tackles the earth; the dusty earth trembles interrupting a foal's approach. The heat from the ground is immense, fleeting the beasts in total -- and to think, it's all from a flick of the palm.

She looks up afterwards, 'how neat.'

The ground shifts; large rock and dirt lift; Zylamort creates a massive female body. With swirling dust, rocks form a giant out of earth.

Evelyn moves backwards. Seemingly, the foal attention had been scattered by the new strength in motion.

'Jale!?' Evelyn yells out in search for him. A war cry brings her nervousness to her creation. The foal retreat, they return to an offensive position in a circle, one large enough to surround the new strength, Evelyn and the two heroes.

'I wonder how Bud is holding up though.' She asks herself, sort lost herself. Maybe she hit her head a little bit *too* hard?

Jale's voice is heard. 'Evelyn!' He appears from the dust. 'They're coming back!'

'Good.' She says.

He gives her a look and then reaches for the book.

'No,' she pulls away. 'I can do this.'

The giant is seen chest up from the dust cloud. It kept them mesmerized for a moment. Jale shakes Evelyn breaking her attention and pulls her to a knee. She refocuses on the task at hand.

A foal reappears form the mists and pounces. It aims for Evelyn; Day shot out from the cloud and knocks it off course. A screech from the foal and together they go rolling. Day kicks his feet, launching the beast up from his spring-like action. Jale shot a bolt of Sophair at it, missing it in the air and another, which lands, hitting the beast in the solar plexus, taking away its breath for a second time.

With unimpeachable power, she cast a spell; one that called upon a source from palms that shot out to collide with another oncoming foal.

The force neglects the foal's tantrums placing it over the ground, rolling it around with shock – literally, lightening.

The two watched as this ancient Aura takes hold of their enemy's last breath. A body bound in light, from head to toe. The foal stops squirming. Its body freezes like a scrapple, shifting from the light into ice. It exhales its last breath as if in a winter's chill.

'Good job.' Jale says, giving her a high five and finds new site, 'Evelyn your arm.'

There is a feeling of vibration within her grasp. She looks down, but it's not from the book, but to find an arm swelling from a scratch.

She frowns hard. 'When did I get that? What does this mean?' She asks him. Their eyes turn site and widen to the distance.

The giant rock body comes swinging to movement around it. That's when they realize these foal are relentless.

Evelyn peers up from the book. 'Riveast!' she shouts the same spell. The bolt crashes. It misses her targeted foal but collides with the giant's reaching arm. Her Aura twists at her arm with wrath – the giant's confusion falls to Evelyn as the giant makes a roar, like a child crying out to its mother. The arm froze in the wake, and shatters, tumbling bits with speed towards them.

'Get to me!' Evelyn yells to her alliance. 'Crekevesk!' water absorbs upward from the earth, forming a dome around them. It freezes with a flash creating a shell-like protection. The wave of rock rolls smashing into it, and damages the structure. Evelyn held her ears to the loud bang.

More foal seemed to have arrived, for they bash at the ice dome. They sneer and tare with loud scratching claws.

Jale can see her fear to what's above, he looks up to the ceiling to find them crawling.

Day, or whatever he is, is breathing heavily, and is the most worried out of the bunch. So he swaps out of Moen to return to human form. This way he can use Aura. The lion-like-Day lights up and the two close their eyes in wait.

She decides to put the heavy book down and reads out loud. 'We've practiced this spell.' She has to yell and does it frantically, flipping through more pages to look for it. 'I can't remember the --' her finger falls to it. 'Here! "May the dome be a casualty to those around".'

'That's it!?' Day asks in naked form, knowing the dome won't last. 'That's all it says?'

Jale's hand falls over hers from anticipation, letting the words reach his mouth, 'Veskekerosh!'

The spell of protection cracks. Everyone in the dome crouches, for it suddenly explodes outwardly. It tosses foe and glittering shards by the fierce hone of Sophair.

A shriek from the giant is heard in the distance. Jale looks up from his shielded stance. The giant seems stunned like the book offered, standing tall with shards of ice in her. Her puzzled look dies down and she moves onto guarding again.

Evelyn skims, flipping through more pages. 'This is it. I hate these damn things you call foals. I am putting an end to this!'

Jale stood watch of their perimeter. He's not sure what else he can do. 'It's up to you now.' He says.

She nods her response. Her bright finger falls to a page under "Summoning" – 'Beliemyth!' she calls out, holding a palm to the distance. Nothing fired. But then, a shake in the earth answered. Nothing happens though... so Evelyn turns the page to find the answers. 'I was sure it would work...'

The giant wards off the foals territory, trampling their wake, crushing bone whenever she could with her only arm.

'Pretty nifty book you got there. Where'd you get a sort of thing like that?' Day asks the two putting on clothes from his pack. They don't respond. 'Nice to know...'

Jale is hunched over her and her lips keep moving. 'Summon thee, Askmith the Unbound -- A legend or it be myth? Refer to Askmith.' She blinks with a resemblance of unknown towards Jale.

'What else does it riddle?' Jale asks, moving to a knee to get a better look. He looks down to the end of the paragraph, reading it. '...Those who run are against thee. Only belief can reveal, Askmith.' Jale looks quiet and something twinkles in his eye. 'Mith?' he asks as if to the air around them. 'Can only belief reveal you?'

A massive quake takes the alliance to the ground. The book tumbles from her grip falling to Jale's feet. The giant stumbles too, when it falls colliding with the earth; it splits in two; shattering its body.

A voice vibrates from beneath and a deep sound came from Thaera. 'Do you believe in me?'

Evelyn tries to get up with her hands, but the constant quake is keeping her down. She yells out to Jale. 'I can't handle this much longer. Use the word backwards to break the spell!'

'I can't reach it.' He yells back.

Day decides to voice his response to the voice below. 'We believe in you!'

'We can't help but believe!' Evelyn cries out as well, hoping Jale can reach the bouncing book.

Something large is born around Evelyn, of bone, seeping from earth. This giant forms rather quickly, also. It takes an easy step backward in the quake of things and suddenly, the shaking stops.

Evelyn looks up at it, squinting to find… a twenty foot human skeleton looking down at her. Evelyn's eyes become watery from fear.

'Don't move.' Jale breathes, 'Htym-eileb!' His voice cracks.

A hard breath is heard from the malediction. Evelyn looks up at the bone-body swaying. Its soul missing from it's now lifeless actions.

'Oh no…' Evelyn says. It replenishes into the earth with a crushing wake around her.

Jale picks up to his feet. 'Evelyn!'

She slowly opens her eyes… what used to be, now forms a ring where it left the rink of Mith.

Jale reaches Evelyn, saying nothing. Instead he's patting the earth off of her. As much as she appreciated it, the flock of dust made it even harder to breathe.

She coughs at him. 'That was fun…'

He grabs her lightly, daring not to let her slip from his grasp again. 'I thought I lost you…'

'You almost did.' She says grimly, pulling away to check for any cuts or bruises on herself.

'Evelyn, I have to heal that scratch.' Jale says.

Day arrives at the two, nudging Jale aside to scan her. 'You're ok -- thank Alas. Nothing hurt, broken? I mean you just came between a fallen… fractal.'

'Day,' Jale jumps in. 'Not now --'

Before she could yell, Miss Dolora collides with Jale, knocking him and Day backwards, putting Jale in a daze and Day to a tumble. The foal gave a blow of dust at the ground and turned to the helpless girl.

'Hesstife!' Evelyn yells.

A look in Dolora's eye, one of furious reacts and the shot of heavy rocks burst in the foal's reaction. She roars, landing someplace behind Evelyn with a thump. It took Dolora longer then Evelyn thought it would for her to get back up.

Evelyn can only hear Dolora's thumps, dashing wherever she goes from pain. 'I... my site,' Evelyn says nervously. Evelyn's mind drifts in and out, and her site comes in and out of focus. There are a few flashes of light and then Jale is at her side.

'Don't move.' He demands.

Evelyn looks taken back at how fast he arrived. Perhaps she's dozing off?

A trampling of feet passes by and then it's gone.

'What was that, was that Day?' She asks, panicky.

'Yes.' He says and lays her on her back.

'Am I dying?' her words could barley be heard. Her site is becoming darker. She can feel her eyelids closing, and then they shut. Jale voice calls out her name, breaking her out of drift. Evelyn shivers and reopens her eyes. She can hardly see Jale, but can feel him checking the wound carefully.

'Evelyn... I'm not going to lie; it's already making its transition.'

Her daze worsens, for the stars are out of focus, a puddle of exaggerated bright spots. She feels energized. It's frightening. Everything is happening so fast, and her thoughts race. Her heart beats faster as well. She goes from hot and sweaty to cold.

'Jale what's happening to me?' She asks calmly, but her words stood out to her. She swore she had been shouting.

The moon clams out from behind the clouds, showing it's pearl. Jale looks up. He looks back at Evelyn. He sees her hand clenched on her heart. He raises her arm. Evelyn reacts grabbing it tightly in her grasp. Her voice moves in and out of tune, becoming deep.

'Jale! It... HURTS, Make it, STOP.' Her grip is becoming fiercer.

Jale yells. 'Evelyn, you must let go.' He struggles with both hands to pry out her hold. Her pupils are dilated, just before they're full black, Jale leans his body forward breaking through her grip. He pushes his hands directed to her chest and says next.

'Blubainic!'

The spell to cure Evelyn's curse reaches her heart. Her body had lifted like a defibrillator, jolting and reversing her transformation. And not a moment later the girl slips away from the darkness unfolding behind black pupils, back to them sea blue.

'It's really cold…'

'Easy now,' he says.

'I just feel… cold…' Then a change in feeling moves through her body, it felt… warm again. She fights to open her eyelids. But Jale reassures her, they're open.

'Jale, I can't see!'

'It's ok. It will come back, you will see again.' He does his best to reassure her. He can see her blinking but there are no recollections of site.

Evelyn leaves the dark place of her mind. There is a slight opening to her -- a brighter world unfolds behind those eyelids.

Jale can see them racing. He's only heard the stories of what goes on behind curtains. It's temporary, until the mind accepts what is happening and what it needs to do to prepare for the next coming changes. Surviving from a scratch is one thing, but to live afterward comes with conditions. The curse will eventually heal into the body, becoming a part of her. Jale only stopped the transformation from completing, so whatever took hold at that time will meld. This cannot be repelled nor be reversed.

Her site found normality and the curtains reopen again; she witnesses the stars. She lay still on the earth, facing the sky.

Jale exhales, and gets up, noticing Evelyn seeing. He bends over to get a better look in her stare, for any signs of shock.

'I'm okay,' staring right back. 'I can see again.' But she doesn't feel the same. She feels physically weak.

He nods. Still, those same beautiful deep blue eyes will no longer see the stars the same way. The trauma of tonight will change her perspective of life, perhaps for forever.

He comes to a sit next to the quiet girl.

Evelyn's eyelids close over her restored eyes. She faints. Her body has gone in a self imposed coma that will begin its transformation process. It's a form of protection that the body requires. Let's hope what she gets from the foal isn't as bad as Jale expects.

He breathes heavily again. He knows what will come next when the coma fades. The conditions will soon be noticeable when she awakens, but one thing is for sure… only time can heal this.

He lifts her unconscious body onto his shoulder, tiredly he moves. He fights to carry her up a hill. Finally, Jale whistles at the top, calling out to Bud. Bud comes to his rescue and arrives shortly after. He taught Bud how to untie himself a few years back, making it more convenient for Jale.

He places Evelyn on the back of Bud, laying her on her stomach. He takes the reins and walks Bud to the spot where the book is, still lying on the ground near the shattered earth by Mith. Jale stares darkly back at the book of Alas. He kneels down and takes a good look around him, just in case that darn Dolora decides to show up unannounced.

He opens the book and does some reading -- finally he finds what he's been looking for -- a binding spell.

Day arrives and moves out of transformation. 'She's gone. You can be sure of this.'

'No scratches on you?'

'No, I'm fine.'

'Good,' Jale says softly.

Day takes off his pack and gets dressed into his wares. 'So what's next buddy?' He asks, as he does this. Jale can't help but keep his eyes on him, noticing his great shape.

'I'm going to take her to my place, in Esmehdar. I'll watch over her, till she's better.'

Day looks at Bud, with the girl hung over his back. 'You don't think… it's going to be bad, do you?'

Jale breathes in deep and releases. 'It'll take some time, my friend. I know of a professional in town who may be able to help me with this.'

Day helps Evelyn up, while Jale mounts. Day sat her up, leaning her against Jale's back. Day stands back.

'Hasu Nuroudra,' Jale's rope binds Evelyn's limp body to himself, and nods next. 'Good bye my friend, hope to see you again.'

'Yes, maybe on better terms?'

Jale can't help but laugh. 'You know... it's going to be alright,' appearing quite confident now, touching the line that connects him to her. He speaks the words and the book of Alas shines and shrinks in his hands. Day moved a little closer to watch. Jale places it in his robe pocket.

'You be careful with that thing,' Day says pointing at Jale's pocket.

He responds with only a smile.

Jale rides the long night, not a howl to be heard and not a memory to be lived. This lonely path stretches into the moonlight. The trees have leafs and the dry earth is beneath him. He smiles. He's the hero of his destiny and he knows it. Tonight was a close call, but he knows better to think of such things. To him it turned out just as it should have. But does she believe in her own fate as much as he trusts in his?

Evelyn's body twitches, and her eyelids slowly quiver. Only to find a scent of sweet sweat, one she admires... She opens up her eyes. She shakes sacredly when the sight of her body is moving above ground. She looks around to see Jale looking grim, but happy to see him safe. Her eyes flash in the night, like a cat's would in the black. She touches the light source around them; there is neither feeling nor heat.

He asks. 'Do you have the strength for me to release this rope?'

'Yes.'

He reaches into the pouch to place a palm on the book of Alas that had been reopened before for this moment and repeats the spell backwards. The rope disintegrates. Evelyn watches bits brush off them and disappear. She peers at the scenery. This is a good change. It's not some massive forestry or a mount of hills, but they follow a single pathway leading forward into a flatbed.

'Where are we heading?' She asks him tiredly, looking at her arm.

'To Erahe,' he responds. 'It'll take some time.'

'Okay.' She says. She pats Bud with her cut arm and feels a slight pain. 'How long have I been out?'

'Thirty minutes, at most.' He says, glancing back to check on her.

'Is that it? Is this a good thing?'

'It implies you didn't have much to heal. It's a good thing. The less time spent means less conditions.'

'Conditions... what do you mean?' She asks, finally moving her site from the scenery back to him.

He's about to speak on another matter, but decides to help her with her question. 'You've gone through a slight transformation stage. It placed you in a coma in order to prepare for the changes your body will succumb.'

Her eyes squint, but not because she's upset but because she's scared. Tears slowly fall down her cheek.

Jale can hardly hear the sniffles with the wind in his ears. But when he did, it wasn't as bad as he expected. For such a traumatizing night, she's sure taking it good. He was expecting her to hit him or something...

There is so much time to think things over, blah, too much time. The silence between them is left alone. The rhythm of the night is felt. It helps keep their thoughts from running.

A bug zips around her. She was afraid to swat it, just in case. She asks. 'Where's Day?'

'Not here, he's gone. He went back to Eslr to help others for more ransoms. That's what he does, remember?'

'Obviously...' She only says, but he could hear the tone, she's lost in thought about all that's already happened. 'I've...' She thought deeply before finishing. 'I went through this really freaky dream and then I woke up.'

'I can only imagine...'

'But you healed my arm nicely,' she replies, admiring his art.

'No actually. I didn't. I didn't think I could with your energy level.'

'Oh?'

He's unsure how to put this. 'The first condition, during your coma, you see. The coma really just pre-paves for the healing process and that of occupying you through dreams. Do you feel... calm?'

'Yeah you could say that. I feel like I'm okay with it. It is strange, this feeling...'

'Yes.' He laughs. 'But I've had stranger things happen.'

She nods, not really sure by what the heck he meant by this, but it was nice to say nothing, nor care for much. Ah, but knowing how old he is, he's must have seen a lot. I bet that's what he meant by it. She examines her arm. 'So conditions... huh? Well this is one of those brilliant times, but it's kinda scary. Will I always be able to heal this fast?'

'Perhaps, and I can't tell if you're being sarcastic or not. Anyways, it will in time.' He laughs. 'I know that sounds redundant. Sorry…'

'No… you saved my life Jale.' She leans in and kisses him on the neck. It was a nice kiss. Man she's so lucky for having someone in her life, someone as great as him and who she really likes. This is just me ranting. But damn, how many of us actually get that? No one, anyways, I'll shut up now. 'I never would have made it this far out on my own. So… really, we will call it a souvenir.'

He scoffs. 'You're taking this better than I expected.'

Now this makes me think about this couple, who're taking things way better than I would have. But you know… fantasy novels got to stay intangible, so the likely hood of this actually happening is rare, about as rare as Evelyn's sea blue eyes.

'Yeah, but I'm not going to turn into a --'

'No.' He says. 'It's never going to change you. You are only parts.' He swallows, 'minor parts.'

'Good.' She says, nodding. Her focus has changed but her emotions remain high. She twitches like a wary animal. The wind is full of scent, more then she would normally notice. 'I smell fire.'

Small houses are in the distance where owners have torches lit near property lines. He slows down to come at a turn. Stakes are lit every hundred yards. Where she sees, barns and more houses come into view having large crop fields.

A lady in the field wore a long brown dress. She looks out towards them waving carefully.

Evelyn waves the same.

More and more homes came into view as friendly ones waved back, but Evelyn noticed a shift in their pattern. Like a new world is beginning to awaken from within these majestic parts.

Evelyn closes her eyes. A far away land was what she pictured. Now bewildering its outer beauty, it is so much… better in the real. She opens her eyes to awaken the pictures she held for so long, of the farmlands.

Children's faces light up as Evelyn and Jale ride by, leaving a fenced gate with the kids rushing over to wave hello, only to rush back into the field again. It left a place in Evelyn's heart, knowing that there are others in this world, beyond her memories; that go and play in the fields.

'I love memories of home,' and then she couldn't believe it slipped her lips. 'I'm so a half-breed now.' It sounded odd as well as overwhelming, like the first time she had mentioned the name of the Rebuin.

He laughs out loud. 'I'm not sure what anyone can call it. I would say... a second chance?'

The crickets sing loud in the fields around them. There are wood fences on both sides of the dusty road, and as they ride in the middle, Evelyn musters in thought. It had been for quite awhile. Of course, she thought about her new life, and what this truly meant to be this "Half-breed". But most importantly, what it truly meant to be alive.

'Are you ok, Evelyn?'

'I'm just really hungry.' She says. 'I'm like salivating.'

'Okay,' and he turns to smile at her. 'I'll stop at the first inn along the way.'

Barns soon surround. They're older buildings, but most peacefully neighboured.

'It's just like home.' She looks around excitedly.

'We're on the outskirts of Erahe. Wait until we reach it and then the inner reaches. Then tell me what you think.'

Evelyn didn't have too, she's already happy she's here. Her emotion is her grace. She could see his eagerness. It didn't take much to see he feels the same.

Two hours into riding. Evelyn holds on, putting her hunger at bay. She wasn't sure what Jale had in his saddle pouches, but she's craving something... meaty. She lifts the lid to find fruits and vegetables. *I'll just have to wait*

They come to a stop at the boarders. It's a great feeling, arriving. There is a feeling of leaving a part of herself behind, once more dropping off her baggage, so to speak, in that she can pick up with a new start.

The post is rather small. It has a simple fence and a few guards. There is a quiet town at its stand in this middle of nowhere. Evelyn and Jale find their seats at a small pub and eat hungrily. It seems all Evelyn wants is protein, having a loss for her regular greenie appetite. Jale is sure happy to be eating.

They wash up at a room he orders for them. They decide to rest here from exhaustion.

435

'I'm glad I'm here.' She says. 'You know, I was never really sure if we'd make it. But now I can see it clearly -- life is only beginning for me. It's got me thinking, maybe you're more like your father then you realize... You saved me, Jalelilian. I don't think your father went crazy with power... I only see a fine boy raised, and for that I'm thanking him.' Her cheek lift and it holds him in the moment.

She passes him into the showers. Under warm water, she cleans herself. Afterward, they jump into their nightgowns and brush their teeth. They get ready for bed, and finally they move their sore bodies onto separate beds. She felt as if she was melting from exhaustion. She was about to say something, but can see he's already fast asleep.

Something smooth covers her mind... as if seeing the blazing sun for the very first time, or knowing it was almost her last... so she watches the kalec sleep. It was almost time to give up, and look at what she would have been missing. Where would she go without him? He's got her escaping into the stars, or however you explain really happy people. I don't really know, because I wish I had what they do. Peacefully is what she has me thinking, and slowly her eyes close to this.

- CHAPTER 18 -

Phases of the Moon

I n a soft bed, sitting against a small headdress; Evelyn opens her eyes. It has a smell of cedar and oak. The cedar brings back memories of her past. It was the sudden awareness that made her mood jump even higher. It's a bright morning and the sounds of carriages are heard, like playing music to her ears. She sits up quickly.

In her nightgown, she places a hand at her brow to sunlight catching her eye, shinning through the room window. She finds herself in a light state of mind. Looking past the window, the horizon couldn't be any brighter. And like this, the room is suddenly darker; this scares her. It's the sudden realization of night and not daylight when the moon is out.

'No way,' she blinks in her amazement and she gets up to move closer to the window. The stars are out. 'Yup, it's night alright… I would have sworn it was daylight. That's freaky.' She looks over her shoulder to see if she missed Jale sleeping under covers. Her fingers sink into the blankets and she crawls over the side. It's empty.

Where could he be?

She looks for her things, peering around. She can't find her robe or pack. Jale's things are missing as well. She hurries out the door and comes to a small hall. She brushes her hair back with her fingers and looks up to see the lady from last night. The lady behind the front desk wore a blue dress and is chatting to a guest.

A voice makes Evelyn jump.

'Up already?'

Evelyn laughed and turns to see the one person she was glad she was scared by. 'Yeah I am.'

'Good. You're awake at the perfect time you know.'

She raises her brows. 'I know... it sort of just happened. It felt like one of those crazy dreams I've been having. I just woke up and I was suddenly looking for you and then you were missing.'

He takes her hand. 'Come outside, there's something I want to show you.'

'Wait.' She breaks from his hold. 'I just had a major moment before now. I awoke and I would have sworn it was day. In fact, I really thought it was.'

He just gave her a look and it said it all.

'Conditions...'

He nods his reply. 'The body is still refreshing from all the change.' He raises a brow to her and then goes on to explain his sudden erg of excitement. 'I've been reading some parts of the book while you've been sleeping.' They pass the lady. Jale pushes the front door open to reveal the night. The warm air hits them with a pleasant surprise. Bud waits straddled up, already set for travel.

'What? What day is it?'

'I don't think you'll believe me, but you slept through the whole day. It's nearly the next morning.'

Evelyn nods not surprised by this. She needed the rest. She asks him playfully now.

'Were you going to leave without me?'

'No, not without you, I was going to wake you, silly.'

She gave him a look as a response.

'Why would I leave you, exactly?'

'I don't know.' She laughs. 'Thank Alas you didn't.'

He smiles and offers his hand to mount Bud.

She asks. 'It's warmer. It's nice. Is that why you're all jittery?'

'No, not exactly,' he faces a road. Carriages pass along, which are lit by their lamps. Jale pointed across him where a sign can be read "Twenty miles from Esmehdar".

Evelyn eyes widen. 'We're here already?' She looks around in joy. 'It's beautiful. I knew something was great about this place! And to think, we were so close.'

'I know, right?'

'Yeah,' she says slowly, getting this feeling of being with home again. It made her stop and look around a bit. Oh, she also has a good feeling that he has much to show her. She gets the most amazing shivers now. She walks out more, mostly nearer the edges of the roadway. It's wide and paved with stone. She wants to get a better view of things. It's what's out here that makes her feel awakened, at the edge of destiny, and to think… another journey lay just miles from this landmark. It's still untypical waking to these sorts of things, she feels. So, as she stares past the sign, not even Jale dared to question her stillness, for all the beauty that waits beyond, to the mystic dawn offering its glow of things.

'It's so warm.' She says, looking back at him. Her gaze awoke his own glory, igniting his own worthy mind. She shouts. 'I did it! I finally made it!'

A carriage passes with much speed. The passengers look out their window to witness the girl's happiness.

'Yes!' Evelyn shouts again, falling to her knees and glances at the waking sun. 'This is the best morning ever…' She laughs out loud, with eyes watery; the girl looks back with that bright smile to witness Jale in patience.

Does he truly know how she feels, about her passion about Alasmieria? The journey that all started with a town called Maesemer and a book? With a Niveus Avis called Willow and a woman that pertained to be Evelyn's mother… turning out to be something so much more… and perhaps, a little badass? Out here, on the leading edge of things, Evelyn's become a true beauty in life, don't you think?

The girl gets to do all the things she wants to, like roam free as a bird. So my question is; what does one with all this excitement and freedom do? Celebrate! But first… she's reminded by Jale to get dressed before experiencing anything radical. She returns back outside. There now, now she's ready.

Still, she wants to get a better view of things, to climb below the cliff and see what lies within the valley of this morning's adventure.

The summer's rays are magnificent, its clever soul shimmering gold and peeking behind Esmehdar, soon to reveal its full face. Or you could call it glory; releasing Evelyn's daunting side and reminding her to let go of past experiences. This sun marks the change of past, present and future self. Evelyn's once sleepy eyes are wide awake.

'All my questions are in that beyond.' She says to herself, smiling. 'Oh how good it feels... how good it feels.'

'Beautiful the world we live in, isn't it.' Jale rather states, already mounted. He arrives to her sides and hands her the book in one hand, and her pack in the other. She flings her pack over her shoulder and straps in. She placed the book into her side pocket and looks up to meet eyes.

He held out a hand. 'So, are you ready?'

'I am.' She says taking his grasp and he heaves her up.

A carriage passes them by quickly, it moved as fast as her racing heart. Its lantern flicker much, from much speed. Oh, but Evelyn's done looking around, she's found her one and only; her Jale.

They join the road. A giant city begins to come into view; bright from the cusp of dawn; just enough to get a picture by the sunlight reaching. For now, mostly tall of towers and wilder creations are viewed.

'Jale, I did it...' She says faintly in his ear.

'I know, we're home,' he replies with enthusiasm.

A town is at the foot of the city. The city walls of Esmehdar tower it. Yet, just beyond Esmehdarian gates, gloating towers of the capital stand even larger then these outer walls. But nothing can out weight the soaring mountains in the backdrop. They are higher and more bulky to the southeast side, holding many lush forestry and grasses. This makes them look a little bit like a row of furry green giants, and hunched over with spines to the sky. And at the mountains tops, there are small snow caps.

To Evelyn's right, the long road stretches till it comes to a straight drop, about... half a mile fall. A waterfall is located in the far, draining into Aspin. It is a sanctioned city at the bottom, nearest Esmehdar. It was built for exporting and gatherer of medicine and herbs to take from the lush of the valley. The crowned Queen's capital calls to it for daily renewals.

More flickering lanterns pass. Evelyn looks out towards the valley, getting a glimpse from the roadway. She cannot get the sunrise out of her mind; this amazing feeling in her gut. It's big orange bubbly self caresses the wild life, into their eyes. If this was a long drive, the headlights would be staring off towards the paradise. They ride, watching the backdrop of sites. The cliff to their left has soaring butterflies near the drop, lingering along the side.

There on the outside of Esmehdar, a town is sanctioned. It has large wooden gates to protect its means.

'That is the town of Hempsvile.' Jale says, pointing to the little houses in the distance, a town in shadow by the towering Esmehdarian gates. 'Obviously it's no Esmehdar, but it still holds plenty to go by. That place reminds me of good memories. I'm not much of a drinker, but I've had some of the best experiences there. But my heart has sunken with the city this time around, and I can see it will catch you too.'

'Good hunting?' Evelyn asks, referring back to his memories with Hempsvile, and he laughs with.

'You could say that, sure.'

'Honestly, I just want to be where you're.'

He is still. And his quiet makes her nervous.

'I feel the same way.' He finally says. And he means it with every fibre in his being, so much so he made sure to turn and smile when he could.

In a world of only mastery, Evelyn can't help but find herself more in a classy film, than a fantasy now, more compelled by today's perfect grace. It feels good to be her own woman and on a mission with an even greater kalec. She loves the uniqueness of life. The skies are their horizon.

Jale makes her feel like an everlasting person. That means no matter what happens; he will bring that other vibe to her life. It reminds her they'll be okay, because his soul is planted confidently in Alasmierian soils. Though there is much to his story, as it's quite easy for Evelyn to be asking questions about it, there comes a time when a look and a saviour is more than enough.

Oh, I should also mention she loves his positivity. They both have that look in their eyes, knowing… that they finally did it. That all along it was themselves they wanted. Each other, I should say. Ha. If you can imagine your perfect partner, than times it by how you feel and double it. That's how they feel. Whew… that's an overload.

She found he was a little light to begin with, but then aren't we all? All that's changed for her, and thank goodness it's him. There's no one she can imagine by her sides right now. A kelec with mean-blood and a girl with bad, can there really be anything better than that? And all she can do now is thank this kalec and the universe that seems to abide by his rule and his father's oath. She realizes now she doesn't have much to choose from, because she has it all. So what does one do? Have a whole heck of a fun with and be thankful for.

Still, life makes her wonderful and chats to her about the basics. It can hold her by the hand or give her that little push she couldn't ask for, better yet, something she wanted so badly. Hey, what can I say, with the most complicated questions out of mind, it only leaves her with a few *how about this* and *that*, and a few *I wonder...*'s.

They arrive to town. In Hempsvile they find themselves surrounded by lit lanterns, but not just from streetlights, but by portable ones that are carried.

They travel into this gothic path, with robes hooded, it helps create the effect. The towers can only get bigger with Evelyn and Jale's arrival outside capital gates. With the sunlight behind it, it cast shadows, reminding Evelyn what resides in Esmehdar -- the very essence to her unknown past.

'What is this place?'

'The major trade district of Hempsvile,' Jale says. 'It's a place sold in chaos.'

'I would have guessed a market always this fast is enticing.' She says. Her eyes watch those around.

'It always makes me want to get off and buy something.' Jale responds.

He's getting waves, and so does she. No, snap out of it, actual hand waves to say hello by humans and other race beings. Not *just* emotional ones. Ha, gotcha. He nods nobly back to the crowds, Evelyn even waved back once or twice. She turns in her stirrups, now holding onto Jale to the commotion around them.

They offer sales, and Jale politely refuses to the sellers.

She can't help but see him in a different world. She knew something was unique that night at the fireplace, him sitting across from her. She gets this feeling he never told her the whole truth, it makes her wonder how much he really hid that night, aside from what she already knows. The feeling pries, it feels like something is missing from the picture.

They leave the trade district and find peace and quiet around this section of town, nearer the gates of capital.

'Wait here. I have to stop at the post office.' His voice grasps her. She watches him leave her side to walk this world with a pace, one that he can still call his own.

'His father's Alas, but his mother's surely not Mieria. I mean, there's no way Jale could live more than five hundred years. That's ridiculous. No... He must be lying.' She knows Mieria died early, long before Reobigheon had. She adds one plus one and her eyes squint. 'So something not right.'

Normally, Evelyn doesn't like to pry in another's business, raised to mind her own but finds this is very much hers. Isn't it? Right, whatever you said.

The area is large, and she waits on Bud near a crossroad. The roads are filled with carriages, and the crosswalks have pedestrians. It's run by right of way and courtesy. Evelyn's attention comes back to the area around her.

Beings pass without attention to her or Bud, it made Evelyn blink; reminding her of Maesemer's town central, dusty and always a crowd during the busiest of hours, only... with thousands of witches and warlocks.

There's no turning back – this really is it, it's happening

Far from home, she's witnessing a new kind of discovery. She looks up to see one of the towers. It's black gleaming. How such a tower could ever be built, is as much a mystery like Jale and his *real* story. One she feels he fails to mention on occasion. Anyways, going back, if one of those fell, it would crush the city below, similarly like the tower that had lay wreck on the forest near the Great Watch. As we already know, she has a bit of an imagination – alright, that's a bad excuse -- reckless boy, me.

She has herself wondering. 'I thought structures of those heights could only exist in Brunon... I wonder if Aura had a helping hand in building such a mass.'

Jale returns, carrying a small sac filled of papers. 'It's easiest if I take it all. I've been away awhile.' He says happily, like a child carrying all his favourite toys.

She says nothing and they exchange looks. He can see Evelyn has something on her mind, but he's just not quite sure what it is. He places the whole sac into his saddle pouch, silently. He glances with a weak smile and mounts once more.

She wants to know more, she wants to trust her gut, yet a dangerous feeling tells her to butt out. He appears calm. It makes her think, would he hurt her if she crossed that line. No, you don't think so either, probably just emotionally eh? Some people just don't have it in them. I'm kidding... relax.

'Why didn't you tell me?'

'Excuse me?' He asks, looking around to see if anyone noticed.

'Your father may be Alas, but your mother is not Mieria, is she?'

His voice lowers. 'Yes, he is. But how did you know --'

Evelyn looks stricken. 'Right, so why didn't you tell me?'

His smile's not visible. 'Because if anyone were to find out who I am...' He stops and smacks his lips. God Evelyn hates when people do that. 'That Alas had a mistress -- those that pray to him would crumble in faith.'

'Who, who was she, Jale?'

He swallows and looks around carefully. He looks like he wants to wait for another time, but she doesn't leave it, 'your mother.'

'My mother... is Tetlas.' He finally says. It was a relief, like the words wanted to fall from his lips the moment he met Evelyn.

'Ah shit,' her face drops. 'I knew it.'

'Her name's Tetlas, alright?' He says again, looking around upset. He knows what's going to happen next. Well, he fears it, all of it. If he lost Evelyn, what would he do? God do we really care anyone?

'Alright,' she says and getting ready to jump off Bud. 'I can't do this anymore.'

'Evelyn.' He hesitates, reaching.

She jumps off landing in time to pull away. 'Don't touch me.'

He jumps off and points at Bud. 'You don't move.' And he turns back to search for the girl. She disappears past the crowd and finds a pair of doors into a building. Jale catches up, 'where are you going?' He grabs her arm and she tugs away, slipping past the door. She thought about holding the door so he couldn't get in, but decided best to keep moving. He reaches her inside. With a grasp he twisted her body and he receives an empty stare back.

'You don't know... do you?'

'Know?' He asks, stepping back.

'That Tetlas killed my birth mother?'

'I,' he hesitates and swallows. 'I didn't know.'

'Let me go.' And he does. She runs away, anything to get a fresh breath of air.

He stands in shock. He's not good a compromising. 'Evelyn.' He calls out again. It was almost in that whiney tone.

In the room of goods, people looked their way. Jale manages to get her behind shelves and out of everybody's site. Evelyn falls to a knee, crying. It's always fun watching something good go to the shits. Funny how it's everything we want and then it's gone. A look in her eyes told him she is unsure about anything he has to say.

Jale comes to his knee also. He's not sure what to do.

Ah, the sweet taste of drama.

She figured it out; Tetlas had to do what she had to, in order to protect Evelyn and this plan for balance -- but it all feels like so much to her, neither Jale or Evelyn wants to admit each other's love for one another, nor admire to the point of pushing each other away, now that they've grown so close, it hurts to separate. Their blooming flowers are becoming dry under this hot heated moment.

'You knew... all this time and you didn't tell me?'

'Alas plan --'

'Alas, crazy bastard, I don't care about a ghost!'

He continues, clearly not caring. '...May have foresaw much, but Evelyn, if my mother -- if Tetlas didn't stick to the plan; you would have died along with your real mother that night, and the whole world would have fallen in turmoil.'

'Oh you have a lot of explaining to do.'

A voice of a shop keeper approaches. 'Excuse me? Are you two alright?'

'Yes,' Jale says, turning to flash his title.

Evelyn literally wanted to say eff off.

The man points and spoke. 'There is a washroom, just over there if you want more privacy, sire.'

'Come.' Jale says to Evelyn and wastes no time moving with her past the looks. He gets them behind the door. For a moment in the stall, there had only been a stare from her.

'Tell me what you know.' Evelyn asks him helplessly, a good one of final surrender. 'I don't care anymore Jale, so just say it.'

'I don't know much, Evelyn.' Jale says near the sink. He moves closer to her near the toilet. 'I'm guessing your real mother would have died, along with you, but Tetlas knew a better way and told me she would save a girl… the one with the book.'

'Nice.' Evelyn pushes past him and he grabs her.

'Evelyn… I only knew what he told me. I never knew anything would come to this. You have to trust me.'

Evelyn just shakes her head. 'I… I don't know what to think,' and comes to a sit on the toilet lid. 'I just don't understand all of this anymore. And it's ok. I've… I'm done.'

He laughs a bit, knowing that feeling. She didn't laugh with. He waits and then he saw her as if it was for the first time. Her cheeks lift, and she shakes off her mood. The life comes back into her face.

She spoke with gloom. 'It's so interesting, all of it. It's funny… when I was younger I always had a different picture of what life would be like. But not like this, funny eh?' She asks him. He says nothing. 'What's it all worth? What's this all for? Then, something tells me there's nothing more than this -- that this is what I would ever want. You and me and this smelly washroom, so at this moment, I'm over all this sadness. This might sound backwards, but I'm with you, you and this plan. I'm in,' her voice picks up. 'What do I have to lose? After all, I have nowhere to go back to. Ha, all I see is you and I guess that's not so bad.'

Jale looks up with brighter eyes, like watching the sunlight coming through -- Her watering his flowers. He says. 'It's funny how the mind rationalizes, isn't it? Yet all this time you've been on the plan. It was the life you had from birth that was finally shaken and then, the real you is brought into motion.'

She just gives him a look. The silence makes her find her words. 'I guess.' She wipes her eyes to signify this. She knows he can't see past her moment. And who cares. It's not for him to follow. 'And to whatever comes next, we'll work it out.'

The door to the bathroom opens and a few stares are met. Jale and Evelyn had to take a few moments to come back to the room. Everyone looks up from what they're doing to see.

We're okay.' She laughs now and the two leave the building with focus on themselves, and a realization of what had just happened.

Two people look at one another. One says. 'I wonder what that was all about, you think their okay?'

The other responds. 'I'm sure it's nothing to worry about, it's no Regalia to fuss about.'

Evelyn and Jale found their day. Bud is looking still as ever. It was nice to see him so peaceful with the busy crowd passing and even patting him.

Evelyn smiles and I hope it never escapes her again. But we both know that can't happen.

'That's my Bud; he's my tamed and disciplined fellow.' Jale says, patting him.

'I think he just likes the attention, like you.'

'Right,' Jale laughs. 'You best get me out of this busy section then.'

'After you,' Evelyn opens her palm to their ride. Evelyn mounts after him. Bud strikes for the gates of Esmehdar!

'Tell me what Alas told you and Tetlas, I want to know the details of your past.'

'No, no more. Let's take a break. How about that? I thought 'done and over with' was in effect?'

'Come on now, that's not fair.'

'Alright,' he says and slows Bud. 'He told me very little, as I was just a boy. It would be later on that I found out the better forces of Reobigheon would collapse. Back when, he only prepared me and my mother for a day that I thought would never come. And one I surely hoped wouldn't, for we'd have to set out and leave the capital in case a "Storm" happens. That's how he put it.

'We knew of his power, but we... we never knew what he had done to change the future, only that he could. One night during a traditional ball, Alas came to us. He told us the time was now, for the day had come. We trusted his words. I... I and my mother fled to the forest like we planned, near the Twin Peaks. We only carried a few things with us, one of which was the necklace, which Alas handed over as a part of the plan to my mother, without my knowing. We were to hide out till the storm passes... even I couldn't have fathomed the Great War, if he had told me... I don't think I ever would have left that night. The rest of the knowledge from that day forward was given to me by my birth mother, Tetlas.'

Evelyn looks away when he finished his sentence. The citizens' have fresh faces, and there is a smell of cooking. Some people wore robes with ranks, some too dark to make out, but the shining jewellery on them isn't. From cold-cut diamonds to silver, but not all are token with silver and gold. Like a carnival, Evelyn's eyes arrive to the most unique figure; aside from the wobbling ears and the odd markings on their robes… it is the very essence of this place that is best.

It's the citizens' expressions that are stricken with wit; a look of readiness, for whatever should come. These people may not have the training of an Errific, or behold their skill sets, yet the Caealon have a power of their own, one focused on unconditional love. With a type of strength and belief system that goes beyond the rigorous Calliskue, love always wins the war.

As far as Caealon's concerned, and in no means referring back to the enemy, they're set free and are moving in the direction they prefer. After today, Evelyn's managed to change more then she can put into words. She feels she fits nicely in the atmosphere of things and has become a contender to say the least. I mean, she was raised by the scariest thing from the south, and walked out of the Twin Peaks for Peat sakes, and I say with only scratches, and entered a land that raised her soul with uncharted nature.

She's faced a beast that comes only from midnight stories and raised spells that can't be comprehend. Still, she survived a foal, fighting near death experiences alongside a Clairic who kept his footing. Now, she is told to hold to a plan, and a book that could be evermore definite, one that may play a key part in restoring a "Balance" in the nature of things. But Evelyn knows better. It's her life and she's going to do things her way.

She has hope in other places, and is ready for something else; for Evaloak to turn over a new leaf and refuse retaliation. It may just be them who could turn the fate of Reobigheon and birth it again. Now isn't that worth thinking about? She would think so, I know it.

The many things could be, but what are for sure, Caealon are a united people, of student and teacher who've come together. With an open hand, they share, and an open heart to receive. This is one thing Caealonians got going on right now. Aside from this, the cities and towns are all so grand to them and all so beautiful to Evelyn, it's worth the mentioning. She can see it on their faces, the way they smile to the power that lies within their hearts. Caealon sure knows how to shine, and they have figured out how to tend to others needs without losing their own centre. They live in a world that is sufficient, beyond the currency gap; the majority of the country is fulfilled and knows there's enough for everybody. Love wins, and they love themselves; because they know *they're enough*. Words I've heard from others. But I have to put my hand down. Is it wrong to call ourselves ugly, or even gross? It sure makes life feel easier to walk around without judgment. I mean, let's face it, and I laugh when I say this, who can judge you if you're already stricken? So I say, enough with the enough and lets play a different game. For some reason this works for me -- Any agree out there? Anyways, it's just a thought and I'm not saying it's for everyone. Alright, let's get back to the story.

Bud continues to throttle through town. Jale moves them toward a massive arch in the face of the wall around Esmehdar. Much higher up a brigade stands post. There are a large number of groups situated on four different levels to the wall. The highest bracket of four in total, has geared infantry mounting weaponry, such as catapults, cannons and crossbows.

And Evelyn thought she looked cool in her wardrobe? She is to find these infantry are certainly suited up for clever appeal.

When Evelyn gets a closer look, the wall is seen differently. It is actually a giant outpost, ringed around the city. The third level has infantry dressed in chain mail. They have a crossbow or longbow in hand.

Clairic and Celestials have the second run of the wall, being nearest to the bottom but not touching ground. They're wardrobe in long draping gowns, silvery and white with many sacs of the many kinds of Burley at disposal.

Infantry weapon a sword and shield at the base of the ring, at ground level.

Further within the arch, Bud passes those with a shield and an offhand. Up ahead, stations are seen. It is a fair site, clean and organized. Let me rephrase that, it's actually a small haven between massive numbers. Esmehdar being on one side and Hempsvile they've only just been through.

There are pubs and restaurants making those under the shade of the arch more comfortable. It's cooler and smells of hay and sod. Evelyn doesn't see any pens nearby. Perhaps the pens are stationed within the wall?

She watches men and woman enter and leave the few doorways to the wall. They move with a close combat weapon in hand. Those that stand guard hold a claymore in front of them, tip to the ground, others with a long sword or broadsword. There are plenty of mounted, with a sword in sheath, throttling past Evelyn and Jale. There is enough space on the road for the mounted to cover a football field, awesomely.

Evelyn catches the feel of the book in her pocket and looks away from a female's guard's gaze. The guard has a claymore supporting her stance, standing right next to a male guard. The woman didn't look twice, nor seem careful of civilian passing.

'They don't seem too worry.' Evelyn rehashes.

'It's because they don't have to.'

'Ah, that's because there hasn't been war to reach Esmehdar?'

'Not since the Wrath of Ages, and...' He says pointing up above -- hoping this would finish his would-be sentence.

Evelyn looks up to see archers from the left windows of the arch, and on the other side, there those cloaks are. Both parties chat, but they're always keeping an eye out. Each window is wide enough for two to fit, and there are hundreds of spots filled.

Back to the base level, lunch time has many eating at tables. Bread loafs, beans, salads, and all kinds of unique foods, but the most recognizable are pastries. There are many fruits left out in bowls too for anyone to walk by and grab for a quick snack.

Guards have to keep on the move with the food constantly needing stalking; it's a large feast. It's an extraordinary site to all, not just Evelyn.

Bud continues through the swallow of the arch, not getting any halts. Let me just stop you, can anyone actually read this book not listening to music? Maybe I should stop interrupting you.

Evelyn notices all the infantry wore the same tabard; art shows a bright yellow star in the middle of a blue and purple background, where a crown is above the sun.

'This is definitely the Royal Guard.' Evelyn says and Jale gave them a wave back.

Jale tilts back. 'Yes.' Many noticed his title and stood up to salute him, others playing card games or just having some good fun are nudged to give attention. They stood up, clearing their throats and salute.

'It's alright.' Jale says, waving his hand of ease. The Calon and Rebuin sit back down.

Hempsvile is looking smaller from the end of the arch. Evelyn looks back one more time and Jale's voice made her turn around.

'Welcome to Esmehdar,' and moves them out of the tunnel.

'Oh my…' She says leaning forward.

This street is spread out, giving it a lighter feel. Some buildings are very unique, marked with colourful paintings and creative symbols. She wonders what they mean. Then she caught a picture of a Niveus Avis; it looks smaller than Willow in actuality.

She couldn't help but look up from memory. It's a clear sky, nothing but bright blue.

The atmosphere is relaxed in the street. I can easily recall the first time I went camping, hiking, and at a water park – it was a place of no responsibility and total freedom. That's what the energy is like in this bustling city. It's exciting. Remember, Esmehdar is a place already housed and they don't have to work, but many work because of joy. That's right, smiles all around, with the best food and life has to offer. Smiles all around, it's hard to say that with a straight face.

Lofty faces pass through the streets in blue robes and purple, wearing odd artefacts. Many have sewed themselves into this comfortable society and never questioning their leave. The happiness on their faces is an emotional site for Evelyn. Finally, there is a place she can rest.

This beats anything I've witnessed yet

'What did all those symbols on the buildings mean?' She asks him. She notices some wear them on their clothes also.

'They're symbols of the Niveus Avis; others were parts to the Caealon flag. I remember mentioning the Niveus Avis's meanings at Telahire. It means hope and freedom.'

'Oh okay, I think I'll have to buy one of those.' Evelyn says blissfully.

Loud chatter bursts to their ears. The sky couldn't be any brighter and this whole place smells of flowers, loathing their rich perfume.

Hempsvile can only compare to a select of Esmehdarians. At first glance, the people of Esmehdar appear soft because of their way of life, but they're much more built; emotionally, and a kindness that supports the morality of the city.

She can see where Jale got his charm, being Esmehdarian. But he's a little different, mostly swift – Evelyn knows if she's not on her A-game most of the time, she'll most likely be swept under the rug by his intelligence. It's nice to know she has this noble in her grace, even when he can be a mind bender. As a mention, he's a life changer.

With all those days spent together, she is finding it harder to keep up with Jale's knowledge. He's intimidating, and this scares her a little. It's good to be scared though. Lately, she can smell more of him; his neck smells... really, really good. Is that a condition acting up? – I hope so.

A large figure with a massive walk is noticed by his shines, by silver armour that gives him a clever appearance. The people are quick to make room for this being to pass. Its male like-face appears pulled back with a thick skull and little ears. Evelyn thinks he looks much like an over grown monger that has a massive amount of weight put on, and has perfectly pearly whites. The figures crest is yellowy, unlike anyone else's blue or purple. He walks with his chest pushed out, a clear sign of prudence.

Jale didn't need to look; his voice sounds of interest. 'You remember that tale about the mountain guardians I spoke of?'

'I do!' Her eyes follow the slow movement of the proud one. 'Ah-ha I knew this would come up again. I was wondering when you would remind me.'

He giggles. 'Yes, they're the ones. They're known as Houllad -- vile ones.'

'Where do they live today?'

'They come from there.' He points to the hunched giants beyond the city, peaking with the same glory as the main subject. The Houllad don't hunch. 'That's the Houllerend Mountain. We just made another treaty with the Houllad kind, to allow them access into our cities. They supply minerals for mining in the mountain, and they've been discovered ever since the Great War. I suppose banging on their door woke them up; Caealon went mining after the Great Separation for minerals and all.' He goes on. 'The Houllad are drawn to fish and teased for eating mongers, cooked... not raw. Thank father. And to answer your question, they live here now. They reside to their own faction, but it is very minute.'

'Thank father eh? And to think I thought there could only be Rebuin and Calon.' She says, watching the figure in fascination.

Is it really happening? I can't believe this is real. They're so... neat... the Houllad

The Houllad disappears into the crowd. She watches him disappear.

'That must have been a large change for Caealon?'

'Yes. It was.' And he takes them slowly through the bustling city. 'This was the treaty I spoke of earlier, at Caszuin.'

'Ah… now I can understand why you expected me to know this.'

He nods.

A young lady about the same age of Evelyn is dressed in purple. It's a simple and tidy gown. Her face lights up eagerly at the site of window shopping on the street. The girl enters into a large building that contains powders pressed up against front display windows. A black wax is dressed across shelves.

Bud takes Evelyn and Jale away from this girl and over a large bridge of white stone. The sun comes out from behind a few clouds, casting its elegance and blush to the streets. They're many levels to Esmehdar and the floors are made of a hard slick rock. It could only come from one place, the Houllerend Mountains.

Jale spoke as they move off the bridge into a brighter pitch of sunlight. 'To the back of the city, a path leads to a place called Canthoull within the mountain. This city was once home to the Houlladians. It's now Esmehdar's storage place for minerals. A passageway marks the end of Canthoull to the back of the city, leading to the mines. When the Great War started that only lasted a night, one crazy one of course… Caealon went to the mountain and mined for minerals to create weapons. We thought the war would last longer…

'In the deep we stumbled across the Houllad mining also, and so a treaty was easily established. We offered them help with a fresher place to stay and they gave us their mountain. It didn't take them long to agree to our terms when they discovered daylight and a more sanitary food supply. It was really as easy as a handshake. I think they wanted to get out of those dark halls of Canthoull ever since their king decided it would be best to start burying their dead near the halls.'

She laughs out really hard.

'Yeah,' he replies. 'They don't like to talk about it much, mind you.' He makes a face. 'So best try and keep our little secret between us and you'll be in their good faith. They might be made of bronze but they're still moving away from the cavern days, so don't go messing 'bout with their emotions.'

'You sound more like me.'

'Yeah, and I said it because I know you have a knack for attracting trouble.'

She makes a face.

Jale turns around in his stirrups to point to a river bend that runs through Esmehdar. Evelyn grasped him around the waist to get a better look. The loud crash of a waterfall can be heard not too far off, draining into the below.

'Now I see your excitement for wanting to come home.' Evelyn remarks.

'I am! I'm so glad to be back!'

The sun is in their eyes. Bridges on different layers of the city are connecting one building to another, glistering in the heat. It appears like a shiny design. Most buildings are is in the shape of a tall rectangle; this gives the city an urban look. The living quarters has less space because buildings are so packed to one another, making it especially hot and sweaty for the ground levels.

The business sections however, are always near a tower, with a fair space for civilians to occupy.

Commoners live near the bottom of the city and the upper class live where the air is cooler and have many balconies.

Rebuin and Calon of all ranks cross from bridge to building. There is little judgment from commoners and vice versa. The one with extra xzena have the option of a better view and a few other exceptions.

Each home falls under classification, form more space to fewer; "Family" three or more, and "Singular" one to two. It gives equilibrium of space. This does push the rich away to Rhion and makes Esmehdar more commonplace.

The difference between Esmehdar and Rhion is Esmehdar celebrates union and difference, whilst Rhion is… well, Calon staples. And their idea of being "Rich" is a rather figurative means. Of course it only pertains to such a mess. A rich person in Esmehdar is not classified with xzena; it is how one treats each other. So it is no surprise Rhion dislikes many Esmehdarians. Esmehdar success is easy, it is based on how happy one is, and that depends on how good one feels in the given moment. It's richness.

Get it? And they don't care for good-looking people either. Ha, what a world. They celebrate all faces and body types, and wardrobes. I don't know about you, but I'd choose to stay behind those walls! Oh come on, you would too.

Anyways, going back to town; the rich are more levelled out, because the Queen taxes at twenty seven percent! She pours fifteen percent into the country and gives two percent for her service and five percent to the Royal Guard and another to the Army. At least working for the infantry is encouraged since it supports a greater means. Can you imagine? Nah, who am I kidding, I'd join the Army.

Large purple or blue sheers and sometimes yellow, hang over the upper class homes creating a colourful bloom on the bottom floor. I think it's quite clear what territory they represent.

I say that, but now that I think back on it. I'm the biggest pansy you'll ever meet. I shake my head, no way to the Army. That shit's crazy! I'm going to be rich and famous one day, I've gotta live.

Jale takes his stead to a stop at a large dome building. A brass Esmehdarian crest is atop. The building connects to an even larger dome that is four times the size. The domes stand out from the regular buildings around the city, they have a unique look.

'Stay here.' Jale says catching the site of a black tower in the distance.

'Okay.'

He dismounts and disappears up the steps to the dome entrance.

Evelyn can feel her frivol, the energy lifting; she too looks to find the tower. The tower is thick at the bottom with a solid tube shape halfway, and the last crop of a spiral. Each tower is made differently, but with similar height. The reason for this happens to start with the spawning of memorial purposes which has been refreshing, reminding each era of present and past accomplishments. Such towers represent a different reign -- but what it's really doing is helping to define change.

A young man with a travelers robe on stops near Evelyn, he has a sac to carry his things. The young one stands out from the crowd around him; he is a little dirty from traveling. You were thinking fairy. Nope. He's definitely got more muscle tone then you and me. Well... definitely me, by far. My mom has more... heck my cat has more – whatever, haters.

'Remind you of someone?' Evelyn reminded herself from under breath.

The wall reaches far up the city, breaking the height of some buildings. The boy looks up at the height, reminding Evelyn of a similar memory of back when. She follows his gaze and got another reminder by his short twirling motion, he's lost. The boy approaches those for help.

Evelyn overhears him talking to a man. The man is tall with a large sword sheathed, a Calon from the Army with a fair rank. A permit allows for the carry of a weapon in Esmehdar, otherwise it must be tucked away for travel, until one is outside jurisdiction.

The man continues his advice. 'You want to go south. That will lead you to the district called Corhonour. Otherwise, if you stay on this course, you'll hit the Royal Road my friend. Best bet is to keep south.'

'Thanks, and best wishes to you, sir.' The young traveler says, tipping a hat and is as quick to disappear in the haze.

Why's it all the skinny gross guys that got to write cool books? Damn. Yo, don't even challenge me; I'll beat you up -- "Scratches neck."

'Royal Road?' Evelyn asks herself. She looks north finding gardens and fountains marking the way. It's an elegant and dressed pathway. 'This could be the way to the Queen's quarters. I'm sure of it.'

A small group clothed in matching robes are moving toward Evelyn and Bud. The group laugh and chatter about a particular professor, one in particular they found amusing. There is a badge on the left hand corner that Evelyn can make out; a letter "A" centre and a symbol of the domes behind the letter are marked.

The students hardly noticed anyone around them being so caught up in conversation.

Evelyn called out to them anyway. 'Hey excuse me. Where does that road lead?' She points past, to the Royal Road.

When they stop, one starts to laugh out loud and the rest join in, moving up the steps instead. They caught Evelyn by surprise. It wasn't a rude laugh; but they must have thought she was joking…

She scratches her head. 'That explains it then.'

Jale returns, coming down the steps. The group saluted to him jokingly but he didn't seem to notice or care, as Evelyn puts it. Well, his head was down, clearly having a focus about him. Still, it scares her how much power he beholds. It makes him evermore so of a good person. I was going to say good looking, but it didn't fall out. It's better to her, knowing he would never use it on anyone out of fear or anger. It's just not his style.

I know this is just a story and it's almost over, but my goodness, I'm so proud of Evelyn and the woman she's becoming. She's found her fulfilled love affair! Oh the feeling, it makes me want to sing. Prosperity... how to explain a feeling... sufficient – again with that word eh?

'Great news, I reported my quest and finished speaking to my officials. I didn't report you on what happened, seeing you're already in good hands.' He smiles largely. 'They were pleased that I made it out alive and really surprised to hear an uprising of foal so close to Eslr outpost. So they're doing what they must, by sending a taskforce to look into this.' Evelyn nods understandably as he went on. 'If reports come back negative, it looks bad on the Queen's management. If this happens, she'll make sure I put an end to it, which I always do. Anyways,' he says easily. 'A few quests assigned to me at this moment, but nothing that requires my immediate attention. I guess I could thank Queen Feira for that.' He looks down at his gold pocket watch hanging from the side of his robe. He wipes some dirt off the glass with a thumb and looks back up. 'Besides, I just got home. Let's head to my place first.'

Evelyn frowns. 'I haven't seen you use that thing in all this time.'

'It's only feasible when I have someone to meet.'

'Like the Queen?'

'Precisely,' he laughs.

'I --' She hesitates. 'Wait, y-you really have to meet her?'

'Yeah, I wasn't joking. I do sometimes, but not today. And you know... I did use it a lot more when I was younger. But I'm outgrowing time.'

Evelyn rubs her face to that – she could easily make a joke out of it. She finds her impression to his humour. 'Look. I know you're a noble and all, but can I come?'

'Of course...' He lingers.

'Really?' She asks excitedly.

'You didn't let me finish... not.'

'Right,' her eyes fall. 'You're silly. Well,' her voice changes pace. 'I got another question.'

'Alright, shoot.'

'Did you see those people who were dressed so nicely in those matching robes?'

He thinks; about to say something else of interest, but finds himself addressing her question. 'Well, you see that bigger one?' pointing to a dome behind the one he just came from.

'Yeah, I do.'

'That's only the grandest school in all Alasmieria. It's the school I graduated at, where I got my degree in Cloradis, a fairly new course, but one all the more greatest.'

'That's fairly dramatic,' she figured the word "Greatest" would slip in there somewhere. 'So that's the school Avel or something? Now I know what a miniature Jalelilian looks like, before all this greatness,' signifying with open hands.

He nods her humour. 'Yes. The school of Avail,' mounting But and they remain put.

'Alright Mr Greatest, how 'bout you to tell me more about how you became so grand.'

He turns in his stirrups. 'You want to know how easy it was.'

She waits patiently.

'Like drizzelwoom to a noullwoom.'

She leans. 'Huh?'

'Ugh, forget it.'

'Wait, now what.' She taps him on the shoulder. 'I want to know how you did it. Maybe I want to be a noble one day too, ever think of that?'

'Then you'll need to know what *she* wants. That's how I did it.'

'Do tell.'

'If I told you that, then I would have to kill you.' He looked back at her after he said it.

He got a squint of her eyes.

He waits.

'So you're not going to tell me?'

He laughs. 'You never take a hint.'

She blinks. 'Nope, can't say I do.'

They ride to a new district, one much smaller then that before, though a cleaner district with higher buildings. There are no drapes to offer any bloom. They come through a tight alleyway. Tall lamps with lit wicks flicker. In this part of town, it is a calm place, away from the haven of central city.

A woman above them wrings out clothes on a rack; she looks well dressed, peering down at Evelyn with one eye, the other's blind. Evelyn nods back respectfully.

'Has everyone seen war?' Evelyn asks Jale.

'An interesting question,' he says, 'depends on your definition of *war*. But no.'

The smell of lofty foods and fresh herbs fill Evelyn's sensation. Somebody is cooking up a brew in the neighbourhood. Also, not too far nords can be heard.

'Evelyn.' Jale touches her hand, a static shock catches them. 'I'm going to move him to the stables; it's just around the corner. Stay here.'

'Shouldn't we unpack?'

'We can do that.' He agrees, laughing from embarrassment.

'What would you do without me?' She teases and they unload their things on the floor. He takes Bud and moves the intended way.

A lantern on the wall flickers close by, it caught Evelyn's attention. It is louder, she can hear it move on the wick. In the calm presence of things, in the still of the alley, she lets her mind silence with the scent of hay someplace far off. The floor is marble, and it sparkles madly in the sunlight.

Her eyes squint.

What does it mean to be half-breed? It's my sense of smell that's completely changed

She looks at her hands – she notices something new about herself nearly every time. Her fingernails are thicker.

But does Jale notice anything new about me?

If she only knew, since he does. He notices her eyes are brighter; her hair is already fuller, even her cheekbones are sharper. It's sexy to him, and to trust this new gift intrigues him. It really doesn't scare him like she thought. Okay... maybe just a bit.

The wind brushes alongside the alley walls, like a mouth, she can feel its warm breath. With Jale no longer in sight, she sought to a pair of steps close by. Sitting on the staircase, she lets her mind relax.

The field and her mother's smiles; she remembers that day, the day when Mom asked her to go to the marketplace alone. How happy it made Evelyn.

Evelyn takes a deep breath in and lets it out slowly, enjoying the alley. The wind crashes her again. She rubs her eyes. All she wants to do is rest now, now that she has sat down. She gets back up and shakes the sleepiness off, hoping that Jale doesn't come around anytime soon. She wants to be fully alert and not miss a thing.

Wind blows leaves down the corridor, their crisp tint brushing along the walkway. Jale returns. She does her best to catch her yawn when he wasn't looking. But he noticed and got the hint. They grab their things, fully handed and move up the steps, balancing a few other objects atop, like fruits and cantinas.

'This is Eventide. My home district,' Jale says. They move beside doors of homes and cross a few bridges. Evelyn stopped on one to look down, making sure not to drop anything. They're three levels up.

In some time, Jale came to a stop at a door. 'Home sweet home,' and puts down his things. He pulls out a key to unlock it. Inside he walks across the room and opens a window. A soft breeze allows the morning to be relived.

Here, in the middle of the living room, Evelyn doesn't notice any picture frames, no resemblance of a family, a friend – but a large bookcase and vase can be found. The room is small and vivid with decadent furniture and other lavishing décor.

'Just put your things on the floor, we can sort it out later.'

'Okay.' She replies.

He gathers the rest of his things from outside and returns, disappearing out of site with them to place them in his bedroom. He calls out from here. 'I'm going to go take a quick shower, why don't you go get us some food, for breakfast and later. There's xzena in the cupboards, in a red container... I believe.'

She shouts back so he can hear well. 'No, no need.' She takes off her pack and digs through her things, past a toothbrush, tooth paste and bumping Burley powder. And a few other things Jale bought for her when they were at Tenor. She pulls out her xzena sacs at the bottom corner of the bag. She looks back up to find he has returned in the living room.

'I'm not the only one loaded. You'll see.' She says and tosses the xzena sacs to him.

He smirks back. 'Hah, and you had me spending?'

She smiles his way and he dumps out the xzena across a polished table. He places his hands on his hips. 'Well then. We will have to get you a bank account for all of this.'

'Really, there's that much, eh?'

'Yeah and where did you get this all, exactly?'

'I took it.'

He gives her a simple look, one that is exemplary, 'really?'

'No,' and moves to the table. She gathers them back into the sac. 'Where do you think I got them?'

'Oh... *right.*' He laughs. 'Oh I almost forgot you also need a port, don't you?'

'Yes, but I've decided I want to go Calon.'

'Ha, brilliant.'

'And later, we will.' She replies. She knew he would be tired. The emotions of the day have been high, and going shopping is a perfect way for him to rest and for her to explore the realm a little more.

'So you can read minds now?' He asks her.

'Only yours.'

'Mhm.' He says looking bored.

'Sometimes I wonder. *What I do*, I wonder what it'd like in there.'

'You can't handle it.'

She rolls her eyes and moves around the intricate complex. 'Are you going to show me around before you leave me?'

'Oh, right.'

He gave her a spin of the complex, and they find themselves in a spare room right next to his. Inside, there are doors to a balcony, but they left the space before they could check outside, because he decides to take her into his bedroom again.

'Decent.' She says, admiring the complex as a whole. His room is identical.

'Really, do you have someplace better?'

'You know what I meant,' she says.

'Come.' He says. 'This is what I wanted to show you.'

He opens the doors to his room's balcony and Evelyn follows him on the platform. The day felt so alive, it held a space of much to venture. It's hearing all the noise of the world that made her heart thumper – she has a much clearer picture of peaked rooftops. To her left, a small opening between buildings shows the landscape where the waterfall tumbles away. 'Wow.' She says, watching it seep off the edge where her site is further blocked, since it drains into the Aspin below. She turns a site from the density of Esmehdar to look up at Jale, who's standing right next to her. 'I really did it. I finally made it.' She says quirkily. 'I know I said it before, but I wasn't so --'

He leaned in for a kiss and landed softly. Their lips intercept. He pulls back to speak, peering around the city one more time. 'You should see Rhion, it's twice the size. Spread out as far as the eye can see.'

With eyes on the scenery her voice lingers for a little, 'I'd like to see that.' Sometimes she has to look up at him from his height, and other times to get the man's attention. 'You think it's odd that we've been sharing the same mother?'

'Hah. It's not like it's by birth or something. But in an odd way, this does make you family.'

'Hmm,' she thinks about it. 'That's not very comforting.'

'Do you think it still counts because you're adopted?'

'Well stolen more or less.'

'Right, but how's your heart?'

She has a frown, 'its... fine.'

'Well, will you letting me steal it also?' And before he let her answer he literally swoops her off her feet, so naturally it made her scream a little. He places her onto the bed.

'Wait.' She says, placing her fingertip to his hip. A sound of banging is heard on the other side of the wall.

He grins and looks up at the ceiling. 'Thin walls, I always thought I should have upgraded.'

She watches him move closer to her and she leans back. Another bang from above them kills their mood -- Evelyn does her best to change the subject. 'It's not like you don't have plans to meet the Queen or something.'

He hesitates. 'Right well, we can do this afterwards.' And he leans in, only to grab his towel off a dresser beside her and he's off into the washroom without another word.

She let her head hit the pillow. She breathes out slowly.

A bird lands on the side railing of the balcony. The avis bites at all its feathers. Evelyn got up and moved nearer. She smiles wondrously at the site. 'Never gets old,' and then watches it carry off and over the cityscape. 'Wow, beautiful. Still, I better head out if I'm to eat something.'

Of all the things she's gone through in life, she's glad she had. It made it better for this moment. She wonders if Tetlas knew how tough the journey would have been from the get-go.

No way had seen the future like Alas

'If Tetlas is right about one thing, it was what to expect. She really did do a good job preparing me. In a large way, she got me this far out. It would have been impossible without... her help.' She stops and thinks. '...And with the help of the plan taking it's every course. Thanks to Alas,' she says whimsy.

And if you can hear me right now, thank you, you're a great man. I mean... kalec!

She leaves the balcony and enters the bedroom. The showers are heard sparking her interest. 'Oh dear,' she says with intrigue. She comes to the sound where the door is left slightly open – just a peek, you know those curtains before the shower? He has none. *And...* her better judgement told her not to.

She leaves the house closing the door behind her. She climbs down the steps and comes back into the streets. Her robe feels heavy on her shoulders. Looking around, she memorizes the area for the way back and follows street signs into a busier district. There are many shops around. She finds what she's looking for, a marketplace and one close to home.

"These are no good, get this" or something on the lines of "I hope you like spicy" are overheard, and a new interest is birthed. She listens to those around and she makes her way inwards. Many chat about prices. 'Alas, this better be one heck of a Babberoll.' A man is overheard saying, lifting a ball of cheese wrapped in cloth, and it being twice the price locally.

What happened to the good ol'days when a basket of Rooberries would buy anything? They're far gone heck much like the smell of pine needles and porridge. Everything is new, everything is different

...And she wouldn't change a sweet thing about it.

There is a rich smell of the ocean. Perhaps that's just the scent of freedom calling a little fish to swim a bigger ocean.

Evelyn leans over the many produce. She's afraid to touch everything, that's pretty scary considering she's been a farmer all life. Her awkwardness glows in this unusual habitat.

Some water-dwellers fillets lay on ice-beds at the left-end of the grocery store. She arrives here. She scratches her head and moves on, finding opal to translucent bottom feeders along rows of ice, too. She moves along and finds a new section. A likelihood of unique seeds and roots brings Evelyn in question.

What is that?

All along new rows of what she can't distinguish between are different vegetables and fruits lining an aisle. To distinguish further she uses her sense of smell. She pulls her nose away from a basket of oval blue shells. It smells ripe, well kind of.

'Blackroot,' a young woman says to Evelyn, noticing the girl's dislike. A differently dressed woman stood before her. Evelyn can't distinguish the fashion here. It seems anything goes. The woman points a finger. 'Best for seasoning stews, this gives it a lively taste.'

'Oh?' Evelyn replies.

'Not from around here, are we?'

'No ma'am.'

'I supposed.' She says and held out a hand for Evelyn to shake. 'Oh, how rude of me, I am Maelise.'

'I'm Evelyn.' She shakes the lady's hand. 'And where in the world are the potatoes?' turning a look around.

The lady stopped and stared for a few moments. 'What are potatoes?'

'Uh,' she lingers. She looks real stupid. 'We use different terms from where I came from.'

'Of course,' she answers. 'I'm assuming you just got in?'

Evelyn questions "In".

'Your arrival to Esmehdar of course.'

'Oh, right. It was just a few minutes ago, actually.'

'Oh wow. Well, I'd love to help you. But I shall warn you, I'm a bit of a blabber mouth, but I'm a local who knows these waters well.'

'Sure. I'd appreciate it.'

They move to a smaller section. 'Well, here are your botany and your rootinus,' pointing another finger to help Evelyn comprehend between the many assortments of fruits and vegetables. The day went on, and Evelyn finished shopping with her. Evelyn had so many questions; she finally gave up for the sake of robbing the lady's time. When they both line up to pay, Evelyn offers to pay the woman's till. The lady happily accepts. They depart with a smile and a goodbye.

Evelyn moves with all the new terms stuck in mind, and four bags of groceries. Two stuck between each arm. 'Rootinus...' Evelyn says, sort oblivious. She climbs the steps home and stops at the front door. She's about to knock.

I think we're past this point. I'm practically family

She pauses and her face drops. 'That's so not what I meant.' Inside she calls out. 'Jale, I'm home.' This sounded odd too; tiredly she moves the grocery bags on the kitchen counter. She comes into the living room and sits on the sofa. Out of the mist of chaos, she can finally relax and enjoy herself.

Jale comes around the corner wearing another Clairic robe on. *Yeah,* just a different fashion with all the same rankings -- he didn't even notice her bored expression and he rolls up his sleeves.

'So, do you even give yourself a break?' pointing. She wasn't going to spell it out.

'Whoa!' He jumps, moving a little closer to the kitchen. 'Evelyn, I am a noble. It comes with the --'

'With the territory?'

He laughs a little. 'Oh. I unpacked your things in your room so you wouldn't trip coming in with the groceries. You can dress out of that robe, if you'd like. I'll make some dinner -- how's that sound?'

Evelyn scratches her head and feels the dirt of yesterday. She didn't have the energy to wash it well. 'Ok.' She replies and wastes no time worrying of cooking; she wants to undress into something softer like he says.

A warm shower felt as good as this day. When she finishes, she comes around the corner all clean, wearing a white cotton robe. It's a bit heavy but she feels it's a good enough fit. She finds him in the kitchen, cleaning.

'You're stunning.' He says giving her a glance over. 'You should clean up more often.'

Her sarcasm found the light of day. 'Stop it; you're making me blush.'

'Is that my robe?' He asks drying his hands from finishing the dishes.

465

The view just outside the kitchen window, over the sink is to be savoured, no I mean marvelled… I don't think I know what I mean.

'You don't mind, do you? I found it on the back of my door.'

'No I don't mind.' He says, admiring her in his clothes. 'I must have left it there before I went on my quest… It felt so long ago.'

She doesn't know what to say, so she moves to a station already set up on the counter. All the food has already been prepared, and placed in a coal oven. It's a glorified indoor barbeque. Smoke passes out of a chimney that goes outside the building. She bends down to get a closer look at the food inside, feeling the heat on her face. 'It's cool how you call vegetables; rootinus and botany; fruit.'

'Yup, but you're doing well, considering all this change.'

She looks away. 'I met a *very* nice lady who helped me out at the grocery store. Otherwise, I would have been in trouble.'

'You're in good hands. You're in Esmehdar, remember?'

'Yeah… yeah I know. We really do live in an *amazing* city.'

He nods.

She leans on the counter, looking up at him.

'What?' He asks.

'I guess that's why we make a good match, you and me.'

He smirks.

She admires a knife, next to her. 'What's the word for this exactly?' She asks with it held upward.

'Hasn't your mother ever taught you to be more careful?' He asks while placing her hand with the cutlery down.

She gave him a look right afterwards and Jale didn't have to read minds; he knew he got the better end of it.

'It's a knife.' He finally said.

She giggles, 'really? It's very *odd* looking.'

'It's the way we do our designs, aren't yours just as well in Maesemer?'

'No, they're rather plain looking.' She leans more. 'And it's even odder seeing that we use a lot of the same terms, isn't it?' It's a moment she'll never forget. She stares past him and gets lost by the scenery out the kitchen window. 'It's love…'

'It's really not.' He replies. Her face drops and he finishes. 'I mean, you said it yourself.'

She found relief. 'It's interesting -- I and Tetlas had a similar talk about this.'

'I miss her.' He says rather looking bored.

She spoke jeeringly. 'Oh, how odd, we don't have the same feeling for our other.'

'Right well, you broke the perfect moment. How many times do you ever see me get emotional?'

She made a face. It meant she didn't care.

They sit down at a long table in the dining room, enough for eight to eat at. She sat with little space from him. There is sautéed botany, cooked Poebeans for protein, which cook under twenty minutes in water. There is bread and Sumslie; a delicious sweet fruit with a thin yellow husk. Candlelight flickers around the room giving their faces a glow. There is one also between them, which is next to an uncorked wine bottle.

'Its smells really great, you're one of a kind, you know that right?' She says.

'Yes, I guess you can say that. I've always been rather classy.'

'Yep you're real magical.'

He scoffs.

I'm just playing.' She nudges him, 'grandpa.'

He raises an eyebrow. 'You're worse then I thought.'

She reaches in for the Poebeans already mixed with the sautéed botany prepared in a white dish.

'So,' he asks, scooping food onto his plate. 'Why'd you come all the way out here again?'

She pauses to think. 'Easy, I came here to figure out more about my family, since I don't have a real identity. I'm what you'd call a *ghost.*'

He raised that brow, unaware of the term *ghost.*

'It's basically a lost soul.' She answers to his look.

'A... now I understand what you meant by that.'

'Yeah, you know... their white and see-through. No?' He looks a little ghost himself. 'They're usually cold to the touch and say "Boo" just to scare you. Oh... how I miss home.' She left him with a teased-look on his face. 'What?' She humours going back to eating. 'I tried explaining it to you.'

'You don't know, do you?'

'Know? No,' she says, being as frank as possible. She takes a spoon and dips it into the inner parts of the husk. The air is warm, and the candlelight flickers in front of them. The living room window is left open, giving some cool air to circulate the room.

'The building we stopped at, you know, the dome one. Does that ring any bells?'

She jumps in her seat. 'Wait... no way... was that the Royal Bibliotheca?'

'What do you think?' He asks and takes a spoon of food to mouth.

She looks away, feeling teased now. There is a look of glory, 'and to think I was right there. All but twenty feet from the door... you should have told me.' She goes back to scooping food onto her plate.

'No way, look at how aroused you are. If I've told you back when, I know we would have never left the building. Besides, this was worth the troubled look on your face.'

She catches her spunk again. 'We have to go tomorrow. Forget everything; I want to know my past. I have to go get my answers. You don't know what it's like not... knowing... Jale.'

He puts his hands up. 'Whoa. Hold on now, Lady of the Forest. We can't just go walking into the Royal Bibliotheca and access information on restricted knowledge. It doesn't work like that.'

She leans in a little closer to him, resting a hand to prop her chin, 'really?'

He makes a face, holding it.

She leans a little closer. She just loves him – a little too much. 'You expect me to like you after that?'

'Hey, you're part of family now.'

'Wait,' she backs off not caring for smart-ass. 'What are you talking about, restricted?'

'Hah. Your mother was the last person on Thaera with the book of Alas. The Queen will have everyone believing it disappeared into oblivion that grand'ol night. If that means finding it for keeps, then so be it.' He says with a little lean himself. 'She's been hunting my mother ever since she found out the necklace was hanging on her neck. That's why the nation knows my mother as the Lady of the Forest. Mostly for the hefty price that hovers over her head, all because Fiera wants that necklace for herself. Funny thing is the Queen had me fooled for so long. If anything, I thought she was only after the book. She holds the title for best kept secret in my opinion.' He toasts his glass as if she's sitting in the room now.

'That's horrible.'

'Why's that horrible?' He catches the look in her eye. 'It's really not. It was an honest mistake. The Queen thought my mother stole it. I and my mother can't come out of the woodworks, not just yet. Who would even believe us? Besides... would you? Look at how long it took you to accept the knowledge, and you're a classy individual.'

She smiles to his badger.

He says. 'Even if people believed us, it would ruin their faith in Alas, and what would that bring us?' He stops to point at a dish on her side. 'Can you pass the beans,' she does so and he continues. 'The Queen is a lassie type, who wants the greater things in life. I can't blame her, not with all the grand ideas she has for this nation. Don't tell her this, but I think she's kinda bossy.'

'Mhm,' she sounds amused.

'I should mind you, which also includes her wanting the necklace to reign as long as she can. It runs in the family.'

'So she's a saint. Assuming she's not interested in potion making and poisoning her fellow mates?'

He says nothing.

She giggles to his unknowingness and gets back to basics. 'So you're pretty much protecting two women in your life?'

'Yeah, you said it.'

'That's pretty much how you're her right hand man?'

'I thought you'd say that. So you do know how evil I can be?' She smirks and he goes on. 'I thought it would be important to stay in her watch, so brilliant right? No wonder why she can't catch my mother, I always have the inside know-it-all.'

She nods her head. 'Only you could make her smile.'

'Well let's not be crude now.' He teases. 'Besides, I think it's best if she stays in power. She is doing a mean job of handling things around here. Look at Esmehdar, it's brilliant. You know, I did help to influence the fairness of evenly dispensed xzena across the nation.'

Evelyn can't help but ignore his last sentence for something rings bigger in her mind. She says out loudly. 'If *she* ever found out we have the book... we'll have --'

'But it won't get to that. Do you really think *she* would allow anyone access to these scarce documents...? Come on now, think about it. If you were the Queen, would *you* want treasure hunters trailing *the book's* whereabouts? Doubtful, and that's why information on your past is kept secret. You're the daughter of the book carrier; and only a handful of nobles know about your existence. Luckily, you're identity is unknown, so you can rest with ease. So naturally, the Queen's eye is on the other prize; on my mother's necklace. The only thing the Queen plans on doing with the book is keeping it safe from the likes of *them*.' His eyes widen. This scares her a bit, reminding her of the enemy -- It was meant to, to satisfy his point.

'Wait.' She puts her hands to his chest, like she heard a noise just outside the room. 'If people were to find out we have the book... would make us...' She looks for the most convenient word. 'Famous?'

'Look, I know you're new, but this isn't exactly the ideal way to make friends.' His expression falters. 'I'm talking more then fame. It'd give us a voice. It'd make us known.'

She relaxes, and changes her mind. This must have scared her some. 'I guess the Queen will never have to know.' He just stares. She looks away awkwardly. 'But it is scary, I mean you're tied to her hip and you're the son of the Lady of the Forest. And then you got me; the daughter of the last known book holder. Forget the son of Alas I'd doubt anyone would believe us, like you say.'

'You're cute when you don't try, you know.' He says.

She makes a similar face.

'Is this something you picked up in the lands of Egerd, trying to impress?'

'You know.' She says cutely, she couldn't help it. 'You're hotter when you do.'

'I don't try.' He says.

'Please, I see the way they look at you, you love the attention. You're a fein for that type of shit.' 'Hah,' he nudges her. 'I'm hardly trying.'

'I wasn't finished, *And*, real with me.'

'Anyways,' he says, returning to their previous conversation, clearly regretting his interference. 'Which makes *everything* that much more appealing... doesn't it? That makes us... legend folk.'

She raises a brow. 'That's silly.'

He shrugs.

She hints at his last statement. 'Wait, were you?'

'A little bit...' He says again and turns his look at his watch, 'which reminds me, I have to get going.'

'But you just sat down,' she whines.

He laughs, 'ha, jealous much?'

'Come on now.' She says, getting back to their earlier conversation. 'Why can't you just go in and get the document yourself?'

'No. I wouldn't dare go near that thing. I have thought about it before, since it is tempting, but only because it's for the good of the nation.'

'For the good of the nation? Okay, now you can go.'

He chuckles and sounds surer of himself. 'That would put me in jeopardy for tampering with *the Queen's* evidence. Even if I requested it, it puts me into questioning; then the Queen will have no choice but to have nobles up my chute and watching my every move. We would have to find another way around, maybe by someone who had direct relations with it, but wasn't supposed to.' Evelyn huddles herself to his talkative self. 'Evelyn.' He pushes. 'You have to go work for the Royal Bibliotheca and get up close with the staff; chances are someone has already read the document and copied it down. This is the Royal Bibliotheca we are talking about here. The chances are high that someone has seen it and read it. If I were them and came across it, I'd do these things. Why else does anyone want to work there?'

Her cheeks lift. 'Well, if anyone would know, it'd be you. I-I could find someone with the knowledge, one who could lead me to finding answers too, that is if I can't get my hands on the documents.'

'Yeah once you get in, they'll likely expect you to stay in. To work for the bibliotheca is more than majesty, it's a passion.'

Evelyn nods nobly. 'Once I'm inside, once I get it, I'll be sure to disappear afterwards. Regardless, I think I am looking for someone in a certain criteria and someone with a little age, no?'

'It could be many things. A bragger is never one of them; it means their rarely trustworthy and don't have anything to give. Would you tell a bragger of your darkest secret?'

She shook her head in response.

He stands, taking his plate and places it in the kitchen. He's tall, Evelyn forgets about that. A tall man always makes her feel safe. But it's sad, because she really can handle things on her own. She doesn't need anything like that. He talks and walks. 'Then you must look for a quiet person instead. And probably a risk taker… usually the last person you'd expect. Of course, you're the investigator and you'll want to get up close and personal. Share something meaningful and take the risk, it usually takes one to get to know one. You do that and you'll win the crowd. If you win their hearts… you'll have their secrets… and maybe a little more then you asked for. Because once you do, they'll start pouring out as fast as you open that floodgate. I think you get the picture. Like a horrisos catching a morr, no?'

She frowns, 'what --'

'What does a horrisos catching a morr have to do with anything?'

'I was about to ask, "What it is".'

'I'm not going to tell you what it is. It's a secret. Now it's up to you to get on my good side in order to get it from me.'

'Don't you have someplace to be?' She reminds his sass. He only laughs, moving closer to poke her. She laughs. 'No, I'm not playing any silly games with you.'

Sometimes she forgets how strong she is. Sucks, something like that.

'Why?' He asks with his pretty eyes.

'Because,' she batters her eyelashes. 'I don't wanna play cat and mouse.'

'What's cat --'

'Ah,' she says suddenly, raising a brow and pokes him. 'So you don't like it either when I cut you down?'

He smiles, toying with her. 'I can't say I notice.'

She rolls her eyes. 'Alright, back to basics. All assuming you'll get me in, that is.'

'Oh I will. Focus Evelyn,' he says and sits down beside her. 'A stickler wants to share their knowledge, assuming they'll find you trustworthy. After all, what good is a secret if you can't share it?'

'Wait, what's a stickler?'

He sighs.

The following days have been much the same, anticipation. Small tasks expected of Evelyn, retrieving groceries, preparing lunch and dinner for them, just small chores around the complex whilst Jale's out, doing his whatever.

When they're together they've been studying the book, but never performing any spells, of course. Instead, they're preparing their knowledge and whereabouts of great ones. It's been four days since and an unexpected change is upon Evelyn.

It's been a later night then most. Evelyn and Jale just got back from getting her a bank account and retrieving an application for her port. She comes to a sit at the living room table with her unfilled document.

Jale leaves her sides and returns with a red candle and a royal stamper, in the other a quill and an ink bottle. He places the writing items before her. He pulls out a Burley sac from his jacket pocket and unties its lace. It's the first time today she's been with him outside his usual wear, and into a more casual fitting and one without his rankings. With a mist of Burley power on the tip of his finger, he blows slowly and it ignites the wick nicely. He is quick to tie the lace and places the sac safely in his pocket.

'You can still become Rebuin if you want.' He gives her a look afterward, hoping she's not just doing it for him. 'You know that right?'

'I like Calon.' She says, dabbing the quill. She hesitates at the beginning of the paperwork. This somehow reminds me of Evelyn being with Mom on the ranch. You know, I kind of liked writing that, but then again, who can really know how far she's come, but me. Sometimes when I write this book, it's like a song playing in my head, and it's so personal I forget I have an outside audience.

It requires a background check on closest family to complete.

'Here, let me.' He says already prepared for this. Where family names are requested, he passes it off as "Exempt" and as with his name; he initials beside it. Next to his initials, he wrote a small piece explaining his reasoning. He finishes and passes the document over.

She reads it, 'a solitude who founded refuge to Caealon. Interviewed and found neither background relations nor relations with Calliskue. Family is unknown.' She looks up at him. 'Will that work?'

'Oh course it works.' But she made him unsure, so he leans in for a second look. 'Yes. There's a thousand misplaced refugees roaming in Caealon; one more won't be a problem.' He watches her write her full

473

name in the name box requested below. 'Evelyn Maelkyn,' he reads. 'You could have done a different last name if you wanted to.' His finger falls to the page, and he finds his humour. 'Well I think it's safe to say that this won't already be in use.'

'Why? I like my surname.' She signs and dates the bottom.

Jale hands her an envelope and she places the form inside. She hands it over. He closes the envelope and seals the tongue with a red wax, stamping it with an intricate "R" letter. He gets up and takes it away.

He speaks from his room. 'I'll send it in the post tomorrow. We will have to wait till then.' He returns in a few. 'Even if I get you into the Royal Bibliotheca, you'll have to wait for your port, firstly.'

She says nothing.

He comes to a sit beside her. Her silence makes him pry. 'Is it the hormonal change?'

'No but the change is getting stronger.' She says and lifts a brow.

He smiles back, seeing his reflection. He knew what it meant for he stopped by the bibliotheca today to check up on any open positions available. And he promised her only after she signed the paper; knowing she'll need his help, would he then tell her the news for later. Otherwise, he figured she would be more mischievous than normal. And that slight detail could be used against her in order to get her a position.

'I'm doing my best.' He says shifting in his seat. 'It's harder to move people around from a royal location. It's seen as rather degrading. I forgot to mention to you that the first time I was there I promised something small. I spoke to the head mistress to pass word; a mention of pay for anyone who was willing to transfer.'

'Awe, you did that for me?'

'Yes. She mentioned it to the staff today, beyond that, still no takers. She thought it was quite odd though, with my nose in all of this.'

'Well it would be, to the outside world I mean. Is all I mean by that,' she giggles, 'what did you tell her?'

'I… might have lied. I said you were a student from a local school-town, called Brishrun. I also mentioned you're a friend of mine. Which is true, you're more than a friend. And you do come from a small town and all, so… I think it makes up for all the lies?'

'Right,' she scoffs. 'If I'm caught, this is going to go down as tragic; the daughter with the book is found guilty of tampering with the *Queen's* affairs, and the son of *Alas* is found guilty of *all* charges.'

He rubs his face, 'sort of ironic really.'

She has a look all to her, one of fun. She rests her head on her upright arm. 'Is this going to cause problems between us?'

He's reading the signs and follows her motion. Her azure is catching and it almost fumbles his speech. 'You're talking about the conditions?'

'Well, you know...'

'Don't worry about that, Evelyn. I won't cross that line, not when the phase of the moon is still blooming.'

It was hard for her to hear this especially with the new change.

'I've never felt like this before.' She says. 'Well, I have, but not so quite profound.'

'Towards me?' he asks.

'No...' She clears her throat. 'Maybe,' she speaks more honestly. 'You know, not everything is about you, you know.'

'Right,' he smiles.

Her eyes are fuller tonight. Her hair is thicker. She can smell the world around her, and sound is newer, too. 'Everything is louder... and...' She says, looking toward the moon. 'I've been hungry -- more energized, and more excited. My urges are a lot more enhanced today. Beyond this, fire is loud.' They both had a pretty good idea for the subject matter was plain to see; an increase in animal instinct. 'Just yesterday it was lower in tone. It started to pick up in the moonlight, but now I can easily hear it, even out of site of the moon's light. It's adapting, the changes. Still, it fills me with a quick feeling, it's... unnerving. Jale, I don't know... you told me these things would affect me... but it's only been three days in. It's getting stronger. The first day was the increase in taste.' She stops when she sees him looking down. 'Look at me.' She says, 'I'm being serious. I'm really afraid of this.'

'I know.' He breathes looking up at her. 'Take it slower. You have lots of time to rest, you know this. The full moon is amongst you, which makes the condition you are in, regardless, a much faster progression. You're starting off with a bang, sort of speak. That's why it's increasing each day.' He says with a hand on her shoulder. 'The phase will get stronger. You only have four more days till the moon breaks its cycle. I promise Evelyn – after that, it will mellow out. I will see to it and get you some remedies, but they're hard to come by, even in my position.'

He gets up from the table to pour himself a glass of water. When he returns he retrieves a book form the bookshelf and sat himself back down. 'I've been reading this for more information then I already know. I picked it up at the bibliotheca the day you said the symptoms were effecting you. It may help further, it had helped me understand a lot more on what you're going through. It showed me steps and preventions. I'm going to be using some of the suggestions to help you.' He rests his chin on his upright arm again. He hands the book over with his free hand. 'Evelyn. I don't really know how you will end up after the final phase. Still, it won't matter -- your conditions aren't classified as "Severe" so you won't turn form.'

Her face drops to the use of that. 'Are you being serious or just plain stupid you?'

'Neither.' He swallows knowing he doesn't want any of that. Evelyn plays hard, doesn't she? 'I'm simply stating what I've learned so far. It's something beyond many, including myself. Not even the book of Alas has anything... I thought it would have.' He was going to say something else on the matter, but decided not to for it could have hurt her feelings.

She nods empathetically and reads the cover. 'Foal Distinctions, are you sure this will help me? It's these sexual urges --'

'Aaah, I don't need to know anymore. I do know what you're going through, believe it or not. I knew a professor who taught me a little bit on the stages of transformation. I can't do much to help, Evelyn. The book told me to stay away, in fact, far away. You're going to have to pull through this first phase till the sun comes out. The good news is the final phase in the next coming days should only be physical pain.'

'*Only?*'

'I have remedies.' He looks sympathizing. 'You're going to be sleeping on the floor tonight, by the way.'

'What? That's *not* fair.'

'Oh *it is*. Otherwise it would be me sleeping with you. And the book is telling me to stop. Evelyn, it's the only thing we've got, so I'm *going* to listen to it. Blame it, not me.' He didn't give her another look, knowing quite well what she'd propose, so he gets up and walks away. His voice picks up someplace in his bedroom. 'I'll stop by the bibliotheca tomorrow to check up on any open positions, or if they've been moved out or not. Until then, the Foal Distinctions will have to do. Goodnight.'

'Great.' She sighs, and looks down at the book. 'Looks to be me and you buddy,' and then at the floor, 'oh and how could I forget you, Mr Wonderful…'

They planned for her to stay on the floor for a few more days, just in case. She's been telling Jale his scent was driving her mad, so she ended up sleeping in the kitchen. Good thing too, because her sexual urges got bad enough she'd have to run the tap to distract all the thoughts.

She comes to a sit at the kitchen table and breathes out heavily, pacing her fingers alongside the surface. She comes to a rest, using an upright arm to prop her cheek.

The moonlight shines onto her empty blanket-bed. All to think, a few days ago this wasn't the case, but now that it has begun, all Evelyn and Jale's time away has made sharing the same bed, and frankly, a bed to climb into, missed.

She breathes out slowly. 'Go to sleep,' she says to herself.

Jale says she has to be close to the light of the moon for the hormones to progress quicker.

She breathes in again and puts her head down in humiliation. The air is a familiar scent that helps to keep the blooming curiosity again. 'You know, I can always sleep in my room…' She knows he warned her about this thing. The temptation of his close proximity would set her mind against her will. A stare to the moon keeps it thrumming. It's a perfect white. Her attention moves to the sound of the bustling night. 'This city doesn't get much sleep does it?'

The open living room window bares scents from the outside, and the loud ambitious world sounds of carriages, loud people and some unlikely noises. She was airing the apartment out because of hot flashes. But now it's just too cold.

She rubs her stiff neck. Blankets and pillows surround her. So she leaves the safe place of the kitchen to close it. She stops, noticing his room door is slightly open. Now she just has to trust herself. On her way to the sound of the city, the wind blows brushing the skin. It feels icy on her sweaty body. It's a perfuse amount. She can't remember the last time she sweated this bad. Perhaps when she was sick – that's been awhile back.

The temptations only got like he said, harder with each day. Why doesn't she just cross that line with him? Because once that itch is scratched... wow, that's a way with words... but Jale says she needs the hormones to propel to the final phase. So if she were to give in... it would only take longer.

She smells herself under the arm pit. 'No wonder why he's been so afraid of me lately. I guess that's a good thing.' She looks over at his room, and decides to shut the window. She shakes her thoughts. 'Ugh. I can't.' She says, fighting another sprawling urge. She comes to the corner of his door and takes a sniff in. She pushes the door to find him sleeping. She takes a deep breath in and finishes her exhale afterwards. 'It doesn't get any better than that.' She holds her expression, feeling lame between the door way and watching him rest. She watches him move. Her fingers twitch. 'Easy now,' she whispers to herself. She fights her grip on the door handle and finally closes it. 'What am I thinking? Only one more night,' she breathes out.

One more

She opens his door again, hesitates, closes it gently and performs a complete U-turn back toward the kitchen. She grabs a glass from the cabinet and fills it with tap water. She imagined pouring herself down with a bucket of cold water to shake these nerves. The whole while, she tilted the glass and gulped it down in one long moment. 'Ahhh,' she breathes out. She stood, waiting as silence came over her, still over thinking her debate.

Then she remembers. She comes back into the living room. She stops. There it stood where she last left it, never getting around to reading it. It gave her the chills that an entire book has been written on her symptoms and preventions. It made her feel... cold.

She rubs her chilly self once more and leans closer to the book's reach. She hesitates, as if words could bite. She takes it out and comes to a sit on his hard living room floor. She opens the cover. As she sat there reading over the introduction, the list went on. She flips past in a hurry and arrives at the first page. It's hard to get past the first few sentences. She scratches at her neck and finally convinced herself of the good it offers. Reading on, she found a rather scary look on her face. It wasn't because of what would happen if she had, but what could have happened if she did.

Why didn't he tell me? – She looks in the direction of Jale's room.

She sighs at the sentence and decided to read it out loud from humiliation. And mostly, it felt like it gave her some sort of control in this defeating moment. But from that moment on, she promised it would be the last thing she would ever read from the likes of this book again.

'There is a chance of transferring the specimen of a bitten host to another if sexual intercourse were committed. The blood dies with the bitten host after their final stage is completed.' She closes the book loudly and laughs, feeling more alien then she ever thought possible. Before the transition, her worst fear was that of an Errific and their terrifying appearances, but now she's becoming her worst nightmare; something changed and unearthing.

How can anyone have let this happen to me? Why the heck would I attract such a mess?

Better, how can she expect to feel ordinary again?

That new is upon her. The night is brighter. She rubs her eyes for a new moments, she thought she was reading in the moonlight. She drops the book and stood up -- she's definitely been seeing in the dark.

'I think I'm going to be sick.'

She leaves the house to bend over the pavement. She thought about tossing her cookies over the ledge, being three levels up, but decided against that. She waited for a moment till the unearthing feeling disappears.

The city is loud with excitement. The faintest sound can be heard – her head snaps in its direction. She sniffs the air. It's like tunnel vision. She looks up at the moon and scratches the back of her neck. She sniffs out again. Instead she hears a trickling of water. She looks further out; now a stone crumbling down a pathway -- leafs scratching down a staircase – more. She moves, she has to, and finds herself tall on this unearthing day. This all started a few days back, with the flicker of the lantern on the wall.

'How could I have allowed this to happen to me?' She whispers to herself. The thrumming moment makes her carry on.

She moves through this alleyway Jale and she walks every day. The girl crosses the street into an unfamiliar territory. Here, streets are brighter; for tonight, the night has alertness. She watches as those in hooded cloaks moves across the plane and disappears into another one of those similar pathways. She watches now, from behind her dark hair in a night robe with her hood up. Her eyes glare like a cat's dots the darkness.

The clouds block the stars, where the towers mark the skyline with a fire lit atop. She looks away from its shadow casting upon her, and is taken aback by those who move around, feeling a bit paranoid of their judgment. She took a step and decides to join a busy crowd across the street, hoping she's disguised enough in her gown.

They smell of food, and other things. They move with this majesty of their own. Sometimes she'll even pass someone without notice of what they look like for the scent takes her attention in full motion.

A turn of a corner leads her deeper into the streets, coming near a lantern. The sound burns louder, she looks away from it; there are many cloaks on the move. She wonders what all the commotion is about; here in the hustling bustling of another district, she finds a large group dancing in the streets. They shake their boots and pound their feet, lifting robes and galloping in rows. They bump and cheer, in robes of blue and purple, smiles of glee and nodding at fellows. The women bang their clap and sound a cheer. But of all the lady and friend, there is only one who is dressed brightly, the Houllad in party yellow.

She looks up at the moon and decides to turn around and go a different way. A sent of dirt and salt lingers the air. She follows her nose and finds herself moving along a familiar road. She stops, because she finds the Royal Bibliotheca across from her.

'Well, there it is.' She says in her decisive ways, a little startled by its site. She stared at it for a few moments, wondering what it looks like inside. Of all the images, she imagines pretty chandeliers, sparkling and hanging low from a tall ceiling. As she found herself lost in time, staring back at this history in the making, which dates back to nearly the starting ages of Esmehdar, she bares a thought in mind.

How in the world would I ever be able to achieve such a mission, to find information on something many don't know exists in the first place? There is change in thought pattern; *Someone's coming*

She turns around to see a guard approaching, but one she never expected to see. This guard is a Houllad fellow, in party yellow. A male one. He watches her for a few moments before making his way over.

Evelyn isn't sure what to do, but what she did find was his scent became stronger. The saltiness thickens and the dirt did as well.

'Excuse me.' He says, with a surprisingly normal tone. He wipes the sweat off his forehead with a large hand. He's got a bulky frame with large plump fingers, but in no means are they soft. His skin is as bluish-grey as clay.

In the heat of the night a small drop fell off the side of his face and landed on the cool cobblestone floor. She heard a "Plop" sound and looked down past his one hand on his side, with another on his unsheathed sword, all to find his boots covered in mud. It's plenty smudged. The Houllad must have gone on a trek in the woods, or he could have stepped into somebody's garden for that sake.

He stops her, pointing the sword a few inches from her. It's as threatening as his mighty fist.

'Are you lost, my lady?' He asks, wiping a foot across the ground. The mud smears.

'No.' Evelyn says, in all sorts of nerves. 'I went for a walk and stopped here. I'm just admiring the building.' She points. 'Beautiful ain't it, don't you think?'

He huffs at her and walks away with boredom.

Evelyn felt a little uneasy, and before she went the way home, she took one last look at that royal building, and thought.

Hey, destiny is but a portal from everything

- CHAPTER 19 -

Destiny

The next morning is bright on her eyes. She squints in the kitchen, hearing sounds of a pan on a stove. She sits up to find Jale cooking breakfast.

'Morning,' he says.

She didn't reply just yet, shaking her head from a large yawn. 'You're up so early?' She says and squints from the sunlight.

'Yeah,' he scratches the top of his head. 'I'm going to head out for a client who asked for me specifically.'

She nods and mumbles. 'I feel a bit of a pain in my legs.'

'Oh really? That means the hormones should be over, the final phase is in transmission.'

'I hope so. I'm just glad I got some sleep.' She rolls on her bedside and pulls her blanket closer to her.

'I have news. It's a good surprise.' He says moving closer, and then notices her eyes are closed. He was going to poke her but decided it was best to let her sleep. So he left her port and a folded gown he picked up for her last night, placing it down on the kitchen table. He rubs an eye from early morning. He had arrived home earlier than usual and hit the sac long before he could surprise her with them.

He eats breakfast alone with a girl sleeping on the floor. He watches, finding it rather peaceful when she does.

When she finally comes to her senses, she opens her eyes.

'I was enjoying that.' He says.

She looks up from her bed. 'Did you say you had news…? I think you did, unless I was dreaming this. I've been dreaming of a lot of things, including you.'

He smiles, and passes her a large blue silky cloth, folded. 'I just got you into the Royal Bibliotheca. When I got the news last night I had to buy you a robe; I was so excited.'

Her eyes widen. She takes it and flaps it open to reveal it fully, with an even brighter crest of the Calon party. 'When, when do I start?'

'Tomorrow,' he says. He watches her admire the robe. 'You like it? It's a classy Calon dress; it twists at the hem and latches to the top.'

'I do, quite a lot actually.' She says, very excited by the look. It's elegant, almost formal for a dinner party.

'You're going to do well.'

'You think?'

'Don't worry about the final condition.' He says and moves to the cupboards. 'These herbs are going to knock you out.' She laughs. 'And any pain that comes your way. Take it with food. You will need lots of sleep, though. Don't go draining that energy and you'll be fine.' He places a sac near her port.

These words were comforting, yet Evelyn felt drawn to go with him. She misses their adventures together. All of his journeys take her to the farthest places of the world. She feels with all his knowledge he shares, nothing could be further from the two.

It will be an interesting challenge being on her own. It's been awhile since she has, and feels it will be an opportunity to put her courage to the test.

'Will you be coming home tonight?' She asks.

'No, doubt it. It's kind of confidential.' He finds she'll sit in silence, and probably over think the days apart, so he tosses her the port and a sac of herbs. Her eyes light up and he couldn't help but smile back. No it's not weed. It's her medicine.

She couldn't seem to sleep through the young night that had surely come, for Jale also had more news before he left this day. He told her she'll be starting tomorrow.

She got her own bed back and got a good catch up on sleep. It was a good thing, because she has been dreading repeating dreams for days now. The foal haunts her. She forgot to mention that.

'It'll be fine.' She reminds herself. The morning made her nerves slip away. Making herself breakfast always seems to get her mind off the thoughts and of what will come, brining her back to the moment.

She opened the kitchen window; the beautiful day is warm and peaceful in all its brilliance. She ate breakfast, next to the warm breeze of today. And took a shower afterwards, getting dressed into the beautiful robe. It's a perfect fit and one that makes her spirits lift.

She takes her port and the sac of herbs to put them in pockets, but she has none. 'Oh shit.' She says. She gets another idea and looks for her bag, when she finds it beside her bed; she fills it with the two items. She slaps the bag and a bit of dirt falls off it. 'I'd better clean this.'

After she bangs it over the balcony and wipes it down with a cloth to reveal the pack's clean face, she latches in and dusts herself off. She's happy in the robe's soft touch, one made for the city and easy travel. It's the first time she wore something this moderate and yet classy, representing a sophisticated and admirable Calon.

'I'm ready.' She says bravely to the day. You know that feeling. Yes you do. Or at least I hope so. I get it a lot, so you must have had it once in your life. It's when you get, really, really upset or the other way around, like when I really, really, get scared. It's literally nerves before heading out for an interview or the first day on the job. Yeah, kind of sucks what god makes us go through. Well, either way, she's ready, feeling anything is possible now -- can't forget the sweat part too.

White marble floors reflect Evelyn's face off its sheen.

An old lady in a blue overcoat with a red ribbon in her hair moves towards her. Her brunette hair is in a soft bun. The lady wares shoes of red.

The building smells a little of dust but in no means has this look. Only someone with a special smell could detect this.

The lady raises her cheeks at Evelyn and her tiny wrinkle of a nose points a little crookedly.

'You must be Evelyn.' She reaches a hand and Evelyn first notices a large ring on her forefinger with a red ruby dead centre. It was so large;

Evelyn couldn't help but find her eyes on its glossy self, cut perfectly, and blood-red.

'I am.'

'You are a pretty thing. I am Miss Glory, your advisor. I will be showing you around today.'

It's much how Evelyn perceived it, an interior of one grand royal space. From a glance, the showcase of items are at her sides, within tall rectangular glass boxes dwell old items and unique craftsmanship. There are statues of Calons and Rebuins of either sex holding quills next to the glass cases, but none of the faces are recognizable.

She moves around astonished, following Miss Glory down the entrance hall. Evelyn can see herself and Misses reflection.

'The royal quarters are at the second level. There are two levels to the Royal Bibliotheca. The first floor is for "Special associates"; where we will be spending our time. The main level is a section above, which is for the "Royal rubies". Only those with this title have the authority to dust the polished bookshelves and nifty books.'

Evelyn finds her eyes on Miss Glory's ring, but looks away to find amour guards who blockade the reach to the second floor's staircase. A sword and shield for each with a crest of Caealon marked on their chest. There are Rebuin in long draping robes. Their hems sweep the floor. They move with eyes on no one. The robed ones are hardly noticeable from such slow and quiet-selves.

Evelyn finds her eyes on the second level again. 'Looks royal,' Evelyn says in agreement.

'The second floor is.' The little lady goes on to explain. 'From the royal vaults to the archives, store extreme potions to special herbs and information. But you probably already know all of this.' She takes Evelyn further in and away from the royal stairway. Miss Glory looks behind a shoulder. 'Such a floor requires a port with a class four strip ranking, of any profession really. There lay different sections for each quarter, though I've never seen the inside of "The core" before. That's what we folk are calling it nowadays.'

'Say,' Evelyn raises a brow, moving slowly with her. 'Could a noble enter the core?'

'Oh yes. Though it's not only for the *highest* of royalty, a four strip is a fair rank in the Army or Royal Guard. Oh, or any graduate of Avail may as well. But only those with a note from officials may enter the archives or the vaults. It's funny you mentioned this, I saw a couple of nobles passing through last night -- Rare as they may be, it was a grand site. A young lady, my what a precious gem she was -- long beet hair, cloaked in silk, shinning blue, like a norish fish; shimmering as they do.' Miss stops to think about this one. 'She was holding files from her majesty the Queen. I stopped and paced a few steps closer to see if I was right, turns out I was. I saw the royal seal.' Miss lost focus on the subject at hand, blinking a little and then continued. 'Then there was this tall fellow. An unlikely hero; not because of his height, but because I saw sure he was a Rebuin, until I glanced over again and found he was actually a noble Clairic, incredible credentials... and all the more rare. Can you imagine what it would be like to meet a *royal*? I bet they all have one thing in common; rare information and royal secrets, to protect the Queen of course... Stunning, nobles really are, their always best in their class. Best mind you, if you do walk into one, just be polite and nod your head. It's keen to give respect to them for they're *her majesty's* representatives.'

Just be easy Evelyn, no one needs to know

Evelyn smiles and replies, 'I've never seen one yet, but I'll be sure to nod and give my respects when I do.' Evelyn does a small twirl in the hall. 'I love this building how it's connected to the school of Avail.'

'Oh yes, and many are from all across Caealon. The standards are high, yes. So unless you have a large bank account and talent in the studies or skilful practice in Aura, it's a tight squeeze to get by. Tens of thousands of students from graduating colleges submit their essay each year, and about seven hundred are accepted. Very few are selected with little compensation. Though, those who have, usually turn out to be just as driven, if not more, because of the considerable opportunity that's presented to them.'

'I thought the school's population was much bigger than that.'

The lady nods. 'I'm quiet new to these things also. My knowledge has grown since my few years at the Royal Bibliotheca. Though we get many students we cannot enter their school of course. I've heard stories of the Oriena Hall. You know, the one filled with glorious stories the students keep to themselves.' Miss really perks this time. 'Sometimes when I'm lucky, I'll overhear the tales of their dungeons and whatnot.' She finds the clock on the wall. 'I'm sorry I'm getting caught up, aren't I?'

'No it's fine, that's why I'm here.' Evelyn replies with integrity. 'I find this place traditional with a unique look.'

'Oh yes, I'm glad you noticed it. The building will grow on you. It's going to be a great relationship, you and it. You'll see.'

Evelyn nods, not sure what to say, so she said what was easiest. 'Thank you.'

They continue a path and one to lead deeper into the hall.

'You have an interesting way about you.' The lady says, and giggles, it is a soft humour. 'Don't let me tell you too much. I can easily get caught in all my blabbering stories. So let me introduce more on our royal rubies. It is for the entrusted associate that has worked for a longer period. A ruby is subject to lavish that come with the second floor, and of course, food and pampering.' Miss raises her brows, 'the works.'

'Can I ask you something? Why do you have a large ringed ruby, did you get it here as a promotional gift?'

'This old thing, no Hun, a ruby is assigned a new outfit in silk red, and a badge made of gold; baring the seal of the Royal Bibliotheca. The seal is beautiful. But the ring so happens to be a gift from my husband, we've been married for ten years now.' Before Evelyn could respond, Miss Glory's finds a larger clock made of dark bark that comes from the swamps from the far reaches of Caealon, the marshes. 'Oh my, we should keep moving.'

The dark bark stole Evelyn's gaze for a moment and she quickly returned to Miss Glory's sides. They walk along and Miss introduces more about the hall.

'This is the White Quartz also known as "The Great Hall," by many who work here. Surrounding it are four quarters, each represents a unique section.'

They leave the premises and enter through the first gateway. Monuments of kings are in this room, statues that hold up the world in their palms.

More guards in steel armour watch from the sidelines, closest to the walls, though it's intimidating, the guests don't mother their notion.

'Don't mess with these ones.' Miss Glory says. This caught Evelyn off guard. She nudges Evelyn, 'I'm just kidding, their mostly for show.'

'Ah,' Evelyn laughs a little, rubbing her face like Jale once had. Evelyn caught a guard watching her in his or her site – it's hard to tell their sex through matching attire. She looks the guardian over, he or she is wearing a blue tabard over their steel armour. Evelyn sees a large sword sheathed. Miss's voice broke her vision.

'The Royal Bibliotheca is of a highest priority, housing not only students of Avail, but the public as well. It comes with very intricate design, as you can see, the building dates back as far as the final tower was built; Maeled's. Yes... this place is very old.'

'Five hundred years, I presume.' Evelyn responds, sounding a little like Jale. She cannot help it; all the time spent with him is growing on her. I suppose it's becoming habitual now seeing how much she admires him...

Evelyn looks up at the ceiling, feeling odd by it. There is an old trim, where statues of Niveus Avis point out from all four corners of the rise. Their snouts closed, with wings down, perched on a plank.

'Yes,' Miss Glory whispers, 'many statues and carvings of our most sacred ones; the Niveus Avis.'

They follow on a blue rug that runs a straight line. Bookshelves are on one side, the other has much more tables for reading. She finally goes on to introduce the quarter. 'This is the first section, The Sapphire. General Knowledge.'

Blue curtains block the site to the next floor. The next floor is much smaller, being further inside the building.

The Sapphire has a tall reach to the ceiling, being curved from the round of the building. It is made with individual and large glass windows. The tables and bookshelves are made with a curve also; they match offering an appeal.

The day brightens the room effectively, showcasing not only bookshelves on the ground level, but to the far reaches of the back wall. There are three large balconies for more use of shelf space. It's quite grand, no doubt. It's an effective use of space all the more. This is where most of Evelyn's attention is around the room.

'Wow...' Evelyn composes herself.

Miss spoke on her own time, looking rather pleased. 'I really love how the outside run of the room is three balconies tall, using effectiveness and showcasing the lower spectrum. Not to mention the design of this place.

At night when the moon is out, the building is most lit up with a more historical feel.'

Evelyn eyes around intelligently. 'Like Apas, one might say.'

'Exactly,' the lady whispers.

A few near the tables look up from a book to see.

'Sorry.' Miss says gently to them, and comes back to a walk alongside Evelyn.

Evelyn notices the bigger lanterns lit on the walls and the small ones are on the tables. It's loud when they flicker. The lanterns are old, for it matches the design of the room. It's all hand crafted, obviously, so it has little gothic metal Crywn and Niveus Avis, with body's stuck in different motions. They cling from the base to the top. The scales are seen, with tongues sticking out from a roaring action, as if flame should produce anytime now. The Niveus Avis are more still, with wings wrapped and heads pointing to the ceiling, as if waiting to see the starry sky.

The room has a black iron look and burgundy glow. But the feelings one gets won't resemble darkness. It's brighter, especially during the beaming sun rays through the ceiling, giving the wood of the tables a fierier glow.

One of the silent dwellers move in those hanging clothes; like a waterfall swishing and seeping out onto the floor, the being moves.

When Evelyn got a look at the eyes behind that dark hood, she saw a flash of green slit irises. Evelyn and Miss wander away from the fellow and slowly, the being drifts off into a different location. Evelyn found her eyes at a squint, not sure if she should ask who these draping ones are. Instead, she finds a wicked subject to come by. 'To bad we can't see past that core, beyond those curtains.'

The lady laughs. Others peek around their book, while a few simply put the book down to stare. The lady never commented further. I guess it was the thing to do around here -- laugh things off.

It was quite unique to walk beside guards lining the wall, some staring out into oblivion, having this tendency to do this.

Miss explains some more. 'The remaining quarters are much the same, of course being different knowledge and a different colour atmosphere. The next room is the Green Zircon, known as the room of "Aura dwellers".' She admires Evelyn's gown, finding a simple gaze, it was a gaze that compliments.

The room and its name made Evelyn smile.

She led Evelyn out of the Sapphire towards the end of the room, to arrive at a green gateway. Green tint is evident on everyone's faces since a green tint is on the top windows. Most commonly, guests with pointy ears are found in this room.

'Many things are found in the Green Zircon, our newest and most profound quarter. It's a site and an attraction. Not many sit and read here, it tends to be a quicker environment.' Miss says.

Evelyn found the maker of spells. A large statue of Mieria is between the tables. Mieria has a quiet look on her face, but it said it all. She's not some Celestial, if that's what one should call her; she's carved Alasmieria and stares back at the plan, holding a smile. Evelyn looked away; it was hard to pull her eyes away from such power, feeling like an extension of her ray of light.

'We don't see too many Clairics, mostly the Celestial kinds who are after a specific act.' Miss says, moving out of the way of a robed girl in purple, holding a stack of books. Miss spoke stupefied. 'Always on the move, Celestials – that's another thing.'

The Celestial gave Evelyn a look and moved on. The girl wore a starry robe and smelled of food. It made Evelyn squint to think about the scent, reminding her of something she might have tried sometime ago.

Bean tortei – This made Evelyn smile, reminding her of Jale back when. It wasn't odd to smile randomly here, not anywhere in Esmehdar in fact.

The two move further into the Green Zircon. 'You'll find the older ones reading, the younger ones normally with the highest emotions. Now-a-days, Celestials are in such high demand; they tend to be quick buggers. So take it easy if they want information as soon as they make a request.' She pats Evelyn reassuringly, it came off as condescending. 'I'm sure you've heard all about them -- one or two in your time. Either way, they always mean best, don't they? Bless 'em hearts.'

Evelyn nods confidently.

A haze of Calons and Rebuins squeeze to get by. The ladders and pedestals are also in use on all stations within the maze. A room with the most diversity, from skin colour, to height and eye. It's speaks glee to Evelyn. Just to think what anyone of these individuals would do if they got their hands on this little book we call Alasmieria. *It* would be a freak out. Like children at their favourite restaurant. I know of one restaurant that I used to scream for pizza and prizes, long when. Starts with Chucky and ends with the yummy melted topping.

It's a good surprise, isn't it? What would you do? What do you think they'd do? I know I'd use it once or twice just to witness one of those big naked giants. Purely academic, all for note taking – alright you got me. *What?* Don't tell me you thought about it too – dirty girl. I'm assuming very few males are partaking in this. Makes me wonder how many actually will hear about this, nonetheless, take any interest in it. No I'm not a drama queen, I'm just having fun. If I was, then I'd be the spider queen and you bitches are in my web.

Evelyn looks down at a cover, one that is held by a girl in a black gown. The little girl put down the book in order to grab a different read from her pile.

The Way of Lyric

Miss Glory's voice picks up catching Evelyn's attention. 'It makes me wonder why you've decided to work for the Royal Bibliotheca.' She asks Evelyn with swiveling eyes, noticing Evelyn peer to all kinds of covers. 'Don't you want to be like them, training yourself with your amendment of sorts?'

'What amendments?'

'Well, I guess it is quite new now that I think about it.' She says warily. 'I would have guessed all Celestials share common knowledge when it gets out. Either way, it has to do with a large bonus. The Queen opened the amendment to spread Celestials and Clairics around. There are a large number of quests to be filled for them now. Strayback's is what the position titles. And then the public watch required Celestials, and the clinics wanted those rare Clairics. After that, it came full circle and the Royal Guard opened their doors and the final spots opened for nobles, too. That's why we opened this section in the bibliotheca; it serves the purpose to arrange the large number of positions required, you see.'

'I see.' Evelyn says. 'I feel well informed. Well, I'm not interested in any of these sorts at the moment.'

Books lay in stacks, without organization, just like some children do when playing with toys and leaving them were they dropped them.

A young man bumps into Evelyn and drops his book. Evelyn bent down in her tight robe and picked it up, reading the title over, 'Lyric and the Power of One.'

He nodded and Evelyn hands it back. He ran off as fast as he came.

Evelyn turns to Miss. 'What happens when we are straight up honest with each other?'

'What do you mean?' Miss asks.

Evelyn thought about it for it a moment. 'Alright I'll just say it. My three biggest secrets are,' her voice is shaky but she shakes herself back to the moment. 'I don't love myself because I don't think I'm big enough.' She hesitates. 'I mean I'm too skinny. And the other one is I sweat when I'm actually nervous. And last but least, I --'

'Why are you telling me this?'

She shrugs, 'I'm being honest.'

'Alright, should we continue on a different subject matter, perhaps on a more professional approach?'

Right, so let's all walk with sticks up our asses. Professional matter, yup, like we have to wait for a different time? Save me form these people. I'm serious. What is up with this professional shit? So let's all just wear suits and ties and do what society tells us. Who? Who is this person that denies our right to be who we want to be at all times? Yeah, it's annoying my rant, but you should see how I really feel about this. Did I make it clear? Okay, good. Oh, I hope my boss doesn't read this.

Evelyn clears her throat, feeling she's out of place. 'To answer your previous question,' being quick on her feet, so to speak, '...what better place for me to learn about the world and all its knowledge then in the finer places of the world?'

'Well then, I love your enthusiasm. You'll love our beloved History Room then. It's brilliant what you can learn just by observation. I always remind myself to take a stand back. It's really a great blessing the changes we've made since the upheaval. My... more change is coming fast.' She says, hinting at Evelyn's mannerism.

'An upheaval?' Evelyn asks, wanting to hug the wall, instead they move away from the traffic and into the maze of bookshelves. They're stepping over books from such a mess, finding the area to be a jungle gym.

Evelyn can hear people reading, she can hear their words that otherwise would be deaf by others. She can smell the fire from the lanterns. She twitches and focuses on the lady's words.

'Oh, you don't know? The rights were once held to the capital, but now we share information with other provinces.' Miss says, lifting a book up to place it on an empty shelve, and carries on. 'Well lucky you are you're the first Celestial associate and much needed for this district. We are glad you've joined us. It'll give a more relevant... appeal to the place. Us ol'gals needed some new-age help, you could say.'

'And maybe just some hands in general.'

The lady smiles with.

The Diamond room is for History. They enter it next. With a stone statue of Alas standing in the middle, being dressed in a starry robe and holding a large book in one hand, with the other, he has a thinking hand on his chin. His robe is silver, matching the drapes to this quarter. He also has white and black dotted stars running down his robe.

Evelyn notices the book in Alas's hand and smiles. It wasn't exactly the same book, but a close replica. A carved name; "Regalia" caught her eye, and the make of the book is a little bigger than that of the actual, and has a lot more glamour and diamonds on the cover and spine.

Rebuin and Calon occupy the tables, chattering on subjects of all kinds. To the back of the wall there appear to be lessons taught with many listening crowds. It gets more entertaining the further in. Evelyn nodded to a few commoners leaning against the shelves having a talk.

The Diamond held mostly folk of female; whether the sex is typical or judicial, Evelyn doesn't know. It made her happy to see such a diversity of both factions coming together so fully. The Diamond is ventured, and the two leave the haze of the past to dwell for a more relative time. The last Gateway is kind of simple and really tidy compared to the last two.

'After you,' Evelyn says, feeling no relevance. 'This must be the study room?' Evelyn asks Miss, who nods.

A lady in a long white dress glides with joy, helping students of Avail and guests alike.

'Yes, also known as The Topaz.' Miss says and opens a palm in the direction to the lady. 'That is Miss Bright. I would introduce you, but she looks a little occupied right now. She is head of the study hall.'

The room is warm and has a brighter feel than the others, with gold-yellow drapes. Evelyn can hear chirping of birds nearby. She looks up to see birds on this quarter of the dome sunroof. Her site falls back to the area in front.

Young people chat, study, read and move along with a steady pace. There are many robes, but not because all are Aura wielders, but Avail first year students. Their robes are half blue with the other crop of purple, with the crest on the chest. Evelyn supposes yellow will be in the works ever since the new treaty.

The students study amongst classmates or student friends, mostly. Here you will find binders, notebooks, ink bottles and *many* moving quills. Oh this reminds me of high school. We didn't exactly have quills, erm, but hey, I'm sure you could find those cool looking ones. Evelyn, beat 'em all up. I'm kidding…

'The *study hall is* my favourite one.' Miss says with an expression brightening up her entire face.

There are a few older and younger commoners who study to their own beat. But all are focused and have a task ready at hand. Whether it is a book between their nose and a document they're reading over, quills cross pages and the chatting is a pleasurable ease.

Evelyn and Miss Glory walk the great length to arrive to the other end. Evelyn looks up one more time to see more avis's on the ceiling. There is much movement up above. She can hear footsteps of shoes and even a fountain.

'Is there a greenhouse above us?' Evelyn finds herself asking Miss.

'My, you're a good guesser. What do you think?'

Evelyn blinks to her sarcasm. Okay, I know what I'd use the book for -- just a tap, nothing too harsh, just a little whack, just one…

'Why we do have a botanical gardens, yes.' The lady finally says to the awkward silence. 'That section is for the royal floor only.' The lady has open palms to The Great Hall. 'Shall we?'

Evelyn smirks.

Hey, at least she's got some spunk – I like this one

A bright glare falls from the ceiling giving the lady in white that much more flash. Together Evelyn and Miss leave The Topaz.

The white glistening floors of the White Quarts comes back to view. The two came full circle and enter The Great Hall.

An old kalec laughs with students surrounding him. It didn't take half-breed ears to overhear his conversation. The kalec joyfully laughs his next words. 'Gaffican, you're always the sharpest tool in the shed. I wouldn't be surprised if you get honours this year.'

'Thanks, Mr Morrowind. I better. That way I can still see you next year.' A young man in an Avail robe says. He has three stripes on his shoulder to resemble a third year student.

Miss clarifies. 'That's Mr Morrowind. He's our newest royal ruby this year. Every four years one is awarded. A ruby retired earlier last month. So it's one year early for a ruby announcement. So we're all so happy for him. He's been working here for eight years and both times the kalec has won ruby.'

'Wait, so why is he still here then?'

'Since the public loved him so much he decided to drop both titles. He's a man always on the move, keeping things in check and tidy. Staying up past hours just to get caught up with projects and helping students.' She spoke with a little whimsical. 'After all these years the kalec is finally going to move on. I really am amazed at how much he's changed. My how time flies doesn't it?'

'How long have you been here, if you don't mind my asking?'

'Oh. Just five years now. I really am going to miss that man.' She used the term "Man" rather figurative here. 'He's really been here the longest out of all of us on the floor. Most retire their position after they miss their chance for ruby. But I'm not going anywhere.'

Evelyn smiles and the two follow their reflection all the way to Mr Morrowind. Evelyn watches Mr Morrowind's little beady eyes twinkle back from the students around him. He wears a clean white suit, with purple buttons and a white gold pocket watch. A royal fitting no doubt. He smiles with the students. And the boy wave's goodbye to the kalec and the students follow the boy, passing Evelyn and Miss Glory to enter The Topaz.

'Why Miss Glory, is it me or is it as a glorious day?' The kalec says, instantly noticing Evelyn.

'Fancy meeting you here Mr Morrowind. I will miss your usual flattery.' Miss replies.

He smiles and turns his attention to Evelyn. 'Well don't you have wonderful eyes, quite astonishing really.'

'Yes, I've noticed myself,' Miss replies on her behalf. 'Evelyn, meet Mr Morrowind. I think we know why he's a little more joy then his usual self... granted we are happy for you, Mr Three times, that's a charm life. I wish I could say so myself.'

'Thank you...' He replies and makes a wheel with his hands, as if to speed up things, but he's actually fishing for something else.

Miss rolls her eyes. 'Yes ...and the chief of the Green Zircon, of course.'

'Of course,' he teases. 'But all the more thanks to you, Evelyn. We could use a little more youth in this establishment.' And gave Miss a wink.

Miss laughs. 'Of *only* those from the Green Zircon, Isn't that so, my gentleman?'

He finds his smirk. He turns his attention back to Evelyn. 'Has anyone seen Evelyn's last piece, I need it to start the engine.' He says as if looking to fit an invisible cog to start an imaginary mechanical engine.

They both noticed a twinkle in his eye but their actions are to themselves.

Miss smiles with her usual charm now. 'He's fishing for your last name.'

'Ah,' Evelyn says in a jeering tone. 'It's Maelkyn,' and reaches in to shake his hand.

'Very good, Miss Maelkyn, we are happy to have you aboard. The Zircon could use a little more... blue.' He meant... Sass and we all know it.

Miss Glory is looking a little more green. 'And what I believe he is *trying* to tell you, is that he likes you and your fitting, alongside those pretty blue eyes, I'm sure.' Miss looked as if she could give him a little whack.

Evelyn notices something else then, that Miss held the same height as him, always kept her eyes on him. She laughed more than usual... Perhaps his charmed life has her in wraps? No, it's something else.

I think Miss has a little crush on Mr Glorious. Well isn't that something?

'How does one say it?' He asks Miss now.

'If looks could kill,' she responds melodramatically.

Both had been staring at her when she said it.

'Ah, but looks remain to the eye of the beholder, do they not?' Evelyn asks the two, wanting to play.

'Quite right,' Miss agrees, taking her eyes off her one and only. Miss nudges Evelyn and quirkiness strings her words. 'If only I had some of your genes, maybe I'd be a ruby by now.' Evelyn wasn't sure what to say, but found a smile between the two. 'Oh, look at the time!' Miss perks, catching them both off guard. 'Evelyn, we better get you in the establishment dress, our royal gala starts soon. I know... cheeky, but... something tells me you're more of a grand scale type yourself.'

'Yes,' Evelyn couldn't resist the flattery. 'Wait, a-a what, did you say a royal gala, tonight?'

Miss scratches the inside of her ear. This was not like her usual lady-like self. 'Oh dear, I suppose I forgot to mention that.'

Doesn't Evelyn bring out the best in people?

Miss replies and turns to him now. 'I'm afraid we will have to postpone this chat of ours.'

'Very well, duly noted,' he winks.

Evelyn couldn't help but make a face.

Miss quickens her steps with Evelyn and the kalec watches the two leave his sides. The two come toward a door in The Great Hall. Miss turns an intelligent key into a large keyhole and presses her way through the doorway.

Evelyn trails behind. They've entered a hall that's small, and tight. They pass a few rooms. One was solely a kitchen, another room was a living room, and at the nearing back, a dressing room. Miss takes her to one last room at the end. Inside this one, there are suits and robes fashioned neatly on shelves. Miss approaches the silk linen and hands Evelyn a silver robe off one of the many shelf's with name tags. This shelf has Evelyn's name on it.

Evelyn gave her a look of surprise and excitement.

Miss replies, handing it over. 'What, did you think we'd start you out in that raggedy mess?'

'Ha-ha funny.' Evelyn says cutely. Miss winks, unravelling it to reveal its full potential. There is a gold hem to the fabric. 'Wow, thank you Miss Glory.'

Miss nods and offers an open palm for her to get dressed in a change room. Evelyn leaves her sides to slip into the dress. Inside the floors are marble and clean. It's a little dark from only candlelight, but there are smells of flowers and refreshing herbs. It brings her back to the moment.

What am I doing here?

'I should be with... him.' She looks down at the robe in hand. It's soft to the touch. She shakes her head and comes to a sit on a bench supplied. She put the robe aside. That's when it hits her... she loves him. She sat there mesmerized. She feels that she has seen the world of Alasmieria, and doesn't need to go any further.

Why the sudden change of heart? It's just happened. A moment ago this all would have been different, but that sent hosted her memories of him. It reminded her of Caszuin, when she awoke in that tall tree... hotel. All this grand attire and all she can be excited about is the memory of his smell... she misses him dearly. All that time spent away, it was driving her mad cakes. She doesn't want to spend one more day apart; she has everything she wants now.

I don't care anymore. I just want that tall man. And he's out there now

She looks up as if to see the moon. 'Oh Alas... What have I done...? I feel lost without him. Tell me what to do. Tell me what the right move is. Does he love me like I do?' She listens to Miss outside, and Evelyn smiles to herself, coming back to herself. Evelyn continues in the ease of now. 'It's amazing how far I've come. And now that I know who I want...' She looks up at the ceiling. 'And you have this geared idea that I should be the one to fix your plan, when the only plan I want is your son. His love for me is purer than anything I've felt.' She comes back out, feeling like she's going to a ball all over again, only in the wrong dress. Don't be confused here; I'm saying she never changed into her silver one.

Miss looks up from fondling with her hair. 'Again it is stunning, Evelyn, but what was wrong with the look of the silver one, you didn't like it?' She looks the girl's face over. Evelyn looked... lost. Miss drops her humour. 'Are you alright?'

'Miss...' Evelyn says and the lady waits. Their silence stirs. Miss can see the girl has a soft expression, one ready to move forward; it's almost a look of determination, to get over this elephant in the room.

'Miss, maybe you should come have a sit down for me.' Evelyn says. Her voice was soft. It told Miss that Evelyn's ready to do something else, to let go and just speak her truth.

Miss finds a seat and sits down.

'I'm sorry... Miss, I've been living this fantasy, and it's all magic --'

'It's what?'

'Just listen.' Evelyn says with her hands in expression. 'But there really is only one fantasy I belong to.'

'Are you going on with another one of your random spurs?'

She watched the girl who laughed. Probably at how odd it would sound out loud, but the girl had a relief about her, for finally saying it.

'Yes, it is. And now I go reaching for something else. That these things keep happening, and now this place. With an even greater night it brings. I've put so much on my plate; so much that I don't think I can eat anymore. But I, I have to go home.'

'Then go,' Miss said, rather simply. 'No wait,' Miss reaches for Evelyn before the girl can slip away. Evelyn smiles softly. She looks towards Miss, feeling a little more reassured. But Miss saw the light when Evelyn tried explaining it; the look said it all; that there's so much more happening in her life that she knew Miss couldn't understand, not in a whole night, and surely not right now.

'Miss, it's not easy for me to explain this. You'd have to walk in my shoes.'

'But I already know... I think,' Miss replies with eyes as bright as hers.

'You do... how? Because I didn't even know until a few moments ago. That's why I came here in the first place. I was hoping to find something to change me.' As she spoke it, Evelyn knew it wouldn't matter, that none of it would make sense. But what mattered was the feeling behind it. 'You see I came searching for answers to a past I don't think I want to know anymore. I don't want to go back to it anymore. I went searching for something that ended up being the last thing I wanted to know, because I found a life with so much more then all of this.' She said, with hands up, signifying the building. 'And now all I want is to go and grab hold of his love.'

The whole time Evelyn spoke; Miss kept her eyes on the girl, watching her every move and the finer details. Then Miss suddenly let's go of her grasp of a typical stereotype, as it fell, an image of Misses awakened memory found its piece to the puzzle. Evelyn was just about to leave when a stronger voice from the lady put her to a halt. 'You... can't be...' Miss says with eyes swishing.

Evelyn knew the lady saw something... for a connection between the two has lit up, and so soon. But this was just too much for anyone to hear, and feel. Then they knew it, what each other saw. Look, I'm saying something definitely hidden for a very long time is about to come out. Oh, but there is so much more.

Just then a man pokes his head into the room. He was about to speak but found himself holding his tongue, as a figure of speech. He's hesitant and decides to listen when Miss began.

'You're her.' Miss says with a smile. She jumps up and down. 'You're!' and gave Evelyn a little twirl as if the change room had turned into the Eslr ballroom. If the girl was to leave because she thought the lady was crazy, Miss suspected the girl would have left by now. 'Evelyn... I should have known.' She puts her hand to her mouth in amazement. The lady drops her hand to speak. 'I knew I was right all along. At first I thought I was going crazy. But now I see it. *You're her*; why else would you be here? You have *the book...* because you're Anna's daughter. You came to find answers to your mother's disappearance, haven't you?'

Evelyn cannot lie; this is the best moment of her life. Only a few moments ago she was thinking out loud in a change room, and suddenly this has come to life. Evelyn stayed put and stood straighter. It was about to seep from her mouth, the question, when something else slipped from her lips instead.

'Are you my sister?'

'No!' Miss laughs. 'I worked with your mother for a short period of time. So I know of you. Your Mother's name was Annie Alastor.'

'I don't understand.' Evelyn says. 'How did you know it was me?'

Just then people pour into the room. A few associates to change into a suitable appearance for tonight. Mr Morrowind is bumped out of the way and the crowed looks lost with his overwhelming look. The associates frown and quickly notice the new girl nearly huddled by Miss.

Miss gave a cheeky smile around the room and the associates moved on. Miss finds Mr Morrowind in the corner of her eye and as quick as he approaches, she pulls Evelyn away and into one of the many changing stalls. She closed the door behind them and spoke instantly. 'I connected the dots. You have the same hair colour, eye colour; that sea blue and... You have the same mannerism as your mother's. Anna said she was going away, but I knew she was hiding something important from me. But I never thought for a second... that it was... *the Regalia*, at the time... I knew she never meant to return. She had a look in her eye, the same one you had before your breakthrough we just started.'

Mr Morrowind knocks on the door. His voice sounds a little mumbled. 'What's going on in there, people are wondering if you're okay.'

Miss pronounces. 'Um – it's nothing; it's just a robe malfunction.'

'Okay...' Evelyn and Miss overhear him say. His next words came out sounding fairly whiny. 'That's what you'll really have me believe?' They can also hear him notifying the crowd to step back and that all was well.

Miss's voice brought her back to the stall again. 'Your mother gave me but a picture of you and the family. Evelyn, she knew you'd come back for answers. She set everything up, just in case she didn't make it across the forest to the Outlands.' Miss goes on to nod to her memory. 'Yes, she also mentioned this to me – just in case her plan went astray and if she would die, your survival would lead you back to me. She knew you'd come searching for answers if this would happen. So I stayed here at the bibliotheca, in case you'd return. Well... not just, but you have the point.' Evelyn looks emotional, but stays her ground, focusing and listening to Misses next detail. 'Evelyn, If only I was listening more carefully, I probably would have stopped her. But I didn't know what to say. She left me with nothing more than a picture... and then she was gone.' Miss stops, and then finds herself smiling largely because she's so happy to bring the information to light.

Mr Morrowind knocks, interrupting something she's about to say. 'Are you *sure* you're okay in there?' He waits, but no one answers his call. Still, a few bickering is overheard in the stall and it makes him squawk. 'Okay.' He opens the door to find Evelyn looking emotional and Miss similar.

'Get in here.' Miss says and pulls him in by the scruff.

The door shuts behind him and he turns to them. 'What is all this fuss about?!'

'It's her.' Miss says plainly.

'Who?' He asks eyeing around, like someone else could be in here with them.

Miss bumps him on the head with her palm. 'Anna's daughter, who do you think?' She turns back to the wary face of the girl's and Miss goes on. 'Me and Mr Morrowind looked into the tragic story and found a document in the vaults explaining your father's death by an Errific attack. It was then that we discovered why she ran, and why your father stayed behind. Why she took all her beloved things to survive. Your mother was running from *them,* but... we found out from the document that your family only had one nord registered in their name. So Anna couldn't take your father along... only the baby they had, with many supplies to survive and the book the enemy wanted. She must have known they were tireless. Tell me Evelyn, w-what happened to your mother. Did she make it out alive?'

Evelyn remains silent, looking down from thought. But it wasn't for long. She gave Miss a stare back. 'She died. The...' Evelyn halts and looks away; she holds back a tear and looks into her eyes again. 'The Lady of the Forest killed my mother. She took the book and played part as her. The Lady of the Forest trained me to come back here. Miss, she's not a bad person. But I don't think I have the time to explain why right now.' Evelyn finds Misses gaze a little worrisome, but continues anyway. 'I let the hard part go. But what you should know is my mother held a legacy with the book and I plan on seeing it through.'

Miss squints and then turns to Mr, 'what do I say to all this?'

He bumps her on the head with his palm, 'nothing.' His eyes light up next. 'This is amazing.'

'*Amazing?!* She just lost her mother.' She bumps him back on the forehead.

He turns to Evelyn. 'Oh, right... I'm sorry about that of course, but the Lady of the Forest, no way!?'

'Shhh,' Evelyn and Miss said together just in case someone outside could be listening.

Evelyn explains. 'I know. It's been that way most my life. Can you imagine? Being raised by the one we all fear? All to find out she's not the enemy we all thought she was.' Evelyn laughs it off. 'It's almost as amazing as having the book.'

Miss gave her a nudge. '*So* you do have it?'

Evelyn figured she didn't really hear much, *but that*. The book is quite a magnificent monument for most Alasmierian times, so Evelyn understood the eagerness.

Evelyn gave her a nod. 'Yes.'

'There is something else.' Mr Morrowind says and he turns to Miss. 'Remind us what we have in our locker.'

She nods and replies. 'Wait here.' And she slips out the door. She finds the room empty. She moves to a locker with her name on it. She unlocks it with her key and opens it. She pulls out a piece of parchment and a large key falls out of it, landing with a ring on the marble below.

Just then the door to the change room opens and a different lady enters. 'Miss Glory, we need you at your station. And where in the world is Mr Morrowind? He's never missing.'

Evelyn and Mr Morrowind overheard. Evelyn turns a look to him. 'Who's that?'

'That's Miss Crowley, she like *owns* me. She's the head of the first floor if you didn't know already.'

Miss Crowley's heels are heard tapping on the floor. 'Mr... Are you in there?' She asks taking a few steps towards the stall. Miss Glory had been pretending to do something of value with her time, untying her hair from the bun. It gave Miss Crowley all the more worry, since the woman never lets her hair down.

'I'm here.' He says and is suddenly pushed out, and acted as if he has a hop to his step.

'Nice to see your chipper self,' she says, a little shaken by the suddenness. He walks with her out of the room. He winks Miss Glory's way before he left with the boss.

Miss bend's down and picks the item that fell. She sat there in her bent knee position, staring at it.

The door to the stall opens and Evelyn moves into the silence.

Miss spoke from her kneel, 'me and Mr Morrowind found this together. We never found the vault or door it opens, but we always would stay a few minutes at the end of the night to find out where it leads. But we never found any such keyhole for that matter. We found it in the Opal Hall, a quarter that was once half resource and Aura material. When the amendment came, arrangements were made to make information on Aura a bigger place. It became the Green Zircon later. This key would belong to your mother if she still worked here. The Opal Hall was her quarter. I found the key only a few days after her departure when renovations were already in stage one.'

Evelyn walks over and the lady stood up. Miss hands the key over.

'It's very old.' Evelyn says with it in hand. 'It's almost... ancient.'

'It's as you say, five hundred years old. I was going to get it studied by a professor, of course... I wouldn't be surprised if the Queen would take it for her own keeping, and in no means would I give it up for a handsome ransom. You best keep it safe, Evelyn. I and Mr Morrowind always considered it your mother's find.' She asks now. 'How does the saying go?'

'You find what you keep?'

'You and your mother are such alike. More than I can say.' Miss relaxes her stare at the key in Evelyn's palm. 'Well, there it is now. I've been holding onto *that* thing for twenty years...'

'Thank you.' Evelyn says, placing it in her pocket.

Miss moves a little closer and hands Evelyn the parchment over. Miss says. 'A face of beauty, with straight black hair, that always fell to her shoulders. You look just like her.'

Evelyn remains still, feeling like it was only moments, but it was much longer. The heat of the day is already making it a sweaty one. Even for noon, it's picking up. Evelyn laughs her next words. 'So I'm not dreaming all of this?'

'Nope,' she shook her head. 'There you hold the only picture you may find on your mother. She also wrote a small note on the back.'

Evelyn nods. The paper is old, and wrinkled, like it had a drink spilled on it. Evelyn touches the stains.

'I know I tend to be a little messy at times.' Miss says, wiping her emotional eyes. 'I never opened it. As you can see,' she points to a seal of white wax.

'Thank you.' Evelyn says and hugs the lady.

The lady found it surprising, but all the more pleasing. 'I better head back now.'

'What was my father's name?'

'Adrian.' Miss smiles. She leans a little closer and asks. 'Is he any cute?'

'Uh, I never met him.'

'No.' Miss hits her. 'Your lover, what, did you think I couldn't tell when a woman is in love with a man?' She has a sheepish smile. 'Or is he kalec?'

Evelyn smiles big, 'yes,' and leans a little closer. 'He's a kalec. And he's quite cute indeed.'

The lady grimaces. 'Well aren't they all.'

'Yes.' Evelyn laughs largely. Her eyes fall to the parchment again. More flowing emotions of happiness are coming out. Like a sun casting its ray for a second time. 'All along... I tried to pretend he didn't matter. And if he ever went away, I would be lost without him.'

Miss is quick to ask, 'your father?'

'No.' Evelyn laughs. 'My lover, his name's Jale.'

'Oh...' And then she made an unorthodox face, 'Jale?'

'I know what kind of name is that right? It's short for Jalelilian.'

'I see.'

Evelyn feels Jale should be here, standing right next beside her, helping her to figure things out.

'What am I supposed to do with this?' Evelyn asks pulling out the key in her pocket. Still with the note in her hand and with the other hand, wiping her eyes with the back of her hand from all the laughter.

'I don't know... I was trying to figure that one out ever since we found it.' The lady shrugs. 'It's pretty exciting the little thing, isn't it?'

Evelyn looks back down at the note and nods to the question. She slowly unravels the parchment. A picture falls out. It lay face up on the floor. Evelyn stares down at it for the longest time. She can see Anna looks Errific. It's rather... shocking. She finally moves till she gets a closer look and then puts her hands to her face. 'There so happy.'

'Yes, they were. Your mother was always happy and quite bold too.'

Evelyn looks up at Miss. 'You have to tell me everything about your time spent with her.'

'I didn't know why she was always so scarce; mostly that's what I thought of her at the time. Most of the time I told her to lighten up...'

Evelyn laughs lightly with her. The girl reaches now and touches the picture, picking it up and flips it over to find writing. Evelyn read it out loud.

'To my dearest daughter Ariana Alastor, be happy. That's what your father always said. He always told me how glad he was to see me happy, that it gave him strength. If you are reading this now, then you know what has happened and you have survived. I will always love you, always... and if you get in a little bit of trouble, than you really are my daughter. If you have this, you've probably met the gentle soul of Miss Glory. Tell her thank you for me. Best wishes, your mother, Anna Alastor and your father's best wishes to you, Adrian Alastor.'

The lady watches, misty eyes.

Evelyn sees something else, looking over the picture again. A baby held in one arm of Anna's, and another baby in the arms of Adrian's, with Adrian's other arm wrapped about his wife.

'One is me... but who is the other?'

'We don't know his name, or where he is for that matter.' The lady answers. 'Anna told me where she was taking you. She couldn't raise him because of his Errific-like appearances. She gave him to someone she trusted in Calliskue, so that way he could grow up safely in a safe location. She figured the enemy would never know, because he's right under their nose. She didn't have any other choice. Beyond that, I and Mr Morrowind couldn't do anything more to help.'

Evelyn looks up from the picture. 'So... I have a brother.' Her cheeks lift to a smile.

And I was wrong... so very wrong about... me. There's nothing more than I'd do for me, to love ones self is the key, it's the answer. And my reality is determined by my focus. How else can anyone love me if I don't love myself? But that's no reason to do it, I love myself now, for the one simple fact that there is. It feels good. I woke up this morning and before I went to work I told myself, 'I'm going to have the best day of my life.' Why? Because I was hurting, I didn't feel like I mattered or belonged. Then it all changed. I am sharing this now because it feels better to be loved. Look. There's only one thing that matters, its how one looks at themselves and honestly, after today, after all the amazing things that happened -- and it's because I changed one simple thought and focused – people do change. I did.

THE END

About the Author

I was born and raised in Hamilton, Ontario. I'm a young author driven by talent. I find the most important things in my life are following my heart and using my emotional compass to guide me. To trust is to receive, and to believe is no truer.

CPSIA information can be obtained at www.ICGtesting.com
Printed in the USA
LVOW11s1601131115

462068LV00003B/3/P